GILDED SERPENT

GILDED
SERPENT

DANIELLE L. JENSEN

TOR
TEEN

A TOM DOHERTY ASSOCIATES BOOK
NEW YORK

GILDED SERPENT

Copyright © 2021 by Danielle L. Jensen

Maps by Jennifer Hanover

A Tor Teen Book
Published by Tom Doherty Associates
120 Broadway
New York, NY 10271

www.tor-forge.com

Tor® is a registered trademark of Macmillan Publishing Group, LLC.

The Library of Congress Cataloging-in-Publication Data
is available upon request.

ISBN 978-1-250-31779-7 (hardcover)
ISBN 978-1-250-31778-0 (ebook)

Our books may be purchased in bulk for promotional,
educational, or business use. Please contact your local bookseller
or the Macmillan Corporate and Premium Sales Department
at 1-800-221-7945, extension 5442, or by email at
MacmillanSpecialMarkets@macmillan.com.

First Edition: April 2021

Printed in the United States of America

0 9 8 7 6 5 4 3 2 1

For H.L.

GILDED SERPENT

1

TERIANA

It was pouring rain.

Monstrous droplets that stung as they struck, like having pebbles thrown against one's face over and over again. A deluge that turned the streets of Aracam to streams, waterfalls pouring from the rooftops. Blackened skies flickered with lightning, the resultant thunder deafening Teriana's ears.

Yet for all the storm's ferocity, the Arinoquians had still come out in the thousands, in the *tens of thousands,* to witness the execution of Urcon.

A platform was set up at the center of the god circle, the great stone towers dedicated to each of the seven gods seeming to watch as the space filled with people. Men. Women. Children. Their faces were twisted with hate and fury and anticipation, their words indistinguishable, but the collective volume rivaled the thunder as they called for the blood of a tyrant.

Motion caught Teriana's eye, and she glanced past Marcus to see Titus cross his arms, his helmet doing little to hide his disapproval of the scene. Not for the first time, she was struck by how much the young commander of the Forty-First resembled his father, Lucius Cassius. And not just in his features.

"If they riot, we'll have more casualties than we did taking the rutting city," Titus muttered. "Every blasted person in Arinoquia is here."

"To bear witness is to strike the blow. It's the closest thing to revenge these people have," Marcus answered, his voice still raspy from his injured throat.

It had been only two days since he and Teriana had stood together on the hill overlooking Aracam. Since he'd committed to whatever it was that was between them: a fragile relationship built on affection and lust and something deeper she wouldn't put a name to. Two days since she'd abandoned reason and committed to the same.

Water sluiced down Marcus's face, but his eyes remained fixed on the crowd, mouth an unsmiling line, the slight flexing of the muscles in his jaw the only sign of emotion. A scrape marred one of his cheeks, and his throat was ringed with dark bruises in the shape of fingers. Injuries that he'd gained coming to her aid when she'd been kidnapped and held prisoner in a failed gambit to defeat the Cel legions.

As though sensing her scrutiny, Marcus turned his head, grey-blue eyes meeting hers with an intensity that made Teriana feel as though they stood utterly alone, despite being surrounded by fifty men of the Thirty-Seventh. The corner of his mouth tilted up for a heartbeat, and warmth flooded her chest, then his attention moved back to the crowd.

Her own skin prickled, and Teriana looked to her left, finding Felix's gaze on her. The second-in-command's bland expression did nothing to hide his anger and hurt at having his place at Marcus's side usurped. Given he was potentially the one who'd paid Urcon's men to get rid of her, standing elbow to elbow with him was unnerving at best. *Was it you?* she silently asked. *Are you the traitor?*

Or are you merely the scapegoat?

The crowd surged, pulling Teriana from her thoughts. A thin corridor formed, leading toward the platform, and several armed Arinoquians appeared, dragging a figure between them.

Urcon.

For more than a decade, he'd lorded over his people with a heavy fist, extorting their wealth, stealing their children for his armies, slaughtering any who stood against him, and enforcing his dominance with terrifying brutality. He was a monster. A villain of the first order.

But it was hard to remember that as she took in the ancient man the warriors were half-carrying, his legs were unable to bear his weight.

They'd stripped him, his naked body scrawny and feeble and showing signs of gout. A few wisps of white were plastered against his skull, and his sunken eyes were wild with fear and confusion. He tripped over his own feet, only the grip of his captors keeping him from falling.

He's a murderer, she reminded herself, remembering the people from Imperatrix Ereni's town that Urcon's men had left slaughtered on the path as a warning for Marcus. Remembering how their blood had coated her bandaged feet, sticky and stinking of copper. Remembering the testimonies of the victims of Urcon's men, who'd committed atrocities in his name. Remembering that it had been this feeble old man who'd employed *Ashok,* one of the corrupted, to exercise his control of Arinoquia and its people.

Yet for all the reminders brought back her terror, they still jarred with what she was seeing with her own two eyes. *Who would follow this man?*

Then the Arinoquians started to throw pebbles.

Teriana flinched as the first struck and Urcon cried out, blood running from a wound on his temple. Another pebble opened a thin line of red across his shoulder. Another a lesion across his thigh. Swiftly she lost count, the air filling with flashes of grey as the people he'd tyrannized for so long rained their hate down upon him.

"They're going to kill him before Ereni has a chance to swing that axe," Titus said. "What a mess this is. We should have handled the execution."

"He's their kill," Marcus answered, and Teriana wondered whether he'd made that decision because he knew Ereni had been displeased about him taking the honor of executing Urcon's men in Galinha. Whether it was a political choice meant to earn the Arinoquians' favor. Or whether it was another reason entirely.

The warriors dragged Urcon onto the platform, where Ereni and the other imperators waited, and the barrage of stones ceased. The old man was bleeding and sobbing, and he remained prone in front of the leaders of the clans.

"The gods have borne witness to your crimes, Urcon!" Ereni inclined her head to each of the towers. "And unless one of them sees fit to stay my hand, let them bear witness to your punishment!"

Everyone in the crowd lifted their hands to make the sign of the Six against their chests, and though she was typically careful never to do so around the Cel, Teriana did the same.

Ereni hefted an axe, the blade wet and glinting from the rain, and the crowd screamed for blood. Her mouth moved, but it was impossible to hear her over the noise of the crowd.

"What did she say?" Titus asked, and Teriana curbed the urge to tell him to be quiet.

"She told him to get up." Marcus's tone was flat. "For Arinoquians, it's a matter of honor to face one's execution bravely in order to earn the favor of the gods. She's giving him the opportunity to regain face before he dies. An opportunity to save himself from being taken by the Seventh god to the underworld."

How do you know that? Teriana wondered. *Who told you?*
Do you believe it?

Titus spit on the ground. "Pagan nonsense. Bastard deserves to die on his knees."

"Titus," Marcus said, "shut up."

At any other time, Teriana would've smirked, but it was all she could do to keep her stomach contents in check as Ereni again shouted at Urcon to get to his feet. Instead, the ancient tyrant attempted to crawl to the edge of the platform, trying to flee his execution.

Expression tightening, Ereni barked an order at her warriors, who grabbed hold of Urcon's ankles and dragged him back to the center of the platform. He managed to extricate himself from their grip, curling into a ball like a frightened child. The warriors forced his body straight, trying to get him into a position where Ereni could swing, but Urcon writhed and twisted.

This isn't right.

Next to her, Marcus rocked slightly on his heels, and when she glanced at him, his jaw was tense, his brow furrowed. *Stop this,* she willed him. *Stop it, before it's too late.*

The crowd was losing its momentum, the noise diminishing as more warriors dragged an execution block onto the platform, tying Urcon to it so that his arms were splayed out. Ereni said something to the other imperators, who all nodded. Then her gaze flicked in Marcus's direction.

He didn't so much as twitch.

The axe blade gleamed as Ereni swung it through the air, slicing through the falling rain, time seeming to slow to a crawl as it descended. But instead of striking true, it embedded in the base of Urcon's skull. The old man screamed in agony.

Grimacing, Ereni jerked the blade free and swung again, but this time hit Urcon's shoulders, the axe sinking deep in the muscle. The old man howled, and Teriana gagged, covering her mouth.

"I'm not watching this," Felix growled, turning, but Marcus reached past Teriana, catching his second-in-command's arm.

"We helped make this happen. So we *will* watch."

Ereni swung the axe a third time, the blade sending droplets of blood flying over the crowd, which was no longer cheering.

This time her aim was true, and the weapon severed Urcon's head from his neck. She reached down and picked it up, holding it high. Blood poured down, glistening crimson droplets joining the rain on the platform, Urcon's eyes dull and sightless. "The tyrant is dead!"

The crowd repeated Ereni's words over and over. Teriana wondered whether Urcon was being dragged down to the underworld with their screams in his ears. And whether he deserved it.

"The tyrant may be dead," Marcus echoed the crowd's refrain. "We shall see about the tyranny."

"Why do you say that?" Teriana murmured under her breath.

"Because," he said, turning away from the bloody scene. "This particular tyrant wasn't working alone."

2

KILLIAN

Despite the cold, the smell of corpse was heavy in the air. The sickly sweetness of rotting flesh mixed with opened bowel, and there was something about it that told Killian it was human, not beast.

Sliding off the side of his horse, he dropped the reins and moved forward on foot, easing over the embankment toward a thicket of dead bushes. The wind howled, tearing at his cloak as he drew closer, heart beating faster and faster until he swore it would tear from his chest.

Please don't let it be her.

Please let it be her.

The thoughts alternated back and forth, same as they always did, fear and grief warring with his desire for this search to be over. To have closure, even if his guilt would remain.

As he reached the thicket, his eyes picked out the familiar shape in the snow. A body facedown, legs splayed and cloak flipped up, concealing the head. A woman, judging from the skirts, which were stiff with dried blood. Small and slender.

Please don't let it be her.

Please let it be her.

Hand shaking, Killian reached down and rolled the body, cringing as the woman's frozen hair peeled away from the ground.

Not her.

"Malahi was wearing a red velvet dress that day."

He lurched upward at the voice from behind him, drawing his sword even as he whirled around. His blade came to rest against Bercola's throat.

The last time he'd seen her was on the battlefield at Alder's Ford, her holding the spear she intended to use to safeguard Malahi's plot to assassinate her own father, King Serrick. The spear that had ended up embedded in Killian's side, the wound nearly the death of him. "You should have stayed gone."

The giantess's throat moved as she swallowed, colorless eyes unreadable as she regarded him. "Probably. But I thought I owed you an explanation."

"There is no explanation good enough!" he snarled at her, watching droplets of blood roll down his blade. Not that she so much as flinched. "You betrayed me."

Because it hadn't been him that she'd intended to hit with that spear. It hadn't even been Serrick.

It had been Lydia. And for that reason, no explanation was worthy of forgiveness.

"I know you think that," she answered. "But I need you to know that I was only trying to protect you. And so was she."

"Bullshit!" he shouted. "You were trying to cover Malahi's tracks so that no one would discover she'd sent an assassin after her own father."

"No." Bercola started to shake her head but froze as his blade dug deeper. "Lydia is corrupted, Killian. Malahi saw her steal life the night of the ball. And if she did it once, she'll do it again. And again. It would only be a matter of time until you had to kill her. And I knew doing so would kill *you*. Better that you hate me for the rest of your life than that."

"She is not corrupted!" He screamed the words, his body shaking. "She's a gods-damned healer, and you should be glad of it, because otherwise I'd be dead by *your* hand!"

She flinched.

"Lydia sacrificed her freedom to save my life. And she wouldn't have had to if not for Malahi's scheming. If not for her lies. If not for *you* enabling her." Fury flooded through him, and because he knew if he didn't, he'd kill her, Killian dropped his sword. "I trusted you."

Silence.

"I won't apologize," Bercola finally said. "I swore to your father to keep you safe, and though he might be in the grave, my oath remains. You may refuse to see it, but there is a darkness in that girl, and it is born of fear. And fears never stay buried."

"I neither need nor want your protection," he said between his teeth. "Go, Bercola. Get out of my sight and out of Mudamora, because if I see you again, I *will* kill you for what you did."

"She's dangerous, Killian. And you and I are the only two living who know it."

"We know nothing! This is all on Malahi's word, and we both know she wouldn't hesitate to lie if it served her ends."

"I saw!" Bercola's large hands clenched into fists. "She healed me afterward, and despite that I was near death, she gave up nothing of herself to make me whole. Because she was only giving up what she'd stolen!"

"The only thing she did wrong was not letting you die!"

Bercola closed her eyes, taking a measured breath. Then the giantess who had watched over him most of his life took one step back. And another.

"They say there is some of the Six in all of us," she said when she reached the top of the slope. "But so is there some of the Seventh. Even in the Marked."

"Go!" he screamed, reaching down to retrieve his sword. "This is your last chance, Bercola. That I'm giving you a chance at all is only because we were once friends."

Her eyes glistened with tears, but the sight only hardened his heart.

"The days grow darker, Killian," she said. "And I think it will be in the absence of light that we all see who we truly are."

And without another word, she disappeared.

3

MARCUS

His head throbbed.

A dull, merciless ache had spread from his shoulders, up his neck, and across his skull to his temples, where it had then begun to squeeze. It was merciless. And it made it so very hard to think.

"Do you wish for me to send in men to quell the mob, sir?" Felix asked as they walked through the streets of Aracam.

Like Galinha, the buildings were made of stone, the entrances small, and the streets narrow. It smelled like rain, rock, and piss, and other than a few dogs rummaging through trash, the streets were empty. Not that it would last. "No. Let it burn itself out."

"There will be casualties."

"Some. But there will be more violence if they perceive us as standing in the way of their revenge. Give it an hour, then have patrols move into the city." He turned his head back toward the towers of the god circle, not needing to push his imagination too hard to picture what was happening to Urcon's corpse. "The people did not receive the satisfaction they hoped for in that execution, and many will look for release in other pursuits."

"Because Ereni botched it."

Marcus shook his head, for the reason was far deeper than that. "Regardless of the reasons, our men are to keep the peace, not add to the violence."

Even though speaking made his injured throat ache, he continued to detail his orders, growing more specific by the second despite the way Felix's jaw tightened, despite knowing that his *friend's* ears would be turning red beneath his helmet the way they always did when he was angry.

Don't act until you have proof, Teriana had made him promise. But the fact of the matter was that either Felix or Titus had stabbed him in the back, which meant Marcus could trust neither of them.

"Anything else, sir?" Felix's voice was stilted. "Or may I go?"

"Go." Not waiting to see if he listened, Marcus turned to Titus. "Start the men with clearing the debris where we blasted the wall. Then get them to work on rebuilding. Tomorrow, I want a call to employ masons and other skilled laborers to take over the repairs of all structures damaged in the battle. Be clear they will be *paid*."

"By whom?" Titus asked. "Our coffers grow thinner by the day."

"The goodwill will be worth the expense. Once the work is underway, I want you to . . ." As with Felix, he delved down into the minutiae, part of him wanting one of them to disobey him in some way, thus allowing him to *act*.

But unlike Felix, Titus only nodded, saluting sharply before departing with his escort.

"I was about ready for you to give them instructions on how to wipe their own asses."

At Teriana's words, several of his men smirked, and Marcus gave them cold stares before turning to her. "A change of regime is a delicate time for any nation. Better that I be specific in my orders, that way if things go poorly, I'll have no one to blame but myself."

"How magnanimous of you." She flipped the braids the wind had pushed into her face back over her shoulder, revealing the bruises on her cheeks. Her split lip. Her right hand was pressed against her ribs, and though he knew they were only bruised, he also knew from experience how each breath hurt, the pain escapable only in sleep.

Which was an escape he couldn't afford to give her. "I've a job for you."

"Oh?" She didn't look surprised. "Do tell, Legatus." Her voice dripped with sarcasm, but whereas once she'd have been mocking him, now her tone served to deceive everyone else. To hide a secret.

"I'll explain once we're in Urcon's fortress."

Under the watchful eye of Gibzen and his men, they made their way to the fortress at the center of Aracam. Like all of the buildings in the city, it did not exceed two stories, but what it lacked in height it made up for in sprawl. Surrounded by a solid stone wall with only one gate, it was a maze of buildings his men were still in the process of searching, but at the moment, there was only one structure that concerned him.

They ducked to enter the building, following Gibzen through the narrow corridors lit by smoking torches. It felt more like walking through a series of caves than a structure built by the hands of men. The ceiling was so low that Marcus had to stoop as they walked, and he idly wondered how Servius was managing.

Ahead, two of his men flanked a heavy door, which they opened at the sight of him, forced to press their backs against the walls in order to allow room to pass.

"I bloody well hate this place!" Servius shouted as they entered. "If you've any kindness in you, sir, don't ask me to stand. It would mean risking what brains I have left to these cursed ceilings."

"Consider yourself at ease while I give Teriana the tour."

She said nothing, following him into the next chamber, which was heaped with gold and silver and gemstones. Chests of coins were stacked haphazardly against the wall, jewelry and silverware mixed in together with sculptures of ivory and bronze, the wealth beyond anything Marcus had ever seen, and there were six more chambers of it. All of it covered with dust. Stolen away and then forgotten.

Teriana cleared her throat. "You'd better not be asking me to swindle Ereni and the other Arinoquian imperators, Marcus. Because the answer is no."

"I'm not." Leading her deeper into the treasury, he stopped only once they were out of earshot, pushing the door to the chamber shut. Dust puffed in his face and he coughed, knowing that he'd be risking one of his attacks if he stayed in here much longer. But he wanted to be alone with her.

"What, then?" Her tone implied that she expected him to ask something of her that she didn't want to give, and Marcus's chest tightened. Would that ever stop? Could it?

"I need you to put a total on this wealth. And I need it within the next two days." And then, because he didn't want it to sound like an order he had no right to give her, he added, "Please."

Teriana's eyes widened, and she gave the room an appraising once-over. "Marcus—"

"It has to be done. We currently have seven armies sitting outside of Aracam—"

"Gods, no wonder you need me to do this. You can't even count. There are *eight* armies outside Aracam."

Despite himself, Marcus laughed, catching hold of her waist and pulling her against him. She slid her arms around his neck, and for a heartbeat, he forgot about his headache. Forgot about politics and traitors and blood. "*My* army doesn't concern me. It's the rest of them."

Tangling his fingers in her wet braids, he rested his cheek against hers, staring at a pile of golden cups, tasting the dust in the air. "The clans united for the sake of ridding themselves of Urcon, but now that he's dead, it's only a matter of time before they start fighting among themselves. If that happens, I'll either have to choose sides or force my own authority down on their heads, neither of which is appealing."

"Don't fancy yourself the new ruler of Aracam?"

Grimacing, he shook his head, then leaned back against the wall so he could meet her gaze. "No. Nor am I interested in another battle on the heels of the one we just won. My men need a chance to breathe."

And he needed a chance to carve out a life for them in this place while at the same time pretending he was still following the Senate's—and Cassius's—orders.

"The clans are expecting to receive a share of the plunder," he continued. "I'd like to give it to them and have them on their way before they start trying to take what they feel they're owed from the people living in this city." He had other reasons, too. Pressing reasons, but they weren't ones he dared to share.

"There's nothing to take. Urcon and his men stripped this city clean as much as he did the rest of Arinoquia."

Letting go of her, Marcus reached down to pick up a woven basket. A tin cup. A leather belt. Not treasure, but items that had had value to someone. "There is always something to take."

A knock sounded on the door, and Servius's voice echoed through. "The representatives from the clans are here."

Time was of the essence, but Marcus still felt a flash of irritation at the interruption. Stolen moments, that was all they ever had. "Tell them to wait."

"More secrets to tell me?" She tilted her head, midnight skin gleaming in the torchlight. Ocean waves rippled across her irises, the color a blue so dark and deep he imagined himself drowning in them. Bruised or not, she was more beautiful than anything in the room. More beautiful than anyone he'd ever seen.

And she'd chosen him.

Bending his head, he kissed her gently, mindful of her injuries. "You are the secret. *This*"—he kissed her again—"is the secret."

Teriana rolled her eyes. "You really need to get some sleep. A secret is something everyone *doesn't* know." Reaching up, she touched his bruised throat. "*This,* everyone knows."

She was probably right. She *was* right, only he didn't want to admit it. "It's one thing for my men to suspect. Quite another for me to shove it in their faces. I . . ." Marcus trailed off, struggling to find the words he wanted. This was untrodden territory for him, and he felt painfully ignorant—not a feeling he was used to. And certainly not one he liked. "*This*," he finally said, "can only happen behind closed doors."

"We live in a tent." She winked. "No doors."

Groaning in frustration, he leaned back against the wall, rubbing at his temples. "You drive me to madness."

"You like it."

He did like it. He liked *her*. But his affection for her had already been used against him with near-catastrophic effectiveness.

Stomach hollow, he forced himself to meet her gaze. "Would you want your crew to know?"

The waves rolling across her irises surged, and for a foolish heartbeat, he thought she might say yes. Then she looked away. "No. It wouldn't go over well."

That was likely an understatement.

"As much as I might wish otherwise, my men talk. To one another. To civilians. To the sailors on my ships. And those are the sailors who supply your crew, so I think it's in both our best interests to keep the rumors in check."

Teriana nodded, but he noticed a slight quiver in her jaw, even these stolen moments dampened by circumstances. Reaching down into an open chest, he picked up a necklace that caught his eye, all sapphires and diamonds and gold. He fastened it around her neck, watching how the gems glittered across the delicate bones of her throat.

Teriana looked down, then unfastened the necklace and handed it back to him. "That gold is steeped in blood. Pretty as it is, wearing it would be bad luck."

"I doubt there's an ounce of gold on Reath that hasn't known blood, one way or another." He dropped the necklace back in the chest, knowing she was right but also that she deserved more than he was giving her. "But blood or no, I need all of this valued. You'll have to stay here while it's done, but you'll be under constant guard. And Servius will be with you."

Opening the door, he led her back in the direction of the entrance. He nodded at the seven Arinoquians, four men and three women, standing with Servius and Gibzen. Switching to their language, he said, "You're here to ensure the inventory of Urcon's wealth is taken honestly and without bias. All will be searched upon departure from this room, and the punishment for theft will be the loss of a finger. Is this understood?"

They nodded, and he said, "Good. Teriana will be my representative, and given her expertise, hers will be the final word. Agreed?"

Everyone nodded, but still he hesitated, searching his brain for a reason to remain. A reason not to leave her presence. But neither Teriana nor this task needed his involvement, whereas there were a hundred other matters that did. "I'll leave you to it," he said, then left without a backward glance.

4

LYDIA

The gates to Mudaire stood open as they approached, soft flakes of snow drifting from the sky to add to the carpet of white. It should've been beautiful, but with the endless streams of black crisscrossing the land, the stench of rot thick on the air, it looked for all the world to Lydia like the flesh of one infected by the blight.

Or a blighter, as she'd learned they were called during their journey back from the battleground of Alder's Ford.

The soft thuds of the horses' hooves turned to sharp clacks as they rode under the open portcullises and onto the cobbles, not a single sentry remaining to guard the city. The door to a house opened and shut on the wind, the hinges creaking, and the shutters on the windows rattled with each gust. Where Mudaire had once been thick with the scents of humanity—food and sweat and urine—now there was only rot, as though the city itself was a corpse laid out to decay.

And yet it was not entirely lifeless.

Lydia noted human tracks in the snow, far too many to be accounted for by a handful of individuals, and she turned to Quindor, who rode silently at her side. As Grand Master of Hegeria's temple, he had authority over all healers in Mudamora and the ear of the King. He'd have answers. "I thought Lady Calorian was able to evacuate the city." Her chest hitched at the mention of Killian's mother, her mind leaping to him as it so often had over the days since she'd turned her back on him at Alder's Ford.

Quindor's gaze flicked to the tracks, his jaw tightening. "There were a good many who refused to go, and there wasn't the manpower to force them. With the battle won, we anticipate more will return."

"Why would anyone in their right mind stay?" There was nothing to eat but vermin and what fish could be caught on the sea, and the majority of the wells in the city were foul.

"Hope. Stubbornness. Fear." His eyes moved to the shadows, and Lydia's went with them, catching sight of motion. Of something human in shape. Her chest tightened, especially when she realized it was following them.

"Blighter," Quindor said softly to the soldiers.

"Would you have me put it down, Grand Master?" one of the men replied. "Or do you wish it captured?"

Before Quindor could answer, *it* stepped out of the shadows.

"Spare a copper?" the child said, her voice high-pitched and sweet. "A crust of bread?"

Instinct had Lydia reaching for her saddlebags to retrieve the girl something to eat, but Quindor caught hold of her wrist. "*Look,*" he said. "Allow Hegeria's mark to show you the truth."

Lydia turned her head back to the child, seeing that the girl's dark eyes were fixed on her. Her skin was pale, but her face bore none of the black veins of blight that marred the flesh of the infected who'd attacked the night of Malahi's ball. Neither was she a mindless thing like those that had pursued them through the tunnels beneath the palace, intent on nothing but slaughter. There was intelligence in this girl's eyes. Thought.

"Look," Quindor repeated.

Lydia stared back into the eyes of the child, her skin turning to ice. All living creatures glowed with an ethereal mist of life that only those marked by Hegeria could see. Quindor and the soldiers, as well as the horses, radiated it, but the girl standing before them had no more life in her than the stones beneath her feet. A walking corpse.

"The blight is evolving," Quindor said, then he nodded at the guard. "Put it down."

"No!" Lydia protested, but the Grand Master grabbed the reins of her horse to keep her from intervening as the soldier pulled his sword.

The girl's eyes widened with fear, and she turned and sprinted toward an alley. But the soldier's horse was faster. A flash of a blade. A gush of blood.

A child's head rolling across the snow.

"Burn it." Quindor's voice was toneless.

Another of the soldiers dismounted to pour oil over the corpse, including the head, and then touched his torch to it. Flames burst bright.

Nausea rose in Lydia's stomach, her skin simultaneously hot and cold, but Quindor's words tore her eyes from the sight.

"The war isn't over," he said. "It has only just begun. And this"—he gestured at the inferno—"is a battle Hegeria's Marked must fight." His gaze fixed on hers. "That's why you are here."

They dismounted in the middle of the city's god circle, and several of the soldiers took the reins of the horses to bring them to the stables at the palace, the only place secure enough to protect them from slaughter.

The doors to the temple opened as they approached, heavily armed soldiers in the company of two young healers inspecting their party before they were allowed to enter.

"Welcome back, Grand Master," both of the young healers said, inclining their heads respectfully, and Quindor smiled affectionately at both as he led Lydia inside.

The last time she'd been here was to deliver Gwen into the temple's care, and the scene was much changed. Instead of the foyer being filled with rows of cots, it was empty of everything except for soldiers, all of the men wearing coats marked with Hegeria's half-moon. What windows the main level had once possessed had been bricked over. The temple was now a fortress.

"Do the blighters try to get inside?" she asked, heart beating a rapid staccato as she remembered the waves of them tumbling through the trapdoor into the palace tunnels, their endless pursuit.

"Not yet," the young healer answered. "But Hegeria's Marked alone see them for what they are, so it's in their best interest to kill us. We think they're waiting for an opportune moment."

"Shush now," Quindor said. "I'd hear a proper report, not inflated rumors. Come, Lydia. I'll show you to your quarters and after you've had a chance to settle, we will discuss the matter of the infected."

The blight is evolving. Quindor's words echoed through her thoughts as she followed him to a curved staircase, leading her upward. They climbed to the fifth floor before turning down a hallway, which circled the tower.

"The dormitories," he said, then led her past a dozen closed doors before stopping before one marked with a 37. "This will be your room. You are responsible for keeping it clean and for your own laundry. Attend me in my office in an hour so that we might discuss your role."

"Yes, Grand Master," she answered, but Quindor was already swiftly retreating up the corridor, so she went inside.

It was small—more cell than room, in her opinion, with a narrow cot against the wall, a rickety wardrobe against the other, as well as a wash table on which a basin filled with water sat. The grey stone of the floor was softened only by the presence of a threadbare carpet, but the blankets on the bed appeared soft and warm. A set of folded white garments sat on the blankets, and Lydia picked them up. A thick robe. A white cotton shift. A woven belt. And on the floor, three pairs of black boots of various sizes.

Lydia methodically stripped off her dirty clothing, leaving it in a pile. Goose bumps rose on her skin as she crossed the frigid floor to stand naked in front of the wash table. There was a mirror on the wall—nothing more than a polished piece of metal—and Lydia stared at her reflection. Her hair was tangled and filthy, her skin marked with dirt. And beneath the filth, her cheeks were hollow, her eyes shadowed and sunken from exhaustion and fear and grief. But what drew her eye was the half-moon that Quindor himself had tattooed onto her forehead during the journey back from Alder's Ford. This was the first time she'd seen it, and she traced a fingernail over the design, reminded, briefly, of how the Empire marked the men in its legions.

And thought of the legions pulled Teriana into the forefront of her mind. Her best friend, who was the prisoner of the young man who'd tried to murder Lydia on Lucius Cassius's orders. *Please watch over her,* she prayed to the Six. *Don't let him hurt her.*

Pouring water into the basin, she picked up the cloth and bar of soap sitting next to it and began to scrub her face, then her body, the water turning a murky brown. She discarded the dirty water into the chamber pot under the cot, then refilled the basin. Bending forward, she immersed her hair as best she could, pinching her eyes shut as she worked up a soapy lather and then pouring the rest of the pitcher of water over her head to rinse it. Reaching blindly for a towel, she wiped her face and wrapped her damp hair. And then she opened her eyes and reached for the basin.

The water wasn't the murky brown of dirt, but rather a deep shade of rust.

Blood.

Killian's blood.

Her breathing accelerated, turning into fast little gasps, the room swimming in and out of focus. She crouched down, pressing her hands to the floor for balance, shivering violently, her skin like ice.

"He's alive," she whispered. "You're alive. And both of you are set to the purposes for which you were destined."

But the truth did nothing to drive away the cold.

5

TERIANA

"This is going to take forever," Servius muttered, wiping sweat from his brow, his brown eyes uncharacteristically shadowed. Whether it was from lack of sleep or other concerns, Teriana didn't know. "We'll need some sort of containers. Half these chests have gone to rot."

No sooner had the words exited his lips, the bottom of the chest he was holding fell out, spilling coins everywhere. All of them gold and stamped with the scorpion of House Rowenes. "That's odd," she muttered.

Servius scooped up a handful, examining them with a practiced eye. "This is the most solid clink I've come across. Looks pure, too. Where's it from?"

"Mudamora, on the Northern Continent." She rubbed her thumb over a coin. The largest gold mines on Reath were on the Rowenes lands, which were near the border of Mudamora and Anukastre. "But they don't trade with Arinoquia, so it's odd to find so much of their coinage here."

And all of it freshly minted, bearing no signs of wear. Which suggested an expensive purchase, and one only a High Lord—or even the King himself—could afford. Shrugging, she tossed it back in the pile and set to work.

It was dusty, laborious work, but there was also something soothing about it. This was what she'd trained most of her life to do—not to sail a ship, but to be a merchant who knew wares well enough to come out ahead in every bargain. If not for the circumstances, Teriana thought her mother would be proud.

At the thought of her mother, Teriana's chest constricted painfully. Was Lydia's father keeping her safe? She'd always believed Senator Valerius a kind and honorable individual, but she'd thought the same about Lydia. And she could not have been more wrong on that front. Part of her wondered if she'd ever have the opportunity to see Lydia again. What she would say to her, if given the chance. If Lydia even cared how much hurt she'd caused.

"Is there any news from my crew?" she asked Servius. "Do you know if they are well?"

The *Quincense* was apparently anchored next to a tiny island off the coast, with men from the Thirty-Seventh, as well as some from the Cel navy, keeping her crew under guard. Before she'd dispatched Bait north, he and Magnius had been running messages back and forth, but now she had no contact with them at all other than what the Cel deigned to tell her.

"Nothing new," Servius answered. "But we'll be sending supplies and some of the injured to join that outpost soon enough. I hear anything of note, I'll let you know."

She twisted a braid around one finger, grimacing at the state her hair was in without her aunt Yedda to put in fresh braids. She looked fuzzy and unkempt, but her appearance hadn't been a priority. What would her aunt say if she knew of all the things Teriana had done? If she learned about Teriana and Marcus? Would she, or any of the rest of the crew, understand?

Was it right to ask them to?

They worked through the day, only pausing when Servius's stomach let out a ferocious growl. "I'm starving," he declared to the legionnaires standing guard. "One of you boys get some grub for us. Buy it from a civilian—I'm sick of the slop we're serving in camp." He tossed one of them a coin. "Enough for all here, plus three. I've a mighty hunger."

Shaking her head to clear her thoughts, Teriana glanced at the ledger she was holding, adding the totals in her head. Already the amount was staggering, and it didn't even include the bricks of precious metals that were piling high in a building near the forge.

When the food arrived, Servius called a halt to the work, leaning against a moldering tapestry, his feet resting on bolts of silk that were marked with dark stains that looked suspiciously like blood. He was easily one of the largest men she'd ever met who wasn't an actual giant, his tunic sleeves stretched around biceps thicker than her thighs. That, more than the hue of his brown skin, spoke to his Atlian heritage, the island province known to breed people of impressive stature. That, in combination with what was undeniably an attractive face, made Servius tremendously popular with Arinoquian women.

"So," he said. "You going to tell me what happened on your way back from Galinha? What we know is mostly what was ascertained from what was left behind, if you get my meaning."

Bodies. Of the young men who'd been watching over her, including Quintus and Miki. Tears pricked in her eyes, knowing they'd died protecting her. "We received Marcus's message recalling us to camp. Set out the next morning. We were about halfway back when Quintus noticed something was off." She shook her head, trying to wipe away the remembered fear rising in her chest. "Was too quiet. And then next thing I knew, arrows were flying."

Her chin trembled, and she took a mouthful of food to hide it, though her appetite was long gone. "Quintus got hit first, but then it was madness. There were so many of them, coming from all sides."

"How many?"

"I don't know." She shook her head. "Fifty. Maybe more. They all wore Urcon's colors."

"Big force to commit to catching one girl with uncertain worth, no?" Servius watched her intently, and she was reminded that he wasn't the third most senior officer of the Thirty-Seventh just because the men liked him. "Especially with two legions camped on Urcon's doorstep."

This was where she needed to be careful. No one but her and Marcus knew about the traitor, and as much as she trusted Servius, it was Marcus's secret to reveal. She shrugged. "They darted me in the neck, and I lost consciousness. When I awoke, I was in the hut where Marcus and Gibzen found me. Their leader—"

"This the Ashok that we're looking for?"

Teriana forced herself to nod, her skin growing cold as the corrupted's face rose in her thoughts. "He told me that they intended to use me to negotiate a withdrawal, but that I was dead either way. That they were only buying time for the mercenaries to arrive."

"It's always helpful when your enemy is a big talker." Servius picked up another skewer. "What did he look like? Marcus passed on a few details, but the bastard has proven elusive."

"Gamdeshian," she answered. "Skin a bit darker than yours. Chin-length black hair. Silver earrings running up his left ear." It was easy to provide the details, her memory of Ashok as clear as though he stood in front of her.

"Eye color?"

Black pits encircled with flame. Like staring into the heart of the underworld.

But she couldn't tell him that—not when she'd kept the knowledge of the corrupted from Marcus. He already knew about healers, and if he learned about the corrupted's powers, he'd inevitably start to wonder what other secrets she was hiding. "Dark."

"I'll pass the details on to Gibzen. It was his men who were killed, so he's taken the hunt on as a matter of personal interest."

He wasn't the only one. Marcus had not taken the news that he'd been betrayed by one of his men well at all, and that the traitor might be his closest friend only made it worse. But as much as it had been Marcus who'd been betrayed, Teriana also wanted vengeance.

"I'm sorry for what happened." She rubbed at her eyes, her chest tight. "Quintus and Miki were my friends. The last thing I ever wanted was them dead."

"Well, then, you're in luck," Servius said, wiping his hands on the moldy bolt of silk he was sitting on. "Because when I heard this story from them, they were still very much alive."

6

LYDIA

Cleaned up and composed, Lydia walked silently through the temple corridors, following the directions a servant had given her to a level with more lush appointments. Her new boots sank into the deep carpets, the air far warmer than it was in the dormitories. Stopping in front of an ornate wooden door, she knocked once.

"Enter," a muffled voice responded, and pushing open the door, Lydia stepped inside.

The room was large, the floors covered with thick carpets and the air kept warm by the flames in the large fireplace to her left. The wall opposite to the door was full of windows, the drapes pulled back to allow in the muted sunlight. Quindor sat with his back to the view, bent over a heavy desk that was covered with papers.

"Take a seat, Lydia." Then he pushed a large box in front of her. "An assortment of spectacles. Hopefully you can find a pair that suits, for I'm afraid there are no lens makers in Mudaire."

"Where did these all come from?" she asked, trying on a gold-rimmed pair but swiftly discarding them, as they made her vision even more blurry.

Quindor gave a soft cough. "They are from those who no longer need them."

From the dead. The contents of her stomach threatened to rise, but she swallowed them back down. Now was no time for squeamishness.

"We need to discuss your role in the patrols."

"Patrols?" she asked, trying on three more pairs of spectacles before settling on a pair that improved her vision satisfactorily.

"The blighters are almost impossible to identify by anyone other than one of Hegeria's Marked," Quindor responded. "The trainees join the guard on their patrols in order to identify and put down those who have succumbed."

"Put down?" She tried and failed to keep the acid from her voice. "They are human beings, not rabid dogs."

"*Were* human beings," the Grand Master corrected. "Now only corpses animated by the Seventh's power. You must vanquish from your mind any notion that they are otherwise, Lydia, or risk madness."

"Is this why I'm here, then?" she demanded. "To be used to hunt down people we should be trying to save?" That wasn't the battle she'd agreed to fight. She had come believing she'd be working to find a cure—a way to save her people. Not . . . *this.*

Quindor leaned back in his chair. "They cannot be saved. Do you think we haven't tried?"

"Clearly not hard enough!" She dug her nails into the arms of her chair. "The blight still mars the land, which means people will continue to fall ill. If the answer is to kill them all, soon Mudamora will be populated by corpses!"

Quindor eyed her for a long moment. "Your passion is commendable, Lydia, if misdirected. The Royal Army is occupied with clearing the kingdom of the remains of the Derin army, but once that task is complete we can begin to discuss what might be done to stop the blight from infecting more people."

"What about the tenders?" She remembered the conversation she'd once had with Killian. His theory that the blight might be caused by individuals marked by the Seventh. "Why haven't they been brought to address the problem?"

"Because they are all dead."

"*All?*" Her stomach dropped. "How is that possible?"

The Grand Master sighed. "The endless toil of forcing the earth to yield in order to provide food for the Royal Army. Our own ranks were decimated by the war. There are more trainees here in the temple than living healers left in Mudamora."

So few . . . And she remembered Killian explaining to her that if the Marked weren't where they were needed to protect the people, it damaged faith in the Six. And that was what gave the Corrupter his power. "If that is the case, then we must find a cure before it spreads."

Quindor folded his hands, watching her over them. "I can see that you'll not be swayed until you've seen the proof yourself. Come."

He took her into the sublevel of the tower, the circular staircase illuminated by candles that cast dancing shadows over the stone steps. Much like the levels above ground, the corridor ran in a circle with doors on the exterior of the hallway, though what lay in the rooms beyond, she had no notion. Ahead, she caught sight of two guards standing outside of one of the doors, both of whom inclined their head to Quindor as he approached. "Grand Master."

"This is Lydia," he said to them. "One of Hegeria's Marked who has recently joined us."

They lowered their heads respectfully. "Marked One."

It was all she could do not to cringe at the honorific, instead smiling at them.

"Before we go in," Quindor said, "I'll remind you that what you will hear is not the voice of a child, but the voice of the Seventh god. And the Corrupter is nothing if not a liar."

At her nod, he pulled a key from his robes and inserted it into the lock, then swung the door open, allowing Lydia to step inside.

She'd expected to find a dungeon cell. Chains. A cage.

Instead, Lydia's eyes fell upon a room with more comfortable appointments than her own. The walls were paneled with tapestries depicting each of the Six, the floor layered with carpets, and the bed at the center covered with thick blankets. Several lamps burned brightly, and a brazier gave off needed heat.

And on the floor, wearing a pink woolen dress and playing with a puzzle, was a little brunette girl. At the sound of them, the child turned, and a gasp tore from Lydia's face as she recognized her as one of the orphans who'd lived with Finn in the sewers. A girl whose life Lydia had saved from illness.

A girl who now possessed no more essence of life in her than the stone floor she stood upon.

"Grand Master Quindor," the girl said, smiling wide. "It has been so long since you visited."

"I've been away, Emmy," he answered. "Only just returned. How do you feel?"

"Well." The girl—Emmy—beamed. Then her upturned grey eyes moved to Lydia, her head cocking slightly. "I know you."

Lydia's blood chilled, her mind recoiling at the idea that the words were coming not from a little girl, but from a dark god.

"You were one of the Princess's guards!"

"Yes." Lydia's voice croaked, and she coughed to clear her throat. "I also saved your life in the sewers. Do you remember that?"

"That was you!" Emmy bounded to her feet, the pink ribbons on her braids bouncing on her shoulders, and Lydia had to steel herself from taking a step back. "Finn told us it was Hegeria herself."

"Finn likes to tell stories. It was me."

"Oh!" The girl darted across the room, flinging her arms around Lydia's waist and squeezing tightly. "I remember your face sparkled like diamonds. You looked like a princess of the north."

Lydia's heart thundered against her rib cage, her fingers like ice as she placed a hand against the girl's back, feeling the measured rise and fall of breath, certain that if she pressed her ear to Emmy's chest she'd hear the beating of a heart. Everything about her appeared alive and vital.

But Lydia's mark told her a very different story.

One could not heal the dead, she knew that. Except abandoning Emmy to the fate of the child she'd watched murdered on the street made Lydia sick.

Quindor was watching, his face grim. "Try, if you must."

She had to. She had to know.

"Emmy, will you sit for a moment?"

At the girl's nod, Lydia led her to the bed, lifting her on top of it and then sitting next to her. Then she took a deep breath and took hold of Emmy's hand, feeling the warmth of the girl's skin against her own.

And she pushed.

It was as though something sank its claws into her and yanked, dragging life from Lydia with painful violence. A scream tore from her throat, and then she was on her back on the floor, Quindor kneeling next to her. "Many others, including me, have tried to bring her back. But one can't heal death." He looked to the girl. "Thank you, Emmy."

A sniffle filled Lydia's ears, and she looked up to find the little girl weeping. Climbing to her feet, she sat next to Emmy again, careful to keep her hands a safe distance. "It's not your fault."

"The Grand Master tells me that I am dead," Emmy whispered. "But I don't feel dead." She looked up at Lydia. "Is he telling the truth?"

Lydia bit her bottom lip, then said, "There is no life in you."

Emmy's chin trembled. She reached into her pocket, pulling out something that glinted in the lamplight.

A gold-and-onyx cuff link in the shape of a galloping horse.

"He told me that he'd protect me," the girl whispered, then she dropped the cuff link on the floor with a clatter. "He lied."

He did protect you! Lydia wanted to scream, but instead bit the insides of her cheeks until she tasted blood.

"Calm yourself, Emmy. We will leave you to your toys." Quindor motioned Lydia to follow him outside, closing the door firmly behind them.

"That"—she pointed back toward the room holding Emmy—"is

cruelty of the purest form. No matter what has been done to her body, her mind is intact. She's a little girl who doesn't understand what's happening to her."

Quindor sighed. "What you were speaking to wasn't human, Lydia."

"But she has Emmy's memories," Lydia protested, wishing she could calm her galloping heart. "How could—"

"The Corrupter know such things?" Quindor interrupted. "Because he is a *god.*"

"But she's nothing like those monsters that attacked the night of Malahi's ball. Those were violent and mindless and terrifying. Emmy . . ." She broke off at the expression on the Grand Master's face.

"Is dead." He caught her elbow, leading her around the hallway. "And what we are seeing is nothing more than a shift in the Corrupter's strategy to win this war. Before, those infected with blight served to terrify and kill, but now they serve a more insidious purpose: to destroy faith in the Six from the inside by undermining the Marked. By making the living followers of the Six believe the Marked have failed them."

The sound of Killian's cuff link falling to the floor echoed through her head, and Lydia's skin chilled.

"Yes, the cuff link." Quindor rose the stairs, his boots making soft pats against the stone. "She said much the same to me when first we brought her here. Truth twisted to a poison in the ears of all who'd listen. How many did she tell it to before we caught her? How many now see Lord Calorian as having failed in his duty to protect the kingdom and its people? How many have lost faith in Tremon as a result?"

A terrifying question, but all Lydia could think of was how much it would hurt Killian to hear it. How he'd blame himself as much and more than anyone else who heard it.

"The blight itself has ceased its spread, but we have no notion of how many of the infected were able to flee during the evacuation. Even now, dozens, perhaps more, of them could be spreading their poisonous words throughout the kingdom—throughout all of Reath!—with no one the wiser. They must be stopped, and Hegeria's Marked are the only ones capable of doing so."

There was logic in his words, but each time Lydia blinked, she remembered Emmy in the sewer tunnels the first night she and Killian had started healing the orphans. How the girl had rallied from her illness beneath Lydia's hands. How the first thing she'd done when she'd recovered was fling her arms around Killian's neck, her faith in him absolute. It was hard to believe that girl was gone, but Lydia's mark didn't lie.

"If the blighters are so dangerous, why are you keeping Emmy alive? Why not just"—she remembered his words from before—"put her down?"

"Because it will allow us to see if the blight continues to evolve," the Grand Master replied as they reached the top of the stairs, the main level full of soldiers, as well as dozens of young healers in white robes and cloaks. "And because she reminds me both of the evil we face and of the goodness we have lost. Something you should keep in mind, because tomorrow morning, it's time you joined the hunt."

7

KILLIAN

"You look like shit."

Killian didn't answer, only poked at the fire with a stick as High Lady Dareena Falorn sat on the ground next to him. Since the battle had ended, they'd both been charged with chasing down what remained of the Derin army, but he'd had little chance to talk to the woman who'd been responsible for most of his training. Who, more than any other, had stood as his mentor. And who had saved his ass, arriving at Alder's Ford with her army right as his lines were being overrun by Rufina's forces.

"Sonia tells me you aren't sleeping."

"Didn't realize you two had met." His voice was raspy, and he coughed to clear it, melted snowflakes dripping down the sides of his face.

"I hired all of Malahi's former guards, since you seem content to abandon them," Dareena answered. "But Sonia has chosen to remain as your lieutenant."

"If she wants to keep the job, she needs to mind her own business."

"She's worried about you, so perhaps don't be an ass." Dareena held her hands over the fire. "She thought I might be able to talk you into seeing sense. I told her that would be hard given that you're devoid of the quality, but she's a persistent one. Am I to assume this is about the girl?"

"Which one?" He gave a violent poke at the fire, sending sparks flying and thinking of Bercola. "I seem to be in the habit of getting the girls I'm supposed to protect killed."

"Lydia," Dareena said, "isn't dead."

"It's a matter of time." Killian flung the stick aside, wishing he had something to drink, but supplies in the Royal Army camp were lacking. "There are fewer than a hundred healers left in all of Mudamora, and you know as well as I do that Serrick has no compunction against using them hard."

"Then why didn't you stop them from taking her?"

The smoke shifted to blow into his eyes, and he closed them against the sting. As he did, a vision of Lydia on horseback filled them. Of her mouth forming the words *I choose this,* then of her turning her back and riding away. "She asked me not to."

"Then she has chosen her fate."

"She didn't have a choice," he snapped. "She knew what it would mean for me to fight her free, and she sacrificed herself to keep me from doing it. To protect me."

"You always did have a way with the ladies."

Anger flushed through him, and he rounded on her. "You think this is something to jest about, Dareena? Something to make light of? I—" He broke off, but he couldn't silence the words within his own head. *I love her.*

The High Lady of House Falorn regarded him with steady green eyes, strands of midnight hair framing her pale face. She wore her armor, snow piling in little peaks on her silvered shoulders, sword resting across her lap. Marked by Tremon as surely as he was himself. The one person who should understand.

"Do you truly believe that the only reason Lydia went with Quindor was to protect you?" she asked. "Hegeria chose to mark her, Killian. And the gods' choices are not at random. Has it occurred to you that this might be the fate she wants?"

He looked away, unable to stop images of Lydia healing orphan children in the sewers beneath Mudaire from crossing through his mind. Her unwillingness to let any of them suffer while she had the strength to save them. Hegeria had chosen well when she'd chosen Lydia, but it was the men in power around her whom Killian feared.

"She was marked to serve the followers of the Six," Dareena said softly. "As were you. And I know it grieves you that her path is not at your side, but that doesn't mean you stop walking. Serrick has put you in a position where you can truly make a difference to Mudamora. Don't squander it."

Before he could answer, a group of armed soldiers approached the fire, their ranks parting to reveal King Serrick himself. It was the first time Killian had seen the man since he'd offered Killian the opportunity to follow in his father's footsteps and command the Royal Army. It had been his dream since he was a child, but he wished it were under the rule of a different king.

Or queen.

Dareena rose, and Killian joined her, bowing low.

"You've both served Mudamora well," Serrick said. "The Derin army is little more than corpses on the ground, and those who remain alive flee back across the wall. The war is won."

It doesn't feel won.

Clearing his throat, Killian said, "I'd like to take five hundred men and press into Derin territory, Your Grace. For Rufina to have brought so many men across the Liratoras suggests they have a xenthier stem at their disposal, and we need to secure it lest she bring more men to make another attempt."

"With thirty thousand dead, I think not even that witch capable of rallying another host so soon," Serrick answered. "And we've more pressing concerns."

How anything could be more pressing, Killian didn't know. "Your Grace—"

"Anukastre has taken advantage of our distraction, and their raiders successfully stole a great deal of gold from one of our mines," Serrick interrupted. "Five hundred men you will have, but it will be to lead south to put an end to the raiders."

Killian stared at him. "You want me to protect your *gold mines?*" Gold mines that sat along the southern border between Mudamora and Anukastre, which meant they were about as far from Mudaire—and Lydia—as one could get.

"*Mudamora's* gold mines," Serrick answered, his face devoid of expression. "And it is gold that the kingdom sorely needs to rebuild. Unlike the remaining rabble of the Derin army, the Anuk are a true threat, which means I must send my strongest to meet them with force."

"But—"

"The gods chose me to rule this kingdom, Lord Calorian. And to lead its marked. Select your forces and do it quickly, because at dawn, you ride for the Rowenes stronghold of Rotahn."

8

MARCUS

Sitting on a stool back in his tent, Marcus stared blindly at the three remaining chests of coins he had in his possession. Two silver. One gold.

The silver would all go to paying the men their next round of wages, the pittance they received for endlessly risking their lives in the name of the Empire. It was in his power to withhold the coin, if needed for other purposes, but he'd never done so and wouldn't now.

"Sir?"

He turned his head to see one of his men step inside, paper grasped in his hand. "Yes?"

"Racker sent a count," the young man answered, approaching to hand Marcus the papers. "And a letter arrived for you, origins unknown."

Nodding, Marcus waited until the soldier had retreated out of the tent, then unfolded the first scrap of paper, recognizing the Thirty-Seventh's head surgeon's precise scrawl.

Two hundred thirty-three.

His chest hollowed, but he shoved away the grief in favor of retrieving a piece of paper in his own hand that sat waiting on the table. He added the number to it, then finalized the mathematics.

It was a start. In truth, a start greater than he'd hoped possible, but only if this gambit worked.

Marcus took several gulps of water from the cup sitting next to him, about to rise, when his gaze fell on the other letter that had arrived. Specifically, on the purple seal stamped in the shape of a flower.

Picking it up, he cracked the wax and unfolded the thick paper, a separate scrap falling loose onto the table as he did. The letter was written in Trader's Tongue, or Mudamorian, as he'd come to know it—the language spread across all of Reath by virtue of the Maarin's use of it. He spoke it well enough, but reading it was another matter, and he sorely wished Teriana was here. For more reasons than just his need for a translator.

Greetings to Marcus, Commander of the Armies of the Celendor Empire,

We have recently learned of your arrival on the shores of Arinoquia and of your desire to facilitate trade between the nations of the West and your homeland. It is our sincerest wish to come to a peaceable and mutually profitable arrangement between our nations. We are desirous of meeting you face-to-face to discuss terms—a meeting we look to with great anticipation.

Her Royal Majesty, Queen Erdene of Katamarca

He'd hoped for this. Katamarca was not a military power, but they were the breadbasket of the Southern Continent. An alliance with them would be advantageous on many levels. Then his eyes went to the letter's postscript.

Please find enclosed a token of our goodwill.

Frowning, he picked up the scrap of paper that had been included with the letter, turning it over. It was written in an unfamiliar language, which he surmised was Katamarcan. But he didn't need to understand what was written to recognize the handwriting. Or the name signed at the bottom.

Teriana, of the Quincense

His stomach hollowed, his fingers feeling the texture of the paper, which was identical to that the legions used. And written in pencil, rather than ink. Supplies taken from his own command tent, which meant it was pointless to hope it predated her capture by Cassius.

What did it say?

Nothing good. For what better way to earn the goodwill of a foreign power than to reveal a traitor in its midst.

What did you expect? a bitter voice whispered inside his head. *She's not here of her own volition. You know she wants you to fail, to be forced into a retreat to Celendor. You know you two are enemies.*

Yet knowing all these things did nothing to ease the pain that replaced the hollowness in his stomach. Even if she'd sent this note when they'd first arrived in Arinoquia, before they'd become involved, she'd still never confessed to having done so. Had been content with allowing the move she'd put in motion to play out.

You can't trust her.

"Do you have time to talk?"

Felix's voice filled his ears, and Marcus lifted his head to find his second-in-command standing at the entrance to his tent.

"About what?" The words came out sharper than he intended, and Felix grimaced before moving farther inside.

"You need to get some sleep."

"Noted. Is there something else you need?"

Silence stretched between them, the tension strange and unfamiliar. While he and Felix had fought many times over many things over the years, it had never been like this. Then again, no matter how hard they'd butted heads, he'd never had cause to question his best friend's loyalty.

"Yeah, I . . ." Felix's brow furrowed. "Are things all right with us?" Then he gave a violent shake of his head. "Don't answer that. I know you're angry at me for advising you to proceed with the battle rather than to negotiate with enemy demands."

"You advised me to allow them to cut Teriana up and send me the pieces rather than to pursue a different strategy."

"Yeah." Felix rocked on his heels. The tips of his ears, just visible through hair that needed to be cut, were bright red. "I'm not going to lie and say that I think what you did was right. That false retreat nearly resulted in us being crushed between two armies, and while we still would've won, a lot of our brothers would've died. It was only luck that you got back in time, and you know what Wex says about luck."

Wex was commandant of Campus Lescendor and Marcus's mentor. He was also famous for saying that a good commander should never rely on luck, because luck always ran out when you needed it most.

"You chose Teriana over your own brothers, and *everyone* knows it, Marcus. They know you gambled with their lives to save a girl."

It was the truth, though he hadn't realized how high the stakes were when he'd thrown the dice. Yet even if he had, Marcus knew his decision would've been the same. "Your point?"

"The men are letting it slide because you pulled a victory out of your ass, the way you always do. But you can't put her ahead of them again. You just . . . can't."

Marcus didn't answer, only stared Felix down, refusing to bend. *Are you a traitor?*

"I don't like her," Felix continued, his gaze fixing on the table between them. "I think she's a smart-ass who believes she can say and do whatever she wants because you have her back."

True, except that Teriana would say and do whatever she wanted even if she stood alone.

"But that doesn't mean I want anything bad to happen to her. I know she didn't ask to be put in this position and is just doing what she needs to do to survive."

Felix was trying to cover his tracks. What other purpose could he have for saying all of this? For trying to make it seem he wouldn't have been delighted if Teriana had died at Ashok's hands? And then trying to cast the blame on Marcus for the mercenary army nearly catching them unaware, despite his actions having put them in that position in the first place. Anger coiled in Marcus's stomach, but he kept it in check, because he could not act without *proof.*

Felix sighed heavily. "It feels like you've forgotten that she's fighting for the other side. I hope you keep in mind that having you wrapped around her little finger is to her advantage, not ours."

Marcus's hand tightened, and Teriana's note crumbled where he gripped it. "Noted. Anything else?"

"No." Felix's jaw worked back and forth. "Everything you asked for has been done or is being done. We're watching the clans to make sure they aren't thinking of moving against us or one another, but thus far, it appears as though they're content to wait for their payout."

"Good. You may go."

"Sir." Felix saluted sharply, then turned to leave. But then he hesitated. "I can't watch your back if you keep pushing me away."

"Then it's a good thing I can watch my own."

Felix flinched, but said nothing else, only strode out of the tent, leaving Marcus alone.

You can't trust anyone.

The thought settled heavily on his mind, weighing him down more than exhaustion. Amarin chose that moment to enter the tent, puttering about and putting things back in their places. Busywork, and having lived with him for eight years, Marcus knew his servant was about to start mothering him.

Sure enough, Amarin said, "Your armor needs repairs. I'll have it done now so you'll have it back when you need it."

Teriana's note still gripped in his fist, Marcus stood and allowed the older man to remove his armor, which was sporting several dents.

"There's wash water in the back." Amarin gathered up all the pieces, frowning at one of the dents. "When should I wake you?"

"Three hours," Marcus answered, his own voice distant in his ears. He went into the rear tent, his eyes flicking to Teriana's bedroll. Her stack of belongings.

Strained muscles moving stiffly, he pulled off his clothes, tossing them in a corner, and glanced down at his body. He was covered in livid purple bruises and his ribs throbbed, but it was his throat, which had been nearly crushed, that hurt worst of all. It ached when he spoke. When he swallowed. When he breathed.

Ignoring the wash water, he lay down on the side that hurt less, staring at the knuckles on his bruised hand, which had been split in the fight and were now crusted with scabs.

And his head. His head felt like it was being crushed between the hands of a giant, every beat of his heart thunder in his ears.

Just go to sleep.

Except everything hurt and his mind kept flipping from problem to problem, refusing to settle. Refusing to give him any peace.

Reaching across to Teriana's belongings, he retrieved a small silk sachet sitting on top. A ship had arrived today from the island where the *Quincense* was anchored, and they'd had a parcel of clothing that her aunt Yedda had sent. Pressing the sachet to his nose, he inhaled cedar and orange blossoms and sea. Scents he associated with Teriana.

But the reminder of her only made him feel worse.

Could he trust her? Or was Felix right that she was only manipulating his emotions to achieve her own ends? Was any of what he believed was between them *real*?

Tossing the sachet back on the pile of her clothes, he squeezed his eyes shut, running through the myriad of exercises he'd been taught to fall asleep, even in the worst of conditions.

But his mind refused to be silenced.

Rolling, he flinched as pain lanced up his side, but then his gaze latched on his pile of weapons, his belt twisted through the mess of metal. He reached out an arm and caught hold of it, unbuckling his belt pouch, fingers moving through the contents until they found a small glass vial at the bottom.

He stared at the foggy contents that he'd had no use for in a long time. Narcotics for pain, which he'd gotten in the habit of keeping on him when the Thirty-Seventh was in Bardeen. When they'd been finishing their training under the guidance of the Twenty-Ninth Legion and its legatus, Hostus.

Old hatred and fear twisted through his guts at the memory of the older legatus. "You're not sixteen anymore," he muttered at himself. "And the Twenty-Ninth is on the far side of the world." Shoving the thoughts away, he unscrewed the top of the vial. Racker kept tight control over his narcotics, particularly this one, but there were certain advantages to being in command, and if Marcus wanted more, he could get it.

Rolling onto his back, Marcus measured two drops onto his tongue, hesitated, then added a third. He'd barely managed to return the vial to his belt pouch when his vision split into two. And then into three.

Curling in on himself, Marcus let out a slow breath, his body relaxing as the pain of his injuries faded, as a haze flowed over his thoughts, slowly silencing the prattle, dulling the emotions. But as he slipped from consciousness, one thought remained, loud and desperate.

Please let it be real.

9

TERIANA

They set up for the division of the treasure in a field just beyond the ridge overlooking Aracam. The same field where Marcus had defeated Urcon's mercenary army as it had tried to attack him from the rear.

Slaughtered was probably a better word.

Though days had passed, piles of dead still smoldered, the rain making it difficult to burn the thousands of bodies, and the stench of rotting meat hung heavily in the air. The mud beneath Teriana's boots was stained a dark red from all the blood that was spilled, and every which way she looked, there were *pieces* that had been missed. Decaying fingers and bits of flesh mixed in with arrowheads and broken weapons, all of it sinking into the damp earth.

It was a place that should be razed and then avoided until the land erased the evidence of the horror, but instead, Marcus had ordered his men to set up a tent in the middle of the field, under which they'd placed a long table. Seven chairs on one side, a singular chair on the other. The treasure she'd helped value sat to the side of the table, stacks of gold and silver bricks, open chests full of glittering jewels, and pieces of artwork wrapped in waxed cloth to protect them from endless rain.

She, Marcus, and Servius stood under the cover of the tent, and behind them were another fifty of the Thirty-Seventh. The legionnaires stood in neat rows, spears upright and shields held just so. Beneath their helmets, their faces were devoid of expression, and though Teriana knew most of their names, they no longer seemed the young men she'd sat around a fire with, but rather fifty killing machines.

"Thank you," Marcus said to both her and Servius, "for accomplishing this task so swiftly."

This was the first time she'd seen him since he'd left her in the treasure vaults with Servius, and she noted the shadows under his eyes were worse than before, his golden skin blanched and waxy. *Has he slept at all?*

"What's the plan?" Servius asked, and there was a slight edge to his voice. As though, improbable as it was, he knew even less about what was going on than she did.

"We agree to the division of the wealth," Marcus answered. "And then, hopefully, everyone takes their cut and returns to their lands."

And then what? she wanted to ask, but before she could, Servius jerked his chin outwards. "Here they come."

From across the field, Teriana saw flickers of motion as the Arinoquian imperators stepped from the trees, each followed by fifty of their own warriors. Ereni was the first to reach the table, the older woman's green eyes fixed on Marcus rather than the gleaming treasure.

The same could not be said of the others, though Teriana could hardly blame them. This was *their* wealth. Wealth that had been stolen from them during the long years of Urcon's tyranny and which they'd fought to get back. It would change the lives of everyone within the clans, allowing them both the means and the opportunity to trade with other nations. Would allow them to thrive, if they were wise in how they used it.

Once all the imperators had reached the table, Marcus inclined his head. "Shall we sit?"

Pulling out his chair, Marcus settled into it, the metal of his armor clinking as he rested his forearms on the table, seemingly entirely at ease. The imperators followed suit, the representatives who'd assisted with the counting moving to stand behind their leaders. Teriana glanced up at Servius, and when the big legionnaire nodded, she took a few steps forward to stand at Marcus's elbow.

"You've all been provided an account of Urcon's treasury?" When the Arinoquians nodded, he plucked up a piece of paper from the table. "As confirmation, then. One hundred sixty bricks of gold. Two hundred forty-three bricks of silver . . ." He continued, voice holding all the emotion of one reading a market list. "Your representatives swear to the accuracy of these figures?"

"I swear it," Ereni's representative said, then stepped back. The chorus ran the length of the table, and then all their eyes flicked to her.

"Teriana?" Marcus asked, not looking up. "Is it accurate?"

Her palms were sweating and her throat felt bone dry, though there was no reason for it. The treasure was all accounted for. She'd watched it be loaded, had counted it as it had been unloaded, and yet unease twisted her guts like bad fish stew. "I swear it."

"Good." Marcus set aside the paper and picked up another. "As is your custom, the profits of this venture will be divided based on the number of fighting men and women whom you contributed to the collective force. Is this correct?"

"You know it is." Ereni pushed her greying blond braid back over her shoulder. "I told you so myself, so let's get on with it." Rising, she rounded her chair and leaned on the back of it, eyes moving over her fellow imperators. "As agreed, we break it into fifteenths." She rattled off the numbers, then said, "It is settled, then?"

Marcus coughed. "With respect, Ereni. I'm afraid I do not concur with your calculations."

All the imperators turned to glare at him, and Teriana's stomach dropped.

Picking up another piece of paper, Marcus eyed it. "You all provided me your numbers prior to the battle, and by my calculation, I am entitled to nine-fifteenths, or sixty percent of the profits of the taking of Aracam. Ereni, you are entitled to—"

Ereni jerked out her sword.

Before Teriana could even reach for her own weapon, the imperatrix had the blade pressed against Marcus's throat, her wiry arm steady. "Stay where you are, girl. And you"—she pressed the blade harder, droplets of blood dribbling down Marcus's throat—"tell your men to stay back."

Behind her, Teriana could hear the legionnaires moving, but she didn't dare look to see what they were doing.

"Servius." Marcus's voice was steady. "Hold."

The men behind stilled to silence. Close as they were, there wouldn't be anything they could do if Ereni decided she wanted Marcus dead.

Teriana lifted her hands, taking a shuffling step closer until the imperatrix's glare stopped her in her tracks. "Ereni, please don't do this. I know you're angry, and I can understand why, but killing him isn't the answer. Put away the sword and let's negotiate."

"Why am I not surprised that you'd try to negotiate for this thieving boy's life?"

"Thieving?"

Marcus's voice was brittle with anger, the first emotion Teriana had seen from him throughout this cursed meeting. He jerked to his feet, and only Ereni pulling back her sword kept him from cutting his own jugular. He rested his hands on the table, leaning across it. And though the rain hammered on the canvas above them, the *splat splat splat* of his blood dripping on the papers was all Teriana could hear.

"Allow me to remind you that you'd have *none* of this if not for my men. That if we had not arrived on your shores and offered you an alliance, all of this"—he gestured at the treasure—"would remain collecting dust in Urcon's palace."

"We didn't need you to defeat Urcon," Ereni snapped, but Teriana didn't miss how her gaze went to the tabletop every time another drop of blood splattered against the papers.

"And yet you were content to *use* us for the sake of achieving it sooner." Marcus tilted his head. "Out of desperation? Out of fear? Out of greed?" He laughed, the tone of it different than Teriana had ever heard from him, and it made her skin crawl. "Or maybe it was because it was *easier* to let me and mine take all the risks while you and yours planned to take all the reward."

One of the other imperators leapt to his feet. "You've got balls, boy, I'll—"

"Sit. Down."

Though he was a hardened warrior, the imperator's sun-darkened skin paled as he met Marcus's gaze.

Splat.

The man sat, though Ereni remained on her feet, naked blade still in her hand.

"Since we arrived on your shores," Marcus continued, "my men have fought to defend your lands and your people from Urcon and his raiders. Bled to achieve the peace you wanted. Though in hindsight, perhaps your goals were less lofty than I hoped." His eyes flicked meaningfully to the treasure before returning to Ereni's face.

Splat.

"Allow me to remind you that you wanted peace as well," she said. "That you wanted to make our shores safe for your *Empire's* trade. You have as much to gain from this as we do."

"I do want peace in Arinoquia." Marcus slowly panned the imperators. "And yet I don't feel that I have it."

Teriana's pulse roared in her ears, her chest tightening as the tension in the group ratcheted up tenfold, the air so thick as to be nearly unbreathable. She understood now why Marcus had chosen this ground for the meeting, surrounded by stinking, smoldering piles of those his legions had slaughtered. Why they stood on ground soaked with blood.

Several of the imperators glanced toward the distant tree line, and Teriana knew what they were looking for, because she was searching for the same. Signs of motion. Signs this was a trap to lure the leaders of the clans to one place and then kill them all.

There'd been no sign of the Thirty-Seventh mobilizing in their camp outside Aracam, but she knew all too well how quickly that could change. That thousands of men could be standing out of sight on the plain beneath the ridge, waiting for the command to attack.

And the imperators knew it, too.

"According to *your* customs, as allies who fought alongside one another as equals, we are entitled to a portion of the defeated enemy's wealth. According to *your* laws, the amount we are entitled to is decided by numbers. For you to stand here and say otherwise tells me that not only do you *not* consider us your allies, but that you consider the lives of the two hundred thirty-three brothers I lost in this fight *worthless*."

Splat.

No one spoke. No one even seemed to breathe. The imperator who'd objected coughed, then said, "Perhaps we've been hasty. Ereni, sit. Let us negotiate so that we might all remain friends."

Neither Marcus nor Ereni moved, blood pooling on the table between them.

Sit down, Teriana wanted to scream at Marcus. *Don't be like this!*

The battle of wills seemed a stalemate, then abruptly, Ereni sheathed her sword and sat. Marcus waited a heartbeat longer, then settled into his chair, revealing that his throat was coated with blood. Part of her was afraid for how badly he was hurt, but the other part wanted to slap him, because it hadn't needed to go this way.

"What amount would you be willing to accept as compensation?" Ereni asked, the words clipped.

"You would treat us as mercenaries?" Marcus huffed out a breath of disgust. "We are legions of the Celendor Empire. We do *not* fight for hire. You, Ereni, should be glad for that, else you'd be very much in my debt."

Teriana closed her eyes, struggling to keep her composure as she realized the depths of his strategy. The legions had paid for *everything* they'd taken in their time here, incurring not a single debt, while at the same time working for Ereni's clan without ever demanding compensation. Not giving the Arinoquians any cause to claim them anything but the perfect ally.

Had he known this moment would come?

Had he planned for this?

And what would he do, given that the Arinoquians were refusing to name him ally in this and he was refusing to be treated as a mercenary?

It was a stalemate that would end in violence if one of them didn't concede, and Teriana's gut told her that Marcus had no intention of backing down. And from the look on Ereni's face, neither did she.

Splat.

10

MARCUS

Marcus felt giddy, and more than a little light-headed, as they trooped back into camp, the horses struggling to pull the loaded wagons through the sticky mud. The wet bricks of gold and silver glinted in the faint sunlight, and his men moved from their camp-fires to watch as he walked toward his command tent.

He'd done it. Against the odds, he'd done it.

The commotion of the men drew Felix and Titus and the rest of those lingering over maps and strategies out into the rain, and his second's blue eyes widened as they lighted upon the procession. "What's all this?"

"I told you not to worry about our coffers." Stepping past Felix, Marcus ducked into the tent, handing his helmet to Amarin, who also took his sodden cloak. Picking up a bottle of rum and a stack of tin cups, he circled the table full of maps and paperwork, setting full cups in front of each of the stools.

The group followed him in, taking their places.

"I was under the impression you were organizing a split of Urcon's coffers among the clans, sir," Felix finally said. "Though it appears you had another plan in mind."

Servius snorted, then reached for one of the cups, which he drained in two long swallows. Slamming it down on the table hard enough to make it shake, he said, "I'm going to get some sleep." Without waiting to be dismissed, he strode from the tent.

Teriana picked up the cup in front of her, then shook her head and set it back down on the table. "I'm going to see after Quintus and Miki."

She was angry with him. Part of him wanted to go after her, to make her understand why he'd done things this way. But the other, spiteful part of himself thought she deserved a taste of how it felt to be deceived. "Gibzen, go with her. And *stay* with her."

The primus made a face but then drained his cup and started after Teriana. Pausing at the entrance to the tent, he said, "I'm neither suited to nor interested in this line of work, sir. You ought to consider choosing someone else from the ranks to guard your . . . *asset.*"

"I'll think on it," Marcus answered, his good mood rapidly fouling. "But for now, *you* will follow orders."

Gibzen gave a sour salute, then disappeared from sight, leaving Marcus alone with Felix and Titus.

Titus picked up his drink and took a mouthful but said nothing. Felix crossed his arms, expression grim, yet he also remained silent.

Which one of you is it? Marcus sipped at the rum but didn't taste it. *Which one of you betrayed me?*

"By Arinoquian custom, we were entitled to a portion of Urcon's wealth," he finally said. "Sixty percent, to be precise."

Titus grinned and shook his head. "Tidy profit for a half a day's work."

"I take it the imperators were not pleased." Felix jerked his chin toward Marcus's bleeding neck. "That needs stitches."

"Ereni doesn't like having things sprung upon her, but we came to an understanding," Marcus answered, curbing the urge to touch the stinging wound. "The allied clans will leave Aracam no later than tomorrow. They have what they came for, so there is no sense lingering. Especially not given the amount of gold they all have in their possession."

"You think they'll go to war with one another over it?" Titus asked.

"Inevitably." Polishing off his drink, Marcus reached for the bottle to refill it. "For more than a decade, they've had a common enemy in Urcon, but no longer. With nothing to unify them, I believe they'll return to raiding one another, as was their custom in their prior homeland."

"Unless you've gone and turned us into their common enemy," Felix snapped. "They believed that gold their due, and you took the lion's share of it."

"We're too big a fish for a single clan to war with."

"What if they unify?" Felix pushed his full cup out of the way and rested his elbows on the table. "I'm not saying we wouldn't win, but it would be heavy losses. Never mind that we're supposed to be focused on broadening our footprint while we search for xenthier paths back to the Empire. That is our mandate, unless you've forgotten. *Sir.*"

It had been the elephant in the room for a long time now that Marcus had taken no steps to search for xenthier stems, but it had been easy to brush aside the matter as a lesser priority than entrenching themselves in Arinoquia.

Except why was Felix bringing it up now?

Was it because his other attempt to get rid of Teriana had failed and he now saw finding xenthier paths as the surest way to achieve that end?

His head began to throb again, the tent pulsing along with it, and Marcus took another mouthful of rum despite knowing he was only making his headache worse. He needed sleep, but he'd only lie awake staring at canvas. And there was so much to be done.

"Well?"

He'd taken too long to answer. Gulping down another mouthful, Marcus set aside the cup. "That's why we'll be allying ourselves with the largest of them before they burn through all the gold and start looking for places to find more."

Felix blinked. "With Ereni? With the woman who, from the looks of it, just about slit your jugular?"

"Yes. I sent a messenger to her camp, so she should be here shortly."

Felix's ears darkened, his jaw working back and forth, but it was Titus who spoke. "It would seem, sir, that you have a good many plans that you haven't chosen to share with your officers."

"Yes, well . . ." Marcus stretched, both hearing and feeling his back crack. "I couldn't risk loose lips."

"Since when has that been a concern?" Felix demanded. "What is going on with you?"

Before Marcus could answer, one of his men stepped inside. "Imperatrix Ereni is here to see you, sir. Do you want me to have her wait?"

Marcus shook his head. "Send her in." To Titus and Felix, he said, "I want to speak to her alone."

Titus left without comment, but Felix muttered, "I'll wait outside in case she tries anything."

Ereni entered, pulling back the hood concealing her face. "You've a lot of nerve, boy. Speak quickly before I lose what patience in you I have left."

"I invited you here to propose an alliance."

The woman barked out a laugh. "Is that so? And what will this particular alliance cost me? I confess that the price of our last *alliance* was a bit rich for my blood."

"It will cost you nothing, for it will be an alliance that puts all the gold you lost to me back in the hands of you and your clan."

Ereni's brow furrowed. "Explain yourself."

Rising to his feet, Marcus drew a map out from under a pile, motioning for her to come closer. "I've marked the territories of the clans. Here, you can see the territory that officially"—he tipped his hand from side to side, because the clans had no firm borders— "belonged to Urcon's clan. I propose that with my help, you take control of his territory, including the port cities of Galinha and Aracam."

She huffed out a breath, then took a half step back from the table. "This—"

"Let me finish," he said, scowling as blood dripped from his neck to stain the map. "True wealth doesn't come from raiding, it comes from trade. From facilitating commerce. Urcon destroyed that opportunity by making the ports of both of Arinoquia's largest cities dangerous and unprofitable. But that could change with you in control."

"And what part would you play in this alliance?" Ereni asked once he was finished explaining his plans to turn Aracam into a center for trade.

"You'll need an extensive military to hold such a large territory, as well as to keep the peace within it," he said. "I can provide that, as well as serve as your advisor."

"In exchange for what?"

"In exchange for fifty percent of the taxes you earn from those in your territory for the next ten years."

"Twenty percent."

"Forty."

"Thirty."

He nodded. "Thirty it is, then. And of course, your understanding that once we have established trade routes with the Empire that your agreement will cease to be with me, but rather with the Senate."

Initially, the Senate would be all smiles and accommodating words. Except once they felt their position strong, they'd begin to push for concession after concession from the Arinoquians until the Empire was firmly in control of both politics and commerce, and then the majority of profit would flow east into patrician coffers.

But that was only a problem if xenthier paths were found.

And if not for the consequences to Teriana, Marcus would dream that they never were. Would dream of an opportunity to give his men a chance at a good life out from under the Empire's thumb. A good life for himself . . .

Picking up the bottle of rum, Ereni drank straight from the neck, her expression thoughtful as she considered his proposal. It wasn't only potential financial gain she was considering, but rather the consequences of declining his offer. What would happen to her clan if Marcus proposed an alliance with another imperator? Or what would happen if he decided to use his newfound wealth and existing military strength and took the territory for himself? She had no choice. He knew it, and so did she.

Slowly, she nodded. "You have your alliance, Legatus. But I will have these terms, and the minutiae of our deal, in writing. And I'll have Teriana's signature as witness. Given she's Maarin royalty, it will hold more weight."

"Pardon?" He gaped at her, not at all prepared for that particular demand. Or that particular revelation.

Ereni chuckled, the gleam in her emerald eyes telling him that while they might be allies, they would never be friends. "It seems your lover is keeping secrets from you, Marcus. As we are again allies, and are therefore aligned in our interests, allow me to bring you into the fold: Teriana is heir to more than just the *Quincense*—she's heir to the triumvirate."

"The what?"

"The Maarin are ruled by a trade consortium made up of the captains of the three ships escorted by Madoria's guardians. Triumvir Tesya of the *Quincense* is one of those captains, which makes Teriana the closest thing the Maarin have to a princess. Her voice carries weight with kings."

Teriana was royalty? The note the Queen of Katamarca had included as a token of her goodwill took on a whole different level of meaning. And also explained how a scrap of paper from a merchant girl managed to make it into the hands of a queen at all.

Inclining her head, Ereni said, "Good day to you, Legatus. I look forward to enjoying the fruits of our alliance."

11

TERIANA

"Did you know?" Gibzen asked.

Teriana shook her head, blood still boiling hot over Marcus pulling such a stunt, though she wasn't certain if she was angrier about him nearly getting himself killed or him taking more than half of the treasure that belonged in the pockets of the Arinoquians. "Did you?"

The Thirty-Seventh's primus shook his head. "Nope. But when it comes to the twisty political parts of command, I'm the last person he's going to confide in." Gibzen laughed. "When it comes to the twisty political bits, he doesn't confide in much of *anyone* until the deal is done. Never been quite sure whether it's because he enjoys the power of having secrets or whether he's just that distrustful of the rest of us. Though he typically keeps Felix in the fold." He gave her a sideways glance, hazel eyes thoughtful. "Yet it looked to me as though the tribunus was just as shocked as anyone to see that gold come wheeling into camp."

"Given I've been locked in a room valuing treasure for days, I've no notion of who Marcus has or has not spoken to," she snapped. Her body ached, and she was exhausted from little sleep and afraid of what she was going to find when she reached the medical tent. "And I'm not all that interested in talking about him, anyway."

"How quickly the hero who risked his own neck, as well as the necks of all these men," Gibzen spread his arms at the surrounding camp, "to save *you* is forgotten."

If only that were the case.

"By way of warning, Quintus is being ... *difficult*." Gibzen's jaw tightened beneath his tawny brown skin. "That's why I'll be going in with you. When he gets in these sorts of moods, he's dangerous."

"I'll go alone." They were her friends and they'd been injured protecting her. There were things she needed to say that she didn't want Gibzen listening to. "If there's trouble, I'll call for you."

Gibzen snorted. "Quintus could kill you before you had the chance to scream, Teriana. It's only because he's injured that I'm allowing you near him at all."

Her pulse sped, because though she knew Quintus was as trained as any of them, it felt strange to call the smiling, laughing young man she knew *dangerous*. "Please."

"Shit, Teriana." Gibzen scrubbed a hand over his shorn black hair. "If I let you get hurt, Marcus will have the skin whipped off my back. Don't think that he won't."

"Tell him I insisted."

"Prisoners don't get to insist." The primus said the words under his breath, but Teriana still heard. And still flinched at the reminder of what she was to the Cel.

Which was possibly a good thing, because it reminded her of what they were supposed to be to *her*.

How had things become so complicated?

"Do I need to bribe you to make this happen?" she asked, reaching into her pocket for some of her gambling earnings. But she paused as his eyes darkened, realizing her misstep too late. The primus was a murderer and not entirely right in the head, but he was also intensely loyal to the Thirty-Seventh. And to Marcus. "Sorry."

He glared at her. "I'm going to pretend you didn't do that and allow you to go in by yourself. But don't say I didn't warn you."

Pulling open the flap of the big tent before he changed his mind, Teriana stepped inside. The first thing that struck her was the smell: sweat and blood and piss and shit mixed in with alcohol and tonics and medicines. And over it all, the sickly-sweet scent of decay.

She bit down on the insides of her cheeks, trying to keep her stomach contents in check as her eyes danced over the rows and rows of injured young men. Some were unconscious on their cots, but others stared at the white canvas above them, their eyes glazed with the narcotics used to numb their pain. Bloodstained bandages and missing limbs and splinted bones. Catastrophic injuries.

The injuries of war.

Several of the medics looked up as she entered, nodding at her before going back to their tasks, but her eyes went immediately to the center of the space, where Quintus slumped on a stool next to the cot Miki rested on, the young legionnaire propped upright by pillows. Quintus had his cheek resting on Miki's lap, the other young man stroking his hair. There were faint creases at the corners of Miki's vibrant blue eyes that hadn't been there before, and her chest tightened. *Not young any longer.*

As she approached, Miki turned his head, a smile rising to his lips. "Good to see you, Teriana."

Quintus jerked upright, turning to look at her, and the anger twisting his face made her take a step back. "What do *you* want?"

"I wanted to see how you were," she said, taking in his injuries. He was stripped down to the undergarments the legionnaires wore beneath their tunics, his naked shoulders and chest wrapped with bandages. Running her tongue over her still-healing lip, she added, "And I wanted to thank you. For what you did."

"Then I suppose you've accomplished what you came for." Quintus's voice was barely recognizable. "Now go."

"You're being an ass." Miki coughed, lifting a hand to cover his mouth as he cleared his throat. "It's not her fault. If you can't be nice, be silent. If you can't be silent, why don't you get some air."

"I'm not leaving you."

"I'll be fine. Go find me something better to eat than the broth the medics are forcing down my throat."

Quintus's jaw worked back and forth. "Fine." Rising from the stool, he leaned over Miki, kissing him once on the forehead. Then again on the lips. "I won't be long."

He pushed past Teriana, heading toward the entrance of the tent.

"Apologies." Miki motioned to the vacant stool. "He's upset and taking it out on everyone he crosses paths with."

"I don't blame him." She sat on the stool, toying with the blanket draped over Miki's legs. Servius had said that he wasn't able to move them—that the surgeon believed his back was broken, paralyzing him from the waist down. Working up her courage, she lifted her face to meet his gaze, searching for the changes the corrupted had wrought upon her friend.

Immediately she understood why no one had yet demanded an explanation from her. Other than the faint creases around his eyes and mouth and a few glints of silver in his short red hair, his pale, freckled face appeared almost the same. It was only because she *knew* what the corrupted could do that Teriana recognized the changes for what they were. Miki, physically, was no longer a nineteen-year-old boy, but a man closer to thirty.

Tell him. It was the right thing to do, but the consequences . . .

"You look like shit," Miki finally said. "Like someone used your face for sparring practice."

"Not inaccurate." Exhaling, she said, "I'm sorry for what happened,

Miki. I hope you don't think I had anything to do with it? I'd never . . ." She trailed off, because wasn't that exactly what she was *supposed* to be doing? Sabotaging the Cel legions? Getting enough of them killed that Marcus was forced to retreat?

"I don't." Reaching out, he took her hand, his palm calloused from a lifetime of holding weapons. "I saw you pick up Quintus's weapon and fight. Saw the look on your face. We might not be on the same side in all of this, Teriana, but I know that you weren't responsible for that ambush."

"Doesn't appear that Quintus is like-minded."

"It's not that." Miki let go of her hand, resting his head back against the pillows, and Teriana's chest tightened as tears gleamed in his eyes. "Surgeon made the call earlier today. I'm not going to get better. I'm never going to walk again, and that means I'm never going to fight again."

And if he couldn't fight, he wasn't any good to the legions.

"The day after tomorrow, I'm being put on a ship destined for that island where the *Quincense* is moored. The island where they keep the *cripples*." He rubbed his eyes, angrily, but one tear escaped to run down his cheek. "The day after tomorrow, I'll no longer be part of the Thirty-Seventh."

12

MARCUS

"I don't trust the imperatrix." Amarin cleared the table of cups, setting the bottle back on the sideboard, out of Marcus's reach. "She's calculating."

"So am I." Marcus rested his elbows on the table, noticing for the first time that Amarin seemed to have aged in recent weeks, the wrinkles in his bronze skin deeper, his hair now more grey than brown. No longer a man in his prime as he'd been when first assigned to Marcus. "And everyone is angry at me, despite my calculations being in their best interests."

"Do you blame them?" Amarin circled the table, coming up behind Marcus and taking hold of the sides of his head. "Breathe."

Marcus obediently took a deep breath, and his servant twisted his head sharply left, making his spine crack loudly, and repeated the motion to the right. Then Amarin dug his thumbs deep into the knots in Marcus's neck, kneading out the tension.

"What I think is that they are rather ungrateful given that I've ensured we have the funds to pay wages and fill bellies for a long time to come, never mind that we now have an ally strong enough to ensure we won't have to go into battle anytime soon."

"Was keeping them in the dark necessary to achieve those ends?"

"If word had leaked of my intentions, I'd never have the chance to negotiate with the imperators. They'd have brought their armies to the meeting and I'd have had a battle on my hands. Or rather, Titus would have had a battle on his hands, because I'd be dead and he'd be in command of this mission."

"Since when have you had cause to doubt that your officers would keep your confidence on something of this magnitude?"

Since one of them betrayed it. Marcus only shrugged, brushing away both Amarin's question and his hands. "They didn't need to know."

"You have to trust someone, or you'll drive yourself to madness."

"Thank you for your words of wisdom."

The older man snorted. "As usual, you'll ignore them."

"Where is he?"

Marcus jumped at Teriana's voice, but before he could rise from his stool, she shoved her way into the tent, the men outside giving him apologetic looks.

"You can't do it!" She leveled a finger at him. "I won't allow it."

"You're going to need to be more specific," he answered, watching Amarin sidestep Teriana as he made his way outside.

"You cannot separate them!"

He stared at her, his brain sluggish. "Pardon?"

"Miki and Quintus!" Casting a backward glance over her shoulder, she came closer, her voice mercifully lower. "Never mind that it will break their hearts, it's cruel!"

All the tension that Amarin had worked away returned to Marcus's neck, and his head renewed its throbbing. "I haven't even seen a report on injuries much less signed off on discharges yet, so perhaps don't berate me for something I've yet to do."

Her eyes, turbid seas of distress, narrowed. "I'm pissed off at you as it is, Marcus, so *perhaps* you should watch your tone."

They glared at each other, and as always, she won.

"Miki's back is broken, and the surgeon says he'll never walk again. He told me that you'll be discharging him from the Thirty-Seventh and sending him to languish on the island with the rest of those who can't fight."

Never walk. Grief, heavy as lead, clamped down on his shoulders, and Marcus slumped back on the stool. "If he can't walk, he can't fight. If he can't fight, he can't serve. I won't have a choice."

"Why can't he stay here? Aren't there other tasks he could do? Not being able to walk doesn't make him useless, you know."

"I never said it did!" Anger flooded through him, chasing away his grief, because though he'd been in this situation dozens of times before, it never got any easier. Back east, when he discharged men who could no longer march, they were returned to Celendor. They were paid out the balance of their earnings, and the Senate's army of administrators ensured they were cared for. At least, for a time.

But sending men back home wasn't an option, so since they'd reached the Dark Shores, he'd made do with other solutions. "It's how it's done, Teriana. If we were forced into a hard march, it would be a burden on the rest of my men to have to carry them. And . . ." He grimaced. "It's bad for morale to have them around camp."

"That's a disgusting reason."

"Doesn't mean it's not true."

Her jaw worked back and forth, misery painted across her face. Then she said, "Let Quintus go with him."

"Quintus will recover."

"Physically, maybe," she retorted. "But being separated from Miki will destroy him. They need each other, Marcus. They love each other."

As if he didn't know that. "Do you think that the other men I discharge aren't loved? That their loss doesn't hurt those they leave behind? I can't make an exception for Quintus or I'll have dozens of other men in here asking for the same! I especially can't do this for him, given that everyone would know it was you . . ."

"That asked you to do it," she finished for him. "So not only were they injured in defense of me, any chance of them being together has been destroyed because of me."

"They knew the risks. And the outcome would be the same if Miki had been injured taking Aracam. I don't make exceptions."

Except for you.

"Please." She met his gaze. "Please don't do this to them."

He wanted to say yes. For their sake. For hers. "No exceptions, Teriana. Don't ask me again."

"Why?" She gave a stool a violent kick, sending it tumbling across the tent. "Why do you have to be this way? Why can't you for once do the *right* thing?"

Exhaustion and pain and frustration slammed down on him, and Marcus felt his temper crack. "Let's not forget that there are those among the Arinoquians with the power to heal Miki. To heal *all* my men who are lying in that tent, injured beyond a surgeon's ability to repair. You could help them, but you *choose* not to in order to protect the people of the West. Just as I choose not to, in order to protect *you.*"

She looked as though he'd slapped her, and Marcus recognized instantly that he'd gone too far.

"I'm sorry." Rising to his feet, he added, "I shouldn't have said that. This is my burden, not yours, and you shouldn't be made to feel otherwise."

Teriana stared at the dirt floor between them, face lowered, but he still saw the glint of a tear running down her cheek. "It's true though, isn't it?" She lifted her head. "Aren't we just a pair?"

"Split loyalties always make for difficult choices."

And it always ended badly.

"Racker hasn't delivered his report on injuries just yet," he said slowly. "Things could change. Miki could improve—I've seen it happen before." He didn't add that the Thirty-Seventh's surgeon was rarely wrong. "I don't want to fight about something that might resolve itself without our intervention."

She gave a slow nod. "Fine. But that doesn't absolve you of explaining that bullshit you pulled with the clans."

Grimacing, he righted the stool, gesturing for her to sit and doing the same once she was settled. "My men need to be paid, Teriana. And they need to eat."

"But you have—" She glanced toward where the chests of coin had once sat, her eyes lingering on the two that remained. "I see."

"It spends quickly."

She was quiet, her brow furrowed. "Fine. I understand why you took the gold. But what I don't understand is why you didn't tell me what you intended to do. Or anyone else, from the sound of it."

The silence stretched between them, tension mounting with each passing second.

"Because . . ." He swallowed hard. "As much as I might wish otherwise, I can't trust you." Reaching into his belt pouch, he dropped the scrap of paper he'd received from the Katamarcan queen in front of her. "Right now, I'm not entirely certain that I know you, *Princess*."

Teriana picked up the scrap of paper, and Marcus felt every muscle in his body twist with tension over what she would say.

"I'm not a princess," she finally answered, setting the note back down. "I don't hold that much power over my people."

"But Ereni said that you *do* hold that much influence. With the Maarin. And with other rulers in the West?"

She bit down on her lower lip, then gave a reluctant nod.

"Is this the only letter you sent?"

"No. I sent one to Gamdesh as well."

His stomach soured, knowing that the nation north of them had the military might to put his legions in the ground. "What did it say?"

"I explained the situation. Your intentions. The Empire's intentions. And I asked for assistance with defeating you." Her chin trembled. "I sent them within days of us arriving in Arinoquia. If that makes a difference."

Some of the tension in his chest released, because it did matter that she'd done it during the early days. Before things had . . . *changed* between them.

"They would've found out eventually," he said. "I can only assume that the Maarin on this side of the sea would make the information known. If not, I assume—given I received a report that Magnius and Bait have disappeared—that the news was destined to reach them."

She exhaled, then rested her head in her hands, elbows on the table.

Her braids rocked back and forth, gold and silver and gemstones glittering in the lamplight. How had he not seen it? No Maarin he'd ever met wore what amounted to a crown's worth of jewelry in their hair—it was a status symbol reserved for the upper echelons of society. And beyond the wealth, all the times she'd spoken of this king or that queen, it had been with the familiarity reserved for individuals one hadn't just heard of, but that one *knew*.

He truly was blind when it came to her.

"Have you done anything else?" His voice was raspy. "Is there anything else I should know?"

Teriana didn't answer for a long time. Finally, she straightened, meeting his gaze. "I need to tell you something about Ashok."

13

TERIANA

Tell him about the Marked.

The truth sat on the tip of her tongue, begging to be voiced. Because this wasn't a secret she could keep, not with the Cel growing closer to the Arinoquians by the day and merchant traffic from other kingdoms destined to begin arriving in Aracam's harbor. And if he found out she had lied about it, especially after this conversation, she didn't think he'd forgive her.

And yet the thought of giving up that secret made her sick. Yes, he'd kept Hegeria's healer's mark a secret, but she thought much of that was due to the guilt he felt over the healer Caradoc dying to save his life. And while the healers were something he could use, they were no danger to him. Unlike many of the other marks.

What would he do if he learned that Bait was capable of turning the tides with such violence as to send the ocean a mile inland, leaving only destruction in its wake? Or of the summoners, who could unleash storms upon them like a weapon? Or perhaps worst of all, what would he do if he learned about Tremon's marked, warriors with unparalleled skill, many of whom had armies under their command? Would he let them live? Or would he see them as the threat they were and send assassins to hunt them down? They weren't just names, but people she *knew,* especially Killian, whom she'd been close with since they were children.

She felt Marcus's eyes on her. Knew he was waiting for an answer. *Make a choice.*

Gritting her teeth, she straightened, meeting his gaze. "I need to tell you something about Ashok."

Marcus's eyes narrowed. "What about him?"

"He's . . . he's not precisely human."

Silence.

"We call them the corrupted," she continued. "They're very dangerous but thankfully also very rare, partially because every nation of the West hunts them down."

"Dangerous, how?" His voice was cold. "I've men hunting him, and if I've put them in harm's way . . ."

"Unnaturally strong and fast," she said. "And if he gets his hands on a person, he can drain the life right out of them, killing them by aging them."

He stared at her, unblinking, then said, "If this creature is as much an enemy to you as he is to me, why keep him a secret? What more are you hiding?"

Her mind raced, desperately seeking a way through this, but there was none.

"I'm going to ask you one more time: What are you not telling me?" His voice was shaking, and fear reared in her mind that she was going to set off one of his attacks. "If you aren't willing to answer, you can pack your things, because I'm sending you back to the *Quincense*. I don't need another backstabber in my camp."

Her heart dropped. Not only because she'd lose any power she had to stop the Empire if she were sent to that island, but because she'd lose *him*.

"Well?"

"I . . ."

He rose in a rapid motion. "Get your things. I'll order an escort to port." He started toward the front of the tent.

"Wait."

He turned around, and she scrubbed the tears from her face. "Every one of the gods grants certain powers to chosen individuals. We call them the Marked. The healers are Hegeria's. Ashok . . . he's one of the Seventh god's chosen."

He listened as she explained the various marks, sitting in stony silence once she'd finished.

Finally, he said, "I want to be furious at you for keeping this from me. For lying to me. Except I know why you did it. And I have no ground to stand on in judging you for it."

There wasn't forgiveness in his voice, only resignation.

"But how can I trust you knowing that you've been lying to my face. Not just before, but after—" He broke off, pressing his hands to the sides of his head as though it pained him. Then he met her gaze. "How do I know what you say you feel for me isn't just another lie? A way to manipulate me into achieving your ends?"

Her chest hollowed. "Marcus, it's not. I swear to you, what's between us is real."

She reached for him, but he took a rapid step backward, holding up a hand as though to ward her off.

"You know me," she whispered, her voice choked. "You know I wouldn't lie about something like that."

"Do I know you?" he asked. "Because it doesn't feel like I do."

"Marcus—"

"I need some air." He turned toward the entrance of the tent. "Don't expect me back tonight."

For what felt an eternity, she stood staring at the entrance to the tent, her guts in knots and head spinning with emotion.

And then she moved.

Heading out into the rain, Teriana stepped through the guards who formed a perimeter around the tent, striding toward the camp gates. Servius was there talking to another legionnaire, but just before she reached them, he exited the camp. The other man turned, and her stomach fell when she recognized Felix.

"I'm going for a walk," she said to him. "Let me through."

"No." He crossed his arms. "You will not leave the confines of this camp. Is that understood?"

"You don't have any right to give me orders, Felix. Move."

"No." He closed the distance between them, leaning down. "This is a legion camp, Teriana, not a harbor alehouse. You don't just get to come and go as you please."

She ground her teeth. "I only want to go down to the water." Though to do what, she didn't know. If she summoned Magnius, it would mean pulling him away from whatever he was doing with Bait, for the guardian's telepathy was limited by distance.

"No. I'm not waking men for an escort so you can go for a midnight swim."

"Then I'll go by myself."

"No."

Everyone was watching them. Waiting to see what she would do. What he would do. And despite feeling more a prisoner than she had in a long time, caution told her this was not the hill to die on. "Fine."

Turning on her heel, she headed along the interior of the wall, circling the camp. To sit in the command tent would mean stewing, so she walked. And walked. The deluge of rain soaked her to the bone, the cool wind making her shiver, but she ignored her physical discomfort in favor of rehashing every choice she'd made since she'd shaken Marcus's hand and agreed to take him and the legions across the Endless Seas. Every single one of them felt like a mistake.

Even trying to warn the nations of the West had blown up in her face, the Katamarcan queen having betrayed her confidence, probably to curry favor with the Cel in the hopes of averting an invasion. All that had accomplished was destroying what little trust Marcus had in her, and the note she'd sent the Gamdeshians had yielded better results only in that it had yielded nothing at all.

Feeling the press of her bladder, she veered away from the wall, heading toward the little privy shack allocated for her privacy. The deluge of rain had extinguished the torches, the only light from the singular storm lantern that hung from a post. Probably to keep anyone from accidentally falling into the ditch full of water and waste.

Peering into the darkness, she reached for the privy door. Then a gust of wind hit her in the back, and what felt like feathers brushed her arms. A second later, a hand clamped over her mouth, pushing her inside the privy.

"Easy, Teriana," a female voice whispered in Gamdeshian. "Kaira sent me."

Kaira. The name of the Princess made her heart leap, because Kaira was not only the Sultan's daughter and commander of the mighty army of Gamdesh, she was marked by Tremon.

Teriana nodded, ceasing to struggle, and the woman let go of her. In the darkness, it was impossible to see her face, but as Teriana turned, her hand grazed a bare thigh. The nudity, the brush of feathers, and the arrival from the sky told her all that she needed to know.

This woman was marked by Lern.

"You're a difficult girl to get alone," the woman said. "These *Empire* soldiers have watchful eyes. They often look up."

What all had she seen from above? The thought made Teriana's stomach twist. "I wasn't expecting anyone to try to reach me."

"You sent word that you needed help. And to warn us."

"For what good it did." Teriana shook her head. "Although at least Kaira didn't betray me like Queen Erdene."

The shifter huffed out a breath. "Gamdesh is *not* Katamarca. And your words did more good than you know. Though your people knew the threat the Empire posed, not a one whispered so much as a word until Kaira approached them with a scrap of paper with your name on it. And since then, the other triumvirs have revealed all that they know of the Empire, its armies, and the young man they sent in search of conquest. Thanks to you, Gamdesh knows the magnitude of this threat, and we will act accordingly."

Fear prickled down Teriana's spine. "Will you attack?" For as good as the legions were, the Gamdeshian army was equally so, and they had the numbers.

"Perhaps," the woman answered. "I left Revat some weeks ago, but as I took to the wind, our fleet was sailing north to aid in the evacuation of Mudaire. On its return, we may turn our eyes to Arinoquia."

"What's happened in Mudaire?"

"Armies from Derin marching under the Corrupter's banner invaded Mudamora, and its capital was under siege. How they have fared since, I have not heard."

Horror filled Teriana, along with the vision Magnius had given her before the crossing of the Twelve's banners being driven into the mud by the boots of soldiers carrying the flaming circle of the Seventh god. The Six have mercy, but it had already come to pass.

"We've no time to discuss Mudamora's plight," the shifter said. "Know only that we heard your call and we are watching. And we will not abandon you, Teriana of the *Quincense*."

"But what should I do?" she demanded, not wanting the woman to go. Not wanting to lose this connection with the world, though it filled her with equal parts hope and terror.

"Watch. Learn. And trust you'll know when the moment to make your move is right, for the best way to win a war is to know your enemy."

"But—"

"You must go. If you linger, they'll notice."

"What's your name?" she asked, desperate for a few moments more with her. For this contact.

"Astara." And opening the door, the woman pushed her outside.

Trying to act normally, Teriana walked toward the camp, but a second later, she heard the rustle of wings.

And a glance upward revealed the shadow of an enormous hawk disappearing into the night sky.

14

LYDIA

Lydia had been teamed with a group of soldiers for patrols. Told to point out anyone they crossed who had no life in them.

It hadn't taken long.

She'd thrown up after the soldiers cut off the first blighter's head. Had fallen to her knees and retched as they'd burned the body, the stink of cooking meat filling her nostrils even as guilt and anguish filled her guts. And in that moment, she'd been certain it couldn't get worse—that this was the greatest horror she'd experience.

She'd been wrong.

The patter of feet running up stairs filtered out from a manor, and the soldiers paused, glancing at the building. "Squatters," one of them muttered as he walked to the door, knocking hard. "Open up in the name of the King!"

Silence.

Lydia clenched her teeth, praying that the group she was with would move on. That they'd make it through today without killing anyone.

But the gods didn't answer.

Instead, the soldier kicked in the door, the rest of the team moving swiftly inside, Lydia forced to run with them. They moved through the house, the men yanking open closets and looking under furniture. Upstairs, they moved from room to room, weapons in hand, until at last, a kicked-in door revealed a starved and filthy family crouching next to a wall. The children were crying softly, the mother and two older women attempting to quiet them. All very much alive.

Except for one.

The soldiers glanced to Lydia, and swallowing hard, she pointed at the mother. "Her."

"You're sure?"

Her throat closed up so that she couldn't speak, but Lydia managed to nod. Yet as they moved on the woman, swords raised, the children screaming as they dragged their mother away, she said, "Wait! Let me . . . let me at least try to help her."

The expressions on the soldiers' faces told her that they wanted no part of such an effort, but she ignored them, elbowing her way to the woman.

Tears flooded down her face, and she dropped to her knees before Lydia. "Please, Marked One," she begged. "They *need* me! They won't survive without me!"

"I'll try," Lydia said, knowing she was talking to the Corrupter but praying if some vestiges of the woman remained, she'd hear.

Removing the thick gloves she wore, Lydia took a deep breath and then grasped the woman's hand.

But the moment their bare skin touched, the Corrupter or the blight, she wasn't sure which, snatched hold, the mist that was her life draining through her hand and into nothingness. Lydia screamed, and the soldiers caught hold of her and pulled her away.

"I'm sorry." Her breath came in great heaving gasps. "She's not alive. There's nothing in her but death."

"Then in the name of the Six and under the laws of the King, we will destroy this abomination," the soldier said.

They grabbed the arms of the woman, dragging her down the stairs and out into the street, the crying children and the older women running behind.

"Please," one of them begged. "You're wrong. She's alive. She's their mother. Have mercy!"

Other squatters came out onto the streets or watched from windows, their eyes filled with horror as the soldiers forced the blighter to her knees. She fought and struggled, screaming for help. Screaming that her family needed her.

Hot tears flooded down Lydia's cheeks because this was wrong. *Wrong wrong wrong.* "Get the children inside," she said to the older women. "Don't let them see!"

But the women ignored her, too intent on struggling against the soldiers to reach the woman. Fighting to save her even as the children sobbed for their mother.

A blade flashed. Blood splattered the snow. A single scream split the air.

Then silence.

One of the soldiers doused the corpse in oil, then touched a torch to it. The smell of cooking flesh filled Lydia's nose and she turned away and vomited. Her guts heaved over and over, and when she finally looked back, it was to find the family watching in mute horror as the flames consumed the woman they loved.

"If you need food, come to the god circle and you'll be provided for," one of the soldiers said.

The older of the women only spit on him before rounding on Lydia, pointing a finger at her. "Murder!" she shrieked. "She's a murderer!"

The rest of the civilians took up the chant, pointing at Lydia and spitting at her feet as the soldiers hurried her away, their weapons in hand.

"This isn't right." She scrubbed at her wet cheeks. "I can't do this anymore."

"You have to," one of the soldiers said. "Else you might as well bend a knee to the Seventh."

Lydia's skin crawled, and she lifted her head to the towers of the god circle. So many times, she'd felt the eyes of the Six on her. Sworn she'd seen the towers move, bending closer to look at her.

This time, it was the black tower of the Seventh that moved.

Her heart caught in her throat as the tower leaned over the city, drawing closer to her, the eyes carved into it glowing red and terrible. She opened her mouth to scream, recoiling backward and tripping over her own feet.

"What is it, Marked One?" he demanded.

"There!" She pointed, then blinked once, because the tower was once again upright. Once again nothing more than inanimate rock. "Was nothing," she whispered. "I'm . . . I'm just tired."

They carried on inside the temple, but once inside, she declined to join the others for dinner, the thought of eating making her ill. Instead, she asked one of the young healers to show her to the library.

The interior and exterior walls were lined with shelves that reached up to the ceiling, the space between filled with regularly set tables surrounded by padded chairs. There must have been thousands of books, and if Lydia had not seen the Great Library in Celendrial, she might have been impressed.

"Is there something particular you're looking for?" the young healer asked.

"No." She trailed her fingers along the spines. "I find the books calming."

Which was true. The smell of leather and paper and ink filled her nose, and her body and mind immediately abandoned the tension she'd been holding since she'd left the Royal Army's camp. Since she'd left Killian standing in the mud and the snow.

This is where I'm meant to be.

15

MARCUS

Ignoring the protests of the men on guard duty, Marcus left camp, heading through the darkness and rain toward the glow of Aracam. It was his men on guard at the city's gates, and he ignored their mutters about escorts and dangers as he stepped through the narrow door to the left of the closed portcullis.

Like most large cities, Aracam never really slept, music and laughter spilling out of alehouses and inns and brothels. Voices spoke in a mixture of Cel and Arinoquian, a good portion of the patrons legion men on their night off, though he recognized several of Ereni's soldiers stumbling down the street, arm in arm. Devoid of regalia and cloaked by darkness and rain, no one recognized him, and therefore no one paid him any mind, which was to his liking.

He strode through the narrow streets toward the center of the city, keeping his head down as he passed a patrol made up of Titus's men. They grunted greetings, their attention more for the shadows between buildings than him.

Lightning crackled across the sky, illuminating the towers of the god circle, and the rain intensified, clinking off his armor and overflowing the gutters that funneled water to the sea. It drove anyone loitering on the streets inside, and soon it felt as though he were alone in the ancient city with nothing but his own thoughts to keep him company.

Reaching the circle, Marcus walked around the perimeter, checking the doors on each, but finding all of them locked. On the Seventh god's temple—made of glossy black stone—he noted there was no door, only a solid base, and he circled it, trailing his fingers against the slick surface, his skin turning numb with cold.

Shivering, he went to the platform at the center of the circle where Urcon had been executed and climbed the steps. Rain had long since washed away the blood, but as he blinked, Marcus saw the axe descending on the man's neck. The spray of crimson. The severed head in Ereni's hand.

A puppet tyrant.

The moment he'd come face-to-face with Urcon, he'd known it was impossible the ancient man was working alone. His body had been incredibly frail and his mind plagued with dementia, but what had troubled Marcus more was that the man was ill-cared for. Filthy and dressed in torn clothing, they'd found him alone in the royal bedchambers surrounded by plates of moldering food and buckets of his own waste, seemingly unaware that Aracam had fallen.

Marcus's first assumption had been that Urcon's underlings had merely carried on as they'd been doing when their master had begun to fail, using his name for authority and keeping his condition a secret lest they lose their power. But with Teriana's confession, he now suspected there had been only one puppet master: Ashok.

With Urcon dead, the creature had lost its power, and Marcus had no doubt that it was not best pleased. Would it seek revenge? Or would it seek to regain the power it had lost?

Sitting on the edge of the platform, Marcus leaned back on his elbows, staring up at the dark towers. Lightning flickered every few seconds, illuminating the faces that had been carved into them; each time they appeared to be in a slightly different position. The effect was unnerving.

"I'm not here to fight you," he said softly, goose bumps rising to his skin with the sense they were watching him. "But I can't go back. I won't."

The familiar clack of steel tread against stone stole his attention from the towers as a lone legionnaire approached him from behind, and a mixture of emotion filled him. Marcus turned, opening his mouth to speak and then stopped short when he saw that the individual was Servius.

"You look disappointed," his big friend said, rising the platform steps.

Marcus shrugged. "I thought you were sleeping."

"I was." The wood creaked as Servius sat. "But then you decided to go on one of your brooding solo walkabouts, and someone had to track you down. Felix didn't think you would want it to be him. He right about that?"

Marcus didn't respond, because he wasn't entirely certain of the answer.

"Men guarding the command tent said you got into it with Teriana and stomped off," Servius continued. "There anyone you *aren't* quarreling with?"

"You?"

"Nope. After that shit you pulled today with the clans, we are most definitely quarreling. And will remain so until you apologize. Sir."

"I don't see why you're complaining," Marcus growled. "You wanted more coin for supplies. I got it for you."

Servius crossed his arms.

"You knowing wouldn't have changed how things went."

"The words you are looking for are: 'I'm sorry for being a deceptive prick and scaring the shit out of you, Servius. It will never happen again.'"

"I'm not saying that."

Servius lifted his shoulders. "That's your choice."

Lightning fractured the sky, and a heartbeat later, thunder boomed. Sheets of rain fell, slapping him in the face. "Fine. I'm sorry."

"'I'm sorry for being—'"

"Don't push your luck."

They sat in the rain for a few minutes, then Servius said, "Don't suppose I could convince you to brood somewhere dry? Preferably a place with food, drink, and pretty girls? I know a brothel—"

"I'm not interested in brothels."

"Then I guess your argument with Teriana wasn't that serious."

"It was serious," Marcus muttered. "She's been holding back information. Important information."

"And this was a revelation to you?" Servius let out a loud laugh, his shoulders shaking. "Allow me to remind you that we are her enemy, Marcus. Well, maybe not us, specifically, but certainly Cassius and the Senate. And whether we want to be or not, we are their weapons to swing as they will. Or, at least, we will be if they get us back under their thumbs. Which is likely why you've been sitting on your laurels when it comes to hunting down xenthier paths."

It took all his self-control not to react. "We've had more pressing—"

"Yeah, yeah. I've heard your reasons why the xenthier isn't a priority. Except I know that you could have a hundred priorities on your plate and it wouldn't stop you from making room for another. So the fact you've done nothing to find xenthier stems tells me you don't want them found."

Marcus knew he should deny it. Should make up a good excuse for his actions that would put Servius off the subject. But he found himself not wanting to. "Do you like it here?"

"Of course I like it here," Servius answered. "This is the closest I've been to a free man since my seven-year-old self walked through the gates of Campus Lescendor. But the moment those paths are discovered, we go back to being nothing more than the identification numbers they tattooed on our backs. And we'll have to do their bidding or we'll find ourselves hanging from the noose."

Freedom. It was almost too much to dream of, but Marcus dreamed of it anyway. And apparently he wasn't alone.

The words sitting on his tongue were treason, and yet he said, "What if we never find xenthier paths, Servius? What if . . . what if we never even start looking for them?"

Servius was quiet for a moment. Then he said, "That would be fine by me. But whether they get found or not isn't entirely within our control."

Marcus knew what he meant. There were dozens and dozens of unmapped genesis stems in the Empire, and the Senate had sent path-hunters through every single one of them a week after the Thirty-Seventh and Forty-First departed, with specific instructions that they were to seek the legions out if they found themselves in the Dark Shores. And the Senate would keep sending men, because there were always volunteers who'd risk everything for the chance at gold and glory.

"We've had no contact," Marcus answered. "Heard not even a rumor of one of those path-hunters having made it to the Dark Shores."

"We're talking about half of Reath, Marcus. Word we are in Arinoquia won't even have reached most places yet. It could take a year for them to make their way to us. Longer."

He hated that uncertainty. Hated knowing that at any moment, an Empire path-hunter could arrive at the gates to their camp. Chewing on the insides of his cheeks, he said, "The Senate's ignorance could be our salvation. Unless we get word back to them that the path-hunter reached us, they'll never know."

A Forty-First patrol—the same one he'd passed earlier—walked by. They saluted, likely recognizing Servius for his size, then carried on.

Only after they were out of sight did Servius say, "That's a big secret. And one not everyone would want to keep."

Titus.

And not just him. There were plenty of men who liked life in the legions, Felix being the first who came to mind. Even those who might wish for something else had obedience so deeply engrained in them that they'd resist going against the Senate's orders. There were more still who'd fear the punishment that would fall upon them if their treason were ever discovered.

And there was Teriana. If the paths were never found, she'd never fulfill her agreement with the Senate, which meant her mother and her people would remain prisoners. Which meant he'd have to keep *her* a prisoner in order to prevent her from taking both the *Quincense* and the information back to the Empire, the thought of which made him ill. As it was, he couldn't silence all of the Maarin.

It was a secret he had no chance of keeping.

"What are you going to do?" Servius asked.

The rain eased, the deluge transforming to mist that ghosted in white clouds through the god circle.

"Keep doing what I'm doing," he finally answered. "I'll play both sides."

"A plan you're well-equipped for." Servius rose to his feet. "With that resolved, you think we might head back to camp? You might enjoy wallowing in misery, but I'm partial to a dry tent and my bedroll."

I told her I wouldn't come back.

The stubborn part of him wanted to stand his ground and refuse to go back. To let her stew.

As though sensing his thoughts, Servius said, "Don't be a petty jackass. Let's go."

They walked elbow to elbow through Aracam, then out of the city toward camp. Servius called out the passwords as they drew closer, and the gates swung open to allow them entrance.

Marcus's eyes went immediately to where Felix stood waiting. Their eyes latched, and Marcus struggled with the mix of emotions that swirled through his mind. When his father had abandoned him to succumb to his illness at Campus Lescendor, it had been Felix who'd kept him alive. Who'd kept Marcus's illness a secret, hiding him and pretending to be him, because even at age seven, he'd known that they weeded weakness out early in the legions. And they'd stood at each other's backs ever since.

Until now.

Something must have shown on his face, because Felix's jaw tightened. Then he gave a sharp salute and strode in the direction of his tent.

"You really throwing away nearly thirteen years of friendship over a girl?" Servius muttered under his breath.

"This isn't about her." Because it wasn't. Not in the way Servius meant. It was because the traitor's actions had gotten six of their brothers slaughtered. Had gotten Miki injured so badly that he'd never walk. And yes, because it had seen Teriana beaten and nearly killed.

And there would be no justification that would allow him to forgive the betrayal: If Marcus found proof that Felix was the traitor, he'd do more than throw away their friendship. He'd see him hang. "Go get some rest. I intend to do the same."

His own tent was lit with a single lamp on the table, everything neat and tidy, courtesy of Amarin, who rose as Marcus entered. He swiftly removed Marcus's armor, then set to polishing it while Marcus walked silently and barefoot to the rear.

In the dim light filtering through the canvas, he could make out Teriana's form. She was lying on her side facing away from him, blanket pulled up to her shoulders. He couldn't tell if she was asleep, the rain loud enough to drown out her breathing.

Creeping onto his bedroll, he sat, silently cursing when his knees cracked.

"I thought you weren't coming back tonight."

Shit.

"I changed my mind." Lying on his back, he stared at the canvas above him, knowing there wasn't a chance of him falling asleep.

Teriana was silent for long enough that he thought she must have succumbed to exhaustion, then she abruptly rolled over to face him, a wet braid smacking him across the chest. "Are we done? Because if we are, I just want to know so—" She broke off, her voice cracking with a stifled sob that made his chest ache. "So that I know."

It didn't feel over. Not with the way he was achingly aware of her presence. With the way he wanted to pull her into his arms. With the way he wanted to kiss her and tell her it didn't matter what she'd done.

Except what if the next time her actions had real consequences? What if they resulted in his men being hurt or killed?

"I can't do this if I can't trust you," he said softly. "And you shouldn't do it if you can't trust me."

Teriana didn't answer, and he felt sick, his stomach in ropes and his skin clammy, because he didn't want it to be over. Didn't want to lose her when he'd only just gotten her back.

Then her fingers interlaced with his, and she whispered, "Then maybe trust is where we need to start."

16

LYDIA

Mudaire was where she was meant to be. And apparently what she was meant to be doing was reorganizing a library.

Dust puffed in Lydia's face as she pulled out another mis-shelved volume and moved it to the correct section, the total lack of order making her head ache. There *was* a system, if not one she would have selected, but it appeared no one had been serving the function of librarian in quite some time. Which wasn't entirely surprising given the war.

And the fact almost all the healers were now dead.

Logically, she knew this wasn't the best use of her time, that she should find a suitable volume and start reading, but diving into the middle of things was *not* how she was in the habit of conducting research. And as it was, she'd yet to even *find* a volume with a subject that related to the blight. Oh, there were endless volumes on infection, but all focused on diseases of the natural variety, and this was decidedly supernatural. There were also volumes on the Marked, including a jaw-dropping 240 editions of *Treatise of the Seven*. They were in many different languages, seeming to tell the stories of the Marked from different nations, and they also dated back centuries. She flipped through the crumbling tomes, struggling to read the archaic Mudamorian, but as with the edition Teriana had given her, none told any stories of the corrupted.

Books moved to piles on the table, then onto their appropriate shelves, her mind slowly cataloging the extent of the collection. She felt herself drawn to the *many* texts written by other healers detailing how they used their marks to repair injuries and remedy illness. Finding one that discussed an outbreak of plague, she sat on one of the chairs and began to read.

What she learned was that Hegeria's mark had its limits.

Symptoms and damage from illness could be remedied, but the sickness itself couldn't be cured. The author likened it to poison: *The illness must be purged through natural means, a healer able only to temper the symptoms and thus allow the patient's body opportunity to expel the infection itself.*

Similarly, natural defects that an individual was born with could not be remedied with a healer's mark, though the author suggested another text that discussed how a mark might be used in conjunction with surgery to remedy such afflictions. Natural degeneration and aging were yet other things that marks could not reverse, and it occurred to Lydia that was likely why her eyesight had not improved when she'd been marked.

She read until her eyes grew heavy with exhaustion, yet while she found answers to many questions, none solved the dilemma of the blight.

"You are supposed to be in your room during the curfew hours, Lydia."

Lydia lurched up from where she'd fallen asleep at the library table. Turning, she saw Quindor standing at the entrance, his arms crossed and brow furrowed.

"Grand Master," she said, leaping to her feet and inclining her head. Then her eyes took in the mess she'd made, stacks of books filling the tables and sitting on the floor in front of shelves, and she internally cringed. "I was . . . The library has obviously not had the resources to see to organization in some time. I thought to remedy that."

"It still does not have the resources," he answered, the furrow in his brow deepening. "This is not a priority, Lydia. Your strength and your mark are required for hunting those infected with blight, not organizing shelves."

Her jaw tightened, both her mind and her heart rejecting the idea that hunting people be the foremost of her mandates. "My goal was research," she said. "To see if I might find something that would help us treat the infected rather than sentencing them to death."

"One cannot heal the dead any more than one can breathe life into a stone." He gave his head a sharp shake of annoyance. "Wasted time, and I have no choice but to allow you to waste more of it to clean up this mess. Which you will do during your free hours, while at the same time, adhering to the curfew placed upon trainees."

Biting down on an argument, she nodded.

"But for now, you need to go make yourself presentable," he said. "King Serrick, as well as several of the High Lords, have arrived in Mudaire in the company of the Royal Army. He has requested your presence at the palace."

The Royal Army. Her heart skipped. That meant Killian was here.

17

MARCUS

He'd slept like the dead, and for the first time in a very long time, he might've slept past dawn.

Except the tent started to leak.

Splat. Marcus twitched as something wet smacked him on the shoulder. *Splat.* Another drop.

"What's dripping?" Teriana muttered, and he realized with a start that he'd curled around her during the night, and his traitorous body was not displeased with the situation.

Face burning, Marcus sat upright and glared upward while he got himself under control, seeing the spot where the rain had soaked into the waxed canvas and several other dark spots that suggested it would soon have company.

And it was no wonder.

Rain hammered in great sheeting torrents, the faint roll of thunder the only sound in the quiet camp.

"Shit." Teriana had sat as well, and she was pointing to the corner. "We're flooding."

"Amarin!" Cursing loudly, he rose and strode out into the main tent, only to find his servant frantically storing maps in their chests as water rained from above, filling the bowls and cups he'd placed under the leaks. "I see you're aware of the problem."

The older man scowled. "Never seen rain like this. What a mess."

Discomfort was one thing, but the endless damp was a breeding ground for disease. Stepping out into the deluge, Marcus shielded his face from the pounding rain, walking barefoot through the mud to the sodden guards. "I need the engineers in my tent, now. And find some dry canvas to tarp over command. Send someone into Aracam to buy it, if needed."

"Yes, sir."

Striding back into the tent, he found Teriana busy helping Amarin. She was fully dressed, and Marcus became abruptly aware that he wore only undergarments, which were soaked through so he might as well have been naked. And despite modesty having been driven out of him by life in a legion camp, his face once again burned red. Fortunately, Teriana was looking anywhere but at him.

"Expect another couple months of this," she said. "When it rains in Arinoquia, it *rains*."

"Noted," he managed to say before hurrying to the back to dress.

When he returned, his head engineer, Rastag, arrived, sparing him having to talk to Teriana. Which was well, because he couldn't think of anything to say and the thought of suffering in silence made him want to run back out into the rain.

A full head shorter than Marcus, Rastag was about as wide as he was tall, his black hair shaved regulation short and a pair of spectacles balanced on his nose. He had light brown skin and the look of someone with more than a few provinces contributing to his bloodline. Rastag was a *terrible* fighter, infamous for his ability to trip up an entire line of men and for the time he accidentally stabbed himself. But he could build anything.

"Sir." Moving to the table, the engineer slapped a schematic down on a dry spot, not bothering to ask why Marcus had called him here. "My proposal for a drainage system for the camp."

Glancing at the detailed illustration, Marcus said, "I think we need more than that."

"Undoubtedly, sir, but it's always best to build on—"

"A good foundation," Marcus finished for him. "You've mentioned that once or twice."

"Wooden—"

"I'd prefer something more permanent," Marcus said, then felt Teriana's questioning eyes on him and lost his train of thought. "Umm . . . Something made out of stone, like Aracam and Galinha—"

"But with more bloody headroom," Servius interrupted, having arrived in the middle of the conversation. "Morning, Teriana."

"Morning, Servius."

A quick glance revealed that she was now sitting on one of the stools, sipping from a steaming cup, her eyes currently swirling seas of turquoise. She twisted one of her black braids around her index finger, gaze fixed on her tea. So deeply and profoundly beautiful that he couldn't help but question his sanity for taking intimacy off the table. *It was the right choice,* he silently told himself. *We need to be able to trust each other.*

If that were even possible.

"Marcus?"

He jumped at Servius's voice. "Right. More headroom. Speak to Felix about which men to use for the construction. And speaking of Felix, where is he?"

"Sleeping off a hangover," Servius said. "He made close friends with a bottle of rum last night."

Unbidden, the memory of how Felix had looked at him when he'd returned filled Marcus's head, along with the knowledge that Felix only drank to excess when he was upset. Shoving away the thought, he said to Rastag, "Give him another hour and then have someone rouse him."

"Understood." The engineer saluted and started for the exit, passing Gibzen on his way out.

"You got Racker's report yet?" the primus asked without preamble.

Marcus took his time answering, sitting on one of the stools and taking a sip of water even as he noted how the scar along the primus's jaw pulled as the muscles beneath flexed. Given Gibzen was alarmingly devoid of empathy and sentiment, his displeasure wouldn't be over the loss of lives. "No. Why?"

Gibzen shifted on his heels, but before he could speak, Racker stepped inside. Casting a glare at Gibzen, the Thirty-Seventh's surgeon said, "I have my discharge report." Pulling out a wax-wrapped sheet of paper, he handed it to Marcus. Eighteen names and numbers, one set of which belonged to Miki. Feeling Teriana's scrutiny, he asked, "And Quintus?"

"Will be in fighting form within a couple weeks."

Gibzen snorted, and Marcus bit down on the insides of his cheeks to keep from reprimanding him. "What of his state of mind?"

"He is distressed, as is expected, but he's steady enough."

"Bullshit," Gibzen snapped. "Everyone here knows he's going to snap the moment Miki boards that ship." He leveled a finger at Marcus. "I want him out. He's too dangerous and too unpredictable."

"That's Felix's call." And as the Thirty-Seventh's tribunus, he should've been here for this conversation.

Scowling, Gibzen turned on Racker. "Discharge him. You know full well what's going to happen."

The surgeon crossed his slender arms, using his greater height to loom over the primus. "If I were to request discharge for men based on what I thought they might do, I'd need stacks of paper to record all their names. If he breaks, I'll revisit the issue. But not a heartbeat before."

Gibzen kicked a stool across the tent. His temper was not good at the best of times, and for him, the answer was *always* violence. Servius rose from his stool, and Marcus readied himself to leap into action if the primus decided to attack the surgeon. "Get yourself under control," he snapped. "And then get out before I consider punishing your behavior."

Gibzen glared at him, but then the tent flaps parted and Felix appeared. At the sight of him, the primus relaxed. "Sir, it's Quintus. I want him out."

Felix took the cup of water that Amarin offered, staring at it as though he wasn't certain whether to drink or vomit. But his voice was steady as he answered. "You've mentioned that. I take it Miki is to be discharged?"

"So says Racker. And you *know* Miki's the only thing that keeps him together."

"I disagree—" Racker started to say, but Felix held up a hand, turning to Marcus. "I'm inclined to support Gibzen in this. His men undertake our most critical missions—it's *stressful* work."

"So you're suggesting we assign Quintus to something less taxing?" Marcus stared him down. "Idle minds have a tendency to go to dark places."

Felix looked away, his golden skin slightly greenish. *How much did he drink?*

Taking a sip of water, Felix said, "As it is, none of the other centurions are clamoring to take him on."

"It's not their call," Marcus said. "It's *yours.*"

Silence filled the tent, broken only by the dripping of water into basins and cups.

"Assign him to me." Teriana's voice cut through the growing tension. "I need a proper bodyguard, and who better than Quintus? He's been with me almost since we arrived in Arinoquia, so I'm comfortable around him and I trust him to keep me safe."

Jealousy flared through Marcus's veins. That she trusted Quintus over him. Wanted it to be the other soldier guarding her back. *Don't be an idiot,* he reprimanded himself. *You can't exactly follow her about, and even if you could, Quintus is twice the fighter you are.*

Gibzen barked out a laugh, stealing Marcus's attention back to the moment. "You sure you didn't take a head injury, Teriana? Allow me to impart a bit of information to you that might change your mind: our man Quintus has the *highest* number of kills in the entire Thirty-Seventh legion. He's an assassin of the first order, which is well and fine when he's on the level, but the second his boy departs,

Quintus is going to snap. Which would be bad enough, but considering that his woe has all come as a result of protecting *you* . . ."

"He's angry with the situation, not with me." Teriana's voice was calm. "I trust him."

That word again.

"He's a murderer, girl. What part of what I'm telling you don't you understand?"

"Pot," Racker said, giving the primus a dark look, "kettle. And his kills were all sanctioned by the Senate, which is more than I can say for *some.*"

Since they'd been boys training together at Lescendor, there'd been no love lost between these two. Racker considered life sacrosanct and refused to take it, under any circumstance. Gibzen killed even when he didn't have to and made no effort to hide that he enjoyed it. Marcus did his best to keep them separate.

"You're just full of opinions today, aren't you?" Gibzen wiggled his first two fingers, pantomiming a figure walking. "Why don't you head back to medical and to playing nursemaid and leave those of us with military minds to make these decisions."

His own temper frayed, Marcus snarled, "Gibzen, shut up and get out! You've said your piece."

Face dark, the primus saluted and then stomped out into the mud and the rain.

Retrieving a pen and ink, Marcus signed the discharge papers and handed them over to Servius. "Get them underway." Then he glanced at Teriana. "If there's a message you want to send to your crew, give it to Servius."

Servius glanced at Teriana. "You want to come with me? We can stop for some grub and you can write a note."

"All right." She picked up a piece of paper and a pencil, then she met Marcus's gaze for the first time since last night and said, "Make the right choice, Marcus."

He didn't answer, only waited for them to depart before turning to Felix. "What do you think?"

Felix's jaw worked back and forth. "Respectfully, sir, I think this is Teriana's call. And yours. Now if you'll excuse me, now that I have a full casualty list, I need to look at reorganizing the ranks."

"Bring the changes to me when you're done."

Felix nodded, then with a sharp salute, exited the tent. Leaving Marcus alone with Racker.

"For what it's worth, I think it's a good role for Quintus," the surgeon said. "Unlike that blackhearted creature you replaced Agrippa with, Quintus takes no pleasure in killing."

It was a struggle not to scowl at the mention of the Thirty-Seventh's only deserter, but Racker wasn't wrong about Quintus. Or Gibzen. "I need to think about it."

Racker was silent for a moment, then he said, "You're in no small way responsible for Quintus's nightmares. Do right by him and give him a purpose, or whatever happens to him is on *your* hands."

Give him a purpose. A thought rolled to the forefront of his mind. Something he'd never considered before and yet now found strangely enticing. "I'll think of something." He stood. "Dismissed."

18

TERIANA

"That was tense." Rain soaked her within an instant of stepping out of the tent, water filling her boots as she followed Servius through the camp, which resembled a giant mud puddle.

"The wet is making everyone cranky."

Undoubtably true, but that wasn't the source of the tension she'd witnessed in Marcus's tent. She'd seen them argue with one another before, but they'd always given off the sense of being unified, their arguments directed toward achieving a common purpose. Whereas what she'd seen in there was anything but unified. "Thought you lot were used to discomfort?"

"We are."

They passed a pair of young men shouting at each other, both their chests tattooed with a 37. They silenced when Servius cast them a dark glare, but it picked right back up again. And it wasn't just them. The half of the camp occupied by the Thirty-Seventh felt sullen and on edge, whereas the Forty-First seemed business as usual, groups not on duty congregating under tarps while they ate, banter and laughter drifting into her ears.

The Thirty-Seventh had taken more casualties, partially because they alone had participated in the battle with the mercenary army, but also because the older, more experienced legion had undertaken the more dangerous positions during the siege of Aracam. Except she'd witnessed their grief, and this . . . this was something else. "It's not the rain, Servius. What's wrong with everyone?"

Her big friend scrubbed a hand through his dark hair, sending droplets flying. "When the top dogs quarrel, it affects the whole pack. I have to hand it to you, Teriana. If your goal was to fracture this legion, you've done a mighty fine job of it."

"You know that's not what I want." The words came out in a rush. And on their heels, she reminded herself that only last night, she'd been visited by a Gamdeshian spy. But while playing with relationships and jealousies might be the way some people created trouble, that wasn't who she was. She had her limits when it came to deception.

"So you say."

"I didn't plan for any of this to happen."

"Sure."

Tentatively, she asked, "Did Felix get angry about the other girls . . ." Because undoubtably there had been others in Marcus's bed before her.

"No reason to." Servius's voice was clipped. "Was always professionals and never the same girl twice. As it should be for any man in service to the Empire."

She flinched, realizing that Servius was angry at her. "It's over, anyway. He says he can't trust me." Never mind that she'd woken last night wrapped in his arms, his heartbeat a steady thud against her back, his breath warm against her ear. Never mind that she'd been a twist of desire and anguish, unsure of whether to wake him with hungry kisses or to extricate herself and weep into her pillow. She'd gotten her answer when he'd woken, horror that had nothing to do with the leaking tent apparent in his eyes.

"Bullshit." Sliding to a stop, Servius loomed over her, his usual good humor absent from his face. "It's not over. At least, not for him."

Her heart skipped, emotion making her stomach flip.

"I want to give you the benefit of the doubt and believe that this isn't an act on your part, Teriana. And if you want to prove that, convince Marcus to reconcile with Felix. Because while the men respect Marcus, they *like* Felix, and right now they're all wondering whose side to take if they split irrevocably."

As if that were so simple. Teriana bit the inside of her cheeks, wishing Servius knew that the source of the conflict wasn't her but the fact Felix might have betrayed Marcus. And that unless Felix could be proven innocent, the rift between him and Marcus would only grow. But it wasn't her secret to tell.

She opened her mouth to say that she'd try, but before she could speak, shouts filled the air. Both of them turned to see a brawl spill out of the mess tent, a crowd swiftly forming as fists flew.

And blood.

"You have to be joking!" Servius snarled at the men, then he leveled a finger at Teriana. "Go back to the command tent and wait there until I get this sorted."

Without waiting for a response, he stormed toward the brawl, roaring curses and threatening to crack skulls.

Beyond the ruckus, Titus exited the mess tent. Cassius's son paused to watch the men pummeling one another, the very faintest smile of amusement growing on his face. Then he walked away.

Teriana watched him go, her skin prickling with unease, because Titus was Cassius's son and she knew he wanted control. And she didn't think there was much he wouldn't do to achieve command of this mission. Even if gaining that control meant ripping the Thirty-Seventh apart from the inside out.

19

LYDIA

Washed, her hair woven into a tight braid that she twisted into a knot at the back of her head, Lydia walked next to Quindor in the midst of their escort as they made their way to the palace.

Emmy came with them.

Bundled in a thick woolen cloak that must have been taken from one of the High Lord's homes, she skipped next to Quindor, his gloved hand clutched in hers. She chattered the entire time, switching from topic to topic in the way children do, appearing for all the world like a happy young girl. And though the Grand Master could see as well as Lydia that she was a walking corpse, he pandered to her, answering her endless questions with seemingly no end of patience. The guards in their escort, however, kept a healthy distance from Emmy, watching her as much as they did their surroundings.

The fortifications of the palace, always strong, had been bolstered in the few hours since the King's return. Archers patrolled the tops of the wall, eyes watchful, and at its base, at least a hundred men stood in the gap between the wall and a secondary barrier that had been built of sharpened stakes pointed outwards. At the sight of Quindor, the soldiers moved a section of it to allow them passage, the guards at the actual gates again confirming their identities before allowing them inside.

The grounds themselves were filled with tents, soldiers and camp followers moving between them, and Lydia suspected the barracks connected to the palace must be full to the brim.

"Do they have water?" she asked Quindor during a break in Emmy's chatter. "Food?"

"The King is aware of how the blight infects," the Grand Master answered, his clipped tone suggesting he saw the same danger as she did. "Food and water are being brought in from Abenharrow."

Even so, having this many in Mudaire was folly. All it took was one of the blighted willfully tampering with a water barrel and the disease would sweep through the ranks like wildfire. And these weren't common citizens, but armed and trained soldiers who knew how to fight. Trying to purge their ranks of blighters wouldn't just be difficult, it might well be impossible.

"He needs to send them away," she said softly. "This is no place for an army."

"It is not your place to give advice to a king," Quindor answered. "You will speak when spoken to and answer only questions posed to you. Is that understood?"

The only thing she understood was that stymieing good advice for the sake of protocol was willful stupidity. But Killian, at least, would listen to her. And the King would surely listen to the man he'd put in command of his armies.

A servant wearing crimson-and-gold livery met them at the palace entrance, bowing to Quindor and Lydia. "The King will see you straightaway, Marked Ones."

While the wreckage and bodies had been removed from the palace, along with the bloodstained carpets, little else had been done to repair the damages inflicted the night of the ball. A strong smell of smoke permeated the air from the fire in the ballroom, the walls and floors bore deep gouges, and there was a strange lack of furniture, though whether it had been stolen by the civilians or removed because it had been damaged, she didn't know.

The servant led them down the hallway to the council chambers, and Lydia's gaze latched on the scorpion gilded onto the heavy wood doors. The armored guards outside eyed her and Quindor, deemed them not a threat, and their attention returned to the corridor beyond.

The servant entered the chamber, Lydia faintly heard him announce them, and then the door swung fully open to reveal the room. She'd seen the inside before only at a glance, but she swiftly marked the changes that had been made. Gone was the large table inlaid with a map of Mudamora and the heavy chairs that had encircled it, each with the symbol of a Great House carved into their backs. In their place was a narrow crimson carpet that led to a dais, on which sat a throne of oak and gold.

Serrick Rowenes, King of Mudamora, sat on the throne, his elbows resting on the arms of the chair, fingers steepled. Standing before him were several men, one of whom she recognized as High Lord Damashere. There was a tall woman dressed in a long tunic cinched at her waist by a sword belt, her dark hair twisted into a knot, the base shaved to reveal a falcon tattoo. Even before she turned to regard them, Lydia knew this must be High Lady Falorn.

But none of them were Killian. *Why isn't he here?*

She and Quindor approached, both of them bowing low when they reached the dais.

"Grand Master," the King said to Quindor. Then his amber gaze flicked to Lydia. "Marked One."

Despite his scrutiny, Lydia found her gaze drawn to the older woman standing behind his right shoulder, instantly recognizing Cyntha, the King's personal healer. Her white robes were pristine, her forehead marked with the half-moon tattoo. Her grey-laced dark hair hung in a simple braid over one shoulder, and her up-turned eyes had deep crow's feet at the corners. The last time Lydia had seen her had been right before Killian had been speared in the side at Alder's Ford.

The healer's nose wrinkled at the sight of Emmy. "That *thing* is dead. Why you keep it as a pet is a mystery to me, Grand Master, but at the very least, you should keep it in chains."

Emmy began to cry, and Quindor patted her absently on the shoulder. "Cruelty is unnecessary, Cyntha. While her mind might be gone, the body you see once belonged to a little girl with a good heart. For that girl's sake, we will treat her with kindness."

Cyntha made a noise of disgust, but the King stepped off his dais, brow furrowed as he inspected Emmy. Reaching out, he wiped the tears from her cheeks, then shook his head. "She appears to me a normal girl, Quindor. You're certain she's dead?"

"Quite. There is no more life in her than the stones beneath your feet, Your Grace."

"I don't feel dead." Emmy wiped her nose on her sleeve, looking pleadingly up at the King. "Please don't let her put me in chains, Your Grace. I'll be good, I promise."

King Serrick's lips drew into a thin line. "I see you," he said softly. "And I will burn every last one of your puppets to ash. I swear it in the names of the Six."

A terrified little scream tore from Emmy's lips, and she twisted away to bury her face in Quindor's robes, her shoulders shaking. And despite *knowing* this was the Corrupter at work, it was all Lydia could do not to demand the King to cease in his cruelty. Mercifully, Quindor gestured to one of the guards that had accompanied them. "Take her to one of the sitting rooms to wait. Have the servants bring her something sweet to eat."

And as the man led the weeping Emmy away, Lydia saw she wasn't the only one moved by the girl. Nearly everyone in the room looked ready to leap to her defense.

"Your return to Mudaire is unexpected, Your Grace," Quindor said once the door closed again. "I was of the belief you intended to travel to Rotahn to address the border war with Anukastre."

Serrick waved a dismissive hand. "Plans change. I've sent my niece Ria instructions on how to manage the situation in Rotahn, as well as the resources she needs to see it done. My place is in Mudaire, for this is where the true enemy resides, lurking behind the faces of my subjects. It must be expunged."

Hunted down. Killed. Murdered.

Burned.

"With respect, Your Majesty," Lydia said, "we should be dedicating our time to finding a cure for those who have been poisoned with blight, because trying to erase it by killing those who have succumbed is a battle we won't win."

One of Serrick's eyebrows rose. "I understand Hegeria's temple does not have adequate numbers of soldiers to hunt the blighters, Marked One. That is why I have brought the Royal Army to Mudaire."

"All that will accomplish is more infections," she argued. "Except it won't be infected civilians, but rather trained fighting men. You need to—"

"Be silent, girl," Quindor snapped. "You overstep."

"She's earned the right to speak." The King gestured to Lydia. "Continue."

All eyes were on her, and Lydia's palms turned clammy. "You need to withdraw all except those required to enforce a perimeter around the city. And instead of hunting those who are infected, we need to focus our effort on finding a cure."

Cyntha huffed out a loud breath. "They're *dead,* you silly little girl. They can't be healed. And if we don't hunt them, how long until the entire city is full of them and your *perimeter* is overrun?"

"They don't die the second they're exposed to the blight," Lydia snapped, then clenched her teeth, knowing she needed to mind her tone. "There are several painful hours between the moment of exposure and the moment they succumb, which means there are several hours within which they *could* be healed, if we could figure out how. But no one is going to come to us for help if they believe we'll just kill them and be done with it."

Quindor said, "I tried to heal the late Princess's horse when it was infected. And likewise, I tried to save High Lord Torrington when he became infected drinking contaminated wine." He shook his head.

"Doing so nearly killed *me*. It can't be done. Heartbreaking as it is, putting the infected down is the only solution—and a mercy, because it prevents the Corrupter from using their bodies for evil. And of course, once they are dead, they are lost to us. One cannot heal death."

"Just because it's not a simple solution doesn't mean—"

"I agree with the Grand Master, Your Majesty," Cyntha interrupted. "The girl is young, inexperienced, and—"

"Compassionate," the King said. "As one of Hegeria's Marked should be. Your many years may have given you wisdom and experience, Cyntha, but they've jaded you as well."

Cyntha's eyes flared, her fingers curling into fists. And out of the corner of her eye, Lydia saw High Lady Falorn's hand close over the hilt of her sword.

"I do not like consigning Mudamorians to death. For that reason, if no other, I see merit in what Lydia suggests."

"Your Grace," Quindor protested. "Already we have too few resources. I understand the allure of Lydia's proposal, but to pull healers from the hunt for the sake of pursuing this task could have catastrophic results."

Serrick held up his hands, making soothing gestures at Quindor. "At ease, Grand Master. I understand the predicament. Which is why Lydia will undertake the research herself."

Herself? It wasn't the amount of work that troubled her, or even the danger, but rather that there were others who knew so much more than she did. What chance did she have of coming up with a solution on her own?

"It's not safe," Quindor said between his teeth. "What if one of the infected kills her? Or one of their family members? I'd ask that you reconsider, Your Grace."

Silence fell across the room, the tension so thick that Lydia could scarcely breathe. Then King Serrick said, "The gods themselves ordained that I should lead Mudamora's Marked to best serve their ends."

Lydia's skin crawled, but there was nothing else to do but to nod.

"I think it best you get underway, Marked One," the King said. "I expect regular updates on your progress."

Despite knowing she was pushing her luck, Lydia asked, "What of withdrawing the majority of the Royal Army and quarantining the city?"

"I shall think on it," he answered. "And speak with my commanders. But military matters are neither your expertise nor your concern. Lydia, you may go. Quindor, remain."

Lydia bowed again, then backed away three steps before turning, it taking all her self-control not to run from the room. Vaguely, she heard a woman say, "Excuse me a moment, Your Grace—I need to piss," but the words went in one of Lydia's ears and out the other, her mind all for her own problems.

What had she gotten herself into? And how in the name of the Six was she supposed to accomplish anything meaningful on her own? And would *any* of it even matter if the Royal Army succumbed?

What she needed to do was find Killian. He'd listen, and he'd have the power to sway the King in a way that she didn't. She started toward the entrance to the palace, intent on seeking him out in the army camp on the grounds, but then a female voice caught her attention.

"He's not here."

Whirling around, Lydia found herself face-to-face with High Lady Falorn. "I . . ."

"You're looking for Killian, I know." She caught Lydia by the arm and towed her up the stairs instead of toward the door. "You think he'll take you seriously where Serrick did not, which is probably true. Unfortunately, he's on his way to Rotahn with a portion of the Royal Army. So you'll have to make do with me."

Killian isn't here. Disappointment hollowed out her insides, and Lydia bit her bottom lip hard in an effort to maintain her composure. Not only wasn't he here, he was on his way to the opposite side of Mudamora.

Stopping in front of a door, the High Lady unlocked it, then motioned for Lydia to go inside.

It was one of the many guest rooms in the palace and, given the upper level hadn't been subjected to the sacking the rest of the building had endured, still possessed all its fine furnishings and décor. The sitting room had two large sofas upholstered in red-and-gold fabric with a delicate wooden table between them. Thick carpets layered the stone floor, and the open windows were flanked by velvet drapery.

In the corner, a suit of armor sat in pieces on one of the chairs, a dented shield with a scraped image of a falcon leaning against it. On the table next to it, she counted no fewer than six daggers of varying length, and underneath rested a bow case and stuffed quiver.

"Have a seat." The High Lady gestured to the sofas. "Care for a drink?"

"Water, if you have it, Your Grace," Lydia answered, perching on one of the sofas and wondering why the woman had brought her here.

"Unless we're around Serrick and his fools, you can call me Dareena." Going to the window, she swung open the glass, the curtains billowing wildly on the breeze. With little regard for the deadly drop to the ocean beneath her, she stood on the window frame, stretching up to retrieve a cooking pot.

As she jumped back into the room, she said, "I don't have much faith that what we're being served is pure." She went to the roaring fire and sat the metal pot over the flames, watching as the snow melted.

"You're marked," Lydia said. "The blight can't infect you."

Dareena turned to look at her, raising one eyebrow. "You positive about that?"

"I . . ." Lydia hesitated. "It hasn't happened yet."

"I tempt fate often enough as it is without drinking poisoned water. Here." She dipped a cup into the pot, then handed it to Lydia. "Drink as much as you like. I've six more basins collecting snow on the ledge."

"Thank you." Lydia sipped at the water, which tasted far cleaner and fresher than any she'd had at the temple, watching the High Lady as she took the seat across from her. She was perhaps thirty years old, and the illustration in *Treatise* had not done her beauty justice. Lydia suspected there wasn't an artist in the world who could, because there was something in the woman's motion, in the weight of her presence, that couldn't be captured with paint or ink. It reminded her of Killian. "If I might ask, why do *you* think the King sent Kil . . . err, Lord Calorian to Rotahn?"

Dareena grinned, her upturned green eyes creasing at the corners. "*Killian* is no more for formality than I am. And I rather suspect you two are past that point already, am I right?"

Heat crawled up Lydia's chest, her cheeks burning. "We're friends."

"It's always good to be friends with your lover."

Lydia felt her eyes pop, and she stammered, "It's not like that. You've misinterpreted . . . We've never . . . I . . ." She clamped her teeth down to stop the babble flowing from her lips. "We are just friends."

The High Lady's shoulders shook with silent laughter. "He reacted much the same way when I pressed him, if it makes you feel any better. Known him his entire life and not once have I seen him lose his head over a"—she smirked—"friend."

Crossing her arms, Lydia leveled the High Lady with a steady stare. "I trust that you had greater reason to abandon the conversation between the Grand Master and the King than to satisfy your curiosity over the nature of my relationship with *Lord Calorian*."

Dareena burst out laughing. "Oh, my. I can see why he values your friendship so highly. Though in truth, I saw why the moment you went head-to-head with the King over the blighted." Taking a sip of her water, the High Lady leaned back against the cushion, resting a booted foot on one knee. "To answer your question, the Anuk have always raided the Rowenes gold mines, but apparently they've taken advantage of our preoccupation with Derin and increased their efforts. Serrick's argument is that Mudamora needs that gold to rebuild and to support those who've lost everything to the war, but I think it's more to do with the fact that it's *his* lands and mines they are thieving from. It's a blow to his pride."

"That's a ridiculous reason." Lydia scowled. "What sort of king makes decisions based on such vanity?"

"All of them," Dareena answered. "And if you think Serrick's bad, you'd have been horrified if you'd met my brother. Kings, as a rule, are a vainglorious lot. And given the Mudamorian monarchy is little more than a popularity contest among the Twelve Houses, our kings are the worst."

"His strategies certainly are." Lydia knew her tone was sour but didn't care. "The method of dealing with the blighted that he and Quindor have come up with is flawed."

"And that"—Dareena leveled a finger at Lydia—"is the reason I'm here. Because I think what you have to say is more important than the words spewing from the mouths of the men we left in that *throne room*." She scowled, then gave a slight shake of her head. "Tell me your opinion of what should be done."

Part of Lydia hesitated. She didn't know this woman, and she was not one to give her trust easily. Especially not to strangers. Except she knew that Killian trusted Dareena, and that had to count for something.

"Cyntha and Quindor are likely correct that there is no cure. The blighters are dead, their bodies nothing more than puppets animated by the Corrupter, although given they retain memory and skill, I think some part of them remains."

"Their souls? If that's the case, isn't Quindor correct that it's a mercy to give them a final death?"

"Maybe." Lydia took a sip of her water. "But there are consequences to us doing so."

Dareena regarded her silently, waiting.

"When I look at one of the blighters, *I* can see they are dead because of my mark," Lydia explained. "But those around them—their friends and family—they don't see that. All they see is the person they love being killed in the most gruesome manner imaginable. By their own countrymen. With one of the Marked who is supposed to be protecting them passing the sentence." She swallowed hard. "And they hate us for it. I don't think it will be long until they start taking steps to protect loved ones they know have been sick, hiding them and attempting to sneak them out of the city. If they haven't already."

"Gods, the Corrupter is insidious in his methods," Dareena muttered, then her eyes fixed on Lydia's. "You're giving me problems but no solutions. And if there is to be hope of Serrick listening to you, solutions are what need to be coming out of your mouth. Remember, he *wants* to win this."

"I don't have a solution." Lydia balled her hands into fists. "But not searching for one isn't the answer. We need to understand *how* the blight infects people and try to find a way to cure people *before* they die from it."

"So you need patients who are infected but still alive?"

"Yes, but no one in their right mind will volunteer."

Dareena rubbed her chin, her eyes distant. "Not unless they were told they'd be safe by someone they trust."

Tugging on her white robe, Lydia said, "Not me. And not you."

"No. It has to be someone who is one of them." Rising, Dareena went and opened the door. Leaning out in the hall, she put her fingers to her lips and whistled sharply. A few moments later, Lydia picked up the sound of boots coming down the hallway.

"I've some girls who might be able to help," the High Lady said. "Double advantage in that you already know them."

A heartbeat later, Gwen and Lena appeared in the doorway, smiles breaking onto their faces at the sight of her. Formerly members of Malahi's personal guard, it had been Lena who'd told Killian of Malahi's plots, and while the results of that revelation had been far from ideal, that didn't change that her friend had sided with her over the Queen.

Rising to her feet, Lydia crossed the room and wrapped her arms around them. "Gods, it's good to see you both. What are you doing here?"

Lena grinned, her copper-colored ponytail bouncing. "We work for the High Lady now. All of Malahi's bodyguard does, except for Sonia. She went with Kil—err, General Calorian, to Rotahn."

The knowledge that the Gamdeshian woman was with him eased the tension in her chest almost as much as having Lena and Gwen with her now.

"I'm assigning you two to assist Lydia in her research, as well as to watch her back," Dareena said. "You'll remain with her at Hegeria's temple until I say otherwise. Understood?"

Both girls saluted sharply.

"I'll leave you to it," Dareena said. "If I stay away much longer, Serrick will send someone to see if I fell in the privy."

She started to leave, but Lydia caught hold of her arm. "Will you try to convince him to send the Royal Army away?"

The High Lady's jaw tightened. "I'll try, but he's not inclined to listen to me."

"Make him listen." Lydia felt her vanquished tension return. "Not only could the King end up with an army full of blighters, without healers to identify them, he might not realize it until it's too late."

20

MARCUS

"I've never had to do this before," Titus said. "At least, not on this scale."

It was late in what had been a very long day that had not been improved by a brawl involving no less than fourteen members of the Thirty-Seventh. The men fought—it was inevitable, given their lifestyle—and he'd heard of fights in legion camps that had seen dozens dead. But never the Thirty-Seventh. Never *his* legion. All the men involved would be punished, but first he needed to drag what had incited the brawl out of them, which might be a challenge, for Servius had indicated all were being reticent.

But that had to wait.

The sun was low in the sky, and they were walking ahead of the stretchers of the men they'd discharged, heading through Aracam toward the harbor, where a ship waited to take them away. Out of sight and therefore out of mind.

At least, that was the idea.

Drums thudded a regular beat, sodden banners flopping on the wind and rain pinging against the golden dragon standards of both the Thirty-Seventh and Forty-First. An honor guard surrounded them, but the procession was also full of men not included in the guard. Brothers. Friends. Lovers. Those who'd feel the absence of these young men more than anyone else.

Marcus didn't think distance would do much to change that.

"Don't let it ever get easy," he finally answered the other commander. "They were injured following your orders and mine."

"It's part of the job."

Casting a cold glance at Titus, he said, "They didn't choose this path. Don't forget it."

They reached the harbor, moving onto the pier. The only ships in port were those from Marcus's fleet, but that would change. One day, he hoped to see it full of merchant vessels, the docks teeming with people rather than devoid of life as they were now.

The men carrying the stretchers stopped, and Marcus started toward those holding soldiers from his legion. Young men that he'd known since childhood. Whether they were conscious or not, he thanked each for their service and saluted them. Then he stepped aside to allow others to say their farewells.

There were many who came to say good-bye to Miki—the Sibernese legionnaire having always been popular—but Quintus never left his side, his face shadowed and drawn. But when the medics nodded at the stretcher-bearers to proceed to the ship, he stood his ground, watching expressionless as Miki was taken away.

Waiting until all were boarded, Marcus nodded once at the drummer, who played a series of beats. Then the air was split with the thunder of hundreds of men's fists striking armored chests in salute.

Marcus saluted as well, then gave the order to return to camp. Moving through the men, he caught hold of Quintus's arm. "We need to talk."

"I don't want to."

"It wasn't a request. Let's walk."

Glowering, Quintus allowed himself to be led a distance from the rest of the men, then crossed his arms over his chest. "What?"

"I'm sorry about Miki." Wiping away the rain running down his face, Marcus added, "And I'm sorry I couldn't send you with him."

"Rules are rules, aren't they, sir?" It was impossible to miss the sarcasm in Quintus's voice.

"Gibzen wants you out."

Quintus snorted. "Ungrateful prick. I've saved his ass more than once. He's a piece-of-shit primus compared to Agrippa."

"He's here whereas Agrippa abandoned us for a girl, so maybe give Gibzen some credit." Scuffing his sandal against the cobbles, Marcus added, "None of the other centurions want you. They all think that with Miki gone, you're going to . . ."

"Lose it?"

"Something like that."

Quintus pulled out a knife and began pruning his fingernails. "So I'm not discharged, but neither do I have a place in the Thirty-Seventh."

"That's right."

"Screw you all."

Quintus started to walk away, but Marcus caught his arm and hauled him back, well aware that if the other soldier decided to fight him, that Marcus would be the one who'd end up bleeding out on the street. "Teriana wants you back as her bodyguard."

"Because I did such a wonderful job of it last time?"

"You did as well as anyone could." Especially given that they'd been betrayed by someone who they all trusted. Except if Marcus revealed that information, Quintus would probably kill both Titus and Felix, never mind that one of them was innocent. "Teriana trusts you. And so do I."

"Your trust is misplaced, Marcus, because I fully intend to desert at my first opportunity. And you and I both know that even if you had the manpower to spare to hunt me down, you'd never find me."

"If you were planning to go alone, that would be the case," Marcus admitted. "But we both know that you'd never abandon him." And seeing the anger rising on Quintus's face, he swiftly added, "Besides, there's another option. A better option."

"I doubt it."

Knowing he was treading on dangerous ground, Marcus took a deep breath. "You keep Teriana safe while she's with us, I'll alter the Thirty-Seventh's books to say both you and Miki are dead. You'll both be free."

Silence hung between them.

"Why can't you just do that today?" Quintus asked. "Don't you think you owe me that much after years of doing your dirty work?"

"Freedom has a price, Quintus. This is the cost of yours. Keep her safe for me and you'll have the chance at a different life."

Wind whistled through the streets, ripping and tugging at his cloak.

"There is no limit, is there," Quintus finally said. "No line you won't cross to have things your way."

There were lines. Except Marcus kept finding himself on the other side of them.

From nowhere, the memory of Lydia's pleading eyes filled his vision along with the sensation of her nails digging into his skin as she fought to hold on. As she fought to survive.

Murderer.

He shoved the memory away, burying it deep with all the others. "Do we have a deal?"

"Yeah." Quintus spit into his hand, then held it out. "We've got a deal."

21

TERIANA

She'd said good-bye to Miki as they'd exited the camp, the resignation in his expression and the hollowness in Quintus's shattering her heart. She'd managed to keep her tears in check, but once she'd stumbled back into the command tent, great gasping sobs had torn from her chest.

The world was so incredibly cruel, and she wanted to scream at the gods for allowing it to be so. Wanted to scream at herself for her part in this particular cruelty, because Hegeria's marked healers had the power to help Miki. And what did it say about her that she chose keeping a secret over her friend ever walking again?

And for what?

The shifter had told her to watch. To learn. To be ready to strike. But what did knowing everything there was to know about the legions matter if she kept hesitating to strike against them?

"Why did you choose me, Madoria?" she whispered to her goddess. "I'm not suited to this. I don't know what I'm doing. *Anyone* would've been a better choice than me."

But no answer came.

Footsteps at the entrance to the tent caught her attention, and she looked up to see Amarin approaching with a steaming cup.

"Some tea, lass," he said, not commenting about the fact she sat on the floor. "You're upset about Miki, I take it?"

Teriana gave a tight nod, knowing that if she spoke, her voice would crack.

"He's known adversity all his life, Teriana. He'll be all right."

"And Quintus?"

Amarin sighed, then sat next to her, toying with the buckle of his sandal. The bronze skin of his hands was marked with age and use, and around his wrists were faded scars that suggested he'd spent time in shackles at some point in his life. "Time will tell how Quintus fares. It's good of you to have volunteered to take him on, Teriana."

"He's my friend."

His mouth quirked. "He's your enemy."

"That too."

They sat in silence for a time, listening to the patter of rain on the canvas above. Then Amarin spoke. "I was part of the last remaining rebel forces in Sibal. Fought against the Empire's legions for years before they finally ground us down. Anyone who survived was forced into indenture. The Senate sold most off to civilians, but they kept me because I was learned and, they believed, young enough to be redirected from my rebellious roots."

"Were they right?" she asked, curious to learn more about this man whom she'd never known to talk about himself.

"No." He huffed out a breath. "And yes."

She waited for him to say more, and sure enough, he continued. "Indenture is nothing more than slavery with the nebulous promise of freedom if only you work hard enough to achieve it; and being prisoner to it only fueled the rebellion in my heart. My belief that the Empire was an evil that needed to be driven out of Sibal, because with the Senate in control, my people would never be free."

To Teriana, that seemed an impossible dream. The province of Sibal was thoroughly under the Empire's control, and even a whisper of rebellion would be immediately curbed, likely with violence. But she said nothing.

"I dreamed of striking a great blow to the Empire, of putting my blade in the heart of a senator. Of showing them that I had not been quelled. So I bided my time and forced myself to become a model servant. And lo and behold, I learned that I was to be given to the legatus of the newly minted legion who had just graduated from Campus Lescendor."

"Marcus."

Amarin nodded. "Everyone was talking about him. The Prodigy of Lescendor, they called him—the brightest mind to have ever graduated. Scores unlike had ever been seen in Lescendor's testing and equally competent in the field. And oh, did they have plans for him. To groom him and the Thirty-Seventh to be the ultimate weapon—one they could use to conquer the last remaining free nations of the East. And one who they could use to quell any rebellion that dared to rear its head. The sharpest weapon in their arsenal."

Her blood chilled, because that was exactly how it had gone.

"Knowing all these things, I resolved to kill him at first opportunity," Amarin said. "And in doing so, to strike a greater blow to the Empire than I'd dared to dream possible."

She gaped at him, barely able to believe these words were coming from the man who'd fought to keep Marcus alive during his breathing attack. Who'd told her that he'd kill her if anything happened to Marcus.

"When the day came that I was to be presented to him, I managed to hide a knife on my person. I was a trained warrior, but they'd either forgotten or believed that I was assimilated. Either way, they'd never see the blow coming." He gave a slight shake of his head. "I was ready, so very ready, and they led me into the room to meet this prodigy, this commander, this warrior that all of Celendrial was talking about, and . . ."

"And . . . ," Teriana pressed, her pulse racing.

"And I found a boy instead." Amarin huffed out a laugh that had no humor in it. "Twelve years old, skinny as a bird, and so short his head didn't reach my shoulder. And though I had opportunity, I didn't reach for my blade."

"It's good that you couldn't kill a child." She couldn't even imagine doing so herself.

Amarin laughed, and there was a coldness to it. "That had nothing to do with it. Celendor's legions *slaughtered* my people's children, and I would have been glad to return the blow. No, the reason I didn't kill him was that I believed it would be a waste of my one opportunity. That they were all mad fools to think this boy such a powerful weapon. That I was better to use the access being his servant would give me to take a life that would make a difference."

"But you didn't." She scowled, anger flooding her. "You, what? Developed so much affection for Marcus and the other boys that you gave up on Sibal? On rebellion?"

"Far from it," he answered. "As I looked for an opportunity to strike my blow, my ambition only grew. Especially when I realized that the Senate had been right about him. And it was then I resolved that my blow would not fall upon a single man, but upon the Empire. And that my weapon wouldn't be a blade."

Teriana's heart skipped, but before she could press Amarin further, sandals thudded against wood, and Marcus said, "We do have stools, you know."

Scrambling to her feet, she muttered, "Uncomfortable stools. When you build your fortress, you should really invest in better furniture. With cushions."

Quintus stepped from behind Marcus. "I hear you and me are to be tight as ticks again, Teriana."

"If you'll all excuse me," Amarin murmured, "I'll see to securing dinner."

"Thanks, Amarin," Quintus said. "I could use some grub. It has been a day."

Marcus glowered at him. "I already regret this decision."

The jaunty salute Quintus gave in response made Teriana's chest tighten, because there was no humor in his eyes, only a haunted hollowness, this all an act to cover his grief.

One of the men on duty chose that moment to step into the tent, immediately looking to Marcus. "Your presence is required, sir."

"I'm in the middle of something. Get Felix to deal with it."

"It's the tribunus who is asking for you, sir. He said to tell you that a magnolia has bloomed, but that the blossom is wilting quickly."

All the blood drained from Marcus's face. "Stay with her," he said to Quintus. "I need to go." Then he all but bolted from the tent.

Turning to Quintus, she asked, "What in the underworld was that about? Do you know the code?"

"Yeah," he answered, expression thoughtful. "It means things are about to get interesting."

22

MARCUS

Heart galloping, Marcus stepped outside the command tent to find Felix standing in the rain with the guards, his face unreadable. "He's in medical."

"How bad are his injuries?"

"He's a dead man."

And would only be the first of many.

Grimacing, Marcus strode through camp as fast as he could without running, both him and Felix ignoring the acknowledgments of the men.

The medical tent was only dimly lit for the sake of the men in it trying to sleep, but the surgery at the far end blazed bright with lamplight. Racker's distinct form was bent over a body on the operating table, his assistants scurrying about.

Pulse loud in his ears, Marcus crossed the tent, his eyes fixing on the naked man sprawled across the table. He was bleeding from several wounds, but what was going to kill him was the gaping hole in his belly. Racker's hands were bloody up past his elbows as he fought to slow the man's bleeding.

The *path-hunter's* bleeding.

For there was no denying what this man was. He had golden Cel skin, which was marked with the tattooed code of the unmarked xenthier stem the Senate had paid him to venture through.

"He say anything useful?" Marcus moved to the man's head. The path-hunter's eyes were rolled back, but he was muttering under his breath. Bending low, Marcus listened. It seemed the man was asking for his wife. Possibly children.

"Not since I've had him." Racker took a clamp from one of the medics assisting him, fixing it over a spurting artery. "He's been mostly unconscious. The men who brought him in have his gear, though."

Which would have all the information they needed, except where the stem had deposited him. With this rain, retracing his steps would be difficult, which meant potentially months of searching for the terminus stem. If they ever found it at all.

Let him die with the answer.

The thought reared in his head, but only for an instant. Then Felix stepped next to the table, along with Titus, who was rubbing his eyes as though he'd been woken from a heavy sleep. The other legatus grimaced at the sight of the path-hunter's injuries. "That's not the work of a blade."

"Obviously," Racker muttered, then he elbowed Titus aside. "If you'd make space, sir. It's rather more important that *I* be able to see than for you to have the opportunity to gape." Then his eyes flicked to Marcus. "Well?"

"Rouse him."

The Thirty-Seventh's surgeon said nothing, only reached out a hand, and one of the other medics handed him a needle, along with a vial. Without hesitation, he injected something into the path-hunter. "Get what you need from him quickly. You'll only have a minute or so before he bleeds out."

Then the path-hunter's eyes snapped open, and he screamed. Bending over the table, Marcus caught hold of the man's arms, meeting his panicked gaze. "Be easy. You are with your countrymen, and we will take care of you."

The man's chin gave a shuddering jerk.

"I'm Legatus Marcus of the Thirty-Seventh," he said. "And you are in a legion camp located within the Dark Shores of the West."

"I found you," the man breathed. "I mapped a path across the world."

"That you did," Marcus kept his voice calm. Soothing. "What's your name?"

"Nonus."

"How long since you crossed?"

"Two days. I think. I lost count."

Which meant Cassius hadn't stopped with the first group he'd sent through the unmapped genesis stems. He'd sent more, and in all likelihood, it had been to their deaths.

The man shivered violently, only Marcus's grip keeping him steady. "Did you travel the entire time?"

"Yes." All the color was gone from the man's face. "I ran until I reached the river. And then I swam. But it kept chasing. Relentless, it was." He reached up to grip Marcus's tunic. "And it wasn't alone."

Despite the heat, prickles of cold ran down Marcus's spine. "What direction did you come from?"

"West." The man's grip tightened. "Deep in the jungle."

"The stem was near a river?"

"Yes." The path-hunter was shuddering, his skin icy beneath Marcus's hands.

"Time's almost up," Racker said. "Thirty seconds, if that."

"How wide a river?" Marcus pressed. "Were there falls?"

The path-hunter's eyes rolled back in his head, then abruptly regained focus. "My girls. You'll make sure they're given the gold? That they're taken care of?"

Marcus nodded, because it was the only comfort he could give. "You have my word."

"Tell them I love them," the man whispered, then he exhaled one last breath and went still.

Marcus stood staring at the man's lifeless eyes. Dead before his time, and all for the sake of gold. All for the sake of giving his children a better life, never mind that his actions could well lead to the deaths of thousands. Of tens of thousands.

How many lives had been taken with love as the perpetrator's defense?

"What was that?" Felix asked.

Realizing he'd spoken aloud, Marcus muttered, "Nothing." Letting go of the path-hunter's shoulders, he reached up and closed the man's lids, then turned to find Felix holding a pencil and a scrap of paper. "Did you get that all down?"

"For all the good it will do us." Frowning at the number tattooed on the dead man's arm, Felix copied it on the paper. "This is going to be a nightmare to find. And obviously the wildlife is a threat."

"But at least we know it's there." Titus's voice was drenched in triumph, and he slapped the dead man's shoulder like a comrade's, jostling the body. "Somewhere, within a few days' journey of our camp, is a xenthier path connecting us to the Empire. Which means we are halfway to having the reinforcements we need!"

The only thing they needed reinforcements for was conquest.

"It does us little good without a return path," Marcus answered. "We have no way of even informing the Senate that one of their hunters was successful, so contain your enthusiasm."

"But Teriana—"

"The Senate will not send us more men without land routes here and *back* again, Titus. *Viable* routes that don't require whirlpools and boons from sea serpents."

"But—"

"I'm not allowing our only route back to the Empire to sail away just to deliver a message. This is a large step for us, but our work is not done."

Titus stared at him, brow furrowed and eyes seeing more than Marcus wanted, so he added, "Go spread the word. Open up casks for a third of the men and let them celebrate."

"And to toast the fallen," Racker said. "This man fought hard to reach us."

Titus inclined his head. "To the fallen." He saluted before exiting the tent, and a chorus of cheers rose a moment later.

"I'll have a tracking party head out at dawn," Felix said. "Not sure what sort of trail they'll find with this rain, but maybe we'll get lucky."

"Maybe."

"Meet you back at command?"

At Marcus's nod, Felix saluted and strode out of the tent, leaving Marcus alone with Racker and the corpse.

"You know what did this?"

Racker's gaze was clinical as he touched the dead man's injuries, fingers delving into the wounds. "Big cat, I'd say. But who knows what sort of creatures hunt the interior."

"I'll speak with Ereni. See if she might have answers."

Racker made a noncommittal grunt, but that concerned Marcus less than the tremor that stole over his head surgeon's hands. Hands that Marcus had never seen shake, no matter how catastrophic the trauma. Hands that without, the Thirty-Seventh would have seen twice the discharges that it had.

"He couldn't be saved," he said, watching the surgeon closely. "It might not have been kind to put him through that for the sake of so little information, but it wasn't what killed him."

Racker's black eyes fixed on him, full of the purest form of condescension that Marcus deigned to opine on a medical matter. "Thank you for your insight, *sir.*"

"Something is troubling you. If not this man, then what?"

Silence hung across the tent, broken only by the faint coughs and moans of the injured men on the cots beyond.

Finally, Racker spoke. "I thought we'd have more time." He shook his head. "I *hoped* we'd have more time."

Marcus hesitated before answering. "We aren't back under their thumbs just yet."

"But soon enough." Racker waved a hand at him. "Get out of my surgery, sir. I'll see what I can learn from the body and have a report back to you at dawn."

23

TERIANA

"A path-hunter has been brought into camp."

Teriana's stomach hollowed, the world swimming in and out of focus. "What?"

"One of the Senate's path-hunters is here." Quintus exhaled. "Which means that there is a way from the Empire to the Dark Shores that doesn't involve a Maarin ship or sea monsters."

"Oh."

He took a look at her, then went rooting around in the cabinets, coming out with a bottle of wine. "Atlian," he said. "Amarin hides the expensive stuff for when we have senators in the command tent."

"Senators?"

"Yeah." He pulled the cork, then filled two tin cups, handing her one. "Soon as we have viable routes mapped, they'll send one, and I can tell you from experience that he'll be a right pain in everyone's asses. Though I suppose you'll be gone at that point. And I'll . . ." He trailed off, shaking his head.

"Right."

He sat on the stool next to her, then caught hold of her wrist, lifting the cup to her mouth. She dutifully took a mouthful of the smooth red liquid, then another. "We're a bad influence on you," he said. "Teaching you to drown your woes."

"I'm a sailor," she said softly. "I was born a bad influence."

Quintus laughed, taking a sip from his cup, eyes fixed on the lamp at the center of the table. They sat in silence together for a long time, drinking the wine. Just after they finished the bottle, the camp filled with shouts and laughter, and then Marcus returned, officers following on his heels. Quintus stood. She did not.

Marcus's clothing was soaked, and rainwater ran in rivulets down his face. Retrieving a towel, he scrubbed it over his hair and dried his hands, not so much as acknowledging her before saying, "Let's have a look, then."

Kneeling before one of the chests that contained maps and other important documents, he moved the pieces of the combination lock, and the mechanism opened with a clunk. He extracted a rolled-up map and a bound ledger, taking them to the opposite end of the table from where she sat, where he unrolled it. Servius used markers to weigh down the corners. "His number?"

Felix handed over a sheet of paper. Frowning, Marcus referred to a page in the ledger, then flipped through the book, pausing when he reached a page near the back. "Bardeen."

Bardeen was on the southeastern edge of the Empire. The *Quincense* did a fair bit of trade along the province's extensive coast during the summer; the winters were too cold for her mother's blood.

Felix leaned over the map, then rested his finger on it, giving a slight shake of his head. "Shit. That's near where we were camped when we laid siege to Hydrilla."

"It was discovered last year," Marcus said, reading from the page. "Underground, after an excavation. Senate had sent sixteen hunters through it, last our records were updated. Who knows how many they've sent since, but surely more than just our corpse."

Gibzen snorted. "Will make it easier to find on our end if there are corpses scattered about it."

Marcus made a noncommittal noise. "I expect they are scattered throughout the jungle, but still, it's surprising that none made it out alive." Glancing toward Servius, he said, "Offer a reward for information about any foreigners having stumbled out of the jungle over the past year."

"Wouldn't they have come to us by now, if they'd survived?"

"Things change. Let's see if a reward will lure them out." He was silent for a heartbeat, then he said, "And offer a reward for any information about known xenthier stems in the area. Titus, start recruiting volunteers to train as path-hunters so that they are ready when we find a genesis stem. Make sure they are clear both of the dangers and of the reward they'll receive if they are successful."

Titus nodded, and though his face was expressionless, Teriana could see the glee in his eyes. He *wanted* to be reunited with the Empire.

"Gibzen, you will head the search for the Bardeen stem's terminus. Racker will provide his report on what he's learned from the body in the morning, but I want you underway before then."

"Yes, sir."

"Good." Rising to his feet, Marcus surveyed the group. "I'll withhold congratulations until we can claim success on our end. Adjourned." Then he turned to Quintus. "Be back in this tent at dawn."

"Yes, sir."

Everyone left, leaving Teriana alone with Marcus. He sat back down on a stool, resting his elbows on the table and rubbing his temples with his thumbs. Then he said, "Are you all right?"

Unfreezing from where she'd sat during the discussion, she moved across from him, eyeing the massive map depicting the entirety of the Empire. It was covered with dots of various colors, most of them red and green. There had to be hundreds of them. Xenthier stems.

"What do red and green mean?" Her voice rasped, and she wished she had a glass of water. Or a bottle of rum.

"Unmapped xenthier stems. Green for geneses. Red for terminuses."

There were so many. So very, very many.

"I shouldn't let you see this." He coughed, and she winced at the slight wheeze to his breath. "It's treason."

As were so many other things he'd said and done. Except things had changed. Now those who'd punish him were within reach. "Then maybe you should put it away."

He stared blindly at the map, then nodded and rose. Rolling up the map, he stowed it and the ledger back in the chest, the lock clicking loudly as he secured it. Picking up a bottle sitting on top of the chest, he jerked out the cork and took a large mouthful. "I've had this headache ever since we took Aracam. It just throbs and throbs and I can't think."

"Rum won't help that."

"Probably not." He took another mouthful, then set it on the table between them. "Even the best-laid plans go awry when the game changes. I know that well, and yet . . ."

Outside, the volume was increasing by the second, the men shouting and cheering and laughing. Marcus turned his head, listening to them, then he said, "If we find the xenthier, your people will be freed. *You'll* have your freedom."

"Freedom that comes with a steep price." For when Cassius had his paths, Marcus and his legions would not be left to sit idle in Arinoquia. It meant war against the West. And against her.

"I don't know what path to choose." He exhaled a shuddering breath. "I don't know what to do."

Neither did she. For everywhere she looked, all paths led to blood.

24

LYDIA

Lena and Gwen walked with her back to the temple, word that the High Lady had sent them ensuring they were given rooms in the dormitories. Not that space was a premium given how few healers remained. And once they'd dropped off their things, the three of them moved into the library.

"What a mess," Lena said. "Who did this?"

"Me," Lydia admitted. "I was organizing."

"An obvious priority in a city overrun by possessed corpses."

Sighing, Lydia moved stacks of books off chairs so they could sit. "I'm hoping to find some clue to how we might combat the blight. Maybe it has happened before. If not here, then somewhere else. I'm not sure exactly *what* I'm looking for, only that the sum of healer knowledge resides within these walls."

"The library at the temple in Revat is bigger," Gwen mumbled, wrapping her thick blond braid around her hand. When both Lydia and Lena turned to stare, her pale, freckled skin turned pink. "What? Sonia told me it was so."

Shoving aside her piqued curiosity, Lydia said, "Be that as it may, we can hardly venture to Gamdesh to visit a library. And I suspect if I ask to send a letter requesting the Gamdeshian healers search for me, that it would be denied. The King seems to have little interest in other nations knowing the full extent of Mudamora's plight."

"Malahi always said his pride would be our downfall." As soon as she said the words, Lena sucked in a breath and glanced at Lydia. "What happened to her . . . It wasn't your fault any more than it was his."

His. Killian. Because he'd sworn to protect Malahi but had left the Queen to come after her.

"Malahi made her bed," Lena added. "She didn't deserve what happened to her, but she caused it."

And yet if Malahi were alive, how different would things be? She'd be Queen, not Serrick, and their differences aside, Lydia knew that the other girl would have shown more empathy for the people. Would have listened to any possible solution that saw them saved. As much as it hurt to admit, the kingdom would likely have been better off if Killian had stayed by her side. "Were you there?" she asked softly. "When Rufina took her?"

Lena gave a reluctant nod. "Not that we did much good. We were riding as hard as we dared back to Mudaire, her at the center of the group. But it was so dark." She bit her bottom lip. "We never saw Rufina coming. Never heard her coming."

The soldiers that escorted Lydia and Quindor back to Mudaire had known a few of the details of what had happened, but Lydia kept silent, waiting for her friend to continue.

"The deimos just dropped from the sky," Lena whispered. "Rufina caught Malahi around the waist and dragged her off the horse. High Lord Calorian was closest to her. He caught hold of Malahi's ankle, but the deimos knocked him off. And then the rest of us were trying to get arrows out. To shoot Rufina without hitting Malahi. But . . ."

But it was a difficult shot. And none of them were good archers. *Killian would've saved her.*

She shoved away the thought.

"Malahi screamed the entire time." Lena's eyes were distant, her face tight with remembered horror. "But there was nothing we could do."

Silence hung like a pall.

"Did they find her?" As she asked the question, it struck Lydia that the King had shown no signs of grief when she'd met him today. It was possible he was enough of a politician that he could hide his sorrow over the death of his only child, but that rationale fell flat in Lydia's mind. Especially given how often she'd seen senators back in Celendor spin the loss of a child to their advantage. To her, it felt almost like he was acting as though she'd never existed.

"No." Lena closed her eyes, her grief for the fallen queen real, and Gwen wrapped an arm around her shoulder, pulling her close. "Though the High Lady has a shifter in her employ who is still searching."

Even if she were a desiccated corpse, Malahi's clothing and jewelry were enough to identify her. And while disposing of a body where no one would find it wouldn't have been a challenge for Rufina, it struck Lydia as more the enemy queen's style to have dropped the body in the middle of the army camp if for no other reason than to make a point.

"Her father's men aren't looking anymore." Gwen's voice was rough. "It's too dangerous for small groups to remain out west, what with the blight. So wherever she is, only chance will ever see her found."

Malahi had blackmailed her. Tried to turn her into a murderer. And yet Lydia wouldn't have wished this fate upon anyone, much less a girl who above all things had desired the best for her people. "The gods have her in their care, now."

Both Lena and Gwen made the sign of the Six against their chests, then Gwen picked up one of the books, flipping through it before tossing the volume back on the table. "So what's the plan, oh *Marked One*."

Rolling her eyes at the honorific, Lydia said, "I want you to find me people who are infected but not yet turned."

"And then we're to bring you to them? And if you don't cure them and they become blighters, we're just going to walk away?"

"Correct."

"That seems . . . not smart."

Lydia sighed. "There's no helping it. Families won't bring me the sick if they hear that we kill my failed experiments."

"But they're already dead," Lena said. "Right? The blighters aren't alive, that's what we were told."

Her tension had worked its way into a headache, and Lydia rubbed at the muscles of her neck, trying to relax them. "Only a healer can tell they are dead," she explained. "To anyone else, they appeared wholly cured and themselves."

Lena made a face. "I preferred when they looked dead. Made it a lot easier to kill them when they were a horde of monsters."

"That's probably why the blight evolved. Before, the blighters were a cudgel." She swallowed hard. "Now they are a blade in the night."

"Then I suppose we'd better get out there." Lena looked down at her Falorn livery. "Probably better to wear something else."

High Lady Falorn was beloved by the people, but given the current resentment toward the Marked, Lydia was inclined to agree. "Be careful," she said. "And be back before dark."

As soon as they departed, she got back to work on her organization of the library, piling mis-shelved books in front of their appropriate sections, stopping only when titles of interest caught her eye. There was so much information—an incredible wealth of knowledge, but the dearth of material on the Seventh god or the corrupted surprised her. They were mentioned in passing only, usually in reference to the impossibility of returning the life one of the corrupted had taken from a victim, as a healer could not *reverse the passage of time or its impact on the body.* Of the blight, or anything like it, there was nothing.

Hours later, a knock sounded on the door to the library. It opened, and High Lady Falorn stepped inside.

Lydia stood, her back and knees cracking loudly. Dareena laughed. "Gets worse with age, but I suppose you are already familiar with the sensation."

"Deeply familiar," Lydia answered. "But advancing age is better than the alternative."

"The Six know, succumbing to old age likely isn't something someone like me has to look forward to," the High Lady answered, motioning for her to sit back down. "Dying young is a hazard of Tremon's mark."

It was impossible not to stiffen, and Dareena's expression softened.

"The greatest danger to Killian *is* Killian," the High Lady said. "But I suspect you know that."

Lydia did; but knowing that she wouldn't be there to put him back together made her ill. "Did you have any luck with the King?"

"Quindor and I both pressed Serrick to move the Royal Army to Abenharrow, but he refuses. He sees Mudaire as the front lines of our ongoing war with the Corrupter, and he believes this is where Mudamora's military might must focus its efforts. He's going to increase the number of patrols hunting for blighters."

"There's no point in having more patrols. Not without more healers to identify the infected."

"Which is why he's recalled all who remain, though it will take time for them to reach Mudaire."

As though Lydia needed more pressure. Once additional healers arrived and the patrols to hunt the infected increased in earnest, she'd lose her chance to try to treat those in the early stage of infection, because Lydia had no doubt in her mind that they'd kill them, too. "He's a fool."

Dareena made a face. "Others are warning him that if we don't keep the blighters in check, they'll grow enough in numbers to be a real threat. Which isn't faulty advice. Serrick's between a rock and a hard place."

"Who is giving this advice?" Lydia asked the question despite having a good idea who it must be.

"Cyntha."

"How is she any more equipped to give advice about the army than I am?" Lydia demanded. "She's a healer, not a soldier."

"She's both. Or was, at any rate." Rotating her chair around, Dareena straddled it, chin resting on the back. "She was born to a minor noble family in Axbridge and grew up in the company of my brother, which allowed her to receive the best military training there was to be had. After she was marked, Cyntha only did cursory training at the temple before returning to be Derrek's personal healer and bodyguard. They were . . . *close.*"

"So you know her well?"

Dareena shook her head, green eyes distant. "My brother was fifteen years older than I was. Our father passed when I was only four, and after he was crowned king, Derrek spent most of his time in Mudaire, Cyntha with him. They parted ways on poor terms after he was married, and I only saw her a handful of times until she joined Serrick's household. She's . . . a hard woman. But not without reason."

Lydia was curious to know the reason, but asking the High Lady for gossip that likely pertained to her deceased brother seemed rude, so she held her tongue.

"Either way, Serrick heeds her advice, so unless you can offer him a compelling alternative to putting all of his resources to hunting the blighters, that's what he will do."

Lena and Gwen chose that moment to appear in the doorway, and though they'd been gone for only a few hours, relief that they were safe flooded through Lydia. Relief that was tempered by Lena giving a slow shake of her head and Gwen muttering, "This is going to be harder than we thought."

Dareena rose to her feet. "I need to get back to the palace." She gave Gwen a gentle slap on the shoulder. "The right path is rarely the easy one. Keep at it and keep safe." Then she left the library.

"We'll keep at it," Gwen said. "The longer we're out among them, the more they'll come to trust us. We just need to be careful to make sure that no one catches us coming and going from here. It might be easier—"

"No," Lydia interrupted. "It's too dangerous at night. I don't want you out there."

"Fine." Her friend shrugged. "But it will take longer."

"I'm not risking you more than I already am. Not unless we're really desperate."

Lena huffed out a breath, a slightly wild smile on her face. "You mean it can get worse than this?"

It can always get worse. "You two should go get something to eat before it's all gone."

"You coming with?"

She was exhausted. Frustrated. Afraid. "No, I'm going to try to get some sleep."

"I'll bring something back for you," Gwen said.

They parted ways on the stairs, Lydia heading to her room and her friends heading to the main level to eat. Once behind closed doors, Lydia pulled off her robes and tossed them aside, then went to the tiny mirror nailed to the wall. Removing her spectacles, she peered at her reflection, noting the shadows beneath her eyes. The gauntness of her cheeks.

It was more than exhaustion, because when she'd been working with Killian in the sewer tunnels, she'd gone with even less sleep. But then she'd been fueled by the sense she was accomplishing something. That she'd been doing good. And she'd had Killian at her side.

At the thought of him, she bit her bottom lip, wondering when he'd arrive in Rotahn. If he'd thought of her since they'd parted ways at Alder's Ford. Closing her eyes, she pulled up the memory of his face as she'd ridden away and knew in her heart that he had. That the connection between them wasn't something to be erased by distance. Or even time.

Gods, but she missed him. Missed him in such a painful, visceral way, it was as though a part of her body had been cut out. A part of her heart. With him, she felt more herself—the best version of herself—though she hadn't realized it until he was gone. Killian would understand why she was fighting to save the blighters rather than kill them, and she couldn't help but think that her chances of finding a solution would be greater if he were here. He wouldn't abandon his people, no matter how much it cost him—it wasn't in his nature.

The cold air bit at her bare skin, her thin shift not enough to keep her warm, so she went to her bed, curling on her side beneath the thick blanket. Closing her eyes, she allowed her mind to drift, building an alternative version of reality where things were as *she* wanted them to be. She imagined the familiar tread of his boots coming down the hall. The firm knock of his fist against the door. How his tall, broad-shouldered frame would fill the entrance, smelling faintly of horses and soap, leather and steel.

What would he say?

A jest? Her mouth curved upward as she envisioned the gleam of wit in his dark eyes and the crooked smile he always gave when something amused him. The sound of his laugh, deep and rich, filling her with warmth.

No . . . He wouldn't make jokes or laugh in such a moment. Casting aside the flawed dream, she started it from the beginning, imagining again his footfalls. The knock. Rising to the door to find him there, dressed in his usual dark coat and trousers, the expensive fabric likely torn in an elbow or knee.

He wouldn't say anything. He didn't need to any more than she did, because they always understood each other. She bit her bottom lip, imagining how he'd push back the dark locks of his hair the way he always did when he was nervous. And when he finally spoke, the deep timbre of his voice would be rough, everything he felt playing across his face for her to see.

I missed you.

Though it was her imagination speaking, it felt real, and her heart flipped, her mind drawing them a step closer together. Though he might protest otherwise, he was a gentleman through and through, and despite how little she wore, his eyes would never stray from her face.

Except she wanted them to.

Her lips parted as she envisioned his gaze running over the length of her body, desire darkening his eyes. How it would feel if he reached out and pushed the straps of her shift off her shoulders, the fabric ghosting down her body and leaving her naked before him. Of her fumbling with buttons and buckles, weapons clattering against the floor as she cast them aside.

Her fingers twisted the fabric of the blanket as she imagined his hands, calloused from use, touching her. Of his skin, hot where hers was cool, pressing against her. What would it feel like when he finally kissed her? What would he taste like?

Her toes curled, an aching need building in her belly as her mind offered her a glimpse of them together. Of falling into this very bed, of his weight pressing down against her, their fingers interlaced.

Her breathing grew more ragged as she descended into the dream, her imagination delivering where reality had failed, going further and further until a gasp tore from her lips and she rolled onto her back, finally allowing the fantasy to slip away.

And then sleep took her.

Along with the nightmare.

She was running through the sewers, her bare feet splashing in the frigid filth, the sounds of pursuit echoing through the tunnels. Her chest was tight, her side cramping, but no matter how she twisted and turned through the maze, the steps of her pursuer only drew closer.

Racing around a corner, she slid to a stop, a bricked wall barring her way. Blight oozed between the cracks of the crumbling mortar like tar, dripping down to form a stream, its rank stench assaulting her nostrils. She stared at the blight, some trick of her eye making it appear to be flowing in two directions, though that was impossible.

Then she heard the scuff of a boot against stone, and a laugh filled the air, hauntingly familiar.

Heart in her throat, Lydia turned, her gaze captured by a set of eyes that appeared like black pits rimmed with flame. But that wasn't what sent terror rippling through her.

It was that the face staring back at her was her own.

25

MARCUS

Mud splashed up his legs as he walked through camp to where Servius had gathered the men involved in the brawl, all of them stripped down to their undergarments in preparation for the inevitable punishment. At the sight of him, they straightened their line and saluted.

"I take it no one has offered an explanation."

"No, sir." Servius glowered at the men, who all had their eyes fixed on the mud. Blackened eyes, broken noses, bruised sides, and split knuckles all abounded, and three of them had arms in splints, which meant they had at least six weeks before they could rejoin their lines. Motioning to one of the men in his escort, he murmured, loud enough for the men to hear, "Tell Racker I have need of him."

The brawlers all shifted uneasily, no doubt wondering what he had in store for them if the surgeon was required. It was three lashes for brawling. Refusing to answer a superior increased the punishment to five lashes. But all of them knew that, so threatening them with it was unlikely to yield results. That they were being so deeply reticent meant that whatever had caused the fight was something that they really didn't want him to know.

Which meant he needed to use a more creative method to get the information out of them.

"I was *deeply* disappointed to hear of the events that transpired at the mess tent yesterday," he said, circling the group. "The Empire holds its legions to a standard of conduct, with laws and protocols which must be abided to ensure strength and unity and order. Yet it is no secret that I hold our legion to a higher standard still, because we are the Thirty-Seventh!" He shouted the last, and all the men slammed their fists to their chests in salute, hollering, "Yes, sir!"

Rounding on one of them, he said, "Is the Thirty-Seventh middling?"

"No, sir!"

To another, he asked, "Does the Thirty-Seventh aim to only *meet* expectations?"

"No, sir! We exceed them, sir!"

Stepping back so as to encompass them all in his next statement, he said, "Is the Thirty-Seventh following in the footsteps of the Twenty-Ninth?"

Their spines collectively stiffened, the barb one that would be effective against any man under his command. The Twenty-Ninth was the legion they'd been assigned to for the completion of their training in the field. Which had been well and good when Dareios was legatus, but the man, as well as his second and third in command, had been murdered not long after the Thirty-Seventh had joined them in the field. The then primus, Hostus, had risen to command, and the Thirty-Seventh's circumstances took an abrupt turn for the worse. The remaining years of their training bordered on torture. If gods existed, then demons must, too, and Hostus was surely one of them. And after how they'd parted ways in Bardeen, Marcus hoped he'd never find himself alone with the older legatus again.

"No, sir!" they all shouted, and as he'd hoped, their eyes were filled with shame.

He stared at them for a long moment, allowing the tension to build. "Then perhaps one of you might offer sufficient justification for why you were acting like them?"

More shifting feet, but no one answered. *What is this bloody well about?* he wondered. *What don't they want me to know?*

"This had better be good, Marcus." Racker's voice filtered up from behind him. "I was about to step into surgery."

It was a struggle not to wince. Turning to the surgeon, he asked, "Can you give me a cost for the medical supplies used to treat these men's injuries?"

The surgeon's eyes flicked over the group, then he shrugged. "Insignificant, for the most part. But most availed themselves of narcotics. In Celendor, the cost would amount to perhaps a gold dragon. But—"

Interrupting, Marcus said to Servius, "Garnish the cost from their wages," his words drawing visible glowers from the men.

"If you'd let me finish," Racker snapped. "Given we have no access to the source here in the Dark Shores and I've been unable to find a suitable alternative, our remaining narcotics are priceless."

"And it was wasted on brawlers." Marcus watched the glowers fade back into shame. "The reason for your actions had better be good. And one of you had better spit it out now. That is an order."

Silence.

And Marcus felt his stomach drop, because in all his years of command, he'd never had men refuse one of his orders. Never.

What was this about? What didn't they want him to know?

Who were they protecting?

He couldn't concede on the matter without looking weak and inviting this to happen again. But neither did he want to follow the protocols of the Empire and accuse them of treason for refusing to obey an order, because that meant he'd have to hang them. Which they all bloody well knew.

His breath was coming too quickly, his chest tightening, because this shouldn't be happening. Not in the Thirty-Seventh. Not to him. "Tell me now or you're out." The words slipped from his lips almost without thought. "I won't have men under my command that I can't trust, so you either tell me what you fought over or you can no longer consider yourself Thirty-Seventh."

"Shit," Servius muttered under his breath. "This is out of hand."

Marcus ignored him, watching instead the horror forming on the faces of the men before him, several exchanging glances with one another. "Well?"

He felt the moment where they mutually agreed, then one stepped forward. "It was over some things that were said about you in the mess tent, sir."

"What things?"

The man's jaw worked back and forth, then he sighed and said, "That you're not following legion protocols, sir. That you're not holding yourself to the standard of the Thirty-Seventh. And that maybe it will be better once we find the xenthier paths, because once the Senate has authority here, things will go back to normal."

Things will go back to normal. The words were like ice water, because they were identical to what the traitor had told Ashok. "Who said that?"

"Was a conversation, sir. More than a few involved, and the argument sparked after the speaker left the mess tent. Men taking sides and such."

"Who wanted things to go back to normal? Who said that part?"

Silence.

"I will have Racker burn the Thirty-Seventh's mark off your fucking chests if you don't tell me!" Marcus shouted.

The tension mounted, then finally the man gave a sharp shake of his head. "Was the tribunus."

Felix.

"Well," Marcus said, all his control going toward keeping his expression in check. Toward keeping from breaking down entirely. "Given recent developments, he might soon get his wish." Turning to Servius, he said, "Three lashes each and garnish the cost of the narcotics from their wages."

And without another word, he turned and walked away.

Teriana and Quintus were mercifully absent from the command tent when he returned, so there was no one to see him slump down on a stool, elbows on the table and his head in his hands.

No one to see the way he scrubbed at his eyes, hating the unfamiliar burn of tears. Hating the way his breath kept catching, not with one of his attacks, but with grief.

It had been Felix. Felix who'd betrayed Teriana's position. Who'd gotten six of their men killed, who'd crippled Miki, who'd ruined Quintus's life. Who'd set Marcus on a path that had nearly seen the Thirty-Seventh caught between two armies. Who'd betrayed him.

A sob wrenched from his throat, and he dug his nails into his scalp, trying to regain control. Trying to shove the twist of pain and hurt back behind the walls that normally protected his heart so well.

Behind his closed eyelids, memory flitted across his vision. Of standing in a tiny room next to a bunk that seemed a sliver width compared to the bed he'd left behind at home, the ache of his abandonment heavy in his chest.

"Top or bottom?"

He'd turned to find another boy standing behind him, golden skin tanned considerably darker than Marcus's by the sun, ears sticking out beneath his freshly shorn hair.

"Pardon?"

"You want the top or the bottom bunk? You were in line behind me for processing, by the way. See?" The boy pulled down the neck of his tunic to reveal a tiny tattooed number. 1518.

His skin still stung from the needle that had left a 1519 on his own skin, and he couldn't imagine how much worse it would be when it was replaced by a larger version when he graduated. If he lived that long.

"Means we'll be standing next to each other pretty much the rest of our lives unless one of us croaks," the boy said. "What did you say your name was?"

Gaius rose on his lips, but he clenched his teeth shut on it, because that wasn't his name anymore. Everything that had been his was gone now. And the thought sent fresh tears spilling down his cheeks as he managed to choke out his younger brother's name. "Marcus."

"Hey, it's all right." The boy patted his shoulder. "Gosh, you're skinny. Good thing you're here—Lescendor feeds us well, I've heard. Clean bedding and new clothes, too. I've bet you've never had it this good."

Marcus opened his mouth to say that he'd never had it this bad, but fear silenced him. Because if anyone learned that his family had sent him instead of his younger brother, he, his father, and his brother would be executed for treason. His mother stripped and exiled, his sisters along with her. Which meant no one could ever find out who he was, and that meant keeping everything secret. His breathing came faster, one of his attacks coming on, because everyone had abandoned him. Everyone. "I'm afraid."

"Hey." The boy slung his arm around him. "Why don't you take the top bunk. That way, anyone who wants to get to you will have to get past me first."

"Why would you do that?" he managed to ask between gasps. "You don't even know me."

"Because we're brothers now," the boy said, gesturing for him to climb to the upper bunk. "I'm Felix, by the way."

"Sir?"

Marcus jumped, his heart flipping at the sound of Felix's voice as it pulled him from his memories, and he lifted his head.

"I've the revisions to the ranks." Felix held two pieces of paper covered in his familiar, messy scrawl. "You said you wanted to see them first."

Taking them, Marcus rubbed at his temples, the names blurring as he read. Nothing sinking in except that his best friend had betrayed him.

"Hard to get any sleep last night with all the noise."

The celebrations of the men had been predictably raucous, but even if the camp had been silent, Marcus wouldn't have slept well. Wasn't sure if he ever would again. "I slept fine."

Felix sighed. "Not sure if you are aware, but Quintus has Teriana pinned out front."

Don't say her name. Don't stand there and act like you care. "I ordered him to teach her to defend herself."

"All he's doing is drowning her in the mud."

Concern that Quintus might actually be hurting Teriana flickered through him, but it was overwhelmed by his grief. And his rising anger. "It's not your concern. I'll review these and let you know if I have changes."

"You don't want to discuss them?"

"I'm occupied." He picked up a pencil, needing Felix gone. Because he needed to calm down and figure out what path forward wouldn't rip the Thirty-Seventh apart. "You may attend to other duties."

Silence. Something that had never been uncomfortable between them before but now felt unbearable.

"No!" Felix slammed his hands down on the table, causing water to splash out of Marcus's cup. "Not until you talk to me."

"Watch your tone." Marcus was on his feet, though he didn't remember standing. "You are not above punishment."

And I will punish you for what you've done.

"Do it, then." Felix leaned across the table so that they were nose to nose. "Have me whipped for being the only one with the courage to call you out on your bullshit behavior."

His temper was an inch from boiling over, because this wouldn't be a whipping. It would be the gallows. "This is not the moment to test me, Felix."

"When, then? When?" Felix's blue eyes searched his. "When the Empire sends a senator over with reinforcements and they learn how you've been carrying on with her? The decisions you've made because of her? When it's you being whipped in the mud for breaking legion law? Or worse, if they decide to string you up for treason? Is that when you'll finally see reason?"

"That's my—"

"I'm not done!" Felix slammed his hands down on the table again. "It's over, Marcus. Our freedom to do what we wanted is over. The xenthier path that hunter came through originated within spitting distance of a fortress *we* conquered. And if there is a way here, there is a way back. It's only a matter of time until we are once again under the Senate's thumb and you are no longer the one in control. You cannot give them any reason to believe you've been anything less than the perfect loyal dog they trained you to be or they'll kill you."

Marcus's breath was coming in rapid pants, his nails digging into his palms. "I have done everything perfectly! We control Arinoquia, which is exactly what I was told to accomplish. What more do you want from me?"

"End it with Teriana. That's what I want."

His hands balled into fists. "I already did."

"That is such bullshit." Felix shook his head. "And the worst is that I can't tell if you're lying to me or to yourself."

"It's. Over."

"Then prove it." Felix leveled a finger at him. "Put her in a different tent. Or better yet, send her back to the *Quincense,* because we don't need her anymore. The only reason for you to keep her around now is because you can't stand to let her go!"

His head was throbbing, pulse roaring, and all Marcus could see was red. "You've been trying to get rid of her from the moment you set eyes on her. So things can go back to *normal*. And don't think I don't know how far you're willing to go to achieve it."

"What are you talking about?"

"You want her dead. Admit it."

Felix stared at him. Then he gestured at the entrance to the tent. "Is that what Quintus is teaching her? To protect herself from me?"

More rain began to fall overhead, pattering loudly against the tent canvas as they stared each other down.

"Thirteen years," Felix said softly. "Thirteen years, we've been best friends. Have stood at each other's backs against every odd. And despite all that, you don't know me at all."

"You're right. I don't." Because if he'd known his friend was capable of betrayal, they wouldn't have been friends in the first place.

Felix raked a hand over his hair. "I'd slit my own throat before I'd turn a blade on Teriana."

"Don't lie to me. I know you hate her."

"It's not her I hate," Felix answered. "It's how you've been acting ever since she joined us. You always put the Thirty-Seventh first, and the men trusted you to keep them safe. But more and more, we're seeing you make decisions with different priorities in mind, and I'm not the only one who doesn't like it. I don't know if she's a symptom or the disease, but if you don't refocus on the men and our mandate, you're going to rip the Thirty-Seventh apart."

"Don't put this all on me. You're the one who caused a bloody brawl, forcing the men to pick sides."

"That's not true!" Felix snarled. "The Forty-First were getting in our men's faces that Titus would already have paths mapped but that you're too busy pandering to the Arinoquians to even look. I told them to shut their traps. That you knew what you were doing and that things would be back to normal soon enough."

That *word*. "Why are you so rutting eager to go back to the way things were?"

Felix's eyes narrowed, searching his. "Why aren't you?"

For a thousand reasons. But the burdens of secrets and betrayal meant Felix was the last person he could trust with them.

"Is it because once the paths are mapped, she'll be through with us?" Felix gave a sharp shake of his head. "Don't bother answering that. Just know that I know hurting her would hurt *you*. And that is something I'd never do, even though if you keep down this path, you'll destroy yourself." He squeezed his eyes shut. "Since we've been children, I've protected you, Marcus. Lied and deceived and *murdered* to keep you alive and to achieve your ends. And for what? What do you give me in return?"

Everything. He gave everything to his legion. To his men.

"Apparently not the one thing that you want." Marcus leaned across the table, wanting Felix to feel as much hurt as he did. Wanting him to know what it felt like to be betrayed. "And allow me to be clear: *that* will never happen."

Felix's eyes widened, color draining from his face. He took a step back from the table, looking anywhere but at Marcus.

Which was the exact moment Gibzen strode in.

The primus looked between the two of them. "Sorry to interrupt, sirs. But I thought you'd want to be the first to know—we found the xenthier. It's far closer than we anticipated. And something else."

"What?" Marcus demanded, nausea rolling in his guts. Because everything he didn't want to happen was happening, and all of it too quickly.

"An abandoned city. And if what my boys tell me is true, you're going to want to see it for yourself."

What he wanted was out of this camp. Away from everything. What he wanted was to be able to breathe. Because only then could he decide how to deal with this.

"They're right," he said, keeping his gaze fixed on Gibzen because he couldn't stand to look at Felix. "Get me an escort ready. We leave in an hour."

26

"I give up," Teriana said, spitting out a mouthful of mud. "This is not how I want to spend my day."

Quintus was ostensibly teaching her to defend herself from a rear attack, but it primarily involved him holding her facedown in the mud. Much to the amusement of all the men standing guard around Marcus's tent.

"Giving up means you're dead," Quintus answered, his weight not shifting off her back.

"Then I'm dead."

The sound of footsteps splashing in mud caught her attention, and she turned her head, peering through her mess of braids to see Felix walking past. He frowned, then asked one of the guards a question. Whatever the young man's response was, it caused his frown to deepen. But he said nothing further, only proceeded into the tent.

"Let's try again." Quintus climbed off her and then caught her by the belt and hauled her upright. Gibzen walked past them then, his face splitting with a wide grin. "Oh, this looks fun. I'd stop to watch, but duty calls."

Flipping the primus a universally insulting gesture, Teriana spit out more mud before reluctantly turning her back to Quintus. This was going to *hurt*. But before Quintus could move, a loud bang echoed out of the command tent along with Felix's shout of "No!"

Instinctively, she stepped toward the tent, but Gibzen held up a hand. "Who's in there with them?" he asked those on duty.

"Just the legatus and the tribunus."

And they were arguing. Teriana could only pick out a few words, but one that kept repeating was her name. And while all those on guard duty held their positions, their heads were turned to listen, their expressions grim.

"What a bloody mess this is." Gibzen gave a sharp shake of his head, then swiveled to look at her, eyes full of condemnation. "Happy?"

Not even a little bit. And neither were all the men in the surrounding camp who'd stopped what they were doing to watch. To listen as their two highest-ranking officers shouted at each other about *her*. Every one of them thought she was to blame for this, unaware that Marcus's grievance with Felix was because of betrayal. Because of treason. "Someone needs to intervene."

"Yeah, but not you." Taking a breath, Gibzen strode between the guards and into the tent. More terse words emanated, but they were too quiet for her to make out.

"Maybe we should—" Whatever Quintus was about to say was cut off by Felix striding out of the tent.

"Fuck!" he shouted, then flung his helmet, the metal slamming against a tent post with a loud clang. No one in the camp said a word, everyone watching in silence as he stormed across the open space surrounding the command tent. Then he slid to a stop, eyes fixing on Teriana.

She held her breath as he stalked toward them, jaw tight and eyes red. "What are you doing?" he demanded.

Quintus stepped in front of her. "Legatus's orders, sir. She's next to useless in a fight."

If she hadn't been sick with terror, Teriana would have taken offense.

"Then why aren't you following them?" Felix asked. "His orders were to *teach* her, but all I see is you drowning her in the mud for the entertainment of idle bastards whose time is better used doing something *useful*." He roared the last, and all the men standing around watching the exchange swiftly departed in opposite directions.

Pulling off his sodden cloak, Felix tossed it at one of the guards. Then he turned his back on Quintus, his eyes on Teriana. "Watch."

Behind him, Quintus shifted uneasily. Teriana didn't blame him.

"Get on with it, Quintus," Felix snapped. "And don't hold back."

"Yes, sir."

Quintus eased forward, making no sound, the stick he'd been using in lieu of a knife held in his right hand.

Then he lunged, his left arm wrapping around Felix's torso, hand clamping down on Felix's wrist.

Yet it seemed Felix hadn't gained his position in the Thirty-Seventh just because of Marcus. In a blur of motion, he twisted his left arm up, hand closing over Quintus's where it grasped the stick. Then he jerked Quintus's arm down, holding the blade tight against his breastplate before slamming his head back against Quintus's nose.

Blood splattered, and Quintus swore, recoiling. He kept his grip on Felix's wrist, but his balance was off and Felix took advantage, twisting to face Quintus and using his momentum to shove the stick away from his chest and toward Quintus's unarmored chest.

Where it came to a stop, the tip resting right below Quintus's sternum. "Dead."

Glowering, Quintus pulled away, spitting blood into the mud.

Wiping at the mud that had splattered his face, Felix retrieved his cloak. As he fastened it, his eyes flicked to Teriana. "You can live without your fingers but not your jugular. Sacrifice the former to buy yourself opportunity to save the latter. Understood?"

"Yes." The word came out as a croak.

Felix's gaze moved to Quintus. "You *will* fall to command or it will be me you answer to, understood?"

Blood ran from Quintus's nose, was smeared across his cheeks and chin, but Teriana could have sworn he blanched.

"Everyone in the Thirty-Seventh is waiting for you to desert, Quintus," Felix said softly. "*No one* wants you at their back. Except for *her.*" He jabbed a finger in Teriana's direction and she jumped. "*No one* trusts you. Except for *her.*"

Silence.

"Prove yourself worthy of that trust," Felix finally said. "Or see yourself drowned in the latrines as others have suggested."

"Yes, sir." Quintus's voice was shaky. "Understood, sir."

Felix moved to walk away, but Teriana caught his arm. "Felix."

His jaw tightened as though drowning *himself* in the latrines might be preferable to listening to anything she might say. "Make it quick, Teriana. I've a thousand men waiting on the field for me and I'd not waste their time. Or my own."

"I'm sorry," she said. "For everything."

He stared at the ground between them for a long moment, then lifted his face to meet her gaze. The grief in them hollowed out her stomach even as she wondered what Marcus had said to him.

"I'd cut my own throat before doing anything to hurt him, including hurting you," he said. "He doesn't seem to believe that, but I hope you do."

Then he jerked his arm out of her grip and strode away through camp.

"I, for one," Gibzen said from behind her, "am looking forward to some time away from this camp. I'm sure you are, too, Teriana."

Whirling around, she stared at him, wondering if Felix wasn't the only one Marcus intended to evict from his life. "What are you talking about?"

"We've found the stem," Gibzen answered. "Get your gear ready. Legatus wants to head inland to see it within the hour."

27

KILLIAN

Cresting a ridge, Killian pulled Seahawk to a stop to survey the dry, rocky plains before him.

And the fortress rising up from them like a mirage in the distance. "Rotahn?"

Sonia had stopped her own mount next to him, one hand shading her eyes from the sun as she peered over the plain. Her clothes were travel-stained and her face shadowed with exhaustion, as were the faces of the five hundred men of the Royal Army that he'd brought with him. He'd pushed them and their mounts to the brink in order to reach the Rowenes stronghold as soon as possible.

Not out of eagerness to deal with the Anuk threat, but rather because the sooner he put an end to the raiding, the sooner he'd be able to rejoin the rest of the Royal Army in Mudaire.

Where Lydia was training at Hegeria's temple.

"Is that it? It's small."

The disappointment in Finn's voice was palpable as he stood up in the stirrups, the orphan, and former ruler of Mudaire's sewers, seeming untouched by the days in the saddle and nights sleeping in the dirt.

Pointing toward the low, brown mountains, Killian said, "Most of the people in these parts live in camps in the hills at the base of those mountains. For dozens of leagues north to south, those hills are full of gold. Sometimes you find bits of it lying around on the ground."

"Truly?" Finn's eyes widened, as Killian had known they would. "For the taking?"

Killian snorted. "Hardly. It's the King's land. Get caught taking his gold, you lose a hand."

Finn rubbed his chin thoughtfully, and Sonia reached over to give him a shove. "Don't even think about it, Finn. You're the squire to a lord now. You can't be thieving."

"I've never stolen anything in my life," Finn protested. "Who spreads these rumors about me?"

Given Killian had needed to steal his own coin *back* from his squire in order to pay for supplies in the last town they'd passed through, Sonia was right to be concerned about Finn's light fingers. Especially given the amount of wealth he was sure to come across in the Rowenes palace. "You're not going to have time for digging around in the dirt, Finn. Not with Anuk raiders taking advantage of Mudamora's distraction."

Gesturing west again, he said, "Anukastre is on the far side of those mountains. During the dry season, they come through the passes and raid, and the Rowenes family has been known to reciprocate. The terrain is treacherous—narrow, rocky paths that are prone to slides—which keeps both in check. And in the rainy season, flash floods make travel through even more dangerous."

"Doesn't look like it ever rains here. Everything is dead."

"Most of the time, it doesn't. But when the midwinter storms come up from the southeast, they break against the mountains and dump rain like you've never seen. The ground can't absorb it, so dry streambeds turn to raging rivers in a matter of minutes, and the front of the floods is more debris than water. They're deadly."

But until it started to rain, the Anuk would be a problem. The challenge was predicting which route they'd come through, because the distance was too great for every possible path through the mountains to be guarded. It was like trying to plug a leaking dam. Just when you thought you'd done it, another leak sprang up. "Hopefully our presence dissuades any further raids."

"Sounds easy enough." Finn thumped his heels against his horse's sides. "Let's go. I'm hungry."

"Your stomach is a bottomless pit," Sonia muttered, but she cantered after him, not liking the boy to be out of sight.

Turning his horse, Killian said to his men, "Another hour and you'll have water, food, beds, and a night of leisure. Move out."

Cheers rang through the air, the soldiers moving past him and onto the dusty road heading toward Rotahn.

But Killian didn't follow. Instead, he remained facing north and east, nearly all of Mudamora resting between him and Mudaire. Between him and Lydia.

You don't deserve to be with her, his guilt whispered. *Your duty is to Mudamora, not to Lydia.*

"Why not both?" he asked softly, imagining he could see across the distance. That he could see her.

You might ask Malahi how well you serve with your loyalties di-vided, his guilt answered. *Though it's hard to question the dead.*

Squeezing his eyes shut, Killian gave a tight nod, then wheeled Seahawk around and broke into a gallop toward Rotahn.

28

TERIANA

The legions had never pressed particularly far inland, their focus on the coastal region of Arinoquia, where the majority of the people lived. The inland areas were wild and uncharted jungle that was rumored to be populated by the original inhabitants of the area, though none of the legion scouts had ever seen them.

The camp they'd made for the night was nothing more than tarps strung between trees to keep off the rain, which meant no chance to talk to Marcus about what had happened between him and Felix without the men surrounding them overhearing. Marcus hadn't even slept near her, leaving her to lay out her bedroll next to Quintus. He'd roused everyone before dawn to continue the march toward the xenthier stem.

Now, it was close to midday, and she was exhausted and drenched with sweat and rain, the waterskin Amarin had given her nearly empty and her concern for Marcus vanquishing any other thoughts. His eyes were bloodshot from too many days with too little sleep, but it was the hollowness in them that worried her. As though despite the significance of what they were going to see, it paled in comparison to his conflict with Felix.

Dodging around the men walking between them on the narrow game trail they followed, she fell in next to him. "You all right?"

"I'm fine."

"You don't look fine."

"I'm tired."

"Marcus—"

But before she could press him, Gibzen appeared, pushing back down the trail toward them. "It's just over the ridge here."

Curiosity briefly outweighing her concern, Teriana followed them to the edge of the ridge, a small gasp pulling from her lips at what she saw.

Below stretched a stone city that was slowly being consumed by the jungle. Vines wrapped around buildings and towers, trees burst through roofs, and foliage consumed the streets. At the center rose the seven towers of the god circle, the stone so eroded that the faces that had once been depicted were nearly vanished to time. And yet it still seemed they were watching—that the gods themselves stood in the center of this ancient city, observing the intruders.

"Any sign of life?" Marcus asked.

"None. Our best guess is that it's been abandoned for close to a decade."

Marcus started down the narrow trail, and Teriana followed at his heels, pausing at what once must have been the gates to this place, the only thing left an arch over the gap in the crumbling wall. There was writing on it, faded from endless rain, and Teriana rose on her tiptoes, squinting at it.

"Can you read the language?" Marcus asked.

"No." She shook her head. "My aunt Yedda might be able to do so, but these people were driven inland by the invading clans when I was just a child."

They ventured into the city, the soldiers flanking them alert, eyes searching the shadows between buildings and watching for movement in the treetops.

Marcus cut left, ducking inside one of the buildings that hadn't crumbled.

"Be careful, sir!" A soldier scurried after him. "Many of these buildings are on the verge of collapse."

Ignoring the warnings, Teriana followed Marcus in, Quintus on her heels with a torch in hand.

Inside, the floor was covered with debris, but Teriana found her eyes leaping to the signs of the people who'd once lived here. A table and chairs gone green with moss. A child's ball in the corner. The remains of woven tapestries too rotten to see the images they'd depicted. The walls had once been painted bright red, but it had mostly flaked away to be replaced by green slime from the endless moisture.

They walked to the rear space, which had once been a kitchen, with an oven set into the wall. Kneeling, Teriana peered through, seeing that it opened into a private yard. It was overgrown with ferns, but in the midst of all that wildness, a bush with large white flowers grew, their perfume filling her nose.

They ventured back out into the street, Marcus saying nothing as he explored, his brow furrowed. They reached the god circle, at the center of which there was a large stone dais. Marcus climbed the stone steps to stand on top of it, but Teriana headed toward Madoria's temple, stepping across the heavy metal door that had broken off its hinges.

"Let me go first," Quintus said, moving carefully across the floor. Both his eyes were blackened and his nose slightly swollen from Felix's demonstration. Yet though there was still a hollowness to his gaze, he'd been more himself since they'd left camp. It was tempting to say his grief had eased, but Teriana's gut told her that it had more to do with what Felix had said to Quintus, though which part had made an impact, she wasn't sure.

"Seems okay." He jumped up and down a few times on the floor.

"Clearly you missed your calling as an engineer." She eyed the dust and bits of stone that rained down from above. The high ceiling had partially collapsed, leaving the structure open to the elements. As her eyes adjusted to the light, she saw the walls were painted in highly detailed images of the sea, vessels filled with brown-skinned men and women drawing up nets full of fish while a great sea serpent swam beneath them. On another wall, there were images of ships with blue sails, and beneath them, a woman with black skin and hair made of seaweed held her hands up to them.

Walking to the table at the center, Teriana pulled a gold coin from her pocket and placed it on top, murmuring a prayer that her goddess continue to protect her people. Glancing at Quintus, who was poking at the artwork, she added another coin, then silently whispered, "Let him find his way back to Miki. They deserve a chance."

Leaving the temple, she blinked in the bright light, noting that most of the soldiers were clustered around Tremon's temple. Frowning, she pushed her way inside and found Marcus examining the artwork, which depicted great battlefields, warriors dressed in leather and bronze, curved metal weapons resembling scythes held in their hands. Many of them rode scaled lizard creatures native to the far side of the Southern Continent. The beasts wore saddles like horses, but Teriana knew for fact that they were known for eating their riders.

At the front lines of the armies rode men and women who wore elaborate masks and who seemed larger than the others. Commanders, for certain, but also likely to represent those marked by Tremon. As she glanced at Marcus, she wondered if any of them still fought for the inlanders, or if they'd all been lost in the war with the Arinoquians.

"I've seen enough," Marcus said, his voice echoing through the temple. "Take me to see the terminus stem."

29

KILLIAN

Thanks to the scouts he'd sent ahead, the Rowenes clan was prepared for their arrival. Soldiers belonging to the fortress garrison took charge of his men and their horses as they came through the gate. Only Killian, in the company of Sonia and Finn, headed on to the palace.

"You sure there's gold to be found on the ground?" Finn muttered as they passed the manned gates of the inner wall. "Because it looks like they used every ounce of it to build their palace."

The boy wasn't wrong. While the building itself was built from sandstone, very little of the rock was visible beneath all the gold leaf, gold plate, and gold paint, the centerpiece a massive central dome that gleamed yellow in the sunlight. And having been here before, Killian knew the interior gleamed just as bright. A testament to Rowenes wealth, but he'd never liked it. Had always preferred his family's home on the coast. Though equally as large, Teradale was built as much from wood as it was from stone, all balconies and open windows that allowed in breeze from the sea it overlooked. Surrounded by horse pastures and orchards full of fruit, Teradale seemed to breathe, whereas the only life to Rotahn was the people living in it.

Many of whom stood on the steps waiting, seemingly unfazed by the relentless heat of the sun overhead, and all of them related in some way to the King. None of them made a move or said a word until several servants approached with bowls of water and toweling. Killian wished he could dump the basin over his head but settled on washing the travel from his hands.

As he passed off the towel he'd used, the dark-haired woman at the head of the group said, "Lord Calorian, we are most pleased to welcome you and your soldiers," then she walked gracefully down the steps toward him.

Lady Ria Rowenes was King Serrick's niece and ruled Rotahn in his absence. Perhaps in her midtwenties, she was small and pretty, her eyes the same amber hue as Malahi's. The similarity sent a jolt of pain into Killian's chest as he looked into them. "We are grateful for your hospitality, my lady."

She extended a hand, and he grazed her knuckles with his lips, extremely aware that he'd not had a proper bath in far too long and reeked of sweat and horse. But to her credit, she only smiled, then turned to Sonia, swiftly closing the distance to kiss his lieutenant's cheeks. "Darling, it has been too long!"

He lifted one eyebrow. "You're acquainted?"

"Yes, of course," Ria answered. "I spent some years in Revat, which is truly the brightest star on all of Reath, and I had the pleasure of making Sonia's acquaintance." Then she gave her head a little shake. "Kaira is a fool to have let you go."

"Kaira's heart belongs to Gamdesh," Sonia answered, tucking her short dark curls behind one ear. "I was a fool to have thought it might ever be otherwise."

Ria made a soft noise. "Her loss is our gain. You and your blade are most welcome in Rotahn." Then she gestured to the steps. "We've much to discuss, but first you must refresh yourselves from the journey."

"Are the war camp commanders here?" Killian asked. "I'd speak with them directly."

One of Ria's eyebrows rose, and she looked him slowly up and down before saying, "It's been a long time since you were here last, Lord Calorian, but allow me to remind you that we've traditions in Rotahn. And *bathing* is one of them."

Pulling off his clothing, Killian handed it to the attendant. "Most of it is beyond repair," he said. "But do what you can."

The man held up Killian's torn and travel-stained garments, his brow furrowing. "I'm sure we can procure something more appropriate, my lord. You did intend to dine with Lady Ria this evening, yes?"

Reluctantly. "Nothing red. And most definitely nothing gold." He glanced over at Finn, who was glaring at the attendant trying to take his clothes from him. "Get the boy something appropriate while you're at it."

Wrapping a towel around his waist, Killian plucked up two bars of soap from the large collection on one of the tables and then caught Finn by the arm, hauling him out of the door and into the cool room housing the springs. It was open to gardens on the far side, the smells of flowers and leafy things filling Killian's nose as he strode toward the pool, which was empty.

"That man took my things," Finn grumbled. "He'd better not pocket anything, or I'll—"

"The only things in your pockets worth taking are things you took from mine," Killian interrupted. Then he pushed a bar of soap and a cloth into Finn's hand. "Scrub. *With* the soap. My horse smells better than you do, and as you might have noticed, the Rowenes clan are an uppity sort about such things."

"I know how to wash." Finn scowled. "And you aren't smelling so fresh yourself, you know."

"Then I suppose we'd both better get to it."

Wading down the steps, Killian clenched his teeth against the chill of the water, then dunked his head under before setting to ridding himself of the grime he'd accumulated, the circulating water whisking away the clouds of dirt and sweat and blood. He cast a sideways glance at Finn, ensuring his newly minted squire was doing the same, and the sight of the boy with his curly hair frothed white with soap foam almost made him laugh.

Almost.

"Rotahn is a nice place," Finn commented, then snarled a string of curses he'd probably learned from Sonia as his soap slipped from his grip, floating to the bottom of the pool. When he emerged with it once again in hand, he added, "How long are we staying?"

"We'll leave in the morning." Killian tossed his cloth and soap on the edge of the pool, and a young attendant scurried forward to replace them with a chilled glass of wine, which Killian drained. The attendant swiftly returned with another, which Killian drank as well. He'd need the whole damned bottle to survive the night here.

"Why so soon?" Finn motioned to the attendant. "I'll have some of that. Where's it from? I've a taste for good vintage."

"He'll have water," Killian corrected. "Or juice."

"Juice? Why?"

"Because you're only fourteen years old," Killian answered, having finally gotten the true number from his young friend on their journey south. "And because you need a level head. And because I said so."

Finn glowered, accepting the cup of juice from the attendant, who also brought Killian another glass of wine. He drank that one, too, exhaling as it finally started to take effect, a buzzing heat filling his veins. "We're here to put an end to the Anuk raids, Finn. Not to laze about in luxury."

"You just don't appreciate it," Finn muttered, and Killian faintly picked up his added mutter of, "Entitled fancy-pants lord that you are."

"Don't forget to wash behind your ears," Killian said, then dodged the bar of soap Finn tossed straight at his head.

Turning his back on his friend, Killian rested his forearms on the edge of the pool, staring at a potted plant but not really seeing it. Being here made him think of Malahi. Made him wonder if her body had been found. Whether it ever would be.

"Killian," Finn whispered, pulling him from his thoughts. "Killian!"

Turning, he said, "What?"

Finn's eyes were wide. "There's women around the corner. I can hear them talking."

The pool was U-shaped, one end for women and one for men, though Killian had heard it was common for both to meet in the middle. "What of it?"

Finn glanced over his shoulder to ensure the attendant wasn't within earshot, then whispered, "I bet they're not wearing clothes."

"It is common practice to remove them while bathing," he responded, pretending not to see where Finn was going with this. His interest in girls had grown, and he'd subjected Killian to endless speculation and commentary during their travels. Only Sonia threatening to drown him in a pond had silenced him on the issue.

"We could go over there," Finn whispered. "If we keep low, they won't notice us."

Killian lifted one eyebrow. "You do know that *Sonia* is over there with them."

"Oh. Right." Finn made a face. "Probably not a good idea, then. She's not interested in men."

"What she's not interested in is skinny little shits who try to peep at her while she's bathing."

"*You* could go over there. I bet they wouldn't mind that at all."

Snorting, Killian shook his head. "Probably. But the reason I can go over there is because they know that I won't."

"That doesn't make any sense."

"Put your head to the task of figuring it out and drink your juice. I'm trying to relax."

Ignoring Finn's affronted glower, he sipped at yet another glass of wine. Now that he was paying attention, he could make out the sound of Sonia's voice, along with several others, including Ria's.

"I'm bored," Finn said. "I'm going to go see what that thief did with my clothes."

"Don't wander," Killian muttered, then pushed away from the wall, swimming slowly toward the far end. Once there, he rested his arms on the edge, watching the sunlight and gardens, his mind drifting to Lydia.

I choose this.

Her voice floated through his thoughts, and he closed his eyes, the vision of the last time he'd seen her filling his mind. How the wind had caught at the loose strands of her hair, whipping them around her beautiful face, those upturned green eyes seeming to see into his soul. He'd have done anything she'd asked in that moment, but what she'd asked was for him to let her go.

Why didn't she choose me? As soon as the thought voiced itself, he shoved it away, annoyed with himself because the answers were clear. Choosing him would've meant him fighting his own people to get her away from Quindor. Them running away and abandoning Mudamora. And neither of them would've been happy with that life, which would eventually mean neither of them would be happy with each other.

"And keep in mind you didn't choose her, either," he muttered to himself. "You chose Mudamora."

It didn't make him feel any better.

"Get your head together," he growled at himself. "Serrick didn't send you here to fret about girls, he sent you here to deal with the Anuk."

Except Anuk raiders and Rowenes gold mines seemed distant concerns, his mess of a mind refusing to focus on armies and strategies and instead leaping back to that *kiss*.

How was it that it wasn't the pain of having a spear wrenched from his side that he remembered, but the soft press of her lips against his? The feel of her hair falling against his face as she gave up her strength to save his life?

You could get to Mudaire in a week if you switched horses often enough.

It wasn't the first time that thought had entered his head. That it would be an easy thing for him to go to the city to see her.

And then what?

His imagination was all too willing to supply suggestions for what he might do when he got there, kissing her being first and foremost among them.

And no part of him wanted to stop there.

Turning his back against the wall of the pool, he closed his eyes and sank under the water, hoping the cold would temper the thoughts running through his head of the times he'd seen her wearing very little, her long legs seeming to go on forever. Gods, what he wouldn't give to have those wrapped around him while he kissed those perfect lips of hers. To rip off her clothes and drink in the sight before losing himself entirely.

Cool it, Killian, he ordered himself, but it was wasted words.

The lust, he could control. But with her, it was so much more than that, and instead of seeing her naked body, he saw her bent over sick orphans, saving their lives. Saw her sacrificing her own body to protect Gwen when the other girl had fallen beneath the mob. Saw her tirelessly fighting to get back to Celendor to free Teriana, no matter the cost to herself. She was the bravest person he'd ever met. The most loyal. The most selfless. A girl worth fighting for.

He needed to breathe.

His heartbeat grew rapid, his chest tightening and muscles starting to spasm. But he didn't want to give up the silence under the water. The darkness. Her face.

It was only when the need was so desperate he couldn't deny it any longer that Killian broke the surface, gasping in mouthfuls of air.

And found himself face-to-face with Lady Ria Rowenes.

30

MARCUS

He could've spent hours in those temples. Days, just picking out the details in the incredible artwork that alone seemed untouched by the endless damp of the jungle. There was so much to learn, so many questions he wanted to ask, so much he wanted to know, but the inlanders weren't his priority. Not when he was going to have to punish Felix's treason when he returned.

His men led them out of the nameless city and through the jungle until they reached the banks of a dry stream, which they followed, the incline growing steeper with every passing minute.

"Well, shit," Quintus said under his breath, gazing skyward. "Didn't expect to see these on this side of the world."

Marcus was inclined to agree.

To either side of the streambed were Bardenese redwoods, some of the trees old enough to tower above the jungle canopy. He imagined that from above they must look like strange sentinels guarding a path through the forest.

"I'm surprised they grow here," Teriana said. "Bardeen is much colder."

"But equally as wet." Marcus walked around a boulder, the stones of the streambed shifting beneath his feet. A stream of size had once run through here, for the banks were high and jagged with rock. Why had the water ceased to flow?

Ahead, a cliff rose out of the jungle, with a dozen or so of his men working near its base. And perhaps fifteen feet above them, a glittering xenthier stem jutted from the rock.

"Explains why none of the other path-hunters survived," Teriana murmured, holding a hand to her brow to shade her eyes from the sun. "Drop like that would kill you if you fell wrong. And even if you fell *right*, most would break a leg or ankle. The man who reached us got lucky."

"His luck didn't last."

At the sight of him, his men stopped working and saluted. The man in charge said, "Nearly got the scaffolding finished, sir."

"Good."

"I know where the stem is in Bardeen," Quintus said. "Remember that stream we had to cross to get to the Twenty-Ninth's followers' camp?"

The Twenty-Ninth was notorious for many things, but one of them was the number of people who followed the legion, providing them services in exchange for the men's coin. Paid company. Those who pandered to vices. *Laundresses.* They always caused problems, so Marcus never allowed the behavior, dispersing anyone who tried to follow the Thirty-Seventh about. "Yes."

"The stream split," Quintus said, "half of it going over the waterfall and the other half disappearing into a hole about ten feet away."

Marcus stared up at the stem, imagining what it must have looked like with water bursting from its tip, a stream originating in Bardeen bringing new life to the jungles of Arinoquia. "Speculation was that the shaft rejoined the rest of the stream at the base of the falls." And given that they'd been in the middle of conquering Hydrilla, no time had been spent investigating. Though apparently afterwards, someone had taken the time to reroute the stream and excavate. Xenthier was often found in streams and rivers, and even legion soldiers were eligible to receive the financial reward if they discovered a stem.

The men were moving the scaffolding into place, and Marcus waited silently until they had it steady before climbing.

"Let's go look," Quintus said, and the wooden frame shuddered as he and Teriana followed.

Reaching the platform, Marcus knelt, casting a backward glance at the jungle and trying to ignore the way his heart skittered at being so high. It wasn't much of a view, the streambed winding its way into the jungle, so he turned to the xenthier, squinting as the crystal reflected light into his eyes.

"I've never had a chance to look at one up close. It's beautiful." Teriana had crawled onto the platform next to him, and his nostrils filled with the scent of cedar and orange blossoms, and inexplicably, the sea.

She reached out a hand to touch it, but Marcus caught her wrist. "*Always* check it's a terminus before touching it." Pulling loose a pebble that had lodged in his sandal, he tossed it against the xenthier. If it had been a genesis, it would have disappeared, whisked away to some unknown destination, but instead, it bounced off, falling to the ground below.

Quintus squeezed between them, the scaffolding swaying from

their combined weight, and Marcus's breath caught, the ground suddenly feeling very far away.

"Smells like Bardeen." Quintus had his face directly in front of the tip, his eyes closed. "And woodsmoke."

Elbowing Quintus out of the way, Marcus leaned closer, feeling the breath of breeze coming from the xenthier brush against his cheek. Inhaling deeply, he nearly recoiled at the familiarity of the scents. None of it brought back good memories. Bardeen had been the last of their missions with the Twenty-Ninth. And the worst of them.

"That's incredible." Teriana's braids brushed his arm as she leaned closer, sending a prickle of sensation across his skin. "It's like Bardeen is right there."

They were within the Empire's reach now, whether the Empire realized it or not. "I've seen enough. Let's go."

Back on the ground, he motioned to Gibzen. "Get something solid in place just in case the Senate sends anyone else. We don't need them falling to their deaths."

If only that path-hunter hadn't survived the fall.

"Yes, sir."

Glancing back up at the stem that had the power to destroy everything he'd dreamed for the Thirty-Seventh, Marcus said, "We'll make camp for tonight." And despite dreading what he'd have to do once they returned to Aracam, he added, "We'll return to the coast in the morning."

31

KILLIAN

"You can hold your breath a very long time, Lord Calorian," Ria said in a low voice, her eyes roving over him in a way that made Killian deeply aware of his lack of clothing. "I thought I might have to rescue *you*."

She giggled as though the idea of doing so was ridiculous, then she bit at her bottom lip, her eyes glinting. Only the swirl of her brown hair in the water concealed her breasts, but he kept his gaze fixed on a tiny mole at the center of her forehead. "Is there something you wanted, my lady?"

"There's only one thing anyone wants when they come to this part of the pool," she said, easing closer to him.

Shit. He'd forgotten about that, wanting only to be away from Finn and the attendants. This was the last thing he was interested in. All he wanted was to be alone with his thoughts, and he silently cursed his reputation. His face. His mark. His own stupidity for allowing her the opportunity to corner him like this. "I only wanted to look at the gardens."

Ria smirked. "I wasn't under the impression you were the sort of man who spent much time admiring topiaries. I'd heard you preferred more . . . *visceral* pursuits."

"Don't believe everything you hear," he said, knowing that the words would do nothing to dissuade her. That she'd see them as him toying with her, as though this were all a game. He'd been put in this sort of position before. It was always the same.

Ria moved forward and he moved back, but his shoulders struck the edge of the pool. Before he could edge sideways, her arms slipped around his neck, her breasts pressing against him. She reached up to kiss him, but he turned his head, feeling her lips catch him on the jaw.

She huffed out a breath. "You're quite the tease, Lord Calorian. Is that how you got my cousin to agree to marry you?"

His pulse roared in his ears, carrying with it a wild fury that he barely managed to keep in check. He wanted her gone, and preferably never to see her face again, but there was no easy way out of this situation.

Not without rebuffing her, which would have consequences. And not by laying hands on her to push her away, which he refused to do.

Then he heard the *slap slap* of bare feet against the tile, and Finn said, "Sorry to interrupt, my lord, but the attendant had some questions regarding your attire for this evening."

From the way that Ria was looking anywhere but at Finn, her cheeks flushing a bright pink, Killian was fairly certain that the boy was still naked as a jaybird.

"Who is he?" she demanded. "And what is he doing in my pool?"

"He's my squire, my lady," Killian answered, resting his elbows on the edge of the pool as she crossed her arms over her chest. "He goes where I go."

"But he's Gamdeshian!"

Killian lifted one eyebrow, about to point out that so was Sonia, but then Finn said, "Half-Gamdeshian, my lady. My father was Mudamorian, and he died fighting against the Derin invaders."

Ria's jaw tightened. "My condolences. May the gods keep and protect his soul."

"Thank you, my lady," Finn said, then without pause, added, "Lord Calorian, they are concerned they have nothing for someone of your considerable stature, and with the dinner hour nearly upon us, I'm afraid they are beginning to fret. Would you condescend to having your bath cut short so the tailor might measure you?"

"If I must." He met Ria's gaze. "Sorry to cut our conversation short, my lady, but it would not do to come to your table without suitable attire. If you'd excuse me."

"Of course." Her voice was strangled, but to her credit, Ria stood her ground in the pool instead of fleeing back over to the women's side.

Nodding at her, Killian swam to the far end, accepting the towel that Finn handed to him.

"They don't need to measure you," Finn said. "I made that up."

"I know." And likely so did Ria. "Thank you."

"Just doing my duty. No different than sharpening your sword."

Casting a glance down, Killian said, "We've talked about this. You touch my sword, I'll—"

"Make me run six laps naked through the army camp, I know. Though as you might be gathering, that's not much of a threat, my lord." Finn took a few strutting steps. "I'd run eight laps naked, just for fun."

"Noted. I'll think up a better threat."

"Or," Finn replied slyly, "you could let me have my *own* sword."

Giving him a weapon would only be the first step. Then he'd be wanting to learn to use it. And then he'd be wanting to fight. And the thought of anything happening to Finn . . . "I just bought you a horse. Don't get greedy."

The attendants were waiting in the chambers with new clothes, Killian's boots polished as shiny as the worn leather would allow and a stiff new pair awaiting Finn. But while Finn's garments were a practical dark brown, Killian's were Calorian indigo with an abundance of white embroidery, and it was all he could do not to make a face. But there was no helping it. Dinner would be when the Rowenes clan discussed strategy, and he needed to be there.

Waving away the attendant, he pulled on the clothes, which were fashionably—and irritatingly—tight, then his boots and weapons, before scowling at the mirror.

Finn snickered. "If we hang you from the battlements, you'd serve as a banner proclaiming the presence of glorious House Calorian."

"I'm taking back your horse. You can walk from now on."

Finn only laughed harder before elbowing Killian out of the way to look in the mirror, smoothing back his wild head of curls, which only sprang upward again. "Shall we?"

They stepped out into the cool corridor, and Killian walked toward the atrium where Sonia sat reading a book, an artfully arranged stack sitting on one of the tables next to her. Before they reached her, Finn said softly, "I wish you'd quit treating me like a child."

Killian's jaw tightened. "You're only fourteen."

"How old were *you* when you got your first sword?"

High Lord Calorian had put a practice sword in Killian's hand almost before he could walk. He'd had a proper weapon before he could read. Had been dueling by the time he was seven. A thousand excuses rose in Killian's head for why his circumstances were different, but they sounded hollow in his mind because none were the reason he didn't want to concede on this. "Fine."

Finn's eyes widened, but before he could say anything, Killian added, "But not until Sonia deems you competent enough with a practice blade that I don't need to worry about you cutting off pieces of yourself."

The brightness faded from his friend's eyes, and irritation flickered through Killian. "Don't look at me like that. I'll speak to the Rowenes armorer and see if he has something that will suit, but you don't get to swing it until Sonia gives her blessing."

"Thank you." Finn's voice was clipped. "The boy with the towels told me that I could eat with them. So unless there's something you need from me . . . ?"

"No." Killian felt suddenly weary, the heat from the wine he'd downed having vanished from his veins. "Go find them."

As Finn trotted off down the corridor, he turned to Sonia, who was eyeing him thoughtfully. Instead of her usual attire of trousers and shirts, she wore a bright pink-and-gold dress cut in Gamdeshian style, golden combs holding back her short curls, glittering jewels running up the sides of her earlobes. Several gold bracelets gleamed against her russet skin, and wide gold cuffs wrapped around the defined muscles of her arms. She was undeniably beautiful, but she was also one of his lieutenants, so he only said, "They gave you everything you needed?"

She nodded. "Your brother and sister-in-law were here, recently. Lady Adra had this commissioned, but it wasn't finished before they departed. And your brother . . ." She inclined a head to Killian's garments, and he cast his eyes skyward, the clothes making abrupt sense.

His middle brother, Seldrid, was notoriously flamboyant in his attire, and he was equally notorious for never wearing the same clothes twice. He left a trail of flashy coats and overly tight trousers everywhere he went, and this was probably the most muted of whatever he'd left behind in the Rowenes palace. Killian made a note to visit the bankers in Rotahn to withdraw enough funds to pay for new clothes or he'd spend every visit here looking like he belonged in a circus troupe.

Offering Sonia his arm, he led her through the palace, heading in the direction of the main dining room.

"It's not about the sword, you know," she said, smiling at the servants that curtsied and bowed as they passed. "Just like it wasn't about having his own horse."

"Then what is it about?"

She muttered something in Gamdeshian under her breath that he was fairly certain translated into, "Why are men so dense?" then said, "They are attempts to spend time with you."

Killian snorted. "He's with me all day, every day. He's just mad that I won't give it to him now. Except that as soon as I do, he'll only want something else."

"I am going to choose to believe the healer didn't do a fulsome job fixing your cracked skull at Alder's Ford, because that's preferable to the alternative!" she snapped. "Your body is with us, but your mind is not. When was the last time you had a conversation with him that wasn't limited to one-word answers and grunts on your part?"

"I've—"

"Been thinking only of yourself," she interrupted, pausing in her diatribe to nod at a servant. "Finn lost *everything* when Derin invaded. His father is dead, what family he has wants nothing to do with him, and all he owns are the ratty clothes the servants are probably burning as we speak. You are all that he has—the only constant, the only person who cares whether he lives or dies, and yet you are behaving as though you barely see him."

"That's not true," he snapped back. "I do care. That's why—"

"You're pushing him away," she said, clearly unwilling to allow him to finish a sentence. "Because you're afraid of him getting hurt. Of losing him, as you have lost others. But fear is the Corrupter's greatest power, and when you let it make your decisions for you, *he* wins."

There was no chance to retort, because they'd reached the entrance to the dining room, the doors swinging open and a servant loudly announcing their titles, Sonia possessed of a few he hadn't known about.

Ria mercifully hadn't arrived yet, but the rest of the Rowenes clan was in full attendance, Serrick's numerous nieces and nephews and cousins, all bedecked in finery and endless, *endless,* gold.

Killian mechanically performed all the courtesies expected of him, kissing the hands of ladies while flattery poured from their lips and allowing the men to pound him on the back while they offered congratulations for his rise to command, all of it holding a false, calculated air.

Servants with trays of delicacies circulated, the expectation that one eat their fill on endless tiny mouthfuls, and Killian's stomach instantly began to ache beneath the onslaught. His constitution was more used to rations than this rich fare.

"Lady Ria Rowenes."

The herald's voice split the air, and Killian turned to watch Ria come into the room. Her hair was woven into a coronet around her head, the dark red gown she wore high-necked and long-sleeved, all the skin he'd seen earlier now covered by brocade. She nodded at those who'd dropped into bows and curtsies, then squared her shoulders and approached him.

What Killian wanted to do was flee the room and whatever conversation was to come, but he stood his ground. "My lady."

She inclined her head. "My lord." And though she wore cosmetics, color bloomed on her cheeks. "I wish to apologize for my earlier conduct. It was inappropriate, and I clearly misjudged your character."

Gods, this conversation was to be worse than he feared. And this time, Finn wasn't here to rescue him. "Put it from your mind."

Her amber eyes were fixed on his chin as she said, "I fear I cannot, for the motivation that pushed me to act remains."

His skin prickled, his mark warning him of something . . . "I take it your actions were not driven by—"

"No." Ria's color burned even higher, but the eyes that flicked up to meet his were uncowed. "Not that I'd be averse."

"You flatter me." A lie, because mostly she made him uncomfortable in his own skin.

Malahi's cousin huffed out an amused breath, seeing the truth he hadn't given. "Will you walk with me? There is something I wish to discuss with you in private."

Part of him wanted to avoid any circumstance that involved being alone with her. But while his mark warned him of a great many things, incoming seductions wasn't one of them. This was bigger than that. So he offered her his arm. "As you like."

Ria said nothing as she led him out of the dining room and through the palace. They exited through a side door, moving through the darkening streets of Rotahn to the exterior wall, where they mounted the stairs to the ramparts. The soldiers on guard bowed low but did not interfere as they walked down its length. Ria finally dropped his arm to lean her elbows on the stone, her eyes on the sun setting in the west.

"The border Mudamora shares with Anukastre is longer than that with any other nation," she finally said. "It's also the most poorly defended."

"It's not the threat that Derin or Gendorn are."

She was silent for a moment, then murmured, "My people who suffer to defend Mudamora's wealth would say otherwise." Turning, she looked up at him. "The King is my uncle and High Lord of these lands, but he does not hold them as close to his heart as I do. And the decisions he's made in recent years might well be good for Mudamora, but they have not favored Rotahn."

"Such is the nature of being king."

"I don't deny that." She sighed. "But my duty is to protect these people. And without soldiers and resources, I can't do that. With every passing week, the Anuk grow bolder in their raids, attacking the mining camps and stealing our gold. Any attempt to resist is met with steel, and those fighting are miners, not soldiers." She wiped a tear from her cheek. "They are terrified. That's why I begged my uncle to send us help."

Guilt twisted through Killian's stomach, because he'd believed Serrick had sent him only to keep his coffers from being harmed. Not once had he considered that it wasn't just gold the Anuk were taking, but lives. "The five hundred men with me know their business, and the Anuk are no fools. Once they've word of our presence, they'll desist."

"And once they do, my uncle will only take his soldiers back to rejoin the main army. And it will all begin again."

Which was precisely what Killian had been hoping for. To spend a few weeks fighting raiders until they decided that the cost was not worth the reward and retreated.

"I thought," she said softly, "that if I gave you reason to want to be here, that you might convince the King to allow you to remain."

Killian's skin was prickling like an army of fire ants marched across him, every instinct in him screaming danger. The Anuk had never been considered a significant threat in the past, their numbers too few, the terrain too difficult to bring large forces across. But that was before Mudamora had nearly lost the war with Derin. The Anuk knew they were weak.

Your duty is to Mudamora. To your people.

What his heart wanted didn't matter.

Taking Ria by the shoulders, he looked into her eyes. "The Anuk have taken advantage of the Corrupter's actions by choosing to attack Mudamora now. They act not only against us, but against the Six. And I think it is high time there was a reckoning."

32

TERIANA

The camp was located not too far from the xenthier, near a water-fall that toppled down the cliff into a deep pool. The crystal water called Teriana's name after a long day of walking through humid jungle.

The camp itself was small, but strangely familiar, the men work-ing to fell trees and build walls to surround the perimeter. A fire burned, and the char of grilling meat filled the air.

Tossing her pack on the ground next to Quintus's, she said, "I'm going to have a swim. And then I want some of whatever it is that's cooking."

"Stay close," Marcus said, then his eyes flicked to Quintus. "Don't let anything eat her or I'll feed you to it next."

Laughing, Quintus led her down to the water's edge, exchanging greetings with the legionnaires they passed.

"Anything swimming in there that we need to worry about?" she asked the men filling pots by the water's edge.

"The occasional snake," one answered. "Though they seem to be making themselves scarce with us banging around."

"Perfect." Pulling off her boots, belt, and vest, she glanced at Quintus. "Come on. You stink."

Shrugging, he unbuckled his armor, tossing it aside, along with his weapons. Then he tugged his tunic over his head and, without warning, gave a loud *whoop* and leapt into the water. Laughing, she jumped in after him, gasping at the bite of cold. The falls had carved deep into the earth, and her ears popped as she swam down, barely reaching the bottom before the need for air demanded she return to the surface.

Quintus was floating in circles on his back, caught in the eddies. "This feels bloody good," he said. "Can't remember the last time I had a proper swim."

Kicking toward the edge, Teriana climbed out to retrieve the soap she'd brought, using it to clean away the filth of travel as best she could while clothed. There wasn't a chance she was getting naked—not when more of the Thirty-Seventh were headed this way, obviously having been granted some time for leisure. Laughing and joking, they all stripped down and jumped in the water, dunking one another and carousing as though they hadn't a care in the world.

Quintus came up next to her, taking her soap. Holding it to his broken nose, he sniffed at it and then made a face. "Smells like girl."

"As if you know." She gave him a playful shove, but then regretted it when the smile fell away from his face. "Sorry. I . . ."

"Not you who should be sorry." He rested his arms on the rocky edge. "I've been thinking about what Felix said. About you trusting me."

Resting her own arms on the edge, Teriana waited for him to continue.

"You should know," he finally said, "that I didn't want to be your bodyguard again. That I planned to leave as soon as I could figure out a way to get Miki off that island. Marcus bribed me into staying. Told me if I watched your back until the Senate released you and your people, that he'd alter the Thirty-Seventh's books to say Miki and I were dead."

Teriana was lost for words, because everything about this was decidedly un-Marcus-like.

"I don't want to do this anymore." Quintus rested his chin on his arms. "I'm tired of fighting. Tired of killing. Tired of being used by a group of rich, entitled patricians who've never done a day of honest work in their lives. I hate them. Hate what they make us do and what they turn us into. Hate what they take from us."

His voice cracked on the last, and Teriana reached over to grip his hand. "It's not right that you're not with Miki."

A tear cut a path down his damp cheek. "Perhaps it's justice for all that I've done."

Justice. Despite having been told several times that Quintus was one of the Thirty-Seventh's assassins, used to perform targeted kills ordered by the Senate, it always felt to her as though Gibzen and Marcus and the rest were talking about a different Quintus. One she'd never met. "If there's anyone who deserves to face justice, it's the men in the Senate who forced your hand."

"They didn't force my hand," he answered. "They only made the choice easy. It's not hard to do awful things when the alternative is your own suffering. Your own life. Yet after, when the guilt is heavy and your dreams are so plagued you can barely sleep for fear of facing your victims, you half-wonder if maybe the alternative was the better choice."

"I'm sorry," she whispered. "I am so sorry for being the reason he's gone."

And for withholding the truth about Hegeria's healers from you.

Quintus scrubbed at his eyes. "It's not your fault. And I just wanted you to know that I intend to be worthy of your trust, Teriana. I won't desert you."

"Neither will I." Leaning sideways, she rested her head against his, not sure if what she was about to do was a kindness or cruelty. "When we're all free, you and Miki find the *Quincense*, all right? I know of people who might be able to help him."

He turned to look at her. "Truly?"

"On my honor," she said. "If it's possible, I'll see it done." Then she looked up at the cliff rising above them. "In the meantime, do you want to jump?"

He smiled, and for the first time, it touched his eyes. "Race you to the top?"

"Not sure that's fair, you being injured and all."

A laugh tore from his lips. "That's the *only* thing that's going to make it fair. For pride or coin?"

Rolling her eyes, she said, "Pride, obviously. You've already lost all your coin to me at cards."

Swimming toward the falls, Teriana examined the face of the cliff, which was rugged and full of handholds, but also slick with moisture. "Go."

Quintus leapt up, catching hold of protruding rock and using his superior strength to haul his way higher. He knew what he was doing, but still, Teriana watched him for a few minutes until she deemed he had a fair head start.

Then she started climbing.

33

MARCUS

"We've come across a few old campsites and a handful of trails that look to have seen recent use," Gibzen said. "But no sign of either Arinoquians or the rumored inlanders."

"Someone built that city," Marcus muttered, slowly following the men he'd allocated a few hours of leisure down to the pool beneath the waterfall. Even with Quintus with her, he didn't like Teriana being out of sight. "And I'm not surprised you've seen no Arinoquians. They stick to the coast."

Gibzen nodded, scanning the surrounding jungle. "We can scout farther inland and see what we discover."

"No." Marcus heard splashing and laughter, and part of him wished he could strip down and join them. But his presence always put a damper on the mood of the men, kept them from fully enjoying themselves. "Already we're on their lands. If we push farther west, they'll see it as an invasion and potentially retaliate. And I'm in no mood to pick a fight with an enemy we know nothing about."

Gibzen shrugged. "Maybe they're all dead. It's been close to two decades since the clans invaded and drove them inland, and they've had no contact with anyone outside the Uncharted Lands since. Hard to keep a civilization alive out here."

"Do *you* think they're all dead?" Marcus's eyes went to Teriana, who had been conversing with Quintus, though now they were swimming toward the falls.

The primus huffed out a breath, then looked up at the canopy. "No," he finally admitted. "I feel watched."

As did Marcus. But given the inlanders had shown no signs of aggression to his men, he had no intention of provoking them. "We have our hands full with the situation in Aracam. Secure the xenthier stem, but otherwise, don't go farther than the city. Understood?"

"Yes, sir."

Loud shouts caught Marcus's attention, and his eyes snapped to where Teriana and Quintus had been moments ago. They were gone.

"Where—" He caught sight of motion farther up the cliff. "*What* is she doing?"

"Climbing," Gibzen answered, as though that much wasn't obvious.

Quintus was known for his skill at climbing, and the heavy muscles in his arms and shoulders bunched as he hauled himself higher at reckless speed.

Teriana was better.

She scampered upward, and though logically Marcus knew to do so took strength, she made it look effortless in her grace. Passing Quintus, she rose higher up the towering cliff, mist from the waterfall gusting over her and making her seem ephemeral. She took no time to test her handholds, seemingly fearless of falling.

Then she was at the top, rolling over only to stand and hold her hands skyward in victory.

"What's up there?" Marcus asked. "Do we have anyone on lookout?"

Gibzen shrugged. "More of the same. Forest as far as the eye can see. I've got a man up there watching our rear."

"Come up here!" Teriana's faint voice reached him. "The view is incredible!"

Gibzen chortled, and Marcus fought the urge to shove him into the pool, instead crossing his arms and glaring upward. Trying to contain his fear as she announced her intention to jump.

She swayed over the edge, and he took an involuntary step forward, but she only laughed, her and Quintus backtracking. Then they raced forward and leapt.

His heart stopped as she fell through the air, braids flying above her head and her face full of delight. She pointed her toes, lifting her arms skyward, and then she hit the water, disappearing beneath its churning depths, with Quintus landing a second later.

Marcus's feet took him to the edge of the pool, and he stared at the place she'd gone under. Quintus rose to the surface, pumping his fist in the air to the delight of the other men. But there was no sign of Teriana.

What if she'd hit a rock? Been caught in the waterfall's undertow? What if she were being dragged unconscious downstream where the rapids grew wild?

"Where is she?" he demanded, searching the water for the glint of the gold in her braids. The men grew silent, their eyes searching, and Quintus dived under the water.

Then a snort of amusement caught his attention. Looking down, he saw Teriana resting her elbows on the rocks below him. "Help me out?"

She reached up, and he dutifully took her hand, readying to haul her out of the water and then give her a lecture on risks. But the second their fingers latched, Teriana braced her feet against the side and pulled. Yelping, Marcus toppled forward, and the water closed over him.

Spluttering to the surface, he was greeted with laughter and Teriana's grinning face. "There's going to be retribution for this," he said to her, struggling to stay afloat with the weight of his armor and gear pulling him down.

"First you have to catch me," she sang, then somersaulted and disappeared into the depths.

Everything he was demanded that he get out of the water. That he not compromise his image of authority for any reason. That he never allow his men to see him as anything other than their commander.

But he was tired of it. Tired of holding himself above them, because above always meant apart.

"Gibzen," he said.

"Yes, sir."

"Establish a rotating watch, but otherwise, the men are at liberty to do what they wish."

A liberty that, for once, he intended to take advantage of himself.

34

LYDIA

The snow-dusted streets were loud with angry voices as the temple soldiers escorted Lydia through Mudaire, civilians shouting and throwing trash in their direction from windows and doors. Broken furniture and belongings littered the ground, looters moving through empty homes to steal anything of value, plumes of smoke rising from at least six locations suggesting they were burning the rest.

But worse were the bodies. Some were nothing more than charred remains—blighters that had been decapitated and then burned—but many more lay rotting among the debris, legs sticking from alleyways and splashes of blood marring the pristine white of the snow.

"They're starting to fight back," one of the soldiers said, obviously seeing her horror. "To defend the blighters when we come for them."

Lydia had known this would happen. Had known that hunting them down and murdering them in front of their families was the worst possible strategy. Yet despite days of searching, she still hadn't come up with a viable alternative. Her research in the temple's library had yielded nothing of use, and although Lena and Gwen had had some success integrating themselves with the civilians, they'd yet to find someone sick with blight who was willing to risk meeting her. And seeing what she was seeing on the streets, Lydia couldn't blame them.

A barefoot woman chose that moment to sprint past them, tears flooding down her cheeks. In hot pursuit were a group of soldiers, naked blades gripped in their hands, but she was fast enough that there was a chance she might get away. Except as Lydia watched, another group of soldiers with a white-robed healer in their midst stepped out from a side street, cutting her off.

The woman slipped and fell, then scrambled to her feet, screaming, "Help! Help me!"

She was a blighter. A walking corpse. But that wasn't what the civilians teeming from buildings and side streets saw. In their eyes, she was an unarmed woman about to be slaughtered by her own countrymen for no other reason than that a healer had pointed a finger in her direction.

A healer who just happened to be Cyntha.

The older woman had a sword strapped to her waist, and as the soldiers she was with moved to fend off the encroaching civilians, she drew the blade, striding toward the blighter. The woman fell to her knees at Cyntha's approach, holding up her arms in defense, begging and pleading for mercy.

But Cyntha only lifted her blade, the wind blowing her hair in silvery swirls around her face, half-moon tattoo stark black against the pale skin of her forehead as she shouted, "In the name of the Six!"

Lydia tried to lunge in their direction, but one of her escort caught her arm, hauling her back.

It was too late, anyway. Cyntha's blade flashed, slicing through the blighter's arm and then her neck, blood spraying as the body slowly fell backward. Taking the torch from one of her soldiers, Cyntha held it to the woman's ragged clothing until it ignited, the awful smell of burned flesh filling the air.

More Royal Army soldiers raced onto the scene, their blades clashing against the cudgels and planks of wood the civilians carried, more blood spraying. More bodies falling. And Cyntha was in the thick of it, cutting people down with vigor that belied her age. Using the strength given to her by her mark to do the exact opposite of what it was intended to. Marked or not, how anyone could see her as a healer, Lydia didn't know.

"We need to be gone." One of the soldiers dragged on Lydia's arm. "If you're noticed, they'll come for you."

She allowed him to pull her up the street, the group breaking into a run until they reached the barricades at the palace walls. The soldiers there allowed her to pass but asked her escort to remain. "They aren't infected," she protested. "Let them through."

"King's orders," the soldier in charge said, the expression on his face telling her that he wouldn't be swayed.

Gritting her teeth, Lydia entered alone, making her way through the Royal Army camp. She scanned the soldiers within to see if any had been turned, but every man she saw was very much alive.

A servant met her at the entrance and escorted her directly to the council chambers. Inside, she found the King sitting on his throne, his eyes closed. His face was drawn and shadowed with exhaustion, his blond braid unkempt and his clothing wrinkled and marked with sweat stains at the armpits.

"You made promises you are clearly incapable of keeping, Marked One," he said without opening his eyes.

"I made no promises," she answered, slowly approaching the dais and wishing they were not alone. "I only offered hope."

He sighed. "Hope, when proven false, is a bitter thing."

Silence that she didn't dare break stretched between them. She'd spent all of her arguments, voiced her pleas that the infected be brought to her rather than killed, but it had done no good.

"There is a ship soon to arrive," he finally said. "It holds all the young healers Quindor had ordered be trained in Serlania instead of adding mouths to feed in Mudaire during the war."

Her chest tightened, apprehension prickling across her skin.

"Unless you are able to provide me an alternative," he continued, "once they arrive, we will begin the process of purging the city and forcing those left onto ships. And then Mudaire will be razed, the gates closed, and what remains abandoned as we retreat to the south out of range of the blight."

Nearly a quarter of Mudamora would be deadland belonging to the Corrupter, the North entirely cut off from the South except by way of ship. "What if the blight begins to spread again?"

"Then we'll know for certain that the Six have turned their backs on Mudamora."

They hadn't. She knew in their heart that they hadn't, it was only that the Corrupter had somehow grown so very strong.

"You have until the ship arrives, Lydia," he said. Then he opened his eyes, and the unflinching determination in them made her stomach twist. "I pray it will be enough time for you to prove that Hegeria still walks with us."

35

TERIANA

"You should be doing this," Marcus said, shifting where he sat next to her. His armor was in a pile in front of him, and he'd spent the past hour rubbing oil into the leather straps and sharpening blades while the rest of them gambled.

"I'm busy." She held up her cards. "But while you're at it, this could use a sharpen." Pulling her knife from her belt, she tossed it on the ground in front of him.

The men laughed, and after casting his eyes up at the tarp above them, Marcus picked up her knife and began sharpening it. He was relaxed, but rather than tempering her own anxieties, his calmness made her nervous.

Glancing at the faces of the other players, she tossed a gold coin into the pile between them, watching as the others met her bet. Scouts made the best gambling companions, because they always seemed to have more coin to wager. Less opportunity to spend it, she supposed, though Gibzen had told her it was because they were risk takers.

"I'm out." Quintus stretched his arms upward. "And to bed."

"Same," two of the others said, one giving Marcus a sly smile. "I don't suppose we get to spend tomorrow swimming, do we, sir?"

"You suppose right."

There were mock groans, but no one argued.

"Ready to call it quits?" Teriana's remaining opponent asked, his eyes gleaming in the firelight.

"And surrender such a pot?" She laughed. "Hardly."

Fishing around in her pocket, she found another gold coin, though it was her last. This game was getting a bit rich for her blood.

Her opponent bit at his bottom lip as he looked again at his cards. Then his eyes flicked to Marcus, who was examining the edge of her neglected knife blade. Teriana's senses perked. "Stakes getting too high? Might be time for you to fold, my friend."

Her opponent snorted, then pulled a coin that glinted gold from his belt pouch, flicking it into the pile hard enough that it all went sliding every which way. But Teriana was a master at sleight of hand, and she tracked which way the coin slid, the sight of the glittering dragon on its face giving her pause. Marcus had forbidden anyone to bring Cel currency across the Endless Seas.

At the sight of the coin, memory danced across her vision. Memory of Ashok holding a handful of golden coins stamped with that very dragon.

Her pulse raced, a thousand questions burning in her mind, but getting the right answers required the right approach.

And the absence of a certain legatus.

Reaching across him for a bottle that was sitting on a log, she turned her face to Marcus, their eyes meeting. *Go,* she mouthed.

Marcus's eyes narrowed, but rather than arguing, he rose to his feet. "Don't drink it all. Dawn comes early."

"Yeah, yeah." She refilled her cup, waiting for him to be out of earshot before turning back to her opponent. Reaching down, she plucked up the dragon, turning the gold coin over in her hands. "Strange to see Cel clink on this side of the seas. Thought it was forbidden."

He made a face. "Before you go ratting me out, I didn't bring it. Won it in a card game in a brothel in Aracam. Off one of the girls who works there."

"Why would I rat you out? Makes no difference to me."

He shrugged. "You're getting a bit of a reputation for stirring up trouble."

It was a struggle not to flinch. "The only thing I've a reputation for is fleecing you lot at cards. And on that subject, let's see what you got."

He flattened his cards against the dirt, revealing a good hand. A very good hand.

But some of her reputation, she'd earned.

Laying her cards down, she smirked. "Better luck next time."

Her opponent swore, his face twisting in frustration as she scooped the pile of coins toward her and shoved them into her pockets, though the dragon she palmed, not wanting to let it out of her sight.

Marcus returned to camp, his eyes questioning as they met hers. But she only shook her head, because the coin was proof of nothing other than that someone had violated Marcus's orders.

"Lights out, boys," Marcus said softly to those who remained awake, unrolling his bedding and climbing into it. She briefly entertained the idea of setting out her own bedroll next to him, but then thought better of it and set it out between Quintus and the fire, climbing beneath the blanket.

All night, she tossed and turned, sleep evading her, and as the faint glow of dawn emerged in the east, Teriana pulled the coin from her pocket, running her thumb over the shiny gold surface and its familiar snarling dragon before turning it over.

And scowling at the sight of Lucius Cassius's face.

The mint had done a fair job capturing his likeness. His profile revealed the weak chin he'd passed on to Titus; the resemblance between the two was marked. Especially given these freshly minted coins bore none of the wear of those that had been long in circulation.

Because *these* coins weren't in circulation at all.

Teriana sat bolt upright, Quintus grumbling and shifting away from her at the motion. But she barely noticed.

Hundreds of coins were minted in honor of a new consul, but they didn't enter circulation until a fortnight after the elections, in conjunction with a ceremony where patricians exchanged a coin bearing the visage of the prior consul for one of the new. Which meant these hadn't been in circulation when the *Quincense* and the Cel fleet had left Celendrial. Which meant these had been taken from the highly secure mint itself.

And there was only one person who could have managed that.

Lucius Cassius.

Tugging on her boots and fastening her belt, Teriana glanced around to ensure the men were still sleeping, then outwards to ensure those on watch weren't watching *her*. Picking up a pebble, she threw it at Marcus. It struck his shoulder and, always a light sleeper, he stirred. But it wasn't until she'd hit him a second time that he lifted his head, blinking blearily as he focused on her.

She tossed him the coin, watching as he frowned at the dragon, giving an annoyed shake of his head before looking to her askance.

Turn it over, she mouthed, and he flipped it over, frown deepening as he held it up to the growing light.

It only took him a heartbeat to come to the same conclusion she had, the muscles in his jaw tightening, the hand not holding the coin balling into a fist. Then he looked back to her and jerked his chin toward the edge of the camp.

Teriana stepped carefully around the sleeping men, Marcus belting on his weapons as he joined her at the perimeter.

"I'm going to take one last look around the city," he said to one of the men on watch. "Start packing up and we can head back to Aracam when I return."

The man nodded. "Give me a moment, sir, and I'll have an escort readied."

"I don't need an escort."

"But—"

"I'm not going far and I won't be long. If I'm not back in a half hour, feel free to come looking."

Obviously torn between what was worse: arguing with his commander or allowing said commander to wander enemy territory alone, the young man said, "A half hour, sir. And don't hold me responsible if Quintus comes looking sooner."

Catching Teriana's wrist, Marcus tugged her into the jungle, nodding at those on watch as they passed. "This is going to raise eyebrows," she muttered.

"Least of my concerns. Walk faster."

As it had the first time she'd seen it, the overgrown city seemed to appear from nowhere. The buildings were crumbling, vines and roots forcing their way between blocks of stone, then pulling them down into the damp earth as though the jungle intended to consume any evidence of civilization. And yet despite that, it wasn't hard to see where roads and streets had once been, and she and Marcus wound their way deeper and deeper into this place that had been lost to time and conquest.

Reaching a spot where there was a break in the tree canopy, Marcus paused in a circle of growing sunlight and turned to her, waiting.

"The coins Ashok had were gold Cel dragons," she said without preamble. "And lots of them. I didn't get a close look, but I remember them being shiny enough that they'd either been polished or were of fresh mint."

"These," he said, holding up the coin, "weren't in circulation when we left. I couldn't even have accessed them—the mint is a fortress to rival Lescendor."

"But I bet the consul could have. And he sure as shit didn't give them to *Felix*."

Silence.

"It wasn't Felix." The words came out of Marcus in a whoosh of breath, then all the color drained from his face. "It wasn't Felix."

He swayed, and worried he was about to faint, Teriana caught his arms. "This is good news."

Marcus flinched, pulling away from her. "I screwed up," he muttered. "What have I done?"

"Titus played you," she corrected. "And not just you. But now we know the truth, and while it might not be proof enough to hang him, at least you know who it was. And who to watch." Her skin abruptly prickled, and she panned the surrounding jungle.

"I know." Marcus looked ready to vomit. "But the things I said . . . He's never going to forgive me. I . . . I don't deserve to be forgiven." He doubled over. "What have I done?"

The sharp *clack clack* of pebbles falling against stone filled Teriana's ears, and she turned away from Marcus, searching their surroundings. "Did you hear that?"

Marcus straightened, hand going to the weapon at his waist, his eyes wet but focused.

"Quintus?" It was possible he'd come after them.

"If it was Quintus, we wouldn't have heard him." Marcus scanned the overgrown buildings, and Teriana's skin crawled with sudden certainty that they were being watched.

And that the eyes doing the watching weren't friendly.

The soft scrape of metal caught her attention, and she looked down to see that Marcus had his gladius in hand. "How long until your men come looking for us?"

"Soon enough." He answered loudly in Arinoquian. "And knowing Quintus, he won't be alone." Then softly, and in Cel, he said, "Get ready to fight."

Fear pulsed through her veins, but Teriana pulled her knife, her fingers flexing on the hilt. "Should we head back to—"

A shadow dropped from above. Screaming, she flung her weight against Marcus, sending them both rolling into a broken fountain. Scrambling to her feet, Teriana whirled around to face their attacker.

Only to find a striped tiger crouched where they'd been standing.

"Run!" The words tore from her lips, and then they were sprinting, weaving through the streets. But behind was the thud of heavy paws. There was no chance they could outrun it.

Leaping over a tree root, she bent to pick up a heavy rock. She twisted and threw it hard, hitting the pursuing cat in the foreleg and sending it tumbling.

"This way!" Marcus hauled on her arm. "We need to get to a place we can defend until my men arrive."

They cut between two collapsed buildings, reaching the towers of the god circle. Marcus sprinted toward Lern's, wrenching open the tarnished door. "Go!" He pushed her through the crack first, following on her heels. But before they could close it, the cat leapt, slashing claws driving it inward.

They retreated into the center of the space, which was faintly illuminated by the sunlight streaming through holes in the roof. The tiger stalked toward them, lips pulled back to reveal fangs as long as her fingers.

"The gods have mercy on us," she whispered.

Then the floor fell out from under her.

36

MARCUS

The floor collapsed, and he was falling.

Marcus hit the ground hard, the rubble from the floor digging deep into his back, his body screaming in pain. "Teriana!"

He searched for her, coughing on the clouds of dust that made it almost impossible to see.

"Here." She was on her hands and knees, struggling to rise. "Where is it?"

A snarl to his left drew his gaze. The tiger had fallen as well but, from the look of it, had landed better. Its muscles bunched and Marcus flung himself between the cat and Teriana, his blade lifted. He'd only have one chance to kill it.

Then the rubble moved beneath them, sinking, the sensation like standing on rocky quicksand.

"What's happening?" Teriana's voice was panicked.

"I don't know." He fought to keep his balance, but the footing beneath him kept changing, and he fell to his knees.

The tiger had its legs splayed wide as the ground shifted beneath it, but then it took one step toward them. Then another.

And that's when Marcus realized the animal was higher than they were. That the ground beneath him and Teriana was collapsing faster, it appearing for all the world like the whirlpool that had brought them to this side of the world.

And understanding dawned on him.

"Climb!" he screamed.

They scrambled, but handholds and footholds fell away, and instead of rising, they slid down.

Farther and farther, a glow appearing beneath them.

Looking between his feet, Marcus saw the tip of a xenthier stem appear, the crystal sucking away any debris that fell against it, moving the rubble to the terminus.

Wherever that was.

"Marcus!" Teriana screamed his name, and he looked up to see several warriors wearing the same elaborate armor as in the paintings throughout the city. Not Arinoquians, but the inlanders. The people the Arinoquians had displaced.

"We were warned of you by one who came before," the lone woman with them said in accented Cel. Which was impossible. How could they know the language? "We know of your Empire. Of what it does to everything it touches. He wore the same mark as you." She tapped the right side of her chest.

"Help us," Teriana pleaded. "Please! You don't understand!"

But the woman only shook her head and said to the tiger, "Kill them."

The massive cat picked its way down, eyes fixed on him and Teriana.

There was nowhere to go.

If they managed to climb up, they'd be met by fangs. And below was a potentially deadly unknown.

Certain death. Or the chance at life.

Catching hold of Teriana's arm, Marcus twisted, and together, they slid down the rubble toward the glowing crystal.

37

TERIANA

The air rushed from her chest.

And all around her was white. White, endless white, and for a heartbeat Teriana believed she was trapped in the xenthier's magic. Trapped between two places. Neither here nor there. Bodiless.

Then the cold hit her. Piercing and bitter and cruel, her sweaty skin screaming under the onslaught.

"Get up!" Marcus shouted, his hands under her arms, hauling her upright, dragging her backward through the rubble that had come through with them. Away from the xenthier stem, which jutted, glittering and black, from the snow.

Where are we?

Then the tiger was in front of her, stumbling to keep its footing. It snarled, head swinging from side to side.

Its gaze fixed on her.

Marcus shoved her behind him, blade in one hand. The animal's muscles bunched, and Teriana lifted her knife, fingers already numb from the cold. Her heart thundered in her chest, pulse roaring in her ears.

Run! her instincts screamed. Instead, Teriana bit down on her terror. "Come and get us, you bastard."

The tiger snarled, but rather than lunging at Marcus, it staggered, skin shifting and moving as though it were made of liquid, the snarl changing to a scream.

A human scream.

It was a gods-damned shifter.

The tiger's form solidified, but it swayed back and forth. Disoriented.

"Don't like the cold?" Marcus started forward, but Teriana caught hold of his arm.

"He's god marked," she said. "By Lern. He can change into any shape he wants."

Except something wasn't right.

The tiger took one step back, then another before spinning around to paw at the xenthier tip. It batted at it with increasing violence, until its body once again turned liquid, flowing in a way Teriana's eyes couldn't comprehend—as though she watched through a piece of glass that distorted everything. She blinked once only to find a naked man where the tiger had stood. He struck the xenthier, screaming curses in a language she didn't know.

Then he froze. Sensing he was no longer the hunter, the shifter slowly turned, eyes landing on Marcus's blade, which was shaking, his hand reddened by the cold.

Gods, it was freezing.

"What is this place?" the shifter demanded in accented Arinoquian. "Where have you brought me? What have you done to me?"

Marcus laughed, and there was an edge to it that made Teriana stiffen. That made her look at him instead of the shifter. "Welcome to the East, you bloody bastard. Let's see how well you fight without your gods to swing the odds."

The shifter took a step backward.

Then a howl split the air.

All three of them froze.

"What was that?" Teriana demanded, turning in a circle, but all around them was snow. A barren landscape of *nothing.*

"Sibernese wolves." There was fear in Marcus's voice. "They're nocturnal. But if they're hungry enough, they'll come before dusk."

And the sun was little more than a glow on the horizon.

As though some of his mark's instincts remained, the shifter turned, peering into the distance. Then he raised a hand and pointed.

In the dying light, Teriana could make out motion. Something—many somethings—racing in their direction.

"Run!"

They struggled through the snow, feet breaking through the crust, which sent them tripping. And there was no escape, the land empty of anything but leafless brush.

Howls filled her ears. Teriana stumbled and fell, and Marcus hauled her up, terror chasing away the burning sting of the cold.

"There!"

Her eyes tracked the direction Marcus pointed, where a small shack had appeared in the distance.

The howls grew closer, and Teriana cast a backward glance over her shoulder.

Racing toward her were wolves with fur as black as night, eyes glittering in the fading sun, wide paws ghosting across the snow despite the creatures being bigger than any wolf she'd ever seen.

"Keep running!"

There was no chance of them outpacing the wolves.

Or at least, not all three of them.

The shifter was taller, his longer legs pulling him ahead.

"I'm not dying so you can live!" Marcus shouted, then threw himself forward. His gladius sliced through the tendon above the man's heel, blood spraying across the snow.

The shifter shrieked and fell, tried to rise, then fell again.

Teriana slowed, but Marcus clambered to his feet and caught her arm. "His turn to be hunted. It will buy us time."

She staggered, the icy air burning her lungs, but the sight of the shifter crawling on hands and knees made her jerk out of Marcus's grip.

"Teriana!"

Ignoring him, she raced back to the man. "May the Six find your soul," she whispered, then sliced her knife across his throat.

"Run!"

She jerked upright, and a sob tore from her lips. The wolves were only a hundred paces away and closing fast.

Adrenaline fired through her veins, and she flung herself toward the shack. Over and over she fell, barely feeling the sharp pieces of snow scoring her bare hands as she regained her feet.

She heard the pack fall upon the dying shifter. Heard them tear into him with excited yelps and whines. Heard the moment when they decided he wasn't going anywhere but that their other prey was escaping.

"We're almost there! We're almost there!" Marcus shouted, pushing her ahead of him.

The wolves' paws made soft thuds against the snow as they continued their pursuit.

The shack was twenty paces away.

Pants from half a dozen muzzles filled the air.

Ten paces.

She felt them gaining on her.

Five paces.

Felt their hot breath on her neck.

She slammed against the door of the shack, jerking up the latch, the door swinging open.

Marcus shoved her inside, sending her tumbling over whatever was hidden in the darkness.

Twisting on her hands and knees, she watched him lean against the door right as the front-runner lunged.

It hit the door, driving it inward, Marcus scrambling to hold it in place.

Teriana screamed as snapping teeth appeared in the gap, the animal's fur stained with the dead shifter's blood.

Marcus smashed his fist against the wolf's nose, and it recoiled with a whine. The door slammed shut. "Get the beam!"

Leaping to her feet, she fumbled in the dim light for the heavy plank. Heaving it up, she wedged it in the slot next to the hinge, but before she could get the other side in place, the wolf hit the door again, opening it a crack.

Teriana's eyes locked with the wolf's, and it snarled, shoving its muzzle in the gap, teeth snapping.

She recoiled as the door inched open enough for it to fit its whole head, and the beam fell against Marcus's shoulder. The wolf was enormous, its lips pulled back to reveal fangs, green eyes fixed on her.

"Hit it!" Marcus shouted. "If it gets in, we're dead!"

Fight.

Balling her fist, Teriana swung hard, catching the animal straight in the nose, her hand scraping along its teeth. It yelped, but didn't draw back.

Marcus's feet slid in the dirt, the door inching open, the shack shuddering as the pack attacked from all sides.

"Kill it!"

She'd lost her knife, but beneath the animal's legs was Marcus's gladius.

Taking a deep breath, Teriana lunged downwards, reaching for the hilt.

The wolf moved with her, only Marcus's weight against the door keeping it from biting the back of her neck. Its paw struck her, clawing along her arm, but then her numb fingers caught hold of the weapon.

Falling backward, she tightened her grip and then slammed the tip of the blade into the animal's chest.

It squealed and scrambled back, taking the gladius with it, and the door slammed shut. Marcus heaved the beam into place. "There's another one. Somewhere. Here." Lifting the beam, he fit it into the brackets, then fell to his knees next to her.

Blood ran warm down her frozen skin where the wolf had clawed her, and she flinched as the animals continued to attack the shack, the wood shuddering with each blow. "Can they get in?"

"No," he said but didn't sound convinced. "They're built for this. But we're going to freeze to death if we don't get a fire started."

He was right.

With her adrenaline fading, the cold was sinking into her bones, the pain worse than the injury to her arm. And Marcus was wearing a fraction of the clothing she was, his arms and legs bare, feet exposed to the deadly chill.

He moved away from her, fumbling around in the dark. "Stove. Is. Here." His teeth were chattering loud enough for her to hear over the wolves. Hers were, too. Her whole body quivered violently, and she shoved her hands into her armpits in a desperate attempt to warm them.

Steel struck against flint, sparks flying.

"Come. On!"

More sparks flew, landing on the kindling in the stove, but it didn't take.

"Light, damn you!"

He struck the flint again, but the knife knocked it from his hands. "Piece of shit!" he screamed at it.

Teriana dropped to her knees next to him, jerking the blade from his hand and fumbling in the dark until she found the flint. She smashed the two together over and over, sparks flying.

One landed on the dry bit of grass, and a flame took.

"Thank the gods," she whispered, though the Six wouldn't have anything to do with it. Not in this place. And even if they could help, she doubted they were of a mind to do *her* any favors.

Blowing gently on the flame with shaky breath, she coaxed the fire to life, holding her hands up to the faint heat.

She was so cold. Colder than she'd ever been in her life. Marcus was on the ground next to her, curled in on himself, eyes shut. He wasn't shivering anymore, but his arm was ice cold when she touched him, and her heart skittered in her chest. He'd die if she didn't get him warm.

Placing slivers of wood over the burning grass, she scanned the small space, eyes lighting on a shelf holding a stack of blankets. Scrambling to her feet, she pulled them down, dust flying everywhere as she tucked two around him and the last over her own shoulders.

"Hang on," she whispered, feeding more wood to the flame until the fire was roaring. Climbing under the blankets, she curled around his body as tears trickled down her cheeks.

He started to shake again, teeth clattering, but it was only when he muttered, "Open the flue," that her chest relaxed and she sat up, tucking the blankets around him. She used a stick to open the flue, the smoke rising up the chimney pipe rather than continuing to cloud the shack.

He needed something warm to drink, but while the shelves were stocked with various supplies, including a kettle and two cups, water was not one of them. What she needed was snow to melt, but that meant going outside.

The wolves had either given up or been driven back by the fire, but over the crackle of burning wood, she could hear the faint whining of the animal she'd injured. Except there wasn't a chance of her opening that door until sunrise. Then her eyes latched on what appeared to be a tiny door at the base of one of the walls, less than six inches square. Dropping to her hands and knees, she unlatched it, revealing snow had banked against the wall of the shack.

"Gods-damned Cel," she muttered. "You think of everything."

She filled the kettle with snow and hung it next to the fire to melt, eyes going to Marcus as he stirred, slowly pushing himself upright.

She shook her head as he stood and pushed him down onto the narrow cot. "And I didn't save your ass only to have you fall into a stove, so sit still."

Lifting the kettle, she poured warm water into the cups and handed him one, then drank deeply from her own. Marcus only stared at his, unblinking. Finally, he said, "Freezing would've been the easier way to go."

"What?" she demanded. "Clearly you need to lie back down if you're spouting nonsense like that."

"It's not nonsense, Teriana." His hands balled into fists, and he rose, unsteady on his feet. "We're in the middle of bloody Sibern! In winter. With no supplies, the wrong sort of weapons, and on the opposite side of Reath from where we are supposed to be!" He threw his cup against the wall, water splattering everywhere. "We should've just laid down for the wolves, because now we get to slowly starve to death while we lose our minds in a shack in the middle of nowhere."

Teriana glared at the fallen cup, the side now dented inward, then she turned to fix her glare on him. "I've noticed that you do this from time to time, Marcus, and I can't say that I like it."

"What's *this*?" he retorted. "Present you with *facts*?"

"*This* is losing your head. And it's not when things get ugly or complicated or hard, but when you aren't in *control*." Picking up the cup, she refilled it and shoved it back into his hands. "You can't stand it when the world isn't marching to the beat of your drums. Now drink."

He scowled and didn't move. "Are you finished dissecting my character flaws?"

Giving him a wide smile, because the alternative was to slap him upside the head, she said, "I don't know: Are you finished with your little tantrum?"

They stared each other down, and Teriana felt no small amount of satisfaction when Marcus looked away first, drinking from his cup.

"Between the two of us, we have a few skills," she continued. "Surely we can figure a way through this."

"We're at least a thousand miles from the coast." His voice was acidic. "And of all the men in the Thirty-Seventh you could've landed here with, I have the *least* practical experience in survival. Possession of skills is irrelevant if said skills are wrong for the task."

Closing her eyes, Teriana took a deep breath, wishing that her cup were filled with rum and not melted snow. "Marcus, if you don't start being more helpful, I'm going to toss you outside to die with that awful wolf."

He crossed his arms, fixing her with a stubborn glare.

"For starts, how do you know we're that far from the coast? How do you know where we are at all?"

"There's a map on the wall behind you."

Teriana's cheeks warmed and she turned, eyeing the framed map nailed to the wall. Taking one of the candles from the supply shelves, she lit it at the stove then held it up so she could see the lines. At the top right corner of the map was written the number 203.

Marcus came up behind her. "We're on the Via Hibernus." He pointed to a line crossing the expanse of the enormous province. "It's the longest road in the Empire, and we are apparently in shelter number 203. Which is here." He moved his finger to a small red dot, which was far closer to the middle of the map than she'd hoped.

A faint flutter of panic settled in her stomach, and because she knew it would be worse if she didn't persevere, she asked, "There's an actual road beneath the snow?"

Marcus shook his head. "There's mile marker posts driven into the ground so that travelers can stay on route. Though even with them, if the visibility is bad, it's easy to lose your way."

"Right." It was late in the year, which meant winter was nearly upon the province. More snow seemed inevitable. "And there's more of these shelters?"

"By necessity. The wolves make it impossible for those traveling in small groups or as individuals to be outside after dark. They're maintained and restocked annually by whatever legion gets stuck with the task. It's shitty work."

Shitty work or not, his words eased her panic. If all the shelters were stocked like this one, they could move between them, living off the supplies, making clothes out of the blankets. They'd be hungry, but it was doable. "How far apart are they?"

"Twenty miles."

Teriana bit her lip. A long walk, especially in the snow, but they were both fit.

"On good terrain, it's reasonable for a messenger to travel three to four miles in an hour," Marcus continued. "In the height of summer, there are eighteen daylight hours for travel. But at this time of year . . ." He paused, then shook his head. "In the depths of winter, there is daylight for less than six hours. Right now, I'd estimate we have about eight hours to travel twenty miles in snow without snowshoes, with little to no food, and with less light each passing day."

Her knees quivered as his words sank in.

They were going to die out here.

38

MARCUS

The night was interminable.

Hours and hours of blackness, the only sounds the groan of the wind, the crackle of the fire, and the endless whining of the dying wolf outside the shack. It ground upon his nerves, inspiring a strange distance from himself that he'd only ever felt in the doldrums.

A sort of madness.

Marcus wanted to go outside and finish the damned thing off if only for the peace it would bring, but he knew the others would be out there until dawn. Either eating the man-tiger or shifter or whatever it was Teriana had called him, or standing watch over their dying pack member.

That would cost them. Would probably be what killed them, in the end.

Kill all or kill none was what they'd been taught about the Sibernese wolves. The creatures were said to hold an almost humanlike grievance against those who killed a pack member. A desire for vengeance that would drive a pack out of their territory, regardless of the risks. Marcus had hundreds of Sibernese in the ranks of the Thirty-Seventh: every one of them had claimed it was true.

He'd brushed the stories off as nonsense—myths told to frighten foolish children away from any thought of wandering.

Now he was starting to believe that in not believing, he'd been the fool.

The wolves yelped and barked outside the shack, and Teriana stirred restlessly in his arms on the narrow cot. After he'd cleaned and bandaged the claw marks on her arm and wrist, she'd wordlessly accepted some narcotic he'd retrieved from the bottom of his belt pouch, the waves of her eyes dull and muddy and entirely unfamiliar in their defeat.

It would've been kinder to give her hope. To lie and say it was possible for them to make it out of here alive. But he'd been cold and rattled and angry, his head spinning from hypothermia, and it had been easier to spout the bitter truth.

You are such a bastard.

Angry with himself, he eased his arm out from under Teriana's neck and stood, feeling the confines of the tiny space pressing in on him. He'd never liked small spaces. Never liked being contained. Had always needed to walk—to get away—to be alone in his own thoughts. A habit that had caused Felix endless consternation over the years.

Does he know I'm gone?

His chest tightened as he envisioned Felix's face when he received the news. In his mind's eye, he could see the thoughts that would march through his second's head. Firstly, that Marcus had gone wandering and that the men had panicked when he couldn't immediately be found. Then, when no runner arrived on the heels of the first pair with news that it was a false alarm, that something had happened to Marcus while he was wandering. Then—

His thoughts scattered as his eyes landed on Teriana's sleeping face, one hand curled beneath her chin.

They'll send word at the same time that Teriana is missing.

Felix will think I've deserted. That I've abandoned him and the Thirty-Seventh to be with her.

And with the things that had been said during their argument, Marcus could hardly blame him.

"No," he muttered, resuming his pacing. "The trackers will find evidence we were attacked. They'll know something happened. That we were killed or kidnapped. They'll tell Felix."

But there was no blood. No bodies. It was possible they'd find the xenthier, but that would be even more damning, because it would look as though he'd discovered an easy escape and taken it. Or worse, they'd send a team after him and they'd end up *here.*

"Shit!" he snarled, then kicked his already-dented cup across the shack with a loud clang.

Teriana muttered and stirred, but the narcotic pulled her back down a moment later.

How much longer until a change of command took place? Two days? Three? Felix would rise to acting legatus of the Thirty-Seventh, but until his rank was confirmed by the Senate, which clearly *wasn't possible,* Titus would be senior to him. He'd take control of the mission. Control of the Thirty-Seventh. Control of *Marcus's* men.

Panic curled in his guts, his chest tightening like a vise at the thought of Cassius's backstabbing traitor of a son being in command of the Thirty-Seventh. Titus didn't care about their lives, which meant he wouldn't blink at sacrificing them to achieve his ends.

I need to get back.
They need me.
I need them.

His breathing was coming too fast, his chest too tight, an attack lurking. "Breathe," he muttered. "Breathe. Think about what you need to do to get back to them."

Turning to the map on the wall, he assessed the situation, knowing there were only a handful of routes out of Sibern. He plucked a charred twig from the stove, added another log to keep the flames burning bright, then began to calculate. Miles they could reasonably travel in a day. Contingencies for weather and injury and the need to hunt for food.

Stretching until his back cracked, he added the number of days, his guts twisting as he arrived at a total.

He'd never been away from his legion for more than a day. His heart rate escalated again, a faint wheeze filling his ears with each breath.

Get it together!

His eyes flicked to the map, going to the jagged ridges demarking the Sibernese Teeth. Calling the damned things mountains was a misnomer, because they were more like shards of splintered rock reaching to the sky. There was a route through, but only experienced climbers dared travel that path, and the Teeth claimed more than a few every year. To go through them would cut their journey's length by weeks or more, but the risks . . . No, the long road it was.

What are the obstacles?

Lack of food. The wolves. The distance between shelters. The cold.

Break it down to increments.

They needed to make it to the next shelter. The wolves would be driven into their dens for the daylight hours, so all they needed to do was run twenty miles in snow in about eight hours.

It's possible. You're both strong. Both fit.

The wolf was silent now, likely dead or near to it, and it would be frozen solid by dawn. Still, they could hack off as much meat as they could carry, which solved the issue of food for a few days.

What about the cold?

He was wearing a tunic, a belt, and sandals. Teriana was somewhat better off in linen trousers, a silk blouse, and a leather vest, but even though her boots came up to her knees, the leather was too thin to provide much warmth. They had the wool blankets, which were legion standard issue, but even if they cut them up, they wouldn't make for enough clothing in this sort of cold. And the temperature would only drop with each passing day.

There will be more blankets in the next shelter. All you have to do is make it that far.

Picking up one of the blankets, Marcus rubbed the fabric between his fingers. Good enough for warmth in a tiny shelter heated with a stove, but out there? In the wind?

Not good enough.

A whine of pain split the air.

The damned thing was still alive.

Frowning, Marcus went to the door, pressing his ear against the wood. Faintly, he could make out the labored breathing of the animal, which couldn't be more than a dozen paces from the shack. He had assumed it would be long dead and frozen before they could reach it, and therefore nearly unusable. But what if it survived the night?

A plan formed in his head, and smiling to himself, Marcus pulled his knife and began cutting the blanket into pieces.

Enjoy your time in command, Titus, he thought to himself. *You won't have it for long.*

39

KILLIAN

Killian dismounted from his horse and handed the reins to Finn, who handed him a rag in exchange.

"You need a healer?" Finn asked, frowning at him. "I can't tell if any of that is yours."

Wiping the rag across his face, Killian frowned at the blood and sweat, then shook his head. "It's not mine."

All of it was from Anuk raiders that he'd fought. That he'd killed.

Sonia fell into step next to him, the light armor she wore as blood-splattered as his own, her eyes shadowed with exhaustion. "Why do they keep coming?" she muttered. "Is their avarice so great?"

Killian hadn't thought so. The raids had always been more like sport for the Anuk. A game the desert people played to see who could steal the most gold out from under the scorpion's nose. But nothing about the battles he'd fought in recent days felt like a game. They'd been vicious, the Anuk refusing to retreat even when they'd lost, fighting until the last of their warriors hit the earth and fell still. "I don't know."

The not knowing was fraying his nerves, because instead of the number of raids decreasing, they were getting more frequent by the day. And until he could find a way to quell them, he would have to remain in Rotahn.

Reaching the building that served as the center of command as well as barracks for him and his officers, he stepped inside, breathing in a mouthful of cool air, the shade a welcome respite from the endless sun.

It was short-lived.

Ria, along with a Rowenes captain named Dwyer, sat at the table in the center, sipping wine. Beads of condensation trickled down their glasses, suggesting she'd brought precious ice with her from the fortress in order to keep her drink cool. At the sight of him, Dwyer rose, though Ria remained seated.

"My lady." Killian inclined his head. "We weren't expecting you."

Ria's eyes flicked over him, her brow furrowing. "Another raid?"

He nodded.

"Then circumstances are worsening rather than improving as we'd hoped?"

"Of course they're worsening," Dwyer muttered. "He's not playing by the rules."

"Mind your tone when speaking to your betters, Captain," Ria snapped. "He is a lord of the realm and marked by Tremon, and you will show him every courtesy."

Killian's skin prickled. "Let him speak his mind, my lady. If he has insight into the Anuk's behavior, I'd hear it."

The Rowenes captain crossed his arms. "It's always been practice to allow the raiders to retreat once they've been repelled, but you've not been allowing them the opportunity. Mark my words, the increase in their efforts is retaliation for *your* brutality. Sir." He added the last after a significant hesitation.

"We *do* allow them to retreat," Sonia snapped. "They won't take it. The deaths are on *them,* not on Lord Calorian."

"I wasn't speaking to you, Gamdeshian," Dwyer sneered. "So keep your mouth shut."

Killian's temper flared, his hands balling into fists at his side. "Mind your tone, *Dwyer.* Not only is she my lieutenant, she's correct. The Anuk show no interest in retreat or surrender."

"Because of your heavy hand!" Dwyer glowered at him. "You've riled them up fierce. With the way things are going, the Anuk are going to cross the border in force, and then Mudamora can place two invasions at your feet."

"Enough!" Ria snarled. "Leave, Captain. I'll hear no more of these accusations."

The other man stormed out of the building, slamming the door behind him.

"My apologies, Lord Calorian," Ria said, smoothing her skirts once. Then again. "We've not seen this much violence in our lifetimes, and it has everyone on edge. But Dwyer is loyal to me to a fault."

So much violence. And apparently the worst of it could be laid at his feet. Killian's stomach twisted. Motioning to Sonia to go, he waited until she'd disappeared into the barracks before asking, "What would you have me do, Ria? I can't stop them from attacking, I can only repel them when they do. And neither can I force them to retreat. This is the only avenue."

"I don't know." She bit at her bottom lip. "Warfare is your expertise, Killian. Not mine. All I know is that every day things seem to grow worse in Mudamora."

"You've received word from Mudaire?" The words came out faster than he'd intended, and he bit the inside of his cheeks.

"Only that the blight remains and that it continues to infect, despite the healers' best efforts."

Lydia was one of those healers.

"Anukastre must sense Mudamora's weakness," she said. "And rather than standing with us against the Corrupter, they aim to take advantage. And that terrifies me, because I don't know how much more our kingdom can take before it falls."

Killian's skin crawled, his mark screaming warning after warning of danger to the point he could barely think. Which was no wonder, because it seemed to be coming from all sides.

Then alarm bells jangled outside, the thud of booted feet filling the air. "More raiders," he said. "I have to go."

But before he could turn, Ria rose to her feet, clutching at his wrist despite it being coated with dried blood. "It is your duty to protect Mudamora, *Marked One*. Please don't fail us."

Killian heard the words she didn't say. *Please don't fail us again.*

The sun was beginning to set as he dispatched the last of the raiders and bent to wipe his blade on the back of the man's sand-colored clothes.

"You want us to start burning them, sir?" one of his men asked, wiping sweat from his brow.

"No," Killian answered, glancing northeast in the direction of Mudaire before turning back to the man. "Drag the corpses to the mouth of the pass and leave them for the carrion."

Where they'd serve as warning for what Mudamora's *weakness* looked like.

40

TERIANA

Teriana rose slowly from the depths of her drugged sleep, blinking at the glowing stove a pace away from her, the smell of woodsmoke heavy in her nose.

Not a dream.

She and Marcus were on the far side of Reath, half a world from the *Quincense* and the Thirty-Seventh. In the middle of bloody frozen Sibern. In a stupid little shack where they were likely to either kill each other out of irritation or be eaten by giant wolves long before they starved to death.

Rolling over and hiding from her misery in sleep seemed an ideal solution, but then her eyes latched on Marcus. He stood next to the door, ear pressed against the wood, his eyes closed and knife in hand.

He was also dressed in what appeared to be clothing made from blankets, complete with a hat that was tied beneath his chin and a pair of mittens. He looked utterly ridiculous, and she would've burst out laughing if it wasn't obvious to her that he had a plan.

Which meant they weren't dead yet.

"Were you planning on saying good-bye?" Her voice was raspy from breathing in smoke all night. "Or were you hoping to sneak out while I was still asleep?"

His attention didn't shift from whatever it was he was listening to outside. "Good, you're finally awake. I thought I was going to have to toss you out in the snow to rouse you. It's dawn."

"We're not in a legion camp, Marcus," she snapped. "Who gives a shit if I sleep in? Who gives a shit if I sleep forever?"

"I do. There's work to be done, and I'm not doing it all while you laze about. Now get up."

Muttering curses under her breath, Teriana sat up. She needed to piss in the worst sort of ways, but the thought of dropping her trousers in the howling wind outside held little appeal. "Are the wolves gone?"

He grunted an affirmative. "All but the one you stabbed."

"The dead ones don't concern me."

"It's not dead."

Marcus sounded positively gleeful, which was not only out of character, but also not a particularly fitting emotion for the revelation.

"At least, I don't think it is." He lifted one of the beams securing the door, setting it aside. "I haven't heard it make a noise since the others left, but we should still be okay."

Teriana shoveled snow from the little trap into the kettle, setting it on the stove. "Okay to do what, exactly?"

Instead of answering, Marcus lifted the other beam and cracked open the door, peering outside. "Come on. Shut the door behind you so you don't let out the heat."

Retrieving her blanket, Teriana wrapped it around her head like a shawl, then stepped outside, blinking against the brightness. The wind pierced through the woolen blanket, and she curved her shoulders inward, ensuring her hands were covered. Her breath made big clouds with every exhalation, and already she could feel the cold seeping through the leather soles of her boots.

Marcus was rotating, one hand shielding his eyes as he scanned the snowy landscape around them. "Keep a wary eye," he warned. "Just because they don't like the daylight doesn't mean they won't make an exception for an easy meal."

Whether he'd intended it or not, Marcus's words directed her eyes to the red stain marring the snow a hundred paces from where she stood. Nothing remained of the shifter other than blood, and Teriana's stomach flipped knowing that it could've easily been her. Or Marcus. That it still could be them, if they weren't careful.

Knife in hand, Marcus circled the shack to where the dead wolf lay unmoving, bloody snow churned up around its still form. It was far bigger than any wolf she'd ever seen, its thick black pelt ruffling in the wind, paws the size of her hand. Instinctively, she touched the bandages on her wrist, the claw marks aching.

The animal's paw moved.

Both she and Marcus stiffened, and it was then she saw its flank still rose and fell; it was somehow still alive. The gladius was embedded in its chest, piercing up into its shoulder, but must have missed both heart and lungs.

Marcus took several steps closer, and the animal opened its eyes, squinting at them in the brightness. They were large, a beautiful emerald shade, and its lips pulled back in a snarl as it focused on them.

"Gods," she muttered, moving to stand next to Marcus's elbow. "Look at those teeth. How do you want to do this?"

"Good question." Marcus reached for the hilt of the gladius, but the wolf moved, mouth snapping at his hand, and he stumbled backward, crashing into Teriana and nearly sending them both into the snow.

"Not like that." Her heart hammered, the memory of this animal lunging at her in the dark all too clear in her mind. "Maybe we just wait for it to die."

"We can't. It could survive all day and then die in the night when we can't do anything about it. Trying to skin an animal frozen solid is impossible, and we *need* its fur if there is to be a chance of us getting out of here."

Teriana tapped her chin. "Wasn't it you who said there was *no* chance of us surviving?"

The wind howled across the snowy plains, tugging at her blanket and burrowing deep into her skin. Down to her bones. Already she wanted to flee back into the shack. To stand before the stove until feeling returned to her hands.

"In a matter of days, it will be decided that I have either deserted with you or that we've both been killed," Marcus finally answered. "Which means Titus will be in command of *my* men and have authority over *your* crew."

So soon. A different sort of chill passed over her, and Teriana's chest tightened. The consequences of her and Marcus dying here had haunted her dreams. But to know that the consequences would be visited upon her crew within *days* made her want to vomit into the snow.

"I'm sure you find that thought as unacceptable as I do," Marcus continued, circling the wolf. "Which means we must get back west to Arinoquia. And this wolf is the key."

"You just wanted us surviving to be your idea."

The corner of his mouth turned up with a hint of a smile. "Speaking of ideas, how do *you* suggest we do this?"

The wolf watched them, green eyes little more than slits against the sunlight. Its flank rose and fell, little gusts of mist filling the air with each panted breath. It was weak from bleeding all night, but it was still bigger than she was. All it would take was one well-placed bite. . . . "You jump on it and hold it down. I'll kill it."

"Justify."

Teriana rolled her eyes, having heard him use that exact word and tone with Felix and Servius countless times. "You're heavier and the stronger wrestler. And we both know I'm better at slitting throats."

"I've never wrestled a wolf."

Teriana shrugged. "First time for everything."

Handing over the knife, Marcus circled the creature, the wolf lifting its head to look back at him as though it sensed what was coming. "Distract it."

Teriana kicked a clump of snow in the wolf's face, and Marcus dived on top of it, arm snaking around its neck.

He pulled it backward, the wolf's head tight against his chest, teeth terrifyingly close to the still-healing knife wound on his throat. The animal snarled and squirmed, but he hooked his ankle under the animal's foreleg, rolling it, free hand grabbing its chin in an attempt to hold its mouth shut. "Now!"

It was a moving target of man and wolf, Marcus's arm barely an inch from where she needed to cut.

Teriana didn't hesitate.

Fresh blood gushed across the snow, splattering Marcus, who held the wolf against him until the creature stilled. Regaining his feet, he scanned their surroundings while wiping the blood from his face with one sleeve.

"You know how to do this?" she asked, kneeling to touch the animal's coat. It was soft and thick, and she buried her fingers into its depths to warm them.

Marcus tilted his head from one side to the other. "Training. Had to skin and gut a rabbit in my third year, though I haven't done it since. And I've read about the process of curing hides. I'll figure it out."

"A rabbit. Over ten years ago," Teriana repeated, eyeing the huge wolf. "And you think that what you've read in a book is going to make up for your lack of experience?"

He jerked his gladius out of the animal's chest and set it aside, not answering. Which was just as well, because her own statement had unleashed a tidal wave of memories. Of Lydia, who'd been of the misguided belief that anything could be learned from a book. A theory that was rarely, if ever, tested given that the other girl practically lived in a library.

Or had.

Teriana wondered if Cassius allowed his new wife the same liberties of occupation that her father had. Not that Teriana cared. "Will we go to Celendrial, first?"

"Yes." Marcus said the word with a grunt of effort as he set to work gutting the animal. "I'll arrange for another legion or two to cross through the genesis in Bardeen to Arinoquia and join our camp, though the Senate might not wish to send them until the path has been confirmed viable, which won't be possible until spring." Then he lifted his head, meeting her gaze. "You fulfilled your contract with the Senate, Teriana. And with me. Cassius will have no choice but to release your people, and once we've crossed back to Arinoquia, I'll do the same for the *Quincense* and your crew. You'll be free."

Just like that.

"Can you please go set some water to boil? I need to get this skin off before it freezes."

His voice was toneless. Utterly and completely devoid of emotion, as though he were a shoemaker informing her a pair of boots would be repaired by next week. Not the commander of the most feared military power on Reath telling her that he now had the capacity to conquer the world if only he could cut the skin off a wolf before it froze.

But her dilemma hadn't changed.

Save her people or save the West. One or the other. If she and Marcus survived this, everyone she loved would be saved. But in the saving, Cassius would regain total power over the legions in Arinoquia, bolstering their ranks with tens of thousands more soldiers. Marcus might regain command, but it would be the Empire who ruled, he nothing more than a tool in its arsenal. War was unavoidable. The Empire's triumph inevitable.

Marcus's hands stilled, his arms elbow deep in the carcass. Then he looked up at her. "As long as you're still breathing, you can keep fighting. Right now, you need to focus on doing whatever it takes to get out of Sibern. Leave the rest for another day."

Fight to live. Live to fight.

"Cut off a chunk of meat while you're at it." Teriana squared her shoulders. "Might as well cook us some breakfast."

She'd never known such toil.

While the sun raced across the sky, they finished skinning the wolf, Marcus working on the hide while she'd turned to butchering the animal, having found the knife she'd dropped the prior night. But *gods,* the cold. It sank into her bones, chapping her skin, numbing her hands, then her feet.

They barely spoke, both of them fixated on their tasks to the exclusion of all else. Teriana found she could barely think, her mind wholly consumed. There was only her knife. The meat. The cold.

Which was perhaps just as well.

"Leave the rest of it. The sun's getting low."

Teriana lifted her head from the icebox at the sound of Marcus's voice, which was raspier than normal.

And as though the pack had heard him, a howl split the air.

"Inside! Now!"

Teriana fitted the lid of the box in place, her numb fingers shaking as she pushed the wooden pieces locking it into their slots. Marcus had already brought the pelt inside, and once she stumbled through the entrance, he slammed the door, lowering the twin beams into their brackets.

"This could be a rough night," he said, tossing a piece of wood in the stove. "They won't be happy with what we've done."

She whirled around to face him. "What are you talking about? They're only animals."

Before he could answer, the air filled with the soft thud of running paws, then something heavy hit the door of the shack.

Teriana threw herself away from the door, nearly colliding with Marcus, who had his gladius in hand.

From all sides, the wolves attacked the shack, the small structure shuddering with each impact. Claws raked down the walls, then a thud echoed overhead.

"They're on the roof," Marcus muttered, barely audible over the noise.

"Are you sure they can't get in?" She'd had a good look at the shack during the day: the walls were made of thick poles that had been set into the earth, beams running across the ceiling and layered with thick planks. It was about as sturdy as a structure made from wood could be, but right now it felt like they were standing in a house made of paper, flimsy and insubstantial.

"They were built because of these wolves."

"That's not an answer!"

Bang.

Bang.

Bang.

Over and over, the wolves attacked the shack, their snarls filling the air. It made Teriana cringe and want to clamp her hands over her ears like a child. There was a viciousness that hadn't been there the night before.

A *fury.*

"They're angry we killed their pack mate, aren't they?"

"I don't know. Maybe. Yes." Marcus pulled another piece of wood from the stack and threw it in the stove. "My men from Sibern told stories. Said the wolves held grudges."

"Grudges?"

The wolf on the roof started digging, claws scraping across the wood as the others flung themselves at the shack. Each attack was louder. More vicious. From all sides, they tried to tear the walls down. To take their vengeance.

Then everything fell silent.

Teriana clenched her teeth, she and Marcus back-to-back with weapons in hand. Waiting. Waiting. Waiting for the attack to resume.

Only the crackle of the fire filled her ears, sweat trickling down her back. "Are they gone?"

Marcus took a cautious step toward the door, pressing his ear against the wood.

The bang from a wolf hitting it on the far side sent him staggering, and Teriana caught him before he fell against the stove.

"Not gone," he muttered. "Merely reconsidering their approach."

It seemed neither of them breathed, listening to the soft thuds of the wolves circling the shack. But no attack came. Finally, Marcus shook his head. "The walls will hold or they won't. Nothing we do will change that. We carry on."

Teriana's eyes flicked to the chunk of wolf meat she'd set out on the dented tin plate for dinner. The thought of cooking and eating it while the pack circled had a distinct lack of appeal.

"Do you think they'd hesitate, if our roles were reversed?" Marcus asked. He had adjusted the cot so that it was standing upright and was in the process of stretching the wolfskin over the frame, brow furrowed with concentration. "You need to keep up your strength. The day after next, we need to make it twenty miles in about eight hours or they'll be the ones eating us for dinner."

As if she needed *that* reminder.

She picked up the plate and began slicing the meat into thin pieces, the process complicated by the fact her hands were still shaking. Taking several measured breaths, she concentrated on stilling them, flexing her fingers. Stretching them. But the shaking wouldn't cease.

"Who taught you to cook?"

Her eyes flicked to Marcus, who was now dragging the cot to the opposite side of the shack from the fire, the wood scratching over the dirt floor. "This isn't cooking. Cooking is an art involving carefully selected ingredients and perfected techniques. This is just

taking a raw hunk of meat and"—she floundered for a descriptor—
"making it not raw."

"I believe that's the definition of cooking."

"Smart-ass," she muttered. Her hands had finally steadied enough
that she could slice without fear of losing a finger. "Polin taught me."

"Not your mother?"

A laugh tore from her throat. "Definitely not. Though I suppose
she knows how." She laid the pieces of meat on the pan and sprinkled them with the bit of salt that had been remaining in the shack's
supplies. "No matter whether you're born into the crew or join it or
what your rank is, you have to take a turn doing every job on the
ship. Teaches you to respect the work of your crewmates."

Placing the pan on the stove, she folded up the one remaining
blanket and sat on it. "My mum taught me how to negotiate. How
to plot a course. How to keep the accounts. How to captain a crew."

But she had older memories. One that was all sunlight and sea,
her mother's face above her, hands gently holding Teriana on the
surface of the water. "Puff your chest out like your uncle Polin does
when he's courting," her mother's voice echoed in her head. "That's
it. That's my girl. You're floating!"

Her eyes burned as more visions played through her thoughts. Of
her mother. Of Yedda and Polin. Of all the rest of her crew, most of
whom had been with Teriana for her entire life. Of Magnius swimming watchfully nearby as she and Bait leapt off cliffs or explored sea
caves. Memories on the *Quincense* or home in Taltuga with its white
sand beaches and azure waves.

It felt like an eternity that she'd been away from them now, but
while there had been days that their absence had made her feel like
she was drowning in grief, she also knew there had been days when
she'd barely thought of them at all. Guilt slapped her in the face,
because maybe if she'd kept her heart and her mind where they were
supposed to be, she wouldn't be here right now. "Will Titus tell my
crew I'm dead?"

"It would be in his best interest not to," Marcus replied. "Your
presence in our camp ensured their continued compliance. He won't
jeopardize that given he has no route back to Celendor if things go
awry."

And there would be no way for them to find out given that she'd
dispatched Bait and Magnius to Taltuga, Gamdesh, and beyond.
They'd be waiting, maybe Aunt Yedda sending her little trinkets and
gifts only for Titus to toss them thoughtlessly into the fire.

"You're burning dinner."

"Shit!" Leaping to her feet, Teriana used her knife to flip over the smoking strips of meat, which were more than a little blackened on the bottom side. "Sorry. Not that you should be complaining. I've never eaten worse in my life than in your camp."

Marcus laughed. "Don't like porridge?"

Rolling her eyes, Teriana said, "Seems to me that Campus Lescendor has a real gap in their curriculum. Your men can build a castle with three twigs and a handful of mud, but they can't even serve porridge without lumps in it."

"A purposeful gap, I think." He inspected the pelt with a critical eye before extracting a whetstone from his belt pouch and setting to work on his knife blade. "I don't think they considered refining our palates in their best interest. Feeding a legion is expensive enough without filling it with fussy eaters."

"You've got an answer for everything, don't you?"

The wind chose that moment to howl across the plains, sliding through the small gaps in the shack walls. Icier than it had been all day, it drew gooseflesh to Teriana's skin, despite the heat of the stove. Sibern's winters were fierce. Deadly. Storms that went on for days, piling up snow until it was deeper than a man was tall. Being outside today had bordered on torture, and this was only the beginning of it. "Don't suppose you've read about making snowshoes."

"I have. We don't have the materials, so you might want to pray that it doesn't snow."

"I don't think the Six can hear me." And even if they could, why would they listen, given what she'd done? What she continued to do. Sighing, Teriana dumped the cooked meat onto a tin plate and set it on the ground between them. "Enjoy."

Marcus sat, one leg crossed beneath him, one knee up, his elbow hooked around it. Picking up a piece of meat, he bit into it, eyes on the glowing fire. His hands were reddened and scraped from labor and the cold, knuckles raw and bleeding in a few places. He'd stripped off much of the clothing he'd made, but what remained was coated with blood, and a red smear bisected the scar on his face. His cheeks and chin were slightly rough with stubble, something she'd never seen on him before, as all the legionnaires were required to be clean-shaven. It made him look older than his nineteen years, and was not, she decided, unappealing. Quite the opposite.

He chose that moment to turn back to her, and her cheeks warmed at being caught staring. "Thank you," he said. "For . . . *frying* dinner."

Taking a bite to cover her embarrassment, Teriana chewed, then said, "Don't get used to this domestic situation, Marcus. You need to hold up your end."

The corner of his mouth turned up. "Domestic?"

Why had she chosen that word? Her cheeks burned hotter. "Aye, domestic. I'm not running twenty miles every day only to have to cook dinner while you kick your heels up next to the fire. Do you even know how to cook?" She shook her head and cast her eyes up to the ceiling. "Never mind, you've probably got six cookbooks committed to memory or some nonsense like that."

He bit his bottom lip, then shook his head. "I'm afraid I have to disappoint you on that count. Lescendor's library didn't have a section on cooking." His eyes fixed on her face, firelight reflecting off them. "I'll have to make it up to you in other ways."

Her stomach flipped. "You're never a disappointment."

Marcus looked away, the muscles in his jaw flexing. Then he froze. "Do you hear that?"

"The wind?" There was most certainly a storm rolling in, the howl of the wind incessant as it hammered the sides of the shack.

"No," Marcus muttered. "*Listen.*"

The wind shrieked, making the stove's chimney moan and sparks fly. It eased for a heartbeat, and that was when she heard it.

Scratch, scratch, scratch.

"What is that?"

Marcus stood next to the wall, head down as he listened.

Scratch, scratch, scratch.

"What?" Teriana demanded, climbing to her feet. "What are they doing?"

He bent to touch the ground, his face growing pale. "They're digging."

41

LYDIA

Sitting in a chair in the library, Lydia stared up at the ceiling, reconciling herself to the fact that she was losing this battle. The ship with the remaining healers had arrived, and tomorrow, the purging of Mudaire would begin.

A purge she'd been told, in no uncertain terms, that she'd be part of.

Sighing, she set to the task of shelving books, having given up on finishing her organization. And as it was, soon this library—and all of Mudaire—would be burned. The loss of knowledge made her cringe, but there wasn't the time or resources to remove all these books, and in order to prevent people from returning to the city—and inevitably falling victim to the blight—the King would have to see it destroyed.

The door opened, and Lena and Gwen walked in, the latter carrying a bowl and a crust of bread. "You missed dinner. Again."

"Sorry." Lydia put a book on a shelf. "I got caught up."

"You do need to eat, you know." Gwen set the food down on the table in front of Lydia. "Not going to save anyone if you waste away."

Lydia dutifully spooned the thin soup into her mouth, which despite being poorly seasoned, sparked an appetite in her, and she found she was still hungry when she reached the bottom of the bowl, using the bread to catch the last few drops. Only then did she sit back in her chair. "We're out of time."

The other girls exchanged looks, then Lena said, "You tried, Lydia. That's more than you can say about anyone else. Gods, all Quindor ever does is hole himself up in the sublevel with his pet blighter."

Quindor was ostensibly studying the girl for signs the blight was evolving or moving toward an ultimate goal, but Lydia believed that Quindor kept Emmy alive to ease his conscience over all those who'd been put down on his orders. "Her name is Emmy."

"Her name *was* Emmy," Lena corrected. "It's the Corrupter the Grand Master is spending all his hours with, and no one should forget that."

"He's well aware," Lydia answered. "He can see she's not alive."

"If all he sees is a corpse, why does he lavish her with clothes and sweets and toys? Seems..." Lena trailed off, her brow furrowing. Then, abruptly, she bent over double and hurled the contents of her stomach onto the library floor.

"Are you all right?" Lydia asked as Gwen pulled the other girl's hair back from her face.

"Must have eaten something bad," Lena mumbled, not able to say more as she retched again, sweat beading on her brow.

Unease rose in Lydia's chest, and reaching out a hand, she caught hold of her friend's bare arm and *pushed*.

And recoiled in horror as the Corrupter's talons dug in.

"What?" Gwen demanded, then her face lost all of its color. "No."

But there was no denying it as Lena dropped to the floor, her face waxen and twisted with growing pain: she was infected with blight. And while this was the exact moment Lydia had been waiting for—to have the opportunity to try to help someone newly infected—never had she dreamed that the individual would be someone she cared for.

Worse, if it were discovered that one of the infected was within the temple, the soldiers were more likely to kill Lena than to allow Lydia the opportunity to try to save her. And neither she nor Gwen could stop them.

But there was someone who could.

"Run to the palace." She shoved Gwen toward the door. "Tell the High Lady what has happened and bring her here. Tell no one else."

Gwen hesitated, her desire to help Lena clearly warring with the fear of leaving her. "I won't let them have her," Lydia promised. "Not while she's still alive—I swear it."

Giving a tight nod, the other girl hurried out the door, slamming it behind her.

Lena was curled up on the floor, and Lydia swiftly retrieved her cloak, tucking it around the other girl. A touch of her skin against Lena's could be enough to trigger her mark, so she pulled on a pair of gloves, the fabric protecting her until she was ready.

"If I die, you need to put me down." Lena was shaking. "While Gwen's gone. I don't want her to see. And I sure as shit don't want her to see me as a walking corpse."

"Don't think about that. I'm not giving up on you, so don't you dare give up on yourself." Unbuttoning her friend's dress, Lydia's stomach flipped at the black lines slowly snaking their way beneath Lena's skin. They were rising on her torso toward her neck, and Lydia knew that when the blight reached her brain, Lena would succumb.

Lena clutched at her gloved hand, pain rising in her eyes. And if what Lydia had been told was true, it was going to get a thousand times worse. "It's going to hurt, but you must try to stay quiet, understand? If they hear you, they'll come."

Warily, Lydia removed a glove and pressed her bare hand to one of the smaller branches of blight. Taking a deep breath, she *pushed*.

But instead of a steady flow of life from her to Lena, it felt like claws digging into her, wrenching life from her body so violently it was painful. Panic flooded through Lydia, and she jerked backward, landing on her bottom. Her braid flopped over her shoulder, and picking it up, she saw it had streaks of grey.

"Did it help?" Lena gasped. "I don't feel better. I feel worse."

"No," Lydia breathed, eyeing her friend, the aura of mist around her unchanged. Which was impossible. Where had the life Lydia had given her gone to? It was almost . . . almost as though the blight had *consumed* it.

Lydia wracked her brain, trying to come up with a way to help her. But her mark was useless against this.

You have to try.

Swallowing hard, she said. "I'm going to attempt something." Something she probably shouldn't with only Lena in the room. "If . . . if my hair turns white, push me away."

"Lydia . . . ," Lena whispered. "Maybe you shouldn't . . ."

Ignoring her, Lydia pressed her hands to Lena's chest, flooding her with life.

Again, it felt as though talons had latched onto her core, ripping her strength from her body, but Lydia only gritted her teeth and kept going. Her vision began to deteriorate as she aged, but not quickly enough that she failed to see that instead of driving the blight back, the life she was giving up seemed to be feeding it. Gasping, she tried to pull back, but the Corrupter's talons wouldn't let her go.

The blackness crawled up Lena's neck, and Lydia could feel her heart beating faster and faster.

Then Lena shoved her away, soft sobs tearing from her lips. "Stop! You're making it worse. It hurts."

And Lydia was nearly drained. Her hands were gnarled, the braid hanging over her shoulder nearly white. And all she'd done was speed along the process.

Think. Think. Think.

What was the blight?

Poison, but not. It was . . . it was death. And Hegeria's mark couldn't cure death any more than it could reverse the passage of time.

Except is that entirely true? A thought teased at the back of her head, slowly shaping itself into something that resembled an idea.

"I'm going to try something," she said. "As soon as Gwen and the High Lady return."

Lena only stared at her, tears rolling down the sides of her cheeks. Then her eyes widened and she screamed.

They were out of time.

Lydia pressed her hands against Lena's heart. But this time when the Corrupter's talons sank in, she didn't push.

She pulled.

42

MARCUS

"How deep are the posts set?" Teriana already had her knife in hand and was on her knees, ear against the ground.

Wracking his memory yielded nothing. "A couple feet, I'd guess. Which is nothing for these animals. They burrow their own dens—digging is what they *do*."

"How long do we have?"

"That depends how long they've been at it." Swearing, Marcus pressed his ear against the wall, attempting to determine precisely where the wolves were digging, but it was almost impossible over the sound of the wind. It was a tactic he'd used himself—using noise to disguise the work of legion sappers as they mined under a fortress wall in Bardeen.

But Marcus had no intention of being out-strategized by over-grown dogs. "Help me get this board off. We need to see where they're digging."

Together, they jammed their knives in between two planks, prying one of the boards away from the posts it was nailed to. Icy cold rushed in, and the wolves immediately attacked the openings.

"Oh, you think you're coming in, do you?" Teriana shouted. Snatching up the frying pan, she slammed it against the muzzles of the wolves trying to force their heads inside, eliciting loud yelps of pain.

Dropping to his knees, Marcus peered through the gaps, trying to get a good visual of where the wolves were digging. But it was black as pitch outside, moon and stars obscured by clouds, and all he could make out were flashes of motion in the darkness. Swearing, he extracted a burning piece of wood from the stove and shoved it through a gap in the posts. Before the flames flickered out in the snow, his eyes found the mound of frozen earth the wolves had extracted from the tunnel, and as he watched, a wolf backed out of a hole, one of its pack mates swiftly taking its place.

"Here." He marked a spot on the ground. "We need to start digging."

Teriana lowered her frying pan, turning to stare at him. "What? You want us to *help* them get inside."

"To lay a siege, one must also understand how one defends against a siege. Now start digging."

It was backbreaking labor. They had only their weapons and tin cups to dig with, and within an hour, Marcus's hands were screaming in pain, nails torn and skin bleeding.

"Stop and let me listen." He pressed his ear to the ground, feeling the vibrations of the animals digging as much as he heard them. "Close."

Teriana shoved her arm back into the hole, then yelped and recoiled. A second later, the pack bayed in excitement. Snatching up one of the tin cups, Marcus scraped it along the base of the stove, filling it with embers, which he dumped in the hole followed by the damp scraps of wool blanket left over from the clothing they'd made. A cloud of smoke billowed up, and he covered the opening with a plate to keep it inside.

The sounds of digging stopped.

Neither he nor Teriana spoke, both of them listening intently between the gusting howls of the wind. Moving the plate, Marcus dumped more fuel on the smoking flames below, which were already dying low.

"Will they give up?" Teriana's whispered words seemed loud after the silence.

It wasn't enough smoke to drive away men. If this had been a fortress under siege, he'd have choked the tunnels with the smoke of bonfires-worth of green wood. If he'd had something poisonous to burn, so much the better. Except they had nothing but bone-dry wood, and giving up their clothing to the flames would only delay the inevitable. But these were animals, so maybe—

The scratching resumed.

"Shit!" he snarled. "They're digging around. We need more smoke."

"It's too narrow to get more fuel down there." Teriana's eyes were wide with fear. "We need to fill it back up. Put the cot or the stove over top."

The stove. Marcus's attention jerked to the cast-iron stove and the tin pipe rising to the roof above. The angle was wrong, but it might work.

Slamming the stove door shut, Marcus wrapped his hands in the blanket, took hold of the sides, and heaved, sliding the pipe out of the hole in the roof.

The shack immediately filled with smoke.

Tipping the stove over on its side, Marcus dropped to his knees next to the stovepipe and cut it with his knife, sawing through the metal even as his lungs filled with smoke, his eyes burning and watering.

He heard Teriana coughing, felt her wrap sodden fabric over his nose and mouth, his fingers burning from the escaping heat.

Beneath his knees, the ground was shifting. Trembling. In moments, it would collapse and the wolves would be in. *Work faster.*

But he couldn't breathe.

Coughs wracked his body, the knife sliding in his grip.

There is no quitting here, only dying.

Wrenching on the stovepipe, he bent it backward, snapping it off and sending choking clouds of smoke into his face.

The world was swimming, everything moving as he tried to angle the pipe into the hole.

Then hands shoved him aside.

Marcus fell against the gap in the wall, sucking in desperate breaths of clean air. The wolves were yipping and running around the shack, several of them slamming their paws against the walls.

Teriana.

She was coughing, consumed by the clouds of smoke, barely visible in the faint light. Grabbing hold of her shoulders, he tried to haul her back, but she pulled away, choking out, "Almost . . . got . . . it. There!"

He dragged her against him, pushing her face against a gap so she could breathe fresh air. Her shoulders shook with coughs, but the sounds of digging had ceased, whatever she'd rigged filtering enough of the smoke into the wolves' tunnel to drive them out.

But not all of it. Smoke rose from the stove, the air of the shack a grey haze. Marcus's eyes burned. His throat felt like it had been scoured by sandpaper, and he wheezed with every breath, an attack upon him although he didn't think it would be a bad one. Pressing his face to a gap in the boards, he sucked in cold fresh air.

"How long until dawn?" Teriana's voice was scratchy, barely audible over the wind.

"I don't know." It felt like an eternity since the sun had set, but with night stretching for sixteen hours, it might be another eternity until dawn. Sweat cooled on his body, a chill setting into his bones, and Teriana shivered in his arms.

"Will they try again?"

The wolves had eased off in their attacks against the shack walls, and while he could still make out the sounds of motion outside, the pack had grown quiet. "They need to eat. Since it won't be us tonight, they'll need to find something else."

Easing his arm out from under her, Marcus went to the stove and added more wood to the fire, keeping the stove door cracked enough that the flames could breathe without choking the shack with smoke. The faint light allowed him to see how Teriana had rigged the stovepipe to fill the wolves' tunnel, using something to create an elbow connecting the pieces of pipe.

Wiping tears from his stinging eyes, Marcus reached out to touch the bend, feeling leather beneath his fingers before he recoiled from the heat. Boot leather.

Swearing, he crawled back over to Teriana, finding her naked foot, which felt like ice beneath his hand.

"Cold," she mumbled.

"I know." He found the bottom of her boot where it had been discarded after she'd cut off the haft, and replaced it on her foot, then tucked the single remaining blanket around her, eyeing the hanging wolf pelt. *That* would keep her warm, but he was rushing the process of curing it as it was, and if he took it off the frame before it had dried and rendered it unusable, they were dead.

You'll both be just as dead if you freeze.

Heat radiated from the stove, but the wind gusting through the gaps they'd made in the wall drove it away. Yet he didn't dare replace the board with the amount of smoke seeping into the shack, and building the fire up higher for heat would only make that worse.

Adding another piece of wood to the fire, he went back to Teriana, pulling her upright. "You need to get up . . . and . . . move," he said, struggling to get enough air to speak. "If you pass out . . . you'll . . . freeze."

"Too tired."

She was nearly deadweight in his arms, swaying on her feet. His own body ached from the chill, his hands and feet numb, only his head warm beneath the hat he'd made from the blanket. Pulling it off, he shoved it down over her tangled braids, the wind biting at his ears. "Come on, Teriana." A fit of coughing stole over him. It was a bloody miracle this hadn't killed him. "Stay with me. Stomp your feet."

Her face rested against his shoulder, cocooned in the blanket he'd wrapped around both of them. She stomped one foot. Then the other. Then she began to cough, and her knees buckled.

"Shit!"

There was no helping it. Lowering her to the ground, he unfastened the wolfskin from the cot's frame. It was mostly dry and had grown stiff and unwieldy. Pushing the cot against the wall, he rolled Teriana up in the blanket and set her on it, her face near one of the gaps in the boards. Then he curled up around her, pulling the wolfskin over top of them and molding it around their bodies as best he could.

It was so cold. So cold. The world swam in and out of focus, his thoughts fuzzy.

There is no quitting here, only dying.

He had never quit. Never given up. And he refused to do so now.

"Stay awake. Stay awake," he wheezed, forcing himself up to add fuel to the fire before retreating back to Teriana's shivering form.

How many more hours until dawn? There was no way to know. But he needed to keep the fire burning until the sun lit the sky.

"Stay awake, stay awake," he repeated, using all the tricks he'd been trained to use to stay alert on a watch. Except his body was leaden with exhaustion, his eyelids refusing to stay open. The dense fur was soft against his cheek, and the painful burn of the cold slowly receded beneath its weight. Time began to skip, the cold and smoke of reality driven away by dreams where tens of thousands of wolves descended on his men and Titus did nothing but stand there and laugh as they were torn apart.

He jerked awake, half-falling off the cot. The fire was little more than glowing embers, so he added more wood. Outside, there was not even a hint of light to break the darkness.

"There is no quitting." He climbed back onto the cot. Curled around Teriana and took hold of her hand. "There is no quitting. There is no . . ."

43

LYDIA

Lydia's hands turned to ice as she pulled the blight into herself.

As she pulled death into herself.

Then the pain took hold. It burned like acid up her arms, and she clenched her teeth trying to hold in a scream as she fought the desire to pull away from Lena.

Black lines radiated up her arms, her skin turning grey, the agony unlike anything she'd ever experienced. Her heart battered against her rib cage, her breath coming in little panting gasps, but she couldn't stop.

Because it was working.

Lena stared at her with wide eyes, then seemed to realize what was happening. She tried to push Lydia away, but Lydia dug her fingers into her friend's shoulders and held on. She dug her heels into the other girl's waist to keep her from pushing her free as she pulled the blight from her friend, searching and digging for the last strands of it, refusing to leave anything behind.

She wrenched out the last little bit, and then an arm closed around her throat, dragging her away from Lena.

"What in the name of the Six is going on?" Dareena demanded, then her eyes fixed on Lydia's face and widened at what they saw. "Gods, girl."

She opened her mouth to explain. To tell the High Lady that she'd done it.

But all that came out were screams.

The blight attacked her from the inside, the burning inescapable, and she fell to the floor, clawing at the stones, clawing at herself in an attempt to get it out. Strong hands caught her wrists, forcing them to the ground, but she fought back.

"Gods-damn it, Lydia!" Dareena shouted in her face. "Fight the blight, not me!"

Her mark *was* fighting, but for every two steps forward, she took one back as death consumed her strength. And she wasn't certain which one would win.

Then she was up in the air, Dareena shouting instructions as she raced down the hall, Lydia slung over her shoulder. "Hold on, girl," she ordered, but all Lydia could do was sob and cry, snot and tears covering her face as they descended the stairs.

"She's infected!" she heard someone scream, but Dareena didn't stop moving until they reached the barracks and dropped her on a cot. She rolled on her side, digging her nails into her arms, barely noticing the soldiers around her. Barely able to see as it was, her spectacles missing.

"Someone needs to put her down!"

The sound of a sword being drawn filled Lydia's ears, along with Dareena's voice, ominous as she said, "By all means, gentlemen, you are welcome to try."

"With respect, Your Grace," one of the soldiers said, "if she's infected, she's dead. All you're doing is torturing her."

"With respect, you idiot," Dareena snapped, "Lydia may have found a cure for the blight, and I for one would like to hear how she did it. So do the whole city a bloody favor and keep your mouth shut."

After that, the world faded in and out of focus, Lydia's throat raw from screaming. Vaguely, she knew Lena and Gwen were near her, could hear their whispers of comfort in her ears and the feel of their hands gripping hers. But it was all distant to the fight going on inside of her. A fight that felt like a war between gods with her body the battleground.

"What's going on?" Quindor's voice. "What's happened to her?"

"I was infected," Lena said. "And Lydia . . . I'm not sure how, but she pulled the blight out of me and into herself."

"You were infected?" Quindor hissed between his teeth. "You need to be isolated. Someone—"

Reaching up from her stupor, Lydia caught her friend's arm. "You don't touch her."

"Don't presume to give me orders, girl. I—"

"Listen to her, Quindor," Dareena said, her gaze still on the watching soldiers. "Because I most certainly *do* presume to give you orders."

The Grand Master gave an annoyed hiss, but left Lena alone to bend over Lydia, pulling open her robes, his eyes unfocused as he examined her. "The blight is retreating."

She could feel the acidic burn fading, the blight drawing in on itself near her heart for one last stand. But she refused to let it win.

Closing her eyes, Lydia bit down on the insides of her cheeks and focused inward, directing her mark at herself, feeling the blight weaken and crumble, and then suddenly, it was gone.

She'd beaten it. Saved Lena and beaten back the blight, but gods . . . the thought of having to do this again. And again and again for all those who continued to be poisoned by the Corrupter. She wasn't certain it was even possible.

But there was hope, because if Hegeria's mark could drive it out of a body, surely one of Yara's marked could drive it out of the land.

Exhausted, she rolled onto her back, staring up at the ceiling above. Then she whispered, "Someone needs to tell the King I've found the cure before he starts the purges. And while they're at it, tell him he needs to find a living tender, because I think I know how we can push back the blight."

44

KILLIAN

A bead of sweat rolled into his eye, but Killian couldn't risk moving to wipe it away. Not when the Anuk raiding party they were about to ambush was drawing ever closer, the warriors' eyes watchful as they scanned the hills and cliffs flanking the path. Other than rocks and scraggly pine trees, there was little cover to be had this time of year, and Killian was relying on the element of surprise.

Below, the first raider's horse stepped past the marker, and a heartbeat later, the deafening roar of falling rocks filled the air. Debris tumbled across their path, and recognizing they'd been ambushed, the Anuk warriors drew their blades, retreating back the way they'd come at a gallop.

Only to come face-to-face with the Mudamorian force trailing them.

There was no way for them to get the gold-laden camel over the rocks, but they could get over them on foot, if they chose.

Go, Killian willed them. *Take the escape route and run.*

But instead, the Anuk pulled their weapons.

Anger flared through him, and Killian shouted, "Attack!" Leaping to his feet, he slid down the steep embankment, hearing Sonia and the rest of his soldiers following behind.

The Anuk drew tight around the camel, large shields held above their heads against the barrage of arrows from Killian's bowmen, their swift desert horses prancing beneath them.

Killian pulled his sword, the bowmen ceasing their assault as the two forces collided.

He crossed blades with a big man, metal singing as they fought, the man's horse squealing and reaching for Killian with yellow teeth. He stepped out of range, then spun and ran the warrior through, not stopping to watch the man fall before rounding on the next.

It was a brutal and bloody dance, the forces well-matched in skill and enmity, but Killian saw nothing but his opponents. Felt nothing but the thrill of the adrenaline coursing through his veins as they fought and fell to his weapons.

"Killian!"

Sonia's voice tore him from the moment, and stepping away from a fallen man, he searched for her.

"The gods-damned camel!" she shouted, pointing.

His eyes tracked to where a lone rider led the laden camel toward a narrow gap left by the rockslide, and without thinking, he caught hold of the reins of one of the horses, swinging into the saddle.

Digging in his heels, he galloped in pursuit, not stopping to look if any of his men followed.

Clearing the slide, his eyes fixed on the Anuk warrior, the small man's sand-colored clothing blending into the coat of his horse, face obscured by the veils they wore to block the endless desert sun.

The camel carried a heavy burden, and Killian rapidly gained ground.

The warrior hazarded a glance over his shoulder, and Killian saw how his eyes widened, but instead of abandoning camel and gold, the man tried to urge it faster.

"Fool," muttered Killian, and he laid his spurs into the small horse's sides and leapt over a pile of rocks the raider was forced to ride around. Drawing up alongside the camel, he sliced the taut leather lead, the camel slowing even as the warrior's mount galloped on.

Catch him, a voice whispered in his head. *Kill him.*

But Killian ignored the voice, instead slowing next to the camel.

The warrior hauled on his mount's reins, the horse wheeling and bucking as the man glared back at Killian. Yet instead of retreating, the idiot dug in his heels and charged back toward him.

"Have it your way," Killian muttered, lifting his blade.

Sword met sword with a clash of metal. The horses sidled next to each other and lashed out with teeth and hooves, as trained to fight as their riders.

The warrior was good. Better than any Killian had fought today, moving with speed and skill. But he was half Killian's size, and in the end, strength counted for something.

With a hard strike, Killian sent the other man's sword spinning off into scrub brush. But in a flash, the Anuk warrior had a knife in hand, ready to throw it.

Killian was faster. His sword sliced through the air toward the warrior's exposed side. Right as the man's veil slipped, revealing the face of a boy.

Too late, Killian tried to alter his strike, but his weapon still slid along the boy's ribs.

A hiss of pain filled his ears, but instead of attempting to flee, the boy lifted the knife, obviously intending to fight to the bitter end.

But Killian had never harmed a child. And he refused to do so today.

Reaching down, he caught hold of the boy's leg and pulled him off his horse, sending him tumbling onto the rocky ground. In a heartbeat, he was off his own mount, pinning the boy's arms with his knees while he pulled up the side of the boy's bloody shirt to assess the wound.

"What are you doing, you Mudamorian piece of shit!" the boy shouted. "Too much of a coward to finish the fight?"

"It's too hot to fight," Killian answered. "And I got what I wanted." He gestured toward the camel, which stood half-asleep in the sun. "Unlike you."

Killian ripped a piece of fabric from the boy's shirt and bound his wrists, tightening the knot as the boy squirmed, trying to get free.

Ignoring the onslaught of cursing that was eerily reminiscent of Finn, Killian stuffed a piece of fabric against the boy's wound, then bound it tight. "Go home," he said. "Tell your people that if they raid again, they will find me waiting for them. And that I will show them no mercy."

"As if we expect mercy from a child-killer like you!" the boy snarled. "Nor do we wish it. What we want is vengeance."

Killian blinked. *Child-killer?* "What are you talking about?"

"You are the Dark Horse," the boy hissed. "The one who attacks our villages in the night."

Unease filled Killian's stomach, his skin crawling. "I've never once been across the border."

"Lies! The survivors said the raiders wore your symbol."

Ria had said the Rowenes army had ceased its raids on Anukastre when the King conscripted the majority of the region's soldiers, which was many months ago. And even if this were vengeance for prior acts of war, why in the name of the Six would they have been wearing the Calorian symbol? Unless . . .

The thunder of hooves rolled through the valley. Hooves coming from the west. And the boy grinned. "It seems I'll have my vengeance sooner rather than later."

Swearing, Killian grabbed the reins of the horse and flung himself into the saddle, catching hold of the camel's lead. Driving both animals into a gallop, he headed in the direction of his soldiers, casting a backward glance as he rounded the bend. A dozen Anuk on horseback appeared, the boy shouting at them to pursue.

Digging in his heels, he urged his mount to more speed, dropping the reins of the camel. His soldiers came into sight, along with a pile of Anuk corpses. His stomach hollowed. "Retreat!" he shouted. "They've got reinforcements!"

His soldiers grabbed the reins of the loose horses, and leaning out of the saddle, Killian caught hold of Sonia's arm, pulling her up behind him. "Go!"

They all broke into a gallop, but Killian felt Sonia twist behind him. "There's only twelve of them!" she shouted. "We can take them!"

Killian only shook his head. Because if what the boy had said were true, the real enemy was much closer to home.

45

TERIANA

There were drums beating. Loud, obnoxious drums that made her head ache like the worst hangover of her life.

Teriana cracked one eye, her gummy lashes pulling apart painfully, the light that assaulted her far too bright. Wincing, she rolled away—

And the bed disappeared from under her.

A muttered *ooof* filled her ears as she landed, and Teriana found herself staring at Marcus, whom she'd landed on. He blinked blearily at her, his eyes swollen and bloodshot, face smeared with soot. Then his gaze snapped into focus and he rolled her off, clambering to his feet, hoarse profanity spewing from his lips as he went to the stove. "The fire. We need to keep it going or—"

"Sun's up."

Marcus ceased loading wood onto the coals and slowly turned to the gap in the wall where sunlight streamed in. Despite her head aching like she'd been hit in the head with a brick, Teriana grinned and pointed a finger at him. "And we're not dead."

"Not dead," he repeated blankly, as though she'd spoken in a language he didn't quite understand.

"How much of that smoke did you breathe in?" she asked.

"Too much." He gave a weary shake of his head, then braced one hand against the wall. "I must have fallen asleep. I'm sorry."

Perhaps he had, but only recently, because the coals were still glowing, a few flames rising from the charred wood. Which meant he'd stayed awake long after she'd passed out, fueling the fire. Keeping her warm. Keeping her alive.

Crawling on her hands and knees, she wrapped her arms around Marcus's neck, pressing her forehead against his. There was no part of her that didn't hurt. No part of her that wasn't exhausted. No part of her that didn't fear the coming night. But together, she felt like they would survive this, no matter what came at them.

And as though he sensed her thoughts, Marcus rose to his feet, pulling her up with him. "We've work to do."

Together, they righted the stove, using the leg shaft of her boot to hold the stovepipe in place once they'd fitted it back through the opening in the roof. Marcus worked on filling the hole in the floor with dirt while Teriana took the kettle outside to collect snow.

The wind had died down, but while no snow had fallen in the night, large drifts had formed, entirely altering the landscape from yesterday. The wolves had done a fine job of fouling up the area around the shack—scat and piss drove her to walk some distance to find some clean snow, her eyes peeled for any sign of motion.

But there was nothing.

And though she knew there must be animals about beyond the wolves, in that moment, it felt like they were utterly alone in this wild expanse of the world, the tiny wooden shack their only refuge. And tomorrow, they'd leave it. Would attempt to cross twenty miles of barren wilderness before dusk fell.

Warmth embraced her chilled body as she opened the door to the shack. Marcus had filled in the hole and replaced the board they'd pried off the wall. A cheery fire now burned in the stove. He had the stiff wolfskin spread on the floor, and on one of the plates sat what she could only presume was the same wolf's brain. "If you think that's what we are having for breakfast, you're mistaken."

"It's not for eating." He gave the brain a poke with his index finger. "It's for the hide. Did you know that every animal possesses a brain large enough to tan its own hide?"

"I've met a few idiots in my day who'd put that theory to the test." She set the kettle on the stove, noticing that he'd also retrieved some of the wolf meat from the icebox, which was currently thawing on a plate. "You read that in one of your books?"

He nodded.

"You know," she said, "I find it interesting that you've apparently read so many books and yet I've never once seen you with one in hand."

"Books are heavy. I don't pack what I don't feel inclined to carry."

Smiling to herself, Teriana didn't say anything, only set to tidying up the shack from the chaos of the prior night.

His sigh filled her ears. "Fine. I had the privilege of being taught to read prior to my move to Campus Lescendor. I was a sickly child, so I spent a lot of time in my father's library, as well as the libraries of his friends."

She'd never pressed him for details about his illness, sensing he didn't want to talk about it. "Sickly . . . ?"

He grimaced. "My attacks were a near-daily occurrence when I was young. The physicians advised my father to keep me indoors and away from strenuous activity. Obviously money was no object, so he indulged me with all the books and tutors I wanted."

She knew from his admission to Magnius during the crossing that he'd been born to the Domitius family, but this was the first time he'd ever acknowledged it. It was a large family, with many branches, but the patriarch and holder of the family's seat in the Senate lived in the villa neighboring that of Senator Valerius—Lydia's father. Which meant it was possible Marcus had known Lydia prior to leaving for legion training.

"Lescendor has a vast library," he continued. "Once I was past the stage of needing to sleep through our set liberty hours, I took to spending my free time there. When I began officer training at age ten, half my days were spent in the library, though of course most of the material I read at that point related to military matters."

"All your liberty hours in a library," Teriana murmured, inspecting the pads of her fingers, which had been scalded while she struggled with the stovepipe. "Who knew I had such a fondness for bookish people."

Marcus lifted his head askance, but she only waved the comment away with one hand. She'd never spoken of Lydia to him, and she didn't intend to. It was possible Cassius had divulged her friendship—that Marcus knew the details of her friend's betrayal—but Teriana found herself not wanting to hear it. What was done was done.

He only shrugged. "I don't get much chance to read for pleasure anymore. Servius picks up books for me when he sees something I might like. Sells them off when I'm through with them." Retrieving the kettle, he rinsed the dirt out of the two cups and filled them. Then he dumped the rest of the water on the back of the hide and began rubbing it into the stiff skin. "Would you mind getting more snow? This is going to take a fair bit of water."

Putting on the wool hat and mittens this time, Teriana ventured back outside, clenching her teeth as the air bit into her warmed skin. How people lived in this gods-forsaken place was beyond her. The unrelenting heat and rain of Arinoquia was paradise by comparison.

The snow crunched beneath her feet, and it wasn't long until it felt as though she was walking barefoot, the thin leather soles affording little protection and snow falling inside her hacked-off boot, though her thoughts pulled her away from the discomfort.

It was strange to hear Marcus talk about his past. Because he didn't. Not ever.

How did a child too sick to do anything but read books in his father's library become the commander of a legion? That fateful day back in Arinoquia, Titus had told her it was genius, but that was only part of it. Willpower, for certain. Ambition. But those were only words, and what she found herself desperately wanting was the stories of those attributes in action, because it had been those events that had shaped him. She wanted to *know* him. Wanted to know all of him, because—

Snow crunched.

Teriana leapt upright, swinging the kettle in a wide arc, missing Marcus by an inch. Heart in her throat, she lowered her weapon. "You startled me."

He opened his mouth, probably to reprimand her for not remaining alert, but then he shook his head and said, "You all right?"

"Aye. Was just . . . thinking."

Squinting, he looked up at the position of the sun. "We've got about six hours until the sun starts to set. We need to eat, deal with this hide, collapse that tunnel, and prepare for whatever tonight delivers upon us."

"Right." She fell into step next to him, the kettle swinging in her grip. And before she knew what she was doing, Teriana asked, "How did you meet Felix?"

"At Campus Lescendor."

Rolling her eyes, she said, "Obviously. I meant, how did you meet him when you were there?"

"Oh."

She could feel him looking at her, but kept her eyes on the snow, waiting for his answer.

"We were delivered on the same day. His number is directly before mine, so we were always lined up together. Were bunkmates in the dormitories. Eight bunks per room, two boys per bunk, so sixteen boys."

"Thanks for doing the math for me."

He huffed out a laugh, then his face tightened. "I . . . I fought with him before we left camp. I was convinced it had been him who'd betrayed me, and the things I said . . ."

"When we get back, you can explain," she said. "He'll understand. He'll forgive you."

"Some things are unforgivable."

"Maybe so. But you won't know until you apologize, and you won't be able to do that if you don't get out of Sibern. So focus on that instead."

His throat bobbed, and he gave a tight nod. And then, to her astonishment, he closed his hand around hers, holding it tightly as they walked. Something he'd never done before. That they'd never been able to do. She smiled at the snow, a soft ache stealing over her.

This is something stupid. This is a mistake. This is folly.

She was going to do it anyway.

Looking up at him, she asked, "Will you tell me about growing up in Lescendor?"

46

MARCUS

Marcus opened one eye, his gaze slowly focusing on the flickering glow of the fire in the stove, the sound of Teriana singing to herself outside the shack easing his concerns about her welfare.

She'd peppered him with questions about his years in training, and he'd found himself telling her things that he'd never told anyone—had never had cause to. They were the stories of the Thirty-Seventh, which meant all of his men knew them. Or had ones just like them, so only the more memorable moments ever came up in conversation over the campfire. And there was something very different between reminiscing with comrades about the tribulations that had bound them together and telling those same stories to someone who stood apart.

It was, to a certain extent, easy to talk about his time at Lescendor, because the lie of his identity came before arriving at its gates and the worst of what he'd done in his life had come after he'd left them. He told her of the many times Felix had concealed his illness, by either hiding him when he had an attack or by pretending to be him to prevent one—for the night of the battle for Galinha had been by no means the first instance. Of how Servius had come to know and the measures his big friend had taken to protect him.

She'd been fascinated with his rise to command, pressing him for details of how he'd recognized that the instructors were always watching, grading and measuring, determining which boys were leaders and which were followers. How the six thousand or so children of their year had immediately fractured into gangs—loners did not fare well at Lescendor—and how they'd warred against one another in the side halls and dark hours, always jockeying for control. How he'd learned to trade in the currency of Lescendor—rations and perquisites and favors—recruiting when he could, using fists when politics failed, creating a gang full of the boys he needed, all of them loyal to a fault.

He'd told her how with each passing year, the gangs grew larger in size and fewer in number. How in their third year, the teachers had split them out that way for war games, gang leaders forced to prove themselves as commanders, not just instigators of hallway brawls. How at that point, he'd started sneaking into the library at every possible moment to listen in on the lessons of the older boys so as to learn the battle strategies earlier. How those same boys had beaten him bloody every time they caught him. How he'd given up his soap ration for months in exchange for the lesson notes of a sixth-year boy in officer training who'd been particularly fastidious in his washing habits.

That had made Teriana laugh, her head tilted back to reveal the long column of her neck, the sound ringing through the shack. "You didn't wash with soap for *three months*?"

"Not quite," he confessed. "Felix got tired of how bad I smelled, so he started to share his ration after a month."

He explained how when the Thirty-Seventh had been in their fourth year, the commandant had selected fifty boys from their ranks for training in advanced strategy and that the number had included Marcus and his inner circle, along with the two other remaining gang leaders and their circles. By the following year, it was down to him and Agrippa, and by their final year of training, Marcus had, unofficially, already been in command of the legion that would be named the Thirty-Seventh.

"Weren't some of those boys angry about their loss of power?" Teriana asked.

"Of course. But most were wise enough to fall in line, especially once they'd taken a beating or two."

"And those who didn't?"

It was tempting to lie, but instead, he said, "As well you know, if a soldier is injured badly enough, he is discharged. And accidents happen." Usually with a nudge from Gibzen, who even as a child had delighted in causing harm.

But it had been Marcus who'd given the orders to see it done.

Even now, he could remember standing back while Gibzen and Felix had beaten Agrippa to within an inch of his life until he'd finally conceded to Marcus's authority. Or pretended to, at least. Part of him had always wondered if it hadn't just been the Bardenese girl who'd driven Agrippa to desert but also the vestiges of rivalry between them. Whether it had always been inevitable.

"If being in command meant making those decisions, why did you want it?"

A question with many answers, all of them true.

"If you're a second-born son in the Empire, there is almost no chance of escaping legion recruitment," he finally said. "And once you're in, the only way out is to die, to be discharged because your mind or body is broken beyond repair, or to desert, which almost always catches up with those who choose to do so. If you want to live, you try to find your place in the legion, whether that is in the rank and file, or as a medic, or an engineer, or a commander. For me, that place was at the top."

It felt as though her eyes, which had been a shade of blue so deep they were nearly black, had dug into his soul when she said, "You didn't answer my question, Marcus."

Because he hated the answer.

"It was a way to survive." Which was true. Even with his illness aside, he'd been small and weak and known nothing about fighting. Having Felix and the others he recruited as defenders had saved his life.

But that hadn't been what had driven him to the top.

Like it was yesterday, he remembered overhearing the conversation between some sixth-years who were about to graduate. About how their leader was being outfitted to go before the Senate in order to be sworn in as legatus. Remembered the moment he'd learned that every legatus of every year had that privilege. How it had gotten into his head that if *he* could win that top spot, it would be *him* standing in front of the Senate. A Senate of which his father was a member.

That was what had driven him: not standing before the men who controlled the Empire, but of standing before his father, Senator Gnaeus Domitius. Year after year. Through exhaustion and pain and terror. The vision of the moment where he'd stand before the Senate and his father would see that Marcus was not only alive, but the top of his year. A peer to those pampered men in togas, not because he'd been born to it, but because he'd earned it. The moment when his father realized that he'd made a mistake in choosing Marcus's brother over him.

Then that fateful day had come. The moment of triumph that had driven him for all those years. Marcus had walked into the Curia with Felix at his elbow, both of them dressed in their new armor and regalia. Facing the sea of men in white, he'd scanned their ranks. Once. Twice. Three times.

His father hadn't been there.

"Once one has a taste of power, it's hard to give up," he finally answered. "And you know I like to be in control."

Truth and a lie rolled into one.

47

KILLIAN

"This is madness, Killian," Sonia grumbled. "Why in the name of the Six would Mudamorian soldiers impersonate you to attack Anuk villages? It doesn't make sense. The whole reason we're here is to defend against them, not incite them."

"Just because it doesn't make sense to us doesn't mean it isn't happening. And the boy had no reason to lie."

Now, he and Sonia were watching the soldiers guarding one of the passes leading through the mountains. Not men of the Royal Army that he'd brought with him, but men from Rotahn. Rowenes men, *Dwyer* among them.

"I'm going to sleep," Sonia muttered, reaching for her pack. "Wake me when it's my turn."

Leaning against a rock, Killian watched the Rowenes men, wishing he could hear what they were saying. But there was a strong southerly wind howling across the hills and through the mountains—nearly gale force in intensity. It filled the air with dust, little eddies swirling between the brush and pines, debris catching in the dry creek bed to his right. Lifting his head, he watched the shadows of the clouds race across the moon, running north along the range toward the towering peaks of the Northern Liratoras. His skin prickled, something about the weather feeling off, but he couldn't spare any more thought for it as the Rowenes soldiers had risen.

They pissed on their fire to put it out, then mounted their horses and started toward the mountains.

Reaching down to shake Sonia's shoulder, he murmured, "They're on the move."

Alert in an instant, Sonia crawled next to him, both of them peering from behind the rock that was their cover to watch as the group headed down the trail, their path illuminated by moonlight.

"Let's go," he muttered.

They kept back as they followed the *clack clack* of horse hooves against rock as they wove through the treacherous mountain passes, riding for hours and well into Anukastre territory before the group dismounted. Slipping off the side of his horse, Killian left the animal and moved forward on foot, Sonia at his heels.

They passed the horses the soldiers had left behind, following the scuff of boots against rock as the men picked their way down a path lined with cactus and boulders, moving onto the dry plains skirting the edge of the desert itself.

Ahead, Killian picked out the lights of fires, which, as they moved closer, illuminated a large grouping of tents surrounding a few small stone buildings. *A village.*

Then a scream filled his ears, and a second later, shadows ran between the buildings.

Swearing, Killian broke into a run, weapon in hand, bursting into the village a heartbeat later. The Rowenes soldiers were attacking the villagers, cutting down defenseless men and women, blood spraying.

"Stand down!" Killian shouted at them, and the men whirled around to stare at him. And that was when he saw the bands tied around their arms. Bands marked with a rough illustration of a black horse.

"Lord Calorian," Dwyer blurted out, the villagers taking advantage of their distraction to escape into the darkness. "What are—"

"Under whose orders are you here?" Killian interrupted, fury coursing through his veins. Because he knew.

Dwyer a step back, lifting his weapon. "An eye for an eye, sir. That's what Lady Ria says."

Lady Ria, whose false tears and pleas to protect her people had turned him into not a protector but a murderer.

"Killian!" Sonia caught hold of his arm. "We've got company."

Hooves raced toward them, and a heartbeat later, a group of Anuk warriors burst into the village, the boy he'd fought in the ambush at the lead.

"Murderer!" the boy screamed, pointing a finger at him. "Kill them!"

The last thing Killian wanted to do was fight the Anuk. But he also had no intention of dying, because that would mean Ria getting away with what she'd done. So grabbing Sonia's arm, he broke into a run.

They tripped and stumbled through the darkness, heading toward the mountain path and their horses. Behind, the screams of Ria's men filled the air, the Anuk cutting them down before giving pursuit.

He and Sonia weren't going to make it.

The Anuk were on horseback, and with dawn beginning to light the ground, the riders were giving their mounts their heads.

"I'll hold them off." He pushed Sonia ahead of him. "Get back.

Tell the people what Ria has done. And if they won't listen, ride to Teradale and tell my mother that Ria's started a war."

That I've started a war.

"You go!" Sonia gasped. "You've a better chance of making it back."

He glanced behind, seeing the riders were nearly upon them. An arrow whistled past him. Then another. And another.

Bending, he picked up a rock and threw it, catching one of the archers in the shoulder hard enough to knock him back.

If he could just get to a place where the path narrowed, he might be able to hold them off. Might be able to buy Sonia enough time.

An arrow scraped across his shoulder, drawing a hiss of pain from his lips. He bent to pick up another rock and threw it.

And when he whirled back around, it was to find six riderless horses galloping toward him and Sonia. He dived into her, knocking her between two cactuses just as the wild-eyed animals passed, and both of them stumbled to their feet and raced up the steep path.

To find Finn holding the reins of their horses at the top of the incline.

"What are you doing here?" Killian shouted.

"Saving your neck, Lord Calorian." Finn bowed, then leapt onto the back of his horse and galloped down the trail, Sonia on his heels.

Swinging into the saddle, Killian looked back to see the Anuk still trying to get around the loose horses on the narrow path. But as he watched, the Anuk boy met his gaze, lifting one hand to level a finger at Killian.

Dread abruptly filled his stomach, sickening and thick as tar, his heart skittering and then plunging into a wild beat of terror.

But it had nothing to do with the boy. With the Anuk. Or even with Ria.

Lydia.

She was in danger.

And there was nothing he could do to help her.

48

LYDIA

Lydia woke with a start, struggling to pull herself from the depths of a nightmare even as she wondered how long she'd been asleep.

Wrapping her blankets around her freezing shoulders, she blinked at the lamp on the table, still exhausted from pulling the blight from Lena's body and from days of little rest.

But it had been worth it.

There was a cure, and once a tender was found, she had faith that the blight could be driven from the land. Not that finding a tender would be an easy task, as none were left in Mudamora. Serrick would have to approach the kingdom's allies for assistance, which would take time.

But at least there was hope.

Rising to her feet, Lydia pulled on her clothing, intent on discovering how Serrick had reacted to the news of the cure. She had wanted to be the one to deliver the revelation, but she'd been too weak, so Dareena had gone with Lena and Gwen in tow as her witnesses. And other than Killian, there was no one Lydia trusted more than the High Lady to ensure the King took this development seriously.

Leaving her room, Lydia walked down the stairs, going directly to Quindor's office.

Once Lydia's mark had defeated the blight she'd drawn into it, the Grand Master had examined both her and Lena thoroughly before deeming them free of the poison. But rather than being invigorated by Lydia's success, he'd seemed to withdraw into himself as though the development was more curse than blessing. And perhaps for him, it was. Quindor was nearly fanatical in his devotion to Hegeria and his dedication to the healing arts. To discover that many of those he'd condemned to death might have been saved was not a blow he'd soon recover from.

If he recovered at all.

She reached his office only to find it empty. Which was peculiar, because he was of a habit of dining in his office at this hour. Going to the main level, she bypassed the dinner hall, which was full of healers and soldiers eating their rations, and instead approached one of the guards manning the main doors, which had already been locked for the evening. "Have you seen the Grand Master?" she asked.

"He went down to see the prisoner an hour or so ago."

A flicker of unease passed through Lydia's chest. Now that they'd found a cure, there was little reason to keep Emmy alive. *She's already dead,* Lydia reminded herself. *That's not the little girl you once knew—just a body possessed by the Corrupter.*

But the admonition did nothing to still the growing trepidation in her stomach as she made her way down into the sublevel, her boots making soft thuds. The air grew colder as she reached the bottom, following the curved corridor to Emmy's room.

Only to stop in her tracks.

The guards who normally stood outside the entrance were gone. Heart in her throat, Lydia crept closer, resting her hand on the door-handle. It turned beneath her grip, and she eased it open, peering inside.

Nothing in the room moved, and her eyes jerked immediately to the prone form on the floor, white robes askew.

Quindor.

She hurried toward him, her stomach turning to liquid as she stared into his sightless eyes. He was unmarked by any injury that she could see, but she knew what had killed him. He'd tried to save Emmy by pulling the blight out of her. But not even Hegeria could bring back the dead.

"Emmy?"

There was no answer, and her skin crawling, Lydia looked around the room for the girl. There was no sign of her. But the stink of blight was thick on the air.

Lowering her head, Lydia peered under the bed, her stomach flipping at the sight of the glistening pool of blight. It had come up through the floor, and as she stared, another flagstone sank into the murk.

Gods, no.

Lydia raced back into the hallway and up the stairs. "The Grand Master's dead!" she shouted at the soldiers by the door. "Emmy's loose in the tower!"

"I'm right here, Lydia."

Her skin turned to ice. Slowly, she turned around to find the little girl standing in the entrance to the barracks, a cup smeared with black held in one hand. "Are you thirsty?" she asked. "All the men were so very thirsty, but I think there might be some left."

Gasping in horror, Lydia shoved past the girl and raced toward the barracks. "Don't drink the water!" she screamed. "It's poisoned with blight!"

But she was too late.

Everywhere she looked, men were doubling over in pain, their faces waxy and sweat dripping down their faces. Those unaffected shoved away their plates and cups, but even as she watched, they started crumpling, falling off their chairs and clutching their bellies, their groans filling the air.

Yet above it all, she heard a loud thump. And then another. And another.

Spinning, she stared at the heavy doors to the temple as they bowed inward, the twin beams that barred them shuddering as something struck the exterior over and over.

"My friends have come!" Emmy squealed, clapping her hands in delight. Then she reached into her pocket, extracting something. Lydia struggled not to retreat as the girl closed the distance between them, holding out Killian's cuff link. And when Lydia didn't take it, Emmy pressed it into her hand. It was warm. "He swore to protect you."

"No, he didn't," Lydia whispered, twitching each time the ram slammed against the door behind her.

"He did. On his knees and in the name of the Six." Emmy smiled sweetly. "But he isn't here. He's failed you, just like he failed me."

The door exploded inward, a battering ram smashing into the guard that had been trying to brace it and sending him flying across the room, where he fell with a wet thump.

And beyond . . . there were hundreds and hundreds of blighters, all wearing the uniforms of the Royal Army. As she watched, they stepped aside to create a path, their movements in complete unison. Like they were controlled by one mind.

Which they were.

The path revealed the center of the god circle and a man writhing on the ground, crimson-and-gold robes stained and torn. Horror filled Lydia's chest as she recognized King Serrick's face, which was twisted with the pain of blight infection.

"Help him!" Lydia shouted at remaining temple guard. But Serrick pushed up on his hands and knees, his eyes fixed on Lydia's. "Kill me!" he screamed. "Do not let him have a king for a puppet!"

And in a blink of her eye, she knew he was right. That the Corrupter would soon possess the King of Mudamora and most of the

Royal Army. An army of corpses, except no one would know it, because it didn't appear the Corrupter had the intention of allowing anyone out of Mudaire alive.

"Shoot him!" she screamed at the guard, who was staring dumbfounded at the horde, seeing them as his comrades, not as corpses the way she did. When he didn't move, she wrenched the bow from his grip along with a handful of arrows.

Her hands shaking, she nocked one of them, then let it fly, but it only skittered against the cobbles. She tried again, and this time, it sank into the legs of one of the corpse-soldiers. He screamed and fell, the Corrupter keeping up the pretense they were living even now.

She nocked her last arrow, knowing that if she didn't aim true that she'd have to go out there and try to kill Serrick with a blade.

If she could.

Her bow twanged sharply, and Tremon himself must have guided her hand, for it flew directly toward the King's throat.

Only to be plucked out of the air.

Lydia's eyes widened at the sight of Cyntha, dressed in black leather, a sword belted at her waist. "Silence!" she commanded, and the blighter army went entirely still, the only noise Serrick's moans of pain.

"Such a shame Killian isn't here," the healer purred. "Though to be fair, even he's never had much luck with this particular challenge."

Confusion twisted through Lydia. That Cyntha, who'd fought so hard to see the blighters killed, now stood among them like she was in command of them. Then realization slapped her in the face, her fists clenching as so very, *very* much became clear.

"How?" The word tore from her throat. But the real question in her mind was *why*.

"You know how, Lydia," Cyntha answered, the breeze pulling a strand of grey hair loose from her braid and sending it trailing out in the wind. "Hegeria might have granted you your mark, but it's your choice how to use it. And the Corrupter rewards those who use their mark to achieve his ends. Strength. Power. Eternal youth." She snapped her fingers.

A moment later, two men appeared, dragging a young man in a Royal Army uniform. With total nonchalance, Cyntha caressed the man's cheek, and Lydia could do nothing as she stole his life, decade after decade marring the man's face until he fell to the ground with a brittle crunch.

And Cyntha was no longer a woman in her fifties, but young and lovely, her hair dark, skin smoothed of wrinkles, and her body lithe and strong. The only thing that remained the same was the faded half-moon inked on her forehead. Hegeria's mark.

Except this creature belonged to the Corrupter.

Cyntha gave a slow clap of her hands. "Age is a nearly infallible disguise, but one I'll be glad to never use again." Retrieving a leather mask, she fastened it over her face, concealing the tattoo on her forehead, as she had when Lydia had seen her the night of Malahi's ball.

"Rufina." The name came out of Lydia's mouth as a croak.

"Named by my master the day I turned my back on the Six," the corrupted Queen of Derin answered. Her attention moved to Serrick, who was writhing at her feet, the blight consuming more of his life with every passing second.

"I had to kill him because of you." Rufina met Lydia's gaze, her eyes burning with the Corrupter's flames. "Had to kill all of them because of you and your . . . *cure.*"

Bile burned up Lydia's throat, fueled by her grief and guilt and fury.

"He broke when the High Lady delivered your revelation. Not because of all those he ordered killed that might have been saved, but because he wished death upon Mudamora's last living tender."

Kneeling next to Serrick, she pulled him upright so that he was looking her in the eye. "Do you remember how you cursed your daughter's name? How you told me she was blasphemous for wanting to rule when her mark demanded that she *serve*? How you said that if the Six still stood with Mudamora, they'd see her dead?" She laughed wildly. "By condemning her, you destroyed Mudamora's only hope. And gave my master what he needed for victory, for once she breaks, Malahi will turn all that she once loved to blight."

Malahi was a tender. But that wasn't the revelation that drained the blood from Lydia's face. It was that the ill-fated queen was still alive. Alive, and Rufina intended to force her to expand the reach of the blight.

"You are a demon." Serrick spat in Rufina's face. "A product of the Seventh's evil."

The Queen of Derin only smiled. "So are you, Your Grace. The only difference between us is that I know which god I serve."

Serrick stared at her, lines of black blight crawling up his face, ripping a final scream from his lips. Then he fell to the ground and went still.

The King of Mudamora was dead.

And Lydia would soon join him if she didn't find a way to flee. But the path before her was filled with an army of blighters, and behind her, the soldiers dying from the blight would soon rise as the Seventh's puppets. There was nowhere to run.

As the direness of her own circumstances became clear, Serrick's corpse rose smoothly to his feet, his face possessed of a cool calmness. Rufina dropped to her knee in front of him. "Master."

"My child." Serrick spoke, but the voice that exited his lips made Lydia's skull ache with the vastness of it. She clamped her hands over her ears, but it was like he spoke inside her head as he turned to level a finger at her. "Capture the Marked One. Do what you will with the rest."

"I live to serve," Rufina said. And as one, the horde of dead soldiers surged through the entrance.

Run.

Terror galloped through Lydia's veins as she sprinted up the stairs, the sound of heavy footfalls close behind her. "The temple is under attack!" she screamed, hoping that any alive who heard would have the wherewithal to hide, for there was nothing she could do for them.

Faster.

Except there was nowhere to run. Nowhere to hide where they wouldn't eventually find her.

Keep going.

She rose higher and higher in the tower, a cramp pinching her side, but she ignored it.

The library.

She hit the floor the library was on, shoving open the door and then slamming it behind her and twisting the bolt.

Except she knew it wouldn't hold for long.

She shoved a table up against the door right as the first blighters reached it, the boards shuddering with the impact of their bodies as they threw themselves against the wood.

Sobs of fear tearing from her throat, she dragged over more furniture, piling it high against the door and then knocking the nearest bookshelves against it. The mess of wood continued to shudder, but there were no shouts outside, only eerie silence.

Spinning in a circle, she searched for a way out, but of course, there was none.

She went to the window and looked down, everywhere she looked, the ground was a churning mass of armed men fighting to get inside of the tower.

Screams echoed up from the windows of the lower levels, the other healers falling victim to the horde, some choosing to leap to their deaths rather than face whatever had come for them, but Lydia wasn't ready to give up.

She circled the library until she reached the window that faced the palace, her chest tightening at the sight of fire breaking out across the city. Of soldiers chasing civilians and cutting them down, screams filling the night. Her worst nightmare come to fruition.

And there was no way out.

Then an arrow shot through the window in front of her, embedding in a bookcase. An arrow with a thin piece of rope attached to it, and terror flooded her veins.

They were coming through the window.

Bracing her foot against the shelf, Lydia jerked the arrow loose and raced to the window, intent on throwing it, but as she looked across at the neighboring tower, her eyes latched on a familiar face.

High Lady Falorn.

Dareena held a finger to her lips, then held up her end of the rope. "Tie it to something."

And then crawl across.

The drop was sickening. Falling would mean certain death, but with the way the furniture she'd piled against the door was moving inward with each slam, there was no other option.

Going to a pillar, Lydia wrapped the thin cord around it twice and then secured it with several knots of a quality that would've made Teriana cringe. But she'd neither the skill nor the time for better.

Going back to the window, she nodded to Dareena, who pulled the rope tight, securing it somewhere within the tower. Then the High Lady motioned for her to cross.

Climbing onto the windowsill, Lydia lay flat across the rope, then took a breath and allowed herself to rotate under it, using her legs to hold her weight as she slowly crept across the gap.

If any of the blighters looked up, she was dead. At this height, she was well within range of a good bowman, and even with her mark, a well-placed arrow was all it would take.

From behind, she heard furniture smashing to the ground, her barricade starting to crumble. Which meant she had only minutes until they were in.

Hurry.

A cold wind whipped at her robes, her hair blowing around her face, but she kept going, moving as fast as she could. And then she felt hands grip her wrists, hauling her across the sill and into the dark tower beyond.

"Someone tampered with the water at the palace," Dareena said softly, untying the rope and allowing it to drop so as not to leave a clue where Lydia had gone. "The whole Royal Army is turned or dead, as are the High Lords. They took Serrick prisoner."

Lydia's stomach dropped. "Lena and Gwen . . ."

"Safe on a ship. One Serrick doesn't know about."

A small relief. "The blighter Quindor kept got loose and poisoned the temple water with blight. They've killed all the healers. And . . . Serrick has been turned. He's a blighter now."

"The Six have mercy on us," Dareena muttered. "Someone coordinated this. Someone is in charge."

"It was Cyntha. Or Rufina, as she now calls herself."

The High Lady stopped in her tracks. "That's . . . that's not possible. Cyntha is a healer. I've *seen* her heal people with my own eyes. She can't be corrupted. That's blasphemy."

"It is possible to do both." Fear slicked her palms with sweat, but this was no time for keeping secrets. "Because I can do it, too."

Abruptly she was against the wall, the High Lady's hands pinioning her wrists to the stone. "What are you saying, Lydia? Because if it's that you're corrupted, you know I need to kill you, no matter how much I might wish otherwise."

"I . . ." Lydia took a deep breath. "Rufina said that Hegeria grants healers our powers but that it is our choice how we use them. And the Corrupter rewards those who use their marks in service of him. And it's not only healers—it's the marks of all the gods that can be corrupted."

It was hard to see in the darkness of the stairwell, but Lydia could hear Dareena's breath, feel the way her fingers flexed as she considered Lydia's words. But she wasn't convinced, so Lydia said, "The tenders in the Royal Army . . . I don't think they all died. I think Rufina captured some of them and forced or convinced them to use their mark to create the blight."

"Corrupted tenders."

"Yes." Lydia's heart was hammering. "That's why Malahi was taken—if Rufina's to be believed, she was marked by Yara but kept her gift a secret. Rufina is going to force her to try to expand the reach of the blight."

"We need to get her back."

"Yes." *They were running out of time.* "But you and I are the only two people alive who know the truth. Which means we really need to get out of here alive. Which means I really need you to trust me."

Wind howled down the staircase, and Lydia felt Dareena shiver, then mutter under her breath, "Yeah, Tremon. Fine. I hear you."

She let go of Lydia's wrists. "Let's go. We can get into the sewers through the sublevel, but we need to hurry. They'll be combing the city soon enough."

They raced down the stairs, finally reaching the ground level in which there was a large statue of a man on a horse, the base covered with dead flowers and other offerings from before the doors were locked. Dareena brought her past it, opening a door to a narrow staircase, which led down to a small cellar. A hole had been knocked in one wall, allowing access to the sewer system, judging from the smell.

Pulling out her sword, Dareena motioned for Lydia to take the waiting lamp. "Let's go."

They moved swiftly through the sewers, heading in the direction of the harbor gate. From time to time, they heard the pounding of boots, and the pair of them were forced to hide in side passages with the lamplight hidden behind Lydia's robes. But she knew eventually they were going to have to climb out into the streets. And when they did, they'd have to fight.

Finally, Dareena stopped. "I have a ship waiting out in deep water. But we're going to need to get to it ourselves, because I've no way to signal them without drawing attention to us. And the harbor is crawling with blighters."

"What about the boats in the cavern at the base of the cliffs?" Lydia suggested. "Is there a way to reach them?"

Dareena rubbed her chin. "Seas are too rough to try to swim. We'd have to go through the palace and down into the tunnels."

"It's not where they'll expect us to go."

"Worth a shot."

They moved closer to the palace, finding a place where they could climb out of the sewers. They hid in an alley as a group of blighter soldiers strode past, none of them speaking a word.

They wove through the dark alleys until they were as close as they could reasonably get to the palace gates, which were open, but guarded by a small force of men.

"Are they alive?" Dareena asked under her breath.

Lydia gave a slight shake of her head.

"I knew them," Dareena said softly. "In life. Sat around a fire and drank with them."

"It's not them anymore."

"I know you can see that," she answered. "But I can't. To me they look very much alive, and I'm going to have to kill them to get through that gate."

"Is there another way?"

The High Lady shook her head, then unhooked a bow from around her shoulder, drawing three arrows from the quiver strapped to her back. "Stay close, but stay out of my way, understood?"

Without waiting for a response, Dareena moved, the bow twanging three times in what seemed no more than a breath and three of the soldiers dropped to the cobbles. The others were trained—or at least, their bodies were—and they immediately dived behind the barrier, shouting the alarm.

But the High Lady was already halfway across the open space, sword raised. Lydia sprinted after her, watching as the woman leapt over the dead men, her blade colliding with that of one of the soldiers. He managed to parry twice and then fell, screaming, but Dareena had moved on to the next.

Lydia had seen Killian fight, his skill and speed beyond anything she'd ever seen, but whereas he was heavy blows and brute strength, watching the High Lady was like watching a dancer moving between men, her violence visible only in the bodies that fell in her wake.

The blighters retreated back against the gate. "High Lady," they pleaded. "Stop!"

But she didn't hesitate, nothing more than a blur of dark leather and steel as she carved into them, parting their heads from their necks one after another until the ground was drenched with blood. Only once they were all truly dead did she stop, and Lydia saw the tears glistening on the woman's face. "Let's go!"

Shoving open the gate, they ran through the camp. It was littered with the bodies of those who hadn't been turned but killed by their comrades, the carnage unlike anything Lydia had ever seen. But there was no time to hesitate, because from behind, shouts filled the air.

"They know we're here," Dareena hissed. "We have to hurry."

Inside the palace, it was dark, blood and bodies littering the floor, but they leapt over them, making their way to the stairs and hurtling downwards, then toward the room containing the hatch that led to the tunnels. Pulling back the thick bolts holding it shut, Dareena heaved it open. "In you go."

Lydia's terror ratcheted higher, the memory of her last time in these tunnels layering old fear upon new until it felt she could scarcely breathe. The torchlight flickered off the walls, casting bouncing shadows as they ran, barely having rounded the first switchback when their pursuers entered the hatch.

The roar of the sea grew, soon loud enough to drown out the shouts of the blighters, and she and Dareena burst into the chamber containing the boats. Lydia's eyes skipped to the opening to the sea beyond. And the gate that barred it.

"Get it open!" Dareena shouted, and Lydia raced forward, shoving the tip of her belt knife into the lock. Her whole body twitched as steel rang against steel behind her, the blighters upon them. Snatching a stone from the damp ground, she slammed it against the hilt of her knife until she broke the lock and the gate swung open.

Only then did she turn, her stomach dropping at the sight.

Dozens of blighters filled the tunnel leading into the cavern, and while Dareena was holding them off, she wouldn't be able to do so for long.

Running to one of the boats, Lydia dug in her heels and pushed it toward the opening. Waves struck the stairs with enough force that she questioned how they'd avoid being dashed against the cliffs. Balancing the boat on the edge of the stairs, oars inside, she watched the timing of the waves, knowing that she had to be precise.

And that there'd be only one chance to get it right.

Now.

"Dareena!" she shouted, then leapt inside the vessel.

The boat slid down the steps, and she twisted, seeing the High Lady—face splattered with gore—racing toward her, the blighters in pursuit.

Dareena jumped off the top step right as the boat hit the water, landing half on top of Lydia as the retreating wave pulled the boat with them.

"We need to row!" she shouted, disentangling herself and trying to get the heavy oars into their locks.

But the water was reversing, the boat picking up speed as the waves flung themselves toward the cliffs.

"Madoria, you might give us some assistance, you waterlogged sea hag!" Dareena screamed, wrenching an oar from Lydia's grip and shoving it into a lock.

Lydia got the other one in, but it was too late. They were too close, the waves too strong. She braced herself for the impact.

Then the water abruptly fell still, the waves flattening, foam floating on the glassy surface. The boat slid forward on its own momentum, striking the rocks, but the thick wood held strong.

"Ha ha!" Dareena crowed, flipping her middle finger at the watching blighters. Then she grasped the oars and leaned into them, rowing the boat out to sea.

"What happened?" Lydia demanded, staring at the still water. "How is this possible?"

"The ship that's waiting for us," the High Lady said, breathing hard, "is not Mudamorian. It's Maarin. And one of Madoria's marked is aboard."

49

KILLIAN

It was a wild gallop back through the mountains, but Killian was only half-aware of the Anuk pursuing him, his mind all for Lydia. She was in danger, he knew it.

And thanks to Ria's meddling, he was on the wrong side of the kingdom to help Lydia.

Please keep her safe, he prayed to the Six. *I don't care what you do to me, just don't let her be harmed.*

It was only as he, Sonia, and Finn galloped out the eastern end of the canyon that the pool of dread in his guts abated. Yet as it did, the void it left behind filled with a new fear. What if his mark wasn't telling him Lydia was safe. What if her life was no longer in danger because she'd lost it?

What if she's dead?

"Ride hard to camp!" he shouted at Sonia. "Tell them to ready for an imminent attack from the Anuk and tell them why it's coming."

"Where are you going?"

"To Rotahn." Digging his heels into Seahawk's sides, he drove the exhausted horse in the direction of the Rowenes stronghold.

"Ria!"

Servants leapt out of his way as he stormed through the palace, hunting for the lady of House Rowenes.

And answers.

"Where is she?" he demanded, catching hold of the arm of one of the Rowenes guards. "Where is Ria?"

"A-bed, my lord," the man stuttered.

"Take me to her."

"But—"

"Now!" He shouted the word in the man's face, not caring that the guard wasn't the source of his wrath. It was because of Ria that he wasn't in Mudaire. Which meant anything that had happened to Lydia would be on her hands.

The guard led him through the palace, stopping beside a door. "Her chambers, my lord," he blurted out, then bolted.

Killian twisted the handle, finding it locked. But rather than demanding she open the door, he stepped back a few paces and then threw his weight against it. Wood splintered, and it exploded inward, slamming against the wall as a scream of surprise filled the air.

As his eyes adjusted to the dimness, they latched on Ria sitting upright in her bed, silken bedsheets clutched to her chest.

"What is the meaning of this?" she shrieked at him.

He was across the room in four strides, his finger leveled at her. "Do you have any idea of what you've done?"

"Nothing that deserves such abuse from you, my lord," she retorted. "So I'd ask that you remove yourself from my chambers and work on formulating an apology."

"You deserve this and worse, Ria!" His vision was tinged with red. "You lied to me. Told me that the Anuk were taking advantage of the war with Derin to attack Rowenes lands, but that wasn't it at all. You provoked them by sending your men to attack their villages in *my name*. To slaughter children in *my name*!" He screamed the words, because the alternative was to tear the room apart.

She stared silently at him, then lifted a shoulder. "We've always raided one another. It is nothing new or of note."

"Of note?" He stared at her, feeling a tremor run through him. "You've started a gods-damned war when Mudamora can least afford it, Ria. People are going to die because of your actions."

"I've started a war?" One of her eyebrows rose. "More like *you've* started a war, Killian. Everyone knows that you've met the Anuk raiders with unprecedented violence. That you've shown them none of the mercy my men cautioned you to use."

"Because I thought—"

She interrupted her with a sharp laugh. "Protest all you like. As far as anyone knows, the only element in Mudamora's relationship with Anukastre that has changed is *you*."

"Bullshit. And when the King hears that you risked his gold and his people . . ." He trailed off, watching the smile rise to her lips. "He's behind this."

Ria clapped her hands together. "Very good. He sent instructions ahead that I was to do whatever it took to keep you in Rotahn. And that if I could discredit you in some capacity, so much the better."

"Why?" Killian felt sick to his stomach.

"Isn't it obvious? You sided with Malahi against him. Made him look the fool at Alder's Ford. And he already hated you. Hated all of your kind."

"My kind?"

"The Marked." Rising, she drew on a dressing gown. "My uncle is a man who craves power and control, and if you think that he doesn't resent the Marked for being raised above him by the Six, then you are truly an idiot. Why do you think he's worked so tirelessly to reduce you all to little more than slaves to the kingdom?"

Belting the gown with steady fingers, she added, "Most of the Marked submitted, but not you. Except with your victory over Rufina's armies at the Ford, he knew he'd lose the favor of the people if he executed you for your treason. Better to wait until you fell from grace. Again. As to why I agreed to help him, well . . ." She shrugged. "With Malahi dead, my uncle is in need of an heir."

Gods help him, but Malahi had been right about her father. Right to see that he was as true a threat to Mudamora as Rufina and her armies. Right to have done whatever it took to see him removed from power. And instead of standing by Malahi's side, as he'd sworn to do, Killian had abandoned her.

But if you hadn't gone after Lydia, she'd be the one dead . . . "You'll be the heir to nothing if the Anuk bring their armies over the border. Your gold will be gone. Your people dead."

"They'll come, but I'm not stupid enough to incite them without insurance." Moving away from the bed, Ria poured a glass of wine and drained it. "The winter storms will be here in another few weeks, making raiding impossible. By the time it's safe again, tempers will have cooled and better judgments will have prevailed. Not that it will come in time to help you."

"I'm not going to let you get away with this, Ria. Nor Serrick," he said. "I'm going to make certain the other High Lords learn what he's done, and they're going to rip the crown from his head."

"On your word?" She chuckled. "With only a foreigner and a street rat to speak in your defense, because you allowed the only other witnesses to be murdered by the Anuk. No one will believe you, Killian, because you've failed before. It's time that you accept that you are nothing more than a pawn being played by higher powers."

His hands balled into fists, the rage in his chest fueled by his fear that she was right.

"A battle is coming, Killian," she said. "Go serve your purpose and prepare our defenses."

"Why should I?" His voice was full of venom. "With what you've done, better to allow the Anuk to cross the border and have their vengeance on you."

"Except it won't be just me they have their vengeance on." She took a sip of her wine. "It will be all the people in Rotahn. And we both know you will never let that happen."

50

TERIANA

They spent another night in the shack, the wolves making only a few lackluster attempts to get in before leaving her and Marcus in relative peace.

"Maybe they've given up." She tried to be optimistic, which was challenging given her exhaustion. Even her hands ached from the effort of softening the wolf pelt enough to use.

Endlessly pragmatic, Marcus shook his head. "They're being patient. Starving your enemy out is an excellent way to lay siege, if you've the time for it. Which I expect they do."

But now it was dawn of the day they'd attempt to cross twenty miles of barren landscape.

Or die trying.

Together, they'd fashioned clothing from the wolf's pelt. Big as it was, it was still not enough to cover them from head to toe, so they'd focused, as Marcus had described it, on the parts most likely to freeze off. Boots for their feet, mittens for their hands, and as she stood next to him, waiting for it to be bright enough to risk opening the door, Teriana rubbed her cheek against the deep, fur-lined hood that protected her head and shoulders.

"Ready?" Marcus turned to look at her, his face shadowed by his own hood. Over one shoulder, he had slung the satchel containing what supplies they'd bring, including the kettle, which was full of hot water. They'd have to drink it before it froze, because there'd be no time to stop to build a fire. And he'd already warned her of the dangers of eating snow. He had one mitten tucked in his belt and was holding his gladius, and thinking this might be prudent, she drew her freshly sharpened knife.

"Grab the meat," he said. "Then we go west. I'm confident the den is north of us, so we'll move fast at first to put some distance between them and us. If you need to rest, say so. This is a test of endurance, not speed."

Though she suspected Marcus was mostly talking to himself, Teriana nodded.

Lifting off the crossbeams and setting them aside, Marcus opened the door and stepped outside, Teriana following on his heels. Both of them looked skyward.

"Overcast," she said, the sun barely visible through the soft grey clouds. It was the first day she wasn't squinting against glare, and her heart thudded rapidly against her rib cage. The sun was the only ally they had. "Should we wait until tomorrow?"

Marcus was silent, and she knew he was considering the odds. "We could. But tomorrow might be the same. We might have weeks of the same. And that wolf meat is all we have unless we stop to hunt, which—" He broke off and shook his head. "Neither of us has the expertise in trapping we need to ensure quick success, and every day, we lose daylight. Leaving is a risk. But so is staying."

She waited for him to tell her what he thought they should do, but Marcus only turned to her. "What do you think?"

Teriana eyed the shelter as she considered their options, none of which were good. "Let's go."

Marcus didn't answer, only scanned their surroundings, fingers flexing on his weapon.

There was no movement in the snowy plains, but the light was flat and strange, making it hard to judge depth. The snowdrifts didn't seem large enough to hide anything, but . . . "What's wrong?"

"I don't know." He shook his head and turned in a circle. "Something . . ."

Teriana's skin prickled as she watched him walk a dozen paces and then stop, searching their surroundings before turning back. "I think maybe—"

Whatever else he said fell on deaf ears as a black shape rose from behind a drift.

The wolf bounded forward, ears pinned and lips peeled back in a snarl. Then it leapt.

"Tremon guide my hand!" The words tore from Teriana's lips, and she threw her knife.

It flipped end over end, past Marcus, who was turning, blade rising.

Then the wolf slammed into him and both of them went down, rolling across the snowy ground.

"No!" Teriana hurtled across the space between them, hooking her arm around the wolf's neck. She dug in her heels, hauling backward, expecting to feel the sharp pain of teeth. It was so heavy—like . . .

Deadweight.

That's when she saw her knife hilt jutting from the creature's eye.

"Shit!" Marcus snarled the word, shoving the dead animal aside with Teriana's help. Then his eyes landed on her blade and he went still. "Who taught you to throw a knife?"

Killian. Killian had taught her. Or at least as much as he'd teach any skill that might be attributed to his mark. "You look like you're playing at darts," he'd laughed at her. "No one has that much time to aim in a fight. Look at what you want to hit and throw the gods-damned blade!"

"A friend," she whispered, watching as he jerked out the knife, wiping the gore off on the animal's coat.

Fear clawed at Teriana's insides as she stared down at the dead wolf. Another pack member that *she* had killed. "What do we do?"

"We go." He started walking west.

"Care to justify that decision?" She mimicked his voice as she asked the question, earning a smile as they broke into a jog.

"They won't give up trying to get in at us tonight. And I expect it won't be only one wolf watching us tomorrow, but the whole pack. They're smart. They *learn*."

Teriana shivered, and it had nothing to do with the cold.

"This is their territory," he continued, stumbling in the snow before catching his balance. "There's nothing to drive them off except for their own need to eat. If we stay, I think we'll be trapped."

"And you think things will be any better twenty miles from here?"

"It's a move in the right direction." He pulled his hood back in place. "Twenty miles west won't get us into another pack's territory, but forty might. Sixty definitely will."

"Great, more wolves," she muttered, wondering how the Sibernese survived in this place.

"More wolves that are likely to take issue with another pack invading their territory." He cast a backward glance over his shoulder. "It's a long shot, but it's something."

51

MARCUS

It was like running in sand.

But worse.

The snow shifted and moved beneath his feet, the crust catching at his toes and tripping him up, making it difficult to tell whether his next step would send him ankle deep or up past his knees.

By the time they passed the first mile marker, Marcus was already dripping with sweat and wishing he could shed some of his clothes, but there was no time. At any moment, the pack might discover their dead scout and decide to give chase.

So they kept the pace.

By the third mile, Marcus's sides were cramping, the muscles in his legs burning and the scent of his own sweat heavy in his nose with each gasping inhalation he took.

"Make it to the next milepost, then we walk a mile."

Keep. Running. Keep. Running. He silently chanted the words with each step, helping Teriana up when she fell only to have her return the favor a few strides later.

Never had he felt more relief as they reached the post embedded in the earth, a three carved on one side, a seventeen on the other for those traveling in the opposite direction, and both of them fell into a walk.

As they trudged toward the next mile marker, the wind picked up, tugging at his hood and piercing through his woolen clothing. But Teriana was shivering, so he moved next to her to block some of the wind.

And probably because she was close enough to hear the faint wheeze to his breath, she asked, "Will running like this cause one of your attacks?"

It was a valid question, given the circumstances, but it still made his cheeks burn hot and his temper flare, reminding him of how it had felt to be the weakest before he'd learned to compensate for his limitations. "If it does, just leave me and carry on. No sense in both of us dying out here."

Teriana stopped in her tracks. "What is wrong with you? Why would you say something like that?"

He kept trudging forward, glaring at the snow and half-wishing the wolves might catch up and spare him from this conversation.

"It wasn't a damned criticism," she snapped, jogging to close the distance. "It's not like you choose for it to happen. It's not your fault."

Bloody platitudes. His temper burned hotter. His sister Cordelia had always said the same sort of things, as though being blameless would somehow make him feel better about his situation when it was the exact opposite. He *wished* he'd done something to cause his illness, because then he'd have somewhere to direct the blame other than bad luck, which only made him feel powerless. "Doesn't mean it isn't a problem."

"Aye, fair enough. But maybe instead of getting defensive, you might inform me how best to prevent it from happening."

He slid to a halt, rounding on her. "How best to prevent it from happening? Do you think if it were so simple, that I wouldn't do just that?"

The eyes staring out from under her hood were the grey of storm-tossed seas, the bow of her lips drawn into a tight line as she glared back at him. "Surely there are certain things that trigger you."

"This conversation, for starts." Turning round, he picked up the pace, feeling an irritating combination of frozen and overheated. It was not the time for this conversation given the wolves could be hot on their heels. Though he supposed it mattered little if the pack came upon them in a full-blown argument or running for their lives.

"Given that I nearly *killed* you with a conversation, maybe that's a good place to start."

"That wasn't your fault. You didn't know."

As soon as the words passed his lips, he cursed at himself, already feeling her smug satisfaction at having won the argument. Lifting his head, he eyed the next mile marker, where they'd again have to pick up the pace. "I don't want you walking on eggshells around me because you're afraid of saying something that will set me off."

She lifted one shoulder. "When have you ever known me to walk on eggshells?"

With him? *Never.* And the last thing he wanted was for that to change. He valued her voice too much to ever want it silenced. "I don't get set off as easily as I did when I was young. Though when it does happen, it's worse."

When he'd been small, anything had set him off. Everything. Climbing the stairs. Pulling a dusty book off a shelf. Being teased by the other children. He'd learned to fear it so badly that sometimes the idea that something might set him off was enough to send him spiraling into wheezing fits. "You do it to yourself!" he remembered his father shouting at him. "Quit fretting, and it won't happen."

As if that were so easy.

"When I was a child, exertion usually did it," he said, feeling her eyes on him. "Climbing the Hill in Celendrial was too taxing for me."

"It's a big hill."

He snorted. "Anyway, once exercise became part of my daily life, it started to take more to wind me and after a few months, it only rarely happened due to exertion. Up until that point, it was happening once, sometimes twice, a day. But it's been ten years since that's done it. Though this cold air won't do me any favors."

"Good to know."

"Dust and smoke and horses and flowers make me sneeze." His cheeks burned hot at the admission. "That can still do it, but the attacks aren't so bad. Not like what you saw."

"So what does it?" Her voice was soft, barely audible over the wind.

Marcus rubbed his chin, which was itchy with stubble, eyes fixed on the milepost because he couldn't look at her while talking about this. "Stress, I suppose."

Though that wasn't precisely it. His life was one stressor after the next. If stress were all it took, he'd never get off the floor. "It's when I feel . . . certain things. Negative things that make me panic."

Things he felt helpless to combat. Things that sent him spiraling down, as though his own body were trying to strangle the emotions out.

"Like what?" *Of course she wouldn't leave it alone.* "What's the biggest instigator?"

He kicked the snow, thinking hard before he finally muttered, "Guilt."

They alternated jogging and walking through the day, moving faster along stretches that had been blown clear by the wind and trudging through places where the snow had settled into dips in the ground. There'd been no sign the wolves were in pursuit, but then again, there wouldn't be. They were nothing if not consummate hunters. Even still, he cast a backward glance over the plain, searching for signs of motion.

"There it is."

Teriana was somewhat ahead of him when he turned back around, stopped with her hands resting on her knees, shoulders rising and falling as she panted. He joined her at the top of a slight incline, sighing at the sight of the ravine below. It was steep and icy, and a frozen stream snaked along the bottom, two logs resting across it functioning as a bridge. But on the far side was a shack almost identical to the one they'd left behind.

Casting a backward glance, Marcus calculated the amount of time they had. An hour, perhaps slightly more. "Let's go. Take it easy, the last thing we need is for one of us to break any bones falling down a hill."

Taking hold of her hand, he braced one leg and helped her slide down until her feet connected with an outcropping, trying to ignore the slight tremor in his leg.

Almost there.

He eased down to where Teriana stood, then gripped her wrists and lowered her to the next solid piece of footing, all the muscles in his body rebelling against the strain. She balanced him as he slid next to her, then motioned for him to follow. "This way."

Together, they picked their way down the steep slope, clinging to rocks and the few scrubby bushes that poked through the snow until they stood at the bottom, which was shadowed from the sun. It was not quite cold enough for the stream to have frozen over, bits of ice floating on the rapidly flowing water. Picking his way onto the logs, Marcus knelt and dipped a cup into the water, trusting it would be clean to drink.

It was frigid enough to make his teeth ache, but bliss against his parched throat. Reaching down to refill it for Teriana, he lifted his head.

And locked eyes with a wolf.

It was smaller than the others had been, likely juvenile, but Marcus suspected it still weighed close to a hundred pounds. Like the others, it was inky black, but this animal's face was frosted with white. Green eyes regarded Marcus intently, ears pricked forward with interest but no aggression. Either a loner or part of a different pack. "Teriana."

"I see it." Her voice was breathy. "I don't see any others."

Easing up, Marcus kept his attention on the wolf even as he scanned their surroundings for any sign of movement. There was nothing but the gurgle of the stream, but that could change in a heartbeat. They needed to get up that slope and into the shelter. "Move slowly," he said. "I don't think it will attack us on its own unless it feels threatened."

Teriana climbed onto the bridge, knife gripped in one hand as she crossed the slippery wood, the wolf watching with interest as they stepped on the opposite bank.

Wind gusted into the ravine, blasting them in the back and ruffling the wolf's fur. Its ears abruptly pinned, eyes looking past them as though searching for the source of a smell or noise.

Then in a flash of motion, it was running, climbing the steep slope that awaited them in great leaping bounds. Not a predator.

But the prey.

Marcus's heart pounded a rapid drumbeat against his ribs, a primal sort of fear filling him. "The pack is coming. Run!"

Adrenaline chased away his exhaustion as they scrambled up the steep slope, losing a foot for every two that they gained. His mittened hands slipped on the slick rocks, his feet finding no traction. Teriana was more nimble, climbing rapidly, but she kept looking over her shoulder at the opposite slope.

"Focus on—"

He was cut off as her foot slipped. On hands and knees, she slid down, colliding with him and nearly sending them both tumbling to the bottom. Catching her around the waist, Marcus held on until she'd regained her grip. "If they come, they come. Watching it happen won't change anything."

But it was nearly impossible to take his own advice as they scrambled upward, his pulse roaring in his ears. It felt like his back was exposed to a line of bowmen, his skin crawling, the need to turn around and *look* almost unbearable.

Climb.

The slope was steepening, not quite vertical but close to it. More like a wall than a hill. And the wolves could be right behind him and he wouldn't know it. He hazarded a glance back.

Nothing.

Teriana was almost to the top, jamming her toes into footholds and hauling herself up. She paused on an outcropping, the lip of the ridge just within reach. But it was capped with a thick crust of snow. She reached for a handhold, but the snow only broke off, slamming her in the face. "Shit!" she snarled, knocking loose more snow that rained down on Marcus as he joined her on the outcropping.

Behind him, the echo of a stone falling down an incline echoed in his ears.

Don't look.

He turned his head. Black shapes poured silently down the opposite slope, moving at incredible speed, built for this terrain in a way he and Teriana weren't.

Grabbing Teriana by the waist, he lifted her. "Climb!"

She scrabbled, hands knocking loose snow that hit him in the face, then she was rising, boots pushing against his shoulders.

She was up.

Her sharp intake of breath indicated she saw the pack. Leaning over the edge, she reached down. "They're almost at the bottom! Take my hand!"

"I'll pull you off." He was already moving sideways, heading toward the tracks the wolf had made when it had climbed. "Get the door open. Get the beams ready. Go!"

Her boots thudded against the ground as she ran, but Marcus's attention was on the path the wolf had taken. A place where the ridgeline had broken, collapsing in on itself. Climbable, but he had minutes.

Maybe less.

Shoving his mittens in his belt, Marcus reached for a handhold, pushing his fingers deep into the cracks, the rock scraping his skin.

Faster.

Toes scrabbling for purchase, he climbed, stones and snow breaking loose to tumble into the gully below.

And he could hear them. The thud of paws against the ground. The soft pant of breath coming from a dozen muzzles. The scrape of claws against rocks and ice as they climbed.

Don't look.

Mist puffed in front of his face with every panicked gasp, his skin crawling with the anticipation of fangs latching onto one of his legs. Dragging him down. Tearing him apart while Teriana listened to his screams.

You're almost there.

He was at the lip of the incline, elbow digging into the snow, reaching with his other hand for something to grip. Anything.

The snow gave.

He started to slide backward.

Marcus clawed frantically for a handhold, but everything broke loose, and he was going to fall.

Then the end of a blanket slapped against the ground in front of him. "Grab hold!"

He desperately snatched the wool, climbing hand over hand, feeling the wolves beneath him. Knowing they were coming.

He rolled over the lip, scrambling to his feet. "Run!"

Teriana turned and sprinted toward the open door, Marcus six paces behind.

Don't look back.

He looked back.

Two wolves leapt over the ridge's edge, ears pinned and teeth bared, racing for the kill.

Two more strides!

He threw himself forward, rolling across the floor of the shack as Teriana slammed the door behind him and dropped a beam into place.

Bang!

One of the animals hit the door, making the whole building shake. Teriana asked, "Are you all right?"

Marcus couldn't get enough breath into his lungs to answer but managed a nod. Every inch of his body demanded that he lie on the floor and never move again, but he forced himself to scan the small space, looking for weaknesses while the wolves flung themselves against the walls, snarling their fury.

It was nearly identical to the shack they'd left behind, but the posts forming the walls were bolted to bedrock rather than embedded in the dirt. Assuming the bolts held against the onslaught, it was a mercy, because it meant the animals couldn't dig their way under.

Shoving off his satchel of supplies, Marcus opened the flue on the stove, hands shaking as he struck his knife against flint. Sparks flew into the tinder that the prior visitor had left set while Teriana stored the meat as far from the stove as possible. "We'll have to keep it cool in here tonight," he said, blowing gently on the flames. "Don't want that meat to thaw and begin to spoil."

"I know." Going to the little trap door in the wall, she opened it and then shook her head. "Wind's blown it back, and I'm not sticking my arm out."

In answer, one of the wolves stuck its nose through the opening, snarling. Teriana leapt back, then with a shriek of rage, she lunged, kicking the animal hard. It yelped and tried to recoil, but got stuck and she kicked it once more before the wolf freed itself.

"I hate you!" She screamed the words not in Cel, which was

what she normally spoke around him, but in Trader's Tongue—Mudamorian. "I wish you'd all burn in the underworld, you filthy beasts."

She slammed the trap shut, then kicked the wall violently enough that she doubled over in pain, resting her hands on her knees as she screamed in wordless anger.

Marcus didn't interrupt. Rage was good. Rage meant she'd keep fighting. Rage meant she was still with him.

Instead, he set the kettle, which he'd thankfully filled with snow earlier, on the top of the stove, then retrieved some meat to thaw for their next few meals. While she swore and kicked and shouted, he smiled when he saw that one of the jars contained a few handfuls of oats and bran, another some salt. The rest, unfortunately, were empty.

Teriana had gone to sit on the cot, the flames reflecting in her eyes and making it impossible to tell what color they were. "Is this what every day will be like? Running not only against the clock but with those animals biting at our heels?" She shook her head, braids swinging back and forth. "I'm exhausted and everything hurts and my guts feel like they are being murdered from only eating meat."

He considered telling her the side effects of a meat-only diet—which were not inconsequential—then decided to pour her a cup of water instead. If the rest of the shelters had scraps of grains and such, they might stave off the worst of it.

"I hate this." She drank the water. "All of it. I'm pissed off, and I want a proper drink, not gods-damned melted snow."

The shelter had grown warm, and Marcus stripped off his extra clothes, wrinkling his nose at the smell as he set them aside to dry.

"I want a bath!" She flung aside her mittens and hood, which Marcus hung up with his. "With soap. I've never smelled this bad in my life. And," she said, casting a baleful glare in his direction, "I want you to shave your face. There was a certain appeal to a bit of scruff, but this"—she waved a hand at his face—"is terrible."

Marcus was inclined to agree, but there wasn't a chance he was shaving it off with a belt knife and no soap. "Keeps my face warm."

She cast her eyes up at the ceiling and called him something in a language he didn't know. He suspected it wasn't flattering.

The kettle boiled, the soft whistle barely audible over the racket the wolves were making outside. Putting the grain into the lone pot, he added water, stirring it until it was an acceptable consistency, then he handed Teriana the other spoon and sat next to her on the cot. "A change for dinner."

Her mouth curved up in a smile. "Thank you."

"You're welcome."

They ate in silence, then sat elbow to elbow watching the fire burn and listening to the wolves. His legs were starting to stiffen, and Marcus knew he should stretch them or he'd be paying for it tomorrow, but instead, he asked, "Were you born on the *Quincense*?"

52

TERIANA

The question was so utterly unlike anything Marcus had ever asked her before that it snapped Teriana out of her misery, curiosity taking its place. "Why do you ask?"

"Just curious. You don't have to tell me, if you don't want to."

"Why wouldn't I want to?"

The muscles in his jaw tightened, less visible now thanks to the facial hair, but enough for her to know that he regretted asking the question. And would use silence as a way to get out of answering hers. But she didn't feel like letting him off so easily. "You've never asked me anything about my past before."

"Haven't I?"

She gave him a long look, smirking when he turned away first.

"We don't spend that much time alone and talking," he said. "Didn't seem like the sort of thing to ask you with others around."

"Interesting. Quintus asked me that very same question next to the fire with at least five of your men present. He's asked me dozens of questions about myself, as has Servius. But never you."

"Yes, well, neither of them have ever interrogated you."

He rose to his feet, refilling his water cup and drinking deeply before filling it again. "Every time I ask you something, you must wonder how I'll use what I learn against you."

"I don't think—" Teriana broke off. Because she had thought that very thought more times than she cared to count. Her past was full of secrets of her people. Of the secrets of the West. And he was too clever not to glean details that would help the legions, no matter how hard she tried to hide them. While he wouldn't use them against her right now, that might not always be the case. "Don't you worry the same thing when you tell me about your past?"

"It's not the same. You've never forced me to tell you anything. Not in the way I forced you."

It was easy to find ways in her head to excuse him. That it had been Cassius who'd ordered the interrogations. That Marcus hadn't had a choice, or at least not one that wouldn't have had significant consequences for him. That she'd have broken under the questioner's torture, so it wasn't as though the Empire wouldn't have gotten the information, with or without Marcus's involvement.

Yet a hard choice was nevertheless a choice, and he'd made his. And she wasn't certain that even if she could forgive him that she *should*.

"I shouldn't have asked you anything," he said, breaking the silence. "Forget I spoke."

As if such a thing were possible.

Not knowing why she couldn't let it go, Teriana said, "But you do *want* to know?"

"What I want is irrelevant."

"That's not what I asked."

He exhaled a long breath, then turned to meet her gaze. "If the story of your life were a book, I'd carry it with me across the world. I'd read it every night. And whenever I reached the ending of what had been shared with me, I'd open it to the first page and begin reading it again."

Teriana's eyes burned and she blinked rapidly. "It would be a very heavy book. I've had a *very* interesting life."

"It would be worth it." He crossed the shack, hands curving around the sides of her face as he bent to kiss her forehead. "Everything you tell me is a gift."

She buried her face in his throat, trying not to cry. "You must think we're about to die if you're saying things like that."

One of the wolves slammed against the side of the shack with impressive force, and Marcus pulled her against him. Held her as she dug her fingers into his shoulders, painfully exhausted but unwilling to sacrifice the moment before she had to. Then she said, "I was born on land. In my grandmother's house with all my aunts present so that the first sounds I'd hear were the songs of our people . . ."

They set out at dawn the following morning, barely making it to the next shack before dusk only to repeat the trial the next day. And the next.

And the wolves never let up.

Each night, they'd take turns attacking the shacks, snarling and barking and howling, creating a deafening cacophony that would've been impossible to sleep through even if she hadn't been in perpetual fear one of them would get inside. Every time exhaustion dragged her under, one of the wolves would shatter the silence, yanking her back into wakefulness, only to repeat the process over and over again, night after night. And like some sort of retribution delivered by the dead pack member she and Marcus were slowly consuming, the constant diet of meat took its toll on their guts, doubling both of them over with cramps that slowed them to a crawl if it didn't send them diving behind barren trees or the nearest snowbank for some semblance of privacy.

It was the purest form of misery, both of them rendered unfocused and irritable. Teriana rather thought that if they were still capable of speaking to each other after this experience, that their relationship might well survive them being enemies on the opposite side of a battlefield.

Now another dawn was upon them. They'd agreed the night before that if it were even slightly cloudy today that they'd stay put and rest rather than risk the wolves coming after them before sunset. But from the gleam of light surrounding the door, Teriana already knew she was destined for disappointment.

Lifting the crossbeams and setting them aside, Marcus opened the door, the brightness of the sun even at this early hour causing Teriana to squint. There was a fresh layer of powder coating the land around them—only a few inches—but enough, she knew, to make the going even slower.

"You indicated," she said, knowing her voice sounded like the rasp of sandpaper on wood, "that we'd be out of this pack's territory and into another's by now. You"—she coughed to clear her throat—"were wrong."

Marcus slowly turned his head, his eyes squinting and bloodshot, the grey-blue irises devoid of their usual sharpness. "By all means"—he sounded worse than she did—"please feel free to contribute any helpful information *you* might have on Sibernese wolves."

"At least I never pretended to be an expert." She glowered at him, noting that his golden Cel skin was chapped red from the wind and dryness where it wasn't covered with dirt, and worst of all, that the beard had grown. "You look like shit, by the way."

He leaned close, their eyes locked, his clearly scrutinizing hers. "You know the color of the water where the river Savio hits the sea?"

The river running through the center of Celendrial was effectively a sewer. The color it turned the ocean was not pretty. "Yes. Why?"

Her sluggish brain answered her own question a heartbeat after she asked it, but Marcus still obliged her with an exaggerated cock of one eyebrow.

"Jackass," Teriana muttered, but he was already turning to the heavy wooden icebox holding their diminishing store of meat, hoisting the satchel containing it and then starting toward the distant mile marker. She fell in next him, elbow to elbow, their feet making soft crunches in the pristine snow.

They didn't speak, each step such an act of will that there was no energy left for anything else beyond the occasional upward glance at the next mile marker.

Step.

Step.

Step.

The muscles of her legs slowly unstiffened even as her stomach cramped. Teriana pressed a hand to her abdomen, feet tripping over themselves with her loss of focus. Only Marcus catching her elbow kept her from sprawling in the snow.

Step.

Step.

Step.

They passed a mile marker, and she glanced up to read the number. *Four.* Sixteen more to go. The muscles of her face tightened with the sudden urge to cry. *Keep going.*

Step.

Step.

Step.

Her lip began to bleed where it had split from the dryness, and she licked it, tasting iron and salt. Licked it again, though she knew doing so would only make it worse. It was like a compulsion, her tongue snaking across the wound every three steps, her mind latching onto the pattern in a manic, desperate sort of way. *Stop it,* she told herself. *Just stop doing it.*

Step.

Step.

Step.

Her tongue ran over her lip, and an angry shriek filled the air. Her mind took far too long to realize the sound was coming from her. Clamping a hand over her mouth, she dropped to her knees, pressing her forehead against the snow.

"Drink some water."

Marcus was tugging on her shoulder, pushing a cup into her hand, the kettle sitting next to him in the snow. She couldn't remember him taking it from her.

"We're halfway there."

"What?" Lifting her head, she tried to focus on the number carved into the post a few paces away, but it swam in and out of focus. "I don't . . . When?" Her skull throbbed along with her abused lip, the pulse the same rhythm her steps had been. "I'm losing my mind."

"Halfway there." He lifted her hand so that the metal of her cup pressed against her lips. "You only need to repeat what you've already accomplished once today."

I can't.

"Drink."

She swallowed the cold water, droplets running down her chin.

"Can you eat?"

She gagged in response, only her clenched teeth keeping the water from coming back up as she pressed her forehead back in the snow. "How do you keep going?"

"I've been marching most of my life." He tugged the satchel of supplies she carried off her shoulders and onto his. "I'm used to it. Now up."

I can't.

"You can." He hauled her to her feet. "One step at a time. One mile at a time. Now *walk*."

The sun flew across the sky even as time seemed to crawl, each step a lifetime.

The world faded in and out of focus, her vision pulsing, her head throbbing, her lip bleeding. She'd lost track of the number of times she found herself on her hands and knees in the snow with no memory of falling. Of the times Marcus had forced water down her throat and then hauled her back to her feet. She couldn't remember when he'd pulled her arm over his shoulder, only that it was there now, him half-carrying her as they staggered up and down the rolling hills.

And behind them, the sun was setting.

Teriana's toe caught on something hidden beneath the snow, and she staggered, dragging Marcus down with her.

"It's only two more miles."

His voice sounded distant, and though she knew he was tugging on her arm, it was as though she were watching it from outside her own body, not feeling it. She was upright, but her knees wouldn't hold, wobbling and bending and buckling beneath her.

"Come on, Teriana!"

She tried to rise, but the effort made her retch, muscles twisting with spasms, her stomach forcing up bitter bile even as the fit consumed what little strength she had left.

"Get up!"

The snow was soft. Inviting. She curled in on herself, knees under her chin, vaguely aware of Marcus pleading for her to keep going, of the fear in his voice. But sleep was beckoning her. If she could just rest for a few minutes—

A howl split the air, pulling her back to consciousness.

"Teriana, they're coming! We need to go!"

Marcus had her under the arms, was dragging her through the snow. But he only made it a few yards before he stumbled and fell, rising to his feet only to repeat the motion.

They wouldn't make it like this. The wolves were too fast.

"Go." She whispered the word. "Just go. Get back to Celendrial and make Cassius free my people."

"No!" He gasped out the word. "That's something you need to do."

"Please." They were both going to die out here if he stayed. And that meant her captured people were doomed. That her mother was doomed. "Please go."

"I'm not leaving you."

"Please!" she sobbed, even as the air once again filled with howls, the noise coming from all directions and none.

"No!" He was in her face, tears running down his cheeks. "It's two miles, Teriana! Are you going to condemn your family because you couldn't find the energy to crawl two bloody miles?"

She looked away, because it might as well have been two hundred. She had nothing left.

The howls were louder now. She didn't know why the wolves were being so loud when before they'd always pursued in silence. Perhaps it was because they knew revenge was in sight.

"Your family needs you." Marcus's lips pressed against her forehead. "*I* need you."

Get up.

She rolled onto her hands and knees.

Move.

She climbed to her feet.

Fight.

The soft thud of paws filled the air, and fear pushed through her exhaustion, adrenaline giving her some strength.

But it was too late.

The wolves were coming up from behind them, minutes away. Seconds.

Marcus pulled his weapon, and Teriana fumbled for her knife, clenching the hilt as she turned.

There were a dozen of them, shapes outlined by the dying rays of the sun. The front-runners bunched their legs, teeth glinting—

Then something shot past Teriana from behind. Wolves, fur black against the white of the snow, raced around her and Marcus, colliding with their pursuers with snarls and flashing teeth.

Another pack.

Teriana stared, fixated on the fight between the enormous creatures, but Marcus pulled on her arm. "This is our chance. Can you walk?"

With the battle raging behind them, Teriana did better than walk. She ran.

53

LYDIA

Being back among the Maarin was both a balm to her soul and a knife to the heart, for as they journeyed, the captain told both her and Dareena what they knew of the fate of the Maarin imprisoned in the Empire, as well as the status of the Empire's incursion into Arinoquia. And for her part, Lydia told them her own story, Lena and Gwen listening with wide eyes as she explained her flight through the xenthier stem, her meeting Killian, and the deal they'd made.

Of Teriana, the Maarin knew little. Only that she was alive and kept under close guard at all times. But not entirely helpless.

"She managed to secrete a letter out of their camp by way of a healer," the captain said. "Took some time, but it eventually reached the right hands in Revat." She gave a rueful shrug. "Kaira rounded up every crew in port at the time and threatened to fill our ships with pig shit if we didn't break Madoria's mandate and tell her all that we knew."

Dareena burst into laughter. "Kaira is a delight."

"She's a force not to be denied," the captain agreed. "Her intent was to turn her eyes to defeating the invaders, but I fear those plans suffered catastrophic disruption with the loss of the fleet in Mudaire's harbor."

"That is no coincidence," Dareena muttered, rubbing her chin. "Lydia, if the legions were to discover and control xenthier paths they could use, how many soldiers could they send to Arinoquia?"

Lydia bit her lip, considering. "They won't be rash," she finally said. "They are methodical and strategic in their conquest, and the Senate won't risk losing control of the provinces for the sake of gaining new territory."

"A number, Lydia."

She cursed herself for not having paid more attention to her father's discussions with his peers. "Ten legions. Somewhere between forty and fifty thousand trained soldiers."

Dareena's eyes went distant, then she shook her head. "Kaira could hold back that many. They only have a handful of ships, which means they would need to go by land, and the terrain is bad." Pointing on the map in front of them, she said, "This is all mangrove swamps, so they can't march up the coast. They'd have to cross between the swamps and the Uncharted Lands."

"And then they'd need to get across the Orinok," the captain said, naming the massive river that formed Gamdesh's southern border. "It isn't bridged, which means they'd have to ferry all their soldiers and supplies across. Seems to me their commander picked a poor location to set down roots."

Unlikely, Lydia thought, shivering at the reference to the man who'd tried to murder her. "He'll probably build a bridge."

Dareena made a noncommittal noise, her brow furrowed, and Lydia quickly said, "Don't discount the young man in command of the legions. He's tremendously clever, known to win as often with guile as with force. He's as great a threat as Rufina, of that you can be sure. And . . ." She swallowed.

"And . . . ," Dareena pressed.

"Ten legions is only the beginning of what they could rally, if they thought the prize worth the risks," Lydia said. "They could send another hundred thousand men."

Dareena's eyes flicked to the captain. "Is this so?"

The man nodded, his black braids swaying around his face. "Why do you suppose we went to such lengths to keep the West secret from them?"

"But a secret no longer," Dareena said. "And unless we unite to fight back, the heart of the West will soon be pinned between an army of the godless"—her eyes flicked to Lydia—"and an army of the undead."

Using a xenthier path located at sea, the Maarin ship had delivered Lydia to a small port town on the southern coast of Mudamora only days after leaving Mudaire. "I'll carry on to Serlania to rally the High Lords," Dareena had said. "You ride fast to Rotahn and track down Killian—it's a well-traveled road, so you'll be safe enough. If your theory about tenders and the blight is correct, we need Malahi. And he's best equipped to get her back."

Now Lydia stood outside the fortress city of Rotahn as black storm clouds raced west toward the distant mountains, the smell of coming rain heavy in the air.

Stone walls encircled the fortress city, with soldiers in red uniforms patrolling the parapets, their eyes watchful. A steady stream of traffic flowed through the central gate, the soldiers inspecting both people and their carts.

Is he here?

Lydia's heart skipped, then her pulse sped at the thought Killian might be on the other side of those walls, and she wasn't certain whether she was excited or terrified. Possibly both.

You're here to tell him about Malahi, she silently reminded herself. *You're here because you need him to help you rescue her.*

But the reminder couldn't erase the countless hours of daydreams she'd had where their reunion had an entirely different focus. Daydreams where she'd felt his lips on hers, desire curling hot in her belly as she imagined his hands on her body, what it would be like to have him peel the clothes from her skin. What it would be like to have *him.*

"He is not yours!" she snarled under her breath. "And falling into a bed with Killian isn't why you're here."

Digging her heels into her horse's sides, she cantered toward the line of traffic, falling in with the people who'd come to market.

As she reached the guards at the gate, she pulled back the white hood of her robes, watching as they inclined their heads.

"Marked One," the taller man said, "you need not have waited with the common folk."

"It was no trouble," she answered, feeling distinctly uncomfortable with the way everyone was eyeing her with reverence. "I need to speak with Lord Calorian. Can you direct me to him?"

The man's face shadowed, and unease filled Lydia's chest. His reaction reminded her of how people had reacted to Killian before he'd won at Alder's Ford. Back when they blamed him for the invasion. "General Calorian is in his camp north of here," he answered. "But you'll need an escort to make the journey."

"I'll manage on my own, thank you."

He shook his head. "The conflict with the Anuk is worse than it has been in a generation," he said. "They've been attacking Mudamorians near the border, and while they wouldn't hurt a healer, they'd take you. You need an escort, which I'm certain Lady Ria would be glad to arrange."

Lady Ria was King Serrick's niece and Malahi's cousin, and Lydia had little interest in speaking to her. But if what this man said were true, perhaps it was the prudent path. "Very well."

The soldier assigned an escort to take her to the palace, which was a monstrous building that would have fit in well in Celendrial. A liveried stableboy hurried out to take her horse as another servant came swiftly down the steps, crimson towel across her arms, a golden basin held in one hand. "Marked One," the woman said as the first drops of rain fell from the sky, splatting against the ground, swiftly turning to a downpour as they moved inside.

"My name is . . ." Lydia hesitated, because the last thing she needed was word of her presence making it back to Rufina. "Gwen. I seek Lady Ria, as I need an escort to General Calorian's camp."

"I will take you to her ladyship directly, Marked One," the servant answered, leading her through the hallways, which were rich with the smell of scented oils. Her boots thudded on the tiles, which were a gold-veined marble, the endless alcoves filled with artwork in golden frames.

The woman took her to a courtyard garden filled with fountains and flowers, though the sound of them was drowned out by the roar of falling rain. And standing out in the middle of it, her hair plastered to her face and her gown soaked, was a woman.

"My lady?" the servant asked hesitantly, this behavior clearly unexpected. "One of the Marked is here to see you. Healer Gwen."

The woman lowered her face from the storm, a smile moving to her lips. "Welcome, Marked One. What a glorious moment for you to have arrived. Gespurn has blessed us with early-winter rains, which mark the end of the season of war with the Anuk. Tonight, we will celebrate."

Rain or not, celebrations weren't in order, because the Anuk were the least of Mudamora's concerns. But Lydia inclined her head. "Thank you for your hospitality, my lady. But in truth, I seek only an escort to General Calorian's camp."

"He is in no need of healers," the woman answered, stepping under the cover of the building and accepting a towel from a servant. "The rains make passage through the mountains nearly impossible for the next two months, so his camp will be idle. You could do more good helping those in need within the city, as we've long been deprived of a healer's touch."

She didn't have time for this. But before Lydia could open her mouth to politely insist on an escort, the bellow of a horn split the air, making her jump. "What was that?"

Ria blanched. "Impossible. They wouldn't dare."

A heartbeat later, a soldier strode rapidly down the corridor toward them. "My lady," he said, inclining his head. "Marked One.

Excuse the interruption, but we've received word that a significant force of Anuk is on the march toward the mines."

"That's impossible."

"They're coming, my lady. Visibility is bad due to the rains, but estimates put their force between two and three thousand."

Ria's eyes widened. "The Six help us . . ."

"General Calorian has moved to intercept, but he's requested reinforcements. I've men gathering, ready to ride at your order."

"Do it. Then have the gates closed and our walls manned in case Rotahn is attacked." Ria turned on Lydia. "If you are agreeable, I'd have you go with our forces with all haste. Our losses are destined to be catastrophic."

Lydia's blood chilled. "Why do you say that?"

"Because," Ria answered. "Until reinforcements arrive, General Calorian is outnumbered three to one."

54

KILLIAN

The scent of rain was thick in the air, the storm rolling in from the south ready to break against the mountains, where it would then dump all the water it carried with it onto the dry ground.

If only it had come a day sooner.

Finn raced toward him, a full quiver flopping on his back, which he handed to Killian.

"You stay here," he ordered his young friend. "If we call for retreat, you head with the rest of the camp to Rotahn, understood?"

Finn scowled. "I can fight. You know I can."

"Not this time." He caught Finn by the shoulders. "You will abide. And if I catch you disobeying me, we're through."

"Fine." The word was clipped, the boy's eyes shadowed.

"We're ready to move out, sir!" one of his men shouted over the thunder. Killian nodded, slinging his quiver over his shoulder. But then in his periphery, he saw a large winged shape fall from the sky. Turning, he watched the enormous hawk land on the ground, its outline moving like liquid until what stood before him was not a bird, but a man.

A man he knew.

"Niotin?" The shifter lived in the north and scouted for Dareena. What in the name of the Six was he doing in Rotahn?

"Killian." The shifter panted for breath, his eyes bloodshot and hooded, one hand braced against a hitching post. "I've fell news from the King."

His blood turned to ice. "What's happened?"

"The blighters overran Hegeria's temple," Niotin said between breaths. "The King and the Royal Army have regained control of the city, but the losses were devastating."

He couldn't breathe.

"The King gave me orders to relay: you are to remain in Rotahn and hold the border against the Anuk at all costs. We cannot afford to lose ground against them."

The words were nothing but noise. "Devastating," he repeated. "The healers . . ."

"All dead." Niotin scrubbed at his eyes. "I was there for their last rites. Rows and rows of them, all dead. And Dareena is missing." His voice cracked. "Serrick fears her lost."

All dead.

A dull roar filled his ears, the world around him growing brighter and brighter.

Lydia is dead.

And he'd known she'd been in danger. Known that she needed his help, but instead of being there to protect her, he'd been caught up in Ria's and Serrick's plots. Had been slaughtering Anuk raiders when he should've been fighting to save everything he loved.

Twisting away from Niotin and Finn, he stumbled to his knees, retching into the mud.

She's dead.

Dimly, he heard Sonia's voice. Finn's frantic explanation of what was wrong. But none of it mattered.

"Killian." Sonia was next to him. "Your pain is my pain, but we must go. The Anuk are less than an hour away."

"She's dead." Tears flooded down his cheeks. "I should've been there."

Sonia pulled him against her, his forehead pressing against her armored shoulder. "I grieve for her. She was my friend. But we cannot abandon the living for the sake of our grief. The Anuk come for vengeance, and they won't care that the harm done to their people was at the hands of only Ria and her minions—all living in and near Rotahn will fall to their blades."

Lydia is dead. He squeezed his eyes shut, seeing her face. Seeing those green eyes that had captivated his soul from the moment he'd first set eyes upon them. "You take the men. You lead. I can't . . ."

"You must." She pushed him back, then gripped the sides of his face and forced him to look at her. "We need you. Do not dishonor everything Lydia fought for by giving up now."

Get up.

The command echoed in his head, and though he wasn't sure who'd given it, he obeyed. "Let's go."

They raced up the steep paths leading into the hills, the mountains forming the border barely visible through the thick clouds, the air streaked grey with the deluge of rain falling upon them. The endless narrow streambeds that wove down from the peaks would no longer be dry, instead filled with debris and water, merging together into rivers as they flowed toward the great washes that drained onto the plains.

"What's the plan?" Sonia gasped out between breaths, struggling to keep pace with him.

"Pick our ground," he replied. "There are two flood paths they have to cross. If we can hold them to the far side long enough for the water to make its way down the mountains, they won't be able to cross. They'll either have to retreat or approach over higher ground, and by then, we'll have our reinforcements."

They hurried along the path, the rain overhead turning the rocky ground slick and treacherous. Lightning flashed, and ahead, he saw his men formed up along the high banks of a narrow streambed, perhaps eight feet across. It was still dry, but with water flooding down from the mountains, it wouldn't be long until it turned into a raging torrent.

Except the water wasn't going to come soon enough.

Racing down the rocky trail were hundreds of Anuk warriors, and they were only the front-runners of the force headed toward Killian's men.

Far more than they could ever hope to hold back.

The Anuk caught sight of his force, screaming their war cries as they pulled their weapons. They were here for vengeance for what Ria had done, and it would take more than rain and floods to hold them back.

His soldiers parted, allowing Killian to move to the front of their ranks. Lifting his weapon, he shouted, "Shields!"

A heartbeat later, his ears picked up a whistling sound, and the sky turned from grey to black, deadly arrows raining down.

The loud *thunks* of arrows striking shields were drowned out by the screams where they'd found flesh, and all around him, Killian saw his men dropping. "Archers, loose!" he roared over the sound, lifting his own bow and taking down three Anuk.

But those coming from behind only leapt over the bodies of the fallen, holding shields over their heads as they sped toward the bank.

"The flood is coming!" Sonia shouted from where she knelt next to him. And when Killian risked looking upstream, his eyes latched upon a dark mass rolling down the streambed. Not water, but a monstrous tangle of trees and branches and debris being pushed by the floodwaters, dark fingers reaching ahead of the main mass like it was some strange sentient beast.

And if this stream were flooding, the riverbed Killian and his men had crossed to get here would flood next. They had to get to the far side of it, or his men would be caught between raging bodies of water.

"Retreat!" He repeated the order, fighting to be heard over the thunder and ominous snapping of branches as the deadly tide surged down the streambed. "Retreat to the far side of the next flood path!"

Holding a shield over his head, he caught Sonia's arm. "You must hold the river, or we're lost. Leave me ten men to buy you time."

"What about you?" his friend demanded. "I'm not leaving you here to get killed!"

"Go!" he shouted, even as he chose those who'd stand with him. Who'd probably die with him. "I'll give you the count of fifty and then we'll follow."

At least his men would.

"Dying isn't going to bring her back!"

If only it would, he'd die a hundred times over. A thousand. "You're in command, Sonia. You let these soldiers die because you're busy arguing with me, that's on *you*."

Indecision rolled across her face, and then she was screaming orders, the Rowenes soldiers moving rapidly backward, shields up against the endless barrage of arrows.

One. Two. Three. He started the count in his head.

"We keep as many as we can to the far side of the stream," he said to those who remained with him, and then he pulled his sword. His shield shuddered, already bristled with arrows. Another thirty seconds and the deadly tide of water and debris would fill the banks in front of him.

Eight. Nine. Ten.

The front-runners raced across the dry bed, screaming their fury as they attacked. Killian met them, hacking and slicing, men falling back into the streambed only to be replaced by more. And more.

Eighteen. Nineteen. Twenty.

Then the flood struck.

The Anuk caught in its way were pulled under the nightmarish mess of shattered trees and mud and water, dashed to death before they could drown. But it didn't stop them from coming.

In twos and threes, they leapt the eight-foot gap between banks, heedless of the danger rushing beneath them despite dozens of them falling into the murk.

Twenty-nine. Thirty. Thirty-one.

Killian kept fighting, taking down those who made it across even as he saw warriors on the far side lifting felled tree trunks, dropping them across the deadly stream to form bridges, the flood flowing just beneath them as they raced across.

Where they met his sword.

Killian lost himself to the swing of his weapon, the crash of steel a music accompanied by the roar of the thunder.

Forty-two. Forty-three. Forty-four.

He'd thought he would be the only one alive by now, but four of his soldiers remained. Fighting. Holding their ground. Waiting for his order.

Forty-nine. He silently cursed the gods, then shouted, "Retreat!"

As one, they twisted and broke into a sprint, racing down the rocky trail toward the distant river, which would be impassable in a matter of minutes. An arrow skipped off his armored shoulder, and next to him, one of his men dropped, fletching jutting from the back of his head. "Run!"

He hazarded a glance backward, seeing Anuk swarming across the makeshift bridges or losing patience and leaping the gap.

His men sprinted down the trail, and in the distance, Killian could make out Sonia and her line of soldiers holding the far bank of the riverbed. It was empty still, but upstream, another, far larger flood of debris was surging its way down. "Run!" he shouted at his men. "Get to the far side!"

One of them dropped, an arrow in his back. Another tripped and nearly went down, an arrow embedded in his leg.

They weren't going to make it.

Skidding to a stop, Killian sheathed his sword and unslung his bow. In rapid motion, he picked off the Anuk archers shooting at his men. Only their eyes were visible between the folds of their scarves, but it was enough for him to see when they recognized him, their determination turning to fury.

Glancing back, Killian saw his men had reached the flood path. That Sonia's force was helping them across. Another minute and the flood would pass through, and this time, tree trunks wouldn't be enough to cross it. But a minute was more than enough time for hundreds of Anuk to reach the opposite bank.

"Killian!" Sonia screamed. "Run!"

Ignoring her, he tossed aside his bow, picking up a fallen shield and drawing his sword.

One after another after another they attacked, more interested in killing him than getting across, all dying beneath his blade, their weapons clanging against his shield, against his mail, though a few found their marks. His body ached with exhaustion, blood running from his temple and down his wrists.

Then a heavy weight slammed against his back.

Killian rolled, nearly losing his weapon as he grappled with the warrior. He punched the man in the face, then pulled a knife and stabbed him twice, but it was too late.

They were racing past, running to get across the river ahead of the flood. To have their vengeance on Rotahn despite there being only one woman within the walls that deserved their wrath.

He tried to gain his feet, but another warrior knocked him down, forcing him to fight his way free.

And when he lifted his head, the riverbed was swarming with Anuk, shields held over their heads to protect themselves from Mudamorian archers.

Sonia was shooting arrow after arrow, fighting to hold them back. But she stopped to meet his gaze, her mouth forming the word *Run!*

He didn't want to.

Climbing to his feet, he turned his back, ready to die fighting. Ready to die with honor.

"Killian!" Sonia's voice sounded strangely like Lydia's, and his chest tightened, the pain almost unbearable. All he knew was that wherever she was, he needed to follow. And that the path wasn't behind him, but ahead.

55

LYDIA

Lydia had never ridden this fast in her life.

She focused on keeping her seat on the back of the horse, allowing it to follow the men rather than attempting to guide it over the unfamiliar ground that was revealed only when lightning lanced across the sky. Then ahead, she caught sight of what must be the mining camp, lanterns swinging wildly on their posts, figures moving at a run between the buildings.

The soldiers bypassed it, heading into the hills at the base of the mountains that were barely visible behind the haze of falling rain.

And that's when she saw it.

In between the flashes of lightning, she could make out clouds of swirling mist drifting up from the hills. More than she'd ever seen at one time, and her chest tightened at the realization of where it was coming from. It was where the battle was being waged, and soldiers must be dying by the hundreds.

And Killian was up there.

"Lydia?"

A familiar voice shouted her name, and she twisted in her saddle to see Finn standing a few paces away holding the reins of several horses, his eyes wide with astonishment. "But you're dead. The message that came today said all the healers in the temple when it was overrun were killed."

"Not all," she answered. "High Lady Falorn got me out."

"He thinks you're dead." Hauling on the reins of the horses, Finn closed the distance between them. "Killian. He entirely lost his head when he received the message."

Lydia's heart skipped, icy fear pooling in her stomach. "Where is he?"

A question with an obvious answer, and yet when Finn pointed at the path the soldiers had taken, toward that terrifying swirl of life and death, a sob still tore from her lips.

Then she dug in her heels, sending her horse galloping after the soldiers.

Her horse stumbled and slid, but she cracked the ends of her reins against his shoulder to drive him faster, heading toward the great swirls of life given off by the dead and the dying.

The rain's ferocity increased, soaking her clothes and turning the ground into a slippery mess of mud. She leapt her mount across narrow streams of brown water, her reckless speed pulling her ahead of the reinforcements, who shouted at her to check her pace. But she couldn't. Killian was in that battle, and the fear she'd seen in Finn's eyes told her that he might not be trying to survive it.

Lightning flashed, revealing a group of men ahead of her. And before the thunder rolled, she made out the screams.

Please don't let me be too late, she pleaded to the gods. *Please don't let him be dead.*

And then she reached the rear of the Mudamorian force, the vantage her horse gave her allowing Lydia to see over their heads. The riverbed was full of warriors dressed in the colors of the desert, their faces veiled and their weapons gleaming with blood.

Then Lydia heard a noise that turned her blood cold.

A roar punctuated by cracks and snaps of breaking tree limbs, and her eyes moved upstream to see a monstrous black mass surged toward them. For a heartbeat, she thought it was blight, then realized it was a tide of deadfall being pushed downstream by the floodwaters.

"The Six have mercy," she whispered, ripping her gaze from the beast to search for Killian, her eyes finding Sonia. Her ears hearing the other woman scream Killian's name.

And then lightning flashed again, and she saw him.

He was bloodied and surrounded by warriors, who threw themselves against him one after another only to drop and die at his feet. But there were so many.

Too many.

"Killian!" she screamed, her voice desperate and shrill. And though the thunder roared and the air was filled with shouts and screams and the clash of weapons, he lifted his head, hearing her.

"Run!" she screamed, knowing he could make it ahead of the flood if he tried. Instead, he turned back to face the enemy.

"Get back!" someone shouted. "The flood is on us!"

Lydia's eyes skipped to the rolling black tide of death. Then to Killian.

She dug in her heels.

56

KILLIAN

A blow caught him against the back, and he fell, fighting to regain his feet, but the Anuk were pressing in on all sides.

And then they were stepping back from him. Flexing his fingers on the pommel of his sword, Killian rose to find they'd retreated to form a half-moon around him, the Anuk warriors using shields to deflect arrows coming from Sonia and the rest.

"So we meet again, Lord Calorian."

A familiar voice reached his ears, and Killian watched as the Anuk boy who'd told him of Ria's treachery stepped out from the ranks of warriors, lowering the scarf covering his face.

Between panting breaths, Killian said, "You neglected to introduce yourself last time, boy."

The warriors shifted angrily, but the boy only shrugged. "I suppose it fitting that you should know the name of the one to kill you. I am Prince Xadrian."

A hundred retorts rose to Killian's lips, but he bit down on all of them. Because this boy had the power to stop the war Ria had begun.

That he had begun.

"This fight will hurt Mudamora and Anukastre both," Killian said. "You need to retreat. We need to resolve this with words, not swords."

"Says the man who's been slaughtering my people!" The Prince lifted his weapons. "You talk of words now only because this is a battle you won't win."

"It wasn't me." Killian lowered his own weapon. "It was the actions of a few who seek to manipulate politics in Mudamora. To manipulate me. These soldiers and the people they defend are innocent."

"The actions of Ria Rowenes, you mean." The boy looked at him in disgust. "Your men told us as much before we executed them for their crimes. They also told us that *you* were her lover and would do anything to please her." He spit on the ground in front of Killian. "You blaspheme your mark, Dark Horse."

Killian closed his eyes, his hatred for Ria making his blood boil. "She lies. As did they."

"This is what you get for allying with the scorpion!" The Prince knocked an arrow from the air with his sword before it could strike him. Marked by Tremon as surely as Killian was himself. "Now let us discover which of us Tremon favors to live."

Not me. "Take your vengeance, then."

Alarmed shouts reached Killian's ears. A second later, a horse leapt up the bank right before a flood of deadly debris rushed past. The horse landed awkwardly, hindquarters sliding sideways on the wet rock, the animal nearly going down. Hooves scrambling, it righted itself, then gave a violent buck, sending its rider flying through the air. She landed on her ass right in front of Killian.

Prince Xadrian stared at the white-robed woman in astonishment as she climbed to her feet, and then Lydia shouted, "If you want to kill him, you're going to have to kill me first!"

Shock froze Killian in place. *She's alive.*

She's here.

Killian vaguely heard whispers moving through the Anuk ranks as they recognized her as a healer. As one of Hegeria's Marked. But none of that mattered, because she was here and she was alive. And gods help him, but she was now in danger because of him. "Lydia, get back!"

Xadrian's eyes narrowed, and then he shouted, "Capture the healer! And then kill General Calorian!"

Killian caught hold of Lydia's arm, trying to pull her behind him, but she resisted. "They won't shoot me," she said between her teeth. "But they seem rather keen on killing *you.*"

"I have armor on!" And the last thing he needed was one of the Anuk archers growing restless and accidentally hurting her to get at him.

"Instead of arguing, perhaps think of a way out of this that doesn't see either of us dead!"

Killian allowed his mind to race, abandoning plans even as he came up with them. He'd caught himself in this trap not thinking he'd need a way out, but now everything had changed.

In his periphery, he could see the Anuk flanking him, could hear them debating whether the deadly river could be bridged. They lifted one of the tree trunks they'd used to cross the other river, but it fell far shy of the opposite bank, catching up against a rock in the middle of the flow.

"You come with us, and you'll be treated with the respect you deserve," Xadrian said to Lydia. "Not as a slave to the scorpion king."

"My thanks for the offer," Lydia answered, as though he'd invited her to a party. "But I'm afraid I'll have to decline."

The Prince gave a frustrated shake of his head, then pulled his veil back over his face so that only his eyes were visible before striding forward, obviously intent on being the one to end Killian's life. "What sort of coward uses a healer as a shield?" he shouted.

Killian tensed, but Lydia snapped, "Don't you dare rise to the bait!" Then under her breath, "Please tell me you have a plan."

He most definitely did not.

Hundreds of Anuk surrounded them, and behind them flowed a river of death.

The tree.

One end of it was caught on the rocky bank, the other against a boulder near the middle of the flow. It shuddered against the pressure of the flood; it was only a matter of time until it broke.

Which meant he needed to be quick.

Killian took a few steps back, pulling Lydia with him. "I've got you," he muttered, sliding his sword into its sheath. Then he stepped onto the bobbing tree trunk, which sank beneath his weight.

All around, muddy water full of detritus surged fast and deadly. To fall would mean almost instant death.

Holding Lydia by the shoulders to balance her, he took step after careful step, feeling her shaking beneath his grasp. Another tree struck the one they were on, and she lurched sideways, but he pulled her upright. "Halfway there," he muttered, then an arrow glanced off his mail, the impact causing him to rock sideways.

"Don't shoot at him!" Xadrian shouted. "If he falls, he'll take her with him!"

Killian took another step, holding Lydia tightly as she eased one booted foot back along the slick wood. Then under his hands, he felt her tense. "Hurry!" she gasped. "The trunk is breaking. I can see the split."

Crack.

Killian twisted, managing two steps before the tree snapped. Flipping Lydia over his shoulder, he jumped.

His boots hit the slick boulder in the middle of the river, and he nearly slid off the far side, Lydia screaming as he struggled to keep his balance, eyes on the deadfall flowing around them. An island of safety, though if the water rose any higher, they'd be swept away.

Setting Lydia down in front of him, he kept an arm wrapped

around her, but she moved so she stood between him and the Anuk. Protecting him when it should've been the other way around.

As if sensing his thoughts, she shouted over the noise. "Don't even think it, Killian! You do anything foolish and I'll push you in the river myself!"

Most of the debris had passed, but now brown water roared around them, surging over the rock and soaking his boots. The battle resumed, arrows flying back and forth, both sides taking casualties. No one could help them.

And the river was rising.

Think! he screamed at himself as the water rose above the boulder, now ankle deep. *You got her into this, now get her out.*

Prickles raced up his skin, and looking upstream, he saw a large tree floating rapidly toward them. Twisting, he looked downstream at the ravine the river flowed into, his eyes fixing on the jagged rocks protruding from the walls.

"Give me your belt!" he shouted.

"Pardon?"

Reaching down, he pulled Lydia's belt loose, then formed a loop with it. And as the tree shot past, he said, "Jump!"

Together, they leapt into the muddy water, catching hold of the tree and hurtling downstream. Debris slammed into his legs, tangling in his ankles, but Killian kept his eyes fixed on the ravine walls, Lydia's belt in his hand.

"Hold on to me!" he shouted, then tossed the loop high, the leather catching around an outcropping.

His arm nearly jerked out of its socket as the belt pulled taut. Lydia shrieked, losing her grip around his neck. He caught her robes, swearing as they slid up over her head, but then her hand latched on his sword belt.

"Hold on!" He discarded the garment in the flow, wincing as a tree struck him, nearly tearing them loose. He had to get them up.

Catching hold of Lydia's belt with his other hand, Killian heaved, dragging them both upward. Hand over hand, he pulled them higher, Lydia clinging to his sword belt, which was sliding dangerously low on his hips.

Lightning crackled and thunder boomed, more water falling from the sky, and he silently cursed Gespurn even as he prayed for respite. His toes found a crack in the cliff wall, and he wedged his foot in deep. Then twisting the belt around his wrist, he let go with his other hand and reached down for Lydia. "Grab hold of me!"

Beneath him, she was still mostly submerged, gasping in pain every time a piece of deadfall struck her, her arms trembling as she fought to keep her grip on his belt.

"Lydia!"

She looked up, eyes full of pain. And determination.

Gods, but he loved her.

Letting go of his belt, she reached up, her hand closing over his wrist.

He heaved, lifting her out of the water, his body trembling until she managed to clamber up him, her bare legs wrapped around his waist, arms around his neck.

"Hold on!"

Reaching up, he caught hold of the outcropping, pulling them higher. Finding toeholds that would support his weight.

And there he stayed.

Twenty paces away, the battle still raged on, the Anuk trying to get across, Sonia and the Royal Army repelling their every advance. But none of that mattered.

She was alive. She was here.

Letting go with one hand, he wrapped his arm around her, pulling her close. Feeling her cheek against his, her hand cold where it pressed against his neck. "I won't let you fall."

"I know." Her breath was warm against his ear. "And you never will."

Though they were still on the brink of death, Killian felt something akin to regret as he heard Sonia's voice from above, a rope falling for them to climb, hands grabbing hold of him and Lydia, hauling them to safety.

57

LYDIA

Her return to Killian's camp was a blur.

After Sonia and the Rowenes soldiers had pulled them up, they'd parted ways. Lydia hadn't wanted to leave him, not when she'd just come so close to losing him. But Killian needed to resume command of his forces, and her assistance with the injured was required, for there were many.

And even more dead.

Dressed only in boots and a rain-soaked shift, her robes lost to the river, she'd gratefully accepted a cloak from one of the soldiers and then set to work stabilizing the worst of the injured so they could be transported back to camp. A strange form of detachment fell over her as she worked, her eyes for the injury but not the suffering, life slipping from her fingertips to stop bleeding and bolster stuttering hearts even as the cloud of swirling life shed by the dead, the dying, and even the living flowed toward her like iron to a lodestone.

As awful a place as it was to work, stepping over severed limbs and pools of blood and still corpses, there was also something right about using the life sacrificed by the fallen in order to save their faltering comrades, and she saw now that her fears of this circumstance had been misguided. This was where she was meant to be. What she was meant to do.

It was what would come next that terrified her.

Rising, she wiped her hands on her ruined shift, then nodded at the waiting soldiers to lift the man on the ground before her, the gaping wound in his guts sealed over, though he'd require more attention if he were to live. A wave of dizziness passed over her, and she swayed.

Another soldier caught at her elbow. "General Calorian gave orders that we bring you to the barracks to rest, Marked One."

"Call me Lydia, please." She'd be glad to be gone from the Rowenes lands if for no other reason than to be free of that ridiculous honorific. "I'll travel with the wounded, then remain with them."

"He suggested you'd say as much," the man answered, still holding her elbow as though she might topple over at any moment. "He asked that I inform you that there are others waiting who are more than capable of helping the injured."

Extracting her elbow from his grip, she crossed her arms. "But no one marked."

The soldier sighed, looking as though he wished he were anywhere other than here, having this conversation. "General Calorian implied you'd say that, too. He said, and pardon my words, Marked One, for I'm merely repeating him, but: 'Tell her if she doesn't listen that I'll come find her myself, haul her back to camp, and lock her in a bedroom until she gets proper rest.'"

There was an aspect of the threat that was undeniably enticing, but Lydia only sniffed and said, "He's welcome to try," then started down the path, following the lantern light of those carrying the injured.

It took over an hour for them to reach the barracks, which were a flurry of activity, but she was greeted by a familiar face.

"Finn!" Closing the distance between them, she wrapped her arms around his skinny shoulders, holding him tight. Though the length of time it had been since she'd seen him could be measured in weeks, it seemed as though he'd grown taller, perhaps slightly broader of shoulder. But the greatest change was his expression, a seriousness to him that hadn't been there back in Mudaire.

"It's good to see you," he said, squeezing her hard enough that her ribs ached. "Things will be better with you here, they always are."

Her skin crawled with unease. Less for his words than for the relief in his voice, making her question what precisely had gone so wrong in her absence.

Then Finn stepped back. "I'll take you to get cleaned up. Arrange for some clothes and whatnot—can't have you walking about a camp full of soldiers wearing *that*. Especially not with old lady legs."

Lydia curbed the urge to kick him in the shins, instead twitching her borrowed cloak more tightly around her body. A quick glance at her braid revealed a mixture of black and silver. The years she'd given up to save the wounded soldiers were coming back to her, though not nearly as quickly as she liked.

She followed Finn through the heavily fortified camp. He led her to a large stone building, pulling open the heavy doors to reveal two narrow rooms to either side full of weapons and gear. Beyond was a large room with several tables littered with maps and papers, and on the far side, a corridor. "This is the officers' barracks," Finn explained. "You can use Killian's rooms to get cleaned up. He won't mind."

Lydia's heart skipped, her skin flushing ever so slightly, but she only nodded as Finn took her to the room at the end, unlatched the door, and pulled it open.

To reveal an absolute disaster of a mess.

There were clothes on the floor and hanging across the backs of chairs, as though they'd been pulled off, tossed aside, then forgotten. The table had no fewer than eight dirty glasses, three empty wine bottles, and a stack of dirty dishes, at least one of which was starting to grow mold. The bedclothes were in total disarray, the wardrobe doors were open, and every which way she looked were bits of armor and weapons, the blades the *only* things in the entire mess that didn't appear in need of a good cleaning.

Finn hesitated, then an apologetic grimace rose on his face. "Umm, sorry for the mess. I haven't had much time to do any cleaning."

Lydia stepped over a muddy pair of boots in the middle of the floor. "Why are *you* responsible for cleaning up after him?"

The grimace turned to a grin. "Because he made me his squire! He's teaching me how to fight, but in exchange, I'm supposed to clean up and whatnot."

From the looks of it, the *whatnot* had taken extreme priority over the cleaning up, but the boy seemed so pleased with his circumstances that she held her tongue.

"I'll get you some wash water," Finn said. "I'll be back in a minute." Then gathering up an armload of filthy dishes, he disappeared out the door. Moments later, he returned with a pitcher of water and a clean basin, the washing of said things obviously someone else's responsibility, for which she was deeply grateful.

"Make yourself at home," he said. "I'll see about getting you something to eat." Then, his arms now full of empty bottles and glasses, he departed, kicking the door shut behind him.

Leaving her alone in Killian's room.

Looking down at her garments, Lydia sighed, seeing that her shift was drenched with blood as well as smeared with mud, as were her bare legs. Circling the room, she eventually found a shirt that appeared clean enough. She set it across the back of a chair while she removed her filthy garments and set to work washing the gore from her skin, making liberal use of the bar of soap on the washstand.

Only once she was through did she glance at the mirror, noting that her face had returned to its usual eighteen-year-old self, her damp hair dark again.

Her skin dry, she pulled Killian's shirt over her head. The costly fabric fell nearly to her knees, the arms long enough she had to roll the cuffs, but the garment covered far more of her than her shift had. Finn still hadn't returned with food, so she went to the bed, righting the linens and furs and pillows before sitting on the edge of it.

She was so tired.

So painfully and exhaustingly tired, and not just because she'd been awake for close to a day and had healed dozens of soldiers, but because of the conversation she and Killian needed to have. Staring at the carpet on the ground, she mentally composed a speech explaining that King Serrick and the Royal Army had been reduced to walking corpses. That Cyntha and Rufina were one and the same. But the part where her mind stuttered was finding a way to tell him that Malahi was alive and Rufina's prisoner, as well as her belief that the Queen was being forced to use her mark to dark ends.

Her eyes burned, and deciding that Finn had been distracted and wasn't coming, Lydia lay down and pulled one of the furs over her cold legs.

The bedding smelled like Killian. Like soap and horses and leather, and she buried her face in the pillow, inhaling deeply, desire and misery fighting each other for supremacy in her core.

It can't be, she silently reminded herself. *Malahi is alive. He's still betrothed to her. Still sworn to her for life.*

Sleep began to steal over her, the world fading away, but then the loud thud of boots along with sharp clangs of metal things being dropped jerked her awake.

"Finn!" Killian's voice, muffled through the door, but clearly him. "I need you to clean the blood off of all of this before it rusts. And please tell me I have at least one clean shirt in the disaster that I know is on the other side of this door."

Said door flung open, and Lydia clambered to her feet, watching as Killian strode in, his face concealed by the padding he wore under his armor as he tore it off and tossed it into the hallway, then pulled the door shut. Turning, his eyes latched on her, and he froze.

Before he could speak, she blurted out, "Finn told me to wait in here. I'm still waiting for someone to bring me clothes."

"Right." His throat moved as he swallowed. "He didn't mention it when I came in."

Her face burned hot. "I can leave."

"Don't leave!" His cheeks flushed slightly pink. "I mean, it's fine that you're here. I just didn't . . ." He glanced down at his bare chest. "I needed a clean shirt."

"You don't have any," she informed him, struggling to keep her own eyes on his face. A thousand times she'd imagined seeing him like this, but what visions her imagination had conjured were pale comparisons to the reality, his body all hard muscle and taut, dusky skin, the weight of his weapons pulling his trousers low enough to reveal his hipbones. "You don't have clean anything. This room is a disaster."

He laughed, scrubbing a hand through his wet hair, the dark locks falling back to rest against his cheeks, which looked as though they hadn't seen a razor in close to a week. "Normally Finn is better at flirting with the kitchen girls to get them to do the work for him. He must be losing his touch."

Silence stretched, the few paces that were all that stood between them so thick with tension Lydia felt she could hardly breathe, much less speak.

Tell him! her conscience screamed at her. *Get it over with!*

Yet before she could work up the courage to open her lips, Killian said, "I thought you were dead. We received word from Serrick that Hegeria's tower had been overrun by blighters and that all inside had been killed."

"It was. And they were." She swallowed, grief for her fellow healers that had fallen rising in her chest. "That message didn't come from Serrick. He's dead and risen as a blighter. The whole Royal Army has been turned. It was Rufina. She and Cyntha are one and the same—using her mark to take lives gives her back her youth, but the effect fades. She's been controlling Serrick this whole time, and when I discovered how to cure those infected by the blight before they turned, she made her move."

"Gods . . . ," he whispered. "How did you get out?"

"High Lady Falorn rescued me when the blighter army attacked Hegeria's temple. We were able to make it to a Maarin ship waiting out at sea, and they brought us south via xenthier. Dareena, Gwen, and Lena are heading to Serlania to rally an army."

He closed his eyes, giving a slight shake of his head before opening them. "I'm in Dareena's debt."

"It was my life. If anyone owes her, it's me." Although High Lady Falorn didn't seem the sort to hold debts.

"It should've been me." In three quick steps, he was in front of her, only inches separating them. "I shouldn't have left you there, knowing the dangers. At the very least I should've been there."

"We both know that wasn't possible. And I don't regret choosing to go." Though she knew she shouldn't, Lydia reached up, curling her hand around the back of his neck. His skin was hot beneath her fingers, his hair soft where it brushed the back of her wrist. "But you should know that I felt your absence keenly."

"Is that why you're here?" His voice was rough, low enough that if she hadn't been so close to him, she wouldn't have heard.

She was here because Malahi was alive and needed to be rescued. Here because an army of possessed corpses would soon march south to make war on the living. But as his hand curved around her waist, warm through the thin linen of his shirt, none of that seemed to matter. "Yes."

And then his mouth descended on hers, words ceasing to matter.

She'd dreamed of this. Gods, but she'd dreamed of it. Of the softness of his lips and the taste of his tongue and the feel of his body against her hands, but again her mind had failed her. Not in its reckoning of her desire, which flowed hot and wild through her veins, but in how intensely she would feel the rightness of his touch. As though his hands had been made to curve around her waist, to slide down her hips, to lift her into his arms and hold her in place as she wrapped her naked legs around him. As though the gods themselves had constructed them to fit together like pieces of a puzzle.

Killian was meant for her. And she for him.

His lips trailed from her mouth to her throat, and she tangled her fingers in his hair, hearing the rapidness of his breath, each ragged exhale ratcheting up her need for more. To have everything. And to give everything in return.

He carried her to the bed, slowly lowering her until her back pressed against the furs, his shirt sliding up her thighs as he kissed her collarbone, then moved down until the neckline of the shirt stole a growl of annoyance from his chest. Reaching up, he caught hold and pulled, sending buttons flying everywhere. A gasp tore from her throat as the fabric fluttered down against her breasts, her sternum and navel rendered bare.

Killian pushed himself back, the muscles in his arms standing out against his skin, his eyes roving down her body. With anyone else, she would've cringed beneath the scrutiny, but his gaze only turned her body to liquid, her head falling back against the bed, her back arching as his fingers brushed the fabric of his shirt away from her breasts.

Then his eyes locked on hers. "There isn't a woman in the world more beautiful than you." He lowered his head to kiss her lips softly. "No one more perfect."

You aren't perfect, an ugly voice whispered from deep in her thoughts.

But the voice was driven away as Killian's lips moved downwards; his tongue teased the tip of one breast and then the other before he continued his descent. She writhed beneath him, digging her fingers into the muscles of his shoulders, trailing her nails down his back, a smile rising to her lips as he groaned, his breath hot where his lips pressed just below her belly button.

You need to tell him.

About Malahi.

About you.

You need to stop this.

But the thoughts seemed distant, because what she wanted was him. All of him. Especially with his fingers trailing lines of fire up the insides of her naked legs, leaving behind prickles of sensation as he kissed the inside of her knee, his cheek rough against her inner thigh.

If you let this happen, you will hurt him.

The thought slapped her across the face, and one word tore from her lips. "Stop!"

She'd meant it for herself, not him, but Killian froze. Lifting his face, he looked at her with concern. "Did I—"

"Malahi's alive." She blurted the truth out before she lost her courage. Before her own selfish desires resumed control. "Rufina has her prisoner in Derin. We need to rescue her."

Tell him the rest. Get it done.

Except she couldn't.

Killian didn't speak, only stared at her, horror filling his dark eyes. Then he whispered, "Malahi's alive?"

"If Rufina's to be believed."

"And she's been a prisoner this entire time?"

Her tongue was too thick, too dry, to speak, so she nodded. "Rufina discovered Malahi was a tender from Serrick. She's trying to force Malahi to expand the reach of the blight."

Silence. The awful crippling sort that made Lydia want to scream, *Say something!*

And then he did, and she wished for all the world that the silence had continued forever.

"Those," he whispered, pushing away from her, "should've been the first words that exited your lips."

And with one violent motion, he turned away and crossed the room, the door slamming behind him.

58

KILLIAN

Malahi was still alive.

Alive, and suffering gods knew what sort of torment under Rufina's hands while Killian had been guarding her reptile of a father's gold mines.

Striding through the building, he ignored Finn as he passed and stepped outside into the growing dawn, boots splashing in the puddles of mud as he went toward the stables. Not bothering with a saddle, he swiftly bridled Seahawk and vaulted onto her back, heeling the mare out of the stable.

Eyes fell upon him with interest as he wove through the fortress grounds, questions rising to lips only to fall away at the sight of his expression. No one attempted to stop him as he passed through the gate and broke into a gallop down the road, heading east as his last conversation with Malahi echoed through his head.

Everything my father touches turns to rot. There is something wrong with him.

How right she'd been. Unwittingly or not, Serrick had been under the Corrupter's control and no one had seen it.

I did what the rest of you were too gods-damned afraid to do.

And how different would circumstances be if he'd helped her rather than hindered? If he'd kept her safe and alive and queen rather than handing the kingdom back to the Corrupter's puppet?

If I lose the crown, everything that happens will be because of you. Because of the decision you made in this moment. And any blood that is shed will be on your hands.

Her words resounded through his thoughts like prophecy. He needed to rescue her. Needed to get her back to the kingdom. Needed to undo the damage his own selfishness had caused.

If only he hadn't gone after Lydia, none of this might have come to pass. Malahi would be Queen, Rufina would have lost her puppet ruler and her power, and all the healers who'd died in Mudaire might well still be alive.

And yet Killian couldn't imagine having done anything different. Couldn't imagine having abandoned Lydia to the fate Malahi had forced upon her. Couldn't imagine having abandoned her to almost certain death.

Lydia.

Images of her flashed through his thoughts. Of her standing her ground against the Anuk. Of her healing the injured on the battlefield.

Of her lying naked on his bed beneath him, her green eyes heavy with desire.

Stop. He dropped the reins, pressing the heels of his palms to his temples, trying to squeeze the image from his thoughts.

But all he could see was her face. All he could taste was her lips on his. All he could feel was the silken smoothness of her skin beneath his hands.

All he wanted was *her.*

"Stop!" He screamed the word, and Seahawk shied violently, nearly unseating him. Then she set to bucking, nostrils flaring, eyes rolling to reveal the whites.

Cursing, Killian slid off the side, letting her go where she willed as he stumbled off the road. Reaching the crest of a hill, he fell to his knees and stared at the rising sun, the brilliance making tears run down his cheeks.

Tell me what to do, he silently whispered. *Tell me how to make this right.*

But as always, the gods were silent. They'd given him all that he should need to be a champion for Mudamora and they'd give nothing else.

He remained kneeling on the sodden ground until the sun was well into the sky, forcing his mind toward honor and duty. And only when his path was clear to him did Killian rise and catch his horse, trotting swiftly back toward camp.

59

LYDIA

"You'll be all right," she said, smoothing the hair back out of the soldier's eyes, giving him a comforting smile. "A few days of rest and you'll be back on your feet."

"Thank you, Marked One," he whispered, catching her hand. "They say Hegeria gave your horse wings to reach us when you did."

"Call me Lydia," she said for what felt like the hundredth time. "And no wings, only a streak of recklessness that I pray won't rear its head again anytime soon."

Smiling, she extracted her hand from his grip and moved on to the next patient, who'd been struck with several arrows, the bleeding having been checked but much of the damage remaining.

Exhaustion hung over her like a pall, but it was better to be here, doing some good, than weeping into a pillow. Sleep was an impossibility.

Goose bumps rose to her skin, and a heartbeat later, Killian said from behind her, "We need to talk."

He'd found a shirt somewhere, but it was untucked and the sleeves rolled up to bare his forearms.

She opened her mouth to argue that she was in the middle of something, but the expression on his face had her instead gesturing to one of the women who helped tend the wounded. "I'll be back shortly."

Killian led her through the maze of buildings making up the camp, then out a side gate, where she found Sonia and Finn waiting. The former smiled at the sight of her, stepping forward to hug Lydia tightly. "It's good to see you, friend."

"And you."

But there was no time for further conversation, Killian having continued onward toward the shadow of the bluff, a grim-faced Finn following on his heels. Only when they were well away from the camp did he stop. "Tell them what you told me."

Lydia swiftly explained, avoiding Killian's gaze as she did, the coldness of his expression making her feel sick.

"Malahi tried to fix the blight," he said when she finished explaining her belief that a tender might be able to reverse the path of the blight. "She couldn't do it."

"That doesn't mean it can't be done," Lydia said. "Blight poisoning can't be cured by a healer in the manner we'd use to repair damage from injury or sickness. I had to draw the blight out. Like a poison." *Into myself.* "If I explained it to her, it might be that Malahi could do the same for the land."

Everyone was silent, then Finn spoke for the first time. "We need to get Malahi back."

"Not *we*," Killian answered. "Me. You three will go to Serlania to join Dareena."

"You can't go alone!" Sonia snapped. "This is the sort of cursed foolishness that always gets you in trouble, Killian."

"The area around the wall is rife with blight, and you and Finn are liable to be infected." He crossed his arms. "As it is, you'll only slow me down."

The last he directed at Lydia and she couldn't help flinching. But she hadn't come this far to abandon her cause over hurtful words. "I'm coming. The blight won't make me sick. And as it is, I understand it better than anyone."

"No. I don't want you along."

There was so much anger in his eyes. And it was her own doing. If she'd only told him straightaway why she was here, none of this would've come to pass. But instead, she'd only thought of herself. "If they've hurt her, you'll need me. If you get hurt yourself, you'll need me."

"I'll manage." Turning to Finn and Sonia, he said, "The last thing we need is word that I'm going after Malahi to reach the ears of the blighters and them warning Rufina. So instead, I'm going to lie and say that those of the Royal Army here with us are ordered to march to Serlania. You three will march with them under the pretense that I intend to follow. By the time Rufina figures out that I'm not with you, I'll have a good head start."

Whether the deception would work or not, Lydia wasn't certain. The Corrupter was a god, and therefore should be able to see *all,* and yet that hadn't seemed the case when she and Dareena had been trying to flee the city.

She opened her mouth at the same time as Finn, but Killian cut both of them off with, "Retrieving Malahi or any of the tenders is a shot in the dark, Finn. They could already be dead, so it's foolish to risk any lives unnecessarily when High Lady Falorn needs everything Mudamora has to fight the blighter army. You wanted a chance to fight? Well, here it is."

"I'm your squire. I'm supposed to stay with you."

Lydia's heart broke at Finn's tone, the pieces fracturing further when she saw Killian wasn't immune, his expression softening. "You *are* my squire. Which is why I need you to join Dareena and fight for her in my stead."

Finn's jaw worked back and forth, but he nodded.

Killian gripped his shoulder. "Meet me back at camp. I've something to give you before I go."

Seeming to sense that any further protest would be for nothing, Sonia tugged on Finn's arm, leading him back to camp. Leaving Killian and Lydia alone together.

"You're a distraction for me," he said, looking anywhere but at her. "And the consequences of that outweigh whatever benefit you bring to the table. Dareena needs all the marked healers she can get, which means with her you can do some good. And as I said before, you'll only slow me down."

Her chest felt hollow, as though his words had carved out her insides and left nothing behind but hurt. "Raising an army to fight the blighters might slow them down, but it won't stop them. Not when the blight will just keep infecting more and more people." She blinked back the tears that threatened to spill down her face. "We have to rid the land of the blight to win this battle, and I believe Malahi is key to doing that. This is my home, and I'll do whatever it takes to save it."

"This is not your home." His voice was cutting. "Your home is Celendor, Lydia."

It was where she'd been raised, yes. But Mudamora was her home now. And she believed with all of her heart that the gods had brought her here to help save it. "This *is* where I belong. This is my fight. And if you don't take me with you, I'll go alone rather than see your pride be the doom of Mudamora."

He flinched, but snapped, "Pride has nothing to do with it."

"What happened between us was a mistake, Killian," she said, wishing to the depths of her soul that it was otherwise. "And it won't happen again."

Neither of them spoke, the tension making her feel sick.

"Fine," Killian finally snapped. "Be ready to leave an hour before dawn."

Then without another word, he strode back to the camp.

She spent a good portion of the rest of the day in the healing tents, the endless work a blessed distraction. But just as it was starting to get dark, Sonia appeared.

"Hungry?" the young woman asked.

Lydia had no appetite, but knew she needed to eat, so she nodded, washing her hands and then following Sonia out of the tent. They joined a queue of waiting soldiers, accepting plates heaped with fresh bread, grilled meat, and steaming vegetables, along with cups of foaming ale.

"Why didn't you go with the rest of Malahi's guard to work for the High Lady?" she asked once they'd found a spot to sit and eat, the fading sun still warm.

"Didn't feel right to leave him." Sonia took a bite of bread, chewing thoughtfully. "Killian won a great victory, but between Malahi's presumed death and your departure with Quindor, he felt far from victorious. It might have been endurable if Serrick had allowed him to continue working to push out the Corrupter's influence but he sent him here"—she gestured at the buildings—"to guard what is for all intents and purposes Serrick's treasury."

Lydia swallowed a mouthful of meat. "It seems to need guarding."

"Cast that blame at the feet of the Rowenes family." At Lydia's frown, Sonia explained all that had happened while they'd been at the border, including Ria's secret attacks on the Anuk. "Though knowing what we know now," her friend added, "I think Rufina was behind the decision to send Killian here."

They ate in silence for a long time, then Sonia set aside her plate. "He's not the same as when you last saw him, Lydia. He's angry. Always, always angry. Quick to temper and slow to laugh."

The food she was eating soured, and Lydia set aside her own plate. "That's not him."

"It is now. He was merciless with the Anuk when he believed they were attacking unprovoked, and learning the truth pushed him to the brink. He was sick with guilt before we learned Malahi has been Rufina's prisoner. Now it's a hundred times worse. It's not you he's angry with, it's himself."

Sonia's words made sense, and yet every time she blinked, Lydia saw the anger in his eyes when he looked at her. The coldness. And she couldn't help but think that Killian at least partially blamed her for all that had befallen Malahi.

Standing, Sonia motioned for Lydia to follow. They discarded their plates back at the mess, then Sonia took her to the rear of the fortress, where she quickly picked up the metallic clang of sword striking sword.

Holding up a finger to her lips, Sonia whispered, "Better if they don't see us." Then she moved behind a series of weapons racks and took a seat on the ground. Lydia sat next to her, peering through the rows of pikes and swords.

Killian and Finn were sparring at the center of the training yard, both dripping sweat from heat and exertion. Though he'd likely never held a weapon before becoming Killian's squire, Finn was already far more adept than Lydia was, his nimble feet serving him well as he danced back and forth.

"You have to hold your ground at some point," Killian said, pressing Finn backward. "If I'd known you only intended to use it as a dance partner, I'd have spent less on that sword."

"I'm wearing you down, old man! As soon as you start to pant, I'll strike!"

Killian laughed, the first genuine smile she'd seen rising to his lips, and Lydia's eyes stung.

Then Finn darted forward in an attack, weapons clashing violently, Finn's expression intent and Killian's devoid of the frustration he'd worn when teaching her. He parried the boy's rapid slashes, then in one quick motion, jabbed at Finn, sword point stopping just shy of his shirt. "Ow!" Finn cried, falling to the ground and rolling around. "I'm dead. I'm dying."

"The dying comes before the dead." Killian reached down to grab Finn's arm and hauled him to his feet. "And you lowered your guard again. Watch."

Lydia sat silently next to Sonia, watching as Killian showed Finn his error before they began anew.

No yelling. No swearing. No weapons tossed aside in irritation.

"This," she said softly, "is not what it was like when he taught me. He's far nicer to Finn."

Sonia made a soft noise, nodding slowly. "For all he claims that he can't teach, Killian is remarkably able to become the teacher each student needs." She turned her head back to watching the pair spar, and then she said, "I like to watch them together. It reminds me that beneath the anger, he's still in there." Then she reached out and took Lydia's hand, squeezing it hard. "You're not just going to Derin to rescue Malahi. You need to bring back Killian, too."

60

MARCUS

They'd covered 140 miles.

It was an incredible feat, given the obstacles they'd faced, but as Marcus stared at the map on the wall of the shack they currently inhabited, he feared it might all have been for naught.

It was snowing.

The lack of visibility had kept them from traveling to the next shelter, but if it continued to snow, it would be the carpet of white flakes on the ground, which was growing thicker by the hour, that would trap them. And with both daylight hours and their supply of meat dwindling, it wasn't a delay they could afford. As it was, they didn't have enough food to make it even halfway to the nearest legion fort, which meant they'd be forced to try to fish or hunt right as the season shifted into winter.

He rolled his shoulders so that his back cracked, then lifted the candle to stare at where the Via Hibernus intersected with the Via Mortis, which was the route through the Sibernese Teeth. The mountain range was long and narrow, passable—in theory—in a matter of days, which was why Empire couriers used it. But only in the warmer months. And the men who undertook the journey were experienced climbers.

"Where are all the Sibernese?" Teriana asked, her head bent over the repairs she was making on her clothing.

"Mostly, they're on the coasts or south of the Teeth where the weather isn't as foul," he answered. "Only a few live on the plains during winter, and they're nomadic. They have to be with such scarce game."

"Don't they have trouble with the wolves?"

"Yes." He scribbled a calculation on the wall with a bit of charcoal and frowned. "But they keep wolfhounds that run the packs off."

"Maybe we'll get lucky and come across a group of them. We've got coin, and I've a few hair ornaments that I'd part with for something different to eat."

"Hope that we don't." He set down the charcoal. "They *might* let you live, but I'd be dead the moment they determined I was Cel. Doubly quick if they figured out I was with the legions."

"What are you talking about?" Out of the corner of his eye, he saw Teriana look up from her mending. "Sibern's been a Cel province for what, two hundred years?"

"One hundred eighty-four."

She snorted. "Right. Specific dates aside, that's quite a few years of peace, no? And wouldn't there be a reward for them assisting *you* of all people? You are fairly important, last I checked."

Marcus hesitated. The situation in Sibern—and in several of the other provinces—was not something the Senate wanted known. But given that the animosity of the Sibernese people toward Celendor was a very real threat to him—and to Teriana by extension—he decided to answer. "There is no peace. Not in the interior, at any rate. They know helping a legion officer would net them a small fortune in gold. They'd still feed me to their dogs if they got the chance."

"We traded down the eastern coast of Sibern last year," Teriana said. "I didn't even hear a whisper of dissent."

"Not surprised. The coast has a heavy legion presence, and the larger cities are more . . . *integrated* with the Empire. It's the places that only see the legions and the Empire administrators once or twice a year that are the problem."

"How so?"

"It started with them refusing to tithe their second-born sons, or rather, claiming that there were no second-born sons." Sitting on an upturned log, Marcus tossed another piece of wood in the stove, wanting to be comfortable as he aired the Empire's dirty laundry. "They refused to keep birth records, hid the boys or pretended they were the children of families with no sons. Sibern's not the only place it's happened—the Bardenese have turned evading child tithes into an art."

"Why is it that no one has ever heard of this?" Teriana's eyes were a brilliant blue; *Curious,* he thought. *And something else.*

"Because the last thing the Senate wants is anyone finding out that evasion is possible," he said, watching her expression. "It's in the Empire's best interest to have its people believe its power is absolute and uncontested, so any rumors to the contrary are vigorously quashed."

Teriana's brow furrowed, but she said nothing.

"But in Sibern, the Empire erred in how it handled the situation. Or rather, the legatus dealing with it erred and the Senate had to go along with his decision in order to keep from looking foolish. Or worse, weak."

Extracting a whetstone, he ran it along the blade of his knife, waiting.

"Well?" she finally demanded. "Are you going to tell me what he did?"

"Can't you guess?"

"Obviously I can guess," she retorted. "But what good is you being a walking encyclopedia of facts if you aren't going to give me the full story?"

"As you like." He sheathed the weapon, stretching one leg out in front of him. "So in circumstances of tax evasion, what one does is to go into the town or village or hamlet and have one of the Empire's administrators estimate how much tax is owed, and then take it. By force, if necessary. Obviously the administrator estimates high, and the legatus in charge will usually turn a blind eye to his men taking a bit more to supplement their own income. The result is that the evaders end up paying more than they would've had to if they'd been law-abiding, thus dissuading them from repeating their crime."

The blue of Teriana's eyes dimmed to grey. "The Thirty-Seventh do much of this sort of labor?"

He made a face. "Hardly. It's for legions on the verge of retirement or weak ones that can't handle a real fight. Anyway, the idiot of a legatus in charge thought that he'd be clever and apply the same practice to the Sibernese evading the child tithes."

"You can't be serious."

"I'm quite serious. In the places that didn't provide any children, he took *all* the boys who appeared the correct age, regardless of their birth order. He took them even in places where it was quite feasible they didn't have any boys to tithe that year. Rounded up *four times* the number of boys Sibern usually tithes and delivered them to Campus Lescendor."

"My gods . . ."

"The Senate couldn't precisely go returning boys without admitting what had caused the problem in the first place," he said. "So they kept them. And since then, the resistance to the tithes in Sibern has only worsened, along with the refusal to pay taxes. Violence against the legions has increased, whole patrols going missing only for their heads to be found staked up for their comrades to find."

It was a bloody mess was what it was. For the number of men it would take to collect the boys and the taxes, it would cost the Senate more than it would receive in revenues. But they couldn't risk ignoring it lest the problem spread.

"When did this happen?"

"About six years ago," he answered, doing the math in his head. "The boys they took—those that survived, anyway—will just have graduated from Campus Lescendor."

Teriana rubbed her chin thoughtfully. "Doesn't the Senate ever stop to consider that arming hundreds of boys with a valid reason to hold a grudge against them might not be the wisest idea?"

Every boy sent to Lescendor had a valid reason to hold a grudge against the Senate, but fear was a powerful motivator. "For that to be the case, they'd have to see us as human beings, not as numbers. And I assure you, the majority of senators do not."

Shaking her head, Teriana returned to her mending. "Your people are awful."

"The Senate is not the sum of the Cel people," he countered. "It's a few hundred men. Even if you count the patrician class, we are talking about perhaps ten thousand out of four million."

"It's those four million people who allow those few hundred men to rule them."

"Those few hundred men control a military with over two hundred *thousand* soldiers, so I'm not sure *allow* is the correct term."

The noise she made was noncommittal, but then she said, "If they did rise up and the Senate ordered you and yours to quell them, what would you do?" She lifted her face to meet his gaze. "Would you fight your own people? Would the rest of the legions?"

He was saved having to answer by the sound of something heavy walking outside the shack.

"Wolf?" Teriana whispered, rising to her feet.

They hadn't had much contact with the creatures since the two packs had clashed, the Revenge Pack, as they'd taken to calling it, having been driven back. The new pack, plus those whose territory they'd passed through, would occasionally sniff around the shacks, but they showed none of the dogged determination to get inside as the Revenge Pack.

Holding his finger to his lips for silence, Marcus listened to the sound of the animal's tread. *Crunch. Crunch. Crunch.* A slow plod over the snow of a much heavier beast than a wolf.

"Bear," he muttered. "Damn thing should be hibernating by now."

"It clearly doesn't agree," Teriana said under her breath. "What do we do?"

Marcus tossed several pieces of wood in the stove, building the fire.

In response, the bear let out a loud grunt and leaned against the door of the shack.

The heavy beams holding the door in place groaned, and with them watching in horror, the brackets began to give, the nails sliding out of the wood.

"Shit!" Marcus flung himself at the door to brace it, knowing that it would do little good. But the second his shoulders hit the wood, the animal grunted and ceased its pushing, returning to its slow saunter around the shack.

Heart hammering in his chest, Marcus moved to Teriana's side, both of them rotating as they tracked the bear's progress.

It circled the shack twice, then stopped. A loud crack of wood split the silence.

Teriana held her breath, waiting.

"Please tell me that wasn't—" Marcus broke off as the sound of chewing filled the air.

Dawn greeted them with clear skies, a foot of fresh powder, and the shattered remains of the icebox that contained their supply of wolf meat. Or rather, *had* contained it, for the bear had devoured every last morsel.

"One less thing to carry, I suppose," Teriana muttered, then started in the direction of the distant mile marker of the Via Hibernus, her feet sinking deep into the fresh snow.

Marcus didn't move. All they had to eat was the wolf meat that had been intended for breakfast and the few handfuls of grain that had been in the supplies at the prior shack. And against his will, his gaze shifted from Teriana to the Teeth in the distance.

He'd read about them, but words on the page did not do the mountain range justice. Unlike other places he'd been, where ranges were made out of peaks and valleys and it was possible to find passes that led through them rather than over them, the Teeth appeared like shards of shale standing on end, all razor-sharp ridges and narrow ravines that he knew dead-ended against sheer walls. There was no pass through them. The Teeth were a maze that consumed men like it were a sentient beast.

Which was why the route through them wasn't on the ground.

It was dangerous, but they could be on the far side of them in days. And on the far side there were forests and rivers, which meant food. On the far side, there was civilization.

"Teriana!" he called. "This way."

Then he started south, eyes on the first mile marker of the Via Mortis.

The road of death.

61

KILLIAN

He and Lydia sat atop the horses he'd taken from the stables—he was unwilling to risk his own to the blight—waiting for Sonia and Finn to arrive with supplies.

The silence sitting between them was the most uncomfortable he'd ever experienced, but he could think of nothing to say to break it. Part of him wanted to argue with Lydia that to come with him was folly, but another saw reason in her words that Malahi might need her help. Though in his heart, he knew the reason he'd agreed to it was because he was afraid to let her out of his sight again.

"What is your plan for finding her?" Lydia asked softly, wiping rain drops from her face.

"If it's corrupted tenders who are creating the blight, it stands to reason that following it back to the source is our best chance of finding them. If we're lucky, that's where Malahi will be as well."

"Do we know where the source is?"

He gave a slight shake of his head. "Somewhere in Derin. Royal Army scouts never pressed past the wall, but they did report that the blight flowed through the gates of the fortress, so that's where we'll go first."

Already he felt sick about having to go there. To the location of his defeat and the place this war had begun.

"How long will it take us?"

"With you along, who knows." His tone was harsher than he'd intended.

"Don't hold back on my account." Her voice was cool. "I'll keep up."

Mercifully, Sonia appeared, carrying supplies in a laundry bag under the guise of doing her washing in the stream. Finn soon approached from the opposite direction carrying the same. Killian had made a show of berating him for shirking his duties earlier, but it was still a ruse with more holes than a sieve given that it was pouring rain.

Dismounting, Killian took the bags and distributed the supplies between his saddlebags and Lydia's. Then he turned back to his friends, unsheathing his sword and accepting the one Sonia carried in exchange. "I've left orders for my soldiers to march to Serlania tomorrow. Assuming they obey, you ride with them. If my orders are somehow overturned, you will leave anyway."

Sonia nodded. He knew she wasn't pleased, but he also knew she'd do it. Finn, however . . . "You're to take my horses home for me, is that understood?" He glared at the boy. "And if anything happens to them . . ."

"You'll hang me naked from my ankles in the middle of Serlania's grand market and pay orphans to throw horse shit at me, I remember." Finn glowered at him. "You'll have to stay alive if you're to carry through on that, you know."

"Count on it." Pulling Finn close, he said, "Good luck. May the Six ride at your side and keep you safe."

Then he mounted his horse and dug in his heels, heading away from them at a gallop. A heartbeat later, he heard Lydia follow, her horse's hooves splattering in the mud.

He kept the speed for as long as reasonable as they headed north, keen to get away from the eyes of Rowenes spies, though he suspected they'd soon be replaced with scouts of darker allegiances. The land north of here and east of the wall was broadly abandoned, the prevalence of blight and the creatures the Derin army had brought over the wall with them rendering hundreds of square leagues uninhabitable. But the rumor was that there was some traffic back and forth through the broken gate and burned-out fortress that had once guarded the wall.

How they were crossing back and forth through the towering peaks of the Liratora Mountains remained unconfirmed, but Killian had strong suspicions that Rufina was making use of xenthier much as did the Empire Lydia hailed from. Either way, he intended to find out.

They rode through the day without exchanging a word, both of them eating in the saddle, stopping only to water the horses at the small streams and ponds they encountered, the water running high.

It wasn't until the sun began to set did Killian start looking for a place to make camp. And for something for dinner.

Retrieving his bow, he kept an arrow loosely nocked, eyeing the underbrush. Motion caught his attention, and in one swift movement, he shot the arrow. Dismounting, he led the horse over to the brush and retrieved the pheasant he'd killed, holding it up. "Hungry?"

They tethered the horses near a small stream, Killian stretching the tent canvas between trees to serve as a tarp. While Lydia gathered wood for a fire, he plucked and dressed the pheasant, making liberal use of the spices he'd had Finn include in the supplies. Starting a fire, he spit the bird over top and left it to cook while he retrieved water from the stream.

When he returned, Lydia was no longer wearing her healer's robes, having changed into a plain woolen dress with a high collar. Sitting next to the fire, she used a comb to part her hair, then extracted her tiny knife.

"What are you doing?" he demanded, turning the pheasant before mixing water with cornmeal in a pan and setting it over the fire.

"Covering this." She tapped the half-moon tattooed on her forehead. "Probably better if no one knows I'm a healer, no?"

She started cutting strands of hair, and after she nearly sliced her forehead open twice, Killian reached over to take the knife. "Let me do it. You keep an eye on dinner."

Kneeling in front of her, he combed her hair down over her face, then began cutting it off just below her eyebrows. It felt like silk beneath his fingers, and her breath was warm against his throat. "There," he muttered, eyeing the glossy fringe that now concealed her tattoo. Instead of softening her face, the style accentuated her sharp cheekbones and the straight line of her nose, the green of her eyes seeming deeper than it had moments before. That a change of hairstyle could make a girl look dangerous seemed ridiculous, but it had. Dangerously beautiful. "That should do it, although once we're into Derin, you might avail yourself of a scarf."

"Thank you."

He shrugged, then gathered up the fallen strands of her hair, tossing them in the brush for the birds before moving on a little farther to gather berries from a bush. They'd need their supplies for when they were farther north, so for now it was better to live off the land. By the time he returned, dinner smelled near to finished. He carefully split the berries between two plates, divided the cornmeal cake and pheasant between them, and sprinkled salt over the food before handing Lydia her share.

Frowning, she tentatively picked up a piece of pheasant and took a bite, juices running down her chin. She chewed, then said, "This is good. Very good. Where did you learn to cook?"

"Picked it up over the years," he answered between bites. "The downside of being born wealthy was that I developed a fairly refined palate that wasn't well satisfied in army camps. Most soldiers can't season food to save their souls, so I decided to learn to do it myself."

Popping a few of the berries into his mouth, he said, "You can't cook, can you?"

Her cheeks flushed. "Not well."

Which he suspected meant *not at all*. "Dish duty for you, then."

"I've never done dishes, either."

"I have every faith that you'll figure it out." He refrained from adding that he *hated* doing dishes—or cleaning of any sort—so he'd gladly catch and cook every meal if it spared him the labor.

They finished the rest of the meal in silence, Lydia gathering the dishes without comment and heading down to the stream with the lantern hooked over one elbow. He gave the fire a few pokes. Added some more wood. Then he decided the horses could use a drink, and untethering the pair, he led them slightly downstream of where Lydia crouched, her sleeves pulled up past her elbows, brow furrowed as she scrubbed vigorously at a plate before holding it up to the light to inspect.

Both geldings snuffled the water, then tried to pull back to the patch of grass they'd been grazing.

"Drink, you bastards," he muttered, glaring at them as Lydia chuckled softly and said, "What's the saying?"

"That horses keep their brains in their balls, which is why geldings are so damn stupid." But the Rowenes soldiers preferred them to mares, so his choice had been limited. He glanced in her direction, the lantern revealing the smile on her face. "What?"

"I didn't say a word."

Glowering, he led the animals back to their patch of grass, where the pair of idiots immediately resumed their grazing. Sitting next to the fire, he stared at it until Lydia returned, stacking the dishes neatly to await breakfast before sitting across from him.

Don't look at her, he silently ordered himself.

But his mutinous eyes immediately abandoned the flames for her face and his tongue, ever a follower, asked her, "Do you miss Celendor?"

For a few moments, Lydia was quiet. Then she said, "Sometimes." Holding her slender hands over the fire, she added, "I'd be lying to say that I don't miss the luxury of my life there, but mostly I miss my father. Bait told me he was alive when the *Quincense* set sail with the legions, and I pray that remains the case. He has Teriana's mother in his care."

"What's he like?"

Her lips curved into a smile, eyes growing distant. "He's kind.

Which might not seem such a special attribute, except that in Celendor, kindness is a rarity. The Cel as a whole are a cruel nation of people, merciless and unforgiving. And while they tout themselves as the epitome of civilization, beneath the golden exterior, they sometimes seem so devoid of humanity as to be more beast than human."

Taking a sip from her waterskin, she continued. "While he had his faults, my father saw the ugliness beneath the gilt and did what he could to enact change. The Valerius family has long been powerful and influential within the Senate, and he pushed for measures that would improve the treatment of those with less means, as well as advocated for the rights of individuals hailing from the conquered provinces, who are not citizens and therefore granted none of the privileges. His greatest wish was to abolish the indenture system within the Empire, which he considered barely a level above slavery, and to that end, all under his employ were free men and women who were paid fair wage and treated well, never whipped."

"Whipped?" he demanded incredulously.

"Sometimes for as little as spilling their domina's—their mistress's—tea. It's common practice to employ a servant whose singular role is to enact discipline," she replied. "If you own someone's indenture, you may do with them as you wish. Beat them, maim them, kill them, though the latter is rarely done because it means a loss on the investment. Most patricians—who are the equivalent to Mudamorian nobility—see punishment as a form of entertainment and go to great lengths to think up creative ways to inflict pain and suffering. The things I have seen . . ." Lydia gave a slight shake of her head as though to clear away visions. "My father abhorred such behavior and attempted to enact laws restricting it during his term as consul. He lost the vote in the Senate, and when he ran for a second term as consul, was not victorious, having lost many of his supposedly high-minded supporters because he'd dared to try to limit their cruelty. When I asked him if he regretted his actions, he told me the only thing he regretted was not fighting harder to see the law passed."

"He seems a good man. What is his name?" It was strange that he didn't know. Had never asked. He knew everything there was to know about Finn's past. Knew the names of Sonia's parents and what they did for a living. But his time with Lydia had always been too focused on the pressing concerns of the present to ever dwell on stories of the past, and he half-wondered if he could claim to truly know her without hearing the stories that shaped her into the young woman he knew.

"Appius Valerius." She sighed, withdrawing her hands from the fire and curling them in her lap. "Once, when I was thirteen or so, one of our servants spilled hot tea on my lap. It hurt, and I was angry at my dress being soiled, so I struck her across the face. I'd seen the other girls I knew do the same, as well as their mothers, so part of me thought nothing of doing the same. And part of me liked doing it. She'd hurt me, so I would hurt her back, but worse."

Lydia was quiet, but he sensed she wasn't through with her confession, so he remained silent.

"I've no notion of how he heard what I'd done, but my father left in the middle of the Senate's session to return home. I'd never seen him so angry. I ran and hid in the library, but he hunted me down and dragged me out into the courtyard, where he had all the servants assembled, including the woman I'd struck. He forced me to stand in front of her, and I thought he was going to make me apologize, so I began in earnest, but he only shouted at me to be silent."

Killian tensed, about to revise his assessment of this Appius Valerius if he'd had Lydia beaten, but then she said, "He told the woman that she could hit me as I had hit her, if she so wished. That she had his word there would be no consequences to her doing so."

Picking up a stick, Killian poked at the fire, rolling over a branch to fuel the flames. "She wouldn't do it, would she?"

"No." Lydia exhaled. "She wouldn't. I could see in her eyes that she wanted to, but it wasn't enough to overcome her fear that to do so would mean a reckoning of tenfold severity. That, despite my father's reputation, this was a trick that would create fodder to entertain our guests while we drank expensive wine and laughed.

"Eventually my father allowed her to go, dismissing the rest of the servants so that we were alone. Then he turned on me and said, 'Lydia, to be good does not mean to be without flaw, for even the best of us are riddled with them. To be good is to recognize the darkness in one's character and strive to remedy it. And if such a thing is not possible, to control it so that it does not harm others.'"

"A wise man," Killian said. "If but there were more like him."

Lydia shivered and she pulled a blanket up over her shoulders, prompting Killian to put another log on the fire. Then she spoke and he realized the shiver had nothing to do with the cold.

"A week later that woman quit her employment with my family to take a job serving drinks to sailors in a tap house for a fraction of the pay. And though the circumstance was my fault, I don't think the reason she left was fear of being slapped in the face again. It was because in his attempts to make *me* understand the power of my position, he'd forced her to face the weakness of her own. And to live every day with that glaring reminder was more than she could bear."

Lydia tilted her face up to the rising moon, its light turning her face silver. "My father is wise. And he is kind. And I love him dearly. But I think it would be a lie to call him *good*." Then she curled up on her side, saddle pad under her cheek. "Good night, Killian."

62

MARCUS

This had been a mistake.

Turn around. Go back. Travel the Via Hibernus instead.

These were the thoughts cycling through Marcus's head as he and Teriana left the shack located at the foot of the Sibernese Teeth, following the marked trail into the maze of narrow ravines between the enormous vertical slabs of rock.

"This place is strange," Teriana said, reaching out her arms so that the tips of her mittens brushed the walls to either side of them. "I've never seen anything like it."

Strange was one word. *Terrifying* was another. "There is nothing else like it. In the East, at any rate."

She turned around, her brow furrowed as she regarded him.

"What?" His tone was sharp though he hadn't intended it to be.

Shaking her head, Teriana carried on through the ravine. She knew something was wrong, but he hoped she was attributing it to his concern over their lack of food stores or his general pessimism about their circumstances. He'd even take her believing he was being an ass for no reason at all over her guessing the truth.

You can't do this, his fear whispered. *You've never been able to do it.*

This time I will, he told it. *I'm not letting her starve to death because of you.*

You'll fail, it answered. *Turn around. Turn around. Turn around.*

No. Marcus gave a sharp shake of his head, shoving away the thoughts, focusing instead on their surroundings.

They'd been in the Teeth for less than an hour, and already he couldn't have said with any certainty which way was south. The path through the ravines was full of switchbacks and places he was certain they were backtracking, and with the towering slabs of rock blocking any vantage of the sun, it would be easy to become turned about without the carved markings to guide them.

Even the wind seemed to switch directions, bouncing off the ravine walls and erasing their tracks, a constant haunting moan that rose to a shriek in certain places. The sound made Marcus's skin crawl.

And it was cold. The sort of chill that bit through clothing, skin, and muscle, sinking its fangs deep into the bone. Yet despite that, sweat trickled down Marcus's back, because he knew the worst was yet to come.

The walls moved in, now barely wider than he was at the shoulder, only a sliver of sky visible far, far above. It seemed they'd reached a dead end, but ahead of him, Teriana made an abrupt right and disappeared from sight. Quickening his steps, he turned the corner and nearly collided with her.

They stood in a narrow chute created by the intersection of three slabs of rock, and there was no way out but to backtrack.

Or to climb.

Looking up, Marcus started counting the spikes set into the chute's wall, stopping when he reached sixty, despite that being nowhere near the top. His heart drummed in his chest, a rapid *thud thud* that might have seemed loud if not for the wind screaming down from above.

Teriana reached for one of the spikes above her head, hanging from it as though to test the metal's ability to hold her weight. Settling her feet back against the ground, she turned to him. "We're going back. We'll take the other route. We'll hunt. Forage. If the Sibernese can do it, so can we."

She's right. Turn around. Go back. "The route through the Teeth takes a matter of days. For us to take the Via Hibernus would mean three more weeks to reach the legion fort, and that's if we travel *every day*. That's not possible if we need to stop to hunt and forage, which means we'll be stuck on the plains in the dead of winter. Do you have any notion of how cold Sibern gets?"

"I've heard." Her face was shadowed by her hood, hiding the color of her eyes. "I still think it's the better choice."

Agree with her.

"Why?" He gestured at the spikes. "The whole route is like this. Spikes and ropes and bridges. And it isn't as though you aren't a capable climber."

Teriana didn't respond. The wind shrieked through what would've been an interminable silence, driving bits of grit and ice into his face.

"Aye," she finally said, pulling back her hood. "I am. But it's not me that I'm worried about."

"I can climb." The words came out from between his teeth.

"You're afraid of heights."

"What makes you think that?"

"Quintus told me when we were cliff diving. Said everyone in the Thirty-Seventh knows it."

He glared at her. "Quintus needs to keep his bloody mouth shut."

"Right." She gave an irritated shake of her head. "Or maybe you need to start being honest about your limitations. We haven't even stepped off the ground and you already look about ready to heave your guts—empty as they are—out into the snow. Exactly how well do you think that's going to go when you're dangling from a hundred-foot cliff?"

"I'll be fine."

"Bullshit!" Her hands balled into fists. "I'm not going to risk watching you panic and fall to your death when there's another route."

His temper snapped. "And I'm not watching you starve to death because of my limitations. Now climb!"

Two steps had her in his face, the seas of her eyes tossing and churning with an emotional storm. "I am not one of your men. You do not tell me what to do."

"Fine. Do what you want." And because if he listened to one more word of her argument, he knew he'd cave to his fear, Marcus started climbing.

His mittened grip on the spikes felt precarious, but even through them, he could feel the cold of the metal, so they'd have to stay. Up and up, he climbed, ignoring Teriana's shouts from below. Her threats to go back without him. Her scathing criticisms of his character.

Focus on where you put your hands. On where you put your feet.

The wind buffeted him, knocking back his hood, and his ears grew cold within minutes, then started to burn soon after. He risked his balance to pull it forward, but the wind only took it off again, so he left it, grinding his teeth against the pain.

Get to the top.

He reached for the next spike and closed his left hand over it. But as he pulled his weight upward, reaching with one foot for the next toehold, the spike gave, angling downwards. His hand slid down the metal.

The wind shrieked even as his stomach dropped and his breath came in fast little pants, his foot searching for the next spike.

I can't find it. Where is it?

His eyes shot down, intent on finding a toehold. Yet it was the distance between him and the ground that made Marcus freeze. That sent the panic racing through his veins.

"Look up, you jackass!"

Teriana's shout snapped him into focus, and his toe found the elusive spike. Heaving with his right hand, he reached for a more secure grip for his left, checking its stability before using it to pull himself to the next. And the next.

Up and up and then he was reaching for the top, scrambling onto the flat rock and rolling onto his back to gasp in breath as he stared up at the sky.

Whether it was a heartbeat or an eternity later, he couldn't have said, but suddenly Teriana was above him, her hands pinning his wrists to the rock.

"We do this on my terms, do you understand?" Tears were dripping off her face, already cold when they hit his forehead. "You follow *my* orders, you do what *I* say, is that understood?"

It had been a long time since he'd taken orders from an individual, but it was surprisingly easy to relinquish authority. Likely because he'd never had any over her in the first place. "Understood."

"Good. Now on your feet."

63

TERIANA

Tightening her grip on the rope, Teriana leaned backward on her precarious perch, trying to get a good look at the next obstacle before heading back to retrieve Marcus.

Beneath her was a two-hundred-foot drop, and if the rope she clung to came loose from its brackets, there would be nothing to stop her from plummeting down and her body shattering on the sharp rows of rock rising up like broken razor blades below. But the thought of falling bothered her much less than the question of how she was going to get Marcus through this.

She'd left him tucked on a ledge, head between his knees and a death grip on the rope strung around this particular tower of rock they needed to circle, shoulders rising and falling in rapid panting breaths that had nothing to do with exertion.

Terror.

She'd seen him face down certain death so many times, but never had she seen him like this. Pale and shaking and unable to speak. There were times she didn't think he could even hear her, he was so lost in the fog of fear. What sort of willpower it took for him to keep pressing forward was not something she could even fathom, but he kept doing it.

Kept following her as they scaled and descended the sharp ridges of rock, going around their edges or over their tops, then over short bridges that crossed ravines with bottoms lost to darkness.

Very rarely was there solid rock beneath their feet. Sometimes it was spikes that had been set into the rock, sometimes ropes snaked through steel loops, one for hands and one for feet. Sometimes it was wood ladders and platforms anchored into rock. Those she hated the most, for they were deceptively sturdy looking. Their wear had become obvious only after Teriana's feet had gone through a rotten plank, nearly sending her falling to her death. It was only by the mercy of the Six that Marcus hadn't seen it happen, because she thought it might have undone him entirely.

Squinting into the bright light, Teriana continued in her progress around the side of the towering ridge of rock, giving each spike she stepped on a good stomp before committing her weight to it. The wind was rising again, trying its damnedest to rip her free from her perch. It forced its way through her clothing, turning the sweat on her skin to ice and chilling her hands and feet despite the thick fur encasing them.

The sun was growing low in the West, casting long shadows across the strange mountain range. Another hour of sunlight, at most, and she had no idea how close they were to shelter. The wolves were not a threat with sheer cliffs on all sides, but she didn't think they could survive the night in the open. Not with the temperature dropping, the wind howling, and next to nothing to use as fuel for a fire.

"Stupid Sibern," she muttered, reaching the opposite side of the ridge and finding a relatively gentle rocky slope leading down to a wind-scraped plateau. "I hate this place. Once I get my ship back, I am never leaving the tropics! To the underworld with lost profits!"

Jumping down the last few feet of incline, she trotted across the plateau, searching for something to indicate which way she was to go next, but there was nothing but rock crusted with ice. Lifting her face, Teriana looking farther afield, stopping in her tracks as the enormity of the view took hold of her.

It was like standing on a platform in the sky, the shadows of towering ridges of rock running east and west as far as the eye could see. The one she stood on now was taller than most, and from it, she could make out a twisting white path running through them: a river.

And rivers had fish.

The thought made her stomach growl, the last of their food supplies having been exhausted that morning, and Teriana picked her way to the edge of the plateau to look down.

Three hundred feet below was a wide river, barely visible in the shadow cast by the mountain on which she stood. It was wide, she could tell that much, and the gaps in the ice suggested the water beneath ran too rapidly to freeze in these temperatures. On the opposite side, perhaps two hundred feet away, rose a cliff as sheer as the one on which she stood, and she searched it for any sign of how they were supposed to get down and then back up again. But there was nothing.

And the sun crept lower.

"Shit," she muttered, and that was when motion between the two cliffs caught her eye, her gaze focusing, understanding hitting her even as her stomach dropped.

Coming here had been a mistake.

64

MARCUS

He was so cold.

Marcus pressed his forehead into his knees, feeling the chill of the rocks beneath him sinking into his bones, the incessant wind pushing through his layers of clothing and freezing the sweat coating his skin. His feet burned and his hands were numb, fingers stiff from clenching the rope mounted on the rock next to him.

He knew he needed to get up. To move and get his blood circulating so that he didn't freeze to death. Yet every time he willed himself to do so, his limbs refused to obey—like they'd been weighted down with lead. His head throbbed, his mouth so dry it hurt to swallow, but he couldn't bring himself to let go of the rope long enough to retrieve any water. Nausea swirled in his gut, the rock beneath him seeming to move like the deck of a ship.

You don't get seasick, he reminded himself. *So even if the mountain is moving, you shouldn't feel like this.*

Do mountains move?

Is this possible?

He tried to shake his head to clear it, but the muscles of his neck cramped painfully, preventing the motion.

"Marcus."

Teriana's voice. But she was gone. Had gone to do something. To . . . check something.

He was imagining things.

"Marcus?"

He ignored the sound of his name. A trick of the wind. A trick of his fear.

"Gods-damn it, Marcus! Look at me!"

His body was shaking. It was being shaken.

"Look at me!"

It hurt to lift his head, the muscles and tendons in his neck fighting the commands of his brain. But he did it.

Teriana was in front of him on her knees, her hands on his shoulders, only her eyes visible between her hood and scarf. "Are you with me?"

He licked his lips, trying to moisten them, but his tongue was dry. "Yes."

The color of her gaze brightened with relief. "Good. I need you to think. What do you know about the shelters in these mountains? About where they are."

Shelters. He tried to focus his thoughts, tried to dig into his memories, to remember the things he'd read. But he kept being pulled back into the moment, his mind refusing to move beyond the cold. Beyond the sheer drop only a few steps from where he sat. "Don't know."

"You do. I know you do." Her voice was soft. "And you don't forget things. You just need to think."

Marcus shook his head, then rested it back on his knees, wishing the world would stop swimming.

"Are they in the ravines? By the water?"

Lunacy. The ravines flooded every spring. Why was she making nonsense suggestions? Scowling, he lifted his head. "They're in places with trees. For firewood."

Her eyes glinted. "A tooth with trees, you say. We might be in luck, because the next one over has the first trees I've seen since we entered these gods-forsaken mountains. Now you need to get up. We're going to go around this column of rock. There are sixteen spikes you need to cross to get to the opposite side, with a rope to hold on to for balance. It's not much of a drop, only fifty feet or so."

Far enough.

"On the far side is a plateau. That's a big flat space."

"I know what a plateau is," he grumbled, flexing his fingers, trying to get sensation back in them. His legs had stiffened, and pain shot through them as he moved onto his knees, keeping as close to the rock wall as possible even as he refrained from looking back at the drop.

"I'll go first. Come on."

She tugged him up, leading him down the path, which grew narrower with each step until it dropped off entirely.

Open space before him. To his left. And the wind clawed at him, trying to drag him off his feet. To send him plummeting down and down.

Cringing, he pressed against the wall, closing his eyes, but that only made it worse. Made him swear he could hear the platform crumbling beneath him, the rock falling away. That he was falling.

Panic, fresh and bright and wild, surged through him. Froze him in place. Tightened the already-painful vise clamped around his chest.

So he snapped his eyes back open.

Teriana stood with one foot balanced on a spike, not even holding on to the rope.

She was going to fall.

He lunged, grabbing the front of her clothing and pulling her back from the edge, sending them both stumbling. She was shouting at him, but he couldn't understand what she was saying. All that mattered was his grip on the rope. His grip on her.

"Don't do that! Let me go! You're going to get us both killed!"

"I can't let you fall."

"Then quit knocking me around, you idiot."

She pressed closer to him, close enough that he could feel the warmth of her body. "I'll go first. You follow."

It was easy to nod. Much harder to force his fingers to relax their death grip on her clothing.

His heart hammering against the walls of his chest, Marcus watched her step back onto the spike, this time holding on to the rope with both hands. In a sideways motion, she moved from rung to rung, pausing with her feet on the seventh and eighth, gaze shifting to him.

You can do this.

He couldn't.

You have to.

His breath was coming in rapid little pants, his whole body shaking.

Do it!

Gripping the rope, he stepped onto the spike, vertigo washing over him as he looked down, the sharp rocks below seeming to rise and fall like waves.

Keep moving.

He shifted onto the next spike, clenching his teeth as he waited for it to give. His arms felt too weak to hold him up if it did, and they shook in response to the thought.

Teriana was humming a song, the melody filling his ears.

He followed it.

Step.

Step.

Step.

His teeth were chattering. Clacking together with enough violence it felt like they might crack.

Step.

Step.

Step.

"Halfway there." She resumed her humming, drawing him forward.

Step.

Step.

His foot slipped on the spike, ripping a gasp from his chest. He pulled tight on the rope, his forehead pressed against it as he sucked in air.

Keep going.

I can't. But he took another step anyway.

It seemed a lifetime before they reached the other side of the ridge, and Teriana led him down the rocky incline onto the plateau. He kept his eyes on her heels, refusing to look beyond.

"We don't have much time before dark," she said between gusts of wind. "But if what you said is true, we only have to cross over this bridge and the shelter will be on the other side. We'll be done for the day. All right?"

He was not all right. "Yes."

"Okay." She stopped.

He kept staring at her feet.

"This is the bridge."

He did not want to look. Because he knew. Knew what was to come. But he had not come this far in life by being a coward, so slowly, Marcus lifted his head.

65

TERIANA

The bridge was made of three lengths of cable, one for walking and the other two for balance, forming a V shape that was held together every few feet by thinner pieces of cord. A fourth rope ran over her head, which she assumed was for baggage, although perhaps it was meant to be a secondary route across if the bridge itself came loose from its moorings.

It wasn't a comforting thought.

The bridge had to be close to two hundred feet in length, hanging above the ravine and the icy rapids three hundred feet below, and with each gust of wind, it swung violently from side to side.

Teriana had spent her whole life in the rigging of the *Quincense*. Had climbed the mainmast in the middle of countless storms to untangle lines and repair sails. Climbing ropes into the heights was part of who she *was*.

But this bridge terrified her.

Marcus had taken one look and turned away, and was now on his knees retching on the bare rock of the plateau.

He was not going to be able to do this.

"I'll go back and cut some of the rope we just used," she said. "I'll tie you to me, that way—"

"No." He straightened, wiping his mouth with the back of his mitten.

"It's my call, remember. You promised to listen to me."

"Not this time."

There was a faint wheeze to his voice that made her skin prickle with apprehension, but he seemed more lucid than he had in hours. More in control of himself. "Marcus—"

He shook his head. "I'm too heavy. If I fall, you'll be ripped right off the bridge"—he took a labored breath—"then we'll both be dead."

"But—"

"The sun's setting. Let's go."

"Can't even go a day without giving an order," Teriana grumbled, because if she didn't say something, didn't tell a joke, she was going to cry. Sweat ran in rivulets down her icy skin and she felt strangely light-headed as she turned to the bridge. It was mounted to an out-cropping a dozen feet back from the edge, allowing her to test her balance on the cursed thing with solid ground still beneath her.

Gripping a cable in each hand, she stepped up onto the lower one, biting her bottom lip as it quivered and moved from side to side. This close to the moorings, it only moved a few inches, but when they reached the center, it would be a whole different story.

Taking a deep breath, she eased forward, humming one of the songs of her people because it forced her to breathe. Reaching the edge, she stopped, the song dying on her lips.

It was so very far down.

"This is not happening," she whispered, then turned back around. Marcus had his hands on the cables near where they were mounted, but had progressed no farther. "Stay here."

Sprinting across the plateau, she eyed the faint glow of sun. Half an hour, no more. Then they'd be stranded in the cold and in the dark. She had to hurry.

Clambering up the incline, she stopped short of the gap bridged by the spikes and pulled her knife. She cut through the fibers, knotting the loose end off so whoever came next wouldn't be without, then took the portion that hung down the incline, looped it around her shoulder, and headed back to the bridge.

"There's only ten feet of it, but it should do for you."

Marcus lifted his head. "What?"

"I'm tying you to this." Climbing the outcropping, she pulled off her mittens and formed a loop around the line stretching above the bridge, double-checking her knot before jumping down. "Up."

He climbed onto the bridge, saying nothing as she fashioned a harness around his legs and torso. Probably because he didn't want her to hear the wheeze in his voice.

"I have to keep slack enough that it won't pull you off when the bridge swings. So if you lose your footing, you'll drop a few feet," she said. "But you won't fall. Climb back up. Then carry on."

"You need . . . the same."

Teriana shook her head. "There's no more rope and no time for me to go back and retrieve more. And if we don't get across this ravine to that shelter, we're as dead as if we fall. Besides, this is nothing to me. I'll be fine."

Before he could argue, she climbed onto the ropes, moving swiftly down them.

And stepped out over the edge.

66

MARCUS

It was a hundred times worse than he'd anticipated.

A thousand.

The bridge bobbed beneath Teriana's weight as she stepped out over the ravine, nothing holding her in place but her own strength and balance. Farther and farther, the wind catching at her hood and pushing it back, sending her loose braids flapping wildly. With her added weight, the bridge swung farther than it had on its own, snapping back in the opposite direction with violent force. Teriana wobbled and clung to the ropes, taking another few steps before another gust of wind caught her, whipping the bridge nearly sideways.

"No." His chest was so tight he could barely get the word out. "Come back."

Either she didn't hear him or chose not to listen, taking another few steps, nearly a third of the way across now.

His breath came in gasping wheezes, his throat tight, his chest worse. His pulse roared in his ears, everything too bright despite the rapidly dying sun. Sweat rolled down his brow, stinging his eyes, but he couldn't let go to wipe it away.

Because he was following her.

The bridge moved beneath him, but Marcus kept his eyes fixed on her. *Please don't fall. Please don't fall. Please don't fall.*

The rope holding him to the baggage line smacked him in the face, but he ignored it and kept moving forward. He needed to catch up to Teriana. Needed to be close enough to catch her if she fell.

Each inhale gave him less and less air as his throat tightened. He had minutes until he passed out. Maybe less.

The wind slammed against him, sending the bridge flying sideways. His foot slipped, only just catching on one of the cords binding the cables together. The bridge rebounded the other way, jerking back and forth like a chaotic metronome.

The ravine was entirely hidden in shadow now, nothing but yawning blackness beneath him. Ahead, Teriana was nearly at the opposite side. Nearly safe.

The bridge swung and the world spun, stars moving across his vision.

Keep going.

But panic was taking over. He was going to pass out. Was going to end up dangling from a rope until lack of air or the cold killed him.

Would that be so bad?

Would it be so bad to be done?

Marcus stopped moving, aware only of his desperate need for air, the cables beneath his hands, and the sound of Teriana screaming his name.

Just let go.

No. He gave a sharp shake of his head, then took another step. Then another.

His vision was fading, the hands gripping the cables feeling not his own but someone else's. He couldn't see.

But he could still hear Teriana's voice begging for him to keep moving. Not to stop.

Then he was falling.

67

TERIANA

She caught him by the front of his clothes, jerking him forward right as he started to fall, only the rope tying him to the baggage line keeping him from knocking her over.

"Marcus?" She caught hold of his head, lifting his face. "Marcus!" But he was still. Unconscious. Barely breathing.

"No." Hot tears ran down her face, soaking into her scarf. "Don't you dare do this."

He couldn't die. Not now, after everything they'd gone through to survive. Not like this.

And there was nothing she could do. No tools that would help him breathe. No healer she could run to find. She was all he had, and that meant he had nothing.

Sobbing, she shoved her fingers inside his scarf, feeling his throat for a pulse. It was weak, but still there. Only his skin felt like ice beneath her hands, and she suspected if she had good light to see by, his lips would be turning blue.

She needed to find shelter. Get him warmed up. Give him a chance to survive.

Unfastening the harness, she dragged him away from the edge of the ravine, laying him down behind two boulders that would serve to keep the worst of the wind off of him.

Then she ran.

Her feet flew over the plateau, the last glow of sunlight fading in the horizon as she raced to the copses of trees.

Darkness fell, the only sound the creak of the scraggly trees around her and the howl of the wind.

She slowed to a crawl, afraid of falling. Of losing her sense of direction and her ability to find Marcus again.

Please let there be a shelter.

Then she heard it. The *snap snap* of cloth flapping in the wind. Moving cautiously, she followed the sound, using the same tricks they used to sail the *Quincense* in heavy fog. Covering one ear. Then the other. Listening and then taking a few steps.

She found the flag when she collided with the pole, her cheek aching with the impact. Feeling around in the dark, she let out a shout of triumph as she found a gap between two tall rocks. Inside, she crawled on her hands and knees, finding a small pile of wood, a rusty axe, and a box of kindling.

With shaking hands, she retrieved her flint and knife, knocking sparks into the dry bits of grass and twigs until one of them caught. The flames revealed she was in a chamber that had been formed by slabs of rocks falling against one another. Other than the wood, there was only a single pot and a heavy piece of canvas that was weighted down by a stone.

After building the fire, she cut a strip of the canvas and wrapped it around a piece of wood to make a torch. Then she ran back out into the night.

"Marcus!" she shouted, squinting up at the few stars, orienting herself. "Marcus, can you hear me?"

There was no response but the wind, and dread filled her chest. If he died . . .

"Don't think about it!" she shouted at herself. "You can't afford to think those thoughts. Marcus!"

She reached the edge of the cliff, moving along it in the direction of the bridge. *Please be alive.* "Marcus!"

In the flickering glow of her torch, she caught sight of the boulders where she'd hidden him, and Teriana broke into a run. "Marcus!"

Skidding around them, she slid to a stop.

He was gone.

"Marcus?" Teriana turned in a circle, searching the darkness for any sign of motion even as she listened for footsteps. The sound of him breathing. Anything.

But there was nothing.

"Marcus!" The shriek that tore from her throat was shrill, her heart battering the inside of her ribs as she searched, her ears filling with a dull roar. Where was he? Where had he gone? Had he moved himself, or was there someone else out there?

Or some*thing*?

Pulling her knife, Teriana held her dying torch low to the ground, searching for tracks. But the bare rock yielded nothing. "Marcus!" She winced even as she shouted his name, knowing that if there was anything out there, her voice would lead it straight to her.

Her torch flickered and flared as the wind gusted. It wouldn't last her much longer.

She needed to go back to the shelter to get more wood. More canvas. And then . . .

"You'll keep looking," she told herself between sobs, heading back down the cliff line. "All night."

But even as she spoke the words, Teriana knew if she didn't find him soon, the only thing she'd be likely to discover come dawn was a frozen corpse.

Tripping and stumbling, she found her way back, aided by the faint glow of the fire she'd left burning, a heavy weight settling upon her chest. This wasn't supposed to be how it would go. This wasn't supposed to be how it would end.

Her torch guttered out as she approached the shelter, and she dropped it to pull off her mittens. To scrub at her burning eyes. And when she opened them, she saw a shadow.

"You jackass!" she shrieked. "I thought you were out there freezing to death, but here you are warming yourself by *my* gods-damned fire while I stumble around in the dark."

Marcus lifted his head, revealing a face that was ghastly pale and drawn, and he blinked once. "I came to and you were gone. I thought—"

"Do you really think I'd leave you?" She glared at him for a heartbeat, then flung her arms around his neck.

"If it comes to it," he said, "you need to. Sit down. I need to sit down."

They both sat cross-legged next to the fire, Marcus taking a few shaky breaths before he continued. "I need to give you some information. Some codes, so that you'll be able to prove your story when you reach Celendrial."

"Piss on your codes," she snapped. "You keep them and use them yourself when we get there."

Shaking his head, he pulled a burning stick out of the fire and ground out the flames on the rock. Then he started writing a series of numbers and letters. "Each path-hunter is given a personal code, as well as provided with the code assigned to the genesis stem he's exploring. This one belongs to the man who found us in Arinoquia. His name was Nonus. And this is the code for the stem in Bardeen. You'll also need to provide them with as much detail as you can as to where the genesis stem we took in the city is located, as well as where it landed us in Sibern." He lifted his head. "It was shelter number 203."

She didn't answer.

"This number"—he wrote 37–1519—"is mine."

As if that number wasn't burned into her soul. Even if she lived to a ripe old age, on her deathbed, she'd be able to close her eyes and see it tattooed across his golden skin. "Thanks for the reminder."

"This code"—he wrote another series of letters and numbers—"means I've delegated you to deliver a message."

"This is stupid. I'm never going to be able to remember all of this."

"You have to."

"And just who am I supposed to be giving these to?" she asked. "Cassius? Call me crazy, but I somehow doubt that he's going to hold to our agreement if I show up without you in tow. He'll probably just have one of his lackeys slit my throat and stuff me in a sewer drain."

Marcus flinched, then tossed the stick back on the fire as though he were trying to hide the reaction.

"Don't go to Cassius," he finally said. "Disguise yourself when you enter the city, and then arrange to speak with my sister Cordelia."

Teriana sat up straight in surprise.

"She's married to Senator Tiberius Egnatius. Tell her everything." He met her gaze. "She's deeply opposed to Cassius. She'll help you."

"Given that the information about the xenthier paths is what Cassius wants, that seems counterintuitive."

"She's against the imprisonment of your people, so for their sakes, she'll help." Marcus sighed. "And if you must, tell her about us. For *my* sake, she'll do it."

"You haven't seen her since you went to the legions, Marcus. You're banking an awful lot on stale sentiment."

"She sneaked into Lescendor dozens of times to visit me while I was in training. And I spoke to her the night before we left for the Dark Shores. If she's alive, she'll help you. Cordelia is no coward."

Realization flashed through her. "That's the woman you were talking to while I was trying to rescue my mother."

"Yes." He turned his head away. "She was trying to convince me not to go, among other things."

What other things?

"If for some reason you can't get to her, travel to Campus Lescendor and ask to speak to Commandant Wex. Don't use my name; just send a note saying that the library mouse needs a favor. He'll help you."

Teriana stared at the codes he'd written, feeling them sink into her memory despite her best intentions. To have them there felt so final, because she no longer needed him to get her people free. But that didn't mean she didn't need him in a hundred other ways. A hot tear dribbled down her cheek, and she brushed it away angrily. "You're giving up, then?"

"No." He rested his chin on his knees, the flames sending shadows dancing across his face. "I'll keep going. But there are"—he coughed— "eight more bridges like that one. Me having another attack is inevitable. Even if I don't fall, having attack after attack is going to kill me. You need to be prepared."

Cool. Pragmatic. Logical.

"You don't need me," he said.

Teriana didn't. Not to survive this, not to make it to Celendrial. Not to force Cassius to hold to the letter of their agreement. But her heart needed him. "Maybe not, but I most certainly want you. And if you even think of presuming to tell me what I do or do not want, I'll push you off the side of a cliff."

Marcus didn't laugh. Instead, he squeezed his eyes shut, his throat moving as he swallowed, cool pragmatism gone and replaced with something that was worse.

"Don't," she whispered, then closed the distance between them, her knees on either side of him, pulling him against her. A shudder ran through him, then he relaxed, his forehead resting against her shoulder. "We'll see what morning brings, all right? We both need sleep, but you especially."

His head nodded against her in acknowledgment, but he didn't let go of her. Instead, he pulled her down into his lap, their bodies pressed together. Lifting a hand, he cupped her face, his thumb stroking her cheek, his eyes searching hers.

Then he kissed her.

It was slow and sweet, pulling a whimper from her lips. But then it turned harder, his tongue chasing over hers, one hand tangling in her hair, the other sliding over the curve of her bottom. She closed her eyes, heat filling her as his teeth caught at her bottom lip, causing her to rock her hips against him. Wanting more. Wanting everything.

But then he paused, both of them breathing the same air, hearts pounding the same rhythm. "Don't stop," she whispered. "Please don't stop."

The kiss he gave her was again sweet. Gentle. And it felt more like a good-bye than anything he could possibly have said.

"We'll make a decision in the morning," he said, lifting her off him. "Get some rest, Teriana."

Her stomach hollowed as she curled up in his arms, silent tears dripping down her cheeks. Waiting. Waiting, for his breathing to deepen into sleep. Only then did she shift, fingers moving over him to slip into his belt pouch, deftly sorting through the contents until she found what she was looking for.

There was no one else in the world like him. No one else capable of making her feel like this. She loved him, and she wasn't going to gods-damned let him go without a fight.

Teriana rose just before dawn, easing Marcus's head out of her lap and resting it on her folded cloak. They'd taken turns at watch, mostly out of the necessity of feeding the fire, and when he'd slept, it had been fitfully, though that was nothing new.

She took stock of the supplies they had that would be of use to her. Considered what, out of necessity, she'd need to leave behind. As she gathered items into various piles, she noticed that during one of his watches, Marcus had scrubbed away the codes he'd written, leaving behind only smears of soot.

A flicker of hope filled her chest that he'd changed his outlook on the day ahead, but then she saw tiny bits of leather littering the floor. Scowling, she lifted up one foot, peering at the bottom where he'd scratched the very same codes into the sole while she'd slept. "You won't win this fight," she told him, but he only muttered something unintelligible and rolled onto one side.

Retrieving the kettle, she went outside in search of ice to melt, then stoked the fire, smoke escaping through the openings in the rocks above as she watched the wood burn. Her stomach growled painfully, and already she felt light-headed and weak from the lack of food. Which, given what she needed to do today, was not ideal.

She'd do it anyway.

Marcus was stirring. Taking the vial she'd hidden in her boot, Teriana carefully measured the drops into a tin cup, which she then filled with water, swirling the contents with her finger before turning around.

"It's dawn," she said, handing him the cup. "We need to get moving."

Marcus didn't answer, only drained the contents of the cup in a few long gulps, then stretched his arms and legs, his face blank and unreadable. Teriana packed the things they needed into their respective satchels, one eye for the task and one for him.

It wouldn't take long.

Sure enough, he swayed sharply, colliding with the wall of the cave. "I'm just hungry," he muttered. "It'll pass."

Teriana stood. "I'm really sorry," she said. "But I'm not going to let you die."

Alarm filled his gaze. "Teriana, no!"

"I'm sorry." She clenched her teeth, watching as the drug took hold, and rushed forward at the last moment as he fell, his weight knocking her from her feet.

A reminder of just how hard this was going to be.

But there was no time to waste. Scrambling round the cave, she bundled him up as best she could, sacrificing much of her own clothing to ensure he didn't freeze. Exertion was going to keep her warm.

Outside, she chopped down two skinny trees with the rusty axe and dragged them into the cave. Using the canvas, she swiftly formed a litter, which she rolled Marcus onto, using ropes to bind one end to her waist so she wouldn't spend the strength in her arms before necessary. Then she loaded the satchels onto the litter, doused the fire, and started walking.

The sky was grey and overcast, the wind mercifully absent, though it would pick up through the day. Teriana dragged the litter across the plateau, sweat coating her skin after only a few minutes, her pulse pounding.

You've lost your mind, a little voice whispered inside her head. *This is impossible. You're in no condition for it. You're not strong enough. You're going to get both of you killed.*

She ignored it.

Reaching the next bridge, she eyed the gap over the ravine, ice and rapids flowing far below. She checked Marcus's pulse and rolled him off the litter, then created a harness for him. Hauling him up on top of a pile of rocks she created beneath the baggage cable, she flung the rope over it, forming a loop much as she had before. Then she pushed him off the rocks.

Marcus dangled limply in the harness, neck lolling to one side as he swung. She swiftly looped the rope around her own body, then after checking her knots again, climbed on the bridge in front of him.

She took a couple steps, then let go of the cable with one hand and reached back to take hold of his arm and tug him forward. Another few steps, another tug.

Each time she had to let go of the cable, her heart skittered, the line beneath her feet seeming to wobble and sway with more intensity as she struggled to keep her balance. She couldn't lean on the cable she gripped with her left hand, nor pull on it too hard or the bridge would tip sideways.

And it was painfully slow.

In the length of time it took her to reach the midpoint, she could have crossed back and forth thrice on her own. And she had to get this done today. Keeping Marcus unconscious for any longer would be too dangerous, and he wouldn't fall for the same trick twice.

Get the job done.

Reaching the other side, she stepped down onto the plateau, pulling Marcus along until they reached the boulder to which the lines were bolted. She pulled loose the knot above him and staggered beneath his weight, falling sideways as she eased him to the ground.

Unfastening the harness, Teriana looped the rope over her shoulders and scampered back across to repeat the process with the litter and the supplies.

One bridge down. Seven more to go.

The day turned into a blur of repeated steps as the sun passed overhead. Harness Marcus. Get him loaded onto the baggage line. Pull him across. Do the same to the supplies. Rebuild the litter. Load Marcus on the litter. Drag him to the next bridge.

By the time she reached the last ravine she needed to cross, Teriana was shaking with exhaustion and nausea, her hands abraded from the ropes and every muscle in her body screaming abuse.

"Only one more," she muttered. "Then you'll be done."

But one more felt impossible as she stared at the expanse of bridge, the longest yet and the late-day wind rising in strength. She needed to rest, to regain her strength, but the sun was setting and Marcus was dangerously cold. Three times she'd had to stop to warm his hands and feet, his skin icy against her overheated flesh. She had given him two more doses of narcotic, but she was terrified to give him any more. Too much was lethal. Would stop his heart. And every time she held her fingers to his throat to check his pulse, she swore it was weaker.

She had to cross now.

It was almost more than she could manage to lift Marcus up and fasten him to the line, her body shaking with the effort. The wind howled in her ears and her fingers were numb from being exposed to the cold while she worked. Knotting his harness to hers, Teriana started forward, bracing her feet against where the vertical side ropes were wrapped around the foot cable, Marcus sliding down the overhead line.

Due to its length, the slope down to the midpoint was more dramatic than that of the other bridges, making Teriana feel as though she were climbing down a ladder rather than walking across a bridge, Marcus's weight threatening to pull her loose with every step.

The wind gusted, sending them whipping from side to side and forcing her to cling to the cables, her bottom pressed against the foot line until the swinging ceased. Her heart thundered, sweat pouring down her forehead and into her eyes, her mouth so dry she could barely swallow.

She reached the midpoint, which was alarmingly far beneath the cliff tops, meaning she was now faced with a climb. And she had almost nothing left to give.

The wind struck.

The bridge swung to the side, then snapped back in the other direction. Again and again, causing Marcus's body to slam against her, nearly knocking her loose. A sob of terror tore from her lips as the wind battered her with no respite, making it nearly impossible to climb.

Finally, it eased, and Teriana clambered forward, locking her feet against the cross ropes and dragging herself up by the cables with Marcus's limp form trailing along behind. Up and up she climbed, breath coming in ragged gasps, her side stitched with cramps. Up and up . . . then, as she pulled on the right cable, it suddenly gave.

A scream tore from her throat as she fell forward, losing her grip on the other cable. She slammed against the foot line, barely getting her arms and one leg around it as her body swung around, back hanging above the river raging three hundred feet below.

Frozen in place, she hung there, the wind blowing her from side to side, Marcus unconscious and helpless above her.

"The Six help me. The Six help me. The Six help me," she sobbed, tears running down her face.

Then a snap filled the air and the foot line jerked.

Tilting her head back so that she could see, Teriana stared in horror at the dangling ropes, the only thing holding the bridge in place the foot line. And if the two cables had already broken loose, what were the chances the third would hold?

Climb!

Arms and legs wrapped around the remaining cable, she climbed, the harness at her waist taut as she dragged Marcus with her.

The incline grew the closer she got to the other side, but she didn't pause to see how much farther there was to go. There was no time.

Hand over hand, her weight resting on the strength of her legs. But they were quivering, her energy nearly spent. Her hands ached beneath her mittens, grip weakening as she reached for the knots where the cables had been linked together, a fiery burn filling her shoulders. Her neck.

Her sides were cramped so badly she could barely breathe, but she was almost there. Almost to the edge. Tilting her head back, she saw the cliff's edge was only an arm length away. Then another snap filled the air.

And she was falling.

The wind rushed out of her lungs as the harness around her body jerked tight, the rope attaching her to Marcus the only thing keeping her from plunging to her death.

She screamed as she flipped upside down, both of them sliding down the baggage line, the world a twist of whites and greys and blacks, wind ripping her hood back from her head as their momentum grew.

They slid to a halt at the halfway point between the two cliffs, the baggage line bowing beneath their combined weight as they swung back and forth.

She couldn't breathe. Rapid little gasps brought no relief, nor the ragged sobs that made her feel like her body was being torn in two. Stars filled her eyes, and it felt again like she was falling. Falling into a darkness that she'd never find her way out of.

You're hyperventilating. Calm down! Some reserve of logic filtered up into her thoughts, warring with her terror. *You aren't dead yet! Think of a way out of this!*

Sucking in a deep breath, she held it, then blew it out. Repeated the process over and over until the stars cleared. Twisting so that she no longer dangled upside down, she shouted, "Marcus! Wake up! I need you to wake up!"

He didn't move. Didn't so much as twitch.

And part of her wondered if he was still alive, or if he'd frozen to death or if she'd stopped his heart with the narcotics. Whether she'd sacrificed herself to save a corpse. And with the thoughts, panic crept back in, so she shouted, "Get your head on straight, Teriana! Hop to!"

Her voice echoed through the ravine, chastising her again and again.

Reaching, she tried to pull herself up the rope linking her and Marcus together, but her mittened hands slipped. Grimacing, she pulled them off and tucked them in her belt, immediately feeling the bite of cold against her skin. She needed to move fast while she still had feeling in them.

And before the baggage cable, which was all that was keeping them from falling, gave way like the others.

Teeth clenched together, she heaved, pulling herself up until she was able to grab hold of his harness. Marcus's back was to her and she couldn't tell if he was still breathing, but she needed both her hands to hold on, so it was impossible to check. Adrenaline fueling her, she snarled and climbed up the three feet of rope between Marcus and the baggage cable, gasping in relief when she was able to hook her legs over it and relieve the strain on her exhausted arms.

You need to check if he's still breathing, logic told her.

And if he isn't?

You'll have to cut him loose to ease the weight on the cable.

Every part of her cringed at the thought. To cut him loose and watch him fall. Watch him hit the rocks and ice below. To hear that sound . . .

If he's dead, he's past caring.

But she wasn't. "Shut your mouth!" she screamed at the voice, hating it because it was part of her that was saying it. An ugly part that she despised and wanted nothing to do with. "He's alive!" she howled at it. "And I'm getting us out of this."

You could at least check.

"Fuck you!" Her voiced slammed against the walls of the ravine. Sucking in a deep breath, Teriana climbed.

Hand over hand, the rope pinched between the bend of her knee and the curve of her foot, she climbed. Her palms burned and bled, her fingers growing more numb with each passing second as the wind assaulted her from all sides, trying to knock her loose. Trying to steal him from her.

I can do this.

Up and up, her muscles stinging as they tore, tendons straining, her head throbbing. Her nose started to bleed, the iron taste filling her mouth and making her cough as it dripped into her throat.

I will do this.

Her body was shaking. Broken and spent. But she kept it going, fueling it with willpower and the desire to live. And then there was solid rock beneath her, but she kept going. Kept climbing until her frozen knuckles hit the stone the line was mounted to.

"Okay." She closed her eyes, tears leaking out from under her eyelids. "Okay."

Unhooking her legs, she dropped to the ground, the world still seeming to move despite the solid rock beneath her feet as she put on her mittens. She couldn't reach high enough to unfasten the knot holding Marcus's harness to the baggage line, so she pulled out her knife. She used her left hand to hold the fingers of her right closed on the hilt so that she could saw at the rope, and wrapped one arm around him when there were only a few fibers left to cut.

She fell backward under his weight, fresh tears welling up as her elbow and head banged against the ground. "Please." The words came out as a whisper, and she coughed, trying to spit out blood, but it only ran down her chin as she used the last of her strength to roll him onto his back and loosen the scarf around his face. "Please."

He was blanched deathly pale, even his lips drained of color. And she couldn't tell if he was breathing.

"No." She sobbed the word, shoving her frozen fingers against his throat. He was still warm, but she couldn't feel a pulse.

A strange whimpering filled her ears, and it took her a moment to realize that it was her. But she couldn't seem to stop making the sound. She held her cheek over his mouth, waiting for the warmth of breath, but her own face was so numb, she wasn't sure she'd feel it even if it were there. "Marcus!"

Nothing.

Rage filled her. An awful consuming heat, but she welcomed it because it was better than the alternative. "Marcus!" She slammed her fists down on his chest.

And he stirred.

Made a soft noise of protest.

Then, very slowly, he opened his eyes. "Teriana?"

68

LYDIA

Though Killian had told her he traveled fast, Lydia hadn't appreciated exactly what that meant. They rode hard from dawn to dusk, only to wake while it was still dark and repeat the process, and she suspected that if not for her mark, she'd have barely been able to walk.

As it was, after eating whatever Killian caught and cooked and then doing the inevitable dishes, she would fall immediately asleep, remaining so until Killian woke her for her turn at watch.

The air grew colder as they progressed north, and they woke one morning to frost on the ground, forcing Lydia to dig out the heavier clothing in her saddlebags, pulling gloves over her hands. The ground grew increasingly barren, the only green the pines they rode through. Yet by midday, even those had turned to brown, the ground thick with fallen needles. So it was no surprise when Killian pulled up his horse and dismounted that what she found him looking at was a narrow stream of blight.

"We need to let the horses go," he said, retreating from it. "The last thing we need is them drinking foul water and becoming infected. The best case would be that they died, but I somehow doubt that's how it would go."

He started untacking his horse, and as she turned to unsaddle her own, Lydia heard him murmuring apologies to the animal for abandoning him, as well as promises that if the animal were clever enough to travel south that he'd surely find someone to care for him.

"Fond words for an animal you referred to as an idiot."

"He's a good idiot." Pulling off the gelding's bridle, Killian tossed the leather straps into the brush. Instead of wandering off, the animal rubbed his face against Killian's chest, receiving several pats on the neck in exchange. Lydia's own horse, by comparison, abandoned her as soon as he was free, going to Killian for what she thought were pats until she saw the sugar they were licking from his palms.

Smiling, she said nothing as he said his good-byes to the animals and sent them cantering back down the trail with affectionate swats on the hindquarters. He watched until they disappeared, then turned to his saddlebags and the tent they'd eventually need, rigging it into something more suitable for carrying on foot. Finally, she said, "Your family raises horses, don't they? That's why it's your house's symbol. How many do they have?"

"Yes. Yes. And a couple thousand head."

"Do you remember your first horse?"

"I've had many. Here, let me do that." Reaching over, he fashioned her gear into a pack, which he lifted onto her shoulders. "Let's go."

It hadn't only been the speed and intensity of their travels that had stymied their conversation—it had been Killian. Since she'd told him about Celendor, about her father, about the servant woman, the words between them had been limited to necessity, and her attempts to get him to say more were met with obvious rebuke.

Was it because she'd allowed intimacy between them while knowing Malahi was alive, or was it because of the story she'd told him?

It was one she'd never told anyone—not even Teriana. Even thinking of it filled her with intense shame. It was tempting to claim she was better than the Cel out of virtue of the way they'd looked down upon her, but they'd raised her, and it had left its mark.

Why did you tell him? an angry little voice whispered inside her head. *Now he thinks you're awful.*

Kicking angrily at a rock, she tried to push the thoughts from her head, but as they walked on and on, her mind stewed and twisted, coming up with things to say only to reject them before they reached her lips, which, given that it was obviously Killian's preference, meant they walked for hours in silence that wasn't broken until they reached a stream nearly large enough to be called a river.

"How do we get across?" she asked as they stopped next to its banks. Ice crusted the edges, and it looked deep enough to reach her hips, if not higher.

Killian pulled off his boots, and she noted one of his woolen socks had a hole in the toe before he tugged it off. "Give me your pack. And wait here."

She handed it off, watching as he waded across the stream, the water rising nearly to his waist. On the far side, he tossed boots and packs on the bank, then returned across.

His teeth chattering, he said, "Hold on." Then he reached down and caught her behind the knees, lifting her into his arms.

"Killian, I can walk!"

"No sense both of us getting soaked." He stepped into the water, and within a few paces, she could feel him straining against the current, his eyes fixed on the flow. But instead of watching the water, Lydia found herself looking at his face. His dark hair had fallen forward, and she had to curb the urge not to reach up and brush it back.

He slipped slightly on the streambed, and she gasped as his hands tightened against her ribs and on the back of her thighs where he gripped her. "I won't drop you," he muttered, regaining his balance and moving on, until eventually, he set her on her feet on the opposite bank.

Shivering hard, he pulled on socks and boots before donning his pack. Then he frowned, looking her over. "Aren't you carrying a weapon?"

Lydia's chest tightened and she shook her head, the only blade she had the tiny one she used for eating.

Extracting a significantly longer blade from his boot, he held it out to her. "Here. Take this. We're moving into territory that is only dubiously under Mudamorian control, so it's best we be prepared."

She stared at the weapon, the blade glinting wicked sharp in the sunlight. "No, thank you."

He huffed out an annoyed breath. "It wasn't a request. Obviously I'll do the bulk of the fighting if it comes to it, but you need to be able to defend yourself."

"A healer is supposed to give life, not take it," she answered. "So I'll run or I'll hide. And if I have to fight back, I'll do it with my fists, but not with a blade."

Then, knowing she was in for an argument, she took several rapid steps to move ahead of him on the path. But Killian caught her arm, hauling her back to face him.

"That is the stupidest thing I've ever heard," he snapped. "I've known dozens of healers over the years who carried blades just in case they needed them, and not a one hesitated to slip it between a pair of ribs if the alternative was them dying."

"I don't care if every other healer on Reath carries a weapon, I'm not going to."

"Then turn around and go back."

She stared at him. "Why are you pushing this?"

"Because it's hard enough to have you with me without knowing that you won't do a bloody thing to defend yourself." His hands balled into fists. "I should never have agreed to you coming at all."

"It wasn't your choice!" She was more upset than angry, because he wasn't wrong. "And I'm not under your authority, so don't even think of trying to give me orders."

Killian scrubbed his wet hands back through his hair, glaring at her. "You've clearly taken leave of your senses."

"Because I don't want to kill people?" She crossed her arms under her breasts, digging her fingers into her sides. "How fortunate that I'm with you, then, *Killian,* because you have no compunction against it!"

He looked like she'd slapped him across the face, and guilt immediately welled up in her chest with the realization that she'd gone too far. Especially since she had no grounds to criticize. She opened her mouth to apologize, but in one swift motion, Killian pulled off her pack and scooped her up.

"What are you doing?" she shrieked at him but got her answer a heartbeat later when he tossed her into the stream.

She landed on her bottom, frigid water closing over her head. Scrambling to her feet, she gasped in a breath and then screamed, "You gods-damned entitled ass!" But he was already striding down the trail.

"Get back here!" she shouted, stumbling out of the water and retrieving her pack. "You *will* apologize for that."

"No, I won't!" he shouted back. "Because you deserved it."

Her body was shaking, her skin like ice, but Lydia didn't care as she stormed down the trail after him. "Killian!"

But he only broke into a jog, keeping ahead of her.

"Killian!" She ran after him, her bag bouncing on her back, her boots making loud squelches with each step. She was going to make him pay for that. Once she caught him, she was going to make him listen to the rough side of her tongue until he was groveling, begging for her forgiveness.

Except he sped up into a run, easily keeping ahead of her as she sprinted after him.

"You are an immature child!" she shouted. "You will stop and listen like a grown man or I'll . . . I'll . . ." She had no idea what she'd do. And as she chased him through the winding trails heading north, her breath coming in great heaving gasps and her side cramping, Lydia eventually resigned herself to the fact she wouldn't do anything at all.

Falling to a walk, she followed his footprints at a slow trudge, wishing the sun would move more quickly across the sky and force him to make camp. Her wet boots were rubbing her feet raw as fast as her mark could heal them, and she focused on the sting rather than the hurt in her chest.

Was this how it was going to go? She'd known there was no chance of them being together. But not once had she considered that their friendship would devolve into spitefulness and hate.

Then she rounded a large boulder and found Killian pacing back and forth across the path, his head snapping at the sight of her. "Thought maybe you'd given up and turned around."

She kept walking past him. "Did you really?"

He huffed out a breath of annoyance, then muttered, "Hope springs eternal."

The sun descended over the mountains, dark settling over the forest, but still he didn't tell her to stop to make camp. And though Lydia knew she was being childish and prideful herself, she refused to ask him to.

Only when it grew so dark that both of them were tripping over roots did Killian stop. "This will do."

From what she could make out, the spot was a wide clearing in the forest, the ground covered with dead grass and brush. Dropping her pack in the center, Lydia gathered firewood without comment while Killian set to clearing a spot for a fire. When she returned to drop a load next to him, he already had a small blaze of grass and twigs burning, but instead of stopping to warm herself, she started back out for another load.

They worked in taciturn silence, Killian cooking dinner and Lydia cleaning up the mess without either of them saying a word. Misery coated her insides as she watched him spread his bedroll next to the fire. "Go to sleep," he muttered. "I'll wake you when it's your turn to watch."

Unrolling her blankets, she took off her boots. But instead of lying down, she said softly, "Do you remember Emmy?" She'd no idea whether this was the right course, but she had to make Killian understand. For her sake.

And for his.

"Of course I do." He was quiet for a moment. "She's dead, isn't she?"

"Yes." Pulling off her spectacles, she set them aside, rubbing at her eyes. "She was infected with blight, but not in the way you saw before you left Mudaire. It evolved, those who rose from the dead no longer mindless, bloodthirsty things, but rather nearly perfect replicas of themselves in life. Only someone with Hegeria's mark can see the truth—that they are walking corpses animated by the Corrupter's power. To everyone else, they both appear and act as themselves."

Replacing her spectacles, she saw that Killian was watching her from across the fire.

"Most often, the infected were killed by soldiers when they were discovered, but Quindor kept Emmy in one of the rooms in the lower levels of Hegeria's temple."

Killian's jaw tightened. "He kept a little girl in a cell?"

"Yes. And no." Biting her bottom lip, Lydia considered her words. "She was kept in every comfort. Fed the best food. Given toys and new dresses. Quindor said he kept her alive to monitor how the infected were evolving, but I think it was that he held out hope she could be cured. That he could bring her back. He . . . he died trying to save her using the same method I used to pull the blight out of Lena. But one can't bring back the dead."

Killian said nothing, and part of her wanted to stop talking, because what she intended to say would *hurt*. But he needed to know.

"When I first returned to Mudaire, he took me down to see her. To prove to me that the blighters were dead and couldn't be healed, but also so that I could witness what the Corrupter was attempting to accomplish. His strategy, so to speak."

As she told him of Emmy and the cuff link, Killian's back bowed and he buried his face in his hands. Struggling to maintain her composure as she watched him crumple beneath guilt and grief, she said, "The Corrupter was using the blighters to undermine faith in the Marked and, in doing so, undermine faith in the Six. What Quindor and the rest failed to see was that killing them wasn't fighting this strategy but playing into it."

Swallowing hard, she said, "The healers were sent out into the streets with groups of soldiers in order to identify the blighters. Once caught, they were killed, most often while their families and friends begged that they be spared. *I* identified blighters and watched families beg for their lives."

"Gods," Killian muttered, then scrubbed his hands through his hair. His cheeks were wet. "Did no one see Quindor was turning healers into executioners?"

"He believed we were at war with the Corrupter and that this was the only way to win." Leaning forward, she added a log to the fire. "Instead, all the civilians in the city cursed us even as they did everything in their power to protect those who were infected, unwittingly siding with the Corrupter every time they did. And Rufina, in her guise as Cyntha, did everything she could to further destroy what faith they had left in the Marked. She slaughtered the blighters she encountered herself, violently and without mercy, and always in places where *everyone* would see." Her lip trembled. "I watched her behead a woman in the middle of the street. A blighter, nothing more than an animated corpse that needed to be put down. But the looks on the faces of the people as they watched one of Hegeria's Marked swing that sword is nothing I'll ever forget. And I vowed that no matter the circumstance, I'd never do anything that would cause them to look that way at me."

"You aren't Rufina." Killian's voice was hoarse. "*She's corrupted.* You are nothing like her."

"Why? Because my eyes don't look like pits to the underworld?" She tossed another log on the fire, watching the sparks fly. "When Rufina wasn't using her mark, she looked normal, too. I *could* be just like her if I chose that path—could use my mark to kill rather than save. I know it, because I've done it." She waited for him to question her, but his silence told her that he already knew. That Malahi had told him about what had happened that night in the tunnels. "I will do whatever is necessary to keep from taking another's life. Even if it means sacrificing my own."

Lying down on her bedroll, she turned away from him. "Good night, Killian."

It wasn't until a long time later that she heard him whisper, "Good night, Lydia."

69

MARCUS

Marcus blinked, slowly focusing on the flickering flames before him, his nose filled with the scent of sweat and smoke, his ears with the *crackle pop* of pine sap burning.

Everything hurt.

From his head to the tips of his obviously frostbitten toes, his body was an aching mass of pain, but worse than that was the fog in his head, his mind sluggish and disorientated. Like he'd been drugged, but somehow worse.

"Teriana?" He could barely get the word out, his tongue thick and his throat feeling as though it had been scoured by sandpaper.

"I'm here."

Her voice came from above him, and Marcus realized his head was in her lap, her hands stroking his hair. Shifting, he looked up, her face swimming in and out of focus. "What happened?"

"Nothing." She gave him a tight smile. "Everything is fine. Have a drink of water."

His muscles protested as she helped him sit and put a tin cup of warm water into his hand. He drank it greedily, and she filled it again from the kettle sitting next to the flames.

There were bandages wrapped around her palms, and her fingers were marked with nicks and cuts, moving stiffly. He sipped at the water and looked around the small cave, the space entirely unfamiliar. "Where are we? How did I get here?"

"Can we talk about it later?" she asked. "I really need to sleep."

His mind was sharpening, clear enough now to notice that her eyes were the color of stagnant pools, her skin ashen, and every move she made seemed an act of will. "What happened to you?"

"Please." Tears flooded down her cheeks, a sob tearing from her lips as she lowered herself to the cave floor. "I have to sleep."

Icy fear built in his gut, and Marcus pulled the blankets that had been covering him over her body, folding one to slip beneath her cheek. She whimpered softly, curling in on herself. *What happened?* His fear was turning to panic, and he rose on unsteady legs.

A flash of memory shot through his head, of stumbling through wind and darkness, Teriana begging him to keep walking, keep breathing, keep living. But before that, there was nothing.

"Think," he growled at himself. "What is the last thing you remember?"

Her face. Her voice as she said, "I'm sorry for this, but I refuse to let you die." And then the world fell away.

Of their own accord, his fingers went to his belt pouch, digging around the contents, but the vial of painkiller he always kept was gone. She'd drugged him.

But why?

Tucking the blankets tightly around her shoulders, he pulled aside the weighted tarp blocking the entrance to the cave. Outside, the sun was rising, bright oranges and pinks burning along the horizon, and he eyed the unfamiliar terrain, noting the dense forest in the distance.

Except that was impossible.

He ignored his aching body and broke into a trot, following a trail. Then he was no longer trotting, but running. Sliding to a stop only when he reached the edge of a cliff, across which was strung a single rope. On the far side, the rest of the bridge dangled, and beyond that, the razor-edged mountains of the Sibernese Teeth.

She'd carried him, unconscious, the rest of the way across the Teeth.

A tremble struck him in the knees, and he sat heavily on the ground, staring. It was impossible. Not only was she half-starved and exhausted, she was smaller than he was.

And yet the proof was undeniable. As was the toll it must have taken on her.

Scrambling back to his feet, Marcus raced back to the cave and ducked inside. Teriana still slept, and when he pressed his fingers against her pulse, it was not half so strong as he'd like. Right now, she needed sleep, but when she woke, she needed to eat.

As did he.

Hunger from days without food bit into his stomach, and Marcus surveyed the shelter for any sign of supplies, but there was nothing but a few jars containing less than a handful of oats and some crumbs from what looked like jerky.

Swearing, he pulled on his discarded hat and mittens, tossed another piece of wood on the fire, then went back out into the cold.

His breath misted as he followed the trail down toward the forest, catching sight of a bird flying in the trees, though that was likely a lost cause. He searched for signs of tracks, for signs of any life at all, but the snow was pristine and untouched. And other than the trees, all the plants were dead. Many of his men probably knew what could be foraged, but he'd been busy learning military strategies and how to kiss the asses of senators while the Thirty-Seventh had been learning to survive anywhere the Senate sent them.

And he'd left Teriana alone long enough. Gathering wood as he walked, he returned to the cave, checked on Teriana, then bolstered the fire.

They weren't far from the edges of civilization. He might be able to walk the distance without food, but there was no chance of Teriana walking anywhere for at least a day. Even if he built something to carry her, drained as she was, he wasn't sure if she'd be able to survive nights out in the open air. But there was no other choice.

Then, out of the corner of his eye, Marcus saw something move.

He turned his head in time to see a mouse scurrying across the cave, and he lunged for the creature.

But it was much too quick.

Pulling a burning twig from the fire, he circled the small space, seeing the cracks and holes that allowed the animals entrance, along with enough droppings to suggest the mouse wasn't alone. They rarely were.

All he needed to do was catch them.

Marcus gathered the supplies he needed and set up the traps, the knowledge of how to do so a relic from his training or a book, he couldn't recall which. After carefully baiting the trap with some jerky crumbs, he moved to the far side of the fire to sit next to Teriana.

Hours passed, and he must have dozed off, but then a loud bang jerked him awake.

Crawling over to the block of wood, he lifted it, grinning at the sight of the dead mouse. "Let's hope you have a large family," he said, picking it up by the tail. And then he rigged the trap once more.

70

KILLIAN

Lydia was nothing like Rufina. She was brave and selfless and kind, and he hated that she felt otherwise. Hated that the Corrupter had gotten his claws into her, even if it had been just for a moment. And it also made him wonder how many other of the Marked had slipped briefly into darkness.

Whether he had himself?

And in asking the question, Killian knew that it was so. That there had been moments where he'd been so consumed by anger that he'd used the strength that Tremon had given him not to protect those he cared about, but to harm. Vividly, he remembered how he'd attacked Hacken in the tunnels the night of the ball. How he'd wanted to hurt his brother as much as his brother had hurt him. How if Sonia hadn't intervened, he might have killed his own flesh and blood. But instead of telling Lydia that, he said, "My first horse wasn't a horse. It was a pony."

"Pardon?"

It was the first thing he'd said to her since they'd started out that morning, and out of the corner of his eye, he could see her staring at him in confusion.

"Before," he clarified. "You asked about my family's horses and if I remembered my first horse. It was a pony. Named Pom Pom."

"Pom Pom?" The first smile he'd seen in a long time lit her face. "*You* had a pony named *Pom Pom*?"

"That's right." Holding out a hand, he helped her over a fallen log, then turned his gaze back north. "And she was the nastiest, vilest-tempered beast I have ever owned. Bucked me off more times than all my other horses combined. My warhorse is a kitten by comparison."

"Your warhorse bites," she said.

"Threatens to bite," he corrected. "Pom Pom actually bit. Constantly and without provocation. She also kicked anything that dared to walk behind her, and despite being only three feet tall, she also was prone to trampling anything and anyone that got in her way, including me."

"And why, given that you apparently own a *few thousand head* of horses," she lowered her voice, clearly imitating him, "would your parents allow their child to be around such a beast?"

"It was my mother's doing. For all she's been a Calorian for twenty-seven years, I've only seen her actually ride a handful of times. My theory is that she dislikes ceding any control over where she's going, but she'd probably box my ears for saying so. Regardless, she was of the mistaken belief that being closer to the ground would make me safer, so when I demanded a mount, she insisted my father procure the smallest pony he could come by. Enter Pom Pom."

"I should think she'd have learned sooner with you having two older brothers."

"*They* got proper horses as their first mounts. Small, of course, but horses nonetheless."

She frowned. "What made you different?"

"My father said she was always more protective of me." He shrugged. "Seems silly, in hindsight. But anyway, by the time she realized her error, I was so deeply enamored with Pom Pom that I refused to give her up. When they tried to take her, I ran away with her and my sword. My father finally tracked me down at a farmhouse a few miles away, me having convinced the family living there that I was an orphan in need of care."

A laugh exited her lips, and it was all Killian could do not to lean down and kiss her. Looking away, he continued, "It apparently became quite a pattern for me. Every time my parents did something that made me cross, Pom Pom and I would gallop off down the road, roving farther afield each time in search of a family to take me in. Of course, everyone knew who I was, and word would be sent immediately to Teradale that I'd been found, which meant my father arriving soon after to lead us back home."

"Would you be punished?"

A memory, so faded as to be little more than an impression of sound and sentiment, filled his head. Of riding on Pom Pom next to his father's stallion, the sun beating down on their heads, listening to war stories. "No. He wasn't much for punishment. Rarely anything worse than being forced to muck stalls or the like. But I was generally so desperate to please him that knowing I'd disappointed him in any capacity was worse than a lashing."

And the last thing Killian had done was disappoint him.

Shaking his head to clear away the rising grief, he said, "Pom Pom was the only one with me when I was marked."

"Will you tell me how it happened?" she asked. "None of the girls in the guard seemed to know the whole of it, and if she knew, Bercola wouldn't say."

It was hard not to stiffen at the mention of the giantess. He'd heard nothing of her since their conversation at Alder's Ford, and he couldn't help but wonder where she was. If she was well. If, maybe, he'd been too harsh in sending her away.

"Very few know the story," he finally said. "My mother, and I suppose my brothers. I was not yet five years old, and I, along with my entire family, had journeyed north to Mudaire. I was supposed to swear my sword to King Derrek Falorn's daughter, Kitaryia, the idea being that I'd be raised alongside her so that my loyalty would be assured. At any rate, the day prior to when the ceremony was to take place, my mother stuffed me into fancy clothes to sit for a portrait, none of which suited me. So I saddled Pom Pom and left the city."

That part was hearsay recollected by his parents, for he didn't remember the clothes or the portrait or riding alone through Mudaire. But clear as day, he remembered what had happened next. "I went galloping down one of the paths along the coast, waving the new sword my father had given me and pretending I was off to slay a beast or some such nonsense. Pom Pom must have been weary of my shouting, because as we entered a copse of trees, she slid to a stop and sent me flying over her ears and into the dirt."

"And you *loved* this animal?"

"Most definitely," he confirmed. "Anyway, I was sitting in the dirt shouting foul words at her, and someone said, 'I believe this blade is yours, Killian.'" He swallowed, his throat feeling suddenly thick. "I looked up, and this enormous man in golden armor stood over me, holding out my sword. I tried to take it back, but he kept it just out of reach, and being the entitled little Calorian shit that I was, I said, 'You give that back or my father will have you lashed, you thieving bastard.'"

"You did *not!*"

"I did. Fortunately for me, Tremon apparently has a good sense of humor, because he only laughed. I was in a right frenzy because he still had my blade, but at that moment, Pom Pom came up to stand at my shoulder, and she stared at him, trembling. Not like she was afraid, but as though she *knew* we were standing in the presence of a god. It was her reaction that finally clued me in to who I was talking to."

He could feel Lydia's eyes on him, then she said, "You don't have to tell me what he said, if you don't want to."

And he never had told anyone, at least, not word for word. When his father and his men had finally caught up with him, all he'd said was, "Tremon marked me," and everyone had believed him, despite there being no real tangible proof.

"You told me what Hegeria said to you the night you were marked." Killian hesitated, then said, "He asked me if I wished to protect the hope of the realm. And I said yes."

Lydia was quiet, and as they continued down the path, it began to snow. At first only a few drifting flakes, but soon it turned thick and heavy, the north wind biting through his clothes. Then she asked, "Do you remember her? Kitaryia?"

"I never met her." But he remembered clearly his father teaching him the words of the oath he'd been supposed to swear to her. So clearly that he'd needed no reminders of them when he'd eventually sworn them to Malahi. "That night, one of the corrupted got into the palace and assassinated King Derrek, and Queen Camilla and Kitaryia went missing. My father organized countless searches, but their bodies were never recovered, and it was assumed they'd either been taken or had been cast off the balcony into the sea."

"Do you think it was Rufina who did it?" she asked while pondering the Falorn queen's given name, which was common in Celendor but not one she'd encountered here.

"Maybe. But they're sixteen years dead, so it doesn't much matter. The truth won't bring them back."

His skin prickled, but when he glanced down at Lydia, she was only staring at the snowy ground. Ahead of them, a narrow stream of blight crossed the path, and as she stepped over it, Lydia said, "Do you believe Malahi's still alive?"

Lifting his gaze to the snowcapped Liratoras that formed the border between Mudamora and Derin, he said, "Yes."

71

TERIANA

The smell of roasting meat filled her nose, and her mouth watered.

Peeling her eyelids open, Teriana focused on Marcus, who knelt next to the fire holding a green branch covered with little forms over the flames, his expression intent.

"Are those mice?" she croaked.

A slight smile rose to his lips. "Yes. Yes, they are. Want one?"

"I can't believe I'm about to say this, but yes." She shifted, trying to sit, but the motion sent slices of agony through her body, and she cried out.

"You've stiffened up," he said. "It'll ease. Let me help you."

Clenching her teeth, she allowed him to pull her upright and rest her back against the wall.

"They take forever to catch, so eat the whole thing," he said, handing her a crackling mouse. Then pulling one off the branch for himself, he winked at her and bit its head off.

"That," she whispered, "is horrible."

"It's not," he said, the mouse's skull making awful crunching sounds as he chewed. "Though I'm partial to the tail."

He bit off the crispy appendage, and Teriana gagged. "Stop."

But for all it was disgusting in theory, the smell of cooked meat had her body singing a different tune. Holding the mouse up to her mouth, she bit into its side, wincing as its ribs cracked. Then drops of grease rolled over her tongue and she found herself taking a second bite. Then a third. "Give me another."

They ate until the mice were gone, and then Marcus leaned against the wall next to her. "You're incredible, you know."

"Says the man who prepared mice for me for dinner." She rested her head against his shoulder, exhausted and sore, but no longer hungry.

"Are you going to tell me how you did it?"

"I captured a giant hawk, and it flew us out of danger."

He wrinkled his nose, then pulled her onto his lap and wrapped his arms around her. "Deus ex machina. I'm disappointed."

"Only because you missed the flight." Closing her eyes, Teriana leaned into him, listening to the steady beat of his heart. The heart she'd fought so hard to keep beating. "Well," she murmured. "It all started when you succumbed to a fit of dramatics and fatalism, and I decided that all decision-making needed to be taken out of your hands. . . ."

Marcus listened in silence as she explained how she'd done it, tensing when she got to the last bridge and the lines snapped. But when she was finished, he kissed her forehead and said, "We're going to survive this."

They were. She knew it.

If only making it out alive meant the end of their woe.

72

LYDIA

Their boots crunched in the deepening snow as they walked down the narrow trail, the towering Liratora Mountains no longer what captured her attention, but rather the towering wall that loomed to her left.

Killian had told her that it ran north and south to protect the only pass between Mudamora and Derin. The rows of jagged mountains did the rest. At least fifty feet high, the wall was made of grey blocks of stone, the seams tight and smooth enough that she doubted even Teriana could've scaled them without rope. The top held fortified guard posts every hundred feet or so, though the lack of motion or brazier smoke suggested that no one—friend or foe—kept watch. A suspicion that was confirmed as they reached the blackened fortress near the center of the pass.

The half-moon exterior wall of the fortress stood whole, but the gate leading into it was gone, the stone stained with soot from where it must have once stood. And running through it was a wide river of blight. Crouching behind dead brush, Killian stared at that gap, his jaw taut. Remembering, she thought. Remembering the last time he'd been here. When the wall had fallen and Rufina had invaded.

Remembering his defeat.

"You see any sign of life?" he asked softly, finally breaking the silence.

Lydia shook her head, having already used her mark to scan the surrounding territory. There was nothing alive. Even the forest around them was dead, leagues and leagues of barren trees as far as the eye could see. "But there could be someone beyond the wall or in the fortress and I wouldn't be able to tell. Should we wait for darkness before we go in?"

"No." Killian climbed to his feet. "Darkness is Derin's advantage, not ours. We'll go in now."

Drawing his weapon, he motioned for her to follow, his gaze sweeping their surroundings as they crossed the clear cut between forest and the fortress wall. He held up a hand as he reached the opening, and she paused as he eased alongside the black flow, peering into the courtyard before venturing inward.

Lydia followed, the stench of blight filling her nose as she searched for any signs of life. But there was nothing but blackened stone, snow, and the endless howl of the wind. Her eyes skipped over the outbuildings, recognizing one as a smithy and another as a large stable, the ceilings of both collapsed. The fortress backed against the wall itself, the opening to the tunnel leading through looking like a gaping mouth, the bottom of the raised portcullis like teeth. And through it the blight flowed.

But Killian went neither through the tunnel nor into the fortress, instead going to the narrow steps that switchbacked their way to the top and taking them two at a time. Setting her pack against the wall, Lydia followed, eyes going east to Mudamora, all greys and whites. The main river of blight broke off into narrower branches that stretched as far as her eyes could see.

Reaching the top of the stairs, she took a moment to marvel at the thickness of the wall, wondering how long it had taken to build, then she went to the far edge to join Killian where he stood, hood back, the frigid wind tossing his hair. "The last time I stood here," he said, "the Derin army filled this pass. An endless sea of blackness and flame."

But now it was nothing but a carpet of white with a black stripe down the middle. The V-shaped pass sloped upward into Derin, the sides of the mountains that formed it holding nothing but snow, rocks, and a handful of spindly trees, all of them as dead as those on the Mudamorian side.

Was this what Derin looked like? she wondered. *Barren and lifeless?* "Are you so sure there is something out there?"

"Yes," Killian said. "Look."

She followed his pointed finger, narrowing her eyes against the glare. In the distance rose plumes of smoke.

They followed the black river up the pass, and she shivered with unease at how it seemed to be both still and moving, pushing east and yet moving west back into Derin, like two opposing rivers merged into one. A trail of footprints ran next to it, all of them headed into the mountains.

"Do you have a plan?" she asked, noting that Killian still held his sword in his gloved hand, eyes prowling over their surroundings.

"Not yet," he answered. "First I need to see what we're up against."

Lydia continued to trudge up the pass, her breath growing increasingly labored as they climbed, her pack heavy. The air felt thin, her lungs as though she wasn't getting enough in each breath. Glancing back, she saw that they were now far higher than the wall, Mudamora visible beyond.

As they reached the crest of the pass, Killian pulled her low, both of them staring into the valley below. The blight flowed into it, then split, each branch leading to one of eight virulently green mounds that seemed to pulse with life. Yet rather than being beautiful, there was something deeply unnatural about them. Something that reminded her of the way the corrupted glowed with such an excess of life as to be gluttonous and foul. *A wrongness.* Armed soldiers stood guard nearby, though they looked more bored than watchful.

"The source," Killian muttered. "The corrupted tenders must be nearby."

It was a struggle to look elsewhere, but Lydia shifted her attention to where the smoke rose—a town. And a large one at that. Even from this distance, she could make out countless figures moving between the rough wooden buildings, plumes rising from dozens of chimneys. Other than the road they were on, the only path leading into town came from a narrow ravine on the north side of the valley. As they watched, a laden cart pulled by a donkey appeared, trundling down the slope into town.

"Xenthier," Killian muttered next to her. "It has to be."

"What do we do now?" Lydia asked. "We can't just walk into town."

"Why not?" Killian gestured to the path in front of them, the snow trodden by dozens of footprints. "Let's go."

Terror pulsed through her veins, but next to her, Killian strode with total nonchalance. "Don't look so worried," he muttered as they approached the town. "You'll give us away."

Though it soon became clear that worried or not, no one in the town paid them much attention. Rough two-story buildings made out of wood lined the muddy streets, nearly half of them seeming to be taverns or tap houses, though with the scantily dressed men and women leaning out the upper windows calling out invitations to all who passed, Lydia guessed that just as many were brothels.

The people themselves had skins of every hue from as fair as Lydia's own to skin as dark as any Maarin, though most wore the same style of clothing, the women in dark woolen dresses, the men in woolen trousers and coats, their cloaks trimmed with fur. The voices that filled the air used different languages and accents, and if not for the fact she *knew* they stood in the landlocked center of the continent, Lydia would have guessed they were in a trading port frequented by ships of a dozen different nations.

Two men rolled out of the front of one of the taverns, fists flying and mouths spewing curses, and Killian tugged her backward as a crowd formed, the watchers cheering the men on as they struggled. "Let's see if we can find an inn of sorts."

Turning down another street yielded rows of quieter buildings, and Killian led her toward one with a sign with gilded cursive writing that said, *The Feisty Donkey.* Pushing open the door revealed a smoky room with several long tables, the benches lining them filled with men and women. A handful glanced up, but then immediately turned back to the platters of food before them.

Approaching the bar, Killian said to the man filling cups of ale, "You have rooms?"

"Aye. It's six coppers a night or a silver for the week. Paid up front."

Killian dug into his pocket, and Lydia clenched her teeth, worried he'd pull out his usual handful of gold and silver, but when he opened his palm it held only a few copper coins. "How much for a meal?"

"Another copper." The barkeep glanced at Lydia. "Each. Unless your lass there can sing or dance, then she can eat for free in exchange for an hour's entertainment. Our other girl's gotten too big with child."

"She sounds like a cat being strangled when she sings and can barely walk two paces without tripping over her own cursed feet," Killian answered. "You'd be paying me to shut her up."

"Can she cook?"

"Nothing you want to eat. You'd lose half your patrons to the latrines from half-cooked meat if you put her in the kitchen."

Both of them laughed, but instead of glaring, Lydia asked, "What about if *he* dances?" Leaning her elbow on the counter, she smiled up at Killian, whose face was filling with dismay. "If he loses the shirt, I assure you that you'll have not an empty seat in the place."

The barkeep looked him up and down. "*Can* he dance?"

"Oh yes. His mother made sure of it."

"Then it's the same deal. You can eat on the house in exchange." He narrowed his eyes, scrutinizing Killian's face. "I'll throw in some ale as well."

Killian's cheeks had turned bright red, and without a word, he counted out the coins and pushed them toward the barkeep.

"Let me know if you change your mind," the man said, then filled two cups and passed them over before retrieving a key with a number eight carved into it. "Second floor. You want water for washing, it's another copper. You want it warm, another copper on that."

"That's bloody robbery." Killian scowled, shoving the rest of his coins into his pocket.

"You want cheap, go next door and bed down with their fleas. Or take off your shirt and start dancing."

Killian gave Lydia a baleful glare, but then he drank deeply from his filthy glass and said, "A bit of dirt never hurt anyone. Let's go, love."

Lydia followed him through the common room toward the narrow stairs, which creaked as they climbed. The hallway upstairs was lit by a single smoking lamp, but it was enough to make out the eight carved into the door they'd been assigned. Unlocking it, Killian stepped inside and glanced around before nodding at her to follow.

As she'd expected, it was small and sparsely furnished, the tiny window devoid of both glass and shutter, leaving a clear view for any in the building across the street. The single bed had a lumpy mattress stuffed with straw, but the blankets were surprisingly clean, as was the floor.

Which was good news for Killian, because she fully intended to make him sleep on it. "This useless lass is claiming the bed," she said, tossing her pack on the blankets and then sitting down.

Killian only laughed, sliding off his own pack. "I'd say you got your revenge already."

She scowled. "What is the plan, Killian?"

"You keep asking me that."

"And you keep not answering."

Shrugging, he pulled out the chair, twisting it backward, then sitting down to face her, chin resting on his forearms along the back of it. "I prefer to figure things out as I go."

She knew that. Knew that he was reactionary, relying on his instincts and his mark to steer him down the right path. But that didn't work for her. "For one, you need an alias. You're too famous, and half the soldiers in this city will have fought against you. That . . . awfulness on your face isn't going to fool anyone if you don't go by something different."

"I think it's coming in rather nicely," he answered, rubbing his scruffy chin. "And I'm curious to see just how long it will grow. Does it make me look wise?"

"It makes you look . . . look . . ." With his dark eyes regarding her like that, all clever retorts abandoned her lips. He was so good looking, it hurt. "No. You don't look even a little bit wise."

He sighed. "Fair enough. But I think it only fair to point out that *your* name is uncommon and your actions on the battlefield saving *my* life well known, so you also need a new name." He reached over and pushed her fringe up to reveal her tattoo before dropping it again. "Gertrude. No . . . no, *Gertie.*"

"Absolutely not. You will *not* call me *Gertie.*"

Killian grinned, and the skin of her chest burned, the heat rising up her neck to her face until her cheeks were an inferno. And knowing that he'd only come up with something worse, she said, "Fine, but that means I get to pick yours."

He shrugged. "Take your pick."

Think of a name. Think of something awful that he'll hate. "Bertie."

Killian burst out laughing, the rich sound of it filling the room as she struggled not to sink to the floor in embarrassment. "Gertie and Bertie? You're not very good at this, are you? How about . . . Tom?"

"Fine," she mumbled. "Tom is fine. Who are we?"

"Married, obviously," he said. "That should serve to deflect any unwanted advances from the ladies, especially if you keep glowering like that. As far as what our story is, I think I need to hear what the story is for all these other people before we come up with one of our own."

Rising, Lydia went to the window and looked out, watching the comings and goings of all the people. This place was a little rough around the edges, but it was also decidedly . . . *normal.* Women with baskets full of laundry or goods walked through the streets. Men gossiped on the corners. Children wielding sticks ran through the puddles, shouting and laughing.

"It's not what I expected."

She jumped, having not heard Killian come up next to her. He rested a hand against the windowsill, leaning out, but his shoulder brushed against hers and she shivered. "Nor I," she admitted, not sure precisely what she'd thought they'd encounter. "I thought all those living in Derin worshipped the Seventh."

"So it is said." Killian's gaze remained on the people below. "Derin isn't easily reached. The mountains defend its eastern borders from Mudamora. The deadlands of the south from Anukastre. The twisted seas and swamps make its western coast unassailable. And the north is frozen year-round, so that border is equally secure. In truth, no one knows what goes on within its borders. And yet . . ."

"There are people here from every nation."

He gave a slow nod, his elbow grazing her upper arm.

"Why are they here?" she mused, watching a laughing pair of drunks walk arm in arm. "*How* are they here?"

"Good questions. But not our priority. We need to learn more about the corrupted tenders who created those mounds. Who they are and, more importantly, where they are."

"And if Malahi's with them."

He gave a slight nod. "Ideally, we'd destroy those mounds, but getting Malahi out is our priority. They'll pursue, and with their deimos tracking us overhead, it will take an act of the Six to reach Serlania alive. But first we need to find out *where* she is."

They made their way back downstairs, finding the common room had filled as the dinner hour approached. Without hesitation, Killian led her to a table, squeezing into a spot between two men. Lydia sat in the narrow gap across from him, the elbows of the women to either side brushing against her. At Killian's raised hand, one of the servingwomen approached, and he ordered, giving her a coin and a wink that made the woman smile and flush, despite being old enough to be his mother.

She returned moments later with two bowls of thick stew and a platter containing slices of still-warm bread smeared with golden butter, along with two glasses of ale. Lydia began spooning stew into her mouth, the bowl quickly disappearing, and then she used a slice of bread to mop up the last few drops. Using her sleeve to wipe away the prior user's lip marks, she drank the ale, feeling her body warm a few moments later.

The room was loud enough that she couldn't talk to Killian without shouting, so instead, she listened to the conversations of the people next to them.

"I'm not staying here any longer," the woman sitting next to her said to her companion. "I'm sick of being hungry and cold and idle."

"You just ate," the man replied sourly. "Quit complaining."

"Yes, because Her *Majesty* deigned to send the vestiges of her army some supplies. But how long until they run out? And how long will she leave us without this time? I want to go home."

"With what coin, woman? It's ten pieces of gold *each* for an escort across the Liratoras."

Lydia blinked at the amount, which was an outrageous sum, but Killian met her gaze and gave a slight shake of his head. *Listen.*

"We could head back into Mudamora and loot," she suggested. "Find some dead lordling's manor and figure out where he buried his gold and his wife's jewels."

The man snorted loudly, then spit on the floor. "Ain't nothing left to loot and you know it. And the land's thick with blight. Here, we might go hungry a day or two, but that's a shade better than drinking foul water and then rising a walking corpse a few hours later."

So those from Derin weren't spared from the blight's effects. Why was she not surprised?

Behind her, a gust of cold air blew in as someone opened the door, then a booming voice said, "Clear my table, you bastards."

Seeing Killian's eyes widen slightly, Lydia turned and looked up.

And up.

Behind her stood a giant, his ruddy head shaved, his colorless eyes unreadable as he watched those sitting with her and Killian clamber to their feet, moving off to find other seats. She started to rise, but the giant smiled. "Not you, lass. You can stay."

"I can move," she replied quickly, but he placed a massive hand on her shoulder, holding her in place.

"Keep your hands to yourself." Killian didn't speak loudly, but a sudden silence fell across the common room.

Almost immediately, the barkeep was at the table, his expression panicked. "They didn't know this was your table." Then he pushed at Killian's shoulder. "You'll find another bench if you know what's good for you, lad."

Killian didn't move, but his eyes went back to her shoulder where the giant's hand remained fixed, despite how she squirmed. "Let her go and we will gladly do so."

"No." The giant closed his other hand over her other shoulder. "She's the prettiest girl in the place, so I want her to sit with me."

Killian rose to his feet, eyes full of anger.

"You're a daft fool," the barkeep hissed. "She's not worth picking a fight with a giant."

"I beg to differ."

"Already?" A new voice filled the silence. "Gods, Baird, could you at least wait until we've eaten before you start picking fights?"

A figure slipped down on the bench next to Lydia, and she turned her head to see a broad-shouldered young man around Killian's age. He rested his elbows on the table and gave her a grin, his teeth white against golden-brown skin, tousled brown hair falling into his hazel eyes. He was exceptionally good looking and clearly knew it. "I'm

Agrippa. The ugly giant who needs to sit his ass down"—he cast a pointed glance upward—"is Baird. You are . . . ?"

Agrippa. A Cel name if she'd ever heard one. And while his darker complexion suggested one of the Empire's provinces had contributed to his blood, the golden hue to it screamed Celendor. Realizing he was staring at her, waiting, she said, "Gertrude."

"That's a pretty name," the giant said, finally removing his hands from her shoulders and sitting next to her, his knees barely fitting under the table. The bench creaked alarmingly.

"Well met, Gertrude." Agrippa took a sip from Lydia's cup, then he looked at Killian. "The only folk who sit at Baird's table are girls with pretty names and those with coin to gamble. Since you're clearly not the former, you'd best have the latter."

Killian's eyes darkened, but then he shrugged. "What's your game?"

"Cards. Thank you, love," Agrippa said to the woman who'd brought ale as well as bowls of stew. She kissed his cheek, and he handed her a silver coin with a wink. "And we don't play for copper."

The grin Killian gave was all teeth. "Neither do I."

"Perfect," Agrippa answered, then he began spooning the stew into his mouth, while Baird tossed the utensil he'd been given aside and drank directly from the bowl.

Lydia glanced surreptitiously down, her stomach clenching as she caught sight of the familiar hilt. It bore no legion marks but it was most definitely a gladius. *Impossible,* her mind kept telling her, except she knew it wasn't. However he'd ended up in Derin, this young man was from the Empire, and she doubted he'd arrived on the Dark Shores via the stem in the baths in Celendrial, which meant there was another path. Part of her wanted to ask him, but that would mean revealing she wasn't from Derin, and she wasn't certain yet if that was a good idea.

Pushing aside his bowl, Agrippa extracted a deck of cards, shuffling them expertly. As he did, two women and a man joined, elbows resting on the table, stacks of silver piled in front of them.

"Blow on my cards, Gertrude," Baird said. "I need a bit of luck."

"She can see your hand, you idiot," Agrippa muttered. "You're going to lose all the coin we've earned for this jaunt across the Liratoras and we haven't even made the trip yet."

So there was xenthier leading here, but potentially not back. That explained why so many languished in this town despite the war being over.

Baird sighed, but pushed Lydia to her feet. "Go sit with your boy, lovely. When he loses all your coin, you can come back." He grinned, revealing a gap where his two front teeth had once been.

The group set to gambling in earnest, coins piling up in the middle of the table, the number of players whittling down as some folded. It wasn't a game Lydia was familiar with, but if it was new to Killian, he mastered it within a hand of play, for soon he and Agrippa were the only remaining players.

"So you're new to town," Agrippa said. "You one of the fools still coming through the xenthier on the hope of making your fortune looting Mudamora or one of the fools who lingered in Mudamora long enough to realize there is no fortune to be had?"

"The latter." Killian glanced at his cards, and Lydia refrained from looking at his hand, having already been informed she had too many tells to be a gambler. Given Teriana had told her the same every time her friend fleeced her of whatever trinkets they'd been playing for, Lydia had decided that maybe it was the truth. "What do you got?"

Agrippa flipped over what was an impressive hand, leaning back in his chair. "Beat that, *Tom*."

Killian didn't answer, and Lydia's stomach sank at the thought of losing what would be a sizable portion of their coin to a stupid game. Then he turned over his cards and Agrippa's smile fell away.

"I think we're done for the night." Killian reached to scoop up the coins, but viper fast, Agrippa caught hold of his wrist. "No one's this lucky! He's cheating. Check him for cards!"

In a heartbeat, Baird flipped over the table, silver scattering everywhere as he lunged at Killian. Lydia screamed as Killian shoved her out of the way. But then Agrippa had her by the arm, his hands going up her sleeve. "It's the girl!" he shouted triumphantly, pulling three cards from her sleeve, all aces in different suits.

"Those are not mine!" she shouted. "You put them in there! You're the cheat!"

But even as she said the words, she knew no one would believe them. That for whatever reason, the pair had set her and Killian up.

"You think you can cheat me?" Baird bellowed. Picking up a chair, he flung it against a wall, then tossed another behind the bar, glass smashing. "There's going to be a reckoning for this, boy!"

"Not in here! Please, Baird!" the barkeep pleaded, ducking as a chair flew over his head. "Do what you want to him but do it outside."

"Outside!" the giant roared. "I'm going to teach this cheating little shit a lesson."

"You are most certainly welcome to try, you lying prick!" Killian shouted back, then he caught Lydia's arm, drawing her with him as the common room emptied onto the street.

Outside, he let go of her, pulling his sword. But Baird only looked at him and scoffed. "Fight me like a man with your fists."

Killian barked out a laugh, but then seemed to see the glee on the faces of the onlookers and realized the giant was serious. "You want me to engage in a fistfight with a *giant*."

Baird grinned. "Unless you're too much of a coward."

Killian was far from a small man, but the giant had to be pushing eight feet tall and was just as thick. And yet Lydia could see he was considering it.

Pushing aside the men between them, Lydia caught hold of his arm. "This is madness," she hissed. "You're going to get yourself killed! He's half again your size!"

"I have my own advantages," he answered. But he wasn't looking at her, his eyes intent on the giant striding up and down the street and inciting the crowd. "And if I don't, they'll run us out of town."

"Better that than you dead!"

"Yes, but better still if I win." He tried to pull away, but she dug in her nails until he looked down at her and said, "Trust me. And for the love of the gods, *don't* interfere."

Unbelting his sword, he pushed it into her hands before striding into the open space, muddy slush splashing around his boots.

Agrippa also moved to the center of the space, catching hold of both Baird's arm and Killian's. "You all know the rules, aye?" he shouted. "No weapons but fists and feet. They go until one of them begs mercy or until one gets knocked out. But if someone dies . . ." He paused, grinning wildly at the crowd. "We'll light a pyre and let the gods fight for the bastard's soul!"

The crowd roared their approval, and Baird pulled his arm from Agrippa's grip. Then he tore his shirt off and threw the fabric in the mud before wrenching off his boots and tossing them into the crowd. "You, too, you little worm!" he shouted at Killian. "I don't trust that you don't have a blade or two hidden."

Killian glowered, but yanked his hand free from Agrippa and circled back to Lydia. Jerking off his boots, he dropped them at her feet, then shrugged off his coat and pushed it into her hands, shirt following suit. The women, and a good number of the men, in the crowd shouted catcalls at him, but Killian didn't react. Instead, he leaned down, his breath hot against her ear. "If this does go poorly, it's all on you." Reaching up, he tangled his hand in her hair. "Find her."

Then he turned away.

Lydia's heart throbbed in her chest as Agrippa again took hold of their hands and held them up. Then he shouted, "Begin!" and dived out of the way as the crowd roared.

Baird attacked first, his fist flying toward Killian's face with crushing speed, but before Lydia could scream, Killian shifted sideways and the giant's fist struck nothing but air. Caught up in his own momentum, Baird staggered, and Killian landed two fast blows to the giant's gut before dancing backward.

The crowd roared in dismay, clearly on Baird's side, but Killian didn't seem to hear them as he paced backward, eyes on the giant. Baird lumbered forward, massive fist swinging, but again Killian evaded the blow, catching the giant's ankles and sending him sprawling.

Instead of attacking, Killian moved out of range of Baird's grasping hands, watching while the giant rose, ignoring the crowd's boos. Again and again, Baird attacked, but Killian anticipated every blow, using his speed to move out of the way and land blows of his own.

Yet he never attacked.

He was wearing the giant down, that much was clear, for while Killian was barely breathing hard, Baird was panting, his massive torso dripping sweat. "Quit dancing around and fight like a man!" he bellowed, the crowd screaming their agreement, but Killian only laughed and circled.

It carried on that way, the crowd growing angrier as their favorite stumbled and bled and failed to land a single blow, and Lydia gritted her teeth, uncertain why Killian was baiting them rather than finishing the fight. What was he waiting for?

Then she got her answer.

Baird slowly rose from the mud where he'd landed after Killian's last blow, and then in a blinding burst of speed that tore a gasp from her throat, he charged.

Instead of dodging, Killian stood his ground, allowing the giant to take him over backward and using his feet to send Baird flying over his head. But the giant caught hold of him as he flipped, and instead of rolling away, Killian ended up on top of him, Baird gripping one of his wrists like a vise.

Killian's fists flew, breaking the giant's nose and then cracking his cheek, but with lightning speed, Baird caught his other wrist. Rolling, they grappled, but as Killian freed a hand, using it to strike the giant in the kidneys, Baird pulled an arm back and slammed his massive fist into Killian's ribs.

Pain washed across his face, and instinct causing Lydia to leap forward, but Agrippa caught her arms, jerking her back. "You getting in the mix will only cause him more trouble, girl."

Both Killian and Baird were bleeding, their bodies covered in livid red marks and their faces swelling, but neither made any move to concede. The crowd was wild with delight and growing in numbers, people lured from all over town by the noise.

And Killian wasn't winning. Even without her mark, she could see his movements slowing down, the pain of dozens of injuries written across his face, and panic filled her because if the giant landed the right blow, it would kill him.

Fear grew in her guts, stealing her control, and she struggled against Agrippa, using the tricks Killian himself had taught her. But Agrippa stymied her efforts easily enough that she grew certain he'd been trained at Lescendor itself, and he only chuckled, forcing her to her knees in the mud. "He won't kill him, lass. He's just teaching the boy a lesson."

Fury mixed with her fear, and she inched her bare fingers over his hand, feeling her mark catch hold of his life. *Take it,* a dark voice whispered in her head. *Silence his laughter, his mockery.*

Her eyes leapt to Killian, who was on his back in the mud, hands up to block the blows the giant was raining down on him. And he turned his head to look at her, his mouth moving silently. *Don't.*

Then Baird's knuckles struck his forearm, and she *heard* the crack of breaking bone. Yet it was her that screamed, the dark half of her mark rising—

But before she could take Agrippa's life, Killian jerked his knee up, catching Baird hard between the legs.

The giant howled, rolling off him and clutching his crotch, his face purpling and tears rolling down his cheeks as Killian staggered to his feet.

"You bastard," Baird groaned. "You truly are a woman to be going after a man's jewels."

Killian spit blood into the mud and grinned, his teeth smeared crimson. "Like any good woman, I was merely checking to see if you had a pair. Given your size, my friend, I can't say that I'm impressed."

"Oh, shit," Agrippa said as Baird's face turned an even darker shade of purple, and then the giant charged, hands reaching for Killian's throat.

How he did it, Lydia couldn't have said, but in a blur of motion, Killian was on the giant's back, one arm around his throat and his legs pinioning Baird's to his sides. Grabbing his broken arm above the elbow, Killian squeezed, Baird's mouth wide as he tried and failed to draw in air.

The giant launched himself backward, landing on Killian hard enough to make him cry out in pain from his fractured ribs, but he held on, ankles locked. Holding tight, even when Baird got one arm free, his meaty fingers leaving claw marks on Killian's arms as he struggled.

And then, finally, Baird went still.

Killian held on for a few moments longer, then relaxed, releasing the giant's throat and rolling him off.

Baird came to a few seconds later, shaking his big head and climbing to his hands and knees, glaring at Killian. Then he grinned. "Not bad, you skinny little bastard."

"We have a victor!" Agrippa shouted, and tugging Lydia to her feet, he pushed her toward Killian. "And to the victor go the kisses!"

Her heart in her chest, Lydia stumbled through the mud, falling to her knees in front of Killian. Leaning against her, he said softly, "I'm going to see what I can learn from them." Then he pushed her back with his unbroken arm. "Go back to the room, woman. You've caused me enough trouble tonight."

Before she could answer, Baird reached down and caught Killian under the arms, lifting him to his feet. "We need some drinks!"

Leaving Lydia to gather up the discarded clothing, they moved back into the common room, the crowd cheering and hammering the men on their backs as they passed. Digging the key out of Killian's coat pocket, she tossed his clothing, boots, and weapons on the table, and ignoring Agrippa's laughter, she strode to the stairs, heading for their room.

Not that she had any intention of remaining there.

73

TERIANA

They spent another two days in the cave, eating mice—along with a rabbit that Marcus managed to catch in a snare—and then they started on their way.

At first walking was agony, every strained muscle in her body screaming that she sit still, but gradually, the pain lessened as she loosened up. It was a relief to be in different terrain, the quiet of the forest broken only by the soft *tromp* of the pine boughs strapped to their feet and the occasional chitter of a squirrel.

But even without the endless wind they'd been exposed to in the Teeth, there was no denying it was getting colder. At night, they made a shelter from the canvas Marcus had taken from the cave, one of them always remaining on watch to ensure that the fire burned high to ward off the chill.

Even with it, by morning she was cold and stiff, and the pain of moving was worse than the first day.

"How long until we reach somewhere with people?" she grumbled. The rabbit was long gone, and her stomach ached with hunger.

Marcus lifted his head and pointed.

Shielding her eyes with one hand, Teriana caught sight of several plumes of smoke rising above the trees. *A village.* "What's the plan?"

He scratched at his chin. "Given this village is on the route to the Via Mortis, it will have lodgings of some sort that we can rent. And those living here will be used to Empire messengers coming through, so they won't be quite as likely to kill me as those on the other side of the Teeth. Still, I think it's best not to mention my legion affiliations."

"Agreed. But *who* are we and why are we coming from the direction of the Teeth at this time of year? We need a story."

Except there was no explanation that wouldn't invite questions.

"We'll tell them that we came from Ygrisia," he said, naming a city on the North Sea that was only reachable by ship during the summer. "And that your family did not approve of our union, so we ran and fell in with the nomads, who helped us reach the Teeth."

Teriana's cheeks colored. She didn't wish to admit that a good portion of this *story* was something she fantasized about in idle moments. "Okay."

"And if they cause us trouble, then . . ." He touched the hilt of his gladius and started walking.

"Don't you dare kill anyone!" She scuttled after him, nearly tripping over her own feet. "The answer is not always violence."

"I promise not to kill anyone who doesn't try to kill me first."

The village wasn't large by any stretch of the imagination, but it was surprisingly full of people given the number of buildings. Many of them seemed to be trappers here to sell their furs to merchants who'd subsequently transport the goods to larger towns and cities for sale. The best of the goods were sent into Celendrial, where the most coin was to be had.

But even accounting for that, the crowds seemed thick, women and children buying cups of steamed milk and sweet cakes from vendors. And the village square was strung with garlands and tiny lanterns, the sight of which caused Teriana to count her fingers, trying to determine the date. "It's the last night of fall, and tomorrow, winter officially begins," she said. It was not lost on her that if she and Marcus had fallen through the xenthier a few weeks later, they'd never have survived. "There's going to be a festival tonight."

Marcus didn't answer, but his brow furrowed, his blue-grey eyes sweeping the town as though he expected to be accosted at any moment. "There's the inn," he said. "Hopefully there are still rooms."

As it turned out, the majority of people were staying with friends or family, so the inn was quiet compared to the bustle outside. But that didn't stop the innkeeper from wrinkling his nose, looking Marcus up and down like he'd rather throw them outside than rent them a room. Though she wasn't certain whether that was because they were dressed in clothes fabricated from blankets and badly cured wolf hide or because Marcus's coloring marked him as quite obviously from Celendor. Perhaps both.

"Late in the year for travel," he said in perfect Cel.

"It is," Marcus answered, not giving an explanation to the implied question. "And we'd rather not sleep on the ground tonight if it can be avoided."

"Looks as though you've spent more than a few living rough. Smells like you've been living rough, too."

"And we grow weary of it. We can pay, if that's your concern."

"That's not my concern." The man rested his elbows on the

counter. "What's a Maarin girl doing this far from the sea in the company of a *Cel* boy?"

"My ship has been keeping to the North Sea to avoid the Cel," Teriana answered swiftly, seeing Marcus's temper was starting to rise. "And they took issue with me taking up with him, so I left."

"Should've listened to your family."

Next to her, Marcus shifted restlessly, so she stepped on his foot. "Believe me, I know. But my bed is made, so I have to sleep in it. Preferably in a room in your lovely establishment." Reaching into a pocket, she extracted a silver hair bead she'd removed earlier, the rest of her hair pulled back in her hood to hide her true wealth. All their coinage was unmarked, which would raise questions. "We'll only be here one night."

"One night," the innkeeper said, his reluctance fading as he examined the silver bead. "But first, you wash up and burn everything you're wearing. Don't want you lousing up my linens." Then he smiled. "For another one of these beads, I'll supply you with clothes that don't smell like rotting wolf hide."

"Gladly." Handing over another bead, she added, "Now point me in the direction of the bath."

Arms full of clothes that the innkeeper had provided, Teriana followed Marcus through the snow behind the inn, heading toward a small structure with smoke rising from a chimney. "I can't wait to sit in a tub. I've never been this filthy in my entire life."

Marcus glanced back at her. "In the interior, the Sibernese don't bathe. That's a sauna."

"A what?"

"It's basically a box that fills with steam and you sweat the dirt off. Or so I've heard."

"That sounds awful." Scowling, she jerked open the door to the little structure, her eyes slowly adjusting to the small front area, which contained only a bench and a few hooks stuck into the side wall from which lengths of toweling hung. At the far end was another door, heat radiating from it.

Behind her, Marcus shut the front entrance and latched the bolt, then began pulling off articles of clothing and tossing them on the floor. "Put anything that needs burning in a pile," he said. "I'll deal with it after we're clean."

She watched him out of the corner of her eye, biting her lip as he shed the last of his garments and wrapped one of the towels around his waist. She hadn't seen him stripped down like this since they left Arinoquia, and filth aside, he made a fine feast for the eyes. He had always been lean, but their ordeal had stripped away what little softness he might have possessed, leaving behind only taut skin over hard muscle.

"I'm going to see how this works." Weapons in hand, he eased past her and opened the door, sending a blast of heat rolling over her. "Come in when you're ready."

Feeling suddenly self-conscious, Teriana transferred her few belongings to the pockets of her new clothes, which she hung on one of the hooks. Then she pulled off her disgusting garments and tossed them in a pile. She examined her own body and made a face at the greyish film of dirt that covered her now much leaner form, her prized curves eaten away by starvation. Taking a deep breath, she wrapped a towel around her body, picked up the soap and cloths she'd bargained into her arrangement with the innkeeper, and then went into the other room.

Marcus was standing in front of a stove, ladling water over hot rocks. Hissing clouds of steam rose to fill air that was already thick with it. Other than the stove, there was only a long bench against one wall, two basins of water, and a large bucket of snow. Mercifully, it was dark, the only light the fire burning in the stove.

Taking one of the basins, Teriana set to scrubbing herself with the soap and rag. The water that ran off her was grey and foul. "It's no wonder he didn't want to give us a room."

Marcus made a noise of agreement from where he was still examining the workings of the stove. Seemingly content he understood it, he took one of the rags from her, tossed aside his towel, and set to work on erasing weeks' worth of dirt.

Her eyes roved over his body, drinking him in, heat rising low in her belly as he squeezed a cloth over one shoulder and the water sluiced down his back. The tattooed *1519* was as harsh and black as ever against his golden skin—something they needed to keep hidden. But that seemed a distant concern.

"Soap?"

She jumped, her eyes jerking upward to find him smirking at her, and with a muttered curse, she tossed the bar, laughing when he fumbled it. They worked in silence, pausing only to ladle water onto the hot rocks. When she was finished, Teriana stretched out on the bench with her towel wrapped around her body, relishing the feeling of being clean. "Not quite as good as my tub on the *Quincense,* but not bad. Not bad at all."

"I don't remember the last time I sat in a tub."

She felt the bench creak beneath her as he sat at the far end, then the silence was broken by the rasp of a blade over a whetstone. "Did you ever go to the baths in Celendrial? When you were young? I've heard they are the purest form of luxury."

He paused in his sharpening. "No. They aren't for children."

The heat was making her mind wander, and she thought of the new baths that had recently been built in Celendrial, the project funded by Cassius, of all people. She'd heard that the warmest pool was filled by a massive dragon made of solid gold. Once upon a time, she might have asked Lydia to take her, but now the only thing she could hope for was that if her traitorous ex-friend availed herself of the waters, that she pick up a nasty foot fungus.

Shoving aside her anger at Lydia, she said, "Keep that up and you're going to sharpen the blade clean off."

"Best you hope not, or the beard will have to stay." Eyeing the edge of the knife, Marcus grimaced. "Not the ideal tool." Setting it aside, he soaped his face, then lifted the blade to his cheek.

"Stop!"

His gaze flicked to her. "Don't tell me you've grown fond of it."

"Hardly." She rolled her eyes. "But I am fond of your face, so I'd prefer you not cut it off. Come here, I'll do it."

"How is it that you know how to shave a man's face?"

There was an edge to his voice, and she smirked when she realized it was jealousy. "Wouldn't you like to know."

He glowered at her, and she laughed. "My great-great-uncle used to sail aboard the *Quincense* with us before he passed. He was ancient as the stones, but even though his hands shook like a boy working up the courage to ask a girl to dance, he insisted on always being clean-shaven, so us young folk had to learn to do it. Was considered something of a punishment, because his breath was bad enough to make your eyes bleed."

Marcus's brow furrowed, and she knew he was trying to determine whether it was the truth or a yarn.

"Come here. Let me dazzle you with my skill with a blade."

Sighing, he rolled onto his back, resting his head in her lap, and she shivered as his hair brushed the bare skin of her thighs. Draping the cloth over her knee and setting the basin within reach, she took up the knife and carefully scraped it across his cheek. "How long will it take to reach Celendrial?"

His eyes were closed, steam beading on his lashes. "We'll head to the Savio where we can hire or buy a riverboat. Then it will be another week or two on the water."

A matter of weeks, and then it would be over. She'd rejoin the *Quincense* and he his legion, and then it would be war. It could be no other way—not with the Senate once again able to exercise control over him and the Thirty-Seventh. More legions would join them, and they'd spread their footprint, conquering in the name of the Empire as they always had.

The thought made her eyes burn, so she focused instead on the task, the hard lines of his cheekbones and jaw emerging as she worked, the scent of soap filling her nose. Marcus kept his eyes closed the entire time, the 37 on his right pectoral rising and falling with each breath. Gods, but she hated that number. Hated the way it bound him. Hated how it would take him away.

"Done," she murmured, setting aside the knife and wiping the rest of the soap from his cheeks.

Opening one eye, he ran a finger down his jaw, then sat up, twisting so that he was facing her. "You do good work, Captain. Thank you."

"I did it for myself."

He laughed, but then they both fell silent, the only sound the rise and fall of their breaths. She wanted to kiss him. Wanted to run her hands over all those hard muscles. Wanted to wrap her legs around him and vanquish the space between them. But she didn't move.

Marcus had ended things between them because neither of them could trust the other.

Except with all they'd been through together, she didn't think there was anyone she trusted more than him. With her life. And with her heart.

As if hearing her thoughts, Marcus leaned toward her, one hand curving around her head.

And then he kissed her.

A soft press of the lips that sent heat coursing through her body, the sensation amplified as her own lips parted, his tongue stroking over hers. His other hand moved to her waist, sending a shiver through her body. This was what she wanted. He was who she wanted. But . . .

Pulling back from his kiss, she reached up to brush his damp hair off his forehead, sandy locks longer than she'd ever seen them. She trailed her fingers down the side of his face, down the hard line of his jaw, her thumb stroking over the scar that marked his high cheek-bone. Gods help her, but he was more beautiful than any man had a right to be.

Meeting his gaze, his blue-grey eyes dilated near black in the dim light, she whispered, "Are you sure?" Her breath caught on the words, and she swallowed hard, her insides a mix of desire and trepidation. "Because I don't want to do this if an hour from now, you decide you wish you hadn't. I can't be one of your regrets."

Marcus closed his eyes, and she could feel his mind turning over her words. Weighing and measuring, and her heart was racing because there was an answer she wanted, but only if he meant it.

Then he opened his eyes and said, "There is nothing in this world that could make me regret you, Teriana. Because there is no one in this world who matters more to me than you."

Her breath caught, her heart racing at a speed she'd not known possible. "Kiss me."

It wasn't soft this time, but deep and fierce, driven by a need too long denied. Never in her life had she been kissed like this, and never would she again, because there was no one else like him. No one else capable of making her blood pound like he did. Who could make her body burn hot like he did. Who could make the world fall away like he did.

He pulled her onto his lap, her knees on the wooden bench to either side of him, her towel falling to the ground. She whimpered into his mouth as his hands slid down over the curve of her bottom, pulling her tight against him before stroking up her spine, the motion sending thrills of pleasure through her body. She tangled her fingers in his hair, her back arching as his lips moved to her throat, his teeth scraping her skin.

"You are so beautiful." His voice was rough, nearly a growl. "Every inch of you is perfect."

Then he hooked an arm under her, lifting her up, his breath hot against her skin as his other hand cupped her breast. The feel of his thumb brushing over the tip made her body buck, only his arm around her hips keeping her from falling back. But the sensation paled as he drew her other breast into his mouth, tongue teasing her, explosions of pleasure jolting through her. Making her sob his name, because there was nothing but him.

"Tell me what you want," he said, licking the condensed steam from her skin. His eyes flicked up to meet hers, the desire in them fueling the heat rising in her core.

Except she didn't know how to articulate what she wanted, none of her fumbling and awkward experiences with other boys having prepared her for Marcus, their one time together feeling a lifetime ago. All she knew was that she wanted him. "Everything."

He gave her a dark smile, and then he lowered her onto the bench, the towels she'd used soft against her back. He shifted onto his knees, hands resting to either side of her as he leaned down to kiss her lips.

Her throat.

Her breasts.

Her navel.

Moving down and down, and Teriana's heart skipped as she realized his intent a second before his hands slipped under her knees, pushing them apart. And then . . .

She sobbed his name, one hand braced against the wall next to her, the other catching at his head, tangling in his hair. Her eyelids squeezed shut, moisture from the steaming rocks of the sauna dripping down her cheeks, each droplet sending thrills of sensation across her skin. Tension unlike anything she'd experienced built in her, every muscle tightening as the feel of his touch moved her closer to the edge of the cliff.

But as she felt herself teetering on the edge, she gasped out, "Not yet!" and pushed him away. Sitting upright, she kissed him even as she slipped her hand between them. Watched as his eyelids drifted shut, as his body shuddered, a smile rising to her lips as he groaned, "Teriana . . ." And then she whispered into his ear, "Everything."

His hands tightened around her hips, lifting her, and then her back was against the wall, her legs around his waist. She dug her nails into his shoulders as he kissed her, trailing her fingers down the hard muscles of his back, the feel of him pressed against her the most excruciating of torments.

"You sure?" he said, pulling back to look at her. "Please tell me you're sure?"

"Yes!" she gasped, needing him. "Now."

The feel of them coming together nearly shattered her. Not just the pleasure but the rightness of it. They belonged with each other. To each other. Even if the rest of the world would never understand and would do everything it could to separate them.

"Don't stop," she said between desperate kisses, her tension once again at the brink. "Please don't stop."

In answer, he let go of one of her legs, her foot dropping to brace against the bench next to them. His hand curved around her hip, moving between them. And sending her over the brink.

She sobbed his name as light burst bright in her eyes, sensation radiating from her core out to the tips of her toes, only to be followed by another wave. Then another. Leaving her muscles shaking and weak.

Marcus kissed her, his teeth catching her bottom lip, his breathing ragged. His body tensing. And only then did her head clear enough to say, "We can't. I might get pregnant," knowing full well that they were already playing with fire.

He caught hold of her hips, lifting her, his head resting against her shoulder as a shudder ran through him, her name on his lips.

Marcus held her for a long time, their breathing ragged, then he slowly lowered her to the ground, their eyes locking.

"You all right?" she said softly, part of her still afraid that he'd pull away.

His mouth curved into a smile that warmed her heart, the reverent way he looked at her making her eyes prick. Lowering his head, he kissed her and she pulled herself against him, the steam having dissipated and a chill taking over the air.

"More hot rocks," she said between kisses. "I'm cold."

"And I'm hungry," he said. "Let's see if they have something better than mice."

74

KILLIAN

Every inch of him hurt.

He couldn't remember the last time he'd been so thoroughly pummeled, and a big part of him sorely regretted not having finished the fight as soon as it began rather than drawing it out. But dropping a giant within a few blows would've raised suspicions, so he'd held back.

Unfortunately, it had turned out Baird had been doing the same, and it took a great deal of self-control not to follow Lydia up the stairs and beg her to take the edge off the pain.

Instead, he took the glass of whiskey Agrippa handed him and drained it, the liquid burning like fire down his throat. "Looks like you're going to be sleeping on the floor," the young man said, his grin wide. "She's being rather unappreciative, in my opinion. She was the one caught cheating."

Killian shrugged and said, "She'll get over it," though more likely he would have to plead for her forgiveness for acting this way. But it accomplished what he needed: Lydia being elsewhere would mean this pair couldn't use her to provoke him.

Because they were clearly after something.

Baird was in the process of shoving pieces of rag up his broken nose to stem the bleeding, his voice muffled as he said, "So what's your business in Deadground?"

Gods, was that truly the name of this place? He accepted a rag from the server and gingerly dabbed at his nose, which was definitely broken. Already his eyes were swelling to the point he could barely see. But that hurt far less than his cracked ribs, which screamed every time he took a breath. And then there was his arm. *Shit.* "I was part of the force harassing the Mudamorians between Mudaire and Abenharrow. We disbanded after the Mudamorians won at the ford, every man for himself. Was tricky business getting back with the Royal Army hunting down and killing every man trying to get to the wall, so I lay low in Abenharrow, which was where I met the girl. Convinced her to come back with me hoping she wouldn't realize it was a bad idea until it was too late for her to turn around."

They both laughed, Baird wincing and gripping his side.

"Deadground ain't what it used to be," Agrippa said. "Our lovely queen is cheap and sends supplies only for those tasked with watching over her weeds, leaving everyone else to feed off one another while we await her next orders."

The mounds. "They've gotten large," Killian said cautiously, not wanting to raise suspicions with questions. Or with ignorance.

"Big and useless," Agrippa said. "Just like Baird." He gave the giant an elbow in the side, laughing when Baird groaned in pain. "And they no longer take orders, if you get my meaning."

Killian didn't, but he nodded anyway.

"Rufina captured fresh talent that she hopes can get the blight flowing in the right direction," Baird said. "What are the odds right now, little man?"

"Don't call me that, you jackass," Agrippa said. "And they're five to one, favoring the Mudamorian Queen continuing to be reticent. Girl's as tough as nails. Pretty too."

Malahi.

She was here.

75

LYDIA

Playing her part, Lydia stormed up the stairs to their room, but once inside, she swiftly pulled on her cloak and mittens, then went back into the hallway and locked the door. Staying in this place any longer than they had to was going to get one or both of them killed, which meant finding Malahi soon.

Pulling up her hood, she slipped back down the stairs, glancing to where Killian sat, still shirtless, with Baird and Agrippa. While obviously in pain, he didn't appear in immediate danger, so, keeping her head down, she fell in behind another group that was leaving the common room and moved out into the street, her spectacles fogging in the chill air.

Despite the hour, the town was bustling as though it were midday anywhere else, though the prevalence of staggering drunks spoke to the idleness of those trapped in this town. Hunted in Mudamora and prevented from returning to their homes in Derin, she could well understand why they'd turned to drink.

Marching along as though she had purpose, Lydia moved through the town, searching for a place that seemed a likely location for keeping prisoners, her strategy to find the only soldiers in town who *weren't* drunk because they'd presumably be on duty doing something. Yet everywhere she walked, all she found was the chaos and wildness of those without *purpose*, the buildings she ventured into filled with people struggling to survive.

Stepping back out into a street, Lydia paused in the shadows to take stock of her situation. Cloud cover blocked what light there was from the moon and stars, the mountains little more than shadows. But the green glow of the mounds was clearly visible.

They were under guard.

Frowning, Lydia walked to the edge of town, stopping to look down the slope at the strange glowing hillocks, the smell of the blight heavy in her nose. Undoubtably the source of it—possibly a fungus or parasitic plant of sorts that stole life from the land to feed itself.

Were they something natural to the land?

Or had the tenders been forced to create them?

Either way, she wanted a closer look.

There were four men standing guard over the mounds, though they seemed more interested in holding their hands over the fire they had built nearby. Lydia kept low as she crossed the empty ground between them and the town, using the cover of darkness and snowdrifts to hide her motion. The wind howled, and the raucous noise of the drunks in the streets easily disguised any sound she made, but relief still filled her as she slipped behind the mound most distant from the guards.

Her relief didn't last.

This close, she could see that the twisting mass of vines making up the mound were shifting and moving, unnatural in every way. She waited to see if the mound would react to her presence. But while the vines continued to squirm, they made no move toward her. So she reached out to grasp one of them.

It throbbed beneath her hand with the same pulsing beat as a heart, but it didn't fight against her as she tugged it aside. Grasping another one, she eased it out of the way, slowly creating a passage into the woven mass of glowing vines.

Taking a deep breath, she eased into the tunnel, making her way toward the center of the mound and pushing aside the vines as she crawled. Soon not even her feet stuck out the side, but the brilliance emanating from the center drew her deeper, the feel of the vines moving beneath her like crawling on a bed of snakes.

Then she saw something. A figure.

Ignoring the chill of fear that told her to *get out,* Lydia eased aside a thick tangle, gasping at what she found before her.

It was a woman.

Far older than Lydia, the woman was wrapped round with vines, thin filaments running through her hair. Her eyes were closed and her skin illuminated by the green glow of the vines. She was kneeling, her hands barely visible where they pressed against the ground, although there was no mistaking the black lines of blight radiating from her fingertips.

Lydia stared at the black murk drawing life away from *everything* it touched, like a parasite. Gagging, she considered withdrawing, but curiosity drew her closer to the woman.

She seemed catatonic, entirely unaware of Lydia's presence, and as she drew aside some of the vines, Lydia saw why. The vines weren't just wrapped around her, they were running *through* her, the woman and the vine parasite merged together. Almost . . . almost as though the woman were now more plant than human.

"Gods," Lydia whispered, trying to understand how such a thing was possible. How it could be undone.

And then the thought fell upon her: *Malahi* could be in one of these mounds.

Wriggling backward, her arms and legs tangling up, she finally tumbled out onto the snow with a soft thud. She sat frozen, waiting to see if the guards had heard her, whether they'd come to investigate, but they never broke from their conversation around their fire. So Lydia moved to the next mound.

Doing her best to stay quiet, she wrenched the vines out of her way, crawling toward the center until she found the tender within: it was a man, his face unfamiliar.

Retreating, she moved on, gasping for breath but unwilling to rest lest Malahi be imprisoned within one of these things.

How would she get her out without killing her? Even her mark had its limits and she'd have to practically tear Malahi apart to get her free.

What would it do to Killian if he couldn't save her?

Tears burned in her eyes, and she pushed up her spectacles to wipe at them before moving onto the third mound. Then the fourth. Then the fifth.

All strangers.

Crawling to the eighth mound, the one closest to the soldiers, she fought with the vines, struggling her way inside, her breath coming in ragged gasps.

Please don't be her.

Please be a stranger.

She shoved aside a tangle of glowing green, and Lydia's heart hitched as she caught sight of blond hair.

No.

Tears flooded down her cheeks as she maneuvered herself around, dragging at the vines covering the woman's face.

It wasn't Malahi.

Wherever the Queen of Mudamora was, it wasn't here.

76

KILLIAN

"How pretty?" It was a struggle to keep his voice steady, his heart thundering like a drum.

Agrippa made a tsking noise, then shook his finger at Killian. "It's a good thing your Gertrude isn't here. What would she say to such a question?" Not waiting for a response, he added, "*Very* pretty. And she's got bigger balls than Baird, although apparently that doesn't take much. Screamed at Rufina that she'd die before hurting her country. The look on our dear queen's face would've had most men, myself included, shitting their pants, but that little lass was pure defiance."

"Leave my balls out of this sad story," Baird grumbled, draining yet another pint of ale.

"Sad?" Killian's stomach dropped. *Please don't let me be too late.*

"Rufina took her back across the Liratoras to her fortress in Helatha." Agrippa took a sip of his drink. "Knowing our queen as I do, my money is on her breaking the girl. And I rarely lose a bet."

Anger and darkness rose in Killian's chest, threatening to consume him. Making him want to lash out at these bastards who'd stood by and done nothing while Malahi was brutalized.

Instead, he picked up his cup and drank until the emotion faded. Malahi was on the far side of the Liratoras, in wherever this Helatha was, which meant that was where he and Lydia needed to go. And these two likely knew how to get there. "That was probably a sight to see."

"One that will stick with me," Agrippa said. "But on a more favorable topic, what's your plan now that you've returned to Deadground?"

"There's nothing here for us," Killian said. "I want to go home."

"That will cost you," Agrippa answered. "Just before we flanked the Royal Army, Rufina"—he spat onto the floor—"blew up the xenthier path leading back across the Liratoras. Didn't want us to have an avenue for retreat."

Killian scowled. "How did she do it?"

"Called down the skies," Agrippa answered, then gave a side

glance at Baird, whose cheeks reddened as he said, "She didn't give me much of a choice, you know."

Confused, Killian stared at the giant for a long moment, and then realization dawned upon him, many pieces coming together, including why the giants of Eoten Isle hadn't started a war since the sacking of Serlania when Killian was a boy—they only fought when they had their even twenty-four Marked. "You're a summoner."

Baird shrugged. "I'm sure there's a darker word for what I am, but aye. Rufina had me call lightning down on the stem, and it shattered the damn thing. Surprised you didn't feel the quake all the way at the coast."

Killian shook his head. "No. And we weren't told."

"No surprise, that," Baird said. "She wants what remains of her army here, ready and waiting for her next move."

"Worked out well enough for us in the long run, no?" Agrippa elbowed the giant in the ribs, Baird groaning and clutching his side even as he nodded.

"How so?"

"In our queen's absence, we've formed a side business," Agrippa answered. "We escort those who want to get home back across the Liratoras. For a price."

"There are better ways to gain yourself customers than accusing them of cheating at cards and challenging them to barroom brawls."

Baird chuckled, tapping his glass against Killian's. "We don't want you as a customer, Tom. That was more of a . . . *trial*."

"Lots lurking in the Liratoras," Agrippa added. "We need good men to get our paying customers through, and thanks to that Mudamorian bastard Calorian, the best are ash on the wind. We've not been able to convince anyone on the Derin side to take up the work."

They were offering him a gods-damned job? "And why would I be interested in taking on such a risk?"

"One," Agrippa said, lifting a finger, "we'll pay you five pieces of gold if you survive to the far side. Two, you've got a girl you're enamored enough with to fight a giant over. Three, a town like Deadground is no place to make a life with a lass like your Gertrude, which is why we'll let you bring her along."

Swirling the contents of his glass, Killian pretended to consider the offer, which was better than he could have hoped for—a guided route into Derin. "I might be interested," he said. "But it will be weeks before I'm fit to fight." He gestured at his broken arm with his glass.

Agrippa gave a sour look at Baird. "Why can you never control yourself?"

"He insulted my balls—would you have had me let such an insult stand?"

"That was *after* you broke his arm, you stupid lump." The young man cast his eyes skyward. "As recompense for Baird's eagerness, we'll get you fixed up well enough to fight."

There's only one way for them to do that.

Killian frowned and took a sip of the whiskey one of the servers had brought over, pretending to be unconvinced. "Maybe I take the girl back into Mudamora. The Liratoras are dangerous."

Annoyance flickered across Agrippa's eyes. "Ten gold coins. And I get you fixed up tonight."

Killian lifted his cup. "Deal."

Rising, Agrippa went to the rear of the room and opened a curtain to reveal a table full of gamblers. He bent to talk to a man whose back was to the main room. Despite not seeing the man's face, Killian's skin crawled, his gut telling him what his eyes did not.

Corrupted.

Shrugging a slender shoulder, the corrupted rose, sauntering over to their table. His eyes were black pits, though the flames that flickered around the irises were muted. He made a soft tsking noise at the sight of Killian, shaking his head. "This will be an *expensive* repair, Agrippa. Are you sure?"

"Just the arm and the ribs," Agrippa answered flatly, slapping a gold coin down on the table. "You get greedy, Sly, and I'll put a knife in your heart."

The corrupted gave the young man a wounded look, then smirked. "We could find another sacrificial lamb."

"No." Agrippa pulled back his sleeve. "Now get it done."

"As you like." The corrupted—Sly—crooked a finger at Killian. "Come here."

It was nearly all Killian could do not to pick up his sword and kill the thing in front of him.

"Get up, Tom," Agrippa snapped. "He's not going to bite a paying customer."

Rising slowly, Killian circled the table to stand next to them, aware that everyone in the common room was watching.

The corrupted's eyes moved up and down his body, then he said to Agrippa, "Are you ready?"

Face souring, the young man nodded, flinching as Sly took hold of his wrist. Then Sly reached out and caught Killian's forearm, hand closing painfully over the fracture. Warmth flooded into him even as the pain abated, then the corrupted moved his hand to Killian's side, fingers trailing down his ribs. "Cracked, but fortunately for Agrippa, not broken."

Realization of what was happening dawned on Killian. Sly wasn't healing him by sacrificing some of himself, but rather was acting as a conduit, taking from Agrippa to mend Killian's broken bones. Killian lurched back. "I'll be fine."

"Bullshit," Agrippa snapped. "I've cracked enough ribs to know. Do it, or the deal is off."

Indecision warred inside of him. This was the opportunity he desperately needed to get into the heart of Derin to retrieve Malahi, but at what cost to his own soul? What would the gods think, seeing him agree to this?

"Well?"

Whatever the cost, he needed to pay it. He owed Malahi that much. "Fine."

Sly pressed his hand back against Killian's side, and the pain rushed away, each breath no longer agonizing. Then he smiled. "All better. Though it's a shame Agrippa won't pay to fix that pretty face."

"Time will do that." Keeping a wary eye on the corrupted, Killian circled back around to take his seat, donning the clothes and weapons Lydia had tossed on the table.

The corrupted sighed, then plucked the coin off the table and slipped it into his coat pocket. "Always a pleasure doing business with you, Agrippa."

Baird watched Sly warily as he retreated back to his table, then muttered, "I can't stand that bastard."

"Nor I," Agrippa said. "But he's got better control than most of his wretched kind, and his fondness for dice ensures he's always in need of coin."

"I've never seen one of them do that." Killian hoped the admission wouldn't out him as not, as he'd claimed, from Derin, but Agrippa only shrugged. "Rufina forbids it. But even one of the corrupted needs to earn a living somehow."

The inhabitants of Derin continued to be not at all what Killian expected. "Thank you."

Agrippa laughed. "Don't thank me just yet—the Liratoras are far worse than cracked bones." Then he picked up the bottle of whiskey and filled all three of their cups. "But enough morose chatter. It's time to celebrate!"

77

LYDIA

Resting on the shifting vines, Lydia struggled to catch her breath, her eyes on the ribbons of blight streaming into the ground from the woman's fingers. Dragging life from the earth in order to feed the strange parasitic plant she'd become.

Was there a way to extract her? To separate person from plant? Shoving aside vines, Lydia examined the places where they grew into the woman's body. She could cut her free, then attempt to operate to remove them from the inside of the woman's body.

Taking a firm grip on her knife, Lydia sawed at a smaller one, cringing as clear liquid spilled on her and trying not to focus on how the woman shifted and moaned, the process obviously painful. But her mark told her the woman's life was strong, so she persevered, moving on to the woman's hands. Twisted vines protruded from her fingertips, digging into the earth like blackened roots, and Lydia's attempts to pull them up yielded no results.

So she started sawing at them with her blade.

Blight spilled from the severed roots, filling the air with its stink and coating her hands, but she didn't allow herself to stop. Not even when the woman started quivering, the whole mound shaking around them as though caught in a storm breeze.

"It's okay," Lydia whispered. "I'll get you out. I'll help you."

Yet as she said the words, the life in the woman began to fade, growing less radiant by the second.

Cutting her free of the blight was going to kill her.

Lydia froze, indecision holding her in place. If she carried on, the woman would die. But if she didn't, the blight would only continue to spread.

What if she didn't choose it?

What if this was forced upon her?

What if she'd stop, if given the chance?

Malahi had once said, *What is one life in comparison to thousands?* when she'd sent Lydia to murder her father.

Lydia had chosen to spare that one life, and *gods,* but she'd had cause to regret it.

Do it! Don't be such a coward!

But her whole body was trembling, tears running down her cheeks. *This woman is a murderer!* She *is killing hundreds! Thousands!*

Clenching her teeth, Lydia dragged the blade across the remaining roots. Then she held her breath, hoping and praying that the woman would survive. That she'd open her eyes and take a breath.

But as she watched, the woman began to wither like a cut flower, the light from the mound slowly fading as they both died.

Panic flooded Lydia's veins, because there was no way the guards weren't going to notice that one of the mounds had gone dark. Scrambling backward, she extricated herself from the tangle of dead vines, only barely reaching one of the living mounds when she heard shouts of dismay from behind her. Casting a backward glance, she saw the guards had approached the dead mound, panic on their faces.

Run.

Keeping low, Lydia raced toward the town, heart hammering as she joined the masses in the streets. Weaving through them, she slipped in the side door of the inn and paused, hearing Baird's booming laugh.

And Killian's.

Peering around the corner, she saw him clicking glasses with Baird and Agrippa, piles of cards and coins littering the table, a half dozen pretty girls squeezed into the benches around them.

Stomach tightening, Lydia spun away and climbed the stairs to their room. Inside, she flung off her cloak and used the water in the basin to clean off the sticky clear liquid she'd gotten covered in while hacking at the vines, angry accusations rising and falling on her lips. That she'd been out searching those awful mounds for Malahi while he'd been carousing. That she'd been trying to save a corrupted tender while he'd been flirting with pretty girls. Over and over, she rehearsed exactly what she was going to say to him when he finally dragged his sorry ass up to the room, her script growing more elaborate and scathing with each revision.

Then she heard a thump in the hallway and a muttered oath, then male laughter. A second later, the handle of the door jiggled.

"Gertrude?" Not Killian's voice, but Agrippa's.

Concerned, she crossed to the door, unlatched it, and heaved it open. To find Killian slumped between Agrippa and Baird, all three of them grinning wildly.

"Are you drunk?" she demanded, crossing her arms.

Killian squinted at her, his eyes swollen and bruised, pieces of bloodstained cloth shoved up his broken nose. "No."

Agrippa and Baird both laughed, dragging him in and tossing him on the bed. "In case he forgets," the former said, "could you remind him that we leave tomorrow? Dawn seems a bit aggressive, all things considered, so let's say midday."

Leave?

Trusting Killian would have answers, she only nodded, shutting and locking the door behind them. Then she strode over to the bed and snapped, "You'd better have a good explanation for why you're jaw-droppingly drunk, because from my standpoint, it appears one of your more shortsighted plans. And that's saying something."

Killian didn't answer.

And when she leaned down to peer at him in the dim light, she realized he had already fallen asleep.

"I don't think so," she snapped. And going to retrieve the washbasin, she tossed the icy contents on his face.

Shouting in alarm, he fell off the side of the bed, then staggered to his feet, trying to extract his sword. But instead, he tripped and fell, landing hard on his ass. Glowering up at her, he said, "What was that for?"

"For being stupid," she said, resting her hands on her hips. "And for falling asleep while I was talking to you. And because I was crawling inside those awful plant mounds while you were . . . carousing and having fun."

"Oh, yes," he snapped back, dragging himself upward onto the bed. "Because getting beaten half to death by a giant is such a delight. And I was doing things, too, so . . ." Then he frowned. "You were supposed to be in *this* room."

"I was looking for any sign of Malahi."

Killian scrubbed a hand through his hair. "She's not in Deadground. Rufina has her in her fortress. A place called Helatha."

"Right." Lydia swallowed, and not wanting to feel as though what she'd endured was in vain, she said, "As we suspected, the mounds are causing the blight. But they aren't just plants . . . the corrupted tenders are inside them. From what I can tell, they are stealing the life from the earth, and it's turning them into sort of a plant-human hybrid."

Killian stared at her. "Pardon?"

Hissing out a frustrated breath, she pushed a glass of water into his hand, then sat on the bed next to him, explaining what she'd seen. "I . . . I tried to cut her free," she admitted. "She died. I left the rest of them alone."

Murderer.

"Ideally, we'd dispatch the others." He rubbed at his temples, seemingly unaware of the guilt twisting through her. "But with one of the tenders dead, they are bound to increase the guards around the remainder. I don't want to do anything that jeopardizes us getting into Derin and finding Malahi."

Relief flooded through her, because the thought of killing the rest had made her stomach twist. "Did you figure out how to manage that?"

"Yes, I got a job." Flopping back down on the bed, he sighed. "As hired muscle for Agrippa and Baird's business—they escort people through the Liratoras for a steep price. Apparently picking a fight with me was an audition of sorts."

"But you can't . . . ," she started to say, and only then realized that he was using his left arm. And a quick assessment of him using her mark revealed that his ribs were no longer fractured. "Who healed you?"

"A corrupted named Sly." Groaning, Killian rolled across the bed to the half that wasn't soaked with wash water. "Agrippa paid for it with some of his own life. Literally. Apparently the corrupted can act as a conduit and take life from one person to give to another. Agrippa's not bad, once you get to know him. The girls around here sure like him."

"He's from Celendor."

Killian turned his head. *"What?"*

"His heritage is mixed, but there is no mistaking that golden hue to his skin. Or his name," she said. "And he's also carrying the style of blade favored by the Empire's legions, so I bet if you get his shirt off, you'll find he's got a legion number tattooed on his chest. That said, he's fluent in Mudamorian and has no accent, so I'd say that however he got here, it was some time ago. Do you think it's too risky to ask him?"

Killian didn't answer, and when she looked up, she saw his eyes were closed. And a second later, he started to snore.

Sighing, she rose and pulled off his boots, tossing them aside. Unbuckling his sword belt, she leaned the weapon next to the bed and then pulled the blanket over him. Courtesy of his broken nose, he was snoring loudly now, and retrieving the lamp, she looked over his remaining injuries, it requiring all of her self-control not to erase them.

Instead, she brushed back his hair from his face, her heart tightening at the silky feel of it against her fingers.

But he was sworn to Malahi.

Part of her wanted to soothe the hurt in her heart with the knowledge he hadn't chosen this path, but she knew that wasn't the entire truth. He might not love the Queen, but he *was* dedicated to her. And would remain so for the rest of his life.

Her eyes burning, Lydia put another few pieces of wood on the fire to keep the room warm through the night. Wet or not, she looked longingly at the vacant space on the bed next to Killian, but instead ensconced herself on a chair, the other blanket pulled around her. Then she stared at the flames until sleep and exhaustion finally took her.

78

TERIANA

Her belly full of thick stew and fresh bread, Teriana pressed her nose against the glass of the window of their room, watching the revelers below. There had to be two hundred of them, all singing and dancing, the contents of their steaming cups probably doing as much to keep them warm as the large bonfire at the center of the square. "Let's go down."

"It's safer to stay up here."

"But going down there will be far more entertaining." Crossing the room, she sat on Marcus's lap, pushing him back against the chair. "And I'm still not entirely convinced that you know how to have fun. This would be a grand opportunity to prove it."

"And if I say no?"

She kissed him until she was certain that distraction had taken hold, then she whispered, "You don't get to tell me what to do, Legatus."

Quick as she could, Teriana jumped up, and catching hold of her new coat, she bolted for the door.

"Teriana!"

She laughed as she heard him scramble to his feet and out the door, fumbling to lock it behind him, then his boots were thumping down the hallway. She paused halfway down the stairs, laughing harder when he nearly tripped over his own feet in surprise at finding her.

Pressed together in the narrow staircase, she silenced him with kisses, then said, "We've cheated death a dozen times to reach this place, Marcus. And in too short a time, we'll be back in the lion's den. What is wrong with taking one night to breathe?"

She could feel his lifetime of discipline warring with her rather excellent argument, but when his grip around her waist tightened, Teriana smiled, knowing she'd won. "Let's go."

Catching his hand in hers, she dragged him down the rest of the stairs, shouting, "Happy Winter Festival!" to the innkeeper as she passed. The door swung open at her touch, and she gasped as icy air slapped her in the face. Keeping a firm grip on Marcus's hand, she wove her way into the throng, grinning when a woman pushed steaming cups into their hands, the drink hot and sweet and fortified with enough kick that it lit a fire in her belly.

Whether it was the booze or the festival or the nature of the people themselves, no one treated them as if they didn't belong. The men plied Marcus with drinks and conversation, hammering him on the back when he coughed after drinking the clear liquor the Sibernese preferred. The women pulled Teriana into dances around the fire, long chains of people laughing and twirling to the musician's music, the beat growing faster with every song.

Children shrieked and laughed as they chased one another through the throngs of their elders, thrilled to be allowed to play at the late hour, and even more thrilled for the seemingly endless supply of candy pushed into their hands.

Then the music slowed, a man with a stringed instrument the only player, and a young Sibernese woman with hair the color of flame stepped onto the platform. The men finally gave up their conversation and drinking, joining the women, wrapping their arms around their lovers and swaying to the music. Teriana stood at the edge, so entranced by the woman's voice that she jumped when arms wrapped around her.

"Sorry," Marcus said, his breath warm against her ear. "Didn't mean to startle you."

She smiled, leaning back against him and feeling the sharp line of his jaw against her temple. "Are you glad I convinced you to come out?"

"Yes. Though I'm going to have the worst hangover of my life tomorrow." He caught her hands in his, holding her tighter. Then he said, "Look up."

Tilting her face back, Teriana gasped, watching as swirls of colors danced across the sky, more beautiful than anything she'd ever seen. A more perfect moment than any she'd ever experienced, and she wished that she could freeze time. Make it last forever.

But it wouldn't.

Grief rose in her chest, and knowing she was on the verge of being overwhelmed, she said, "Let's go try the games."

Holding his hand, she led him to the booths set up with games of chance and skill, the prizes for winning ranging from toys to furs to jars of sweets. Spying a ring toss, she made her way over, her mood improving as she examined the rows of colored bottles with necks of varying sizes. "How much is it to try?"

"Copper for three tosses, miss."

Teriana fished one of the coins she'd exchanged a hair ornament for out of her pocket and handed it over, and the man gave her three rings of yarn wrapped around iron beads to give them weight. She pushed them into Marcus's hands. "Try to win."

Brow furrowed, he eyed the bottles and tossed the rings, his scowl increasing each time he missed. "This is rigged."

"You just don't like to lose!" she laughed.

The man running the game smiled at her and handed her the rings. "Perhaps the lass will have more luck."

Grinning, she threw the rings, groaning each time she missed. But on her third toss, the ring slipped over the neck of a bottle and she shrieked, dancing in a circle. The man handed her a doll with bright red hair, and she passed it to a girl who ran past, the child's face widening with delight. "Let's play another!"

"They're all rigged," Marcus grumbled, glaring at the bottles as though they'd personally insulted him. "What's the point?"

"The point is that it's fun."

"How is losing a game you have no chance of winning any fun?"

She considered pointing out that she *had* just won, but instead said, "Sometimes it feels like you know everything except how to *live*."

Marcus was quiet, then he looked away. "I never felt there was much point."

Why? she wanted to ask, because she knew it wasn't a trait that could be wholly blamed on the legions. Not given most young men in the Thirty-Seventh lived and laughed as well as any civilian. Instead, she wrapped her arms around his neck and rested her cheek against his. "Do you still feel that way?"

The silence stretched for long enough that she thought he wouldn't answer. And then he said, "No, I don't."

79

KILLIAN

He had never been so hungover in his entire life.

"I'm never having a drink again," he groaned, rolling into the pillow to block the sunlight and then yelping as his broken nose protested, forcing him to instead pull the blanket over his head.

"An admirable goal." Lydia's voice was tart. And as he peered out from under the blanket, he saw she was packing their bags. "We're to meet Agrippa and Baird prior to midday, and assuming you didn't lose all our money gambling, we need supplies."

He opened his mouth to say that he always came out ahead when gambling, thought better of it, and instead pulled a handful of silver from one of his pockets. "Here."

"Get up, *Tom*." Her expression was cool. "Some breakfast will make you feel better."

The thought of eating did not make him feel better. "Can't you—"

"I am *not* healing your hangover, so don't even think of asking."

Groaning, he dragged himself off the bed, wondering where she'd slept. If it had been next to him. The thought of it appealed to him more than it should have, but then he caught sight of the blanket draped over a chair near the fire, and disappointment flickered through him.

Guzzling down a few glasses of water, he asked, "Am I recalling correctly that you told me last night Agrippa is Cel?"

"I'm surprised you remember."

He scratched at his beard. "Did you also tell me to take his shirt off?" He remembered her saying something to that nature, but *why* he'd want to do so, Killian had no notion.

Lydia exhaled an aggrieved breath. "If he's from the legions, he'll have a tattoo of his legion number on his chest and then his identification number across the back of his shoulders. Not that it really matters—just an uncanny coincidence."

She was upset. He could see it in the stiffness of her body. Hear it in the clipped tone of her voice. "The gods are meddling, Lydia. There are no coincidences—not for us."

"Then I suppose time will tell why we've crossed paths with him." She slung her pack over her shoulders. "Let's go."

Downstairs, the common room was infinitely quieter than it had been the prior night, with only a handful of patrons, Agrippa among them.

"Good morning," he said, looking remarkably well, all things considered. "I'm surprised to see you down here so early."

Killian shot a meaningful look toward Lydia, who was speaking with one of the serving girls, and Agrippa laughed. "My sympathies. Spent too much of my life forced to rise at dawn, so now I find that I can't sleep a minute later, no matter how hard I try. Baird, however, will sleep the day away if I let him."

Killian slipped onto the bench across from him and accepted a glass of water from one of the girls. Knowing that this young man was from Lydia's homeland—a homeland that had invaded Arinoquia with an eye for conquest—made him more interested in taking Agrippa's measure.

He was much shorter than Killian was, perhaps shorter than Lydia as well, his skin a golden-brown hue. His clean-shaven chin had a dimple in it, and Killian supposed he was good looking enough. He was broad-shouldered, and the flex of the muscles beneath his shirt suggested they saw some use. According to Lydia, these *legionnaires* were trained from childhood to be soldiers, and though he'd seen no proof yet of such skills, there was something about Agrippa that warned Killian he'd be dangerous if provoked.

"Eat." Lydia shoved a plate containing runny eggs and dry toast in front of him, then sat down on the bench. "Good morning, Agrippa."

He gave her a slow smile that had Killian revising his good opinion of him. "Good morning, Gertrude. I understand you'll be journeying with us across the Liratoras."

"So I was informed." She took a mouthful of the runny eggs, and Killian nearly gagged, pushing away his plate. "I expect I'll be needing some warmer clothing for such a trek. Could you point me where I might go to purchase such garments?"

"You'll be fine dressed as you are," Agrippa answered, resting his elbows on the table as he studied her. "But you might want to get yourself a few more weapons, because the wildmen *are* an issue."

She cast a sideways glance at Killian, then asked, "Wildmen?"

"As the story goes, Mudamora used to exile its criminals over the wall. Most died, of course, but some survived and made a life for themselves in the mountains. But doing so turned them a touch . . . feral."

"Are they the only threat?"

"If they were the only threat, I wouldn't be charging ten gold pieces a head to escort people across the mountains. But don't worry, love, I'll keep you safe." Agrippa winked, and Killian *would* have hit him, but Lydia's steely expression was quickly wiping away the other man's smirk. Having been subjected to that very same glare, Killian almost pitied Agrippa. *Almost.*

"How many people do you take at a time?"

"Ten, usually," Agrippa answered. "But we've some children with us this time, so it's to be twelve."

Then a loud series of thuds filled the air, and Baird tumbled down the stairs, landing in a heap at the bottom.

Agrippa winced. "He does that with shocking regularity. He'll be fine."

But Lydia was already on her feet, hurrying to the giant's side. "Are you hurt? Let me help you."

"You're a sweet lass." Baird nearly pulled her over as she tried to help him stand. "It's the cursed ceiling—it's too damned low!"

"It's not the ceiling, you jackass!" Agrippa called. "You're still drunk."

"Am not, you ugly little shit," the giant answered, circling the table and sitting next to his friend. Reaching across the table, he took Killian's plate and started eating. "We ready?"

"Yes, though it's not thanks to your lazy ass," Agrippa answered. "Customers are meeting us at Meril's in a half turn, so finish up."

80

MARCUS

Living had always felt dangerous.

Like tempting fate, given how much he had to lose. How much he'd lost already. A far better thing to focus on what would allow him to keep breathing, to keep his men breathing, than to set his sights on *more*.

Except now *more* was what he had.

Teriana in his arms, her lips pressed to his, her laughter in his ears. Going back to the way he'd been before would be like seeing color for the first time only to blink and find the world once more cast in shades of grey.

So he shoved away practical thoughts about wasting precious coin and allowed her to drag him from game to game, the delight on her face as she tried her luck greater than any prize.

"Look at all that candy," she murmured, stopping in front of a booth that had a table with a large jar of colored jellies, before which sat a puzzle made of twisted pieces of metal. As they watched, the Sibernese villagers paid copper pennies for a chance to win the jar, all of them eventually giving up in frustration.

"I'm going to try," she said. "Give back one of the coppers I gave you. I've spent all mine."

He gave her the coin and then leaned against the post holding up the canvas over the booth, watching her dark brows knit with concentration as she worked the pieces of metal this way and that, attempting to solve the puzzle. As the minute glass ran down to its last grains, she scowled, tossing the puzzle on the table with a metallic thud. "This one's definitely rigged. There's no solution."

The owner of the game only chuckled, having already pocketed her coin. "Anyone else care to try?"

Everyone around shook their heads, muttering that there was no solution and that the man was conning them out of their coin. Giving Teriana a wink, Marcus said, "I'll try."

She shrugged. "Your copper."

Handing the coin to the man, Marcus waited for him to turn over the timer. Then he stepped closer to the light, his eyes running over the pieces of metal, the sounds of the festival growing distant as he considered the puzzle.

"Not going to solve it by standing there staring at it, boy," the man said. "You'd have been better off—"

Marcus twisted the puzzle and gave it a little shake, and the pieces came apart in his hands.

The man gaped at him, then laughed. "Seen this one before, have you?"

"No." Marcus handed over the pieces. "Just a knack for finding solutions. You can give the candy to the lady."

Teriana's eyes shifted to the vibrant turquoise of tropical seas as she accepted the jar, then she untwisted the lid, allowing those around to take some before grabbing a handful. "Try them," she said around a mouthful of candy. "They're good."

"They're bad for your teeth," he informed her, but when she cast her eyes skyward, muttering that he was hopeless, he laughed and took a handful, eating them one by one as they walked.

"It hardly feels as though we're in the Empire," she said. "This place feels . . . uncorrupted."

"Most of the people here speak Cel," he said. "And they use Empire coinage. And if it were summer, I'm sure there'd be Cel merchants here. Definitely messengers traveling the Teeth."

She huffed out an annoyed breath. "You know what I mean. It doesn't feel like Mother Empire is looming over their shoulders, policing every move. Like in Celendrial, where there's legionnaires on every corner glowering at everyone."

"Would you prefer they smiled at everyone? Because sometimes people take smiles the wrong way."

"You are driving me insane. And I need to go find a privy," she said. "Hold my candy. But don't you dare eat it all."

"Not a piece," he promised, then lowered the jar, pretending not to notice as giggling Sibernese children took the rest of the jellies and shoved them into their mouths before racing off.

Leaning against a wooden post wrapped with garlands, he watched the Sibernese dance around the fire, holding his hands up in defeat when two men tried to push another of the little glasses of liquor into his hands. And instead of joining in the conversation, he observed. He rarely saw groups of people like this—relaxed and happy and entirely at ease. The presence of legion men always put people on edge, his presence worst of all, though he'd never realized how much so.

This was a good place. A good life. Hard, but honest. He envied them in that.

Teriana had reappeared from across the square but was waylaid by a group of young girls. One of them asked her something, and from the way Teriana's smile broadened, her eyes growing wide and expressive, he knew she was telling them a Maarin yarn.

Then his skin prickled, some sixth sense telling him he was being watched.

Lifting his head, Marcus scanned the festival before turning to the darkness beyond the village, trying to determine what had triggered the sensation. In the distance, a dog barked, then whined, the sound abruptly cutting off.

And he knew.

He lunged in Teriana's direction, pushing into the crowd, but before he made it two paces, legionnaires burst from the darkness.

"On the ground! On the ground!"

The Sibernese villagers screamed, dropping to their stomachs in the muddy snow. Marcus kept going. He couldn't let them catch Teriana.

Then a blow caught him between the shoulders, sending him sprawling.

"I said on the ground!" A deep voice sounded from behind him, and a foot came down hard between Marcus's shoulders, pressing him into the mud. Lifting his face, he searched for Teriana, relief flooding him as he caught sight of her beneath a wagon, hiding with the little girls.

"Now what do we have going on here?"

A voice speaking in clear Sibernese cut through the night, and Marcus turned his face to watch a legionnaire stride into the center of the village square. A centurion was his best guess, though the men wore heavy garments that covered their armor. He wracked his brain, trying to recall which legion was stationed in western Sibern.

Not that it mattered.

The centurion pulled back his hood, revealing the face of a man in his late thirties with ivory skin and bright red hair. Sibernese by birth, though Lescendor and decades of service had likely stripped him of any loyalties he had to the province and its people. Even so,

Marcus grimaced, knowing that the choice to send someone of the same blood as these villagers to lay down the law had been purposeful.

"Varro!" the centurion called out. "Remind me, what hour does curfew begin?"

"Fourth hour, sir!" one of the men called back. "Sundown."

"And what hour is it now?"

"Near on midnight, I'd say, sir."

"Midnight." The centurion circled the bonfire. "I relaxed the rules for you lot, I'll have you know. Tarried, so that our arrival would come late, giving you some few hours to celebrate the end of the season. My gift to the people of this village."

Pausing, the man tossed another log on the fire. "Not in my wildest dreams did I think to arrive at midnight to find you fools still flaunting the Empire's order. Spitting in the face of my generosity."

Marcus scowled, knowing that the centurion had waited until it was late enough that the villagers had believed there no chance of a patrol showing up. Had waited until the villagers had drawn in those tasked with keeping watch before approaching. That they'd orchestrated this moment so as to catch as many individuals in violation of curfew as possible. Individuals who would now have to pay the fine. He shifted, but the legionnaire with his foot on Marcus's back only ground his heel down harder.

Fury rose in his chest. He could have the bastard whipped within an inch of his life for this. If they knew who he was—

"And it need not *be* like this!" the centurion shouted. "You could have your freedoms and your festivals and your fun if only you'd just *fucking* abide!" He screamed the last few words, and several of the people around Marcus began to cry, their faces full of terror.

The centurion bent low over a prone man. "Pay your taxes!" Then he rounded on a woman. "Tithe your second-born boys!" Straightening, he circled around the bonfire again. "Live by the same laws as *everyone else* in the Empire, and all will be well in your lives."

He paused only a few feet from Marcus. "Would that I could forgive your actions tonight, but alas, I am charged with maintaining the law, so it is to me you will pay the cost of your transgressions." He lifted a hand in signal. "Varro, line them up. Take the names of any without the coin and explain they are now in debt to the Empire and will be charged interest until they pay their fine."

"Yes, sir. And the children?"

The Sibernese centurion tilted his head from side to side. "I am feeling benevolent. Allow the children to return to their homes."

"Get up!" A hand caught Marcus by the belt, hauling him to his feet, and Marcus found himself face-to-face with a grizzled legionnaire, a long scar bisecting an empty eye socket. The man's brow furrowed. "You a citizen, boy?"

"Yes," Marcus said from between his teeth, wiping mud from his face. "I am."

"Why didn't you say something?" The legionnaire brushed mud off Marcus's back. "Don't see too many citizens this far north at this time of the year. What's your business?"

"My father believes the Sibernese are withholding choice fur from Celendrial's markets," Marcus lied. "He sent me to purchase from the source."

"Smart man." The legionnaire slung an arm around Marcus's shoulders. "We've got a citizen here, lads. I'll get him settled before we carry on with business."

Shit. How was he supposed to get Teriana back to the inn with this bastard at his elbow? Marcus glanced toward the wagon where she'd been hiding, intending to signal at her to stay put.

But Teriana was gone.

His pulse roared, panic rising in his chest as he searched the shadows for any sign of her, but she and the children had disappeared. What he did see was the eyes of those he'd been celebrating with moments before, all of them fixed upon him. They'd shared their food and drink and hospitality with him, yet while he'd broken the same law as they had, his blood ensured he'd never pay a fine for it.

"You didn't get this far north without discovering the Sibernese were under curfew. While you are exempt from the restrictions, you'd be wise to abide by them anyway," the legionnaire said. "Get caught up in a scrap and you might find yourself on the wrong end of a gladius, Cel or not. Get my meaning?"

"Wise advice." And because Marcus knew how these men thought, he added, "The alcohol and pretty girls got in the way of my good sense."

The big man laughed and slapped Marcus on the back hard enough that he staggered. "Can't fault you that. But next time, coax the bottle and the girl up to your room *before* sunset. Here we are."

They'd reached the inn, and the legionnaire pulled open the door, gesturing for Marcus to enter. "My apologies again, citizen. And good fortune with the rest of your business in Sibern."

"Gratitude." Marcus gave the man a smile, then headed toward the stairs, taking them two at a time. *Please be here.*

Hitting the top of the stairs, he turned to look down the hallway, his stomach plummeting when Teriana wasn't waiting at the door. Which meant she was still out there.

He needed to find her, but he had no intention of going unarmed. Jamming the key into the lock and twisting it, he flung open the door.

And found Teriana standing by the fire.

"Thank the gods!" She crossed the room, shoving the door shut. "I thought they'd rounded you up with the others."

"Cel citizens are exempt from the curfew," he muttered. "How did you get—"

"The children," she interrupted. "They were able to sneak me out of the square, and they showed me a back way into the inn. But you need to get out there and make this stop. These people can't afford the fines—it will put half of them in debt to the Empire, and you know as well as anyone the rates of interest it charges."

He did. Just as he knew that the Empire was more than happy for them to be indebted to it for the rest of their lives. "There's nothing I can do."

"Bullshit!" Teriana snarled, glaring at him. "There's not a man out there who outranks you. And don't give me the excuse that you don't want Cassius to have warning we are coming. These people showed us kindness. We owe them."

Marcus bit the insides of his cheeks, struggling to keep his anger in check, because Teriana wasn't the cause of it. "We do owe them, but if I intervene, it will only make circumstances for them worse." Striding across the room to the window, he scraped off the frost so that he could see the lines of Sibernese being fined in the square. "I can go down there and order them to allow the villagers to go back to their homes, and yes, because I outrank them, they'd have to abide. But I do *not* outrank their legatus, and his orders come directly from the Senate."

He rested his forehead against the glass. "In a matter of days, these men would be back, and I assure you, they'd show no *benevolence.*" Just saying the word made his tongue sour. "I only have power when the Senate is unable to countermand me, and on this side of the world, that means I have no power at all."

Her hands were balled into fists. "I hate them."

Watching the legionnaires carrying out commands that he himself had been forced to give in a different time, in a different nation, Marcus felt guilt rise in his chest, bitter and foul. Especially knowing that he'd be forced to do so again. "So do I."

81

KILLIAN

Meril's, it turned out, was the general store. The proprietor seemed to have a deal with Agrippa as the provisions they'd need for the journey were already packed.

And the customers were waiting.

They were a mix of folk. Three men and one woman who looked like they might have been soldiers, given the way they wore their weapons. Two couples of varying age who bore only belt knives, a family of four that included two children. The boy and girl were perhaps six and eight by Killian's reckoning, and they had wary looks in their eyes and kept close to their parents' sides.

"Time to pay up your balance, travelers," Agrippa announced, holding out his hand as he circled the group, collecting coins.

When he was through, he said, "This here is Tom—he works for me now. That's his girl there, goes by the name of Gertrude. Don't bother her or you'll end up looking like Baird."

"It's true," the giant said mournfully from where he was gathering up sacks of supplies.

"You all got the explanation of how this goes and the risks we face before you signed up, so I won't waste words," Agrippa continued. "But before we head out, I'll remind you: we leave at dawn each day. If you're not in the boat, you get left behind."

Boat? Killian cast a sideways glance at Lydia, but her expression was equally confused.

"Being on the river gives us speed and makes it harder for the wildmen and other predators to get at us, so we don't stop the boat for any reason. So you have to shit, hold it or stick your ass over the side, because I don't stop for *any* reason."

What sort of mad trek was this?

Yet for all Killian's confusion, every customer nodded, then lifted their bags onto their shoulders.

"Then let's go."

Agrippa led them outside and around to the back lane, where Baird was loading the supplies into a sturdy wooden boat. It sat on skids, and a pair of mules stood chewing on their feed where they were hitched to the front of the contraption, a bored-looking boy next to them.

"Got everything?" Agrippa asked Baird, and when the giant nodded, he gestured at the boy. "Get them going."

With the boat leading the way, they progressed through the streets of Deadground, then out of the town, heading west.

Lydia moved closer to Killian as they walked. "Did you know about this?"

"No," he admitted. "I assumed we were going by foot."

"It sounds dangerous." Her head swiveled in the direction of the children. "Maybe you could find out more details about what we've gotten ourselves into. I'm going to try talking to the women to see if I can learn anything helpful." Then without another word, she marched up to where the female soldier walked and introduced herself.

Rubbing at his aching head, Killian lengthened his stride until he fell in alongside Agrippa. "You didn't mention the boat."

Agrippa grinned and threw his hands up in the air. "Surprise!" Then he laughed. "Don't look so worried. The rapids get a little wild in a few places, but it's better than going by foot. And a damn stretch better than fretting about wildmen ambushes every ten paces."

"If you do this with regularity, then don't they try to ambush you on the water?"

"Oh, they do. And they will. There's a reason I wouldn't do a run with just me and Baird." Agrippa shifted his pack on his shoulder. "But the river's fast and long stretches of it run through ravines with sheer cliffs, so there is no way for them to get at us."

"And at night when you make camp?"

"At night they hide behind fire to protect themselves from the mimics, just as we will be." Agrippa glanced up at him. "The journey is brutal. Don't expect to get much in the way of sleep."

"Good to know." Moving closer to the boat, Killian looked inside, eyes running over the four rows of benches and two sets of oars. The supplies were sitting at the far end, along with several quivers stuffed with black-fletched arrows the Derin army had used.

"You a good shot?" Agrippa asked, reaching up to touch the bow strapped to Killian's pack.

"Not bad." Knocking his knuckles against the thick wood of the boat, he asked, "How do you get back to Deadground?"

"The river runs past the xenthier genesis that leads to Deadground's terminus. Rufina, bless her black heart, hasn't asked Baird to blow that one up yet. Still needs it to bring across the new army she's rallying."

Another army. Killian's chest tightened.

"Though it will be about as piss-poor as her last," Agrippa added, his voice sour. "Farmers with swords are *not* soldiers. It's no way to build an army and certainly no way to win the war. My homeland has its ugly side, but at least we train our soldiers before sending them to fight."

"You're not from Derin?"

Agrippa made a face. "Do I look like I'm from Derin? No, I'm from a place called Celendor. Heard of it?"

Yes. "No."

"No one ever has." Agrippa laughed. "It's on the far side of the world. Only the Maarin know anything about it, but the few I've chanced to encounter since my arrival took one look at my Cel self and tried to slit my throat. Some sort of nonsense about how East must not meet West. Unfortunately for them, I'm not so easy to kill."

Apparently the lengths the Maarin went through to keep the halves of the world secret from each other were greater than either he or Lydia had realized. "How did you end up here?"

"An unplanned tumble into a stream resulted in me encountering a xenthier stem. It tossed me out in the Uncharted Lands along the border of Arinoquia. I was half-dead when a band of warriors found me and saved my life."

Arinoquia. Killian's heart skipped, then raced, his trepidation building. That's where the Cel army was now with Teriana. "How did you come from there to Derin?"

"Same as everyone else. All who walk a dark path find themselves in Derin." Agrippa snorted at whatever expression he saw on Killian's face. "I spent two years hunting for a xenthier stem to take me home. Did a stint in the Gamdeshian fighting pits, but I was winning too much, so the bet-masters put a price on my head and I had to run. Traveled up the coast of Anukastre and figured I'd have a look around Derin to see if I could find a stem that would take me back east. No luck on that count, and by then, my winnings had run dry, so when Rufina started recruiting, I enlisted. Worst decision of my life, which is saying something. You?"

"I prefer fighting to farming."

Agrippa grinned. "Until you met Gertrude."

"Something like that. Isn't Rufina taking issue with you depleting her army with your little side business here?"

"If she does, it's her own damn fault." His voice took on a falsetto. "'I'm not paying you to gamble and whore, Agrippa. Do what you want, but be there when I need you to resume command or I'll hunt you down and make you beg for death.'"

Agrippa had been in command of Rufina's army?

Killian stared at the ground in front of him, it taking all his self-control not to react. Not to pull his sword and run the bastard through, because this young man had commanded the army that had killed *thousands* of Mudamorians. Had used the skills taught to him by the Empire to serve the Seventh. And in one blow, Killian could prevent him from ever doing so again.

Except he needed Agrippa to get to the other side of the Liratoras. Given what Lydia had seen of the corrupted tenders, any delay would be to Malahi's detriment. "You're a brave man to risk crossing her."

Agrippa made a noncommittal grunt. "I'm scared shitless of her. But as it is, she's got bigger issues to consume her fanatical mind than us and our boat."

"Do you know what she's planning?"

"Nope." Agrippa pulled the waterskin loose from his belt and took a swig. "All she told me was to be prepared, because when next she marched, it would be with an army unlike the world has ever seen."

An army of the dead.

They had traveled for several hours, rising higher and higher into the mountains, and the mules were beginning to drag their feet when, finally, they crested the slope to find a glacier spread out through the valley. They led the mules and the boat down the edge of it, heading to where a small, partially frozen river flowed from its base.

"Here we are," said Agrippa. "We can have a spot of lunch while we wait for Baird to finish his performance."

Most of the customers sat down on rocks, but Killian approached Agrippa. "What do you want me to do?"

"Get a fire going," he answered, and gestured to the pile of wood. "Baird will take a bit of time."

"What precisely does he plan to do?"

"You can ask him if you can watch, if you want." Agrippa shrugged. "It's not as exciting as you might think, but maybe I've just seen it too many times."

Curious, Killian quickly built a fire, and leaving Lydia talking with the other women, he ventured down the frozen river in search of the giant.

Baird had built his own fire, but instead of standing next to it, he was currently perched on a rock, staring at the sky.

"What exactly do you intend to do?" Killian asked.

"Can't very well paddle a boat down a frozen river, now can we," the giant answered. "And we are sure as shit not using it as a giant sled."

Killian knew as much as anyone about summoners, but no one really knew the extent of their power. The summoner his mother had brought to aid with evacuation had raised wind to help the speed of the ships, but that had wreaked havoc on the weather. He couldn't begin to imagine what sort of fallout so much warmth would have. But he supposed he was about to find out. "May I watch?"

"If you want." Baird ceased his assessment of the sky. "But keep your tongue still. It takes some concentration to pull a wind from as far as Anukastre."

Killian took a seat on the rock the giant had abandoned, wrapping his cloak more tightly around his body against the chill. In the distance, he caught sight of Agrippa speaking to Lydia. But she had her arms crossed and was looking through her spectacles at the young man as other women might a dead rat left on the doorstep, so he decided she had it in hand.

Then the sound of a deep humming drew his attention back to Baird. The giant was circling the fire, his arms held up to the sky, feet moving to the same rhythm as his humming. As Killian watched, Baird's steps turned to great leaps, the enormous man displaying a speed and agility that would have shocked Killian if he hadn't seen firsthand what the giant was capable of.

Then Baird began to chant, speaking in the language of Eoten Isle, which Killian only knew a few words of. Bercola had been reticent to teach him, and Killian was not the best with languages as it was. But from what he gathered, Baird was asking Gespurn's permission to do whatever it was he was doing, and Killian idly wondered, given Baird fought on the side of the Corrupter, if Gespurn might say no.

He got his answer a few minutes later as the pressure in the air shifted, causing Killian's ears to pop. Glancing up, he saw the few clouds in the sky were swirling above, and then a hot wind smelling of sand struck him, growing in intensity and heat with each gust. His head throbbed as it increased in force, the chill long gone from the air, the snow around him melting.

Removing his cloak, Killian turned his head, listening to the glacier groan and crack, meltwater running off its edges. And slowly, the stream running away from it grew wider. Deeper.

Faster.

"Let that blow for a time and then we'll get underway," Baird announced, kicking slush over his fire. "Dancing always gives me a hunger."

Somehow, Agrippa had gotten the information out of Lydia that Killian knew how to cook, and he was tasked with roasting the chickens. When it came time to eat, he motioned for Lydia to join him on the rock where he'd watched Baird.

"How is your head feeling?"

Her voice was tart enough that he determined she'd not forgiven him for getting blindingly drunk the prior night. Which he really didn't think was fair given it had yielded impressive dividends. "It's fine. And on a more important note, Agrippa likes to talk. He told me he came through a xenthier stem that put him in Arinoquia."

Lydia's eyes widened.

"It gets more interesting, and not in a good way. He's Rufina's general." Swallowing a mouthful of chicken, he added, "He was the one in command of the Derin armies. And he will be again."

Her face went still. "Then why is he still breathing?"

"Given Baird can call lightning with enough accuracy to hit a xenthier stem, picking a fight with his business partner could be risky."

"Then don't pick a fight with him. Slit his gods-damned throat and the giant's, too."

The tone of her voice as much as the words made Killian's hackles rise. Or rather, the lack of it. Entirely emotionless, as though she were asking him to pass the salt, not to murder a man. "That's not really my style."

"Your style?" Lydia stared at him, green eyes bright. "How many of our people died because of him? How many more will die because of him? Killing him will protect Mudamora, and isn't that supposed to be what you *do*?"

Unease filled his chest, because none of this sounded like Lydia. "According to you, Malahi's our path to saving the kingdom, and to reach her, we need to get through these mountains. We need Baird for that, which means we can't do anything to Agrippa. Once we're on the other side, my feelings on the matter might change."

"Might?" Her hands balled into fists where they rested on her lap, her eyes fixed on Agrippa, who was regaling the two children with some sort of story, their faces rapt.

"He's not her commander by choice," Killian said, hoping to temper her rage before she did something both of them would regret. "She threatened to kill him if he didn't comply."

"Better to die than to do what he has done." A tear trickled down her cheek, and she scrubbed it away furiously. "You didn't see what it was like in Mudaire. You didn't have to watch Mudamorians hunting Mudamorians in the streets. Didn't watch the dead rise up, the Seventh in control of their bodies. That's the army he'll lead next, and with his training, it's going to be close to unstoppable."

"That's the blight, not Agrippa."

"The Empire is a blight! Why can't you see that?" she snarled, then gave her head a sharp shake, rubbing at her temples.

It occurred to him that she wasn't seeing Agrippa as just Rufina's minion, but also as the enemy that had tried to have her murdered. That had her best friend kidnapped. That was invading just as surely as Rufina was. "Can you do this?" he asked softly. "There is no shame in saying no. I can take you back, then return on my own."

"I'm fine. And even if I wasn't, we can't afford the delay." She rose and walked to the edge of the glacier, gravel crunching beneath her boots as she inspected the melting ice.

"Tom!" Agrippa's voice caught Killian's attention. "Time to start earning your keep!"

Killian and the other men pushed the boat off its skids and down the gravel to the banks of the now roaring river.

"No refunds, but this is the last chance for any of you who've lost your nerve," Agrippa announced to the group. "The boat stays on the water until dusk, and if you try to turn around at that point, you won't last ten minutes. Anyone?"

No one spoke. Killian glanced at Lydia, but she only shook her head.

"Then, let's go."

He, Agrippa, and Baird pushed the boat halfway into the water before pausing to let the customers climb in and casting off.

Baird sat in the middle and took hold of the oars, Agrippa taking position at the front and Killian at the rear, and everyone else arrayed between as they sped downstream, the giant deftly steering them around any obstacles. The two children giggled and shrieked whenever there were rapids, the boat bucking and plunging, icy spray misting over the group. It was all in all an enjoyable way to travel, but like all good things, it didn't last.

After a couple hours, Agrippa moved from his place in the front, stepping over people until he reached Killian. "We're entering wildmen territory," he said, keeping his balance easily as the boat bobbed over rapids. "There aren't many good ambush points along the stretch we'll cross today, but keep a keen eye. They know I'm a good shot, so they don't usually come down onto the banks of the river. But they also know we have gold, and many of them are good shots themselves. Kill them on sight, understood?"

"Understood."

Agrippa moved back to his position, then he cleared his throat. "We're about to hit some rougher water. Not the worst we'll encounter but rough. Here's the deal: if you fall out, try to swim to the boat and we'll pull you back in. But most likely, you're dead. While I'm sorry about that, there will be no refunds." He laughed, but everyone on the boat only stared at him with wide eyes. "It hasn't happened yet, but if the boat flips, swim to shore. We'll try to right it, but again, it likely means we are all dead. So hope that doesn't happen. Questions?"

No one said a word.

"All right, then." Turning to face forward, Agrippa retrieved his bow from the case mounted next to a full quiver, his posture alert as he scanned their surroundings.

Holding his own bow, Killian eyed the land they were passing through. Dense forests covered the steep mountain slopes to either side, the mountains so tall that their peaks were lost in the clouds. Frozen waterfalls zigzagged down the naked rock above the tree line, and it occurred to him that he'd seen nothing living—not even a bird—since they'd left the glacier.

Then he caught sight of a glint of metal in the trees. Squinting, he finally picked out a figure dressed in white furs, almost impossible to see in the snowy terrain. It watched the boat pass without moving, but turning backward, Killian didn't miss the arrow that shot into the sky. "Agrippa!"

"I saw," came the grim reply. "Everyone down between the benches. Keep low and hold on."

"Bloody bone-collecting bastards!" Baird snarled. "Can't even give us one day's respite." Then he let go of an oar and retrieved a helmet from between his feet, jamming it on his bald head.

Taking up two arrows from the quiver fixed to the side of the boat, Killian nocked one, seeing the white water ahead and knowing that was where the ambush would be. The ground to either side was devoid of cover, but the wildmen wouldn't be standing on a bucking boat when they made their shots.

Dropping to one knee on the bench, he reached down to touch Lydia's shoulder. "Stay low." She turned her head to nod, and he saw she'd wisely tucked her spectacles away in a pocket.

The boat rose and fell, bucking like a bee-stung horse, water splashing in over the sides as Baird kept them to the center. Killian held on to the edge to keep his balance, knowing he'd have no such luxury once the attack began.

Then over the roar of the river, he heard shouting. Close to two dozen fur-clad figures rose from where they were hiding in the snow and raced toward the river, bows in hand.

"Get us to the west side, Baird!" Agrippa called, and Killian's skin prickled. *Trap.*

Rising, he ignored the force waiting to rain death upon them as they passed, and looked downriver. Saw the series of boulders jutting out of the water that would force the giant to bring them right against the west bank, as well as the twenty feet of overhang. A perfect spot for boarding. "It's a trap!" he shouted. "They're going to try to board us from that overhang."

Agrippa's gaze jerked downstream, then he shouted, "East bank, Baird!"

"Shit!" the giant swore, his massive shoulders bulging as he fought to change course, nearly running them up on a boulder. Killian hissed between his teeth as wood scraped against rock, but they slid around it, dropping into a dip on the far side.

The boat floundered in the swirling churn of water, then bounced free, shooting toward the waiting wildmen. "You'd better be right about this, Tom!" Agrippa shouted.

But before Killian could answer, arrows thudded into the side of the boat. Swearing, he loosed three arrows of his own, hitting two wildmen and missing a third, while Agrippa hit another two.

Then the boat rolled over another dip, Agrippa nearly going over the edge and Killian barely managing to grab hold as the vessel tipped.

"Paddle!" Agrippa hollered as arrows whizzed past their faces, the people hiding in the bottom screaming.

Baird's shoulders strained as he fought to extract them from the recirculating flow, the wildmen taking advantage and moving right up to the water's edge.

Fletching sliced along Killian's cheek as he fought to keep his balance. Snatching up two more arrows, he braced a heel against a bench and felt Lydia holding on to his leg as he aimed at the nearest attacker, taking the bearded man in the chest. Then another in the leg.

The boat bounced free, and only Lydia's grip kept him from falling backward into the churning swirl of water. It spun in the current, he and Agrippa scrambling for position. They both hit two more, but then a scream of pain from inside the boat caught Killian's attention.

One of the arrows had caught a woman in the back of the shoulder, but there was nothing to be done about it.

Except Lydia had let go of his leg and was crawling across the benches toward the woman.

"Stay down!" he shouted at her, but she ignored both him and the arrows that rained around her, sinking into the benches and supplies. It was only a matter of time until one found its mark.

Balancing on one knee, Killian shot arrow after arrow, his aim better as the water steadied, but the wildmen were moving off the bank and out of range.

But the ambush was yet to come.

Killian turned his attention to the rapidly approaching overhang. They'd no longer be running right beneath it, but the wildmen would have the advantage of the higher ground, those in the boat sitting ducks for their arrows.

A figure shifted, and he lifted his bow to aim but the wildman was mostly hidden behind a rock. *Shit.*

"Back paddle!" he shouted at Baird. Grabbing a handful of arrows, Killian leapt off the side of the boat and landed with a splash a few paces back from shore.

Ignoring the freezing water that filled his boots, he raced down the edge of the river, rising the incline opposite to the overhang. There were four of them crouched in the brush and snow, and their eyes widened in surprise as he appeared on the far side of the river from them.

He killed one before they had a chance to react, then was forced to find cover himself as they shot arrows in his direction.

"Hurry!" he heard Agrippa shout, and leaning out from behind a rock, Killian hit another. But he could hear those who'd survived the first attack racing through the trees toward him. There wasn't much time.

He shot three more arrows, killing one of the men, but the fourth remained. And Killian had nothing left to shoot at him.

"Go!" he shouted at Baird. "As fast as you can!"

The giant rowed hard, the boat skipping over the rapids. The fourth man grinned in triumph, nocking an arrow and aiming at Baird, but Killian didn't need a weapon to kill him.

Picking up a rock, he took advantage of the man's distraction and threw it hard. Grey flashed over the water, then the wildman fell backward, bleeding from the forehead.

But the others were now upon him.

Outnumbered, Killian took three running strides and jumped off the edge. Cold air whistled past his ears as he fell, then he landed with a heavy thud on one of the benches, the boat rocking. Wordless shouts followed him, but the river was already veering around the bend, taking them swiftly out of reach.

"Wasn't that fun?" Agrippa announced, hooking his bow over one shoulder. "You can all sit up now. Daylight is nearly spent, so they won't attack again today."

Ignoring him, Killian stepped over Baird to where Lydia was working, her face grim and her gloved hands coated with blood. "How bad is it?" he asked over the woman's sobs.

"Not good. I need to take this arrow out and stitch the wound up, but I can't do it with the way this boat is bouncing around."

"Then she'll have to keep until we stop for the night." Agrippa leaned between two men to run an experienced eye over the bleeding woman. "She'll last another hour."

Lydia gave a tight nod, then murmured comforting words to the woman as Killian edged around her to talk to Agrippa. "You said they don't attack this far upstream."

"They never have before," Agrippa muttered, his eyes on the western bank, watchful. "I always figured they didn't get enough warning we were coming to do so, but they must have someone watching the water levels. Maybe spies upstream."

"These people need shields to hide behind when we come under attack," Killian growled. "They're completely exposed like this. Half of them will be dead by the time we're through the mountains."

Agrippa shook his head. "They'll need both hands to hold on. Those rapids we just passed through are nothing compared to what's to come."

Frustrated, Killian scrubbed a hand through his wet hair, not certain why he even cared. These people were from Derin—half of them had fought against him at Alder's Ford—which meant they were the enemy. And yet he still felt obligated to keep them safe.

"I was honest about the risks, Tom," Agrippa said, breaking away from his scrutiny of the surrounding mountains to stare Killian down. "They all knew what they were getting into. They all deemed the chance of getting home worth the chance they might lose their lives."

Killian glanced down at the two children huddled between their parents, no longer laughing when the boat bounced and the water sprayed. "And them?"

"Hopefully not a mistake I'll have cause to regret."

Killian retreated to his spot at the rear, stowing his bow and keeping an eye on their surroundings as the sun slowly settled in the sky. True to his word, it wasn't long until Agrippa called out, "Here's our stop for the night!"

Baird rowed the boat to shore, where Killian and Agrippa jumped out first, the rest of the group following with Baird carrying the injured woman.

"You got that in hand, Gertrude?" Agrippa asked, and when she nodded, he motioned to the rest of the group. "First rule of this voyage is that we protect the boat. Without it, we are all dead, so we put it before any one individual. Now let's get it out of the water and into the center of camp."

Killian was dripping sweat by the time they had the heavy vessel settled in the middle of the camp, which was surrounded by a circle of charred wood. Agrippa handed him an axe. "We need six good-size trees felled for our perimeter. Venturing out in the dark to get more isn't an option."

"What attacks at night?" Killian asked, eyeing the growing shadows warily.

Hefting an axe of his own, Agrippa's jaw tightened. "Fear."

82

LYDIA

Coming here had been folly.

Lydia used what remained of daylight to finish wrapping a bandage around the woman's shoulder, then helped her lean back against the side of the overturned boat. That she'd been the only one injured was pure luck—luck, and Killian being his lunatic self, jumping out of the boat the way he had. Her heart had been in her throat the entire time, certain he'd be shot. Or if not shot, then left behind by the boat, because of a surety, Agrippa would have abandoned him.

Then the Cel devil himself was kneeling next to her, holding out a small pouch. "Have her chew a pinch of this, and it will help her sleep through the pain. We won't be going anywhere until dawn."

"What is it?"

"My own special concoction," he replied. "She'll sleep like the dead, trust me."

Not a chance.

But the injured woman held out a pleading hand, so Lydia grudgingly gave her a pinch of the green leaves, watching as Agrippa rejoined Killian and Baird to fell trees.

The location they'd chosen for the camp was unremarkable as far as she could tell. The ground was packed-down dirt and rock covered with fresh snow, but in a perimeter around the camp were built up piles of charred wood.

What sort of creatures prowled these mountains that a group this size needed to surround itself with fire? That the wildmen, who appeared nothing short of fearless to her eyes, went to ground every night in order to avoid?

An answer to be had soon enough, as the shadows stretched longer, the women joining the men in helping to drag the felled trees inside the perimeter.

"Not these," she heard Agrippa say to one of the women, tossing a nettled branch back into the woods. "The smoke is toxic. Puts you to sleep right quick. Here, drag this one over to Baird instead."

Baird methodically chopped the trees into firewood, which Agrippa then used to create equally spaced fires until the group was surrounded by roaring flames. The heat, at least, was welcome, her clothing soaked from being endlessly splashed by the rapids.

Retrieving a large pot from the pile of supplies, she stepped between fires, going to the edge of the river to fill it. She also took the time to rinse the blood from her gloves, the water like ice against her skin.

"You all right?" Killian knelt on the rocks next to her, dipping a hand into the river and using the water to wash the sweat from his face.

"Yes." Sitting back on her haunches, she dried her hands on her skirts. "*You* need to quit showing off, though. Normal people can't do that sort of thing, and eventually, they are going to start to question why you can."

He frowned, scratching at his beard. "I wasn't showing off—I was saving our asses."

"Next time, do it with less flair."

Her tone was more cutting than she intended, but instead of snapping back at her, Killian caught her arm. "What's wrong?"

I killed a woman. Her chin trembled, because every time she blinked, she saw the corrupted tender's life fading into nothingness. "Nothing beyond the obvious. I'm fine."

A whistle cut the air, and she glanced over her shoulder to see Agrippa motioning them back. Climbing to her feet, she reached down to pick up the heavy pot of water, but Killian picked it up first and carried it back to the cook fire.

"No more venturing out," Agrippa warned the group. "Not for any reason. You're going to hear all sorts of strange things tonight, but no matter what it is you think you hear, don't step outside the perimeter unless you want to end up in a stomach."

The little girl started to cry, and Lydia was surprised to see a look of guilt flash over Agrippa's face. "You're safe within camp, little one," he said, then to her mother, "Stuff her ears with scraps of fabric. Stuff your own if you can't handle the noise."

With the ease of much practice, they continued setting up the camp, using a large piece of canvas fixed to the edge of the boat to create a tent of sorts. Killian was relegated to cooking once again, though she noted he kept a watchful eye on the trees, his expression telling her that his mark was warning him of danger.

The group had only just finished dinner when the last glows of the sun set, plunging the mountains into darkness. No one spoke, the only sound the rushing of the river and the crackle of flames, and Lydia held her hands up to the fire as the temperature dropped.

Then she heard it. Only faintly at first, the sound barely audible over the fire: crying.

"I hear something," one of the women said. "Crying. There's someone out there."

"Not someone," Agrippa clarified, poking at the fire. "Something. And I told you before you paid me what to expect from these creatures. Just ignore them."

"Help! Help!" A child's voice cut the air, full of terror, and Lydia clambered to her feet, searching the surrounding trees for motion. But she could see nothing but darkness.

"Try something new, you bastards!" Agrippa shouted. "I've heard this one before."

Lydia ignored him, walking slowly to the perimeter, allowing her vision to go out of focus so that she could see the life of whatever was out there. Then hands closed over her shoulders, drawing her back.

"Don't listen," Killian said, his breath warm against her ear. "It's a trick to lure you out."

"I know." She resisted the urge to lean back against him. "But . . ." She trailed off, her eyes latching on a small glowing form huddled perhaps a dozen paces away.

"Help me," it whimpered. "I'm scared."

"There's a child out there! I can see it!" She tried to pull out of Killian's grip, but he hauled her back, arm around her waist.

"Gertrude, it's not a child." Agrippa had come up next to them.

"Then what is it?" she demanded. "What sort of creature can speak with a child's voice like that?"

"I suppose being from Mudamora, you wouldn't know of them." He exhaled a long breath. "We don't know what they are, exactly. They're called mimics because there isn't a sound or voice they can't replicate. Whatever they are, they have an uncanny ability to choose just the right thing to set people off. I've lost more travelers to their tricks than to the wildmen."

"Have you seen them?" Killian asked, still holding her tight, his heart throbbing steadily against her back.

"Yeah." Reaching down, Agrippa picked up a burning stick. "Let's see if we can get a look at this one."

He cocked his head, listening to the sound of the child crying, then threw the branch. Lydia held her breath as the flames flew end over end before striking a tree. An enraged shriek cut the air, and for a second, Lydia saw it. White fur and claws and a mouth full of needle-sharp teeth, and then the flames flickered out.

"Gods," one of the men whispered from behind them. "I've never seen anything like it."

"Nor I," Agrippa said. "Lern must have been in a foul mood the day he made these beasts, if he can be credited with creating them at all."

All around her, the travelers made the sign of the Six against their chests, and as she did the same, Lydia was again struck that these people were not at all what she'd expected.

Killian drew her backward toward the cook fire, and Lydia felt a stab of disappointment when he let go of her, her back growing swiftly cold away from the press of his chest. The family had followed Agrippa's advice and wrapped fabric over the ears of the children to muffle the mimics' voices, the four of them already readying to fall asleep inside the makeshift tent. The other travelers were wrapping themselves in blankets and joining them, the space tight enough to be unappealing.

Going to her pack, Lydia unfastened her bedroll, grimacing at the dampness of everything. It was going to be a cold night.

"I'll take first watch," Agrippa said to Killian. "Then Baird, then you. Try to get some sleep. Tomorrow will be far worse."

The giant was already snoring loudly next to the fire, clearly unconcerned by the mimic, which had returned to the trees around camp, whispering and crying in a child's voice, although it was easier to ignore it now that she'd seen it.

Killian was unrolling his own blankets next to the fire. He looked up right as she looked at him, and her face warmed as she considered just exactly how to manage the sleeping arrangements given the story they'd told Agrippa.

As if hearing her thoughts, the Cel legionnaire said, "Don't hold back on my account. I've seen it all at this point."

Killian scowled at him, but Agrippa only laughed and pulled a blanket over his shoulders, eyes roving the trees beyond the fires.

Biting her lip, Lydia laid out her bedroll between Killian's and the fire, rolling up her cloak to serve as her pillow. Lying on her side, she pulled her blanket up to her chin and watched the snowflakes fall into the flames, acutely aware of Killian moving behind her.

Of him rolling up his own cloak, then lying down. Close, but not touching her.

Then the loud screech of a deimos split the night.

Lydia jerked upright, turning to see Killian already had his sword in hand, his eyes skyward.

"Mimic," Agrippa murmured. "Too cold for the deimos."

Lying back down, Lydia curled in on herself, trying to calm the racing of her heart. But it was impossible to relax with the mimic imitating the deimos's screams, the pounding of wings. Not with open sky over her. A cold wind blew down the slope, piercing through her blanket, and she shivered, clenching her teeth.

Then Killian's arm slipped around her waist. His hand pressed against her abdomen, he pulled her back against him.

Instantly her body went as stiff as a board, fear fleeing as her mind fixated on each place they were touching. Her shoulder blades against the hard muscle of his chest. Her bottom against the flat planes of his stomach. The heels of her boots against his shins.

She could feel the heat of his breath against her hair, and instinct caused her to lift her head so his other arm could slide beneath her neck. It was not lost on her that this was the position she'd dreamed of finding herself in night after night when she'd slept alone in her room in the temple. Fantasies of being wrapped in his arms, except it had never stopped at just that. And part of her was afraid to relax lest her body betray her with desire for what she couldn't have.

"Try to sleep." His voice was low, something in the tone of it causing heat to flood into her belly and her chest to ache. "I'll watch your back." His fingers interlocked with hers. "So will the Six."

And though the thought of sleeping seemed impossible with the mimics screaming and her nerves thrumming, eventually, exhaustion took hold of her and she slipped into darkness.

"You were the last person I expected this from."

A cool, polished voice filled her ears, and Lydia's heart leapt into a gallop, her skin turning to ice as she recognized the voice of her would-be murderer.

"How can you live with yourself? You betrayed your brothers. You betrayed *me*."

Her eyes snapped open, moving from the fire before her to search her surroundings. Killian still held her close, his slow, measured breath telling her he was asleep and unaware of the danger.

"You *deserted* us."

"No, I didn't."

It was Agrippa who'd spoken, responding to the accusation in Cel, and realization dawned on her that it wasn't Marcus she was hearing, but one of the mimics. Except how was that possible? How could the creature replicate the voice of a young man it had never crossed paths with? Speak a language it had surely never heard?

How did it know which voice would cut a person to the core?

"Didn't you?" Marcus's voice was bitter. "How long has it been since you tried to find a way back?"

"There is no way back. I searched."

"You gave up. You're a deserter."

"I'm not." Agrippa's voice was hollow, and her eyes finally found him, pacing around the perimeter of camp, his hands balled into fists.

"You are. And when we find you, 2483, we'll make you bleed for it."

She heard Agrippa's breath catch, saw the way he was looking to the opposite side of the fire with what looked far too much like intent. And as much as she longed to see this young man dead, Killian was right. They needed him.

Drawing his weapon, he took another step toward the fire.

"Decisto!" The word tore from her lips, and she silently cursed her error as his shoulders went rigid. Slowly, he turned to stare at her.

Shit.

Killian stirred, and as she sat up, he opened his eyes. "What's wrong?"

"Nothing." *Or possibly everything.* "Go back to sleep."

He watched her for a few seconds, then tightened his grip on her hand and closed his eyes. A few minutes later, his breathing deepened.

"Interesting choice of language," Agrippa said quietly, his eyes fixed on her face. "Other than the Maarin, I thought I was the only one on this half of Reath who could speak it."

Because there was no way to backtrack on her error, she said in Cel, "Did you really believe you were the only one to accidentally cross the world?"

Silence.

Then, his voice ragged, Agrippa asked, "Do you know a way back?"

"No, I don't."

His shoulders slumped. "Doesn't really matter, at this point. I can never go back."

With all the things Agrippa knew about the West, him going back to the Empire would be catastrophic, but curiosity still demanded she ask, "Why not?"

"Because they'll execute me as a deserter."

"But you said you didn't leave by choice," she pressed. "Surely once you explain the circumstances, they'll understand."

"That the xenthier took me to the far side of the world? To a place that doesn't even exist in their minds?" He snorted. "Thanks to some choices I made about a girl prior to my unplanned departure, no one in my legion would believe me, most especially not my friends. I'd be dead long before anyone would corroborate my claim."

You might be surprised, Lydia thought. "The Senate does not execute individuals without trial."

"The Senate doesn't execute deserters—the legions do."

"But—"

Agrippa held up a hand to forestall her. "I know what the law is, Gertrude. But I also know what actually happens when a deserter gets caught. I've seen it." Sheathing his weapon, he came back over to the fire, taking a seat. "It's an unwritten rule that if we catch a deserter, we bypass official channels and return him to his legion for justice, and I assure you, there is *no* trial. And the execution isn't a hanging, either. The deserter gets beaten to death by his brothers."

Lydia pressed a hand to her mouth, horrified by the visual. Logically, she knew that legion training fostered violence, but she'd been raised to believe their obedience to the Empire was unquestionable. This smacked of something entirely different.

"You're a civilian," he said. "No one outside the legions understands— desertion is the absolute worst thing you can do. Worse than even murdering one of your brothers, which happens a lot more than desertion, in case you were wondering."

"Why?" she demanded. "Surely they, more than anyone, could understand why someone might choose a different life?"

He made a face. "Because . . . because it makes those left behind feel weaker, and no one likes that. Especially given the things we face." Scrubbing a hand through his hair, he added, "The reason the legions do what they do so well is that we rarely fight as individuals. So it's not only your own strength bolstering your nerve, but the strength of the men to either side of you and your certainty that they'll hold their ground. Having a man desert is like having a man abandon the line and leaving your flank undefended. It rattles your certainty that the man on the other side of you won't do the same, leaving you all alone. It's terrible for morale, and catching the deserter and killing him is like . . . like cutting out the weakness."

He was right. She didn't understand. Refused to understand how boys raised to be like brothers could kill one another because one decided they didn't want to kill at all.

As though reading her thoughts, Agrippa said, "I can tell you don't get it, so you'll just have to believe me when I say it's true. And by the time a deserter is caught, they are so vilified that nothing they say matters—guilt has already been decided. We were with the Twenty-Ninth when they got ahold of one of their deserters. What was left of him wouldn't have filled a jar. After nearly four years of me being gone, the Thirty-Seventh would do the same to me in a heartbeat."

Though she'd known that must be his legion, hearing it from his lips still made her shiver. Especially given the legion's relative proximity.

"No one escapes the Empire's net." Marcus's voice filtered across the fiery perimeter of the camp. "Nowhere on Reath is beyond our reach."

"Oh, shut up," Agrippa snapped. "Choose someone different."

The mimic fell silent, and Lydia asked, "If you could go back, if they'd accept your story, would you?"

"I don't know." Rising to his feet, he moved to add more wood to the perimeter, then came back to sit across from her. "Most of my life I've been doing what I've been told because the alternative is death. By noose. By Rufina's mark. If I had a choice, it might be to walk a different path."

"You've always had a choice, Agrippa." A young woman's voice filled the air, speaking in Cel but with a heavy Bardenese accent. "And you've always chosen to be the villain."

As Lydia watched, Agrippa's face twisted with grief, and he reached up to press his hands against his ears. "Go to sleep, Gertrude," he said. "She's going to berate me for the rest of the night."

Lying back down, she curled up against Killian's warmth. He stirred, pulling her closer. "Sleep, love."

Her heart caught in her throat, but instead of heeding him, she lay awake for a long time listening to the mimic whisper in the Bardenese woman's voice. The last thing she remembered before falling asleep were tears trickling down Agrippa's face.

83

KILLIAN

Killian had slept heavily, barely stirring until Baird shook his shoulder in the wee hours of the morning, muttering, "Keep the fires burning and don't let anyone leave the perimeter," before flopping back on his bedroll, snoring within minutes.

The last thing Killian wanted to do was move.

Lydia was wrapped in his arms, her backside tight against his stomach and her hand gripping his where it was pressed between the soft curve of her breasts. Her head was tucked under his chin, the clean scent of her hair filling his nose. He could feel the soft throb of her heartbeat, and though he knew he should get up, should check the fires, instead he focused on the rhythmic beat.

What he wouldn't give for her face to be the last thing he saw every night and the first thing every morning. To be the first thing *she* saw every morning.

Lifting up on his elbow, he regarded her in the glow of the fires. Her spectacles were clutched in her free hand, and without them, she seemed younger. The lashes framing her eyes were inky against her ivory skin, and her pale pink lips were slightly parted, her breathing steady. She'd always been slim, but the recent weeks had taken their toll, her cheeks hollowed and the skin beneath her eyes darkened by shadows. Exhausted, and yet she pushed forward. Not because she had anything to gain from this venture, but because she'd do whatever it took to save their people.

Gods, but he loved her. Wanted her more than breath. More than life. But she'd never be his.

Because he could never be hers, no matter how much he wished otherwise. He'd sworn an oath to Malahi to stand by her, to protect her, to be her champion, and he'd failed miserably on all counts. He owed his queen more than just fighting to get her free—he owed her his fidelity.

She might already be dead. You might be pushing Lydia away for nothing.

Shoving away the thought, Killian carefully disentangled himself from Lydia, murmuring that all was well when she stirred, then tucked the blankets around her. Other than the crackle of flames, the only sound was the weeping of the pair of mimics lurking outside the perimeter. The rest of the travelers still slept within the makeshift tent, a quick glance inside revealing that all of them had scarves wrapped around their heads to ward off the noises.

Adding a few logs to the fires, Killian extracted one of his knives and a whetstone, working it over the edge. His gaze flicked to where Agrippa slept, one hand gripping the hilt of his weapon, his brow furrowed. Killian still hadn't decided what he was going to do about him. Agrippa was integral to Rufina's plans for the future—killing him would damage those plans. Except he found himself recoiling from the thought of stabbing Agrippa in the back. Even stabbing him in the front had little appeal.

"Why?" Lydia's voice cut the air, making him jump. "You've never shown any compunction against killing men before."

His gaze jerked to where she lay, but her eyes were closed.

The mimic.

"You're supposed to protect people," it said in Lydia's voice, her tone cool. "But the whole cursed kingdom knows you're a failure at that. The only thing you're good for is killing."

Though he knew it wasn't her, Killian still flinched. Not only because of the words, but the fact that these creatures could obviously see inside his head. Which meant they knew who he was. All it would take was one of them calling him by name and someone overhearing, and he'd have a fight on his hands.

"How fortunate that you like to fight so much." Her voice dripped with sarcasm, cutting and cruel. "But at least I know you'll put my life first—you always do. Never mind that that's what got us in this predicament in the first place."

Scowling, he rose to his feet, shoving the whetstone into his pocket and sheathing his knife. Retrieving his bow and an arrow, he stalked toward the ring of fire, searching the darkness for the cursed creature.

It fell silent.

"Start up that yammering again and we'll find out how you like an arrow between the eyes, you little bastard!" he snarled softly, searching for signs of motion.

"I don't know why you are even here." Malahi's voice came from the far side of camp, and Killian whirled, lifting his bow.

"You never bothered making me a priority before," Malahi

continued, her voice moving through the trees. "There was always something else that mattered more: First the children in the sewers. Then *her.*"

"That's not true," he whispered, then cursed himself for answering the creature. For allowing it to know it was getting to him.

"Isn't it?" Malahi's laugh was bitter. "You swore yourself to me. You agreed to marry me. But when I needed you most, you were riding off to rescue her. I hope it's been worth it."

"You didn't give me much choice." *Why was he answering it?*

"Is that what you tell yourself so you can sleep at night?" she said. "You had a choice. And everything that has come to pass, all the blood that has been spilled and will be spilled, that's on *you.* Because I was right. I saw the enemy clearly when no one else did, and if you'd only believed in me like you promised, none of this would be happening."

His heart was thundering, his breath coming in too-fast gasps. "That was a mistake. I'm here now. I'll get you back."

"Oh, yes. Because it was *me* you were thinking about while you held *her* in your arms. I see right through you, *Tom,* I know she consumes your thoughts. I know that you dream about being with her. That you imagine how things would be different if I'd *stayed dead.*"

"That's not true!" he snarled, hating that it was.

"I trusted you!" Malahi was sobbing now, the sound like a knife to his chest. "I loved you and you betrayed me."

Dropping his bow, he wrenched out his sword, determined to silence this horror with steel, then Agrippa said loudly, "Jilted lover! That's a new one. About time you little bastards showed some creativity."

Whirling, Killian found Agrippa standing behind him. "They'll do whatever it takes to lure you out. Fear. Guilt. Anger. They see straight to your soul and use what they find against you."

Shoving his sword back into his sheath, Killian scrubbed a hand through his hair, wondering how much Agrippa had heard. "How do you keep coming back to this place?"

"Greed," Agrippa answered. "It's hard for them to bother you when all you care about is gold. Now what do you say to a bit of target practice?" He held up a full quiver. "Make the furry bastards work for their dinner, right?"

They spent the rest of the night shooting at the mimics whenever they made a sound. Likely a waste of arrows, but there was an undeniable catharsis to it, especially when one of them struck true. Yet when dawn lit the sky with a faint glow and Agrippa moved to wake the others, Killian found himself hesitating to wake Lydia, reluctant to touch her.

"You should've woken me earlier," she murmured, rubbing at her eyes. "Those things are pure evil—no one should be on watch alone."

"It was fine," he said quickly, avoiding her gaze. "I don't need your company."

She was quiet for a moment, then said, "It doesn't have to be me." Without another word, she rolled up her bedroll and went to see to the woman who'd been shot the prior day.

84

LYDIA

He was upset with her, that much was obvious. But trying to speak to him about it was an impossibility. Agrippa and Baird had them hurrying to be on the water as soon as the sun was in the sky, snapping at them the entire time that the wildmen didn't sleep in, so neither could they.

Frost had coated the trees overnight, the landscape sparkling and silver as they floated down the frigid river. Chunks of ice rode the rapids to either side of the boat, and the wind was not as warm as it had been the day prior. Baird was once again at the oars, guiding them through the safest route with the ease of someone who'd done it many times before. Killian was in the rear, but Lydia refrained from looking back, discomfited by the growing tension between them. Instead, she focused on Agrippa, who stood watchfully at the front, his eyes scanning the trees for any sign of motion, his bow held loosely in one hand.

He had to have questions about who she was, yet he hadn't asked any, which in the light of day struck her as strange. Given how much she and Killian were keeping from him, his disinterest should've been a relief. Yet instead, it pressed upon her and would've consumed her thoughts if they weren't so twisted up with creating increasingly elaborate scenarios for why Killian was avoiding her.

Although logically Lydia knew she couldn't have said or done anything, given she'd been asleep the majority of the time, as the hours passed without incident, she grew increasingly convinced she'd said something in her sleep. Or made some sort of inappropriate noise. Or moved against him in a way that was indecent given they were on their way to rescue the girl he was supposed to marry. By midday, her cheeks were aflame with all the things she'd imagined herself having done to provoke him, so she almost missed it when Agrippa called, "Ravine's ahead, Baird!"

The giant released a world-weary sigh. "I hate this spot."

Curious, Lydia wiped spray from the lenses of her spectacles, noting that the river narrowed as it flowed between twin cliffs, the water white with the violence of the rapids.

"It's going to get rough," Agrippa announced. "So hold on. If the boat gets turned over, try not to drown while the current takes you downstream. When the river widens out, there's a spot we can get righted. Unfortunately, it's also a spot where the wildmen like to ambush us, so if you aren't drowned, try not to get shot while Baird gets the boat sorted."

Murmurs of concern passed between the other travelers, and Lydia's heart skipped as she saw the size of the waves formed by the rapids, water exploding against the boulders protruding from the surface.

"Please tell me you can swim." She jumped as Killian spoke in her ear, the first words he'd said to her in hours.

"Well enough," she answered, turning her head to look at him. "Can *you*?"

He lifted one eyebrow as though the suggestion he *couldn't* do something was utter lunacy. Then he said, "Take off your cloak. Put your spectacles in a deep pocket of your dress where you won't lose them." Then he lowered his voice. "If we get turned over, I'll try to get to the far side of the rapids to deal with the wildmen. You stick with Baird and the boat."

"You think they'll be there?" she whispered.

"I know they will." He pointed, and she looked into the trees to see a bearded face staring back at her. The wildman lifted his bow to the sky, but before he could shoot a signal arrow, he dropped, a black-fletched arrow protruding from his throat.

Killian lowered his bow, his expression grim as he slipped onto the bench next to her. "Spectacles."

She pulled them from her face, shoving them deep into the pocket of her skirt and fastening the button to close it. The world turned to a blur around her, but the growing noise of the rapids filled her ears. Fear flooded her gut as she caught hold of the rope fastened to the edge of the boat, and Killian did the same.

The turbid water hurtled them toward the gap in the cliffs, the boat bucking across the rapids like a wild horse. Water pooled around her legs, and at Agrippa's shouted instructions, she caught hold of a bucket with her free hand, bailing it out as best she could.

Then there were cliff walls to either side.

The roar was deafening, the boat surging over water more violent than she'd seen in all her life, waves washing over the sides. Agrippa screamed at them to bail, but Lydia could barely keep her seat, her body tossed left and then right as the boat plunged forward.

The boat lurched sideways, and she slid into Killian, screaming as they nearly tipped, but Baird hauled on the oars, dragging the boat out of the backward flow of the current and sending them hurtling forward.

Down and down they flew, and there was nothing but dark frothing water and threatening rocks, her ears filled with shouts and screams and Baird's curses as he fought to keep them from smashing into the cliff walls.

They rolled over a monstrous wave, then the boat shuddered and slipped backward, water pouring over her and Killian, dragging the boat beneath the flow.

Killian caught her around the waist, hauling her forward in the boat as Agrippa howled at everyone to move, to bail, to *listen*, but it was chaos.

The boat spun, somehow leaping free of the backflow. Except now they were traveling backward down the river, Baird barely in control as they bounced from wave to wave.

Recovering her bucket, Lydia bailed, heeding Agrippa's shouts that if they didn't, the boat would sink. The water was up to her knees, the vessel sitting deep in the water and scraping over submerged rocks.

Next to her, Killian twisted, and she glanced up to see him peering downstream. Then his body tensed, and he shouted, "Agrippa! They're going to try to flip us!"

Heart in her throat, Lydia tried to see what he was seeing, but to her it was only a blur of river and rock.

And then her eyes caught motion: a rope looped just above the surging river.

"Hold on!" Killian shouted.

The loud slap of rope hitting wood filled the air, and the back of the boat lifted up, spilling the passengers on top of one another. Killian lunged, knife in hand. But the rope slid along the hull and he missed, Baird barely managing to get the oars out of the way before it caught on them.

The opposite end of the boat lurched upward, and Lydia somersaulted, barely catching herself on the sides of the vessel, her legs dangling in the water. Someone fell past her as she dragged herself in and her breath caught until she saw Killian hanging from a bench, one of the children clutched in his arm.

The travelers were screaming, barely holding on to the boat as it dangled, the rope having snagged on the prow, the stern bouncing on the waves. But above the noise, Lydia heard a woman scream, "My girl! My little girl!"

It was a child that had fallen in.

"Shit!" Agrippa shouted, then he dived into the water, swimming hard downstream.

"Hold him!" Killian shouted, pushing the little boy into the arms of one of the men, then he reached down and caught hold of the back of Lydia's dress. "Wait until I'm up, then count to a hundred and cut the rope!"

Up?

But before she could ask questions, he was climbing the side of the bouncing boat. Balancing on the prow, he jumped, caught hold of the rope, and climbed, knife gripped between his teeth.

Clenching her own teeth, Lydia started climbing the benches, struggling to get around the other passengers. "You are insane!" she hissed as Killian reached the top of the cliff. But instead of rolling over the edge, he caught hold of the rocks and went sideways, keeping out of sight. There was nothing she could do but follow his lead. "One," she said, freeing her belt knife, frozen fingers clutching the hilt. "Two . . ."

85

KILLIAN

It was hard to grip the rocks, his hands were so numb from the freezing water, but Killian ground his teeth and ignored the pain as he worked his way farther along the lip of the cliff, keeping a count in his head as he went.

Lifting himself up, he peeked over the edge and saw a dozen wildmen holding the end of the rope, their faces tight with strain and focus as they fought to flip the boat over.

But they weren't his concern.

He rolled over the edge and kept low until he was into the brush, then pulled his sword and clambered over the rocks and through the trees, his boots sliding in the slush as he raced downstream.

Reaching the end of the ravine where the river widened, he grimaced at the sight. Agrippa had caught the little girl, but he was clinging to a rock in the middle of the river, his eyes fixed on the wildmen standing on the banks with bows in hand. If he tried to reach the edge, he and the child would be shot, but if they remained in the water much longer, they'd both freeze to death.

And Killian only had another thirty seconds before Lydia freed the boat.

Moving at speed, he jumped down the steep incline, hitting the ground and rolling to his feet. The wildmen heard him and turned, but he'd already cut one of them down. Holding the man's body in front of him like a shield, he sliced the arm off another, then shoved the dead man at the archers before attacking.

It was a dance of blood and steel, his skill against their numbers as they pulled their blades and threw themselves at him with utter fearlessness.

Killian fought to maim rather than to kill, needing to whittle down their strength before the boat appeared.

He left screaming men in his wake, their weak blades shearing beneath Mudamorian steel. Blood splattered him in the face, his and theirs, but Killian ignored the pain.

From the corner of his eye, he saw Agrippa swimming to shore, the girl still in his arms, but he couldn't afford to think of that now.

Fight.

One of the wildmen got under his guard, weapon slicing along his ribs, and Killian stumbled back. The other man grinned at him with broken teeth and lunged, but Killian skipped sideways, stabbing him as he passed.

But the wildman's momentum wrenched his sword from his grip.

Cursing, Killian pulled a knife and barely caught the downward swipe of another blade, his body shuddering under the impact. He kicked the man in the knee, not pausing to watch him crumble, instead twisting and throwing his knife at another man who ran screaming toward him.

It sank into the wildman's left eye and he fell, landing on Killian's legs.

Struggling to get free, he jerked sideways, an arrow embedding next to his head, and he looked up to see another man with an arrow trained at his chest.

And then Agrippa was there.

He slashed open the archer's back, then turned to punch another in the face, fighting with impressive skill.

The boat flew from the ravine, full of the sprawled forms of the soaked travelers, Baird fighting to get into position to row. And Lydia, her eyes wide with terror, clinging to the prow.

Back-to-back against Agrippa, Killian crossed swords with what seemed endless fur-clad warriors, his clothes as much soaked from blood as water. But he could sense Agrippa faltering, his skin cast blue with cold, his sword arm wavering.

Out of the corner of his eye, he saw the boat reach the shore. Saw Lydia on her feet, racing toward the still form of the girl lying on the bank. Saw one of the archers train an arrow at her back as she knelt next to the child.

A massive wildman came charging at Killian, the man nearly as big as Baird. He parried the man's blow, but the force knocked him backward. Punching the man in the gut, he twisted in time to see the archer's bowstring snap forward.

"No!" he screamed, lunging.

But Agrippa was already there. He threw himself forward, colliding with Lydia and then sprawling over both her and the girl, an arrow embedded in his back.

Killian's skin burned, his panic rising as he saw more wildmen crossing the river, racing to reinforce their brethren, because he knew this wasn't a fight he could win. Gutting the big man, he sped toward Lydia. "Get the girl in the boat!" he screamed at her, then slid in the slush and gravel, bending to get an arm under Agrippa's shoulder and hauling him to his feet.

Arrows flew past him, and he snarled in pain as one scored along his upper arm, but he kept himself between Lydia and the attackers. The other travelers hauled her and the child into the boat.

"Start rowing!" Killian shouted, then half-threw Agrippa into the arms of the others.

Rock and gravel crunched as the wildmen pursued, arrows flying, and Killian leapt into the vessel. Seeing Agrippa's bow still miraculously fixed at the prow, he grabbed it and a handful of arrows, balancing on one of the benches as the boat surged downstream.

An arrow shot toward him. Killian leaned sideways to avoid it, then loosed three of his own, his aim true.

Then the boat surged around a bend in the river, leaving the wildmen cursing in their wake. But it wasn't their shouts that stole his attention. It was the sob that came from behind him.

"My baby!" a woman howled, and as he turned, he saw the mother clutching the girl's still form. Lydia knelt next to them, the wet fringe of her hair parted and plastered against her head, clearly revealing the half-moon healer's mark tattooed there. She lifted her face to meet his gaze, her intentions obvious.

And the ramifications equally so.

86

LYDIA

The girl was alive, but only barely. If Lydia didn't help her, death would come. For her, as well as for Agrippa.

She turned to look at the young man who commanded Rufina's armies. His arms were braced against the side of the boat, face twisted in pain, his eyes fixed on her face. "Help her," he said from between clenched teeth. "I'm fine."

"No, you are dying."

"Your bedside manner is shit, Gertrude. Anyone ever tell you that?"

She shrugged, then turned back to the girl's mother. "Give her to me. I can help her."

With obvious reluctance, the woman handed her the still form of the little girl. She was battered and bruised, but the cold water had done worse, her pulse so sluggish as to be nonexistent. Taking a deep breath, well aware that all eyes were on her, Lydia pushed life into the child, healing her injuries and bolstering her strength even as she felt her own diminishing.

"Healer," one of the men murmured, and it was a struggle not to flinch, because this revelation would put any chance they had of rescuing Malahi at risk.

The child opened her eyes and began to cry, and Lydia allowed her mother to pull the girl from her arms. "Do what you can to keep her warm."

Then she turned back to Agrippa. His forehead was pressed against the side of the boat now, his breathing rapid. Rubbing her now age-spotted hands together in an attempt to warm them enough that she could work, Lydia took the knife that was strapped to his belt, as her own had been lost to the water. The sharp blade easily sliced through his clothing to reveal a well-muscled torso with four numbers tattooed in black across the backs of his shoulders.

Ignoring the tattoo, she bent to examine the arrow, which was embedded just below his shoulder blade.

Not bothering with a warning, she caught hold of the shaft and yanked. Agrippa screamed and thrashed, forcing Baird to drop the oars to hold him steady, but Lydia already had her hand pressed against the injury.

I know he's the enemy, she silently whispered to Hegeria. *But help him anyway.*

Then life flowed from her fingers, her heart fluttering as she repaired the internal damage before moving outwards, the feel of muscle and flesh knitting together beneath her palm unnerving no matter that she'd done this a hundred times or more.

"Enough!"

Hands closed over her shoulders, pulling her back, and she stared up at Killian. His voice was dark as he said, "If any one of you even thinks of selling her out to Rufina, I will hunt you down and your death won't be swift. Understood?"

However the other travelers reacted, it must have satisfied him, because he nodded and moved to the back of the boat. Lydia turned on her hands and knees, intending to follow so that she could deal with the deep slice across his ribs, but then his eyes latched on hers. "No."

"But—"

"I said no." He sat on the back edge of the boat, eyes on the forest they floated past. "We've another two hours until nightfall. Baird, are we going to make it to your next camp?"

"It's going to be tight," the giant said, eyeing the sun, which was nothing but a faint glow through the growing cloud cover, droplets falling to splatter against his face. "And this rain is not our friend."

"Can you stop it?"

Baird gave a slow shake of his head. "If I meddle any more, I risk bringing worse down on our heads."

"So we're going to be in for an interesting night," Killian muttered. "The rest of you start bailing. We need speed if we are going to survive this."

But as the rain shifted to snow, a cold wind whipping down from the mountains, Lydia couldn't help but wonder if there was any chance of them surviving the night at all.

They reached the camp just as the sun was setting. Everyone silently followed Killian's orders, dragging the boat to the center of the charred perimeter, the rest working to fell trees to use for the fires they'd need for tonight. Not that Lydia had any idea how they were going to get them started.

The wood was soaked from rain and snow, and the oil that had been in their supplies had been lost when the boat had upturned, along with a good portion of their food.

"You need to rest," Lydia snapped at Agrippa, catching him dragging a tree back to camp. "That wound is only partially healed."

"The mimics like this spot," was the only answer he gave, dropping the sapling and then striding back into the woods, his ruined clothing flapping around his body.

Ignoring her own exhaustion—her mark was taking longer than it usually did to regather her strength—Lydia checked on the little girl, who was sitting with her mother next to the cook fire Killian had managed to get started.

"You've made a mistake coming into Derin, Gertrude," the mother whispered under her breath. "I don't care how pretty that man of yours is, leaving Mudamora was a mistake."

"I can't very well turn around now," Lydia answered, holding her hands over the flames. They ached, the pain reaching all the way up to her elbows, and she idly wondered if this was how they'd feel when she'd actually aged. If what she felt was her future, if she lived long enough to know it.

The woman glanced in Agrippa's direction. "Rufina hunts the Marked," she whispered. "And he's her general. If you were smart, you'd have let him die."

"We need him and Baird in order to survive this," Lydia replied, knowing her tone was flat but unable to help it. Unsure of whether saving Agrippa had been a mistake or not. Only that he'd taken that arrow for her and that letting him die hadn't been something she was willing to do.

Killian chose that moment to reappear, helping one of the other men carry a tree over to where Baird was chopping wood. Her eyes went immediately to the slice in his coat, the fabric gaping to reveal the bleeding wound beneath. He had injuries on top of injuries, and marked or not, he had limits. Climbing to her feet, she moved to intercept him before he went back into the forest. "Let me stop the bleeding."

"No." He moved to step around her, but she shuffled into his path. Scowling, he bent low. "You're not recovering as swiftly as you should. It's been hours and you still look old enough to be your own grandmother when you should be looking your normal self. Is it this place? Or is it something else?"

"I don't know." She bit down on the insides of her cheeks. "At the very least, let me stitch it up."

"Agrippa said he'll do it once the fires are lit."

Agrippa? Logically, she knew that the young man would have received training to do it, but that didn't mean he was good at it. And even if he were, why would Killian choose him over her to do it? Hurt flooded through her chest, but Killian had already stepped around her and was heading back into the forest.

Pulling off her spectacles, she rubbed at her stinging eyes before shoving the wire frames back over her ears. She needed to do something to keep busy, so she carried the wood Baird was chopping and set it at regularly spaced intervals around the perimeter while others worked to get them lit. And only when the last silvered rays of the sun disappeared into dusk did Killian reappear.

"All right, let's get this done," Agrippa said, digging into what remained of their supplies and extracting a medical kit. Killian pulled off his shirt and coat, and Lydia clenched her teeth at the sight of the wound, which was crusted with drying blood, more seeping out to run down his sides. She watched Agrippa like a hawk as he prepared, both grateful and annoyed when he did everything as he should.

"You sure you don't want her doing this?" he asked, but Killian only gave a sharp shake of his head, lying down next to the fire.

"Need something to bite down on?"

"Quit stalling and get it done," Killian snapped. "I've a bad feeling about tonight."

Agrippa's brow furrowed, and he glanced toward the dark woods through the smoke and steam of the fires. Then he set to cleaning the wound, focus entirely on his work.

Lydia's hands balled into fists and she forced herself to look away, asking the children's father, who was putting together dinner from what remained of the supplies, if he needed help. But all he said was, "You've done enough, Marked One. Rest by the fire."

The camp, which had already felt too small, all of a sudden felt like a prison, and Lydia fought the urge to pace the perimeter like a caged animal in a circus fair. Sitting on a rock, she held her hands out to the flames, willing them to return to youth, hating this sudden loss of strength.

Was it being in Derin? Or was it her? The question circled her head as a plate of food was placed in her hand, as she mechanically spooned the tasteless porridge into her mouth. The life shed by those around her drifted toward her, the skin of her hands slowly smoothing, but she wanted it to happen faster.

Wanted to take it.

She recoiled from the thought right as Agrippa said, "I'd say try to take it easy, but there's little chance of that."

"Thank you." Killian sat up, pulling his shirt over his head and accepting the plate handed to him, staring blindly into the fire as he shoved the food into his mouth.

Why are you acting like this? she wanted to scream, but it wasn't a conversation that she could, or would, have with all these people listening in. She was torn between wanting to flee this situation and wanting to stay, between anger and distress, and *why wasn't her mark working?*

Then there was a rustle in the trees. The sound of something, no, *many* somethings, circling the camp.

"Good evening, you little bastards!" Agrippa called. "You couldn't wait to see me until *after* I finished eating?"

Uneasiness filled Lydia's chest, and her eyes flicked to Killian. His spoon was halfway between the plate and his mouth, then slowly, he set both on the ground, his eyes fixed on the darkness.

Tension seeped off the group as they waited to see what the mimics would do. Who they would target.

What secrets they would reveal.

"What sort of father stays in a boat while his child is drowning?" the mother's voice snarled. "What sort of father clings to safety while a stranger saves his little girl?"

The father in question turned to stare at his wife. "It wasn't me," she whispered. "I said not a word."

"It's the mimics." Agrippa scowled. "Ignore them. And if you can't ignore them, muffle your ears so you can't hear them."

"Coward!" the mimic shrieked. "You've always been a coward. Would that it had been you who'd drowned so I might find my children someone better. A real man. Like Agrippa."

The father blanched even as Agrippa let out a belabored sigh. "*Ignore them,* you twit. They're only trying to rile you up. And if it eases your mind, I'm really not interested."

Except rather than being pacified, the man pointed a finger at the ex-legionnaire. "*You* said they took the thoughts from our minds—that they didn't make things up." Then he rounded on his wife. "Which means they might be saying it, but you're the one *thinking it.*"

"I'm not!" Her eyes were wide. "They speak false!"

"I always knew you were unfaithful," a mimic hissed in the father's voice. "Ungrateful little chit—the only reason I married you was because you were pregnant, and this is how you repay me?"

The woman's shock turned to fury. "I have never once even *looked* at another man, you pig! How dare you."

In a heartbeat, the pair devolved into a shouting match, half their words from their lips and the other from the mimics until it became nearly impossible to tell who was saying what.

"Enough!" Agrippa shouted, stepping between them and pulling them apart. "Will you two calm yourselves?"

Another mimic added fuel to the fire, saying in Agrippa's voice, "I had her half a dozen times before we left Deadground. And every time, we had a good laugh about you."

"Why you little—" The father swung his fist at Agrippa, who caught his wrist and twisted, sending the other man face-first into the ground. But then the mother flung herself at him, screaming curses even as the mimics chattered in the voices of all three.

Killian and Baird dived into the fray, pulling everyone apart even as Lydia scrambled to the children. "They are all just upset," she whispered, wrapping fabric around their heads to hold pads against their ears, the tears on their faces making her chest tighten. She pulled them against her so they couldn't see, and only then looked up.

And saw the couple weren't the only people the creatures were going after. The rest of the group were all standing at various points around the perimeter, eyes wide as they listened to whatever the mimics were saying, the noise of voices deafening.

Then one man stepped between a space in the fires.

"No!" she shouted, letting go of the children and running after him. Through the smoke, she saw him fall. Saw the splatter of blood even as she heard his screams, and Lydia lunged between the flames, catching hold of his wrist.

She tried to haul him back, but the mimics had hold of him, and instead, she was dragged between the stacks of burning wood, barely feeling the heat.

Then hands closed on her ankles, jerking her to safety.

The man came with her. But only half of him.

Gagging, Lydia fell back against Killian, staring first at the dead man's sightless eyes, and then the ruined mess of flesh at the bottom of his torso. His legs were gone.

"How many are out there?" Killian asked in a low voice, and she tore her eyes from the corpse to look beyond the fire, seeing the life surround the mimics' forms.

"Dozens."

Another of the group ran screaming into the trees, shouting, "I'm coming! I'm coming!"

"Everyone needs to calm down!" Agrippa hollered, but it was to no avail. The camp was in chaos, everyone fighting with one another as the mimics riled frayed tempers and exploited fears.

The couple were tied up, but there was no more rope. Agrippa and Baird struggled to restrain people, Killian going to their aid. But they couldn't hold down everyone, and the other travelers flung themselves at them, attacking.

And the sun had only just set.

Lydia's mind raced, then a solution occurred to her. But it was one not without risks.

Picking up a burning branch, she tossed it outside the perimeter. Driving the mimics back. Then she took a deep breath, and ran between the fires, snatching up an armload of needled deadfall from the shadows and then stumbling back inside the ring.

No one had noticed her go, the mimics' volume growing by the second. So no one noticed when she went to the cook fire at the center of camp and dropped the branches on the flames, a great cloud of smoke filling the air. Hurrying to the edge of the perimeter, she sucked in a deep breath and then pressed her face to the ground, watching as the group unwittingly inhaled the smoke.

Slowly, they stopped fighting, looking around in confusion, only Agrippa seeming to realize what she'd done. Holding his breath, he raced in her direction, then stumbled and fell to the ground, unconscious. Everyone else dropped to the ground, and Killian fell to his knees.

His eyes locked on hers as he gasped, "Keep the perimeter fires lit!" Then he swayed and fell on his side.

The need to breathe was becoming nearly painful, but Lydia kept holding her last clean breath of air in her lungs. She stumbled over to the fire and tossed water on the flames. Gouts of smoke and steam rose into the air, but flames still flickered, so she threw dirt on the fire. Only when she couldn't take it anymore did she race back to the perimeter and suck in a deep mouthful of air.

Though it was much dissipated, she still tasted the acrid smoke of the nettles, and a wave of dizziness swept over her.

Stay conscious, she silently pleaded. *Otherwise we are all dead.*

On hands and knees, she crawled around the perimeter, adding fuel to the fires in case she succumbed. Only then did she check the others, going to Killian first. His pulse was strong, and she prayed he'd be the first to wake, because she didn't think she'd get away with this trick twice.

Only once she was certain everyone was all right did she sit next to the children, lending them her body heat against the mounting cold. Through all of this, the mimics had been quiet. She prayed the smoke had knocked them out, too, but even as the thought crossed her mind, she heard a voice. Unfamiliar and yet . . . *not*.

"What a strike of fortune, the Calorian boy being marked," a man said, then laughed. "The gods favor our girl, there can be no doubt. Once the boy has sworn himself to her, I'll speak to Liam about a betrothal. It's a good match—will please the people."

Liam was Killian's father's name. Lydia shook her head in confusion, her eyes going to Killian, but he still slept. Were the mimics stealing from inside his head, even now?

"Kitaryia is not yet three, Derrek," a woman said softly. "Wait until she's older. Until we see if she favors his company or not before rushing into these things. We've time."

A child babbled in the distance, the words unclear to Lydia, but she heard the *click click* of heels, then the woman said, "Let me help you, love," and she abruptly could see the scene playing out before her. A woman's face, hazy, looking down at her, and beyond, a tall man in a green coat, his face equally blurred.

He said, "Best hope she favors him, for he'll be at her side the whole of their lives."

The woman laughed, and Lydia felt the strange sensation of being lifted. Of being carried, and she gave her head a sharp shake. "He's not a boy to be led anywhere he does not wish to go. His parents can scarce keep him seated through a lesson without him escaping off into the wilds."

"He'll settle."

"I don't think so, so best hope he favors our girl as well."

A loud bang echoed through the night, and Lydia jumped, trying to pull her head from the fog. But it was impossible.

"What is the meaning of this, Cyntha!" the man snarled. "You've no business being in here."

"Which is strange, given this was *my* bed for more than a decade, Your Grace." A new voice purred the words, a younger version of Cyntha's voice.

Rufina.

Whose mind were the mimics taking this from?

There was no time to dwell on the question, because Rufina was speaking again.

"My bed, until you cast me aside for *her*."

"Get. Out!" the man shouted, his anger palpable, and Lydia tried to see, but her vision was obscured by the woman's body. But she heard the gasp, heard the man say, "Gods . . . your eyes." A flurry of movement, then, "Guards!"

"All dead, I'm afraid," Rufina answered. "Revenge is a thing best savored, and I could risk no interruptions."

"Camilla, run!" the man shouted, and then steel rang against steel. "Run!"

The woman sobbed, but then she was running, and Lydia realized with a start she was seeing through the eyes of the child. The child that was wailing in terror for her father.

"Run, run, run," Rufina sang from behind. "There is no escape!"

Terror filled Lydia, her body turning to ice, and she muttered, "It's not real, it's not real, it's not real." But it felt real, as though she were truly the child in the woman's arms, father dead and the murderer chasing them through the hallway and into other rooms, nowhere to go and no time to hide.

"Would you like to die first or wait as I strip the life from your get?" Rufina called, her voice closer.

"You will not touch her!" the woman screamed. "You will not have her!"

A door latch clicked, and Lydia stared out over the ocean before being turned back to face Rufina, who prowled closer, eyes midnight and flame. "You stole my life," Rufina hissed. "You took *everything* that was supposed to be mine."

"It was never yours," the woman said, her voice steady as she backed up, climbed on a balustrade. "And it never will be."

"You'll kill her yourself instead?" Rufina laughed. "How noble of you."

"I will save her."

"There's nowhere to go. Nowhere that I won't find you."

"Yes, there is," the woman answered, and then Lydia was falling.

She screamed, grasping at the air around her, wind whistling in her ears, a hand closing over her mouth just before they struck.

Cold, frigid water surrounded her, everything black and disorienting.

"Hold on, love! Please hold on!"

They were flung forward, and Lydia sobbed as something scraped along her leg, tears flooding down her face to join the seawater. She was dragged onto rock, then up again in the woman's arms, and they moved through total darkness.

"Shssh, love," the woman whispered. "They must not hear us."

Voices and thundering boots reverberated through the dark tunnels beneath the palace, growing light coming toward them, but the woman turned away and into another tunnel.

More darkness, the only sounds the woman's feet shuffling over rock and the child's muffled sobs. And then a glow filled her eyes, a crystal xenthier stem appearing, illuminating the blackness. Holding tight to the child, the woman reached out and touched it.

White light.

Lydia wept as the light cleared, the sounds and visions fractured and strange, but also painfully familiar. She knew where the woman and the child had escaped to.

The woman was faltering, falling over and over, each time struggling harder to rise. "Walk, my love," she finally whispered. "We are so close. Here, she cannot harm you. Here, you will be safe."

The remembered scent of flowers filled Lydia's nose, the drone of insects in the foliage and distant sound of waves crashing in her ears. Higher, they climbed, and she was so tired. So afraid.

Then the woman fell.

Lydia pulled on her arm, pleading at her to get up, but the woman's eyelids only fluttered, so she started to scream. A clang of a gate and voices speaking over top of her, shouting, "Get the senator!"

And then a man was kneeling next to her and the woman, her father but not the father she'd left behind. And the woman caught his wrist, speaking in Cel. "Care for her, Appius. Keep her safe."

"Where is the physician?" Lydia's father shouted, and she saw the tears on his face. "Get someone! Knock on every door!"

"It's too late," the woman whispered. "Her name is Princess Kitaryia Falorn. Tell her that her mother loved her."

And then the spark faded from her eyes and she went still.

"Mother!" Lydia screamed, grabbing at her body, hands coming away covered in blood. "Mother!"

And then hands were shaking her, Agrippa's face inches from hers. "Gertrude!" he shouted. "Snap out of it. It's only the mimics playing with your head."

Only it wasn't the mimics. It was real. It was her memory.

"Let her go!" Killian shoved Agrippa away and knelt before her, still swaying from the effect of the smoke. "Are you all right?"

All the connections clicked in her head, a thousand realizations, and an awful mix of grief and bitterness and loss welled up in her chest. *I know who I am,* she thought, staring into his eyes. But all she said was, "Dawn will come soon enough. Everyone should get some rest."

87

TERIANA

They left the village at dawn, backs weighed down with the supplies Marcus had purchased with silver taken from her hair.

It was the last time they slept in a proper bed, neither of them willing to risk encountering a legion patrol. Their nights were spent huddling together in a tent. When they needed supplies, Marcus went into the markets alone, leaving her to worry until he reappeared. And to continue to worry as he silently brooded, even more sparing on conversation than he normally was.

As much as the events in the village had grieved her, they seemed to have a more lasting impact on Marcus, despite them being no revelation to him. But no matter how much she pressed him, he refused to say anything beyond that all individuals living within the Empire were subject to its laws, just as they were subject to the punishments for breaking them. But though he said the words with conviction, the way he'd go silent for hours afterwards, his eyes distant, made her certain that he was questioning those laws.

Or perhaps his own role in enforcing them.

Except what choice did he have? Grand title he might possess, but she knew he was nothing more than an indentured servant to the Senate, doomed to work off the debt that had been forced upon him as a child, his freedom withheld for another twenty-five years, if he lived that long. To defy the Senate's orders meant punishment—if the offense were great enough, he'd be hanged for treason. He was a slave to the will of a group of men he hated, and there was no escape, other than death.

Except, perhaps, for one.

The thought burned in her mind as they traveled south, each passing day growing warmer even as it brought them closer to Celendrial. Closer to the moment when Marcus would once again be a legionnaire. To the moment he'd again be the Empire's tool for conquering the West. To the moment when they'd part ways and she and her freed people would join the armies of the West in the fight against the Cel incursion.

To the moment he'd cease to be the young man she loved and once again be the enemy she needed to defeat.

"The Savio," Marcus said, rather unnecessarily, as they stopped next to a wide river. "We'll travel west along it until we reach a village, then we should be able to buy a boat that will take us the rest of the journey."

Sliding down the bank, Teriana pulled off her coat and stuck her hands in the cold water, relishing the feel of it running over her skin. The weather had improved with each passing day, and it was warm enough for a bath to be possible without risk of freezing to death. Especially given that this far upstream, the Savio was clean enough that she could see the rocks under its swift running surface, though it would grow fouler the closer they got to the ocean.

Closing her eyes, she imagined she could feel the strength of the sea reaching out to her, calling her home. It had been months since she'd stood on a beach. Longer still since she'd stood on the deck of a ship, and though a riverboat was a far cry from the *Quincense*, she rose and eagerly started downstream.

It didn't take long to find one of the countless small settlements that made their living off the river. "Circle round and wait downstream," Marcus said. "We can only assume that Cassius is still capturing any Maarin he can, and now that we are in Celendor itself, we shouldn't risk anyone getting close enough to see your eyes."

Grimacing, she nodded. And after giving him a list of supplies, she circled round the town and sat down on the bank to wait.

Perhaps an hour later, Marcus drifted downstream toward her, awkwardly steering a riverboat that had seen many years and looked ready to retire on the bottom of the river.

"Nice boat," she said, wading out and then pulling herself aboard. "I hope it was free."

"Was all I could afford after buying your supplies," he countered, handing her a package. "So don't complain."

Taking hold of the rudder, she waited as the current took hold of them before easing toward the center of the Savio.

A temperate wind caught at her hair, sending her ragged braids streaming out behind her as they sped downstream. Only once she'd had her fill at the helm did she say, "Think you can manage this without crashing us for a few hours?"

Turning from his contemplation of the passing landscape, Marcus shrugged, then walked carefully to where she stood, taking the rudder. After giving him a few instructions, she retrieved the package of supplies he'd purchased. Then, sitting with her legs crossed, she went to work on unraveling her hair.

It wasn't a task she ever did herself. Only her aunt Yedda touched her hair, and that was one of the reasons she'd delayed removing the braids for as long as she had. Because it would be like giving up the last thing she had of her family. Except not only were they grown out and fuzzy and unraveling in several places, it wouldn't be long until she was reunited with the *Quincense* and her crew. And she knew that if her aunt saw the current state of Teriana's hair that she'd never hear the end of it.

It was arduous work, and her back and neck and arms ached by the time she finished unbraiding. Her muscles protested as she set to combing out the handfuls of hair that had come loose, tossing it into the river to float away. She could feel Marcus's eyes on her as she worked, and as always, she had to fight the desire to go to him. To wrap her arms around his neck and lose herself in the pleasure of his touch, because it was the only time she could forget that they were racing toward the moment they'd part ways forever.

Her eyes burned at the thought, and she rubbed at them furiously before filling a bucket with river water and setting to the task of washing her hair with soap that smelled like lavender, then massaging its length with oil that smelled of the same. Rebraiding it herself wasn't a remote possibility, so instead, she wrapped it tight to her head with the scarf of indigo cotton that Marcus had selected, hoping it would serve to keep her hair out of her face until her aunt could set her to rights.

"You look like your mother."

She jumped at Marcus's voice. They often went a long time without talking, but the silences were easy and comfortable. Made more so by the fact neither of them went long without touching each other, the brush of his hand against hers as they walked never failing to make her heart skip, then race, always, always wanting more.

I don't want to give you up.

"You'll see her soon," he added. "And the rest of your people."

She'd been separated from them for so long . . . "If she even wants to see me. Not sure if you recall, but she wasn't overly pleased at some of the decisions I made."

"I remember."

Chewing on the insides of her cheeks, she said, "When you told me I'd lost my chance to see her the morning we left, I wanted to kick you in the balls I hated you so much. But that wasn't the reason, was it? She told you she didn't want to see me, didn't she?"

Marcus's throat moved as he swallowed, his eyes on the river before them. "People say things they regret when they're angry, Teriana. She's had a lot of time to think, and she may see your choices differently having spent so many months a prisoner."

"You don't know her. She's stubborn."

"Sounds like someone else I know."

Teriana frowned, never having considered herself anything like her mother except in appearance. Captain Tesya was rigid and married to their people's ways, whereas Teriana had always felt drawn beyond the confines of her ship. To people who were different than she was. It had caused endless conflict between them over the years, and some days, she wondered if her mother had the right of it. If Teriana had never befriended Lydia, none of this would be happening.

And I'd never have met Marcus.

It was a selfish thought, and she shoved it away. "With my luck, I'll have gone through all this to get my people free, and they'll cast me out for it."

"You didn't do it because you thought they'd appreciate you for it," Marcus said. "You did it because you believed it the right choice. Because you wanted to protect them."

"Or because I couldn't stomach having my fingernails ripped off."

He flinched, then shook his head. "I think if you'd believed your mother's path the right one, you'd have stomached far worse than that. It's easier to suffer for something you believe in."

She opened her mouth to ask when the last time was that he'd been tortured but paused.

Marcus had suffered tremendously as part of the Empire's desire for power and domination. Yet she knew that he didn't believe in it. Did he endure it simply because he had no other choice, or was there another reason? Not for the first time, she wished she could see inside his head because every instinct told her that there were secrets that he kept, and not just from her. "When they send you back with more legions and more resources, what will you do?"

"What I'm told." His jaw tightened. "If I don't, the Senate will execute me, and someone equally qualified will take command. My defiance changes nothing."

She remembered what Amarin had told her in the command tent. About not striking a blow against one senator but against the Empire itself. Was such a thing even possible? "Have you ever wondered," she asked, "what you might achieve if you fought for something you believed in?"

Marcus didn't answer for a long time, then finally said, "I don't know what I believe in anymore." He pulled on the rudder, sending the boat drifting into one of the endless tributaries of the Savio. "It's starting to get dark. We should find somewhere to make camp."

88

LYDIA

The rest of the journey through the mountains had been mostly uneventful, the greatest threat the rapids of the river, but even those eased after that night. And it wasn't long until they were into the foothills, the forests dense and full of wildlife that had been nearly absent from the mountains themselves.

Baird eased the boat against shore, and Agrippa and Killian climbed out to drag the battered vessel up onto the gravel, holding it in place while the survivors climbed out.

Lydia climbed up the bank, taking a seat in the thick grass covering the slope and resting her head on her knees, silently telling herself if she ever saw a boat again, it would be too soon.

"Thanks again for traveling with us," Agrippa said loudly to the backs of his passengers as they wearily climbed the bank, faces drawn as they walked past Lydia with nothing more than the clothes on their backs. And their lives. "Do recommend our services to your friends!"

"Don't get many repeat customers, do you?" Killian asked, helping Baird drag the boat farther out of the water.

"Not a one." Agrippa scowled at the boat. "And after this last trip, I think it's time I passed this business opportunity on to someone else. Gold in the pocket does me little good if I'm floating facedown with wildmen arrows in my back."

"I've been saying that for a month, you skinny little shit," Baird said. "'Bout time you saw reason."

Agrippa shrugged. "Was good while it lasted."

"No," the giant replied. "It was not."

Lydia was inclined to agree. No amount of gold would entice her to take another journey through the Liratoras, although it wasn't lost on her that if they were successful in retrieving Malahi, they were going to need to find a way out of Derin.

"What will you do now?" Killian asked, trying, and failing, in Lydia's opinion, to look disinterested.

"Go see if Rufina is ready to put me back on her payroll, I suppose," Agrippa answered. "Commanding an army is easier work."

"So you're going to head to Helatha, then?"

"Yeah."

Killian's gaze flicked to Baird. "You?"

The giant shrugged. "I go where the little man goes."

"I am *not* little." Agrippa glowered. "You are merely profoundly large."

The pair bickered back and forth, then Killian said, "Gertrude and I are heading that way as well."

Lydia struggled not to scowl at him. Agrippa and Baird had seen too much for them to *not* be suspicious of her and Killian. They needed to part ways with them now, not venture into the underworld with the commander of its armies. What was he thinking?

"You could travel with us," Agrippa said. "Rufina could use a man with your talents."

"He's not looking for a job soldiering," Lydia said loudly, glaring at Killian. "He's going to take up farming. Or become a merchant."

"Honorable, safe professions." Agrippa smirked. "But don't sit there and pretend that's what you're interested in, Gertrude. You like the excitement. Admit it."

"You are mistaken." She injected as much frost into her voice as she could.

He held up his hands. "So sorry, beautiful. Farming is a wonderful profession, and I'm certain you will both have a fulfilling life growing potatoes together."

Killian laughed, and Lydia glowered at him.

"Either way," Agrippa said, "the road to Helatha is far from a safe one, so perhaps you'll allow me the courtesy of ensuring you arrive in one piece."

There wasn't much she could say to that. "I hope it will be less eventful than the first half of our journey together, Agrippa."

He grinned. "No promises." Then he rounded on Killian. "Though don't let me tie you to me with coin, Tom. You more than earned your wage."

Digging into his pockets, he counted out glimmering gold, Killian looking more and more delighted with each coin Agrippa dropped onto his palm. It was probably, she thought, the first time he'd ever received a wage, and the novelty clearly overwhelmed his good sense, for he said, "We'd be glad for the company."

"Perfect." Agrippa stretched, cracking his back. "Let's get underway. There's a village about an hour from here with an inn that makes the most excellent stew. . . ."

He continued prattling as he walked down the path next to the river, Baird following at his elbow.

"Have you taken leave of your senses?" Lydia hissed under her breath as Killian came up next to her. "We can't trust them."

"I'm aware." Killian shoved the coins in his pocket. "Agrippa fully intends to turn on us. But us parting ways isn't going to stop him from doing that."

"You think he wants his gold back? If that's the case, why in the name of all the gods did you take it in the first place?"

He gave her an affronted look. "Because I earned it. Several times over."

Crossing her arms, she waited for him to give her a proper answer.

"It would've looked strange if I hadn't," he finally said. "And no, I don't think it's the gold. He repaid everything he took from those people. I saw him slipping it back into their pockets earlier—no one but me noticed."

Which seemed both entirely out of character and also exactly what she'd expect from the ex-legionnaire. "Why—"

"I don't know. But I'd rather have him where I can see him than have to constantly watch over my shoulder," Killian interrupted. "Keep your wits about you. I expect he'll do it soon. And he's not stupid enough to take me on without help."

They fell into silence after that, both of them staring at Agrippa's back as he walked and sang bawdy alehouse songs, Baird occasionally joining in with his deep baritone. They reached the village he'd spoken of without incident and partook in what was, in fact, very good stew before carrying on down the road, Agrippa never ceasing his endless chatter.

It was nerves. With what Killian had told her sitting in her head, Lydia noticed the tension in Agrippa's posture, how he was no less watchful for them being out of the Liratoras than he had been when there was fear of wildmen and worse.

And yet nothing happened.

"There's a town up ahead where we can get rooms for the night," he finally announced as the sun was beginning to set. Turning to walk backward, he grinned at Lydia. "A hot bath, Gertrude. With soap."

"You three availing yourselves would do me more good than soaking myself," she answered, wrinkling her nose.

"Tubs are always too small," Baird grumbled. "Haven't had a proper bath since I left Eoten Isle."

"When did you leave?" Killian asked. It was the first thing he'd said in hours. "And why?"

"Fifteen years ago, give or take," the giant answered. "Lost my woman to a life debt during the last war with Mudamora, which was a bitter tonic to swallow. Decided I wasn't interested in a life spent sitting on some rock keeping the Endless Seas still and took to the road, which my people took issue with. Gespurn won't mark another summoner until I'm dead, so they put the hunt on me. Derin proved the best hiding place. That's where I met the little man, here. Sorry. I mean the *average* man, here."

"Nothing about me is average," Agrippa said. "Especially not—"

"What made you decide to fight for Rufina?" Lydia interrupted before he could finish.

"No one *decides* to fight for Rufina," Baird said wearily. "You obey or you die."

"I hate to add another sorrowful note to this dismal conversation, but I'm afraid I have bad news, Gertrude," Agrippa said. "It doesn't look like you're going to be getting that bath after all."

"Why?" she asked, then yelped as Killian pulled her closer to him, his weapon in hand and eyes on the surrounding trees.

Agrippa stepped away from them, tugging Baird with him. "Because it appears I'm not the only one who recognized your boy. And his worth." Then more loudly, he said, "Allow me to remind you all that while he's only worth a thousand gold coins dead, he's worth five thousand alive. Choose wisely."

89

MARCUS

Marcus lay on his back on the deck of the boat, Teriana's cheek pressed against his chest and his eyes on the endless stars above them. The boat swayed and drifted, moored to a tree along the bank, the air filled with the sound of cicadas and the scent of freshly tilled fields. Despite the darkness, it was still hot enough that sweat dampened his brow, not even a breath of breeze rustling the trees to cool his overheated skin.

He was home.

They'd been in the heart of Celendor for some time now, floating down the Savio and past Cel cities and towns and villages, the landscape devoted to the agriculture and livestock that dominated the nation. It was hot and humid, the winter rains warm as bathwater as they fell from the sky. But tomorrow, they'd arrive in Celendrial, and he'd have to face the moment he'd dreaded for so very long.

Teriana shifted in her sleep, her naked legs entwining with his. He ran his fingers down her back, soothing her into the restfulness that he denied himself.

Tonight was their last night together. The last time he could listen to her wild tales over a campfire. The last time he could lose himself in her beautiful body. The last time he would see dawn with her in his arms.

He didn't want to let her go. Didn't want to lose her. Didn't want to go back to being the Empire's weapon for many reasons, but one of the biggest was that he knew one day it would mean meeting her across the battlefield.

But what was the alternative? If he didn't go to Cassius and the Senate with the locations of the xenthier paths, Teriana's mother and people would remain imprisoned. And the Thirty-Seventh would remain under Titus's control believing he was a deserter. Which he would be, having abandoned his brothers. Having abandoned Felix with those last toxic words.

Have you ever wondered what you might achieve if you fought for something you believed in?

Teriana's question floated through his mind for the thousandth time. A thought that he'd never allowed himself to have and never could, because the moment he stepped out of line and crossed Cassius, the consul would reveal Marcus's secret. That he was first-born, not second. That his father had sent him in his brother's place because he wanted to keep his healthy son as heir and in doing so had broken one of the Empire's most sacrosanct laws. He, his father, and his brother would be hanged in the Forum, his mother stripped of even the clothes on her back and sent into exile, his younger sisters along with her. Cordelia's husband would be encouraged to cast her aside, which would mean her children would be taken from her forever. He couldn't do that to her. Wouldn't let her be hurt in that way.

Unbidden, another girl's words filled his head: *Which sort of man are you, Legatus? The sort who desires to save the world? Or to save himself?* The voice of the girl he'd murdered to protect both his families.

And to protect himself.

How much worse would he have to do? How much further would he have to go?

His head was a throbbing mess of pain, his breath coming too fast. Shifting Teriana off his chest, Marcus sat up and moved to the edge of the boat. Eased carefully off it, the water cold against his overheated skin.

Reaching the bank, he stumbled up it, already gasping for breath, panic setting in. He fell to his knees, forehead pressed against the rocks and mud, feeling his throat close. Feeling the darkness take over, pulling him down and down, tears soaking his cheeks because he knew someone like him wouldn't be granted such an easy end.

And that when he woke, exhausted and aching and ill, the decision would remain.

90

KILLIAN

Ambush.

His skin had started crawling the moment they'd entered the clearing, but he'd thought it would be Agrippa who'd make the move. Or Baird.

Instead, a group of armed men, one of which he recognized from the village alehouse, stepped out of the surrounding brush. They had bows, but instead of shooting, the men all pulled their swords, obviously heeding Agrippa's words.

Good. Their greed would be their downfall.

"You can make this easy. Or you can make this hard, Calorian," one of them said. "Put down your weapons and we'll let the girl go unharmed."

"Lydia," he said softly.

"Yes." There was fear in her voice.

"Run."

For once, she didn't argue, hauling up her skirts and bolting toward the trees even as he threw himself at the men, meeting the front-runner with a clash of steel. The man met his blows twice, then Killian got past his guard and stabbed him in the chest, whirling as he extracted his bloody blade and throwing a knife at one of the other soldiers.

One of the attackers raced after Lydia, but Killian dived forward, hamstringing him and then leaving the man to scream while he engaged with the others.

They came at him three at a time, forcing him to rely on speed to dodge their blows.

One of them caught him across the forearm with the tip of his weapon. Killian ground his teeth against the pain, gutting the man and then shoving him into his fellows while he backtracked to gain better ground.

Across the clearing, Agrippa had his weapon in hand, face expressionless as he watched the fight. Where Baird was, Killian didn't know.

He'd deal with them both later.

Dancing around a swipe of a sword, Killian punched the man in the face, then twisted to block a downward strike of a blade. But another soldier lunged into the mix, forcing him to drop and roll or take the weapon in the gut.

On his feet in a flash, Killian threw a knife, striking a soldier in the face as he rushed toward him, but they were coming at him from all sides. Blood ran down his hand, slickening his grip as he engaged with one, the man's face determined as he parried every one of Killian's blows, not good enough to win, but good enough to distract while his fellows attacked from the rear.

Killian sensed the blow coming and ducked, a blade whistling over his head. He turned and stabbed the soldier in the leg, but another only took his place.

There were too many of them.

Cursing, Killian stumbled back, his eyes on the men warily stepping over the bodies of the fallen even as he heard the footfalls of those circling around.

"Gods-damn it!" Agrippa swore from across the clearing, and then he was racing toward the fight, weapon raised. He carved into the back of one of the men, twisting to stab another in the guts, and Killian didn't stop to question what the Cel bastard was doing.

Instead, he lost himself in the fight.

Blood splattered and men screamed, dying under the onslaught of steel. They held their ground for a time, then Killian felt the balance shift, and two of the attackers bolted.

Picking up a fallen sword, Killian flung it, taking one of them in the back, and chased the other at a dead sprint. Sensing he was about to be caught, the man whirled, raising his sword. But Killian's downward strike sheared through the blade. The man screamed, and fell, pleading for mercy.

Killian cut off his head. And then he turned.

Agrippa was resting with one hand against a tree, breathing hard as he watched Killian approach.

"Finally showed your true colors."

Agrippa made a face. "That's a tad rich coming from you, *Lord Calorian.*"

Killian paused, seeing Baird approaching through the trees, a struggling Lydia gripped against his chest. *Shit.*

The giant paused upon reaching the clearing, both his eyebrows rising. "This," he said, gesturing to the dead soldiers at Agrippa's feet, "was not part of the plan, little man."

"Yes, well, my conscience got the better of me. I'll try not to let it happen again, but in the meantime, let the girl go."

The giant heaved a deep sigh, then dropped Lydia at his feet. She scrambled out of reach, eyes wide as she took in the scene.

"Did you really think no one would figure out it was you?" Agrippa said, dropping his hand from the tree. "For days, we stood on the far side of that ravine watching you stride about in all that shiny armor, refusing to die no matter what we gods-damned threw at you. The image of your blasted face is burned onto my brain—I'd have recognized you anywhere."

"So why not turn on me in Deadground?" Killian snarled, stepping between them and Lydia. "Why bring me through the Liratoras when you could've killed me surrounded by your own damned army?"

"Gold, you jackass!" Agrippa shouted, his face twisted with anger. "There's a bloody reward for your head, that's why. And an even bigger one if I delivered you to Rufina alive. Big enough that maybe Baird and I could finally be free of her."

Killian allowed the tip of his blade to drop. "What do you mean, free of her?"

Agrippa scrubbed a hand through his hair, spiking it with streaks of blood. "I don't want to fight for her any more than anyone else does, but that viper gives no one any choice. It's fight or be given to her minions to have your life stripped away. But you"—he leveled a finger at Killian—"if she had you, she wouldn't need me. And maybe as a reward, she'd allow me to leave. Baird too."

"I'd never fight for her."

A bitter laugh tore from Agrippa's throat. "That's what everyone says, and yet we all find ourselves doing so." He lifted his head. "That's what your queen said when she first arrived."

Fear and anger twisted in his guts. "What do you know about Malahi?"

"I know exactly what I told you back in Deadground. That she's a tender. And that Rufina needs her to keep pushing the blight across Mudamora. That she's both pretty and defiant, but that Rufina is unlikely to allow her to keep either attribute."

"Has she hurt her?"

"I avoid Helatha like the plague," Agrippa said. "But last I heard, Rufina was making use of the tried-and-true practice of torture to try to break her to her will."

Anguish flooded through Killian's chest, because everything

Malahi was enduring was his fault. If only he'd stayed by her side like he'd sworn to do, she'd be safe.

"Why stop now?" Lydia's voice cut through the air. "Why turn on your own soldiers?"

"I don't know." Agrippa dropped his weapon, sitting down in the blood and the mud. "I changed my mind."

"What's to stop you from changing your mind again?"

"Only my conscience, I suppose."

Lydia glowered, and Killian lifted his sword. "Give me one good reason why I don't kill you both now and save myself the trouble later?"

"Because"—Agrippa leaned back on his hands, his usual shit-eating smile returning to his face—"you need my help to get your queen back."

91

TERIANA

"We'll have to identify ourselves if we dock the boat in Celendrial, so it's better we get out here and walk the rest of the way," Marcus said.

Teriana nodded, and though the river ran fast enough that she needed to pay attention to what she was doing, she found her gaze fixed on the massive city in the distance. The sun beat down on the endless white-walled structures, the only green to be seen that on the villa-crusted hill rising up from the north side of the city. Though she couldn't see the harbor, the towering statue of a legionnaire in full regalia was clearly visible, as were the towering public buildings, their columns rising high to support roofs decorated with detailed reliefs. The paved roads the Empire was famous for converged on the city, full of travelers and rivaled only by the dozen towering aqueducts that delivered clean drinking water for the million or more people contained within the city's low walls.

Their boat ground against the shore of the river, jerking Teriana from her thoughts, and she jumped out, helping Marcus drag the vessel farther up, where they abandoned it. Neither of them speaking, they made their way through the brush and trees into a clearing, where Marcus paused, setting their gear on the ground.

"Feels strange to be back here," she said. "A lifetime ago that we sailed out of that harbor."

Marcus only nodded, a deep furrow marring his brow.

Then there was a scuffle of noise in the brush. Both of them whirled, and a second later, a large lizard with yellow scales appeared, pausing as its golden eyes fixed on them.

It was about the size of a dog, but more sinuous, its feet tipped with sharp claws and its mouthful of teeth clearly visible as it hissed.

"What in the underworld is *that*?" she demanded, pulling out her knife and stepping back.

Appearing unconcerned, Marcus said, "It's a dragon."

The symbol of the Celendor Empire. She'd known they were real creatures, but, "I've never seen one. It's . . . sort of ugly."

"They're rare, especially this close to cities," he said. "People think they're poisonous, but they're not. They just have filthy mouths, and their bites turn foul within a day. They follow whatever they bite until it dies."

"Gods," Teriana whispered, watching as the dragon wove from side to side, sizing them up.

"They're considered vermin. Farmers kill any they come across."

The dragon hissed, and to her surprise, Marcus took a quick step toward it and hissed back. The lizard stared at him for a minute, and then with shocking speed, spun in a circle and disappeared from sight.

"Bit strange that Celendor uses something considered vermin as its symbol," she said, sheathing her knife.

"It's a fitting choice." He stared at the dirt, mouth drawn into a thin line, and she knew that he was about to tell her their plan of action for meeting with the Senate. And with Cassius.

Her heart was galloping so hard in her chest that she could barely breathe. But she had to do it. Had to ask. "Don't go into the city."

Marcus's face snapped up. "But if—"

"I'll go," she said. "By myself. I'll meet with the Senate—with Cassius—and I'll tell them about the xenthier. I'll tell them everything. And I'll also tell them that you're dead."

He opened his mouth, but she couldn't let him interrupt her now. "I might have to wait until they can prove I'm telling the truth, but then Cassius will have to honor the agreement. He'll release my mother and my people, and then I'll cross over with whatever legions he sends and get Titus to give me the *Quincense* back. And then I'll . . ." She swallowed hard, but she couldn't ask him to give up so much without making sacrifices of her own. "Then I'll come find you."

The only sound was the wind in the brush and the distant sound of the rushing Savio.

"Why?" The word sounded torn from his throat. "Why are you asking me to do this? Why are . . . why are you *willing* to do this?"

Twin tears rolled down her face. "Because I love you."

And there it was: she'd said it. The words that had been sitting on her tongue for a long time now, and if she was truthful, even longer in her heart. She was in love with him, and if living apart from her people was the only way to be with him, then she'd do it.

But would he?

"You shouldn't." His voice cracked. "I don't deserve it."

"That's not what I asked." Catching hold of his hands, she squeezed tightly. "I love you and I want to be with you, but the only way that's possible is if you leave this life behind. Will you do it? For me?"

He didn't answer, only stared at the ground between them, his breathing shaky. "I . . ." He pulled his hands from her grip. "I need a minute. I need to think. I . . . Just don't go anywhere, all right?"

"All right," she whispered, watching him disappear into the brush, heading down to the river. Bending her legs, she rested her forehead on her knees, trying to hold back the sobs that threatened.

What did you think? a dark voice whispered inside her head. *That he'd give up everyone he cares about just for you?*

She squeezed her eyes tighter, hating the flush of fear and embarrassment and hurt that burned her skin.

He's spent his entire life fighting to get where he is, the voice continued. *Why would he give that power up? What can you possibly offer that will compare to what he's got now?*

"Shut up," she muttered, reaching up to wipe her nose with her sleeve. "You're underestimating him."

Except he hadn't come back. What did that mean? Was he considering her offer or trying to think of a way to let her down gently? Should she go find him?

"He told you to wait," she muttered. "Maybe for once, you might listen."

Then hands closed over her shoulders, hauling her upward and dragging a scream of surprise from her throat. She was spun in a circle, finding herself face-to-face with six legionnaires, a 29 stamped on the metal of their breastplates.

"Well, well," one of them said, grinning. "What do we have here? A Maarin girl."

"Thought we'd caught the last of you," another said. "Though I'm sure the consul will be more than happy to add you to his collection."

"Let me go!" She tried to jerk free, but the hands gripping her were like iron, squeezing hard enough to bruise. She lifted a foot, intent on slamming it down on his instep, but he kicked her in the back of the legs, sending her sprawling.

"Touch her again and all six of you will be whipped until I can see the ground through your rib cages." Marcus's voice cut through the air, calm and cold in a way she hadn't heard in a long time.

Lifting her face, she saw the legionnaires' faces darken, and one said, "Who are you?"

"Taken a few blows to the head since Bardeen, Carmo, or is it the drink that's turned your memory to jelly?" Marcus strode toward her, and miraculously, the men moved. "Get up."

Part of her cringed at his tone, but she understood the necessity, rising swiftly.

"Well, I'll be damned," one of them said. "It's the Thirty-Seventh's legatus. Aren't you supposed to be on the other side of the world?"

Marcus fixed the legionnaire with a cold stare, and the older man rolled his shoulders and looked away first, muttering, "Sir."

"Mine is the business of the Senate and none of your concern."

"We're under orders given by the Senate and the *consul* that all Maarin are to be arrested, sir," the one called Carmo said. "So while your business may be your own, the girl must come with us."

"She's my asset, and she has an agreement with the Senate and the *consul*," Marcus countered. "She will remain with me."

"Then I'm afraid you'll need to come with us as well, sir," Carmo replied, a slow smile working its way onto his face. "If all is as you say, I'm sure it won't take long for this to be cleared up."

"As you like." Marcus's voice was flat. "Lead on."

He said nothing to her as they followed the legionnaires through the brush, then up a well-trodden road. And the men, perhaps realizing they'd pushed the limits far enough, said nothing to them. It didn't take long for a camp to come into view, the orderly white tents and campfires at equal intervals eerily familiar. Flags snapped on the wind, the Cel dragon glittering in the sunlight, seeming to watch them as they approached.

The men on the perimeter nodded at the group as they passed, eyes going first to her, but as several of them recognized Marcus, it was he who garnered all the attention. Word spread ahead of them as they walked through the camp, men getting up from their leisure to watch them pass, their faces not particularly friendly. A large tent loomed ahead. The dragon standard, a 29 beneath its claws, gleamed where it was embedded in the ground by the entrance.

"If you'd wait a moment, *sir*," Carmo said, "I'll see if the legatus has time to see you."

Marcus didn't answer, only scratched at his cheek, expression furrowed with annoyance. A crowd of soldiers had gathered now, none of them saying anything as they watched on, but there was a feral quality to their eyes that made Teriana's pulse race faster. They shouldn't be in any danger from these men, and yet . . .

Carmo stepped back out. "He'll see you now."

While the camp itself was identical to that of the Thirty-Seventh, it was like stepping into a different world inside this commander's tent. The furniture was heavy and ornate, the chairs well-padded, and the ground layered with thick carpets in vibrant colors. Rather than maps spread across the table, there were platters loaded with food, the plates porcelain and the flatware polished silver. Crystal decanters of wine were set among the platters, and lamps of colored glass illuminated the scene. It was like being in the tent of a king or a senator, nothing like the spartan furnishings Marcus kept in his own command tent.

"Well, look what the cat dragged in."

Teriana's eyes shot past the laden table to the large chair on the far side of the tent. Though to call it such was a misnomer, because it looked to all the world like a throne.

A man dressed in a red tunic and legion armor lounged on the chair, one leg slung over the arm, a glass of wine held loosely in one hand. Judging from his golden skin, this legatus was Cel by blood. His white-blond hair was shaven almost to the scalp, his eyes a vivid emerald green, and his face not at all hard on the eyes.

"Hostus," Marcus said, his expression bland. But his fingers flexed at his side and his hair was darkening with sweat at the temples, both of which betrayed to her his nerves. "It's been a long time."

"Did you miss me, my little apprentice?"

"No."

The man laughed, and Teriana struggled not to take a step back, though she wasn't entirely certain why. There was something about him that screamed *danger*. As she glanced again at Marcus, she saw a bead of sweat roll down his cheek and realized that he wasn't just nervous around this man. He was afraid.

Apprentice . . . The word rolled through her mind, and it dawned on her that this was the legion that had trained the Thirty-Seventh after they'd left Lescendor. That this was the man who'd trained *Marcus.*

"Aren't you supposed to be conquering the Dark Shores in the name of the Empire?"

"That's not your concern."

"Oh, but you know me, Marcus." Hostus took a drink from his glass. "I'm endlessly curious." He gestured at one of the men in the room. "Pour the boy a drink. Let's see if he holds his wine better than he did at sixteen."

The man splashed crimson wine into a glass and held it out to Marcus.

"I'm not thirsty."

"Drink!" Hostus screamed the word with such fury that Teriana stumbled backward, nearly falling.

Marcus stood his ground. "I don't have time for power games, Hostus. My presence is required in Celendrial, so while your hospitality is as pleasing as I remember, we will be on our way."

"We?" Hostus rose from his chair, and for the first time since they'd entered, his gaze settled on Teriana. She forced herself to meet his emerald eyes, tracking his progress around the table. "Of course. This is the Maarin girl you cut a deal with." He made a tsking sound. "Always negotiating when you should be *taking*; did you learn nothing in our time together?"

"Did you?"

Hostus huffed, then his lip curled up. "Aren't we brave now that we're all grown up." He stopped next to Marcus, leaning close enough that his lips were practically brushing his ear. "But I still remember the sound of your screams when I beat you bloody on the floor of this tent, boy." He swayed from side to side. "Like music. Like poetry."

Marcus's jaw tightened, but he said nothing.

Then in a flash, the older man reached out and caught Teriana by the back of her shirt, dragging her sideways and forcing her to her knees.

"Let her go!" Marcus snarled, reaching for his weapon, but the other men already had theirs out and leveled at him.

Hostus slid his hand under her scarf, fingers catching her hair. Then he twisted his hand, pulling her head back to reveal her throat, and she clenched her teeth at the sight of the knife in his hand.

"Neither Cassius nor the Senate will be pleased if you kill her," Marcus said. "Satisfy your pleasures elsewhere."

Chuckling, Hostus pressed the tip of the knife against her throat, scoring a burning line in her skin as he slid it down to her collarbone. "Cassius will be just as happy to see this one dead, and what the Senate doesn't know, they can't gripe about. I'm willing to bet a fair bit of gold that *no one* knows that you're even here, Marcus. And I think we both know that Cassius wouldn't weep to learn you'd met an untimely end."

He was going to kill them. Or more likely, torture them and *then* kill them. They needed to escape, but how was that even possible in the middle of a camp ruled over by this man?

"I think it will be you who does the weeping if Cassius discovers you killed me and therefore lost his chance at learning the location of the xenthier stems leading to the Dark Shores. And the stem leading back." Marcus's smile was cold. "We two are the *only* individuals with that particular piece of information. It will be hard to claim Titus's glory if no one ever learns of it."

Hostus shifted his weight, his blade digging into her flesh and then easing up again. "Here's the thing, *boy*. I heard a little rumor that you couldn't stomach this one"—he pulled harder on her hair—"being put to the question the first time. So I think you'll tell me everything I want to know if I get to work on her. Am I right?"

Marcus shrugged. "You'll only kill her anyway."

Negotiating with this bastard was a waste of time, and Teriana knew it. The commander of the Twenty-Ninth *wanted* to kill them far more than he feared the consequences of doing so. There wasn't a chance of him letting them go.

"That's true," Hostus replied. "But I think you'll tell me what I want to know anyway. Carmo, get me my tools."

Taking a deep breath, Teriana envisioned Felix's instructions.

And she *moved*.

92

MARCUS

Teriana reached up and caught hold of Hostus's wrist, and Marcus's stomach plummeted. Because Hostus was trained, and Teriana—

She dragged his arm down, pressing it against her chest and then twisted, pushing the blade into Hostus's chest. It clanked against the metal of his breastplate, but it was enough to startle him backward. Teriana hooked his ankle with her own, Hostus landing hard on his ass.

Hostus cursed, but Teriana was already behind him, blade against his throat.

"This is how it's going to go." Her voice was cool and composed, but the wild waves of her eyes betrayed her fear. "You lot step away from Marcus. Then you clear a path out of this camp, or your legatus is going to find himself bleeding out all over his fancy carpets."

"If you kill me, they won't let you go." Hostus spoke to Teriana, but his eyes fixed on Marcus, the rage terrifying in its familiarity.

"Won't make you less dead." Teriana pressed the knife harder. "How much farther do I have to slice to hit your jugular? Not much, is my bet."

Hostus didn't reply, only stared Marcus down. Because they both knew this wouldn't work. The older legatus was devoid of fear but flush on pride—he'd die before conceding. Marcus and Teriana would both have a dozen crossbow bolts embedded in their backs before they were halfway across camp, and if she slit Hostus's throat as she fell, it was a risk the other man was willing to take.

There was no way out.

"What is going on here?" a familiar voice barked from behind him, and it was all Marcus could do not to twist around and give a smart salute.

"Commandant." Hostus didn't give the order for his men to stand down. "I'd salute, but the girl here has me in a delicate position."

"One you no doubt earned." Commandant Wex circled in front of Marcus, his eyes widening in recognition. "Get your weapons off him, you bloody fools! And sheath them while you're at it."

"Yes, sir," they all responded, sheathing their weapons. Wex rounded on Hostus and Teriana. "Put down the weapon, lass. Whether the fool earned the cut or not, you kill him and you'll hang."

Teriana didn't move, her eyes flicking to Marcus. He nodded. "It's fine."

For a heartbeat, he wasn't certain she intended to listen. Then she skipped away from him, moving to Marcus's side. "Nice blade," she said. "I think I'll keep it."

Hostus said nothing as he rose, but his eyes promised death.

"I'm no small amount surprised to find you here, Marcus." Wex crossed his arms, looking him up and down. Mostly up, because the commandant of Campus Lescendor was a good head shorter than Marcus, his hair brilliant white against his dark brown skin. But what he lacked in height, he made up for in undeniable authority.

"I succeeded in the first stage of the mission to the Dark Shores," Marcus answered. "I'm here to give a report to the Senate."

"Yourself? Alone?"

"Not by choice."

Wex frowned. "I'm sure that's a story to tell." His attention went back to Hostus. "And for what reason was he not given an escort to Celendrial?"

"Look at him, sir. We thought—"

"Oh, be quiet." Wex spit an impressive glob onto the Bardenese carpet. "I know the answer, and I'm not interested in your lies." He stared at Hostus, then shook his head. "I need to have a discussion with you about other matters, but it will have to wait in favor of this." Then he offered Teriana his arm. "Come along, lass."

She blinked, then slipped her arm through his, allowing him to lead her out of the command tent.

"There will be a reckoning for this," Hostus hissed, his eyes full of hate.

Marcus didn't look away, only allowed his own demons to rise to the surface. "Yes, Hostus. On that, you can count."

Outside, ten boys wearing armor stamped with a 51 waited, and they all fell into step around Wex and Teriana as he escorted her through camp, Marcus following. He could feel them looking at him out of the corners of their eyes, curious who he was but too well-trained to overtly show it. They passed through the perimeter of the camp, where the group's horses waited.

"Now which two of you lads fancy a walk back to Lescendor?" Wex asked. "I'm afraid we are in the need of some speed, so I'll be taking your mounts."

Teriana's eyes widened in alarm, and having seen her on a horse, Marcus said, "Better Teriana ride with me."

Taking the reins, he swung into the saddle, then reached down and hauled her up behind him. She wrapped her arms around his waist, her cheek pressed against his back, and Marcus had to force down the ache that rose in his chest as he remembered what he'd been on his way back to tell her when they'd been caught by the Twenty-Ninth.

It didn't matter now. The choice was out of his hands.

"Lescendor first," Wex said. "We need to talk." Then he frowned. "And *you* need a haircut."

Not answering, Marcus dug in his heels and headed down the Via Lescendor at a gallop.

93

TERIANA

She clung to Marcus with a death grip as they rode at what felt like reckless speed down the road, the horses' hooves leaving a cloud of dust in their wake. Her neck stung from where Hostus had cut her, but that was the least of her concerns.

Marcus said nothing, and neither did the tiny old man who galloped next to him, their escort riding ahead and behind. The young boys couldn't have been more than thirteen, though judging from the number stamped on their armor, they'd already graduated. Children, and yet for all they were skinny and speckled with pimples, half of them probably still devoid of facial hair, she knew they were dangerous. Trained killers, even if they'd yet to take a life.

They rode for close to an hour, and then in the distance, a massive fortress loomed out of the countryside, the ground for miles around it nothing more than churned-up dirt. Hundreds, possibly thousands, of children stood in neat lines in the field, men on horses watching from the rear. She heard the familiar whistles and horns, the boys changing position, following the orders of their commanders as they played at war.

Yet as her group passed, and someone recognized the banner they carried, the ranks all turned as one and the thunder of salutes filled the air.

They approached the gates to the fortress, the towering walls patrolled by more children, their expressions serious as they watched. One of the boys in their escort shouted a code, and a heartbeat later, the portcullis rose, a deep horn bellowing from within.

Relaxing her grip, she looked upward as they passed into the long tunnel, seeing the murder holes in the ceiling and wondering if they were armed. *Likely,* she thought, for it seemed Lescendor conducted itself as though it were in the heart of enemy territory, not within the heart of the Empire.

And she was about to see the inside.

The gates at the far end of the tunnel swung open, and they rode back out into the sunlight.

The buildings were all columns and elaborate porticos, everything carved in swooping patterns and scenes of battles throughout history. Fountains depicting famous commanders spewed water to either side of the group as they rode down the wide lane, which split at the end, circling around a gleaming gold fountain carved in the shape of Celendor's dragon. On the far side, a large domed building stood, crimson-and-gold banners flapping from poles that jutted out from the base of the dome itself.

There were boy children everywhere, all seemingly engaged in various sorts of training overseen by either older boys or men with silvered hair. All of them stepped into neat lines as they passed, small fists hitting their chests in salute.

"How many children are in training here?" she asked, wishing she wasn't the one to break the silence.

The commandant turned to look at her, his grey horse frisking beneath him. "Thirty-five thousand at present. And the Fifty-First remains, and they have 5,197 legionnaires in their ranks."

An army larger than nearly any other, and that was just those in training.

Stopping in front of a large building with towering columns holding up a wide portico, the commandant dismounted, handing his reins to one of his escort. Marcus let go of the reins and gently tugged her hand free from where it clutched his stomach, lowering her to the ground, then dismounting swiftly himself. They followed the commandant up the steps and into the shade of the building, six of the boys following suit.

The interior was as fine as any senator's home, the tiles polished and the tables holding delicate glass vases filled with flowers. Marble busts depicting young men graced the alcoves, and when Teriana looked up, it was to find the ceilings painted with a battle scene, dead and dying littering a burned field with Celendor's banners rising above it all.

The commandant led them up several flights of stairs, then down a hallway, pausing next to a door. "Teriana, you can get washed up in here. A medic will be along shortly to see to the injury to your neck, and we'll also see if we can't find you some fresh garments."

"I want two of you with her at all times." Marcus's voice cut the air, the first thing he'd said since they left the Twenty-Ninth's camp, and Teriana twitched at the tone of his voice. "Under no circumstances is she to be left alone, understood? The other four of you will remain outside her door."

The young centurion frowned, clearly aware that Marcus was someone important, if not of his precise identity, but at the commandant's nod, the boy answered, "It will be done, sir."

Without saying another word, Marcus and the commandant strode down the hall to the next room and disappeared inside.

"This way, miss," the centurion said, swinging open the door, and she stepped inside.

Judging from the furniture, which included a narrow bed, this was sleeping quarters of some sort, but it was devoid of any personal items, the linens tucked tight around the thin mattress.

"What's your name?" she asked the boy.

"It's centurion Pullo, miss," he answered. "This here is Norin." The other boy who had entered bobbed his head, his eyes skipping to her chest and then back to her face. "Miss."

Gods, but they were young. "You can call me Teriana."

An older servant woman entered carrying a jug of water, which she set on the table next to a basin, along with a cloth and a small piece of soap. "I can get you a dress," she said. "If that will suit you, miss."

"My own clothes are fine, thank you."

The woman departed, and after she shut the door, Pullo blurted out, "Who's that man with the commandant?"

"The one ordering you about, you mean?" She winked at him, as much to diminish her own nerves as his. "Not rightly sure if I'm supposed to tell you."

Holding the silence and enjoying the way they clearly wanted to press her, but were refraining, she said, "That's Legatus Marcus of the Thirty-Seventh Legion."

Both boys' jaws dropped. "You can't be serious," Pullo finally said. "*That's* the Thirty-Seventh's legatus?"

"Why?" she asked. "You heard of him?"

"Have we heard of him?" Norin demanded, his voice cracking. "He's only the most famous—"

Pullo gave him a shove. "She's teasing, you dunce." Brow furrowing, he said, "The Thirty-Seventh's supposed to be conquering the Dark Shores. The Maarin—" He broke off, giving his head a shake. "Thought I recognized your name. You're the girl who was supposed to show them the way."

"Guilty."

She could see that they were desperate to ask her more, but there was a knock at the door and an older man entered, carrying a medical kit with him.

"I hear you fell afoul of Hostus," he said, setting out his supplies and then gesturing at her to take a seat.

"Aye. He's a right prick, that one."

Pullo and Norin both smirked, but the medic gave her a steady look. "He is that. But he's also the consul's right hand, so best you keep your opinions to yourself."

Though it should come as no surprise that Cassius would keep a man like Hostus about to do his dirty work, Teriana's stomach still soured. For months, Cassius had been a distant threat, and while out of sight had not meant out of mind, now she was within easy reach. And the only thing standing between her and him was Marcus.

And he no longer had the Thirty-Seventh here to back him.

She sat still, clenching her teeth as the medic silently cleaned the cut on her neck, muttering that she was lucky she only needed a few stitches. He bandaged the wound, then departed, leaving Teriana to clean herself up as best she could with two thirteen-year-old boys in the room. She'd only just finished when there was another knock, one of the boys standing guard in the hallway leaning in. "The commandant has asked the legatus to attend him in his office. You are to accompany him, miss."

Trying to curb her unease, Teriana stepped into the hallway.

Marcus was waiting.

And it was as if all the months they'd spent together had been erased and he was once again the devil who'd watched her be tortured. Who'd used everything and everyone she loved to force her to take him and his men across the world in search of conquest.

They'd shorn his hair, and his cheeks were freshly shaven. He was once again dressed in the tunic and armor of a legionnaire, a crested helmet tucked under one arm and his weapons belted at his waist. The breastplate had a 37 stamped on it, looking as though it had come fresh from the forge, which she supposed it probably had. And as he turned away to stride down the corridor and his crimson cloak drifted out behind him, the golden dragon glaring at her, eyes malevolent.

They stepped out into the sun, where a relative mob of young boys waited, all of them scrambling into straight lines at the sight of Marcus, fists pounding chests as he strode past. Nodding at them, he headed toward the center of the fortress city where the largest building loomed, its wide copper dome having gone green with age, and with every rank of boys he passed, there was a thunder of salutes.

"Your fame precedes you," she said, but he only glanced down at her, saying nothing as the doors to the building swung open ahead, the boys guarding them standing straight.

You were such a fool, she silently whispered to herself. *Such a fool to believe he'd give all this up for you.*

Where the leather of her boots was silent against the marble floors of the building, Marcus's sandals clacked loudly, the echoes reverberating off high ceilings painted with scenes of legion conquest. Through another set of doors, and despite herself, Teriana gasped as it was revealed to be an enormous library.

Four stories high, the shelves were full of books and scrolls, the main level encircled by twin layers of shelves full to the brim with more volumes. At the center, there were six large wooden tables, next to which stood perhaps a dozen boys wearing only their tunics and weapons. Marcus nodded at them as they stood to attention but carried on to the door at the far side of the room, only then pausing. "Wait here." His blue-grey eyes flicked to Pullo. "Do not let her out of your sight."

"Yes, sir," the young centurion said, and Marcus disappeared into the room, shutting the door behind him.

"Right," she muttered, then turned to find all the boys staring at her. "Hello."

They all nodded their heads, eyes full of curiosity. "This is Teriana," Pullo said. "She's the Maarin girl that took the Thirty-Seventh and the Forty-First to the Dark Shores." He frowned, then turned to look at her. "You *did* get them there, didn't you?"

"Pullo," a boy at the center of the group said, "it's not your place to ask such questions."

"Sorry, sir."

Stepping away from the door lest she be tempted to eavesdrop, Teriana circled the room, staring up at the seemingly endless shelves. On the second level, the shelves were broken up at equal intervals with nine enormous golden plaques. They each had a different symbol on top, and beneath the symbol were ten smaller plagues with numbers engraved in them, the one at the top given more prominence than the rest. And on each of the nine save one, a familiar number held that prominent spot: 37–1519.

Marcus's legion number.

"They're there," she finally answered. "They have control of a nation called Arinoquia." Then she pointed. "What are those?"

The boy who had chastised Pullo cleared his throat. "There are nine tests potential legates undertake prior to graduation. Those numbers belong to the highest-scoring individuals over the past one hundred forty-two years."

Teriana whistled between her teeth. "No wonder you're all tripping over yourselves to make Marcus's acquaintance." Though she noticed Titus's number was on a few of the boards as well.

"You're very familiar with the Thirty-Seventh's legatus." The boy tilted his head, the comment holding no criticism, only interest.

Familiar was an understatement, but Teriana only shrugged. "You spend every waking minute with someone, and you get to know them as well as they can be known." She smiled at him. "And I'm not one of his underlings." Pointing at the one test where Marcus's number was ranked second rather than first, she said, "That's one of you boys in the top spot, isn't it?"

He nodded.

"It's you, isn't it, Legatus?" And when he nodded, she said, "Well done." Especially well done, given his number was on more plaques than not.

"Thank you."

Pausing in her circling, Teriana hopped up to sit on one of the tables. "What's your name?"

"It's Austornic." He glanced at the closed door, then came a few steps closer. "Have there been many battles?"

Too many. And from the looks of things, many more to come. "There have," she answered gravely, and because the alternative was to cry, she asked, "Would you like to hear the story of how Legatus Marcus of the *still*-undefeated Thirty-Seventh Legion tore the tyrant Urcon from power?"

94

MARCUS

Hating himself for the way he was treating her, but knowing that it was necessary, Marcus closed the door in Teriana's face.

Then he turned around.

It had been more than seven years since he'd stood in this space, and yet nothing was changed: the walls still hung with maps, the desk still cluttered with books and half-drank water glasses, cucumber slices and crushed mint leaves settling to their bottoms. Commandant Wex sat on the chair on the far side of the desk, and with a smile, he said, "I supposed you've finally earned the right to sit."

Shaking his head, Marcus lowered himself onto the stool, resting an ankle on his opposite knee. The stiff leather of his new sandals was already giving him a blister. "Seems strange to do so."

Rising, Wex went to the sideboard and filled two glasses with water, dropping several slices of cucumber into each.

Accepting the one he was offered, Marcus frowned at it.

"I recall you don't like cucumber," Wex said, taking a seat. "But it's good for you, and you'll need something to wet your tongue while you give me a full report."

Though it had been years, it was still engrained in him to obey this man, and so Marcus started at the beginning, giving the pertinent details of the crossing and an account of what had occurred once they'd landed. He kept some choice information, such as the Marked, back, but otherwise was thorough.

"Bardeen." Wex rubbed his chin. "And Sibern."

"Yes, sir."

"Couldn't be much worse placed if they were at the bottom of the sea." Rising, the commandant went to a framed map of the Empire on the wall, staring at it silently for a long moment. "Sibern is more of a logistical challenge, but Bardeen . . ." He shook his head. "It's a pot on the verge of boiling over. Supplying you via that stem will require a significantly larger legion presence in the region, which will incite them further, I'm afraid. And Cassius won't hesitate to quell them using force. It will be nothing short of a massacre."

"Nonus was the only path-hunter to make it to us," Marcus answered, then took a sip of water in an attempt to wash away the bile rising in his throat. He already had one massacre to his name, and the last thing he wanted was to be part of another. "The rumor is that those in much of the West are partial to entombing terminus stems, so any further men the Senate sends might be walking into their graves."

Wex made an aggrieved noise, scrubbing a hand over the white bristles of his hair. "Madness. I'll see if we can pause the process until you've had further opportunity to make safe the stems in your area, but . . ."

"Cassius."

Wex nodded. "His popularity with the peregrini has never been worse, but it's a different story with the citizens. He favors them, and those with influence have found themselves making a great deal more money since he gained the consulship." Wex's eyes turned hard. "Don't think I didn't notice your complicity in his rise to power, boy. Was it a bribe or a threat?"

"Both."

The commandant grunted. "He's recently appointed Hostus to command of the city guard—that's why the blackhearted bastard is here. The Twenty-Seventh is being moved to Timia, and once they're gone, the Twenty-Ninth will take up residence in Celendrial's barracks."

Marcus's hands turned to ice. "You can't be serious. Hostus? Celendrial will boil over."

"Then its streets will run with blood, because Cassius won't curb him."

Staring at the cucumber floating in his water, Marcus allowed the weight of this development to settle onto his soul. *This is your doing,* his conscience whispered. *Your fault.* "Is he favored to win again in the next election?"

"He wasn't." Wex sat back down at his desk. "It's believed by most that you and yours were lost to the high seas to some Maarin trick. Cassius spent a small fortune on your campaign to the Dark Shores, and until now, it has yielded nothing. He always had a strong opposition in the Senate, and that has grown. Those are not men who like to have their gold squandered. Even with Hostus's legion sure to pull the same trick as yours, he wouldn't have won. Not against Tiberius Egnatius."

That was his sister's husband. Marcus curbed the urge to ball his hands into fists, because Cordelia was treading on dangerous ground.

"Of course, with your arrival back in Celendrial, that will change." Wex leaned over the desk, and Marcus forced himself to meet his gaze. "You've just won him another term, whether you willed it or not."

His chest grew tight, a wheeze rising in his breath, and Marcus drank the contents of his glass, trying not to gag on the taste. "He'll have to let the Maarin go, now, which won't make him look good."

"We'll see." Wex rested his elbows on the desk. "Speaking of the Maarin, do you care to explain how the enemy caught you alone with the girl?"

Not in the slightest.

"I needed to speak with her about something alone and we went too far afield." He lifted a shoulder. "It was a mistake."

Silence.

"It's not like you to get involved," Wex finally said. "Less like you to make mistakes. Put an end to it, or you're going to make more."

"There's nothing to end," Marcus lied. "And even if there were, with Teriana having delivered on her end of the bargain, she'll be out of my camp and back aboard her ship."

"With how much more knowledge than she had before?" Wex gave a slow shake of his head. "Better for you to slit her throat than to let her live, though I know that's not your way. You'll live with your mistakes no matter how much they cost you."

Marcus didn't answer, only met his mentor's gaze with as much dispassion as he could manage. "She's not a threat."

"Time will tell. Either way, it's time we're off. The Senate sits today, and my messengers will have reached their recipients by now with news that you are at Lescendor, so all will be there."

Fastening on his cloak, Wex opened the door, and both of them stepped out.

To find Teriana standing on one of the tables, surrounded by boys, all who wore rapt expressions.

"And he stood at the front lines himself," she said. "Only him and a hundred men against an army of seven thousand strong. Or at least," she whispered the last conspiratorially, "that's what the enemy *thought.*"

No one noticed his and Wex's appearance, the boys' eyes fixed on Teriana as she took a long pause, surveying them. "The enemy emerged from the jungle, racing on foot and on horse across the open field, *murder* in their eyes."

"She's got a gift for storytelling," Wex murmured softly as Teriana carried on with a somewhat exaggerated version of the battle for Aracam, ending with a triumph of drums and horns and the men chanting Marcus's name.

"One of her many talents," he replied, his chest tight. Then more loudly, "Be mindful of what you believe." All the boys twisted in surprise and fell into line. "Half of what she says is fiction."

Teriana hopped off the table, lifting one of her shoulders. "Just telling it as your men told it to me."

He didn't answer, only surveyed the library that had been his solace for most of his youth, his eyes skipping over the leaderboards for the officer tests. When he found one where he'd lost the top spot, he smiled. He turned on the boy—Bardenese, judging from the hue of his brown skin—standing close to Teriana. "You're Austornic." Wex had told him of the boy earlier while Marcus was getting his hair cut, the commandant not so subtly suggesting that Marcus take the newly minted legatus under his wing.

"Yes, sir."

"Well done. The commandant speaks highly of you."

The boy swallowed, clearly fighting a smile. "Thank you, sir."

Marcus looked the boy over, thirteen and all gangly limbs and elbows, though his eyes were full of intelligence. Not the cunning sort, but thoughtful and observant. And the boys behind him radiated the sort of loyalty that was earned, not forced upon them. "The Fifty-First have any interest in crossing the world?"

Austornic's eyes widened. "With you, sir? To the Dark Shores?"

Marcus nodded. "It's a dangerous place, but there is a great deal to learn."

"Yes, sir. I'd be honored, sir." He glanced sideways at his officers, who were all grinning. "We'd all be honored to learn from the Thirty-Seventh."

"Good." Marcus turned to Wex. "Send them when you're ready."

The commandant nodded, then gestured to Austornic. "We are off to see the Senate. I'm putting Teriana here in your personal care, understood?"

"Yes, sir."

"Shall we?" Wex strode through the library, Marcus at his elbow, trusting Teriana would follow. Hating the questioning look in her eyes, but it couldn't be helped. She was in danger enough without anyone believing she meant anything to him.

Not that it was a secret he'd be able to keep for much longer.

The boys guarding the doors swung them open, and Marcus stepped out into the sun.

Only to find the space full to the brim with the Fifty-First, all of them lined up in neat ranks, banners flying above their heads, their armor polished to a shine. And in the center of them waited a golden chariot pulled by two horses, their trappings gold and plumage crimson.

"What nonsense is this?" he asked under his breath.

"Cassius has a habit of making decisions behind closed doors," Wex answered. "I think it best that all of Celendrial know you are here and why. And what better way to accomplish that than a triumph?"

95

TERIANA

With their helmets on, they didn't look like children.

They looked like soldiers.

That was the first thought that struck her as she stepped out of Lescendor's library to see the Fifty-First lined up in neat rows, their dragon standard bearing their number glinting in the sun. And Marcus had just agreed to take them to war.

To his credit, he appeared not the slightest bit pleased as he glared at the golden chariot that awaited him. "This is unnecessary. A horse will be fine."

"The citizens love their traditions," Wex answered. "I assume you remember how to drive one? And how to follow an order when given one?"

"Yes, Commandant." Striding down the steps, Marcus stepped into the chariot, taking up the reins. Two young legionnaires on horses followed, carrying crimson-and-gold banners with Celendor's dragon wrapped around a 37.

"Do you know how to ride a horse, Teriana?" Austornic asked.

"Not well."

"I see." He frowned. "Is your preference to ride behind me or for me to lead your horse?"

Her preference was *not* to cling to a child's back while she rode to meet the man she hated more than anyone on Reath. "I'll manage myself."

Wex appeared next to her, holding armor identical to that the legionnaires wore, along with a hooded cloak. "Cassius will be aware of your presence by now. Put these on."

Her skin turned to ice, but she managed a nod, accepting his help buckling the breastplate rather than revealing her shaking hands. The cloak went over top, the laces down the front hiding the metal protecting her torso, the hood shadowing her face. It was uncomfortable and hot, but better than the alternative.

Between Austornic and Pullo, they managed to get her on the back of a horse that looked about a hundred years old and required her to thump her heels against its sides half a dozen times before it deigned to start moving. The boys mounted easily, the young legatus trotting his mount to where Marcus stood glowering in his chariot. "They are yours to command, sir."

Marcus gave a slight nod before barking out orders that Teriana barely registered, her stomach hollowing at the tone of his voice. That cold authority that she hadn't realized she hated until today. *This isn't who you are,* she wanted to scream.

Except maybe it was.

Everything they passed on the short trip to Celendrial was a blur, her horse walking in the correct direction by virtue of Austornic and Pullo keeping her between them, their eyes watchful. Her gaze never left Marcus's back where he drove the chariot ahead of them, his red cloak fluttering on the wind, the gold dragon embroidered on it glittering in the sun. Half the boys marched ahead and half behind, the noise nearly drowning out the drumbeat.

Ahead, Celendrial appeared in all its filthy glory, sprawling far outside the walls of the inner city. At the sound of the marching men, people poured from their homes, lining the road to watch the parade pass. This was a poorer area of the city, populated primarily by the peregrini—the people from the Empire's provinces—with only a few Cel faces mixed in among them. At first they cheered and shouted, throwing flower petals at the boys of the Fifty-First's front ranks.

But then, seemingly in an instant, the tone shifted.

The cheers ceased, a hush rippling its way up the road toward the arches of Celendrial's eastern gates. Unease prickled along Teriana's skin, and she searched for what might have triggered the change in mood, because now the hush was being replaced with murmurs of anger.

Not at the boys forming the Fifty-First. But at the man driving the chariot in the midst of them, the flags marked with a 37 flying above him.

"Austornic," she said, leaning closer to the boy. "What's going on?"

Beneath his helmet, the young legatus's jaw tightened. "The consul's policies are not favored by the peregrini. There is a great deal of ill will toward him."

Toward Cassius, and by extension, Marcus. Because it was the Thirty-Seventh that had put Lucius Cassius in control of the Empire. Which meant many would see him as complicit in everything Cassius had done since, regardless of the Thirty-Seventh having spent most of his term in the Dark Shores.

The parade ground to a halt at the gates, and a legionnaire with armor bearing a 27 trotted through the parting ranks to stop in front of Marcus's chariot.

"The Thirty-Seventh legion requests the right of triumph for our victories across the Endless Seas." Marcus's voice carried across the crowds. "Will Celendrial open its gates?"

"Do you recognize the authority of the Senate?" the other man replied. "Do you swear your life and loyalty to the Empire?"

"I do."

Teriana shivered, looking away even as the soldier declared, "The Thirty-Seventh is granted its triumph."

Horns blared and drums thundered, their music filling Teriana's ears as the men marched through the gate. She looked up as they passed beneath the dragon mounted atop of it, the gilded serpent that poisoned all it sank its teeth into, and she wasn't certain whether she wanted to vomit or scream.

Instead, she whispered, "You haven't won yet," and then turned her eyes to the streets ahead. To the path that would take her face-to-face with her greatest enemy.

96

KILLIAN

"Welcome to Helatha, city of the damned," Agrippa said, sitting on his heels on the ridge.

"You make it sound more exciting than it is," Baird muttered, taking a seat on a rock, but Killian ignored him in favor of getting a look at Derin's capital city.

And Rufina's stronghold.

It was larger than he'd expected, unwalled and sprawling, the west side of it resting against a lake so large, he couldn't see the far side of it. But the enormity wasn't what made his stomach lurch.

It was the broken god circle at the center of it, only the black stone tower of the Seventh god remaining upright. The other six were leveled, long lines of rubble crisscrossing the city like fallen corpses.

As though sensing his thoughts, Agrippa said, "It's forbidden to take the stones from the collapsed towers. They're something of a monument to the Seventh's supremacy here."

"How long have they been like that?" Never in his life had Killian seen a god circle felled, and seeing the sacrilege toward the Six filled him with simmering anger. But also with fear, because if the Six held little power here, what did that mean for him?

"A thousand years, it's said," Baird answered. "This is an ancient place—older than I've ever seen. But for all they are broken, the stones the towers were made from never crumble, which many say is a sign the Six have power here, still."

"Let us hope," Killian muttered, wondering what it would feel like to fight without Tremon guiding his hand. How much weaker he'd be. How much slower. "That's Rufina's fortress, I take it?"

He pointed to the structure rising out of the lake. It was made of the same black stone as the Seventh's tower, and though the sun was high in the sky, a shadow seemed to hang over it.

"The Pit," Agrippa answered. "It's as much a prison as a fortress. The dungeons beneath it are full of those who've crossed Rufina or her minions, and every day or so, she selects a few to sate her appetite for life. Sacrifices to the Seventh, she calls them, but in reality, the corrupted are no better than a drunk with a cellar full of wine."

Next to him, Lydia twitched, and Killian turned from his appraisal of the city to look at her. Her jaw was tight, hands balled into fists, but her expression was determined. "They can control themselves if they want to," she said. "Rufina would have gone weeks, perhaps even longer, when she was at Serrick's side posing as Cyntha." Then she turned to fix Agrippa with a stare. "Did you know that's where she was? What she was doing?"

A good question.

Agrippa shook his head. "I came to her attention somewhat more than a year ago and have only seen her a handful of times in the intervening period. Usually when there was something she wanted me to do. She never told me where she was the rest of the time, and I wasn't stupid enough to ask."

"You mean brave enough." Lydia's tone was cutting.

Agrippa only shrugged. "Take pity on those of us who don't have gods at our backs, *Marked One*. Human bravery has its limits, especially when one's life is held in the fist of a sociopathic queen."

Lydia's eyes flared, and sensing that Agrippa was about to hear in great detail what she thought about *that*, Killian said, "It looks exceptionally well-fortified given that Derin has never been invaded."

"A ruler will do that when their own people are constantly trying to kill them," Agrippa answered, though his eyes were still fixed on Lydia. "She's utterly reviled by the common folk, and more than a few have made attempts to slit her throat. But she's hard to kill."

"I've noticed." Knowing Rufina was Cyntha, that made more sense. The woman had been trained alongside King Derrek Falorn from childhood—even without a mark, she'd be a force to be reckoned with.

"At any rate, that's where Rufina is keeping your queen," Agrippa said. "Rumor has it that she's made more than a few attempts to escape, so she's well-guarded at all times, typically by at least one of the corrupted."

"Not an issue. Can you get me in?"

"Probably. But it will be the getting all of us out that will be the challenge. And even if we manage it, there will be immediate pursuit by the full force of the garrison here. Deimos will fly ahead to warn the border patrols and then hunt overhead during the night hours, likely with corrupted in the saddle. Getting into Derin is one thing, but getting out is an entirely different story. Not to diminish your skill, Lord Calorian, but even you have your limits."

Killian exhaled slowly. "So . . . we need a way to get her out that won't raise any attention. That won't even be noticed until we are well away from Helatha."

"I don't suppose you've any grand ideas?"

"Maybe," Killian answered, his skin prickling. "How much did you say that reward on my head was?"

97

LYDIA

"This is a terrible plan!" Lydia snapped, struggling to control the crippling fear constricting her chest.

"No," Killian answered. "It isn't. So quit arguing with me and get your things ready. You're going with Baird to a safe place of his selection, and you will remain there until they meet up with you. And then the three of you are going to get Malahi safely back to Mudamora."

"While you sacrifice yourself." Even saying the words made her feel sick.

"I'm not just going to lie down and die, if that's your concern," he answered, handing Baird his weapons, one by one. "I have every intention of trying to kill Rufina. And if I survive that, of escaping myself."

Except with the plan he and Agrippa had concocted, there was almost no chance of Killian getting out alive.

Handing over his sword, Killian said to the giant, "Give us a minute, would you?" And when the giant was out of earshot, he turned to her. "Time and again, I failed Malahi. Put her second to concerns that I considered more important. I owe her this. And even if I didn't, we both know her life is more important than mine."

"Killian—"

He held up a hand, pressing his index finger to her lips. "We both know the best chance Mudamora has at healing the blight is a tender. But beyond that, Malahi is the rightful queen. The High Lords will again rally behind her, and with the kingdom united, there might be a chance of Mudamora surviving this. That's hundreds of thousands of lives that might be saved, and if it means sacrificing my own, then I'll gladly do it."

Tears spilled down her cheeks. "I'm not leaving you to die. Agrippa and Baird can get Malahi out. I'll stay and help you escape."

He gave a slow shake of his head. "This is what I'm meant to do. This is what I was marked to do—to protect the hope of the realm."

"I can't lose you." A sob tore from her throat, because she knew nothing that she might say would change his mind. "I love you, Killian.

And I don't care if I'm not supposed to or if you'll never be mine, but I refuse to let you die."

His shoulders bowed, but not before she caught sight of the glint of tears in his eyes. "Except that I am yours." His voice was rough. "From the moment you walked into my life, my heart, my soul, belonged to you, even if my sword did not. And I'd say that I felt torn in two because of it, but that would be a lie, because every moment I've spent with you has felt right."

Twin tears slipped down his cheeks, and Lydia's heart felt like it was shattering, the sharp little pieces cutting into her soul.

"I love you." His eyes searched hers. "More than life. More than duty and more than honor, and it's because I love you so much that I'm going to do this. I know your heart, Lydia, and if I let Mudamora burn in order to be with you, you won't just despise me for it. You'll despise yourself."

No one on Reath understood her like he did. But it wasn't fair that to be true to themselves, they had to be apart.

"You are my heart." His hands curled around the sides of her head, his tears falling to mix with her own. "And I will love you until my dying breath, that I swear to you. But you have to let me go."

There were no words in any language that could convey the emotions in her chest, so she lifted up on her toes and kissed him. Felt him flinch, and then his grip on her tightened and the kiss deepened. Her lips parted, her knees shaking as his tongue chased over hers, her shattered heart throbbing as he pulled her against him. As she pushed the strength of her mark into him, vanquishing injury and exhaustion, hoping that he'd feel her with him through this.

That he'd know she'd never give up on him.

"Hate to break this up, but time's a-ticking," Agrippa said, and Lydia tried not to sob as Killian relaxed his hold on her. As he stepped away.

"Baird's got the chains," he said. "When you're ready."

Nodding, Killian wiped at his face, then strode to where the giant was standing next to their packs, manacles and lengths of chains held in one hand.

"Baird's going to take you to an abandoned farmhouse about two miles from Helatha," Agrippa said to her in Cel. "You wait there until we come with the Queen, and then we're going to hightail it to Mudamora."

She didn't answer.

"He might get out, okay?" Agrippa scrubbed a hand through his hair. "Bastard's got a lucky horseshoe shoved up his ass, I swear it."

"What is it that they teach you at Campus Lescendor about luck?" she murmured, staring at Rufina's fortress—at the Pit.

He coughed, then cleared his throat. "To make our own."

"If you betray Rufina, she'll never stop hunting you," she said. "She needs to die."

"We've been through this, Lydia," Agrippa said. "This is the only sure way to get Malahi free, and for Killian, that's the priority over killing Rufina."

"What if we can do both?"

Curiosity blossomed in his eyes. "I'm listening."

"Are you familiar with the sacking of Hypaxe in Denastres Province?" she asked, naming one of the more famous victories in Celendor's history, one won by guile rather than brute force. The Denastrian king had taken several influential Cel hostages and threatened to kill them if the legions didn't pull out of the area surrounding the city. The legatus in command sent an offering to the gates on the condition that one of the hostages be released, a gift of food and drink, fabrics and spices, all of it carried in by dozens of young boys, their indentures included in the offering. Little had the Denastrians known that the boys were all students from Campus Lescendor. During the night, the boys freed the prisoners, helping them escape over the walls into the arms of the legion waiting below. The next morning, the legions sacked Hypaxe, leaving no survivors. And when that legatus returned to Celendrial in triumph, it was those boys who held the chains of the Denastrian king.

"Everyone in the Empire knows that story," Agrippa said. "But Killian's an obvious danger, even in chains. She's not going to let her guard down around him, that's why Baird and I are going to rescue Malahi."

"I know," Lydia said. "But she *will* let down her guard around me."

98

MARCUS

The sun overhead was merciless in its heat, and by the time they reached the Forum, Marcus was drenched with sweat, the effort of driving the blasted chariot greater than if he'd been marching alongside the boys of the Fifty-First.

Dropping the reins, he stepped out of the back of the chariot and fell into step next to Wex, it requiring too much of his self-control not to look over his shoulder at Teriana, who walked with Austornic. Her face betrayed no emotion, but her eyes were violent swells of inky black, betraying her terror over what was to come.

Climbing the steps where he'd watched his men put Cassius into power, Marcus stepped under the shade of the portico and then into the Curia itself. The halls were nearly empty, the Senate in session, and his palms turned to ice as they approached the golden doors leading to the chamber that contained the most important men in the Empire. And though it wasn't his chief concern, Marcus couldn't help but wonder if *this* time, his father would actually be seated in their ranks.

Wex paused, turning around. "Teriana, you will have to wait outside. Austornic will stay with you."

And though he knew he shouldn't, Marcus looked over his shoulder, his eyes locking on hers. *I'll see this through,* he silently promised her. *To whatever end.*

She gave the slightest of nods, then Austornic was tugging her over to one of the benches lining the hallway, more of the young legionnaires surrounding them and blocking her from Marcus's view. Which was just as well. He needed to focus on the challenge at hand.

The doors swung open, the golden dragon splitting down the middle to reveal a narrow corridor between the tiered bleachers. On the opposite side of the open space was a dais holding an empty golden chair. And looming above it towered a painted map of not just the Empire, but all of Reath.

"Commandant Wex of Campus Lescendor," the speaker announced. "And Legatus Marcus of the Thirty-Seventh Legion."

Striding into the open space, both he and Wex came to a stop in front of the dais, a quick scan revealing that while the bleachers were packed full of senators, Cassius was not among them.

"The consul is delayed, Commandant," said a legionnaire with a 29 stamped on his armor. "He had other pressing matters to attend to."

"I've no doubt," Wex answered, then he stepped closer to Marcus, murmuring softly, "This is Cassius playing games. Don't be baited."

Being made to wait was not what had Marcus's skin crawling. It was what Cassius might be doing that made him uneasy, and he fought the urge to leave the room to ensure Teriana was safe.

"Austornic might be just a boy, but he's a well-trained one," Wex said softly. "Trust him."

When it came to Teriana's safety, Marcus didn't trust *anyone* but himself.

Especially in enemy territory.

99

TERIANA

It was cool in the Curia.

Almost cold. Teriana shivered, shifting her weight on the hard stone bench on which she sat, part of her tempted to go outside into the sun to warm herself.

But there was not a chance of her doing so. Not when her fate, and thus the fate of her mother, her crew, and all her captured people was being decided on the far side of the door.

Clack. Clack. Clack.

At the familiar sound of the tread of legion sandals, she lifted her head, feeling a wave of icy cold wash over her. She climbed to her feet, her heart in her throat, pulse racing. Not at the sight of Hostus, his grin feral, but at his companion.

"You are a survivor, I'll give you that, Teriana," Lucius Cassius said, stopping in front of her. Reaching out a hand, he ran a finger along the scarf holding back her hair. "You look like your mother."

"Don't touch me!" She wished she could retreat, but the bench pressed against the back of her legs.

"The commandant and the Thirty-Seventh's legatus are waiting inside, Consul," Austornic said, edging between them. "As is the Senate."

Cassius reached out to ruffle his hair. "Wex hasn't favored a young commander like he favors you since Marcus was at Lescendor." Then he glanced over his shoulder at Hostus. "Remind me . . . it was you and yours that completed the Thirty-Seventh's training, was it not?"

"Yes, Consul."

"Forgive my poor memory . . . You had an interest in taking on the Fifty-First, didn't you? These boys?"

"We'd be honored to do so."

Austornic paled slightly. "We will abide the commandant's decision as to where, and with whom; we are deployed, sir."

"Of course," Cassius answered. "The Senate always takes Wex's suggestions into account." He brushed an invisible speck off Austornic's armor. "I don't know about you, Teriana, but I think that the young Maarin boys we are currently hosting would cut fine forms as legionnaires. I, for one, look forward to seeing them march under the Cel dragon."

Visions of her people's children being torn away from them and forced into training at Lescendor filled her mind. Of them being turned into killers who'd slaughter their own without thought, all loyalties and love for their people destroyed. "You'll be waiting a long time, Cassius, because it's not going to happen. I delivered on our bargain. Marcus is about to tell you as much. By the end of the day, I expect my people to be released."

"*Marcus*," Cassius emphasized his name, "is remarkably gifted at earning loyalty."

"Probably because his word is worth something." She balled her hands into fists. "Unlike yours."

He leaned in close, a wave of frigid air washing over her. "Be wary of where you place your trust, my dear. Not all people are worthy of such a gift."

And without another word, he strolled toward the doors, which opened to allow him and Hostus to enter before slamming shut behind him.

100

MARCUS

The doors swung open and Cassius strolled in.

He wasn't alone.

Hostus sauntered at the consul's elbow, a cold smile on his face, his too-green eyes glittering like a reptile's.

"Apologies." Cassius swept a hand so that the word encompassed all present. "And gratitude for your patience."

The consul looked much the same as he had when Marcus had set sail for the Dark Shores, his lank blond hair perhaps a touch longer, his golden skin greasy and the air around him cloying.

And cold.

As Cassius passed Marcus, swatting him companionably on the shoulder, a wave of chilly air came with him, receding only as he climbed the dais and sat on the golden chair.

"Legatus," he said as he settled himself against a crimson cushion. "I confess, I was stunned to hear you were in the city. We had feared the worst."

"Allow me to vanquish those fears," Marcus answered. "My legions have the nation of Arinoquia"—he gestured at the map—"under our control, and we have successfully found xenthier routes between the Dark Shores and the Empire."

The chamber broke out into murmurs, silencing only when Cassius lifted his hand. "An incredible feat. And you came here yourself to deliver the news, requesting the right of triumph."

"Am I not triumphant?" Marcus could feel the eyes of the senators on his back, but he kept his gaze on Cassius, noting a slight souring of his expression.

"So it would seem." Cassius tilted his head. "Now tell us, where are the stems located?"

"The path-hunter—a man by the name of Nonus, who regrettably succumbed to injury—crossed a stem near Hydrilla in Bardeen, which terminates about a day's march inland from Arinoquia's capital of Aracam. There is a genesis stem in an abandoned city nearby that terminates in Sibern, within eyeshot of the Via Hibernus and shelter number 203."

"I see." Cassius rose, turning to look up at the map. "Not ideal locations."

"No. But if there are two paths, there are bound to be more."

Questions broke out from behind him, but Cassius waved them off. "Tell me, Legatus, how is it that you, in the lone company of your Maarin advisor, came to be the one to cross into Sibern? It seems ill-advised for a young man of your importance to take such an extreme risk."

"Not by choice, Consul." Shifting his weight, Marcus added, "We were separated from my main force by hostiles in the Arinoquian interior and happened upon the xenthier stem by accident rather than design. I had the choice of risking an unknown destination or certain end, and I chose the former."

Cassius clapped his hands. "What a delightfully exciting tale, Legatus. I should love to hear the particulars at a future time. Tell me, do your men know what befell you and the Maarin girl? Are they aware of the existence of the stem?"

"To answer those questions would be speculation."

"Hmm, of course. Who would be in command in your absence?"

"Legatus Titus of the Forty-First and the Thirty-Seventh's tribunus."

More whispers from the senators seated on their benches, along with the rustle of them shifting to bend closer to one another's ears.

"I will resume command once I'm returned via the Bardeen stem," Marcus said. "I'd request the addition of another legion to bolster my ranks, which will allow further expansion of our footprint. And while I'm here, there is the matter of the Maarin." He hesitated, the sudden silence behind him unnerving. "Teriana of the *Quincense* has fulfilled her end of our agreement, and as such, we must uphold ours."

"The Maarin, of course." Cassius held out a hand, and a lawyer stepped forward to hand him a document. "Allow me to refresh my memory."

He slowly read through the pages, nodding from time to time. "On the surface," he murmured, "it certainly seems that Teriana of the *Quincense* has gone above and beyond what she agreed to, but . . ."

Cassius shook his head, and Marcus's stomach dropped, because he'd *known* it wouldn't be so easy. That Cassius would find a way to wriggle out of the bargain.

"It specifically says here that the xenthier stems are to be *viable*," Cassius continued. "I believe that was your own addition to the document, Legatus, and for good reason. A stem that delivered into the bottom of a lake or off the side of a cliff would be no means of retreat for your men." Lifting a finger, he leveled it at Marcus. "As always, you show great foresight."

Foresight was not the word Marcus would have used in this moment. Not when he could see just how Cassius intended to use Marcus's own words against him. Against Teriana.

"The question we must ask ourselves," Cassius said, stepping off the dais to circle the space, forcing Marcus to turn, "is whether we consider these stems in Bardeen and Sibern *viable*."

"Has Bardeen slipped our grip so badly that we should not?" Marcus asked. "Do you doubt the Empire's ability to provide supplies and reinforcements?"

"Bardeen has been restless, to be sure." Cassius rested an elbow against a railing. "But it is the lesser concern. What I fear is a circumstance where we, in giving up your access to the Maarin, deprive you of an avenue of retreat. For while it isn't the bottom of a lake or the side of a cliff, what is two legions of young men finding themselves in a Sibernese winter but a slower way for them to die?"

It was the truth. But Marcus had banked that Cassius's desire to increase the Empire's hold on the Dark Shores would be greater than his desire to keep the Maarin prisoner. Judging by the way the consul's piggish eyes gleamed, he'd been wrong. And unless he could convince the Senate that he was satisfied with the stems, Teriana, her crew, and all the Maarin prisoners would pay the price.

"Our position in Arinoquia is strong. A need for retreat is unlikely, but if it were to occur, we would be prepared for the elements." As if it were possible to be prepared for the dead of Sibernese winter. Half the legion would starve, and the other half would freeze to death. Those who got out alive would probably wish they hadn't. "And the majority of our fleet is intact, which would allow us to move positions within the West should I deem our position compromised."

"I don't doubt you believe that to be the case, Legatus, but it feels irresponsible to leave you so exposed. In either event," he turned to face his fellow senators, "this is a matter on which we must vote, do you not agree? We are responsible for these young men and must treat this decision with the gravity it deserves."

The senators thumped their heels against the ground in agreement, and Marcus ground his teeth in frustration. "This is a tactical decision, not a political one, and as such, it should be mine."

And what would your decision be if Teriana weren't involved?

He shoved away the thought, adding, "I will accept the Senate choosing not to commit more resources to the campaign until additional paths can be mapped, but refusing to honor our agreement with the Maarin means the Senate's word is worth less than the paper that agreement was written on. How am I to negotiate with the nations of the West given they will surely hear of this?"

Cassius stared him down, and in his eyes, Marcus could see the truth: *We didn't send you to negotiate.* "I applaud both your enthusiasm and your honor, Legatus. But this, my friends"—he gestured to the senators—"is a much-needed reminder that despite all he has accomplished, the legatus is only . . . nineteen? Or is it twenty now? Regardless, he's little more than a boy and speaks with a child's passions."

Incredulity filled Marcus, followed quickly by fury. But before he could speak, Wex said, "Consul—"

"It isn't meant as an insult, Commandant," Cassius interrupted, waving his hands in pacifying gestures. "Only a reminder that those of us with age and experience have a duty to the Empire to guide the passions of young men lest they be our downfall."

Marcus heard what Cassius was truly saying: this was not a reminder for the Senate but for him. A reminder that he had power only because the Senate gave it to him. Which meant in this room, he was powerless.

"Direct your minds to this difficult decision, my friends!" Cassius shouted. "All who deem the path to Sibern *viable,* and are of the opinion we should consider the contract with the Maarin fulfilled, please cast your vote."

He didn't want to look. Didn't want to see the moment where he'd failed her. But this situation would be no better for his cowardice, so Marcus lifted his head. And his stomach dropped at the sight.

No hands. Not a single one.

"And we have our answer," Cassius said, holding his hands out wide. "The Maarin girl, Teriana, will remain your *advisor* until a better route can be mapped."

"As you say, Consul."

"What of the matter of sending the Thirty-Seventh and Forty-First additional supplies?" Wex's voice cut through the muttering of the senators, and all fell silent. "They've long been without the support of the Empire."

"The route through the Bardeen stem is yet to be confirmed," a voice answered from the benches, and Marcus's heart skipped as Senator Valerius stood. "Surely we shouldn't risk resources until it has been proven safe."

"It has—" Marcus started to say, but Cassius cut him off.

"A difficult thing to prove in a timely fashion with Sibern falling into its coldest months. Is it not worse to refrain from resupplying the Thirty-Seventh and Forty-First when we surely are capable?"

"What is it that they say in commerce?" Valerius retorted. "Do not throw good money after bad? Surely that's a metaphor that speaks to you, Consul?"

The room burst out in an uproar, Cassius flapping his hands until they quieted. "You speak good sense, as always, my friend. We must ensure we have all the information there is to be had before making a decision. Shall we adjourn today and revisit the matter tomorrow?"

There were nods of agreement, and then Cassius turned on Marcus. "Obviously you will remain in all comfort in Celendrial while we make our decisions. And if we deem it too dangerous to proceed without confirmation of the path's safety, you will remain until we can be certain your life won't be put at risk."

Leaving Titus in control of his men. "My preference is to return straightaway, Consul."

"We will decide tomorrow. Not before." Cassius's smile was cold. "I'd of course—"

"I'd be happy to offer the legatus the hospitality of my house. It will spare him traveling back and forth to Lescendor."

The familiarity of the voice sent a shiver down Marcus's spine, and he looked up into the crowd of toga-clad men to find his father standing, one hand resting on the railing. "If you are amenable, that is, Legatus?"

His heart was racing, but Marcus managed a stiff nod.

"Where is Teriana?" Valerius was again on his feet, his eyes fixed coldly on Marcus.

"She's waiting outside." And gods, but the last thing he wanted to do was tell her that despite everything they'd done, everything *she'd* done, that her people remained imprisoned by the Empire.

"I'd offer her the hospitality of my own home," Valerius said. "She will be eager for news of her mother, and that is something I alone can provide. Among other things."

"I'd prefer—"

Cassius clapped his hands. "Then it is settled. Domitius will host the legatus for his stay, and Valerius will ensure the Maarin girl is taken care of. Adjourned."

101

TERIANA

Silence filled the hallway, and Teriana slumped down onto the bench before her knees could betray her. "He's not going to let my people go."

"It's not his choice. The Senate has to vote." Austornic said the words softly, his eyes distant, and she wasn't certain if he was talking about the freedom of her people. Or his.

Seconds passed. Minutes. No one spoke, the boys of the Fifty-First standing entirely still, eyes watching the corridors though their minds must have been on their own futures.

Then the door swung open and toga-clad senators strode out, all of them eyeing her with interest but saying nothing. Leaping to her feet, she peered through the crowd, searching for Marcus, but he was surrounded by senators, all of them trying to talk over one another.

Then a familiar voice said, "You can't imagine my relief to learn that you were well, Teriana."

Focusing on the man in front of her, Teriana took a step back at the sight of Lydia's father. "Senator," she managed to stutter out, but all she wanted was him out of her way. To get to Marcus. To find out what the Senate had decided.

"I'm afraid I have news that will disappoint you," Senator Valerius said, taking her arm. "It has been ruled that the path terminating in Sibern is not a viable route of retreat for the legions in the Dark Shores, and as such, your contract is not yet fulfilled."

She swayed on her feet. "What?"

"You'll need to return to the Dark Shores with the Thirty-Seventh's legatus until another path—one deemed viable by the Senate—has been discovered."

"But . . ."

"I'm sorry, Teriana. I know this must be a crushing blow."

She barely heard his words, her gaze going past him to lock with Marcus's. He was still surrounded by senators, but he mouthed in Arinoquian, *I'm sorry.* Then Lydia's father tugged on her arm, leading her out of the flow of traffic.

"The Senate has agreed that you will stay with me until you

depart," he said. "And of course, I'll be able to give you an update on your mother."

His words jerked her back into the moment. "She's well?"

"Quite well, I assure you." He led her down the corridor, away from Marcus. "For her safety, it won't be possible for you to see her. Though I'd be happy to arrange for a message to be delivered."

A message that would say what? That Teriana had given the Cel everything they wanted and gained nothing? That all she'd endured, all that she'd accomplished, had amounted to nothing thanks to a singular word in a contract?

A scream of fury and frustration and sorrow began to boil up in her, and she clenched her teeth, her eyes burning.

"Senator." The commandant appeared in their path. "Legatus Marcus has requested that she remain under guard at all times, even on your property, which I understand will be an inconvenience. Legatus Austornic"—he gestured to the boy—"will be in command. Address any of your concerns to him."

"Of course." Senator Valerius nodded at the boy. "Shall we, then?"

"Marcus," she started to say, but the commandant interrupted. "The Thirty-Seventh's legatus will be hosted by Senator Domitius."

His father.

A thousand thoughts and emotions were rolling through her head, and yet she allowed herself to be led out of the Curia and into a waiting litter. Lydia's father sat inside with her, pulling the curtains closed as the bearers rose, the litter swaying from side to side.

"You are under a great deal of scrutiny, my dearest girl," he said softly, "So it's best we save conversation for a place with fewer ears."

Which was just as well, because she could barely think. Could barely breathe. She'd thrown all the West to the Empire's wolves and had nothing to show for it. Her people were still imprisoned, and if Cassius followed through on his threats, soon that would be the least of their concerns. "Did he try?" Her words sounded distant in her own ears. Like they weren't hers at all. "Did Marcus try to free us?"

Lydia's father was quiet for a time, the only sound the tread of the Fifty-First surrounding the litter. Horror filled her stomach, because if Marcus hadn't at least tried, what did that mean?

"Yes, he did," Valerius finally said. "Vehemently. But in doing so, he revealed a bias toward your people, which called into question his judgment on the matter." He hesitated, then added, "Cassius has no desire to see the Maarin freed, but in this, his actions have merit. We cannot abandon those boys without a way to retreat, and being dropped in the middle of Sibern in the dead of winter is not acceptable. That Marcus argued otherwise raised many eyebrows, mine included."

Had he always known this might happened? she wondered. *And if so, why didn't he tell me as much?*

The litter was climbing the hill now, the men bearing it breathing hard from the effort of the climb. Moving aside the curtain, Teriana looked out at the walls and gates enclosing the vast villas, the scent of the sea drowned out by the endless flowers filling the gardens, an army of servants tasked at attending to them. Everything about this place catered to the lives of the few, and gods, but she hated it. Hated how once she'd loved coming here, had loved being surrounded by wealth and luxury unlike any other on Reath, had loved one of them like a sister, only to be betrayed by her.

Because if there was one truth she knew above all else, it was that this was *Lydia's* fault.

And so as they entered the grounds of the Valerius manor, Teriana didn't hesitate in demanding, "Where is she?"

Not waiting for an answer, she strode into the house where she'd spent so much time it felt like a second home. Teriana pushed past the waiting servants and took the stairs two at a time. Walking down to the library, she flung open the doors.

Only to find the room empty.

Which made sense. Lydia didn't live here now: she was Cassius's *wife.* And therefore unreachable, because as furious as she was at her ex-friend, Teriana wasn't stupid enough to go after her in Cassius's house.

Faint panting filled her ears, and she turned to find Senator Valerius leaning against the door frame, a hand pressed against his chest.

"I want to see her," she demanded. "Send her a message to come here immediately and explain to my face why she betrayed me."

His shoulders slumped, and he heaved in a deep breath. "I'm afraid that's impossible."

"Why?" She balled her hands into fists, half a mind to take her rage out on him instead.

"Because," he answered. "Lydia's dead."

102

MARCUS

On numb feet, he walked next to his father as they exited the Curia, Senator Domitius heading toward a large litter carried by eight servants.

"I'll walk."

His father glanced at him, and Marcus realized with a start that he was now taller than him. That his father, who had once held unquestionable authority in his eyes, was slender and fragile, his eyes marked with wrinkles and his hands with age spots.

"Of course you would," he answered. "How silly of me. I shall walk with you."

"Do not feel obligated, Senator."

"A brisk walk clears the head, and it will give your—" He broke off. "My *wife* time to prepare the house." Gesturing at one of the litter-bearers, he said, "Run ahead and tell Drusilla that Legatus Marcus will be our guest tonight."

The man sprinted up the street, leaving Marcus and his father to follow, the litter and a dozen men of the household guard trailing after.

Lifting a hand to his mouth and coughing, Senator Domitius murmured, "We are being watched. Though I suppose you know that."

"It's no surprise."

They walked in silence for several minutes, passing under dripping aqueducts, civilians and peregrini alike stepping aside at the sight of them.

"What are the Dark Shores like?" his father asked abruptly. "They are the focus of so much of our attention, and yet you're the first to have actually seen them."

Not answering the question, Marcus instead posed his own: "Cassius hasn't gotten any of the other Maarin to talk?"

"No. They've remained reticent, I'm afraid. Though he has left off in executing them."

"Good. I gave my word, and I'd be unhappy to hear it had been broken against my will." Even so, Marcus suspected that Cassius was still availing himself of dark rooms in the slums in the attempt to extricate more information from the captive Maarin. It was the currency with which he did business, more so than even gold.

"Valerius has been militant in their defense."

"Do you know why?" The mention of the senator's name caused uneasiness and guilt to rise in his guts, a reminder that the girl he'd murdered had friends. Family. And given Marcus hadn't been arrested upon arrival, they likely had no idea what had become of her.

Before his father could answer, a rotten apple flew past Marcus's face.

"Cel pig!" a peregrini woman shouted. Then she threw something else in his direction. Marcus stepped out of the way, but his legs were still splattered with overripe tomato as the mess struck the paving stones.

"Apologies," his father murmured, snapping his fingers at the guard to clear a path. "The peregrini grow bold of late. They do not favor Cassius and strike out against his supporters."

Which he, no matter how much he hated Cassius, was one of. And Marcus found himself wanting in equal parts to fall to his knees and beg for the woman's forgiveness and to scream in her face that he had no more power in this than she did. But instead, he walked forward, refusing to look at any of the people who shouted insults and threw rotten food in his wake.

They wove through the narrow winding paths leading up the Hill, the overhang of the trees providing respite from the beating sun, though Marcus couldn't help but notice that his father was panting, sweat running in rivulets down the sides of his face. "Do you need to pause, Senator?"

"No, I'm quite fine." His father glanced back at the litter trailing him, then started up a series of steps. "I remember when you—"

"Things change."

"Indeed."

The path forked. To go to the left would lead eventually to Cassius's home, but they carried upward to the top of the Hill, a place Marcus hadn't been since he was eight years old.

And yet it was as familiar as though it were yesterday.

The trees were somewhat taller, but the ancient walls between trees were identical, as were the bits and pieces of the grand villas visible through the dense gardens, the air thick with the scent of flowers. And faintly, Marcus could make out the sound of the surf pounding against the shores at the base of the cliffs far below this last row of homes.

"This is Valerius's home," his father said between breaths. "In case you were concerned over the welfare of the girl."

Marcus started, for a moment believing his father spoke of Lydia before realizing he meant Teriana.

His chest tightened painfully as he glanced through the closed gates, faded memories of sitting on a library floor, looking at the illustrations in books with a small girl with long dark hair and green eyes. She'd been his friend—perhaps his only friend at that age. And he'd murdered her. "I remember."

Continuing down the path, they reached the gates to the Domitius property, which sat at the very pinnacle of the Hill. One of the litter-bearers hurried ahead of them to unlatch the gate, swinging it open and then lowering his gaze as they passed.

A path made of tiny squares of white stone wound through the towering trees, past fountains featuring nude women that sprayed water from their fingertips and toes, filling the air with a tinkling music that he'd recognize a hundred years from now. Pots of bright blooming flowers buzzed with bees, and the path branched again and again, a maze he'd explored daily as a child.

"Please be kind to your mother," his father said softly as they rounded a bend and the villa appeared, all columns and porticos and colored marble. "It was my decision, not hers. And I don't think she'll ever forgive me for it."

"Do you regret it?" The words exited his lips before Marcus had the chance to think about whether he truly wanted to hear the answer.

Senator Domitius paused, staring up at the wide doors, the metal inset with twelve squares depicting famous moments of family history. "No," he finally answered. "For I believe the legions saved your life. And that they would have consumed your brother's."

It was an answer that denied all culpability for what he'd endured, and Marcus balled one hand into a fist before forcing it to relax. The past could not be undone.

Although it seemed he was about to face it whether he wanted to or not.

Pushing open the door, his father stepped into the atrium, a square opening in the ceiling revealing blue sky. Beneath it was a large golden basin that collected water during the rains. Marble benches sat between alcoves that contained busts depicting Domitius patriarchs, potted ferns providing splashes of green against the white walls.

But Marcus's gaze went immediately to the two girls standing at the far end, one of them arguing vehemently with an older female servant.

"I don't wish to go," she said, stomping a sandaled foot. "There is nothing to do in the country villa."

"Your mother says you must, domina," the servant pleaded, then her eyes snapped to Marcus and his father. "Apologies, dominus!" She dropped to her knees. "We were to be gone before your return."

"Ah, yes. The legatus walks more swiftly than is my custom, so you are not to blame." Marcus's father waved a hand to the girls. "Legatus, these are my daughters Faustina and Julia."

His younger sisters. Neither of whom he'd seen in nearly thirteen years. Julia had been only a baby when he'd left for Lescendor and Faustina an irritating toddler who'd ripped pages from his books, now twelve and fourteen.

Both girls inclined their heads, echoing each other with, "Well met, Legatus."

"Well met," he replied, unnerved when two pairs of blue-grey eyes fixed on him, for it was like looking into a mirror.

"They are off to the country," his father said. "It seemed a . . . *prudent* choice, given tensions within the city."

They could be sent to the far side of the Empire and it still wouldn't be enough to keep them safe if Cassius decided to turn on Marcus's family, but all he said was, "Wise decision."

"Off with you," his father said. "Already the hour grows late."

The girls obediently followed the servant woman out the front door, and as it closed, Marcus asked, "Do they know who I am?"

"No. Only that they had an older brother who went to the legions. Telling them more was unnecessary."

The words stung, though Marcus wasn't entirely sure why. Shoving aside the emotions, he followed his father down a corridor. Sconces of perfumed oil scented the air, but beneath it, the faint breeze carried the smell of the sea, and he inhaled deeply, hoping it would steady his heart for what was to come.

But nothing could have prepared him.

His mother sat straight backed on a couch, ankles crossed beneath her, hands folded in her lap. Her blond hair, which hung in long ringlets, was held back from her face with combs made of gold and pearl—exactly how she'd worn it when he was a boy, although now it was shot through with silver. She wore a gown typical of a patrician woman, tourmaline silk that left one shoulder bare, the other crisscrossed with delicate golden chains that matched the belt cinching the waist. Though she must have heard their approach, she did not move from her study of the tiled floor.

Then she took a shuddering breath and rose, lifting her face to meet his gaze. "We are pleased to have you in our home, Legatus."

"Thank you for your hospitality." It was a struggle to get the words out. A struggle to breathe.

Silence fell between them, the tension of far too many things unsaid keeping anything from being said at all.

Then she stumbled across the few paces between them and fell to her knees in front of him, pressing her face against Marcus's shin. "Forgive me, please forgive me. I should never have let him take you. Should have protected you, run away with you, whatever it took to keep you safe."

The world swam around him, details of the room—new and old—coming in and out of focus. "Domina . . ." He didn't know what else to call her. Couldn't bear to call her Mother.

She looked up at him, face streaked with tears, her pale blue eyes swollen and red. "He told me the physicians said you would die no matter what we did. That if we allowed you to go instead of your brother, that at least we'd have one son who survived. But I have regretted it. Every single day."

He felt dizzy and ill, nausea rising in his stomach, every inch of him wanting to escape the situation. To escape this *confession*.

"For the longest time, I thought you were dead." She was sobbing, her fingernails digging into his legs. "That you were buried in a numbered grave at Lescendor. And *he*"—she spit the word at his father—"never deigned to tell me otherwise."

"It was for your own good," his father protested. "I feared you'd lose yourself and go after him if you knew the truth, and we all know what the consequences of that would've been."

"Damn the consequences!" His mother screamed the words, and Marcus flinched. "I deserve them. You deserve them. He is our son, and we sacrificed him because he was sick."

He was going to pass out. Blindly, Marcus reached out and caught hold of a table, the vase on it rocking. Then he heard the measured click of heels, and his sister's voice cut through the air. "Oh, get up, Mother. Don't subject him to your dramatics."

Swishing past him, Cordelia reached down and hauled their mother to her feet, pushing her bodily down on the couch. Picking up a decanter of wine, she poured a generous glass and forced it into their mother's hand. She filled another glass with lemon water and finally turned to face Marcus, pushing the glass onto him with the same authority she had their mother. "Perhaps some refreshment before we unearth the family skeletons."

He drank deeply, the room slowly ceasing its rotations, allowing him to focus on his elder sister. She wore her blond hair in a tight coronet of braids, her blue-grey eyes rimmed with kohl, and the silk of her dark blue dress curved outwards over her stomach. *Pregnant.* Yet another life whose safety he needed to worry for.

"It's good to see you alive, brother." Cordelia's jaw trembled, then she wrapped her arms around his neck, her necklace clanking against his armored chest. "I'm not sorry for the things I said to you, but I did come to regret that our last meeting ended in anger. I thought that would ever be how you'd remember me."

"How is it that you two had opportunity to speak?" their father demanded.

Cordelia let go of his neck, stepping back a pace. "Not your concern, Father." To Marcus, she said, "Perhaps you'd care to take a moment before dinner to rid yourself of the city's dust and change into"—her brow furrowed—"more comfortable attire. I noted a young man from Lescendor was here delivering a package, so I assume they sent you what you might need."

"Thank you." Inclining his head to his mother, he said, "Domina. Senator," then followed Cordelia out of the room.

She led him through the corridors and up to the second level, by-passing the room that had once been his and stopping in front of one that had belonged to his brother. "My husband is keeping Gaius occupied, but they'll both be along shortly." Her fingers on the latch, she hesitated. "I'm sorry for her behavior. I'd hoped to arrive before you to prevent her dramatics."

"It's fine."

She gave a slight shake of her head. "It's not. She behaves as though she were not culpable in the decision—as though she were blameless. I half-think she's managed to convince herself that she's the victim."

He hated that word. "I don't need you to protect me, Cordelia. Not from her. Or anything else."

"Habit." She opened the door. "I need to speak with you alone after dinner. There are things you need to know that by necessity must be kept between us."

"Concerning what?"

Her jaw worked from side to side. "The Valerius girl. Lydia. She—"

A servant appeared up the corridor, and she broke off. "Later. You need a clear mind for the conversation ahead."

Unnerved in every possible way, Marcus entered the room, closing the door behind him and flipping the latch. The space was filled with every possible luxury, but he ignored it all, going instead to the open window, which faced Valerius's property.

Where Teriana was, even now.

He hated being away from her. Not only because he couldn't ensure her safety, but because without her, he felt not himself. Around her was the only time he felt he could truly breathe, and deep down, he knew that a selfish part of his soul was *glad* Cassius and the Senate had refused to accept the Sibern path. Because it meant more time with her.

Lowering himself onto a bench, he rested his elbows on his knees and his face in his hands, finally allowing himself to think about the moment when she'd asked him to give it all up. To forsake his legion. To be with her.

To remember the decision he'd made.

Not that it mattered now. The decision was out of both their hands, and the only path was forward.

Unbuckling his armor, he left it scattered on the floor, then availed himself of the basin of wash water, his nose wrinkling at the perfumed soap that had been left for him. Sitting next to the bed was a chest, and within, he found several small knives suitable for hiding away, along with folded formal attire. Grimacing, he pulled it on, hating the bulk and bothersome folds of the toga, but knowing he couldn't very well go to dinner in a legionnaire's tunic.

There was a mirror on the wall—not the cheap polished brass used by the masses, but silvered metal covered with flawless glass, and he stepped in front of it, staring at his reflection.

This is who you might have been. Who you should *have been.*

Not a soldier. Not a commander. But the heir to one of the most powerful families in the Empire. Destined to take his father's seat on the Senate and, when the time was right, to run for consul and win.

A patrician.

A politician.

One of the pompous pricks he hated more than anything on Reath.

Twisting away from the mirror, Marcus pulled on the leather sandals that had come with the clothes. Then, with a knife tucked in his belt, he exited the room and made his way downstairs.

Faint conversation, along with the scent of food and wine, filtered their way into his nose, and he entered to find his parents and Cordelia lounging on couches.

They weren't alone.

A man in his twenties perched on the corner of Cordelia's couch, a glass of wine in one hand. Though his skin was the golden hue common to those of Cel heritage, his hair was such a dark brown as to verge on black, and his eyes were a dark hazel. He rose at the sight of Marcus, extending a hand. "Legatus. I'm pleased to finally make your acquaintance—when she isn't cursing some of your recent decisions, Cordelia speaks highly of you."

Grasping the man's forearm, Marcus glanced at his sister, who lifted one shoulder. "Tiberius and I don't keep secrets from each other—he knows everything, so speak as freely before him as you would me."

"You shouldn't be sharing family secrets, sister," a voice said from behind, and Marcus turned to find his younger brother lurking in the corner. "No offense, Tiberius."

"None taken." Tiberius sipped at his wine. "You have a great deal to lose, Gaius. I understand entirely."

Pushing away from the wall, Gaius crossed the room to take a seat on an empty couch, and Marcus noted he took care to keep a healthy distance between them. "Tell me, brother, do those living in the Dark Shores curse your name the way they do in Chersome, indeed the way they do across the entire Empire, or have you not progressed so far yet in your conquest?"

"Gaius, shut your bloody mouth," Cordelia snapped.

"Cordelia! Language!" their mother said, sitting upright. "You've the foul mouth of a soldier." Then she blanched, glancing at Marcus. "Your pardon. I meant the rank and file, of course. Not an officer."

This night was going to be the purest form of misery.

"Drink?" Tiberius asked. "I'm afraid it's a serve-yourself affair. Even the most loyal servants tend to have loose tongues, especially when it's about matters that might earn them some coin."

"I'm fine with water, thank you."

"I'd heard that about you." Tiberius filled a glass and handed it to him. "Straight-headed, they say. Stickler for the rules. Not one for unnecessary chatter."

Marcus met his gaze, not answering. He didn't like this man

knowing his secrets—not when he'd sacrificed so much to keep them that way.

"Perhaps we might address the matter at hand." Having been silent the entire time, his father finally spoke. "Cassius holds a great deal of leverage over this family, and insight into how else he might use it against us is worth knowing."

"I suppose that depends on what his end goal is." Marcus leaned against a column, then took a sip of his water. "You and Tiberius here know him best, so perhaps you might provide me with some insight."

His father and Tiberius exchanged uneasy glances.

Marcus made a face. "You sit with him on the Senate. Hear the policies he proposes. The gossip. Whereas I've been living in a tent on the far side of the world, entirely cut off from all of this."

"Power," Tiberius answered slowly. "And all that comes with it. He's had a taste of being in control, and I think there is little he wouldn't do to retain it."

"So he'll run for another term as consul."

"Undoubtably," Tiberius answered. "And as much as it pains me to say it, with your successes, he will very likely win. If your arrival had come after the coming summer's election, he might well have lost the consulship."

Not unexpected, but Marcus still struggled not to grimace. "My intention was to refrain from contact with the Empire until after his term was through, but circumstances conspired against me."

"You truly expect us to believe *that*?" Gaius snapped. "You're here because you want more men. So you can conquer more of the world and increase your own fame. And don't think for a second, *brother*, that we don't see you doing it as an attempt to make a point to us."

Marcus's temper flared, his fingers curling into a fist. But beating Gaius bloody last time hadn't solved a damn thing. "Every time you open your mouth, useless words pour forth like shit from an ass, *Gaius*. Do us all a courtesy and remain silent unless you have something helpful to add. Because I assure you, *choosing* to travel an unmapped stem into the depths of Sibern is something only an idiot or a madman would do. And I am neither."

"You overstep." His brother's face purpled as he turned on their father. "Are you truly going to stand there and allow him to speak to me in such a crass and offensive manner?"

"Oh, be silent," their mother snapped. "Or if you cannot, take this"—she shoved a bottle of wine into his hand—"and go complain to the flowers in the garden. Perhaps they will care about your petty jealousy."

Gaius glowered, but remained silent and took his seat.

"How was it that you crossed with just the Maarin girl?" Cordelia asked, her brow furrowed.

"We were separated from my men by hostiles," he answered. "We took refuge in some ruins, and the floor collapsed, revealing the xenthier. It was either die by their hands or risk the path."

"Ah," she replied, but the furrow in her brow remained as though she knew he wasn't giving the whole of the story.

"But that is irrelevant," he added. "What's done is done. All that matters now is what Cassius is going to do with this victory, which he is sure to claim as his own. And how he's going to use this family to hold on to his consulship."

"He'll push us to campaign for him, there is no doubt of that," his father answered. "And for the coin to fund it. I wouldn't put it past him to bankrupt us in pursuit of his goals, knowing full well that we are in no position to deny him the funds."

"I'd say it's better to be broke than to hang from the gallows, but you would handle destitution very poorly, Father," Cordelia said, shifting on the couch. "For your own sake, you might grow a pair and stand your ground against him."

"Cordelia!" their mother snapped, but his sister only ignored her.

"Marcus is Celendor's golden boy," she continued. "He is making Cassius look *very* good, and if Cassius reveals that you broke the laws of the child tithes, it won't only be Father and Gaius who swing, it will be Marcus, too. I don't think he'll risk it."

Marcus wished he had her confidence. "I'm replaceable, Cordelia. With Titus, who, I'll remind you, is Cassius's son. Or if he can't get the Senate to agree to it, then one of the many other men who have the same training and skills as I do." He turned to his father. "My advice is to do what he asks."

"No matter the consequences?" Cordelia demanded. "He's a tyrant, and if you think he doesn't have grander ambitions than two terms as consul, you are an idiot."

"Ambition or not, the law limits him."

Tiberius cleared his throat. "Laws can be changed. Already he's amended those related to the child tithes to the legions. In a year, families will either have to pay or give up fourth sons as well. The coin is nothing to those who have it, but those without means will lose another child."

Marcus's chest tightened, the hate that had been directed at him by the citizens becoming all too understandable.

"And his argument for the need of expanding the legions has only been strengthened by your return," Tiberius continued. "As soon as a path—one more viable than that to Sibern—is discovered, he will send more legions through without delay. To make a name for himself and to secure the wealth that Maarin ledgers show the Dark Shores has."

"There are limits," his father argued. "You make him sound as though he aims for the power of an emperor, which the Senate will never grant. Celendor rid itself of such a position for a reason."

"And yet what are we but an empire without an emperor?" Cordelia said. "I think that's exactly how Cassius envisions himself."

"You're being emotional, Cordelia, which is no wonder, given your condition," their father said. "You are caught up on semantics and speak of that which you don't understand."

"Half of Celendor's power rests on the strength of semantics," Cordelia retorted. "And unlike you, I see clearly and without fear for my own neck."

"Exactly!" Gaius rose. "Easy for you and Tiberius to stand on principal when neither of you risk being sent to hang."

"Even if our lives were on the line, it would change nothing." She rose to meet him. "You're a coward."

Gaius lifted a hand to slap her and Marcus moved to grab it, but Tiberius had already stepped in front of his wife. "Enough. This quarrelling yields no dividends. Let us turn our heads to how we might mitigate Cassius's control over us without catastrophic consequences."

"If you mean, can we assassinate him and solve our woes, the answer is likely no." Marcus drained the rest of his water. "He's too clever not to have contingencies in play to make us pay if we move against him. Otherwise, I'd have slit his throat while he slept."

Rather than the brutality shocking them, their faces only registered disappointment it wasn't an option.

"He holds all the cards in the game between us," Marcus continued. "And even if he did lose the consulship, he would not lose his ability to play them. So make your choice: accommodate him or live with the consequences of crossing him. This conversation is a waste of breath."

"I take it you've made *your* choice?" Cordelia asked.

He surveyed them, these people whose blood he shared. Whose lives he'd protected, though they hadn't given him the same courtesy. They were sly and conniving and ambitious—Cel patricians to the core—but he'd known that even as he'd backed a tyrant in order to keep them safe.

Why?

They didn't deserve it, not really. Their lives weren't worth more than those who'd suffer and die as the result of Cassius being in power. And part of him wondered if Gaius hadn't seen to the heart of it in that he'd had something to prove. "I made my decision a long time ago," he said. "Do what you will, but I won't have this family's blood on my hands."

"Then you're just as much a coward as the rest of the family."

Marcus stepped closer to his sister, shoving Tiberius back when he tried to move between them. "Allow me to remind you, Cordelia, that *you* could end this. That *you* could go before the Senate and confess this family's crimes. That *you* could bear the burden of this family's destruction. After all, you have the least to lose." He searched her eyes, so similar in color to his own, then leaned down so they were nose to nose. "But it's easier to get me to do the dirty work, isn't it?"

Cordelia didn't so much as blink. "If it were my secret to tell, I would fall on my knees before all of Celendrial and confess. But more than anyone else, Marcus, it's *yours*."

Scowling, Marcus turned away. "I need some air."

He strode out into the gardens, barely seeing the greenery and statuary, and went to a large fountain depicting nude lovers entwined in an embrace, water spraying from their mouths. It hadn't been here when he was a child, and he stared at it, wishing with all his heart that he'd never come back here.

"I need to speak to you in private."

He turned to see Cordelia standing behind him, her expression grim. "About what."

She hesitated, then met his gaze. "About the Maarin girl . . . Teriana. You need to part ways with her."

His irritation that yet another person was raising this issue clouded the more pressing question of how she knew. "Talk to the Senate. Or Cassius. Neither seem inclined to allow me to part ways with her."

Cordelia huffed out an annoyed breath. "I'm talking about her role as your wh—"

"You even think of calling her that and this conversation is over."

"And there's the proof. You're not usually so easily baited. Especially not into revealing your secrets."

Scowling at her, Marcus said, "It's none of your blasted business who is or isn't in my bed, Cordelia."

"Except that it is. Everything you do, every choice you make, impacts our family, and so I'll make it my business." She shifted her weight, fussing with the folds of her dress. "Especially when what you're doing gives Cassius more leverage."

"What difference does my relationship with Teriana make?" he demanded, despite the question being woefully naive: Cassius wielded information like a weapon.

"Tiberius told me that eyebrows rose during your meeting with the Senate. You've a reputation for never unnecessarily endangering your men, but despite the Sibern path being a woefully ill-equipped avenue for retreat, you argued in Teriana's favor. Your bias toward the Maarin is apparent, and that undermines everything you say on the matter."

He knew that. But what else could he have done? "We'll be gone again soon enough."

"You still need to end it. Your being with her is immoral, Marcus. She's your prisoner, and all the sweet words and passionate embraces in the world won't change that."

His jaw tightened, and he didn't answer. This was always the way with Cordelia: she used the truth, knowing it would do the fighting for her. "I didn't make her do anything, if that's what you're accusing me of. It was her choice."

"Which doesn't excuse you in the slightest."

As if he didn't know that. As if he hadn't been willing to give up everything in order to make what was between him and Teriana *right*.

"End it."

"No!" The word tore from his lips, and he jerked to his feet, pacing back and forth before leveling a finger at his sister. "I have given up *everything*. I won't give up her unless *she* wills it."

Cordelia looked away, lowering her face and rubbing at the side of her belly as though soothing the child within. "I didn't want to bring this up, but you give me little choice."

"Why stop now?"

"Fine." She squared her shoulders. "Did you kill Lydia Valerius?"

Of all the things for her to say, he hadn't expected that. "You know the answer."

"I *suspect* the answer. You've never admitted it."

Because it was easier to pretend it had never happened that way. "Yes, I killed her."

"Personally? By your own hand?"

Between his teeth, he said, "Yes. I drowned her in Cassius's baths and put her down the drain. Happy?" Not entirely how it had gone, but the result was the same.

She flinched, lifting a hand to press her fingers to her mouth. Softly, she said, "He thought it was something like that. Not you, specifically, but that she'd been killed in the baths."

"Who?"

"Her father."

Senator Appius Valerius. The man who even now had Teriana in his home. Marcus's blood ran cold.

"We've become close in recent months," Cordelia continued, "unified by our mutual hatred of Cassius, though Appius believes our motivations entirely political. But he confessed to Tiberius and me his belief that Cassius, having used his betrothal to Lydia to secure the consulship, decided to have her killed rather than to go through with the wedding."

"He's not wrong."

"I know." Cordelia's jaw worked back and forth, then she said, "Did Cassius tell you why he wanted her dead?"

"No. Only that she was a liability and that he wanted it done." And he hadn't pressed for more details. "From what he said to her in her final moments, Lydia had clearly been publicly disparaging him, so I assumed that was the reason."

"Oh, Marcus. *Everyone* disparages Cassius, even his followers. Even if she'd loathed him, he wouldn't have cared enough to kill her."

His pulse was galloping, his stomach hollow. "Why, then?"

"Because she was connected to the Maarin." Reaching up, Cordelia caught hold of his hand, pulling him onto the bench next to her. "Lydia had few friends. Never mind that she was bookish and peculiar in her pursuits, her blood wasn't patrician, and you know how we can be."

It felt like a vise was closing around his chest, his breath coming too fast.

"Appius told me she had one close friend. Closer than close, in truth, for Lydia loved this girl like a sister. A Maarin girl."

"Teriana." He could barely get her name out.

"Yes." His sister squeezed his hand tight. "That's why you need to end it, Marcus. Because imagine what it will do to Teriana if she discovers she's sleeping with the man who murdered her dearest friend."

103

TERIANA

"What do you mean Lydia's dead?" She gaped at Senator Valerius, unable to decide whether the sudden hollowing of her chest was because revenge would be denied her or grief that Lydia was gone.

"That's is what I believe to be the case." Stepping outside, he said something to Austornic, who'd ventured up after them, then shut the door behind him. Crossing the room, he sat on a bench, motioning for her to take the seat across from him. "And I believe that Cassius was the one who murdered her."

Gagging, Teriana pressed a hand to her lips, trying to keep her stomach contents in check as she stumbled into the chair. Putting her head between her knees, she said, "Why would he kill her? She gave him everything he needed to capture my people."

"Lydia didn't betray you, Teriana."

She lifted her head. "But he said she . . ." She trailed off, because Cassius had never overtly said that it had been Lydia who'd given her up. Teriana had only assumed that to be the case because he'd had her copy of *Treatise*.

"Vibius is the traitor," Senator Valerius answered. "In more ways than one. He found where Lydia had hidden the book you'd given her and showed it to Cassius. When she discovered Cassius was using it as leverage to arrest your people, she tried to warn you, but I—"

Breaking off, he rose and went to fill two glasses with lemon water, handing one to her. Resuming his seat again, he met her gaze. "I am the one you have cause to be angry with, Teriana, because I was the one who prevented her from warning you."

Her hand trembled, water spilling over the rim of the glass. "Why?"

"To protect her." He took a large swallow of water, then set the glass aside. "Vibius would have told Cassius she'd interfered, and I feared the consequences. Feared I'd be unable to keep her safe from him, should he try to do her harm in retaliation for upsetting his plans. I sacrificed you and your crew in order to keep her safe, and yet she's still dead."

"How?" She could barely get the word past her lips.

"The morning the *Quincense* was towed into Celendrial's ports, Cassius requested a sojourn between him and Lydia at the baths. I did not wish for her to go, but she did anyway, likely hoping to intercede on your behalf."

The world spun in and out of focus, but Teriana forced herself to concentrate. To listen.

"She went into the baths, that much I know is fact. But shortly thereafter, Cassius sent word that she'd never arrived. A search began, but the servants working in the bath's gardens revealed that a girl fitting her description was seen sneaking away. Others spoke of seeing her in the city. And more still that they'd seen her boarding a ship destined for Sibern. But I don't believe it was her."

Reaching across the space between them, Senator Valerius took her hands, his skin hot against her icy fingers. "Teriana, she fought against him so hard. And I know in my heart that she'd have died before abandoning you. She went into those baths, but I don't think she ever came out. Not alive."

A whining sound filled her ears, and she realized that it was coming from her lips. That she was shaking, tears flooding down her face, and a gasping sob tore from her lips.

Lydia was dead.

Lydia was murdered.

Lydia was gone.

She screamed, wrenching out of Senator Valerius's grip and falling to the floor, where she pounded her fists against the wood, harder and harder, seeking the pain. Relishing it.

Dimly, she heard Austornic and the other boys burst into the room. Heard the senator murmuring that it was only grievous news, to give her space, and the doors shutting behind them.

And then he was kneeling in front of her.

"I grieve with you," he said, drawing her up. "She was my child. The light of my life and the blood of a woman who saved me in my darkest hours. But tears will not bring her back. Which means revenge is the only thing left to us."

"How do we hurt him?" she asked, her tongue thick. All this time, she'd believed Lydia had been the cause of her woe, but it was the opposite. It was because of her that Lydia was dead.

"Powerful as Cassius is," Senator Valerius answered, "he is still subject to the law. If it can be proven that he arranged Lydia's murder, he will be stripped of the consulship. And if I have my way, he'll hang."

"I don't see how I can help." She scrubbed at her eyes, trying to stop more tears from forming. "I didn't know she was even dead. When I saw he had *Treatise,* I thought she'd betrayed me because we hadn't helped her escape the betrothal."

And looking back, she felt sick to have believed such a thing about her friend, who didn't have a petty bone in her body. Who'd gladly suffer to save anyone she loved anguish.

"You have the ear of the Thirty-Seventh's legatus."

She stiffened, looking up.

"I know the boy was involved with Cassius's scheming." He shifted off his knees so he was sitting on the floor next to her. "Lydia sneaked onto Cassius's property and overheard a conversation between the two. Learned that Cassius blackmailed the boy into ordering his legion to vote for Cassius in the elections."

"Didn't order them," she muttered. "He gave them the choice. But the blackmail part is accurate enough. Cassius told Marcus that he'd have the Thirty-Seventh sent somewhere awful if they didn't do it."

Lydia's father's brow furrowed. "At worst, it would've been only for the length of Cassius's term. And even then, Cassius doesn't have total authority over such matters and he'd have had a hard time arguing a legion of that caliber be underutilized. Any legatus would know that, him especially."

Teriana rubbed at her temples, trying to sort through the mess of politics and lies and intrigue, unsure of what she should say. Not wanting to betray Marcus's confidence out of hand. "He wanted to escape."

"What do you mean?"

"He's tired of being under the Senate's control—of being told where to go and who to conquer without any respite." Biting her lip, she added, "I've seen firsthand the horror of what they do and what it costs them—he wanted the opportunity to give his men a better future, and he thought the Dark Shores was a chance for that."

Senator Valerius was silent, finally saying, "He's darkened the future of a good many living in the Empire to achieve that freedom."

"He knows. But something *you* should know about Marcus is that he'll do whatever it takes to protect those he cares about, and that legion is everything to him."

"Not everything, now is it?" The senator climbed awkwardly to his feet, pacing up and down the room. "From the way he conducted himself today, I can only assume he's quite taken with you."

She squeezed her eyes shut.

"If he knows anything about Lydia's fate, he might be willing to tell you."

Her eyelids snapped open. "Are you suggesting he was involved?"

"Charming as I'm sure he can be, Teriana, please keep in mind that the boy is a trained killer with an entire legion of trained killers at his disposal. And Cassius would not have done the deed himself—it's not his way."

Was Marcus involved? Her blood chilled. *Had he sent someone like Quintus to kill Lydia while she sat defenseless in the baths?*

Bile rose in her throat, but then she shook her head. "No. His involvement doesn't make any sense. By the time Lydia was killed, the Senate had already agreed that Marcus would be in command of the mission. He'd have no reason to do Cassius's dirty work."

"Teriana, he's been doing the Empire's dirty work for a good portion of his life." His voice was soft, as though he were breaking bad news to a particularly naive child. "He's arranged assassinations before—I know that for a fact."

As did she. And maybe she was naive, but still she said, "There's a difference between doing it on the orders of the Senate and to satisfy the personal grievances of a single senator. He wouldn't have agreed to it, especially given he *hates* Cassius."

"You seem to have come to know him well."

Lydia's father fell silent, and when Teriana glanced in his direction, she saw that his eyes were considering. Then he asked, "Why does he hate him?"

She opened her mouth to point out that the answer was obvious, then closed it again. Because it wasn't.

"The question remains: If he knows anything about Lydia, do you think he'll tell you?"

Swallowing hard, she nodded. "He trusts me."

"Do you think he'd be willing to testify against Cassius in the courts?"

For the sake of taking away the consulship from Cassius, she had to believe it was so. Except if he'd always had knowledge, why wouldn't he have used it before? "I can ask him."

Senator Valerius reached down for her hand, drawing her up. "I'll arrange for you to see him tomorrow. Cassius seems eager to have him out of Celendrial, and perhaps this is part of the reason why."

Allowing him to lead her out of the library, she avoided the curious eyes of Austornic and the other boys, though they followed. Senator Valerius took her to Lydia's rooms. "You can rest in here,

Teriana. They are as she left them. I'll have the servants bring you something to eat."

Shutting the door, she crossed the room and climbed onto Lydia's bed, burying her face in the pillows and inhaling, searching for the familiar scent of rosewater and perfume.

But they smelled stale. Lifeless. Not like Lydia at all.

A strange desperation filled her, and Teriana fell off the bed, stumbling into the closet and grabbing dress after dress, searching for the scent that would trigger her memory. That would pull her back into a time when Lydia had been alive and well.

Her best friend.

Her sister.

But it was as though she'd never lived in these rooms. As though she'd never lived at all.

"I'm sorry." She dropped to her knees, pressing her forehead to the tile. "I'm sorry!"

Great heaving sobs tore from her lips. Her chest ached, and her face was slick with snot and tears. The world swam around her. A world of loss and hurt and pain. And betrayal. Not Lydia's but hers. If only she'd taken Lydia away that day, none of this would have happened.

It is your fault.

You did this.

And maybe that was so. But it was Cassius who was the villain.

The wild twist of emotions running through her demanded that she go in search of his blood, but the odds of her success were slim. Which meant she needed a better weapon.

She couldn't wait for tomorrow. Not when she knew for a fact that Marcus was in reach.

Easing open the window, she leaned over the edge, searching the darkness of the gardens below for signs of the young legionnaires tasked with watching over her. She caught sight of a flicker of motion, the gleam of light against a metal breastplate, and she watched as the shadow navigated the pathways. When he was out of sight, she climbed up on the sill, and taking a deep breath, she jumped.

Air whistled through her hair as she fell, her boots making a soft thud against the dirt as she fell into a roll. On her feet in a flash, she hurried through the gardens in the direction of the Domitius villa, pausing from time to time to ensure she wasn't being followed.

The wall between the two properties was ancient, the stacked stones green with moss but easy enough to climb. Rolling over the top, she glanced to ensure the footing was good, and then she jumped.

"What are you doing here?"

A gasp tore from her mouth and she whirled, drawing her knife before it dawned on her that it was Marcus who'd spoken.

He was dressed in the garments of a patrician man, a long tunic and perfectly draped toga, though she noted he had a knife in one hand, which he swiftly slipped away. In the moonlight, his face looked pale and drawn with exhaustion, his eyes slightly swollen, and faintly, she heard a wheeze to his breath. "Are you all right?"

"It's been a trying evening."

Belatedly she remembered that this had once been his home. That these people were his family. "What are you doing out here in the dark?"

He was quiet. Then he said, "I was coming to see you."

"Fairly certain you could've come through the front gate." Though in fairness, she probably could've done the same.

Tension hung between them, as though a chasm had split the earth and they stood on opposite sides.

"I'm sorry." His voice was so soft, she barely heard it.

"Valerius told me you argued with Cassius. Tried to get them to free my people but that the Senate wouldn't agree to it." She bit her lip. "I know you did everything you could."

He didn't answer, only reached out to take her hand.

"We'll just find another path." Fear was rising in her chest, but she wasn't sure why. "A better one. Then they'll have to let my people go."

"Teriana—"

"There's something I need to ask you," she interrupted before she lost her nerve. "Valerius believes his daughter was murdered by Cassius—she was supposed to marry him. Do you know anything about it?" Her jaw trembled, and she sucked in a deep breath before adding, "Lydia was my best friend."

104

KILLIAN

The worst part was not being able to see.

Agrippa had bound his wrists and ankles, but it was the black sack he'd pulled over Killian's head that was driving him mad, his vision reduced to flickers of light and shadows as the pair led him through Rufina's fortress. "Best to keep her unaware for as long as possible," Agrippa had said, and though there was merit to the thought, Killian was starting to wonder if he'd stacked the odds so far out of his favor that not even his mark was going to get him out alive.

"We weren't expecting you, General," a voice to Killian's left said. "We were under the assumption you were to remain in Deadground."

"You know what they say about assumptions." Agrippa's voice was light, but Killian didn't miss the edge to it. "Now tell Her Majesty I'm here. And that I've brought her a gift."

"Who is he?"

"Not for you, you pus-filled pimple," Agrippa answered. "Now open the bloody door."

There was a thud, then the faint creak of a heavy door being opened, and a moment later, Killian heard the speaker say, "General Agrippa is here to see you, Your Majesty. He has a prisoner with him."

"It had better be a prisoner of note," Rufina's voice purred. "He's not supposed to be here."

"Walk," Agrippa muttered, jerking on Killian's arm. Then he said loudly, "Rufina, my queen. You are a vision, a delight for eyes that have too long been deprived of true beauty."

"And you are as tedious as always, Agrippa. What are you doing here? I told you to remain in Deadground, though I've heard you've been doing a fine job ignoring my commands, as usual."

"I've expensive tastes that require funding," Agrippa answered, and Killian's arm lifted as the other man shrugged. "For me to remain at your beck and call required some creativity on my part."

Rufina huffed out an amused breath. "You're lucky I value your skill set, because removing your tongue holds a certain appeal."

Killian turned his head, tracking the sound of Rufina's voice, which came from the far side of the room. A large room, judging from the way their boots echoed.

"All the girls in Deadground thank you for your restraint, Majesty." Agrippa gave Killian a shove, sending him toppling to his knees. "And as a sign of my continued loyalty to your crown and cause, please accept this gift."

Boots thudded against the stone floor as Rufina approached, and Killian's skin crawled with the knowledge that the corrupted queen was within reach. And him powerless to do anything about it. Then a hand caught hold of the sack over his head and yanked it off.

"Well, now," Rufina said softly. "You really have outdone yourself, Agrippa."

Blinking against the bright torchlight, Killian's eyes fixed on Rufina standing before him. Though he knew she was much older, the corrupted queen appeared in her early twenties, with pale skin and black hair that hung nearly to her waist. Her eyes were set at the upturned angle common to those of northern Mudamora, though hers were dilated black pits rimmed with crimson flame. And on her forehead was the mark of Hegeria, the tattooed half-moon faded with age.

"Where is Malahi?" he demanded between his teeth. "What have you done to her?"

"Ahh, but of course. That's why you're here." Rufina smiled. "The Princess. Or is she the Queen? I confess, I can't keep track of whose head wears the crown of Mudamora these days. Though I do know who *rules*."

Her fist caught him in the face hard enough that Killian saw stars as he fell backward.

Then Agrippa was standing between them. "If you could hold on to your restraint a heartbeat longer before you kill him, Majesty, there's the matter of my compensation."

Rufina huffed out an aggrieved breath. "You're the commander of my armies, Agrippa. Bounty hunting is beneath you."

"Very little is beneath me, Majesty," Agrippa answered. "Which has long been to your advantage. And I'd add it would also be to *your* advantage to be seen holding to your word lest your word cease to have any meaning at all."

The flames around Rufina's eyes flared, but she reached out and patted Agrippa's cheek, smirking as he flinched away from her touch. "Very well, Agrippa. What was it I said? A thousand gold coins?"

"Five thousand," Agrippa answered. "Getting him here alive was no small amount of work."

"An expensive life." Rufina knelt in front of Killian, her eyes roving over him, her palm curving around his cheek. "But well worth it."

He felt the pull and recoiled, but Rufina caught him by the back of the head, holding him in place. "This will be a pleasure," she whispered. "I think I'll do it slowly. Savor the thrill of consuming one of the Marked."

Another pull, and there was nothing he could do to get away from her. It had always been a slim hope that he'd survive this, but all that mattered was getting Malahi free.

Then Agrippa caught hold of his shoulders, wrenching Killian from Rufina's grasp. "Before you get too far along there, Your Grace . . . I want something else on top of the gold."

This wasn't part of the plan.

A frown creased Rufina's forehead, her eyes flicking away from Killian. "What?"

"I want an end to our arrangement." Agrippa rocked back on his heels. "I wish to be free to go my own way."

"Tragically, I have need of you," she said. "I've not found another commander with your . . . *prowess,* so I'm afraid you'll have to content yourself with gold and women."

"I told you I brought you a prize, and I meant it," Agrippa said, and Killian's blood chilled. "Who better to lead your armies than the man who beat them on the field?"

"He won't fight for me," she answered. "My master says he can't be turned."

"In my experience, it's all about finding the right incentive. Or the right threat."

No. Please, no.

Rufina cocked her head, eyes glittering with interest, and Killian lunged, trying to grab Agrippa, desperate to stop him, but the other man only stepped back.

"You give me what I want, Rufina, and I'll give you the reins to the Dark Horse," Agrippa said. "I'll give you the girl he's in love with."

Rufina laughed. "He's not going to destroy his kingdom for some girl."

"I wouldn't be so sure about that," Agrippa answered with a smirk. "Because the girl who possesses his heart is none other than Kitaryia Falorn."

105

MARCUS

Marcus had been on his way to find her. To tell her that she needed to remain in Celendrial and to make arrangements with Valerius to hide her away with her mother. To keep her safe.

"Lydia was my best friend."

The pain in Teriana's voice was like a knife to his heart, and he wanted to fall to his knees. To beg her forgiveness, though he didn't deserve it. To hand her a knife and tell her to kill him herself, if that was what she wanted.

She deserved the truth.

"Marcus?"

And if it were only him who would suffer for it, he would confess everything. Would walk to the gallows and allow them to string him up for murder, because he deserved it.

But his family would also pay the price for what he'd done. Valerius would use the information against Cassius, and the consul would take the loss of his power out on Marcus's family.

He felt her tense. Knew he'd been silent too long, but neither truth nor lie would come to his lips, so he said, "I knew her. When I was a small child. I used to play with her in her father's library. She was . . ." He trailed off, faded memory washing over him of a dark-haired girl who sat patiently with him while he gasped and wheezed. Who'd held his hand and told him that he'd be all right. "She was kind."

"Yes." Tears rolled down Teriana's cheeks. "Did he hurt her?"

"He was using her to gain Valerius's support in the elections."

"I know that much." There was an edge to Teriana's voice, as though she knew he was stalling. "I'm asking if Cassius had her killed, Marcus. If you know anything, you owe me the truth of it."

He owed her everything, the truth most of all. Except giving it to her wouldn't bring Lydia back from the dead, but it would condemn the living. And while some of them didn't deserve his protection, his younger sisters did. The unborn child in Cordelia's belly did.

"I don't know." The lie slipped off his lips. "Cassius only told me the things I needed to know—he doesn't trust me."

"So you weren't involved?"

He could hear the hope in her voice, the silent plea. "I didn't order her assassination, if that's what you are asking."

I did it myself.

"If you'd known something, it might have been enough to strip him from power. Maybe have him executed." A tear ran down her dark cheeks, glistening in the moonlight. "But as always, he wins."

Without thinking, Marcus closed the distance between them, pulling her against his chest. Her shoulders shook as she cried, but still she wrapped her arms around his neck.

End it. Tell her she needs to stay in Celendrial. That you'll deal with finding the path and then free the Quincense.

Except what he really wanted to tell her was that he loved her.

"Teriana—"

Shouts from his family's home filtered through the gardens, and he turned, unease rising in his chest. And then a woman screamed.

"Get back to Valerius's villa," he said. "Tell Austornic and his men that something's wrong. To be ready."

"What's going on?" she demanded, but Marcus only caught hold of her waist, lifting her up the wall. "Go!"

Another scream cut the night, desperate and terrified.

Trusting Teriana to take care of herself, he sprinted back through the gardens, knife in hand. Only once he was close did he slow, crouching low as he made his way toward the rear of the home.

Inside, his mother was on her knees, a man he knew to be one of the Twenty-Ninth holding her by the hair, a knife to her throat. His brother and father, as well as Tiberius, were bound at the wrists, and another man was holding Cordelia down on the floor, his sister violently struggling. They wore civilian clothing, nothing about them, not even their blades, suggesting this was a legion kill.

"Where is he?" one of them growled, and Marcus recognized his voice. Carmo, the Twenty-Ninth's primus and Hostus's favored man for dirty work. He was Atlian by birth and nearly as big as Servius. "Give him up, and we'll let you go unharmed."

His mother lifted her chin, expression defiant. "I don't know where he went."

"How sweet," Carmo crooned. "A mother protecting her son to the bitter end." When she blanched, he laughed. "Yes, love. We know. And *you* should know that there isn't anyone alive the Twenty-Ninth hates like your little prick of a son. He embarrassed us to achieve his own ends, and we've long awaited this opportunity to see him dead."

Just tell him, Marcus silently willed her even though he knew that Carmo had no intention of leaving any of them alive.

But instead, his mother spit at Carmo's feet. "If you know who he is, then you know I'll die before giving him up. So get on with it."

Silence.

"From my experience, mothers can be difficult to break," Carmo finally said to his men. "There's really only one way to do it, and that's to make them choose between their children. Kill the pregnant one. Slowly."

Tell him! If they came after him first, he could better ambush them in the dark.

A sob tore from his mother's lips, then she said, "Don't hurt her. Marcus is in the gardens."

"Kill everyone but the pregnant one," Carmo said. "We might have need of her yet."

The man holding the knife to his mother's throat started to smile, but the expression fell away as he looked down to see Marcus's knife embedded in his chest. He staggered backward, clutching the hilt, but Marcus was already moving on his next target.

Sliding across the tiled floor, he caught hold of the man's fallen knife, lifting it in time to deflect a downward blow from the third man. He kicked him in the kneecap, breaking his leg. The man hissed in pain, but that didn't stop him from tackling Marcus against the tile.

They rolled, crashing into furniture, glassware shattering around them. Dimly, he heard his mother screaming. Knew that Carmo could be taking the opportunity to kill her. To kill Cordelia.

Panic flooded through him, and Marcus slammed his knee down on the man's broken leg. He screamed, but instead of trying to pull away, the man took advantage of the position and twisted, his arm going around Marcus's neck.

He gasped for breath, clawing at the man's arm, kicking his broken leg. But even as he did, his eyes latched on Carmo, who had his sister on her knees, a knife to her stomach. Tiberius was trying to crawl on his bound wrists, pleading she be spared. Offering any amount of gold for her safety.

But Carmo only kicked him in the face before turning his gaze back to Marcus.

"Hostus wanted to do it himself. In his honor, I'm going to take my time. I'm going to make you watch while I kill every last one of these useless patrician sots. I'm going to—"

His mother flung herself at Carmo. Snarling, he backhanded her with his knife hand, sending her toppling into a table, but Cordelia took advantage, twisting in his grip and sinking her teeth into his wrist. Carmo cursed, slicing at her with his knife. Blood blossomed along her rib cage.

White-hot fury boiled up inside Marcus, and he slammed his head back, feeling the nose of the man holding him shatter. Snatching up a fallen knife, he shoved it between the man's ribs and then flung himself at Carmo.

His shoulder took the primus in the stomach and sent him falling backward into a potted plant. Screams filled the air, but he ignored them, catching Carmo's wrist to keep him from stabbing him in the throat.

They rolled, knocking into tables, a marble statue falling and missing Marcus's face by a hairsbreadth. Catching hold of it, he slammed it against Carmo's arm, hearing the crack. But the primus only grinned with bloodied teeth and knocked it out of Marcus's grip. "While you stand behind lines, the rest of us have been fighting, boy. Pain is an old friend."

He rested his broken arm against Marcus's throat and leaned. "Go to sleep, Legatus. And when you wake, the fun will begin."

His vision darkened, stars bursting across his eyes as he fought against the bigger man. Too many people depended on him for him to die. Too many lives were at stake. But Carmo was so much stronger.

Then pottery exploded, raining shards and dust down into Marcus's face. And his sister's voice, howling, "Kill him!"

Coughing, he kneed Carmo in the balls. The primus screamed and reared backward, and Marcus rolled out from under him. Grabbing the statue, he twisted and slammed it into Carmo's face, hearing bones shatter.

Blubbering and screaming, Carmo fell on his back and tried to crawl away, but Marcus was on him. He struck him again with the statue. Then again, his fury blinding him from all sight. All sound. All reason.

He beat him with the heavy marble, blood splattering him in the face, Carmo's skull shattering and then turning to pulp, but he couldn't seem to stop. Then a hand caught his arm, wrenching backward. And a voice full of authority said, "Stand down."

Jerking free, Marcus raised the weapon, ready to fight the new attacker.

Only to find Commandant Wex staring down at him.

"They're dead," his mentor said. "But Cassius has ordered your assassination. You need to get back to the Thirty-Seventh, and you need to leave tonight."

106

LYDIA

"I believed Derin was only a level above the underworld," Lydia murmured as she followed Baird through the city of Helatha. "But other than the towers, it seems little different than Mudamora."

The streets were lined with homes and inns and businesses, the squares filled with vendors selling foods and fabrics and tools. People of what seemed like every nationality in the West went about their business, and besides a lack of men—probably mostly dead in the war—and the fallen towers of the god circle, Helatha felt normal.

"Appearances can be deceiving," the giant answered. "Darkness flourishes here because darkness rules. Those who don't embrace it suffer for it."

As though to confirm his point, one of the corrupted passed in front of them, the sickeningly bright glow of life around him telling Lydia he'd recently used his mark. Had probably killed with his mark, and she highly doubted there were consequences.

"Rufina isn't the first of them to style herself as queen," Baird added. "But she's the most ambitious in generations. The first to cast her eyes outside the border with a mind for conquest, though it was the knowledge she took from Agrippa that saw it come to fruition. The Celendor Empire fascinates her in its reach and dominance, and she's using its strategies."

Even as the Empire did the same on the Southern Continent.

"Enough chatter," the giant muttered. "Keep your head down and look servant-like, all right?"

Lydia lowered her head, but her eyes flicked forward as they rounded a bend and Rufina's fortress came into view. The black rock seemed to grow from the lake itself, the only way to reach its gate a narrow bridge that rose high above the water. The battlements were patrolled by armed soldiers, and she noted several catapults trained at the city.

She followed Baird onto the bridge, the only sound the flap of banners bearing the burning circle of the Seventh. The men guarding the gates allowed the giant to pass uncontested, all of them saluting as he passed.

"The general just came through with a prisoner," one of the soldiers said. "You know anything about that?"

Which meant Killian was with Rufina now. In chains and entirely helpless. Bile rose in Lydia's throat, and she swallowed hard, fighting to keep her terror in check.

"What?" Baird bellowed. "The little shit was supposed to wait. Bet my last coin he's taking all the credit. And all the gods-damned reward."

"Who's the girl?"

"Not your business. Come on, you." Baird pulled on Lydia's arm and led her inside the fortress. "This way."

They ascended a polished set of onyx stairs that split halfway up, Baird going left, his boots making heavy thuds that echoed the beat of Lydia's heart. *They needed to hurry.*

Sconces illuminated the corridor, the air thick with the scent of burning oil, the chill of the building at odds with the temperature outside: cold enough that mist formed with her every breath.

Ahead, she caught sight of two soldiers standing to either side of a doorway, and her pulse leapt into a gallop. Both saluted Baird, but neither moved from the door

"Her Majesty wants the girl cleaned up," Baird said. "Has a special sort of pain planned for her."

"This is the first we've heard of it," the soldier said. "We're under orders that no one goes in or out without Her Majesty's express permission. We'll need to confirm."

Baird shrugged. "The general's just brought her Killian Calorian in chains, but by all means, please do go interrupt the moment. I'm sure she'll handle that well. Our queen is known for her even temper."

The soldiers exchanged glances, then one said, "Agrippa caught Calorian? How'd he manage that feat?"

"By being smarter than you two knuckleheads. Now let this one in so she can do her job."

All of this rested upon the giant's authority and credibility. If they didn't trust that he was telling the truth, this entire plan was going to go straight to the underworld for all involved.

The soldiers shifted, then one shrugged. "You'll stay with her?"

"Obviously," Baird replied. "I saw her in Deadground. She's a looker."

"Was," the soldier answered, taking a key from his belt. "But not anymore."

Dread filled Lydia's stomach as he unlocked the heavy door, and she took a deep breath, gripping the pile of clothing she carried. *You can fix her. Whatever Rufina has done to her, you can fix it.*

Even as the thought trailed through her head, Lydia knew she was lying to herself.

The door swung inward, Baird going inside first, but as Lydia followed, her eyes went immediately to the small form sitting on a bench. The light rendered the individual as nothing more than a dark shadow.

But she'd recognize the rightful Queen of Mudamora anywhere.

The door thudded shut behind her, and giving a quick glance to ensure that the soldiers hadn't followed them in, Lydia took a deep breath and said, "Malahi?"

The figure didn't answer. Didn't so much as move.

Lydia met Baird's gaze, and he mouthed, *We don't have much time.*

"Malahi? It's Lydia. We're here to get you free of this place, but I need you to listen to me."

The figure twitched, then a rasping voice whispered, "Why should I listen to the girl who is to blame for me being here in the first place?"

Swallowing hard, Lydia stepped forward, setting the clothing on a table before moving around the side of the bench. Even with the warning from the guards outside, it still took all her self-control not to gasp at what she saw.

Despite the frigid air, Malahi wore only a rough shift, and her sand-colored skin held an alarming blue cast from the cold. They'd cut her long blond hair into a ragged mop, but there were bald patches where it appeared to have been torn from her scalp. And her face . . .

It was crossed with a livid red wound that stretched from her hairline to her chin, the black stitches holding it together sloppily done. Her arms and throat were crisscrossed with claw marks and burns, and her fingers were raw where the nails had been torn from their beds. Lydia could barely stomach imagining the pain Malahi had endured. And would continue to endure every time she looked in the mirror.

Sunken amber eyes met hers. "She wanted me to steal the life from Mudamora. I refused. She did this to me—" Malahi rose in a sudden movement, her face inches from Lydia's. "I still refused."

Lydia flinched at the accusation, but there was little she could say in her own defense. "Killian's here—"

"Given you're here, that's no surprise."

Anger flared in her chest, but Lydia left it simmering, knowing she'd need it later. "He's given himself up to Rufina in order to save your neck, so curb your vitriol."

An emotion Lydia couldn't name flickered through Malahi's eyes, then she turned away. "Then he's given himself up for nothing."

"Mudamora is falling beneath the blight as we speak," Lydia said, the way Baird was watching the door telling her she was running low on time. "It needs a tender to repair the land."

"I tried." Malahi's voice was bitter. "I couldn't do it. Mudamora is lost."

"Then why are you bothering to resist Rufina?" Catching hold of the other girl's shoulders, Lydia spun her around. "Why not just give her what she wants and spare yourself the pain?"

"Because I refuse to betray the gift Yara gave me!"

"Isn't staying here and doing *nothing* just that?"

They glared at each other, then Malahi looked away. "There is no escape. Do you think I haven't tried?"

"He's going to take you back to Mudamora." Lydia gestured to Baird. "You're going to leave this room disguised as me." Opening the satchel, Lydia pulled out the cheap wig Baird had procured at a brothel and pulled off her cloak. "Put these on."

"This will never work. You're almost a foot taller than I am, and we look nothing alike."

"It will, because the guards out there believe Baird on their side."

"And what about you?"

"When they discover it's me in here and not you, they'll bring me to Rufina. And I'm going to kill her." She could only pray that Rufina, like the Denastrian king, wouldn't see her as a threat until it was too late.

"And just how do you plan—"

The rest of Malahi's words were drowned out as the door exploded inward. Terror surged through Lydia's veins as Rufina stepped into the opening. Malahi screamed, scrambling to the far side of room, where she cowered, rocking and sobbing.

"So it is you, little healer." Rufina smiled at her like a cat who had caught the canary. To her left, Agrippa leaned against the broken door frame, his eyes glittering with amusement. And beyond, Killian was chained and on his knees between a pair of corrupted, one of his eyes swelling and his lip split. And he was staring at her like he'd never seen her before.

"You traitor," she hissed at Agrippa. "You gave your *word*."

Rufina chuckled. "You'll find, Kitaryia, that Agrippa's word isn't worth the rag he wipes his ass with. The *only* thing one can trust in is his own self-interest."

Lydia's blood turned to ice at the *name,* because no one, least of all *Agrippa,* should know her identity. "How . . ."

"Those in Derin call them mimics," Agrippa answered. "But what I never told you was that I call them reflections. Not only because they see who you are, but also because they see who you once were." He gave her a lazy shrug. "Sorry, Princess, but she wasn't going to give me what I wanted unless *I* sweetened the offering. And for Her Majesty, you are the sweetest prize on all of Reath. She really does *not* like your family."

"You're a bastard!" Lydia clenched her fists, but Agrippa only laughed and said, "Guilty."

"Enjoy your gold and your freedom, pet," Rufina said, stroking his cheek. "Although don't expect either to last forever." Then in a blur of motion, she grabbed Lydia by the hair, dragging her across the floor toward the door. "Put Calorian in the dungeon, and for the love of the Seventh, do ensure he's secure."

Killian moved.

He twisted behind the corrupted soldiers holding his chains and wrapped them around the man's neck. A loud crack filled the air as he twisted the links, breaking the corrupted's spine. The man dropped and Killian lunged toward Rufina, but the other corrupted soldier yanked on the chains, snapping him onto his back.

Lydia screamed, struggling, but Rufina only pushed her to the floor as Killian fought against his chains.

Cold steel pressed against her cheek, and Rufina said, "Healers can endure a remarkable amount of abuse, Lord Calorian. More, even, than you."

Killian froze.

"Good boy," Rufina purred. "Remember who holds your reins or Kitaryia will feel the whip."

"Don't listen to her," Lydia pleaded. "Don't let her use me against you."

His breath was ragged. "You weren't supposed to be here. You were supposed to be safe."

Lydia's heart felt cleaved in two. "I couldn't leave you."

And she didn't regret that choice. The only thing she regretted was placing her trust in someone born of the Empire.

Twisting in Rufina's grip, she hissed at Agrippa. "I'm going to rip your gods-damned heart out for this."

"It's nice to have aspirations." He crouched next to her. "It was a good plan, Princess. But plans only stay good until the battle begins, and then everything changes. You adapt, or you die, and I've always been a survivor." He patted her cheek. "Good doing business with you."

"Don't touch her!"

Killian lunged upward, but Agrippa only grinned and said, "This is for Alder's Ford," before swinging his fist.

Killian dropped like a stone, and Lydia sobbed, trying to get out of Rufina's grip to reach him.

"Take him to the dungeon," Rufina ordered. "Ensure he is well secured. The Princess and I need to have a little chat."

"Sounds lovely," Agrippa said. "Hate to miss it, but it takes time to count out five thousand gold coins, and I want to be gone from Helatha. Too many people want me dead." Then he gestured to the doorway. "After you."

107

TERIANA

She stood frozen on the far side of the wall, listening to the screams coming from the Domitius villa.

He told you to go.

"Since when do I listen?" she growled, then reached up to climb back over.

Only for a hand to close on her wrist.

"What are you doing out here?" a young voice demanded.

"Let me go." She tried to haul herself loose, but the young legionnaire's grip was strong. "There's something happening at the Domitius home."

"I know." The moon peeked out from behind a cloud, revealing the face of Austornic. And behind him half a dozen more young legionnaires. "The commandant is on his way there now. You need to stay here where you can be protected."

"I don't need protection! Especially not the protection of children!"

Unfazed, he shook his head. "You need to return to Valerius's villa, and I'd prefer you did it of your own volition."

Marcus was in danger. She knew it in her core, but she also knew that these young soldiers were more than capable of subduing her. Better to go with them and then try to sneak back out. "Fine."

Under their watchful eye, she returned to Lydia's home only to find Senator Valerius pacing back and forth across the tiles. "Have you lost your mind, Teriana?" he barked at the sight of her. "With the number of people who want to see you dead, one would think you'd show more care."

"There's something happening at the Domitius house!" she snarled back. "I heard screams."

"And you thought to interfere yourself rather than to enlist the service of those trained for such matters?" He threw his arms up. "Your mother is right about you, girl. Act first and think later. It's amazing you are still breathing."

Heat rose to her cheeks at the reprimand, the words sounding precisely like something her mother would say. "At least I try." Her throat tightened. "All the rest of you do is sit on your laurels and allow those like Cassius to carry on as they would. The world will not be saved by the likes of you and my mother."

"Teriana!"

Marcus's voice cut through the air, and then hooves clattered against tile. Marcus, mounted the commandant's horse, rode straight into the room. His face was splattered with blood, one eye swelling shut and his bottom lip split open.

"What is going on?" Senator Valerius demanded. "Have you lost your head, Legatus?"

"Not yet." Marcus swung off the animal, tossing the reins at Austornic. "Cassius sent assassins after me. Twenty-Ninth men disguised to look like disgruntled peregrini."

"You're hurt." She reached for him, but he stepped back.

"I need to leave tonight."

"I'll grab my things." She started toward the stairs, but Marcus caught hold of her wrist.

"You're staying here, Teriana."

Her skin turned icy cold, and slowly, she met his gaze. "What?"

"You've done enough." His expression was unreadable, but his fingers squeezed tighter around her arm. "Valerius can keep you safe. I'll return to Arinoquia and find another xenthier path—one whose viability the Senate will be unable to deny. Just as they'll be unable to deny the freedom of you and your people."

"But you need me."

"I don't." He dropped her arm. "Not for this. It's over, Teriana."

Pain sliced through her chest, her knees wobbling beneath her. "Marcus . . ."

But he'd already turned his attention to Valerius. "Can you keep her safe?"

"As safe as anyone can," Lydia's father answered. "This is the right choice, Legatus. She's just a girl—you should never have used her like this."

"Quit talking about me as though I'm not here!" she shouted, fighting to keep her composure. "It was my choice to make the bargain. My choice to take them across the Endless Seas."

All of it had been her choice. Maybe her options hadn't been good, but that didn't absolve her from her decision to walk this path. "You can't keep me here. You have no right to make that call."

There was a commotion outside, and Marcus grimaced. Catching hold of her arm, he pulled her into a side room, slamming the door shut.

"What happened tonight?" she demanded. "What's changed? Why are you doing this? Why—"

"Because I love you, that's why."

All the rest of her questions died on her lips. For so long, she'd wanted Marcus to say those words. And now he'd said them but was leaving. She stepped toward him, but he retreated, holding out a hand to stop her. His knuckles were bleeding.

"I love you," he repeated. "More than you could ever possibly know. But allowing myself to be with you was selfish. And allowing it to continue would be—" His eyes glittered with unshed tears, and he scrubbed at them fiercely. "You need to be away from me."

"Why?" She reached for him, but Marcus jerked away, stumbling over his own feet.

"Because we are enemies, Teriana. And while you might think you love me today, one day soon you are going to come to hate me." He sucked in a ragged breath. "And I'm too much of a coward to watch it happen."

Maybe he was right, but if he was selfish, she was equally so, because she refused to let him go. Not like this. "You don't know that. You aren't a god—you can't see the future."

"Some things are inevitable." He went still for a heartbeat, then squared his shoulders. "Good-bye, Teriana."

And without another word, he opened the door and strode from the room.

Teriana dropped to her knees, great heaving sobs tearing from her chest, her face slick with tears as grief poured from her.

It had been less than a day since she'd slept in his arms. Had dreamed about walking away from everything for a chance at a life with him. Since she'd told him that she'd loved him.

And now it was over.

Screaming, she slammed her fists against the floor, anguish and fury twisting through her veins, her insides feeling carved out by a sense of powerlessness.

And then the tears stopped.

She remained with her forehead pressed against the cool tiles, just breathing as she allowed reason back into her thoughts.

And steel into her heart.

It was *her* ship imprisoned on the far side of Reath. *Her* crew. *Her* people locked in Celendrial's prisons.

And she'd be damned if she left their fate in the hands of a Cel legatus.

Rising to her feet, she wiped her face with her sleeve, then took a deep breath and left the room.

Senator Valerius, as well as Austornic and the rest of the Fifty-First boys waited outside, all appearing more than a little discomfited. Not that she could blame them.

"So," she said to the young legatus. "Now that you've seen that it's not all grand battles and strategy and victory, you still of a mind to cross the world?"

Austornic inhaled, his eyes distant as he considered. Thirteen years old, and already responsible for the lives of the thousands of boys in the Fifty-First. There was much about him that reminded her of Marcus: the methodical intelligence, the loyalty to his men. But whereas Marcus was tarnished by ruthlessness, this boy exuded a sort of kindness.

She wondered how long he'd keep it.

"Yes. Yes, I do."

"You want to wait the year the Senate will likely take to decide the path is *safe*?" She injected as much scorn into the word as she could, casting a sideways glance at Valerius.

"Safety is relative," Austornic replied. "If we stay, Cassius will give us to the Twenty-Ninth for the rest of our training. I think you understand why I might be of a mind to avoid that fate."

Fresh fodder for a sadist. Teriana's belly soured, because as was so often the case, these boys were facing a dearth of good options. "Let's see if we can't get you out of reach, then."

Valerius shook his head. "Teriana—"

"I need you to get me a meeting," she said before he could start telling her what she should or should not be doing.

"You want to meet with *the Senate*?"

"No." Gods help her for asking this. "I want you to set up a meeting between me and Lucius Cassius."

108

LYDIA

Lydia fought Rufina, kicking and screaming, down the corridors, but the corrupted queen only laughed and dragged her onward until they reached a cavernous room with a large throne at one end. But that wasn't what captured Lydia's gaze: it was the circular hole at the center of the space from which freezing air emanated.

Rufina hauled Lydia toward it, and she screamed, panic rising as the woman hung her over the opening, only her grip on Lydia's hair keeping her from plummeting into the endless dark depths. An icy wind blew, making her skin burn, and as she stared down, Lydia swore she could see the Corrupter himself staring back at her.

Then Rufina hauled her upright, dropping Lydia on the floor. "Someday," she whispered. "But for now, I've need of you."

The silence that followed was deafening.

Then Rufina said, "The last time I saw Princess Kitaryia, she was little more than a babe in her mother's arms, the pair leaping off the balcony of the Royal Palace into the ocean below. Even with my knife in her back, I knew your mother had survived the fall. The gods have always favored the Falorn family. And no bodies were ever found."

Lydia didn't answer, only met her cold stare with one of her own.

"I was certain one of Madoria's had intervened and spirited the pair of you away, but Agrippa tells me that Camilla took you to the far side of the world. To the . . . *Celendor Empire*." She said the name with relish. "Out of reach of both me and the gods. Is she alive?"

"No," Lydia whispered, hate rising from the embers of her anger like curls of smoke. "She bled to death on the street."

A soft chuckle exited Rufina's lips. "If she'd stayed, a healer could have saved her. But neither gods nor their marks have power in Celendor, or so Agrippa tells me."

Logically, Lydia had known that. But it still hurt that her mother had died to protect her. "He's quite the source of information."

"Isn't he just," Rufina murmured. "He opened my master's eyes to a world of opportunity, for my master looks back at those who gaze into the darkness, whether they know his name or not."

Cassius. Lydia's blood chilled, but she kept the reaction from her face. "Like you did?"

"Even so." Rufina sat on the ground in front of her, resting her chin on her knees, watching Lydia. "You want to know why, don't you?"

"I already know why, Cyntha." Lydia spit her name. "Because you were jealous and spiteful that my father chose my mother over you. And rather than getting over it like a rational person, you gave yourself to the Corrupter in order to have your vengeance."

Rufina smiled. "You make me sound so petty."

"Because you are."

"No, I was just a woman who grew tired of being powerless. Tired of being used." Tilting her head, Rufina added, "Hegeria marked me to save your father's life, did you know that?" Then she laughed. "Of course you don't. He quelled that story, disliking the thought of anyone's fame eclipsing his own. But no one knowing it doesn't make it less true."

There was a part of Lydia that hated Rufina speaking about her father in such a way, but another part of her was loath to silence her, because this was her story as much as Rufina's, and she rather thought the corrupted queen might be the only one who'd ever give her the whole truth.

"I was the warrior healer who guarded his back and pieced him together whenever he got in too deep, which was often. I was also in his bed for ten years, which is the *only* thing anyone remembers about Cyntha, if they remember anything at all." She sighed. "And I *loved* him more than life itself, which was my true downfall."

How much evil has been done in the name of love? Lydia wondered as she stared at Rufina's flaming eyes. *How many people have been hurt?*

"For most of my life I was his in every possible way, and then one day, he decided it was time to take a wife. To give Mudamora a queen." The flames around her irises softened into a faint red glow. "But it wasn't to be me. He needed someone fit to produce heirs, and Hegeria's mark is . . . *parasitic*. And all my pleas that I'd refrain from healing anyone until a child was born fell on deaf ears because he didn't want to give up my capacity to heal *him*."

Lydia could hear the remembered pain in Rufina's voice, the hurt. Could all but feel the powerlessness she must have felt in that moment. And there was a part of her, deep down, that understood the woman's choice more than she ever cared to admit.

"The mark I accepted to save his life was the same mark that made me unfit to be his queen. Because it's a mark that *takes and takes and takes* but gives nothing in return. Yet there is no power on Reath that would allow me to get rid of it, so instead, I resolved to change it. To make it serve me and protect me and make me strong, and it has delivered in abundance."

Strong enough to protect herself. Strong enough to never be hurt by another. Lydia closed her eyes, entranced and terrified by the allure of the woman's words.

A knock sounded on the door, and a moment later, one of the corrupted entered, the life around her blazing with unnatural fierceness. "My queen," she said, bowing. "We've urgent need of your presence."

"I'm occupied."

The woman's gaze flicked to Lydia, then she stepped closer to Rufina, murmuring something she couldn't make out in the woman's ear. But whatever it was, it caused Rufina's eyes to widen in fury. "That little prick dares to steal from me?" she hissed. "I'm going to rip out his heart. You stay here and don't let this one out of your sight."

In a blur, Rufina raced from the room, leaving Lydia alone with the corrupted. "Agrippa get greedy?" she asked, her voice hoarse.

"Something like that." The corrupted moved to lean against the wall. "And she won't forgive him this time. Not now that she's got something better."

Killian.

Lydia's eyes burned, because Rufina was going to use her against him. And she knew it would work. Knew that if the Queen of Derin did to her what she'd done to Malahi that he'd agree to whatever she demanded of him.

And maybe at first it would be little things. Things that cost him nothing to concede. But well she knew how small concessions led to bigger ones, and how long until Killian stood at the front of Rufina's army as it marched across Mudamora?

It would destroy him.

Tears flooded down her cheeks, her chest so tight that she could barely breathe. Her plan had been to remain to rescue him, but because of that traitorous bastard Agrippa, she'd be damning Killian to something worse than death. And it had been for nothing. Malahi was still a prisoner, and given the terror she'd shown toward Rufina, how much longer would she hold out against the corrupted queen's torture?

You have to get them out.

But how? The corrupted guard stood only a few paces away, watching her with interest.

Kill her.

The corrupted was stronger than she was. Faster than she was. Probably far more skilled at combat than she was. How could Lydia possibly get around her?

Even the odds, the voice whispered. *You know how.*

Her mind recoiled at the thought. But her heart lurched, recognizing hope where before there had been none.

You could make yourself strong enough to save him.

You came back from it before. You could do it again.

You wouldn't be killing anyone who didn't deserve it.

Lydia's pulse throbbed in her throat, a desire that she'd buried deep rising like a dark tide, washing over her. Claiming her. Freeing her.

"Might I have some water?" she asked softly. Piteously. "I'm so very thirsty."

The corrupted eyed her for a moment, then shrugged and went to a table off to the side holding glasses and a pitcher. She returned swiftly with a wineglass filled with crimson liquid. "Rufina's not one for water."

"Thank you." Lydia waited for the corrupted to bend over her, holding out the wineglass.

Closer.

She closed her fingers over the glass and gave the woman a weak smile. Then Lydia jerked her hand up, smashing the glass into the woman's face.

The corrupted shrieked, clawing at her eyes, but Lydia was on her in a heartbeat, twisting behind to clamp a hand over her mouth, her legs and other arm wrapped around the woman's body. She could feel the excess of life spilling from the woman. Life stolen from what were probably innocent people.

But this creature was not innocent.

And neither was she.

Digging in her fingers, Lydia *pulled.*

109

MARCUS

He urged the horse through the rear of the Valerius property, heading toward the back gate where the commandant was waiting.

You did the right thing, he silently told himself. *To have kept things going would've been the worst thing you've ever done.*

If only it felt that way.

But he couldn't think about that now. Not when Cassius and Hostus had their sights set on killing him. Not when the Thirty-Seventh remained under Titus's control. Not when the Maarin remained as prisoners of the Empire.

Wex stepped out of the shadows, and Marcus's stomach clenched when he saw his father and sister were with him. Cordelia had a cloth pressed against her ribs and her face was pale.

"You shouldn't be on your feet," he said to her. "You need to see a physician."

"It's not so bad that it can't wait. And you didn't say good-bye."

She stepped toward his horse, but feeling Wex's eyes on him, Marcus drew the animal back. "Good-bye."

Her jaw tightened, but she gave a nod before retreating into the garden.

Wex stepped forward, handing Marcus a piece of paper with Lescendor's seal on it before stuffing supplies into the horse's saddlebags. "My name should get you through any resistance you meet, though your own should do well enough."

His father held up a heavy purse. "Gold, in case other measures fail."

Marcus took it without answering, shoving it into his saddlebags.

"Cassius will anticipate that you'll head to the Bardeen stem to return to your men in the Dark Shores." Wex rocked on his heels. "He'll have Hostus send men to Bardeen to stop you, and if they succeed, it's over. They'll claim to be returning you to Celendrial on some farce of a reason, but we both know they'll leave you in a shallow grave. The same if they catch you along the way."

"They won't catch me."

Wex was quiet for a heartbeat, then he said, "You won't be able to outrun him forever."

Maybe not, but Marcus intended to try.

"If you'd give us a moment, Commandant," his father said. "I wish to speak to my son alone."

Wex leveled him with a long stare, then finally said, "There's a reason we take them young, Senator. A reason we cut them off from their families. A reason we force them to forget. You are a *liability* they can't afford."

"You overstep, Commandant."

"No, I don't. These boys are *mine* to protect the moment they walk through the gates of Lescendor. And while I might not be privy to the details, I expect that it is because of *you* that much of this has come to pass, Domitius. Why else is your wife cleaning blood off your floor and your son dragging bodies down to the water to be fed to the sea? The peregrini curse Marcus's name in the streets for raising Cassius to power, but I think if the truth were known, it would be the Domitius name they'd drag through the mud. And that maybe you'd deserve it."

"Wex," Marcus said softly. "It's fine. Go ensure everyone is safe."

"Just because you were born to them doesn't make them your family," Wex said. "Look to those who guard your back, not those who throw you to the wolves. Look to the Thirty-Seventh." And without another word, he retreated into the garden.

The horse frisked beneath Marcus, sensing his apprehension as he waited for his father to speak.

Senator Domitius was silent for a long time, and then he said, "I should never have given you up to Lescendor. It is the greatest mistake of my life, and I will die regretting it."

Staring at the black sea, Marcus allowed the words to sink into his soul. For most of his life, he'd dreamed of hearing them, but now that they'd been said, he found they changed nothing. Taking a deep breath, he dug his heels into the horse's sides.

And he didn't look back.

He rode at reckless speed, the horse sliding on the trail and nearly sending them both plunging to their deaths a dozen times, but Marcus couldn't afford caution. Not with Hostus hunting at his heels.

He hit the beach and pushed the animal into a gallop, heading north, where he'd go around the outskirts of the city and head inland.

A hard two-day ride would take him to a genesis stem that led directly into the heart of Bardeen, only an hour's gallop from Hydrilla and the stem that would take him back across the world. But Hostus would have contingencies in place in case his men failed in their assassination, and watching the road to that xenthier stem would be one of them. Which meant not only did Marcus need to come up with a different route to Hydrilla, that route needed to get him there faster than Hostus. And it needed to be one the other legatus would never predict.

Giving the horse its head, Marcus sank into his memories, drawing up a map of the Empire marked with the countless xenthier stems, the paths zigzagging across the continent.

And with that map in his mind, he plotted a route only a madman would dare take.

Dawn was glowing in the East when he reached the town of Alsium, his horse's flanks drenched with sweat. He'd paused along the way only long enough to rid himself of the bloodstained formal attire and to don his armor, his red-and-gold cloak hanging over his mount's hindquarters, the helmet signaling his rank heavy on his head.

The men on watch at the town gates saluted as he passed, and he trotted through the quiet streets, heading toward the fortress.

The gate was closed, but a man with a 13 stamped on his breastplate stepped out, yawning as he asked, "Number, rank, name, and the nature of your business?"

"37–1519," he answered. "Legatus Marcus of the Thirty-Seventh. Passage to Timia."

The legionnaire blinked once, then he peered at Marcus's breastplate as though to confirm he was of the legion he claimed. A thousand questions formed in the man's eyes, but his training did its duty. "Yes, sir. Open the gate!"

There was a scuffle of motion inside, then the gates swung open, revealing a large space, at the center of which stood a glittering stem of xenthier. Twelve more men of the Thirteenth encircled it, backs as straight as the spears they held, but they stepped aside as he approached.

Dismounting, he handed the reins of his horse to one of them, knowing he'd need a fresh mount once he reached Timia. Then, ignoring the prickle of fear creeping up his spine, he reached a hand out toward the stem.

White light flashed across his vision, then he was stumbling across sand instead of earth, in broad daylight rather than dawn.

"Welcome to Timia, sir," a man with a 21 on his breastplate said.

"I need a horse." Marcus shook his head to clear it. "A fast one, as my business is urgent."

Mounted on the fresh animal, he galloped down the road, groves of fruit trees on either side, heading inland. It took less than an hour for the fortress to appear, and those manning the gates were infinitely more watchful than those back in Celendor. "37–1519!" he called in answer to their query. "Legatus Marcus of the Thirty-Seventh Legion. My business is in Denastres."

The gate swung open, revealing a scene made different only by the smells in the air. Handing off his horse, Marcus passed those guarding the stem, took a deep breath, then reached out to touch it.

White light. Then rain splattered against his forehead as he staggered, a wash of dizziness hitting him.

He'd known this would happen.

Traveling through stems in swift succession was avoided because it caused unpleasant physical symptoms that could leave a man debilitated for days.

But that was a risk he needed to take.

"Welcome to Denastres, sir."

Lightning crackled, and Marcus lifted his face to watch the storm overhead, a fierce wind driving sleet into his face. "I need a horse. Faster the better."

He rode through the wildness of the storm, his horse splattering through rivers of mud. But he kept the pace until the fortress appeared.

"Welcome to Faul."

"Welcome to Sibal."

"Welcome to Atlia."

"Welcome to Bardeen, sir." Marcus barely heard the words. Falling to his knees, he heaved up the contents of his stomach, the ground around him lurching and swaying.

"You all right, sir?" The legionnaire dropped to one knee, hand resting on Marcus's shoulder. "You need a medic?"

"No." Marcus wiped his mouth with the back of his hand. "It's just been a long day." Less than a day since he'd left Teriana in Celendrial.

It already felt like a lifetime.

"I need to get inland." He climbed to his feet, though it was only the older man's grip that kept him from falling over sideways. "Urgent business."

"That's a dangerous journey, sir. You'll need an escort."

Marcus shrugged the man off, knowing if he stopped even for a moment that he'd pass out. And that it would cost him everything.

Might cost *her* everything.

"Horse." He coughed, his chest aching. "Now."

110

KILLIAN

They'd dragged him down into the dungeons beneath Rufina's palace, the air stinking of moisture and rot and waste, and thrown him into one of the cells with the chains on his ankles and wrists still firmly in place.

If they'd left him alone, he might have had a chance of extricating himself with the pick he'd hidden in the heel of his boot, but instead, the three soldiers remained, their eyes never moving from him despite the shrieks and cries of those locked in the surrounding cells.

Even then, he might have gotten free, except all three of them were corrupted.

Not that Killian didn't intend to try. He had to.

He should've known that Lydia had given up too easily with the way she'd marched down the trail at Baird's side, never once looking back. Should've known that she'd risk herself to save him. It was who she was.

And who she was, was Kitaryia Falorn.

Which was impossible. And yet . . . *not*.

While King Derrek Falorn's body had been discovered in his rooms, drained of life by one of the corrupted, the bodies of his wife and daughter had never been found, the blood splatter found on the balcony suggesting the worst. And Killian's own father had searched for them for months, for years, never finding a whisper of a rumor that either survived.

But they had. Or at least, Kitaryia had. On the far side of the world, hidden away in the heart of the Celendor Empire. Until chance or fate or some act of the gods had brought her back.

Grinding his teeth, Killian again assessed his options for escape, but he'd not gotten himself into this expecting to have to extricate himself right away. Or at all. But thanks to that traitor Agrippa, dying was not an option. Not with Malahi and Lydia both prisoners.

Think.

The moans of the other prisoners were abruptly drowned out by the sounds of running feet, and a second later, someone shouted, "Has Calorian escaped?"

"No," one of the corrupted, a short man with a greasy mustache, answered. "He hasn't moved since we tossed him in there."

"You're sure?"

"Of course I'm sure," the corrupted snapped. "Come see for yourself."

A soldier appeared in front of Killian's cell, peering in at him. But instead of relief filling his gaze, the man swore. "Shit! It wasn't him."

"Wasn't him that did *what*?"

"Someone's taken the Rowenes girl. Her guards are dead. We're searching the palace, but . . ."

Killian's shoulders started to shake, and though he knew it was probably better to stay silent, no amount of control could contain the laughter that spilled from his lips. Especially as realization of *who* the culprits were dawned on their faces.

All of them were staring at him, then the mustached corrupted said, "Someone needs to tell the Queen."

Taking hold of the bars, Killian leaned against them and smiled. "Which one of you lucky bastards will be the one to tell her that her own general just stole her prize out from under her very nose while all of *you* guarded the decoy?"

All of them gaped at him, their dismay palpable.

Stepping back, Killian laughed even as his focus turned entirely to Lydia. To what might happen if he didn't get to her soon. "That's what I thought."

111

MARCUS

Bardeen was a pot that had already boiled over, and as he galloped down the muddy road to Hydrilla, passing patrol after patrol, Marcus saw endless signs of the violence that had come as a result. Violence that, once upon a time, he had predicted would come.

Bodies of Bardenese rebels left where they'd fallen and turned a grotesque purplish black, blood in pools around them. And Marcus knew that the only reason there wasn't legion dead surrounding them was because the legions buried their own.

It took him close to a day to make the journey to Hydrilla, the fortress city that he and the Thirty-Seventh had defeated what felt like a lifetime ago. His eyes took in the familiar ramparts, the echoes of catapults and drums and screams filling his ears, and an old guilt bit at his stomach.

But it wasn't to the fortress he went, but rather to the ground that had once held the camp the Thirty-Seventh had shared with the Twenty-Ninth. To the worn path leading to a bridge that had once stretched across a violent river of water. But now the ground beneath was nothing but rocks and mud, the river rerouted by a thick dike.

Sturdy walls made of Bardenese redwoods surrounded the spot where the river had flown over its falls, mounds of dirt still piled outside from the excavation. And at the base of the hole they'd dug was the xenthier that would take him back to Arinioquia.

That would take him back to the Thirty-Seventh.

He was so close.

Dismounting, he abandoned the exhausted horse, walking on wobbling knees toward the men posted outside the gate. They saluted, their eyebrows rising at the sight of the number on his chest.

"This stem has been mapped," he said to them. "It leads across to the Dark Shores where the Thirty-Seventh and Forty-First have established themselves. I wish to inspect the stem's position, for it will soon be supplying us."

"Yes, sir," the centurion said, fumbling with the lock, which was already rusting from the damp.

And that was when Marcus heard a commotion in the distance. His head, as well as those of the soldiers before him, turned, eyes going immediately to the group of men sprinting in their direction, weapons in hand. On their breastplates, he could just make out a 29.

"What's this all about?" the centurion muttered.

"Not my concern." Marcus stepped into his line of sight. "Now get the lock open."

Frowning, the man twisted hard on the key, the lock popping open with an audible click.

"Stop him!"

Shouts from the Twenty-Ninth men filtered up to them, and the centurion's eyes widened. "Apologies, sir, but perhaps—"

Marcus shoved the man out of the way. Shouts of alarm filled his ears, but he ignored them, pushing open the gate and then slamming it shut. Catching hold of a piece of lumber, he braced it against the gate, knowing he was buying himself only seconds.

Ahead, a dark pit loomed, ropes anchored to posts dangling into its depths. He raced toward it even as wood splintered behind him.

"Stop, sir!" someone shouted. "They say it's not safe!"

Lies. Especially given that hesitation would cost him his life.

He slid to a stop, his stomach flipping as he gazed into the blackness, unable to see the bottom.

You've been through the Teeth. You can do this.

And if he didn't, he was dead.

Catching hold of one of the ropes, Marcus swung over the edge, his feet scrambling against the wet earth as he lowered himself down into the darkness.

Down and down.

The stream had carved the path, but though it had been since widened by human hands, it felt too narrow. Too close.

Like he was climbing down into the underworld Teriana so feared.

"Pull him back up!"

He was rising. Men hauling on the rope, dragging him back to the surface.

No.

He had come too far. And too much depended on his success.

So Marcus let go.

Air whistled past his ears, and he tried to slow his descent by dragging his arms against the walls, roots and rocks cutting into his arms and hands. Then his feet struck the ground, the impact twisting one of his ankles and rattling his spine.

Ignoring the pain, he dropped to his knees, feeling the walls for an opening.

There.

It was a narrow tunnel that sloped downwards, and he crawled into it, trusting it would take him where he needed to go.

Trying not to imagine being buried alive down here.

He could see nothing, could hear nothing, though he had no doubt that the Twenty-Ninth still pursued. He had to hurry.

Sweat poured down his face and into his eyes and Marcus blinked, realizing he could now faintly see. The glow of a xenthier stem—it had to be!

But a faint draft that stank of male sweat drifted past him.

Hurry!

Heart pounding, he crawled forward, rounding a slight bend. And then it was there. Glittering crystal that was equal parts alluring and terrifying.

What if this isn't the one? his terror whispered. *What if they made an error in the codes? This could take you anywhere!*

A hand closed around his ankle, hauling him backward.

Shouting, Marcus kicked hard, whoever it was behind him cursing in pain as his foot connected.

Go!

Scrambling, Marcus reached forward and closed his hand over the stem, bracing himself.

The world turned white, and all around him was nothingness. And it seemed to go on forever, as though he'd been lost in some in-between space. Marcus screamed, but there was no sound.

There was nothing.

"*Ooof!*" He landed on his back with a thud, but before he could orient himself, nausea took hold, offering him barely enough time to roll before his guts rose. He dug his fingers into the cut stone beneath him, stomach heaving, the world spinning. And he had only the briefest moment to note that the air smelled of jungle before everything went dark.

112

KILLIAN

Like a trio of bloody cowards, the corrupted had drawn straws to see which one of them should tell Rufina that Agrippa had spirited Malahi away. The woman drew the short straw and hurried off in the company of the soldier who'd brought the news.

Leaving Killian with two corrupted, a set of manacles, and a prison door to contend with.

Taking his time wasn't an option.

Although thanks to Agrippa, at least time was something he had.

In hindsight, Killian realized that it had only been when Rufina was about to kill him that Agrippa had revealed Lydia's presence in the fortress and her true identity, the clever bastard banking that Rufina would be enticed enough by the prospect of turning Killian into her general to spare his life. That Agrippa had thrown Lydia under the cart wheels would still earn the smart-ass a punch to the face when Killian got out of this mess, but he did have a level of grudging admiration for the ruthless effectiveness of Agrippa's plan. And for his ability to think on his feet.

Sitting on the filthy floor, Killian stared back at the two men watching him, shifting restlessly so that they wouldn't notice when he finally took hold of the heel of his boot and extracted the lock pick wedged into the leather.

"Do you think Rufina killed the messenger?" he asked. "She doesn't seem the sort to take bad news very well."

Mustache spit through the bars. The glob struck the molding straw in front of Killian, giving him a good excuse to jerk farther backward into the shadows. "The Queen does not harm the chosen out of hand."

"You so sure about that?" Killian asked, resting his wrists behind his bent knees, slipping the pick into the lock. "Because quite a few of you died in the battle at Alder's Ford."

"That was Agrippa's doing!" Mustache snarled. "Not the Queen's."

"Ahh, Agrippa." One lock came loose, and Killian chuckled to muffle the noise. "I confess, I have trouble keeping track of whose side he's on."

"His own!" Mustache stepped closer to the bars as Killian freed his other wrist, then started on his ankles. "If you think he's going to take that girl and hand her over to your people sweet as pie, you don't know him."

His ankles were free.

"He'll probably hide her away and then ransom her back to the Rowenes family for twice what Rufina offered him," Mustache sneered. "So don't go thinking he's on your side, *Lord Calorian*. He's just using you like he uses everyone else."

"Thanks for the warning," Killian said, giving Mustache a smile right before he struck.

One end of the manacle whipped through the air. It passed between the bars, striking Mustache in the face and shattering his nose. The man screamed in pain and fury, fumbling at his side for a weapon, but Killian was already on him.

Reaching between the bars, he pulled loose the knife at the man's belt and threw it, the blade punching into the other corrupted's eye just as the man was leaping to his feet. He wavered, then dropped, but Killian's attention was back on Mustache.

As the man recoiled, one hand clutching at his face, Killian caught hold of the front of his shirt and jerked, slamming the corrupted into the bars, blood splattering him as he looped the manacle around the corrupted's neck.

And pulled.

Mustache screamed, bracing his arms against the bars and trying to push himself back far enough to get free, but the chain was pressing hard against the base of his skull, crushing his spine.

Grinding his teeth with effort, Killian braced his boots against the bars, pulling until, with a loud crack, Mustache's neck snapped. The flames illuminating his eyes went dark, and he slumped against the bars.

Drawing in a gasping breath, Killian clambered forward, using the man's sword to slit his throat just in case before digging around in the black leather of his coat for a key to the cell.

It wasn't there.

"Shit!" Killian dug through his memories of being locked inside, cursing himself for being so rattled about Lydia's capture and identity that he hadn't been paying attention. *Who had unlocked the cell?*

The woman.

Who was probably lying dead in Rufina's throne room for delivering bad news.

Falling to his knees, Killian searched for the lock pick he'd dropped, sweat running in rivulets down his forehead.

Hurry. You don't have much time.

A wave of prickles ran over his skin, and he looked up from his search to find a pair of burning eyes staring at him.

"A good effort, Lord Calorian," Rufina said, shoving aside the corpses of her men with a booted foot. "But not good enough."

Rising to his feet, Killian took a wary backward step, knowing she was a far greater threat than either of the two dead men had been. Not just corrupted, but a warrior.

"Where are Agrippa and Baird?"

He huffed out a laugh. "A good question. Wherever they are, I suspect that it's with a chest not nearly heavy enough to be full of gold. Though knowing Agrippa, he probably stuffed in as many handfuls around Malahi as he could fit."

"Tell me the route they plan to take to get back to Mudamora. You obviously planned to get out of here alive to rejoin them, so you must know it."

"Part of the plan was that I didn't." He smiled. "Just in case."

Rufina's jaw tightened, her eyes flaring. "A plan that didn't include Kitaryia being my prisoner, is my guess. You aren't the sort to risk the people you love to achieve your ends, though Malahi should be thankful that Agrippa is more ruthless."

Fear churned in his stomach, because although he'd known it would come to this, Killian hadn't realized how swiftly a threat to Lydia would paralyze him. How easily it would make him agree to anything just to ensure her safety.

"How long will you stay silent when I start to cut her apart?" Rufina purred. "How long will you stay true to your kingdom and cause when I take her fingers? Her hands? Her pretty green eyes?" She smiled. "She'll heal. But they won't grow back."

His breath hitched, his stomach twisting in ropes, because he knew he'd crack the moment Rufina put a knife to Lydia's flesh. "What do you want?"

"Agrippa's route."

Malahi might be able to stop the blight.

"Shall I fetch her now? No sense tarrying . . ."

Malahi might be able to save tens of thousands of lives. Might be the key to winning the war.

"How long do you think it will take for me to make her scream?"

Killian took a deep breath. "They . . ."

His words were cut off by the rapid thuds of boots against stone, then a blur of dark hair and black leather struck Rufina in the side, sending her toppling down the aisle in front of the neighboring cell, the two figures grappling until one came up on top.

Pale skin splattered with blood, her spectacles gone, and her hair come loose from its braid, Lydia looked up at him.

But instead of the green eyes he loved staring back at him, all he saw was darkness and flame.

Panic surged through his veins, but Killian barely had a heartbeat to come to grips with how far she'd fallen before Rufina threw Lydia off, both of them rolling and coming to their feet.

"Well, well." Rufina drew her sword. "What would your dear gods-fearing parents say if they could see you now, Kitaryia?"

"Don't call me that," Lydia hissed. "It's not my name."

"But Kitaryia is the girl Killian is sworn to protect." Rufina danced forward, swiping playfully at Lydia with her sword. "What do you suppose he thinks of you taking up the Corrupter on his offer for power?"

"Doesn't matter."

Lydia picked up one of the dead men's swords, and Killian cringed even as Rufina laughed, the corrupted queen recognizing what he already knew: that Lydia was no warrior. He had to help her.

Falling to his knees in the moldy straw, he searched for the gleam of metal. Rufina was toying with Lydia, like a cat would a mouse, but that wouldn't last.

Where is it?

"Your father begged for his life, you know," Rufina purred. "Did the mimics echo his pleas? Did you hear his sobs for mercy as I drained his life? Did you hear him piss himself in the end?"

"Shut up!" Lydia screamed. "You're a liar."

"I'm not." Rufina laughed. "For all his skill with a blade, Derrek was a coward. That's why he took weak, submissive Camilla for a wife. A woman with no family, no history, no name of importance so that nothing about her would ever challenge him."

"Then it must have really ground your nerves to know she escaped you!"

"Except she didn't escape, did she? Dead in a gutter on the far side of the world is still dead, Kitaryia."

"Don't call me that!"

Killian's heart pounded with desperation, knowing Rufina was baiting her. Hearing Lydia's hisses of pain when Rufina's blade found its mark.

Hurry.

He fumbled bits of straw, then his fingers brushed against something cold and metal. Triumph flushed through him as he held up the pick, then he threw himself at the cell door, reaching around to insert the metal into the lock.

Focus.

But it was impossible when his eyes landed on Lydia, her stolen disguise sliced open in half a dozen places, blood slicking the leather. And Rufina with not a mark on her.

Help her.

His hands shook as he struggled to trip the mechanism, his breath coming in ragged little gasps.

Click.

The locked popped open, and Killian took a step back and then kicked the bars. They swung out with violent force, striking Rufina in the back. She stumbled, and he caught hold of her sword arm and yanked, sending her toppling head first into his cell, her skull cracking against the floor.

"Close it!" he shouted at Lydia. But instead of listening, she tried to go after Rufina.

Panic surged through Killian. He threw himself at Lydia, sending her flying across the aisle and into the bars of the cell opposite. Rolling on his back, he struck out with both feet, hitting the swinging door of his cell. It flew shut, the latch activating a heartbeat before Rufina slammed into it.

The corrupted queen screamed in fury, flinging herself over and over against the bars.

Then she went still, and it felt for all the world to Killian like the Corrupter himself stared out of the black pits of her eyes.

"It doesn't matter if you escape this place, Lord Calorian. With every sacrifice Kitaryia made to my master, his hold on her grew. She'll never be free. It's only a matter of time until you'll have to kill her. Or risk her turning on innocents."

"The only life I want is yours," Lydia hissed, then flung herself at the bars.

Rufina only stepped back, laughing. "Let me loose, then, Highness. Let's see who comes out victorious."

A dull thunder of boots filled the air, growing louder by the second. Dozens of men—likely with more corrupted among them—racing to the aid of their queen. Too many of them to fight, and Killian couldn't risk Lydia taking more lives. Couldn't risk her descending lower than she already had.

He had moments until the soldiers would be upon them. The water dripping from the ceiling splattered him in the face, falling to join the rivulets pouring down the corridor.

Which meant it was draining somewhere.

He dragged Lydia away from Rufina's cell, it taking all of his strength to do so. "I need you to come with me."

"I'm not leaving her alive!"

"We don't have time, Lydia. We need to go."

Gripping her hand, he dragged her down the corridor, handing off his lock pick to one of the men in the cells. Giving them a chance.

Cell doors slammed open behind them, the prisoners racing out and opening other doors, a horde of men and women running toward the stairs and the coming soldiers. Screams split the air, and Killian fought the urge to turn around and fight. But he needed to get Lydia free of this place before he lost her entirely.

They skidded in the slime, stopping at the grate over a drain in the floor. Just big enough for a person, though for him it would be a tight squeeze. "We need to get this open. It has to lead to the lake."

But Lydia wasn't, listening her gaze on the fleeing prisoners.

"Lydia!" he snapped. "Help me!"

Giving her head a shake, she bent her knees, gripping the grate even as he took hold himself, praying to all the gods their combined strength would be enough. Her hands were pale against the rusty steel, fingers and wrists slender, but as she jerked on the grate, it immediately began to give. The unnatural strength given to her by the consumption of gods-knew how many lives.

Please let her come back from this.

Killian clenched his teeth and pulled, and slowly, the grate ground out of its casement. Setting it aside, he bent to look in the hole, which angled downwards, but there was nothing to see but blackness.

"She's free."

Lydia's breathy whisper caught his attention, and Killian looked back to see the soldier who'd opened Rufina's cell withering in the corrupted queen's grasp as she drained his life to bolster her strength. Lydia took a step in her direction, and sensing her intent, Killian kicked her feet out from under her. A snarl of fury tore from her lips as she fell into the drain, fingers slipping in the slime as she disappeared from sight.

He sensed a surge of motion rushing toward him, every instinct in his body screaming that he should turn and fight.

Killian jumped.

His shoulders were crushed inward by the walls of the drain tunnel, but the coating of slime and filth did their duty, and he picked up speed. Looking upward, he saw Rufina's shadow crouched over the opening, but she didn't follow.

She didn't have to.

He shot out of the tunnel and flew through the air, barely sucking in a breath before he plunged beneath the tepid surface of the lake. Kicking hard, Killian swam upward, gasping in a mouthful of air.

All around him was mist and darkness, the lake surface still.

"Lydia?" he whispered, treading water, listening for any sound of her. She didn't answer, and his heart flipped with the certainty that something had happened. That she was drowning. Or worse, that she was already swimming to shore intent on taking lives. "Lydia?"

Then his skin prickled.

It was so dark he couldn't see his hand in front of his own face, and the only smell was the reek of everything draining from the city. But he knew she was there.

The water rippled against him, and almost the same moment he saw the faint glow of her eyes, he felt her breath against his cheek.

"Why didn't you let me kill her?" The fury in her voice made him want to back away. "Why didn't *you* kill her?"

"Because we couldn't kill her and get out alive."

"She murdered my parents! Stole every drop of life from my father and stabbed my mother in the back. And you might have cost me my only chance at vengeance!"

They didn't have time for this. Already he could hear shouts of alarm from the fortress they'd escaped, which were spreading down to the edge of the lake.

"Agrippa told Rufina what he overheard the mimics saying to you." He cast a glance toward shore. "Your mother died to save you, Lydia. Do you think she'd wish for you to die in pursuit of vengeance?" And though he knew it was cruel to say, he added, "Wouldn't that make her death for nothing?"

She sucked in a breath, and his skin crawled, warning him that he was treading on dangerous ground. That like this, she might attack. And in the water, he might not be able to fight her off.

"Agrippa and Baird didn't betray us. They have Malahi," he said as the alarm bells rang through the city. "But getting her out of Derin will be next to impossible—they need our help. Mudamora needs her—and it needs you—far more than it needs Rufina dead. You need to fight for the living."

"I'm no good to anyone now," she whispered. "I'm corrupt."

He'd seen it. Knew it. But hearing it from her lips carved out his insides because he couldn't lose her. Not again. "Only if you want to be."

She didn't answer.

"We need to go," he said. "Need to steal a boat before the beaches are crawling with soldiers."

"You should leave me." Her voice was choked. "Go. Get Malahi back to Mudamora. It's what you were meant to do."

"What I was meant to do was be with you." Reaching out, he caught her around the waist, drawing closer. "To never leave your side and to guard your back until one of us ceases to draw breath."

"You swore that to Malahi."

"I swore it to you first, even if you weren't there to hear it. Swore it a hundred times with you in my heart. And even if I had not, I love you. And if this is where you choose to make your stand, I will be at your side until the bitter end."

"I'm not getting you killed, Killian—" Her voice cracked on his name. "Go!"

"No."

"Damn it!" she snarled. "And damn you and your bloody honor."

"Curse it all you want, I'm not leaving you."

He could feel her thinking, trying to decide what to do. Then she said, "Fine. How do you propose we steal a boat?"

Relief flooded him. "First we need to find one."

They swam silently toward the shore, which, judging from the noise, was already crawling with soldiers.

"Can you see them?"

"Faintly. The fog is obscuring them."

Hopefully water would do the same. Squinting toward the bobbing torchlights, Killian examined the dozens of fishing vessels tied up to the docks, a small one catching his eye. "Can you swim underwater that far?" he asked, pointing.

"Yes, but the second we climb into that boat, the corrupted are going to see us. Me, especially."

"That's why we're not going to get in. Let's go."

Taking a deep breath, he dived under the water, swimming hard toward the vessel, trusting his sense of direction to keep him on course in the blackness. The brightness of the torches grew, and he flipped on his back, swimming until he saw the boat's shadow overhead. Setting his feet against the ground, he braced his hands against the bottom of the rowboat, then slowly tipped it.

His chest grew tight with the need to breathe, but Killian didn't dare move faster. Not when the slightest splash would alert those hunting them. He sensed Lydia next to him, felt the water push locks of her hair against his face as she reached up to help him turn the boat.

And then they had it over.

Rising into the pocket of air beneath it, he sucked in a deep breath, hearing Lydia do the same. He moved to the front and untied the knot holding the boat to the dock, then whispered, "We'll walk it out as far as we can, then head down the shore a bit before flipping it over."

"This is insane," she whispered back, her eyes glowing in the darkness. "Someone will see us."

His gut told him otherwise. "Let's go."

Holding on to the edges of the rowboat, they eased it out between its larger neighbors and headed into deeper water, Killian's water-logged boots catching in the twist of weeds. Only once they reached the drop-off did he turn the boat south, ignoring the temptation to stick his head out from under the water to see if they'd been spotted.

Only when he was certain that they were truly hidden by the fog did he slip into the open, but all there was to see was darkness, even the lights of the city lost to the thick grey mist. The water rippled, and Lydia emerged, her eyes no longer glowing. "You see anything I don't?"

"Nothing." Her voice was tight. Strained.

"Let's flip the boat."

Together, they dragged it closer to shore, then eased it over, taking care not to make any noise. Climbing in, Killian untied the oars from where they were fastened and set them in the locks, heading first into deeper water and then south.

Lydia didn't speak. Didn't say a single word until the faint glow of the sun lit the horizon, illuminating her face. "It doesn't last very long."

He knew what she meant without asking. "Wouldn't serve *his* purposes if it did. The Corrupter isn't giving you anything, Lydia. He doesn't give anyone anything, only takes."

"If only that were true."

Her fingers drummed against the edge of the boat, the rhythm frantic and uneven, the motion reminding him of addicts deprived too long of their drug of choice. And it had only been a matter of hours. A matter of hours, and already she was craving more. "It's his tool for controlling you. He comes out ahead."

"As if *you* could possibly understand!" she snarled, twisting in the boat to face him. "No one ever accuses you of being weak or incapable. No one ever accuses you of being a *liability*."

She threw his own words in his face, and he flinched. "You found a cure for the blight, Lydia. That makes you many things, but a liability isn't one of them."

"What it makes me is something to be used. A tool for others to achieve their ends." Fury rendered her voice almost unrecognizable, the coming dawn illuminating eyes that remained dark pits into the underworld.

He wanted to say that it wasn't her that was speaking—that it was the Corrupter's influences—except Killian knew that wasn't entirely the case. It was the fear of helplessness that lurked in her heart that was speaking. The same fear that had driven her to want to learn to fight all those long months ago, despite his warning that no amount of skill with a blade would erase it.

And now the Corrupter had offered her something she believed would vanquish her fear. Except all it did was bury it, the cost of keeping it from clawing its way up so very high. "You sound like Rufina."

"Perhaps she has the right of it, after all." Lydia leaned toward him, her gaze feral. And hungry. "You should've left when you had the chance. We will both have cause to regret that choice."

Killian kept rowing, but every muscle in his body was tense. "You can control this, Lydia."

"I don't think I can." Her tongue chased over her bottom lip. "I don't think I want to."

I've lost her.

She lunged, and he only just got his foot up in time to knock her back, nearly sending her overboard. But in a heartbeat, she was on her feet, pale fingers reaching for his throat.

And he swung. The oar was little more than a blur in the air, connecting with the side of her head with a loud crack. A blow that would've killed anyone else, but had only gained him a few seconds of respite.

Dropping to his knees, he used her belt to bind her wrists and strips of fabric to hold her ankles, trussing her tight so that she wouldn't have the leverage to break them. He was gagging her when her eyes flickered open, fury filling her gaze as she realized her state.

"I'm sorry for this. You know the last thing I want to do is hurt you," he said, pushing her hair back from her face, the wet strands tangling in his fingers. "But you also know that I don't give up without a fight."

And neither did she.

With that thought in his mind, Killian glanced at the sun to get his bearings, the weight of all that was to come heavy on his shoulders.

But for now, all he could do was keep rowing.

113

MARCUS

"Wake up, wake up," a familiar voice said, and Marcus flinched as water splashed him in the face, dragging him into consciousness.

Blinking, he tried to wipe his eyes clear, but his wrists were bound, coarse rope digging into his skin. Then his gaze focused, and Titus's face loomed in front of him.

"Well, if it isn't the most wanted deserter on this side of the Endless Seas," the other legatus said, a smile that reminded Marcus of Cassius rising to his lips. "You should have stayed gone, Marcus."

"I didn't desert." His throat was painfully dry, the words coming out barely louder than a whisper.

"That's not what the Thirty-Seventh thinks. That's not what Legatus Felix thinks. They all believe you abandoned them. For a *girl*."

"No." Marcus licked his lips, trying to moisten them. Trying to push the fog from his head. "We were attacked. Had no choice but to take the xenthier stem we found, but it landed us in Sibern." He coughed. "I've been to Celendrial."

Titus picked up a cup, holding it to Marcus's lips as he desperately swallowed the water. "I believe you, Marcus. But you know how legions are about deserters—I'm not sure they'll listen."

Marcus choked on the water, turning his face away from the cup. "I have new armor. A letter from Wex."

Titus shook his head. "You were found in civilian clothing." Then he turned his head and said in Arinoquian, "Was there a letter on him? Armor?"

An ancient man with the mahogany skin of a Gamdeshian moved forward, lamplight glinting off the multitude of rings piercing his left ear. "No letter. No coin. Nothing but the clothes on his back."

A chill ran down Marcus's spine, his stomach twisting into knots. "Path-hunters are coming to confirm the route, Titus. They'll confirm my story."

Or would they? He was no longer certain.

"I want to believe you," Titus said. "But you've been charged with desertion, and protocol demands that I give you over to the Thirty-Seventh. And to Felix."

Who he'd left on the worst of terms. Who likely hated him. Who had no reason to believe anything other than that Marcus had deserted for Teriana.

And *someone*, probably Titus, had gone to great lengths to ensure Marcus had no proof otherwise.

The Thirty-Seventh was going to kill him.

"I'll speak on your behalf," Titus said. "Ask Felix to hold off on sentencing you. But . . ." He shook his head. "Unless those path-hunters arrive soon enough to corroborate your story, I might not be able to stop the Thirty-Seventh from having their revenge on you. They're angry, Marcus. And they're not the same legion as when you left."

What else had happened?

Standing, Titus said to his men, "Time to head back to Aracam. Let's give the Thirty-Seventh back their deserter." Then he leaned closer, his breath hot against Marcus's ear. "And when they turn on you, I think you'll be wishing I'd slit your throat instead."

ACKNOWLEDGMENTS

Gilded Serpent is easily the most challenging novel I've ever written, not only because of its length and complexity compared to my other books, but because holding the minds of four different point-of-view characters at once often threatened my own sanity! A huge thanks to Spencer and my daughters for putting up with me constantly in front of a computer screen, because work-life balance is something I'm a bit of a failure at. The biggest thank-you to my parents for the endless support of my writing and for listening to my endless chatter about my imaginary worlds, as well as all the childcare you provide. Thanks to my brother for never letting me take myself (or my work) too seriously. A huge thanks to my mother-in-law for taking care of my girls so I had time to write and for always being there for my family.

All the thanks to my editor, Melissa Frain, who went through this beast of a novel so many times and who loves these characters so much. To the team at Tor Teen, Lindsey, Rachel, Devi, Saraciea, and Isa (as well as all the others behind the scenes) thank you for your hard work getting this story into the hands of readers.

I'd be lost without my agent, Tamar Rydzinski, who supports my work in so many ways—thank you!

To my Turtles (you know who you are!), you are all huge inspirations and I appreciate the knowledge you've shared with me more than words can say! To my bff Elise Kova, knowing you have my back makes the hard days so much easier! To Amy, thank you for always pushing me to add more emotions to every page and for your love for these characters! To Shimrit, thank you for your help with timelines because we both know how bad I am at them! To Eileen, all the hugs for both your support and for sending me photos of your adorable baby to brighten my days.

And the hugest of thanks to the bookstagrammers, especially #teammarcus and #teamkillian, who fill my DMs with so much love and encouragement on a daily basis. You are my legion, and I'd be lost without you.